LOVE'S AWAKENING

Oliva walked out on the small gallery and looked up at the sky. Somewhere a dog howled mournfully, and the sound was as much a part of this night, this place, as the crickets and frogs were on the bayou.

She sighed. So this is marriage. When she thought of the pleasure he gave her in the darkly private nest of their bed, she knew that she was now part of a great mystery. She could feel the tendrils of tenderness wrapping around her soul like insistent spring vines, tugging her gently to lean towards him, as a flower turned to light.

She walked back from the gallery, dropping her clothing in the darkness, approaching the door to the little bedroom her bare skin prickling in the night air.

"Blow out the candle," she said softly.

"What?"

"Blow it out."

He leaned over, blew, and the room was suddenly, overwhelmingly dark.

"Olivia?" he asked, his voice a whisper.

She did not reply.

He sat up, but she knew he could not see her. Her heart was pounding as it did their first night together, the way it did when she woke in the night in the bayou and wondered what creature had made that noise so close to her bed and waited to hear it again—and she moved silently across the room towards him. Her husband.

BAYOU

PAMELA JEKEL

ZEBRA BOOKS
KENSINGTON PUBLISHING CORP.

ZEBRA BOOKS

are published by

Kensington Publishing Corp.
475 Park Avenue South
New York, NY 10016

First Zebra Books paperback edition: June, 1992

Printed in the United States of America

For my mother,
Delorse Patricia Jekel,
Who would rather sing than spade,
Dance than dream,
And wing than root.

And who, to her firstborn
At a fissionable age, said,
"Let's go to the library,
I don't feel like cooking."

Preface

The history of civilization is written along the riverbanks of the world. The Mississippi, called the *Meche Sebe* by the early Indians, has been a magnet and a mirror for man since he first walked this land. Draining half a continent, thirty-one states, and much of Canada, the river's waters create the fourth largest drainage basin in the world, yet the legend of the Mississippi comes less from its size than from its impact on the American soul. The river flows through our music and our folklore, sings in the images of our painters and poets, and for four centuries has lured those who were inclined to set themselves adrift.

Most of these waters and many of the drifters eventually find themselves in the deep delta country of Louisiana. Called a birdfood delta, the river's estuary provides this nation with our largest and most fertile wetlands ecosystem. Larger than even the vast Okefenokee, Louisiana's half million acres of swamp make her the quintessential bayou country of the continent, and likely the next great conservationist battleground.

This deep delta estuary is a tumultuous mating between sea and river, belonging to both and teeming with life. The mixings of the two waters produce habitats unmatched in richness and diversity. Over four hundred species of birds make their home here, the take from Louisiana's waters is larger than anyplace else in the United States except Alaska, and the bayous provide a nursery for all sea life in the Gulf.

But change is as relentlessly inevitable as time and the river. For the past five thousand years, the Mississippi has been hammering away at its geological destiny. Through the ages, it has selected first one then another route to the sea. Each change has wreaked havoc and, in time, created a new fertile delta. Together, these deltas make up the land of Louisiana.

In the same way, history has selected first one and then another band of sojourners as its new route to the future. Under ten different flags and from a rich gumbo of German and Irish, Spanish and French, Cajun and Creole, African and Caribbean, Yankee and Southerner, Louisiana has built her destiny. Whether it was planter or pirate, aristocrat or slave, each culture surfaced for a brief shining moment of power—only to give way beneath the flotsam and froth of newcomers.

In a sense, this deep delta land of amorphous goo is the most Southern of all our landscapes because here, south of the South, perhaps more than anyplace else, our past is at its most primitive and least homogenized.

The deep delta has a deceptive calm, like that of an Eden where time seems to stop; where breezes waft, easy and warm, through great trees and swaying mosses; where streams are gentle; where nearly everything that moves, moves slowly; and where nothing promises to happen—until it happens. Until, that is, the wind rises and this land of slow motion becomes a place of sudden and violent change. Here in the bayou, where a man often wears his heart on his sleeve and a chip on his shoulder, you can still hear America becoming, as richly diverse as the vast patternless bayous in this, her Southern heart.

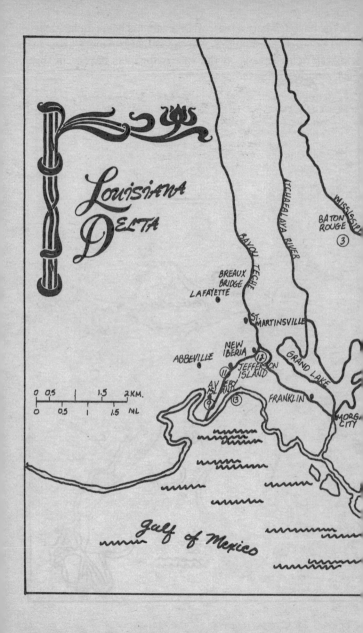

North

Bayou

1 – DOUCET CABIN
2 – WEITZ BREWERY
3 – CHOCTAW VILLAGE
4 – POPICH OYSTER BEDS
5 – LAFITTE STRONGHOLD
6 – BATTLE OF NEW ORLEANS
7 – BEAUSONGE AND BONREVE

8 – LAST ISLAND RESORT
9 – BIRD SANCTUARY
10 – IRISH PALACE JAZZ CLUB
11 – SHADYOAKS
12 – BAGATELLE
13 – SALT MINE

State of Mississippi

DONALDSONVILLE

AINCOURTVILLE

POLEONVILLE

LABADIEVILLE

THIBODAUX

RACELAND

HOUMA

LAC DES ALLEMANDS

Lake Pontchartrain

NEW ORLEANS
6

10

DE LA CROIX

BAYOU TERRE AUX BOEUFS

Brenton Sound

LAKE SALVADOR

BAYOU LAFOURCHE

BARATARIA BAY

MISSISSIPPI RIVER

CHENIERE CAMINADA

GRAND ISLE
5

GRAND TERRE

ISLES DERNIERES
8

PART ONE
1786-1815

They were approaching the region where reigns perpetual summer,
Where through the Golden Coast, and groves of orange and citron,
Sweeps with majestic curve the river away to the eastward.
They, too, swerved from their course;
and entering the Bayou of Plaquemine,
Soon were lost in a maze of sluggish and devious waters,
Which, like a network of steel, extended in every direction.
Over their heads the towering and tenebrous boughs of the cypress
Met in a dusky arch, and trailing mosses in mid-air
Waved like banners that hang on the walls of ancient cathedrals.
Deathlike the silence seemed, and unbroken, save by the herons
Home to their roosts in the cedar-trees returning at sunset,
Or by the owl, as he greeted the moon with demoniac laughter.

—Henry Wadsworth Longfellow, *Evangeline*

To begin . . .

The Mississippi is one of the oldest rivers of the North American continent, and its bed has changed over the past million years with the comings and goings of each ice age. We do not know the exact age of "The Father of Waters," but about three thousand years ago, when the sea level stabilized at its present height, the bayou waterways were already three thousand years old and had been carrying land to the sea for all these eons.

Man came to the river as soon as he could walk upright. The early Indian tribes had a flourishing fishing industry when the Spanish explorer Hernando De Soto discovered the river in 1542. Their culture was already dying by the time the French colonizer, La Salle, claimed all the lands around its mouth for King Louis XIV in 1682. Calling it Louisiana, despite earlier names and claims, the first French settlers were to leave a cultural imprint on the bayou lands that continues to this day. In fact, it was they who coined the word "bayou" from a Choctaw word *bayuk,* which means small, meandering stream.

And so any saga of the deep delta should begin with these French refugees. Exiled French-Canadians, they were banished from their Nova Scotia farms by the British in a fit of tyrannical paranoia. Families were divided, children lost to parents, and small wretched bands of these Acadians were forced from their homes in this "Grand Dérangement" of 1755, to shuttle from Massachusetts, Georgia, Virginia, New York, Maryland, and the West Indies, repulsed by many colonies, forced into servitude on labor-hungry Yankee farms in others. A few groups finally managed to make their way to Louisiana, where they were given lands along the bayous and welcomed by French colonists as kin.

From a land of prairie, slate gray skies, and cold Atlantic winters, they came to the deep delta country. Here were drooping willows, shadowy cottonwood, pendant branches of live oaks, and masses of creeping vines. Jagged Spanish daggers and scrub palmettos hid six-foot water moccasins and alligators larger around than cattle. Rank vegetation gave rise to clouds of biting insects at dusk, and the raucous bullfrogs joined with the weird cries of vultures, the eerie hoots of the owl, to drown out the strange stillness of the swamp. Children of those first refugees would be marked by their parents' memories, their priorities forever altered, as were children of Depression parents nearly two centuries later. Thirty years after the first Acadian arrivals, stragglers were still making their way to the colony. Some of them found news of family long-dead, still others rushed gratefully into the arms of relations who had somehow managed to survive in this land, so different from what they had known.

They called it the *la prairie tremblante*, the trembling prairie, and they set about to make it home.

It was the year of her mother's long torment. And in that year, Oliva Doucet came to understand that every belief she ever held about some day being wife to some man, was gradually growing as ravaged as her mother's once-vital body. Until that year, her father's cabin seemed a sure refuge in a world of fearsome change.

The little cabin was set on a rise out of the swamp water, at the end of a twisting black-water stream that wound among the tangled palmetto clumps and cypress. All about the place, the earth was hidden in growth, but the high ground around the Doucet home was cleared for a struggling garden patch, lily roots, and Lebanon Doucet's cape jessamine bushes and crape myrtle trees.

The sun was late to reach the cabin because of all the moss-draped live oaks around it, but the slant-floored gallery (built wide and inviting in the Acadian style) was sheltered from the winter rain. The two sleeping quarters were behind the big room; the cookshed was a few steps apart, past a covered walk from the back door; and the smokehouse was beside the cookshed.

The well was close to the kitchen, thanks to luck and Simon Doucet's good planning. A view of the cabin from the bayou took in the corncrib, the cow lot, and the pigpen used in the fall for fattening the shoats. Out in the clean-swept yard, the wash pot stood, not too far from the well. The wash shelter was built to hold one trough and one woman at it. There were a thousand burnt-out fires under the old iron

17

wash pot, and before Oliva, Lebanon, her mother, had stood at the wash trough hollowed from a cypress block, battling the clothes clean, boiling and wringing and rinsing again, to banish the bayou mud.

But now, Oliva Doucet did that chore alone for herself, her mother, her father, and brother, and her hands were growing larger and stronger than they should have been for her fourteen years.

She finished wringing her mother's underlinen, and carried it with the basket of damp clothes to where a single line was strung clear of the dripping trees, under the shelter of the little cocked-roof privy. Along the walk, Oliva noticed the pinks were already readying for spring blooming, though the lily clumps looked dead under the last frost.

Every root along the path had been a burden in some woman's hands, Oliva thought, for men will scarcely trifle with such things. Every leafing, every flowering bush about the cabin had a history. The parent of that quince was planted in a tub in Baton Rouge and came by pirogue to Lafourche, when her mother saw it and had to have it for her own. This crape myrtle bush lived in Massachusetts once, she'd heard her mother say, and this cape jessamine came from Virginia; *grandmère* dug the root herself and bundled it for the journey. These lilies were from England and were brought over dried in a chest.

As she bent and reached with the wet clothing, she could see out beyond the garden and across the water to the little isle where the Doucet graveyard rose on a hill of dry ground. There, the four cypress tombs of her two sisters and two brothers lay in shaded silence. She only remembered one loss, of course, her baby sister, Cleoma, who had died of the fever at two. All the others were dead before she was born. But Valsin remembered them all, for he was the oldest. Perhaps this was why her brother was sometimes *mélancolique,* like a brooding turtledove. All those losses in a narrow, shadowed row.

Oliva had wept and mourned for days when Cleoma was taken, sorrowing for those laughing dark eyes and plump little hands, so soft. Even the bottoms of her feet had been pink and perfect. But Lebanon only looked much older than the day before, her eyes more deeply etched with grief, her shoulders lowered, as though she carried Cleoma on them invisibly. Death, her father said, may come at any time to anyone, even the creatures in the bayou know as much. Therefore, he said, they live each day as though they'll know no other. Surely, *le bon dieu* meant for us to do the same. Let him continue to grieve who can be sure he will not die tomorrow.

Oliva pulled her eyes from the graves and finished hanging the linen on the line, squeezing out the rinse water as best she could. The girl knew that in this weather it well might take two days or more, and even then she would likely have to move the clothes by the hearth to dry completely, smoke smell or not.

She went up the gallery, scuffing her bare feet for pleasure on the well-worn cypress boards. A sleeping fire winked and smoked on the kitchen hearth. She swung out the pothook to be certain the dried peas did not lack water. Old Juno, her father's hound, rose lazily to greet her, yawning cavernously. His bitch, Jolie, being much younger, jumped up to paw at Oliva as though she hadn't just seen her the hour before, danced on two feet, now on four, wagging fiercely, whimpering, and laughing, her eyes bright with worship. Papa always gave away her litters, and Jolie would grieve a week, having no explanation for so monstrous a loss. Then she would come to Oliva, who alone would take time to pet and fondle her, and lick her hand as though she pleaded apology for all manner of things gone wrong.

Oliva straightened from the flurrying dog and went resolutely back to the room where her mother lay still under the feather tick. An hour was long enough to be gone, even if there was little she could do to ease Lebanon's suffering.

Oliva settled quietly into her mother's rocker, which seemed to have already molded itself to her smaller frame in this last fortnight of watching. The lean figure under the blanket had not stirred a mite in her absence. Of a sudden, Lebanon Doucet's sunken eyes opened, and although Oliva could not see her mother's mouth under the bedcovers, she knew she smiled. Oliva reached over and burrowed under the feather tick until she found her mother's hand. She held it, stroking her thumb absently, as soothed as she hoped her mother was by the touch of their fingers.

Her mother moved her mouth out from the linens and whispered, "My feathers, *cher?*"

Oliva squeezed her mother's hand and dropped it, rose and took from the pig-hide chest in the corner, the robe of feathers Lebanon Doucet had made two years before. She laid it across her mother's chest, pulling the edges up around her ears as she liked. Now, she could clearly see her smile of pleasure.

Oliva took her mother's hand again and smoothed the feathers down, their two hands together moving over the robe as one. Her hands were not as clever as her mother's, Oliva thought. She knew how to fox a shoe tongue, and even at fourteen, her basket stitches were close and nigh perfect, but perhaps she would never have the magic in her fingers that her mother had.

Simon Doucet had been offered a fine sorrel brood mare for the robe if he would trade it, but he would not. Lebanon had made it with waxed thread and a needle made of a heron's leg bone, and Oliva could scarcely see the work in it. Small and cunning, the stitching was set about the barbs of glass green feathers, around each fiery puff of breast down, each sheened quill of purple softness. Using all manner of feathers, her mother had made the ruff a mingled rainbow of colored down, and in the robe itself, every color one's eye could see on birds shimmered throughout: tawny gold from the grosbeak, ruby from the tanager and the throat of the

20

hummingbird, gawdy green from the wood duck, pale pearl from the egret, and snow-ice blue from the wild goose.

Oliva could remember when her mother would stoop and find a lost bird feather—even a sparrow's wing quill had a light in it, she said, that was as rich as a storm cloud. But then, the walking and the stooping would bring on one of Lebanon's coughing fits. Oliva would watch her mother leaning there, holding onto a tree for support, while the cough racked her, and when the coughing was over, leaning her head wearily on the tree's body as though on an old friend's breast. She remembered the times she saw her mother spit blood on the mossy earth, and the sight of it was ugly and frightening.

Lebanon treated her cough with butterfly weed and moonseed roots flavored with cumin. But the slow croupiness in her chest only worsened. If she could get away to the north, out of the winter damp and the summer fevers, maybe she could have healed. But she would not leave the bayou and her husband's bed. At last, her bright eyes grew dull, and she walked wearily in smaller and smaller circles around the cabin. Then Oliva took over her care, and the clean-swept pine floors grew more dark, for she had less time to clear away the mud old Juno and Jolie tracked in, and someone must make the flenses of salt pork infused in honeywort, and the doses of fermented mulberry juice which kept Lebanon's cough from ripping her chest in two. Someone must spoon down the sweetness which quieted her and let her sleep. Sleep was all she seemed able to do for so many weeks now.

And sleep was what was overtaking Lebanon once more. Oliva carefully moved her rocker closer so that she could continue to hold her mother's hand as she drifted into what seemed to be a dream as long as winter. The only sound in the cabin was the rain hissing and dying in flame down the chimney, and the occasional soft rumbling snore of Juno as he waited patiently for the men to arrive.

Old Juno rose and bayed mournfully, his nose pointed out the cabin door to the bayou beyond. Oliva went to the door and saw a pirogue approaching, with a tall figure poling easily into their cove. Her heart jumped once in her breast like popped corn, and she flew to the glass to smooth her dark hair and be sure her teeth held none of the noon meal. She glanced down with dismay at her worn workshift, but there was no help for it. At least, she vowed, the tattered day bonnet could stay on its hook.

A voice hallowed and Old Juno settled back down to the hearth with a harrumph of resignation, for he knew that voice well enough.

Oliva stepped out the door and smiled at the boy who was settling his pirogue at the cypress planks which made the Doucet landing. She lifted a hand in greeting.

"*Bonjour,* Oliva," Emile Arceneaux called out, fending off the wild advances of Jolie who had raced to greet him. "Is your brother at home?"

Oliva's smile deepened. Emile would know—as would any man in Lafourche—that these days were unlikely to find either Valsin or Simon Doucet under their own roof in the middle of the day, not with traps to set and skins to harvest. "Not until dusk," she said, her voice low and gentle. "You can wait by the fire, if you like."

Emile stepped onto the gallery, his large boots making what seemed to be more noise than any three of Juno, and she shrank back slightly at the tallness of him. Emile was

22

eighteen—she knew for she had asked, wondered if he knew she asked—and the second-oldest son of Pierre Arceneaux, a shrimper in Lafourche. Thrice he had waltzed her at Le-Bleu's *fais-do-do,* and his dark eyes had sought hers across the crowded dance floor, even when he had let her go to another. Twice before he had come to call, but Papa and Valsin had claimed him for their talk by the fire, and he scarcely spoke to her at all.

But smile he did, and when she saw his unspeaking smile, she felt that no matter how dull or bitter a day might be, he would soften its edges by his presence. He spoke slowly around her father, and she found herself listening for anything he said. His presence before her now made her heart feel swamped, like the sudden spilling of cool water when she tilted the well bucket too far, and splashed her feet in a puddle of startling pleasure on a hot day.

He held out a damp bag. "*Papa* sent these along, he says he wouldn't mind some fresh squirrel, when Valsin finds the time." Emile spoke some in English, some in French, as did many of the young men in Lafourche. The combination of the two tongues made her feel they spoke almost a secret language together.

She looked into the bag at the mound of fresh shrimp, gray and glistening. "*Merci bien,* I'll tell my brother when he comes in."

"Your mother any better?" he asked quietly, glancing behind her into the open door.

She shook her head. "But no worse, either. She's sleeping now."

"The rain's stopped," he said, gesturing out to the bayou with a wide-sweeping hand. "I thought to maybe get a buck, there's good sign upriver." He glanced away at the water casually. "You want to come along?"

She looked back towards the gloom of the sleeping quarters and heard no sound within. She hesitated.

"Just awhile," he added softly.

23

She gazed up at him and saw the least lifting of his left eyebrow, the little crooked quirk his lips took on of hope. His beard was none too heavy, and it seemed as though it might be silky to her hand. "Just awhile," she repeated, and whirled to catch her cloak off the nail. Juno rose expectantly, but she said to him, "No, you must stay and watch *maman, ami,* and make no noise."

In moments, she was settled in the bow of Emile's pirogue, and he was poling out of the little cove, Jolie yapping mournfully on the bank.

"I passed a nesting of egrets on my way," Emile was saying as he moved the pirogue skillfully out into the current. "Want to see them?"

"Oui, vraiment," she said, glancing over at the shore. He was right, there were many small heart-shaped stampings where the deer had come to drink. It suddenly seemed like a month since she had been out of the cabin! Fresh sign so near meant good hunting done quickly.

Deep through the overhanging trees, Emile poled the pirogue through the sleeping bayou where now and then a loon cried sharply or a gust of ducks took wing before them. Little by little, the sky was clearing, and it looked as if it would be a scarlet sunset to the west. She glanced at his musket, lying on the bottom of the dugout. It was a well-polished weapon. You can always tell a man by the care he takes with his guns, papa said. His guns and his boots. Where he had been today, where he would go tomorrow. Oliva could make Valsin's and papa's boots from the tanning of the hide to the stitching of the top laces, but Emile's boots were seamed so that the awl marks did not show, likely foreign-made, and the leather was finished more expertly than she knew to do. She pulled her camlet cloak closer about her, watching him.

"The trapping goes well this season, *hein?*" he asked slowly.

"Well enough. Papa says that he's seen better years. Valsin says he must be careful to leave enough for the other trappers to take."

Emile grinned and nodded with easy understanding. He knew Valsin's bragging tongue was no better nor worse than the tongues of most swampers along Lafourche bayou.

"The shrimp nets are full?" Oliva asked, fetching around her mind for more questions, once he answered this one.

"Never full enough to please *mo' père,*" Emile said rue-fully. "But me, I say the catch will be better when the weather turns."

They moved along now in silence, and she felt a current run between them like the moving water beneath them, almost as irresistible and even less evident to the eye. He moved the pirogue deftly, easily, balancing the stern end, watching for submerged stumps and overhanging branches, yet his eyes were on her often.

She was keenly conscious of her face, her hair, her breathing which moved her breasts under the cloth of her bodice. Usually she wore her hair braided and bound in a sleek black coronet, held to her head firmly by shining walnut pins which Valsin had carved for her and rubbed to a gleam with oil of olives. Today her hair was unbound and loose around her throat, and it made her feel both free and shy before him.

Suddenly he said, "You're a small thing to hold." He said it then he glanced away.

She flushed and looked down at the water.

"When we waltzed, I all but spanned your waist with my two hands—me," he added, more boldly.

"I'm not so small," she answered softly, *"mais* you are *vraiment grand."*

"Not to hear my brothers tell it," he laughed. "They say I'm the runt of the litter."

She looked up at him with her eyes clear and shining. "Not to me. You are taller than Valsin, and he a half-score older! Taller than *papa, aussi."*

They came upon the shore of a crowded cypress knoll set

low in black coiling water. Suddenly, she lifted her hand with a cry and he turned his eyes from her face. There, a little distance from them, the egrets rose in spirals like blown snow. They circled high in the trees over them, calling low to one another. For long moments they dipped and swayed, dancing up and into the trees and down again, swirling plumes of dazzling white against the darkening sky. The pirogue was stilled now, and nothing moved but the leaves and those white birds.

"No matter how many times I see them," she said, "I never tire of it. Like lace and smoke on the wind."

He smiled. "Your words are near as good as the birds, for truth."

She sighed happily. "I know a place where the deer come to drink. I'll take you there." She stood up and began to move towards the stern of the boat.

"Do you think I let you pole me while I take my ease?" he teased. "My brothers would shame me out of the village."

"Your brothers will never know," she said pertly, reaching for the pole.

He took her shoulders to ease past her in the narrow dugout, balancing carefully with a wide stance. But when he touched her, he stopped, facing her while the boat swayed gently in the still water. Gazing down at her, he seemed to hesitate in wonder for an instant. She felt his shyness, and it calmed her.

"Close your eyes," he murmured.

She obeyed him, her hands half-reaching to balance on his waist.

He kissed her eyelids softly, gently, one by one, lingering at each for the smallest instant, as though to feel what she saw through those eyes. Her eyes trembled open, and his face was very close. "I want to do that for a long time, me," he said.

She tilted her chin up towards him unconsciously, without plan or preamble, as though her body moved under its own signal. He touched his lips to hers very softly, lingered there an instant, and his hands stole around her shoulders to pull her slightly closer. She felt her lips tremble as though a cry wished to escape her, felt his lips tremble, too. And then he pulled back, almost reluctantly, and let go her arms.

"Shall I pole then?" she asked quietly, reaching for the staff beside him.

"If you think you can," he said, suddenly himself again and teasing.

"Watch me, M'sieu," she said, moving into position at the stern and dipping the pole into the water.

"I will," he said, lounging in the bow where she had sat. He shoved his long legs down the length of the dugout to stretch them, and Oliva screamed when she saw it. His boot toe touched the musket barrel while her hands were still helpless on the pole. His weight turned the barrel of the gun towards him. She heard the sharp explosion before she could move to stop it.

Emile crumpled his right hand against his chest, his mouth open in agony, and where his fingers had been, where his hand had been, blood pumped from a mangled, blackened stump. She dropped the pole and gathered his arm against her, but he groaned and pulled away, his eyes already darkened and dull with horror. Moaning, she ripped a long tear from the footing of her skirt and reached over the side to snag a branch which drifted alongside. She snapped the branch in half, scarce noticing her strength, and bound the wood on the inner curve of his handless wrist with the cloth. Murmuring to him with quavering voice, she laid him down on the floor of the pirogue, and then dipped her skirt in swamp water to rinse his pale face, for he was near to fainting.

"Lie still, *cher,*" she said as firmly as she could, "lie still and keep your heart from pounding no matter how it pains you. I will get you home as fast as I can."

She held her hands against his jaws for a moment to try to still their chattering, then she picked up the pole, gathered

27

her fists on it, and leaned with all her might, with all her love, into the current.

Simon Doucet poured clear turpentine over the stump of Emile's right hand and rebound it tighter, making a sling which held the mangled arm close to the boy's body. Oliva brought the gallipot of goose grease and the green ointment to soothe the burning, but Simon scarcely looked at her. Valsin had poured laudanum down Emile's throat, followed by a dram of rum. Emile seemed half-in, half-out of their presence, and he had said only, when he saw Simon and Valsin come to the gallery to meet them, "We were just gone awhile, M'sieu. To see the egrets." With that, he collapsed in her brother's arms and never saw Simon's fierce scowl at her, never heard her flurry of panicked explanation.

Simon caught and tied the ragged artery, tied up the loose places with horse hairs, cut away the torn flesh, and seamed the edges with a waxed thread and a needle cleansed in flame. As Valsin carried Emile out to the pirogue, he was too weak to even lift his head. His eyes were blue-lidded, his brow pasty pale and wet in sweat. As they gently laid him in the dugout, covering him with blankets, he murmured something.

She bent to hear and, when no one saw, she pressed her cheek warm for a moment against his own. When she lifted her head, she saw that her father watched her darkly.

"You might now give some thought to your mother," he said, trying to keep his anger in check.

Oliva gasped and turned to stare at the cabin. She had bumped the pirogue into the landing, screamed for her father, had hurried to bring him what he needed to save Emile, had never given her mother a thought since she stepped across the door.

Valsin stepped into the pirogue and lit the lamp, for by now the swamp was dark as the night. "There was a gator under the house when we got back from the traps."

She moaned aloud. An alligator under the house was a sure portent of death.

"I hope she's still alive," Valsin added coldly, "by the time I return." With that, he swiveled the pirogue and pulled away towards Lafourche.

Oliva knelt at the grave, pulling at the stiff winter weeds, her mouth set with indignation. There was no time in this land of rank growth when weeds would not root. Even now, in the cold month of January, her mother's grave needed tending.

She sat back on her bare heels, scanning the sky for a break in the clouds. High in the wet gray, a swamp buzzard spiraled slowly, stiff-winged, waiting. Not a good sign, she thought. He should be with his kin, drooped high in a dead cypress crown, oiling his feathers, watching for any little death on earth below. His ceaseless hunt meant the rain would probably continue without pause for at least two more days.

The birds were stilled as well. Papa always said, watch the birds. The birds say it best, what *le bon dieu* will bring on the wind. Do not be too busy to listen to what they say, eh?

Oliva began the private confession she had with her mother at every visit, a ritual she had gradually perfected in the two years since Lebanon's death. Sometimes she spoke aloud, low and murmured admissions which she could no longer tell Father LeBlanc. Other times, she merely thought she spoke, but did not. Either way, she knew her mother listened. As she always had in life.

When she stopped to think of it, the confessions had actually started that first night, after Valsin rowed Emile out of her life. She had wept over her mother's bed, taken her hands and repented for her neglect, but her mother could scarcely hear her. The coughing had returned in Oliva's absence and shaken her mother fiercely, as proved by her sweaty, matted hair and disheveled bedlinens. Sometime in the struggle, she had let go her water, and the bed was as wet as her hair and skin. So sunken was Lebanon in her own pain and weariness, she hardly knew that Oliva had left her alone . . . and hardly realized that she was now at her side. Oliva wept as she washed her mother, pulled off her sodden linens, and tried to make her as she had been before.

"*Maman,* I am so sorry," she sobbed, "I did not mean to be gone, I did not mean to sin, papa will scarcely look at me! And now Emile may die for my disobedience! *Maman,* his hand, his *right* hand! It is blown from his body! How will he live? What will his people say?"

Lebanon Doucet opened her eyes. They wavered towards the cypress beams, to the door, and finally to Oliva's face, as though they were only lightly anchored to this earth. "Emile?" her mother murmured weakly.

"Emile Arceneaux, *maman,* he came and he asked me to see the egrets. So I went with him, but only for a short while. He wanted some squirrel, he brought some shrimp from his father. *Maman,* he"—and here, Oliva's voice dropped to a quivering whisper—"he kissed me."

With that word, Lebanon seemed to struggle to some semblance of her self, some consciousness of her daughter's dilemma. "He will marry with you?" she asked, almost indignantly. "He has spoken to your *papa?*"

Oliva bent her head to her mother's breast, and her voice

was muffled in the linens. *"Maman,* he may die before the morning!" She added miserably. "And even if he lives, his life will never be the same."

Her father's voice from the door jolted her upright. "If you mean to add to her suffering, you must keep away from her completely." He spoke in French, which only underscored the coldness of his tone.

Her mother's voice rose weakly from the bed, and she put one hand on Oliva's head. "Have you given yourself to this man?" she asked gently.

"Only my heart," Oliva whispered.

Her mother gathered her strength and her voice was loud in the room. "You will not punish her further," she said to her husband in his own tongue. "She has suffered enough, *vraiment.*"

"She forgot her duty to you and she forgot her duty to God. To leave her mother alone, to go with a man, a maiden—!"

"I forgive her. God will forgive her. You must do the same," Lebanon said wearily. "Now, both of you leave me. Must I come from my bed to make peace between you?" She closed her eyes.

Simon frowned and left the room. As Oliva pulled herself away from her mother's breast, Lebanon murmured weakly, "Do you love this boy?"

Oliva was silent, turning her eyes from her mother's. Finally she answered, "I think I will die if he does not love me."

To her great surprise, her mother smiled. "That is not the same as loving him, *cher.* But I do understand." As Oliva began to weep once more, she patted her hand gently. "I understand. And so does God."

Her mother died two days later, drifting away from life as gently as the ebb of the waters around the little cabin. One moment Oliva was listening to her breathe from the rocker, the next moment, there was only silence in the room. For the next two nights, she sat up with her mother, saying the prayers and keeping the candles burning. Whatever angers her father and brother had harbored melted away in their mutual grief, and together, they stood by Lebanon Doucet's cypress tomb, as it rested at the head of the four smaller tombs which held her lost children.

When Father LeBlanc came to make the burying, he brought news also of Emile. "His arm will heal, *cher,*" the priest told her gravely, "but *naturellement,* he cannot stay in Lafourche."

"Why not?" she asked, her mouth stretched in horror.

The priest shrugged. "And shrimp with one hand? Farm the crops, perhaps? *Non, cher, c'est impossible maintenant.* His father has sent him to his *oncle* in Baton Rouge, there to learn the law. For that," Father LeBlanc smirked, "a man does not need two hands, eh? The lawyers can thieve you well enough with only one."

At the distress in her face, the priest added, "It is hard, this loss? He was a *bon ami?*"

She nodded, mute with grief.

"Then you would wish the best for him, I know. And here, he can make no life." He appraised her gently. "It is time for you to think of making a marriage, my daughter. Now, with your mother gone, you must make a life as well."

"My father needs me," she could only say, her throat too thick for speech. She would not go by the priest again that day.

She stood by Valsin while he cut and carved the wooden tomb which would hold their mother above the ground, away from the spring and winter floods, away from the creatures and the damp mold which soon enough covered all things in the bayou. She gathered the herbs and collected the ashes which would line her tomb, to help keep off the snakes and the beetles. She bathed Lebanon and dressed her gently, lovingly, taking as long at the task as she could. This body, she thought over and over, lay with my father, gave birth to me, suckled me, held me, and wept with me, laughed with me—and perhaps no one will ever love me in that way again. Sometimes her eyes blurred so from the tears, that she had to stop her laving and layering until she could see more clearly.

The funeral itself gave scant comfort. Perhaps if Simon Doucet had allowed his wife to be buried in the chapel cemetery, then the rows of friends who would come to mourn might have offered at least a feeling of fellowship in their grief.

Oliva could recall when the Widow Antony lost her husband. A large group of neighbors gathered for the funeral dinner, as was the custom. She made a table with three long planks set on sawhorses, cooked six ovens of rice, and the widow's brother who lived only a half arpent away came with his wife and ten children, as did most of the village. This was the custom. And though the guests disposed of every single one of her flock of thirty chickens before it was over, the widow was pleased that her neighbors showed their friendship.

Because they lived so far from the village, Oliva had seen few funerals. It was not the first time she had wished that a rutted road—even a cart path—wound from their cabin to Lafourche.

At least Father LeBlanc had come. It was a comfort to have him read the prayers out of the book. But Oliva's father would have less and less to do with the priest and his church these days. "She should sleep with her children," he said gruffly to Father LeBlanc, when he said that Lebanon should rest in the Catholic cemetery. "God can find her as easily here as he can anyplace."

Oliva had draped the wooden tomb with boughs of greenery and lit the four candles at each end, but her voice was too thick to send her mother into eternity with the proper hymn. She could hardly speak, much less sing. After the funeral, when she could decently slip away, she ran to the bayou and

33

wailed her despair to the skies, screaming so loud that the birds rose in answering shrieks from all sides and the frogs were stilled into shocked silence. Throwing herself to the ground, she sobbed for her mother, for Emile, for the sad face of Valsin, the haggard eyes of her father, for her own pitiful life as it stretched before her with no hope. Oliva wept until she could not lift her head from exhaustion.

Then, as now, the bayou itself seemed to mirror her loss, and the black water and damp air made the swamp seem as sad and heavy as her heart. Only at the water's edge did she feel free to let loose all her anguish and rage. When she crept back to the cabin, barely able to stand, she stumbled to her bed and then could not find rest. For a long night, Oliva had repented that she had not buried her mother in her feather robe. But finally, come morning, she knew that she would have been wrong to do so. Though she could not say she could ever bring herself to wear it, neither could she bury such beauty in the ground. Her mother would never have wished such a fate for the work of her fingers, of that Oliva was certain.

Now she was finished at the grave for another week. She stood and wiped her hands on a fist of ferns, tucking her hair back under her *garde-soleil*. The bonnet was one of the last things she had of her mother's, and she always wore it to the grave, rain or shine. Often she had to stop herself from bringing out the feather cloak to lay over her mother. She crossed herself, whispered a brief, "*Notre Père, je vous salue Marie,*" and turned away from the burial isle. She had come thus each Sunday for almost two years. The pain was beginning to ebb, but not the emptiness.

Oliva stepped into the pirogue, settling the little dugout with her pole in the shallow water. Across the bayou, smoke came from the chimney. Papa and Valsin were back early, which meant full traps and empty plates to fill. They'd be up late, skinning by firelight, and it would be many hours before she could give in to her sadness. By then the relief of the emotion would be past, and likely she would not give in at all. But for just a moment, the silence was a small soothing.

She stood motionless, easing the boat past an open space of black water. Overhead, the live oaks and cottonwoods met in a canopy, dripping on her slowly. The air was so hushed, she could sense the fall of the raindrop before it hit. She could hear the silence of the swamp.

It did not sleep through the winter, but only drowsed. And like a drowsing body, the bayou breathed around her. With silence, it spoke, like the soft sigh of a deep rolling fog, or the closeness of mists, or the murmur of deep water flowing unseen beneath heavy lands. She turned to hear the sudden muffled flight of wet wings, hidden by the trees. Then, on the other side, the plop of caught rain, from a leaf tired of holding the burden of it.

The creatures of the swamp, she knew, were sensed more than seen. The eye had to be quick to catch the signs. A slither of green, as a snake slid through a patch of duckweed, just under the shallow bank water. The dark, barklike head of the alligator, partly submerged, his slow-winking eye just breaking the surface, then easing soundlessly away. The bobcat and the bear, who could melt away into shadow without bending a fern tip. That was the bayou in winter. Lonely, ghostly, and waiting.

A sudden rustle caused Oliva to turn and face the forest, and then she smiled, remembering one of the sole exceptions to the swamp's solitary season. A white-tailed buck moved into the clearing, the points of his antlers glistening with the rain.

It was nearly the end of rut, so this one must have been unlucky, she thought, slowly turning her head and keeping her body still. He's got a hot heart, and he's careless.

These were the few months when the whitetail stalked the woods with impudence, sometimes many bucks after the same doe. When rivals met, they battled raucously, goring each other and snorting furiously, stamping and crashing through the palmetto. Sometimes bucks would lock horns, and then they would starve, if they weren't taken by alligators or muskets first. When they found a doe, they stayed with her only a few days, then they began the restless search again, to find and fight for another.

In that short season, the bucks were the only threat to the stillness all around. This one looked worn out from his long campaign.

The buck moved from tree to tree. In his winter coat of gray—in the blue, the hunters called it—he was almost invisible among the ash-colored moss hanging from the branches. All at once, he stiffened and bent his head, staring directly into her eyes.

Don't never shoot the buck with the chair on his head, *cher,* she could hear her father's voice in her mind, and this one had a rack, though small. But then her eyes widened as the buck moved further out into the clearing to see her.

Around his leg, he dragged a trap. High up, it had caught him, and now she could see that his eyes were not the normally timid eyes of the whitetail, not even the more defiant stare of the rutting bucks in this season. This one had eyes of torment. She moved her hand slowly to her musket, thinking surely he would whirl away.

He did not. The buck moved slightly closer to her, still gazing into Oliva's eyes.

Without hesitation, she fluidly shouldered her gun, sighted, and waited—still the buck stood, unflinching. Though Valsin had taught her well and she was never without her musket, she had only rarely shot a creature. She instantly thought of her mother, who had never, for twenty winters in the swamp, taken down game. That was a job for the men. But her mother was dead.

She squeezed. The sharp crack of the musket shattered the silence of the swamp, and far away she heard the alarm cries of herons as they took flight. She wedged her pirogue back again in the mud and went to the fallen buck. His eyes were still open, but the torment was gone, already glazed over in sightless opacity. She knelt at his side.

The trap had caught the buck between knee and hoof, had rubbed away the flesh from countless old wounds and scars, until the leg looked less like fur and flesh than dead bark. His hoof was larger than prairie whitetails, for like all marsh animals, he needed extra support in the spongy ground. The trap around him was worn thin from miles of grass. It was shiny, silver-delicate, like a wrought pendant for a lady's bodice.

No doe'd have you, Oliva thought, with that rattling horror hung on like a harness. Thoughts of Emile stung her deeply, coming as they often did countless times, when she was undefended against them. The old women of Lafourche had whispered the same thing about him, that no woman would have a one-handed man. She had not seen him again, but she knew he was in Baton Rouge. Despite their whispers, he had married almost a year ago. Perhaps in the city, a man's hands mattered less. When she pictured him, often in the night, she recalled how he had looked with his face so close to hers.

She shook the memory away, taking sure strong hands to the trap and removing it. Your quest for a mate has been surely a torture, she thought, smoothing the soft guard hairs on the buck's throat. But perhaps Valsin can make something beautiful from your pain, yes? She released the boat again from the mud and poled across to tell her father and brother that there was fresh venison to be hung.

That night she stood by the stove frying the *grillades* the way her father liked them, with plenty of pepper and bacon fat. A pot of boiled crabs simmered, seasoned as her mother showed her with bay, thyme, onions, and the little red peppers. Simon Doucet was honing his skinning knife on the whetstone. Valsin was picking a duck. He sat with his broad thighs apart before the fire with the fowl between his knees, softly ripping away fingerfuls of down.

"He makes rain for the hunt tomorrow, papa?" her brother asked her father, glancing up at Oliva with a grin.

Simon did everything with a certain solemnity. Oliva could scarcely imagine her father a young man like Valsin. Surely he had frowned in such a serious way, when at *grand-mère's* breast. Even when he told a joke to men at a cockfight, he brought a dignity to the telling. Now he considered his only son's question as though there were a hundred likely responses.

"Possible," he said. "Possible He makes rain."

With a teasing twist to her mouth, Oliva set down the platter of grilled venison liver before her two men. "Perhaps I should go along with you, then. Somebody needs to be sure we get our larder full." She spoke half in French, half in English to her father, which was her habit. He, as usual, pretended to understand only the French.

"One buck, and she's a hunter," Valsin said, reaching for the plate. "Maybe she should take her musket to the next

38

fais-do-do. With luck, we might see more than a buck in rut this winter, *hein?*"

Oliva put her hands on her hips and tossed her thick black hair back from her shoulders. "Yes, and when I need advice on the rutting, *mo' frère,* I know where to come for it."

"Oliva," her father grimaced, "enough." He added gently, "Let us have some peace this night, eh?" He gestured to the pile of muskrats waiting to be skinned. "Lest they curl up before we can take the knife to these."

"Her tongue'd dry the thickest pelt," Valsin teased, pulling a mock-mournful frown. "Nobody will ever rid us of her, such a hot mouth."

Oliva moved swiftly to cuff her brother, but the knock at the cabin door stayed her hand. Her eyes questioned her father, but she moved quickly back to the stove, her back to the caller, as was fitting. Simon nodded to Valsin to loose the lock. Now a familiar voice called out, and she knew why old Juno hadn't bayed.

Father LeBlanc bent his head in the door. The priest said, "Ah, good, you're all here. Can a man get a cup of coffee on this evil night?"

Simon pulled out a chair near the fire while Valsin took the father's wet oilcoat. Oliva added more grounds to the hot water and set him out a tin cup.

"Where else would we be?" Valsin asked, settling himself again.

The priest replied, "Well, you might be sitting at Guidry's fire these days, from what I hear. Or is it Hebert's you still favor?"

Oliva grinned and turned away. Everyone in the parish knew that Valsin couldn't make up his mind between Marie Guidry or Caroline Hebert. Both fathers had begun to frown at her brother with impatience when at the Mass, and the girls were entirely too cordial to each other for belief.

Valsin said, *"Bénissez-moi, mo' père.* And bless my bride

when she comes." He added in English, "Whoever the wench will be."

Oliva reached past him and poured them each a cup of the readied coffee, nodding shyly to the priest. She hadn't seen him within the cabin walls since her mother's burial, and his black frock made her feel unsteady all over again.

"So did you come out on this wet night to talk about my wretched weddin' day?" Valsin was asking.

Simon set aside his cup and tilted back in his chair. Oliva could tell by his manner that he'd known the priest was coming and why.

"Actually," Father LeBlanc said gently, "it's not your banns I'm thinking of tonight, *mon fils.*" He looked point-edly up at Oliva with a smile. Simon and Valsin followed his gaze. "Paul Bellard has come to me once more, asking me to offer his suit. The year of mourning is far past, and he feels it is proper now to speak."

Oliva crossed her arms. "He has spoken before," she said.

The priest shrugged. "This I know. As does every soul in the parish. But he had hoped you'd reconsider, my daughter, and accept him at last."

She frowned and turned away.

"He is a good man, yes?" The priest turned to Simon with open hands of supplication. "He has a solid house with thirty arpents of land. Good stock, fat hogs, a fine stallion, and two brood mares—"

"He is old," Oliva said softly. "Nearly thirty, they say."

She could feel the tension in the room and knew that Simon must finally be the one to break it.

"Not so old," her father said at last. "No older for a man, than you are for a woman."

Even though she knew it was coming, it hurt nonetheless. She was nearly seventeen. Two years past, she should have wed. Most her age had two children. If her mother hadn't died, perhaps she would have posted banns by now, but with the death, her father needed her, Oliva thought, her mouth turning stubborn, and Paul Bellard has old eyes, whatever his age. "He is a farmer," she said, and her voice crisped with scorn. Her sadness made her shorter than she should have been, she knew, but it suddenly seemed that there was no refuge anywhere from the eyes of the men.

"So what do you want then, a fine merchant?" her brother laughed. "A fisherman, perhaps? A prince?" He looked to his father for support. "If she won't take a farmer, she won't take nine men of ten in the village. And then she can live on the bayou all her life. Is that what you want for her? A life like our mother had?"

Oliva's jaw jutted out like a plough. "*Sacré nom!* Would that be so bad, then?"

"Not if you want to end up in your grave by thirty-five, as she did. Too far away from the simplest comforts, even a doctor, so that the damp of the swamp became part of her bones. Not if she wants," he added solemnly in French to Simon, "to be *une vieille* by the time she's a mother once."

Oliva said sharply, "An old woman! *You're* older than I am, you should tend to your own life, brother, and let me tend to mine."

"That's what I do, me," Valsin said. "I post the banns next Saturday. Marie Guidry will be my wife."

Oliva smiled, her whole face softening. "For true? Ah, Valsin, that is good news. She is a fine girl. A good choice."

"This is good news!" Father LeBlanc said heartily. "And you will move to the village?"

"Her father will have it so. We will take the side parcel, ten arpents on the bayou, and her brother and I will shrimp." He gestured to the pile of pelts on the cabin floor. "Except in the season, when I'll trap with the old man here." He leaned across and slapped his father on the back. "Don't want to leave all the rats in the world to one pair of hands."

"This is fine. A good woman, a good choice. Next year, you watch, I'll be christening your first son. The good God knows we must change to grow. Which is why," the priest said, turning his gaze back once more to her, "you must make a choice as well, Oliva. Even the Holy Mother did not grieve so long. You cannot stay out here in the bayou with your father all alone, it's no life for a young woman."

"And who will tend to him if I do not?"

Simon spoke up then. "Perhaps I shall post the banns as well."

With that, both brother and sister turned to their father in amazement. He shrugged. "Is possible. Perhaps in the spring."

Valsin grinned. "The Widow Broussard?"

Simon allowed himself the smallest of smiles. "Possible."

Valsin laughed and slapped the table hard, jolting the coffee cups. "That's the way, *mo' vieux,* the fires are not out until they're buried in the ground, eh? She will have you?"

As the men continued to discuss the widow and her holdings, Oliva turned from the table with sorrow. Her mother had not been buried two years, yet so soon her father was talking of a new wife! Everything would be changing. Papa would move away from the little cabin, Valsin would have a new family in the village, and only she stood like a crane with her feet trapped in the mud, unable to move forward into spring.

The priest was making ready to leave with congratulations all around. As his hand touched the door, he turned back to her. "Shall I tell Bellard you'll receive him, my daughter?"

She kept her back to the door. *"Non, mo' père,"* she said quietly.

Simon began, "We will think on this more, perhaps talk on it, eh? In a few days—"

She turned. "You may tell M'sieu Bellard that I will most likely attend the *fais-do-do* at LeBleu's. I will save him a waltz."

Father LeBlanc bowed once, with a sideways smile she thought most inappropriate for such a holy man. "Amen,

42

cher. Since you first took communion, I knew you had a mind of your own, yes."

Oliva swiftly remembered the old nun who had taught her, the pale wrinkled face nestling in the white fluted bonnet, the thin drying lips sharing the story of Christ's fate. The nun's hands, too, dry and bloodless. With a strong vindictiveness which seemed meant for Oliva alone, she had said, "And a foul burly soldier stepped from the crowd with a long spear, the kind that will pierce a wild boar. He looked upon the Good God of Heaven, bruised and torn by the nails, and he put the spear to Our Savior's side. Then he drew back his arm and with all the weight of his shoulder, he leaned on it, until the spear slipped between Jesus' ribs and deep, deep into the sacred flesh."

Oliva had shuddered, her eyes wild and defiant with horror. Later, when Father LeBlanc asked, she refused to say she hated the soldier on Calvary.

"You think on the gifts of the good God, yes," Father LeBlanc was saying now, "and what He wants for His children."

After the priest left, Oliva's anger simmered higher, as she pictured first Emile's white face when last she saw him, then her mother's pale face in death, then her brother leaving, then her father standing in the chapel next to the pinkly-plump Widow Broussard. When she remembered her mother as she was at the last, she recalled most her painfully thin arms, with the muscles a lifetime of work had hardened gone loose and slack; the gray hair, scanty over the angled skull; the eyes fevered with pain from the lung disease which ate her from within.

She scowled. Yet some women wore fine shoes, kept thirty laying hens, and got fat on the profits. Oliva lifted one bare foot and examined her heel for any tinge of yellow, as she had every night since she was ten. No yellow yet. Yellow heels were a certain sign of spinsterhood. Tante Thérèse told often and mournfully of first seeing the fatal tinge of yellow on her heels at the age of seventeen—and now she was in her thirties and, of course, without hope, since no man on the bayou wanted such an old woman. Not unless she was a widow and came with fifty arpents of land along the river. Oliva slammed the stove lid in place and yanked off her apron.

Valsin kissed her cheek absentmindedly, already absorbed in his new plans. Her father watched her jerk her apron onto its hook and said, "Always I will have only one wife, Oliva. No matter how many widows I wed." He touched her elbow lightly. "But it has been two years. It is not good for two old ones to be alone, if they can care for each other, yes?"

"I could care for you, papa," she said, her voice suddenly thick with pain.

"You want to care for me? To make me happy?"

She nodded.

"Then make a marriage with Bellard. Have a fine grandson who will set the traps when your papa's knees ache with the winter wet. Make a good home I can come to, when the widow grows cold."

She rolled her eyes.

He shrugged. "Colder, then." He squeezed her elbow gently. "That will make me happy, *cher.* Save me a place to sit in the sun. That will be the kernel of my life. This is only the rind."

Oliva stayed awake for many hours, far past the time when Valsin's snores had steadied themselves into their nightly rhythm. Usually, the night noises of her father and brother thrummed through the little cabin and kept away the cold in her heart. This night, she could only think of traps and frozen waters, dances which whirled into corners, and Paul Bellard, the best indigo farmer in the village of Lafourche.

She said her rosary, thinking of Bellard. Perhaps it would be best, after all. It was so hard with only Valsin and her

44

father for company, as bleak and grim, sometimes, as the gray sky and the drip, drip, drip of the water on the roof from the sodden trees. Sometimes she wished she might never wake, might never have to kindle another fire in the stove, might never have to wring another load of wash, might never clean another catfish, might sleep in peaceful, untouchable, unsorrowing invisibility next to her mother and her sisters forever. But then, the dawn came, a bird called, and she felt its every note in her limbs and her heart, filled with a wild restless urge to run anywhere, to anyone, so long as it was away. Papa said that the best time to scorn pain was when it was boundless. His words had haunted her, and somehow comforted her during the last two years.

She heard thunder far away on the river, a gentle neighborly sound in bed. It came like something thickly padded, bales of cotton dropping. Or like the distant collapse of heavy walls. When the cross reached her fingers, she balled the beads in her hand and smiled secretly in the dark. It was the last effort she made each night, to end her day with a smile, so that she would not make unhappy tracks across her face. She closed her eyes and imagined she was lovely.

Oliva had often heard her father say, A man is among friends when he lives on Lafourche. The bayou, which ribboned out from the Mississippi and wove its way through small villages and communities, tiny hamlets, past swamp cabins and fishing pirogues, was the lifeline of the people, whatever their business. Often you could not say where Lafourche began and ended, for all the weaving, crossing waters. And so it was with the bayou people, too.

In the bayou, Simon told her, a man who is an *ami* of one is an *ami* of his family, from *bébé* to *grandpère* to *cousin secondaire*. A relative is more than related, he is blood and will stand to the blood against all outsiders. If Jules has done insult to one close to Alcée, then he will have Alcée to answer to. Has Alcée lost his money? Then Alcée's friend will feel sad with him and share what he can.

And children? It was said that you could stand anywhere on the bayou, throw a stick, and you'd hit a child. Likely a cousin. Oliva knew of four different families with more than a dozen children each, who took *le bon Dieu's* advice to "be fruitful" to heart. Everyone knew that God smiled on big families, and a husband and wife with only one or two, like her own parents—? A sad shrug. *Ah, c'est triste.*

The idea of children both lured and frightened Oliva. Sometimes she felt that having a child of her own would be the only way she would ever feel that she belonged to anything, that anything belonged to her forever and completely. Other times she was sure that a child would be the end of whatever freedom she might find, the death of that fierce spark within her that made her believe she was somehow worth more than simply the sum of her parts. A child meant life eternal. A child also could mean death.

"But *maman* was never well," Valsin often reminded her. "You're stronger, *cher*. Your husband will need plenty of beds, *hein*? You don't never turn him away, him."

Maman never turned against *papa,* Oliva thought in wonder. She could scarcely recall a time when the word *non!* came from her mother's lips. Perhaps, had she said no more often, she might have counted fewer graves in the little island across the bayou. Never once did she refuse. She stood by the stove every day of the year, helping to dress the skins, to bring in the firewood, to care for the chickens, to weave, to sew, to fish from her pirogue, to harvest the small vegetables in their time, and to keep her family warm, dry, and fed. She wiped at the moisture that dripped from the cabin walls, killed the ants and lizards and spiders which always found their way into every niche, and axed the snakes she found round the cabin door. When she had no soap, she used bayou mud. She gathered the blackberries and figs, washed out the boats, patched the nets, and cleaned the traps. She scraped away a life for them in the swamp, and she did not complain.

But Lebanon died an old woman. And in all her memories, Oliva could not search out a time when she had seen her mother waltz with her father at a ball or sing while she cooked.

And yet, and yet . . . the sound of her laugh came easily to Oliva's mind, as familiar as the cry of the geese overhead.

Come to think of it, few *femmes* danced after they were wed, for few husbands thought it seemly. Make a marriage and give up the promenade? It was a poor bargain, that, to be planted at every *fais-do-do* like a cypress.

When you love, her mother told her, no trouble seems too great, no task too hard.

But if there is no one to love? she had asked wistfully.

Marry, and the love will come.

To Oliva, that was the same sort of promise that the priest made. Be worthy, and peace will come. Be peaceful, and faith will come. Be faithful, and paradise will come forever. Always the promises. But no one could tell her why many of the worthy seemed less happy than the less worthy. And why many of the married showed less bent towards love than those who were still unwed. Why was it always the married who said that love did not matter? Why did a man rush to waltz with his favorite until he wed her—and then he never yearned to dance with her again?

Oliva sometimes suspicioned that she learned more at *le promenade* than at *le catéchisme*. The last three *fais-do-dos* had been at LeBleu's stable, for his land rose higher from the water, and the horses dragged through less mud to be hitched. Each Saturday, Acadian families from the bayou's farthest reaches made their way by pirogue or calèche to meet their neighbors, wherever a hall was large enough to hold them.

Those families with the most land on the river usually came by calèche, the wooden carriages with rawhide seats which could be raised or lowered to keep the skirts of the daughters from the mud. In the pockets of those skirts, they carried shot bags full of silver to gamble at *vingt-et-un.*

Babies were put in a back room where an old woman watched them, murmuring, *"Fais dormi, mes enfants,"* go to sleep. The weekly ball took the same name, and the *fais-do-do* became the place where married love and would-be-married love could grow under the watchful eyes of *les vieux,* the old ones who kept the old ways intact.

Now, as Valsin poled the pirogue upriver towards Le-Bleu's, Oliva sat a little straighter in her seat. She liked to believe that anyone on the bank would know it was Simon Doucet's daughter by her figure, even if they did not recognize the boat.

Her black dress fit neatly, her slim back was erect, her neck was proud. Though she was still in half-mourning, if they looked they might see a glimpse of ribbon at her throat, another matching one at her waist. Something of assertion in the crispness of her *garde-soleil,* which did not hang down limp and meek like the sunbonnets of the old women.

They might say to themselves, "This one will have her way, *hein?* She will make all winds blow in her chosen direction. She will please herself and be her own good luck."

Luck. The priest did not believe in luck, but said that all plans were God's. Oliva could remember her mother telling her that she had found peace once she believed that. But such an uncertainty seemed horrifying to Oliva. If she were to believe that her own life was not in her control, she could not rest. Fortune was a gamble, it seemed to her. There were those in the village who could never win, no matter what cards they drew. Others, no more worthy, rarely lost.

Oliva put one hand on her clean dancing shoes, wiping off

the night dew, and tucked the other into a fold of her skirt, lest it become spotted like a guinea egg. She settled the large pot of shrimp gumbo more securely at her feet. Fortune, she decided, must be tracked, baited, and trapped, just like the rarest creature in the deepest woods.

Her father caught her eye and nodded at the pot. "Plenty of peppers, *'tite?*"

She cocked her head. "I make it like always, papa. Like you like it."

He glanced towards the sky as though checking for clouds. "I hear M'sieu Bellard likes his gumbo with plenty of peppers, him."

She glanced skywards also, as though the clouds themselves held some sudden fascination. "Perhaps he best eat from Adele Naquin's pot, then, she puts enough peppers in to fell a mule." She dropped her head and smiled slightly. "At least I heard this, me."

Valsin laughed back from the bow, "You better be sweet to the old man tonight, *cher,* you may have to make the last waltz with him."

Simon Doucet said softly, "Is possible that dance is taken."

"Is more than possible, papa. Is sure as dogs will bark at the moon," she replied. With one hand, she flipped her bonnet sides back so that her face would show and smoothed her throat ribbon.

Valsin bumped the pirogue among the others tied to the bank, more than thirty boats in all moored before LeBleu's long hall. Nine buggies were already hitched, more were coming up the levee, and the cluster and welcoming cries of arrivals at the door rose over the waters and made her lift her head and set her mouth to a smile, conscious once more that every face marked its own trail.

I might be seventeen, she thought calmly, I might be a trapper's daughter, but I am worthy of any man on Lafourche.

LeBleu's was a large cabin, the biggest on the bayou, with a special hall attached to the front for fêtes. A bride and groom who did not count themselves friends of LeBleu were forced to make a sorry *bal de noces* indeed, for few homes along the river could accommodate as many guests or dance as many feet.

As always when she walked through the wide door of LeBleu's towards the back where the food table stretched long and full, she was struck by the number of trees that must have fallen to build the place—and how quickly the big floor was filled by so many shoes.

Their little cabin in the swamp never looked so empty and meager to her as when she came to Lafourche. Its split cypress walls were held together with daubed mud, the three rooms had only one window each, and always the head room was taken with drying skins, so that she must almost stoop to stand by the stove. In the good seasons, she could bake in the rounded outdoors mud oven, but now with the rains, she must do all she could with a balky black stove and sooty irons.

But at least she could sit on the broad gallery facing the bayou when she had finished, and the breeze was soft.

LeBleu's kitchen was three times the size of her own, and still the women finished some of their cooking outside, standing about and nattering like mockingbirds. The Alidores had three *bébés,* all at the one time. But yes, for true! Who would have thought ol' Alidore had it in him, that skinny lil' fellow, eh? . . . They say the Spanish fight the British . . . *Mon Dieu,* not more war! *C'est bon,* I hope they kill every last mother's son . . . Was it true one of the Babin boys shot his brother by mistake for a deer in the swamp? The talk rose up with the good cooking smells, drawing the children who darted about, snatching at this morsel or that, pulling on their mothers' skirts.

In the other corner of the levee, the men shared the news, their heads together earnestly, occasionally interrupted by a sharp laugh and a slap on the back. Only the young had eyes for each other, as they lounged in tight groups about the side of the house. Oliva stopped and spoke to Edna, Eudora, and Eunice, the daughters of old Baptiste, hailing other *jeunes filles* who passed, kissing the cheeks of a few. She resolutely kept her eyes from the gaggle of young men at the corner of the house, though she noticed that hardly any of the girls who spoke to her could keep their eyes from drifting over her shoulder to one boy or another.

LeBleu's was more barn than house, truth be known. But with its wide cypress floor, wooden benches all round, the room with the beds to one side for the *bébés,* the two others for the men to play cards and the women to gamble their chicken money on *vingt-et-un,* it was perfect for the *fais-do-do* or the wedding feasts which would fill it every Saturday night in the spring.

She rounded the corner and found the usual group of spectators, mostly men and boys, watching the snakefight. When the season turned drier, horse races would draw the crowds, but in this time of damp and mud, cockfights and snakefights were common.

A large drygoods box sat in the yard. A king snake and a cottonmouth lay within. She could smell the strong odor of the moccasin, and she stopped to peer inside over the shoulders.

They looked as though they would never fight. Each lay neatly coiled, head pillowed on its body in a state of what seemed to be serene repose. The men and boys watched silently, careful not to move abruptly or jostle the box. They made their bets only when they moved back from the snakes, almost as if the snakes could hear the sums being offered.

The snakes lay motionless, each coiled like a freshly painted ornament made of metal. Oliva felt lulled herself by the heat of the cooking fires behind her, the curious, almost medicinal smell of the cottonmouth, and the hypnotic effect of staring into the quiet box.

A group of *filles* went giggling behind her, lifting neat bonnets off their heads, their hands to their mouths in joint mirth. She turned to wave to one or two, and when she turned her head back again to the box, she blinked.

Only the eyes of the snakes seemed alive, but there was a different air about them now. Suddenly, all the heads of the spectators came up at once. One of the snakes moved. The cottonmouth lifted its tail less than half an inch. Short, thick, black, with a spade-shaped head, the snake looked as if it knew that it carried death with one bite.

When the moccasin twitched its tail, the king snake moved its head slightly. The moccasin then lifted its own head, and the two snakes seemed to actually see each other for the first time. The king snake was a handsome, sleek cord of black and gold. His delicate tongue wickered in and out almost dreamily. The moccasin smell grew stronger. Then, as though in agreement, the two snakes lowered their heads once more and gazed at each other calmly.

Oliva drew back from the box when a girl called her name, gesturing to her to come and help carry a platter of sausages inside. As she moved, there was a sound like a quickly drawn sigh from the box. She looked back and saw that the king snake had the moccasin—or the other way around. She could not tell which, it had happened that swiftly. The two reptiles were an indistinguishable mass of writhing muscle, black and black and gold. Emile Benoit was doing a kind of excited dance behind her, shouting at the king snake to finish off the cottonmouth.

The king snake, with the cottonmouth's head between his jaws, was now carefully taking his hold, wrapping himself around the moccasin's body. There was a muffled snap, like a twig breaking under a man's shoe. The moccasin lashed its tail a few times, then died with its dazzling white mouth open. The men laughed and cursed, according to their luck, and Oliva turned to help carry the sausages into LeBleu's, picking up her own kettle from between her feet.

She nestled her pot of gumbo down among the platters of fish fritters, chicken fricassee, and sausage and rice. The oily rich smells of the food made her stomach feel suddenly hollow. But it was the end of the table which drew her closer.

There, all in a row, were a dozen *gâteaux*, white and yellow and spice cakes, topped with apples, cinnamon, spiced cherries, and cream. Sugar was something Simon seemed to forget to buy when he went to the village; there was rarely ever more than was needed for the sweet, strong coffee he and Valsin drank morning, noon, and night.

One cake was slightly off center on its plate, as though it had been set down in a hurry. Just a slight nudge with one knuckle would right it, would only dislodge a little of the sugar frosting—

Oliva pulled her hand back abruptly as Marie Guidry swooped upon her from a flock of chattering girls. "Oliva!" she cried, embracing her quickly, kissing first one cheek then the other. "I'm so happy you came, and you look *très charmante* in that red ribbon. Did you make your gumbo? Papa says he will eat no one else's tonight!"

Marie's arms were on hers, her face all smiles, but her eyes scarcely left the wide-open door.

Oliva smiled and took both her hands, lowering her voice. "He's out with the men, *cher*, he'll be in to ask for the first waltz in time."

Marie colored redly, squeezing her close. "Ah, you are too wise for one so young, *'tite cousine.*"

Oliva whispered in her ear, "Soon, you will call me little *sister*, yes?"

Marie pulled back, her eyes wide and hopeful. "For true?"

Oliva put a finger to her lips and turned the girl around, pointing her towards the door where Valsin was just coming in. Gently pushing her towards him, she added, "Me, I would not have him. But maybe you can make something worth wearing out of such a sorry skin."

Marie's face glowed when she saw Valsin come towards her. Oliva could see that he kept his hands to his sides with an effort, kept his face bland with only the strongest will. The two of them walked docilely to the punch barrel, unaware that twenty pairs of eyes followed them, twenty mouths turned up in knowing grins.

Oliva felt a happy pang at the obvious joy in her brother's face, the stiff formality of his shoulders as he almost, but not quite, reached down to touch Marie on her bare arm. She had never felt such giddy excitement, that painful longing she sensed in Marie when she saw Valsin come through the door. Even with Emile, her feelings had not had enough time to ripen to that yearning. Cut off at the bud, she would never know what might have flowered from his first kiss.

Just once, Oliva vowed, I mean to feel that passion. And then I'll chop some farmer's cotton, cook some farmer's gumbo, and carry some farmer's *bébés* till my arms ache. But not until. By the Holy Virgin, not until I feel what Marie feels now, me.

The music men were stepping up on the playing platform, three of them with their fiddles and a new man Oliva did not know. The usual fiddlers were familiar: Herman Bourque played at LeBleu's every Saturday night, and his high, loud voice led the other two *secondaires* in the rhythms that kept the dancers moving.

But this new man held an instrument Oliva had never seen. There were always strangers at any *fais-do-do,* for news of a fete went up and down the bayou easily. LeBleu's was wide, and strangers were welcome, so long as they made no trouble. But few of *les autres* ever joined the music men—and never before could she recall seeing such an odd box among the fiddles.

"Who is this one?" Oliva asked, as Adele Naquin set down her pot, a huge cauldron which she could scarcely lift to the table.

She glanced back over her shoulder and wiped her upper

lip, where a faint fuzz was turning darker with moisture. "Ah, that is the *Allemand* from Vacherie, he makes a visit with old Bourque, they say."

Poor Adele better have some miracle within her pot, Oliva thought privately, for she's not as old as I am, and already she looks as weary as a biddy with too many chicks. "You make your good gumbo, *cher?*" she asked politely.

"With enough peppers to curl a black moustache," Adele said grinning, rolling her eyes.

Paul Bellard had a black moustache.

Before Oliva could recover, the music men struck up the first tune and dancers flooded past her to the floor. There old Baptiste's daughters, all three of them very pretty, whirled with partners quickly chosen when the first notes began.

Like most of the young girls, their arms and hands were bare, and Oliva smiled to herself when she remembered what they had to do to look so lovely.

Old Baptiste's daughters were dark-haired, slender, and *piquantes.* Alas, they were also all of cotton-hoeing age. This last was what old Baptiste prized above all else, because his boys were too young to work the fields. In the spring, the girls chopped cotton from sunup to sundown, with only a few hours to rest when the sun was hottest. Each time Oliva came to Lafourche, she could see Edna, Eudora, and Eunice going up and down the rows, hoeing Baptiste's cotton.

But on Saturday night, they blossomed like the crape myrtles before their front door. They always took care to wear long sleeves and gloves while hoeing, because they knew all the young girls let their arms and hands go bare at the dance. And because they wore shoes and stockings to the fete, it was all right to go barefoot in the fields.

No young women could risk the complexion of an alligator, so they fixed their *garde-soleils* with curtains, protecting their shoulders and the shields which stuck out stiffly on each side, narrowing their field of vision so that a stranger might walk up to them and they would never know until he faced them!

Of course, even facing them, he would scarcely see them if Baptiste's daughters did not wish to be seen. Their disguise was complete.

But how different the girls looked on Saturday night! So sweet and fair was the lace at their necks, so flouncing their skirts. Their soiled and tanned feet of the weekdays might be pinched in dancing shoes, but it never showed when they danced.

Oliva guessed that more than one of Baptiste's daughters took off her shoes and stockings the minute she left the hall for home, savoring the cool mud of the levee.

And then on Monday morning, they were back to the cotton patch, camouflage complete once more. She was grateful poling a pirogue did not make for such hard callouses on the hands. She would rather tan skins than pick cotton any day.

The fiddler was singing the second verse now,

> J'ai passé devant ta porte,
> J'ai crié, 'Bye-bye la belle,'
> Y a pas personne qu'a pas repondu
> Oh y yaie, mon coeur me fait mal!

It was the saddest, sweetest song, and the dancers loved it most. "I passed in front of your door, I cried out, 'Bye-bye, beautiful one,' no one answered, oh, my heart hurts me!"

To her surprise, the German man moved forward on the platform with his box, and a strange new sound changed the old song forever. Some of the dancers stopped, amazed and delighted. Others whirled even faster, urged on by the new music which cried like a baby, moaned like a bullfrog, and shrieked like a hawk with a rabbit.

In that moment, Paul Bellard stood before her, bowing stiffly from the waist. *"Allons promenade,"* he said, taking her hand almost before she had offered it. She felt a swift flurry of mingled hope and anxiety—and something else: the stiffening of her spine which presaged annoyance.

He turned her into the current of dancers expertly, with a decade of dancing showing in his touch, his grip round her waist. And then the music caught her and for a full chorus of the song, her feet sang along, skipping over the cypress floor effortlessly, and she never cared who held her or why.

But then Paul Bellard began to speak, and her heart fell from the swirl of dancers, her feet felt once more confined in heavy shoes. "I be putting in four more arpents of corn this spring, me," he said bravely, watching her face. "Four more of cotton, too. Got me a good dairy cow."

Oliva smiled vaguely, straining to hear above him to the music of that strange box.

"She's freshenin' good."

"What?" Oliva almost stumbled, she was so suddenly out of step with Bellard.

The man flushed slightly. "She's a fine milker."

They were close to the music now, and the German man smiled down at her, tapping his foot in time to that wondrous noise he made. "What is that instrument the stranger plays?" she asked Bellard.

"Accordion, he says. From the *Bayou des Allemands.* I seen a squeezebox like that in Baton Rouge last year, me. You like it?"

"It's a miracle," she said wonderingly. "I never knew music to speak so."

The musicians were finishing the song now, and many of the dancers were singing along,

> Moi, j'ai été congner à la porte
> Quands ils ont rouvert à la porte
> Moi, j'ai vu des chandelles allumées,
> Tout le tour de son cercueil.

Oliva sang with the squeezebox, her eyes almost closed in joy, for the delicious yearning in the song. "I had been knocking at the door, when they opened the door, me, I saw some lighted candles all around her coffin . . ."

And then the music ended, the dancers stopped, and couples broke up, men to one side, women to the other, as was their custom. Only the married women and the old ones sat on the benches, though; the young girls and the men stood round, waiting for the music to send them back out on the floor. Some of the married men waited, at least as many as sat in the card room, for it was acceptable for a married man to dance with a young girl, so long as it was not too often, but never could a woman dance once she was wed. No husband could allow such a thing.

Oliva returned Bellard's bow, escaped to the edge of the women, and took up the punch ladle. She sipped, watching him over the edge. He was well liked by the others, it seemed, for when he approached the men at their bowl, they spoke to him, slapped his arm, and laughed. Perhaps they laughed because he danced with her. Perhaps they felt her destiny was already decided, just like Bellard's milk cow.

She wondered if Valsin talked with Marie of his muskrats and his traps, and how many of each he hoped to have by spring. She handed the ladle to the next girl in line, smoothing her red ribbons. Well, she had promised a waltz and he had it. Let Father LeBlanc dance the next one with him, if he thought him such a man of parts. Farmers! Did they think of naught else but brood stock and crops?

The fiddles sprang to life with a flurry, and just as Oliva noticed that her father was leading Widow Broussard to the floor, a hand touched her bare elbow. She turned to see the German stranger at her side.

"Will you dance?" he asked, the accent sounding almost as strange as his music box.

She hesitated, glancing around for her brother or father. One held Marie's plate for her, watching her nibble at rice as though each grain were a flower; one danced the widow in a weaving ring, his face pink with pleasure and pride. Her feet itched to join the rhythm, and she knew if she stood long enough, Bellard would come to claim her. Few others would ask, if they saw her in his embrace too often.

She laid a hand on the newcomer's arm, glancing up at him curiously. "You know *L'Avance?*" It was the five-part dance done only by her people, and she doubted he could even recognize the music. Perhaps that was why he had left the music men.

"Mais oui," he grinned down at her gaping mouth. "You try me, yes?"

He spoke French to her! Not well, with an accent which sounded as though it curbed his tongue like a bit, but still, he knew enough to say the words.

And he knew enough to lead her into the first of the five parts of *L'Avance* as well, she quickly saw. They moved in the intricate square dance, in and out with the darting, swooping couples, into the second part, the *Petit Salut,* and he asked, "Your name, if you please?"

She gripped his arm a little more firmly, for he was moving her swiftly, surely, and she dared not stumble. She felt eyes on them both, caught a brief glimpse of Valsin and Marie staring at the German as he whisked her past, and replied, "Doucet, M'sieu."

He was not watching the dancers, but looked only at her. When she saw how insistently he gazed down, she averted her eyes, and then saw her father watching them also, holding a cup for the widow, whose plump face was petulant and incredulous all at once.

Her heart was hammering wildly with the reel and also the stares, but she lifted her chin defiantly and returned the German's gaze. "And yours, M'sieu?"

"I am called Joseph. Joseph Weitz. I come from the *Bayou des Allemands,* you know it? I come to play *die Zieh-harmonika,* eh, the accordion, you call it. Did you hear?"

The man had the reddest hair she had ever seen. Next to the Acadian men who surrounded him, he looked like a blaze of light with his fiery hair and his lighter skin; clearly not a farmer, his hands were not rough and calloused like Bellard, not a trapper neither, not a scar on his thumbs anywhere. Yet he obviously was used to work, his arms and shoulders told her that. "I heard," she smiled up at him, "and I thought it was cries of the angels."

He smiled broadly, a slow, warm grin that she felt to the roots of her hair. "Cries of the angels," he murmured.

"It made me want to promenade myself, me!"

Now he whirled her around for the third part, the *Grand Salut,* and the music went faster still, with all of the couples facing each other toe-to-toe in two lines. Weaving in and out, her bare hand grazing the bare hands of twenty other girls, her bare arms embraced by twenty other men, she kept her eyes on this German, and felt his eyes on her even when she turned her back. When he claimed her again, clutching her firmly, she said, "And what do you do besides make music with angels, M'sieu?"

"I make beer, *M'amselle* Doucet. The finest in all *Lousiane.*"

She laughed low in her throat.

"This is funny to you?" he asked in English.

She shook her head, still laughing. "Papa makes whiskey, him," she replied in the same tongue. "Valsin say it is so bad he must shut his eyes to drink it."

The German laughed with her, squeezing her tighter, as the music went into the fourth part of the reel, *Les Visites.* "Well, to tell a truth, I make the *only* beer in *Lousiane, hein?* So if it is not so good, nobody care. Is Valsin that angry-looking fellow next to the pretty girl?"

She peered over his shoulder as they whirled past, drawing her mouth down so that she might not look too happy. "My brother. Why should he look angry, him? He's got *un amour* of his own."

60

"And you?" her partner asked quickly, his voice suddenly more intimate "With your otter eyes, dark and warm as café. Do you have a love of your own as well?"

Her mouth gaped open for a second time. These Germans were certainly bold enough. And a stranger, besides! All she knew told her to toss her head, refuse to answer such a scandalous question, and perhaps even walk away, leaving him open-armed on the floor. But something made her speak instead. *"Non, M'sieu,"* she took refuge in her own tongue. *"J'ai rien."* And then that same something made her add, "None which I want."

The final fifth of the dance was ending, the *Grande Chaîne* which led all the couples round the floor in a weaving pattern, each man holding fast to his partner at both wrist and waist.

"I used to live further north," he was saying now, "past Natchez. You know it? It is different up there, yes. Down here, the air is softer. And sweet."

"Sweet?" She loved the bayou, but she never thought of it as sweet. Perhaps, though, in the spring—

"Ah yes, up there the air gets a tang! I guess from all the pines. The turpentine. All your trees are sweet in the sap. The cypress, the orange—good trees, but different. Your water is different too, *non?*"

"How different?"

"Our rivers are too shallow for boats, full of colored rocks—"

"What colors?"

"Green and gray and black. Some are red. Like your lips."

She heard that in every tissue.

"I must go back to play now," he said, "but I wish you to save me another waltz, eh?" He passed her under his arm and out again with a stylish flourish. "The last one, perhaps?"

Paul Bellard came out of the card room then, leaned against a bench, and watched her turn past. She could not read his face. At the thought of the farmer claiming her for the last waltz—a sign to all who watched that she accepted his suit—she felt her feet go cold and leaden with dread. The German tucked her under his arm, seemed to fit her next to his heart, and when she looked up at him, she saw a small raw flicker of light in his eyes, a hunger which made her stomach lurch in response. "Is possible," she said softly.

The music stopped, the dancers exploded in applause, and partners hurried to the punch bowls. Joseph Weitz bowed deeply before her, a formal and graceful salute. "Anything is possible, *M'amselle*. You have only to wish it."

Dazed, Oliva hurried to the punch bowl, taking refuge in the laughing crowd of girls, pressing back against the wall where she could not be seen. Her hands trembled as she smoothed her hair and straightened her ribbons. When she peeped around Adele's shoulders, she saw Valsin still staring at her, Bellard still watching her, though papa was turned away, speaking low to the widow. She colored and turned her back.

Holy Mary, did she not have the right to dance with a man of her choice? Was she betrothed without even her say-so? Did what she want mean nothing at all?

"You have only to wish it," he had said. And wish it, she did, by the Good God! It seemed to her in that instant that she was balancing on the edge of a high and perilous peak—and at no other time in her life would she have so much power over which path she might take. Once she chose, her way would be set for the rest of her days. But so long as she refused to choose, she still had control over her own fate, at least as long as someone wanted to choose her . . .

She walked to the front of the covey of girls, took up a platter, and defiantly helped herself to a slice of one of the fattest *gâteaux*. Oliva watched her brother and father, half-expecting them to walk to her end of the room at any moment—but the music began, the floor filled, and neither approached.

She ate the cake hurriedly, barely noticing the pleasure of

its sweetness. When she set her plate down, Bellard was once more at her elbow. Again, with scarcely more than a bow and a good grip, he began to move her out among the dancers.

After two circles in silence, he said, "The good Father said that he declared me."

It occurred to her in that instant that she had never once heard him speak her given name. "He did," she replied, dropping her voice so that few would hear.

"He said that you would need more wooing." His voice seemed to boom over the music, making her wince.

Oliva pulled back and gaped at Bellard. "He said that?"

"He did. And so, I ask your permission to—commence," he finished awkwardly. "If wooing is what you want."

At his obvious embarrassment, she felt a mix of pity and irritation. Surely, these were not the feelings she should have for a would-be husband! He pulled her slightly closer and she dropped her eyes in confusion. "I—I do not know what to say," she murmured.

"Say you will have me," he said, his voice firm, his eyes averted over her head.

"M'sieu," she began anxiously, "I cannot. I'm sorry, but I cannot accept you if I do not have—feelings for you, can I? Would you want such a union?"

He glanced down at her and then away again, never missing a step in the dance. "Do you speak of love?"

"Yes," she said gently, "I do, M'sieu. I do not love you."

"That is of no moment," he said formally. "I do not love you as yet, either. But we will learn to love. And we will make a good partnership. You are a fine and comely woman. You need a home, and I have a good one; I need sons, and you—"

"You do not love me?" she asked, shocked at his admission.

"I care for you, of course, but I cannot love what I do not know, can I? I expect to love, in time. So will you, likely."

Still he did not say her name! The pity began to dissolve,

and her irritation rose higher and flushed her cheeks. "This is a fine wooing," she said shortly.

"Well," he replied blandly, "I haven't started yet. Tell me I can start, and I will."

She pushed herself out of his arms suddenly, throwing them both off balance. They were stopped in the middle of the whirling couples, who parted around them with curious glances, like frothing water around a rock in a torrent. "M'sieu, you must ask another," she said angrily, "I will not marry with you."

He glanced around sheepishly, still clinging to her arm. Now it was he who lowered his voice. "Maybe we should speak of this another—"

"No, no, no!" she said, her voice rising in despair. "I don't wish to speak of it at all, not here, not anyplace else! Find another brood cow for your barn, it won't be me!" She whirled away from his hands, struggled through the dancers, her face contorted with half-sobs of embarrassment, and rushed outside to the cool night air.

Marie followed her quickly, Valsin glowering behind her. "Go back," Marie said to him softly, "and let her alone for a moment."

"For the whole village to hear—!" he started to bluster, but Marie only held up one small hand to silence him. He turned with a frown and went back inside LeBleu's, glaring over his shoulder.

Marie embraced Oliva gently and pulled her into the shadows. Her pity made Oliva's eyes well up and spill over, but she kept her voice firm. "I cannot marry that farmer," she said miserably, "I cannot make myself."

"And so, you shouldn't," Marie murmured gently. "But neither should you shame him before the village."

"But he would not leave me alone! He takes my hand as though he's already lain with me!"

"Hope makes men do that."

"Carelessness makes them do that," Oliva snapped,

angry all over again. "Would you marry without love? Can you truly counsel me to do such a thing, Marie?"

Before Marie could answer, Simon Doucet's voice cut across the darkness. He stood in the doorway, the noise and the lights behind him, looming large and black with folded arms. "Oliva," he said quietly, "come back inside now."

Marie shrank away, pressed Oliva's hand once, and disappeared past Simon's shoulders into LeBleu's. As Oliva walked closer, he said, "I am shamed you saw fit to treat M'sieu Bellard so ill before all eyes. Your mother must be weeping as she watches you this night."

"Truly," Oliva sighed resignedly, "my mother would weep, *vraiment.*"

"You have grown wild as a weasel," he said firmly. "I have not done my duty as your father. Perhaps a husband can teach you your duty better than I. Now go inside and see if you can behave properly before our neighbors."

"Oui, papa," she whispered, passing behind him.

As she went through the door, a hundred eyes looked at her and then away. Bellard was nowhere to be seen. Marie and Valsin watched her as she approached the table of food, Marie smiling hesitantly, Valsin frowning big as a quarter moon.

The fiddler leaped into another tune, and the dancers crowded the floor again. Mercifully, they no longer stared. To her great relief, old Benoit came and bowed before her, smiling gently. "You will waltz, *cher?*" he asked. Gratefully, she fell into his arms and whirled away from her father's eyes, her brother's frown. Then another asked, and another.

And each time she whirled past the music platform, at least a dozen times, Joseph Weitz grinned down at her as if applauding her audacity.

Finally, the fiddler held up his bow and shouted, *"La dernière valse!"* and now the floor filled once more with couples whose eyes fastened most firmly on each other. Valsin strode by with Marie on his arm, and right behind him, a German redhead shouldered through the throng.

He held out his arm to Oliva. "Will you?" he asked, his eyes searching her own.

She did not trust her voice. Smiling, she took his arm and preceded him onto the floor. After an evening of other shoulders, so many sets of feet, his at once felt familiar and safe. But that's not true, she thought swiftly. In fact, of all of them, his are the most strange. *Les autres,* we call them. The others. Not of us, not like us, not *for* us.

But he moved her so well in his arms!

"I would like to escort you home, *M'amselle* Doucet," he was saying, snapping her back to attention.

"That is not possible," she murmured.

"Why is that not?"

"Because I only go home *en famille, moi.* That is our way."

"Then," he said, smiling so that his eyes crinkled up at the corners, "I will take *maman* home as well."

Oliva glanced around to see Valsin dancing past her, his eyes pegged to Marie. Simon was leading the widow to the floor. Something she said made him laugh aloud, his head back in delight. *"Maman est morte, "* she said softly. "Almost two years now."

Joseph pulled her a little closer, but gently. "That is sad," he said, "too sad almost to bear. It is not good to be alone."

"I'm not alone." She pulled back slightly.

"*I* am. My parents are gone, as well. Soon as we come to this coast. *Die Grippe, yah?* You call it *l'influenza,* I think. So I know what a sadness this is." He pulled her a little closer again. "So," he said, more briskly, "I take papa home, as well. *Nous allons,* we three, *chez Doucet.* You say yes."

She thought quickly, as the song came to an end, yes, Valsin could see to Marie in the pirogue, that certainly would not be a problem, and the German could take papa and me home. If I wish it so, it could be. He turned her around a final

66

time, tucking her once more inside his arm and under his heart. His tenderness was almost womanish. Oliva was accustomed to men and their ways, but those attentions had always been playful, sportive, never proffered with such soft earnestness. She said, "You could ask papa." She tried to keep her voice unconcerned. It was a cold, clear night, and the cabin would look well by moonlight.

The fiddler took out his musket and fired it into the roof. *"Le bal est fini!"* he shouted, the traditional end to the *fais-do-do,* which precluded the crowd demanding yet one more dance.

She hurried to snatch her shawl and bonnet from the hook, watching through the gaggle of girls to see Joseph waiting by the door. A quick detour to pick up her gumbo pot—empty, thank the Good God—and as she returned to his side, Valsin and Simon were there in a blink.

"This *Allemand* pays you court, Oliva," her father said. It was not a question. He was watching her carefully.

"It's a wonder any man here tonight would consider it," Valsin said sourly.

Before she could speak, Joseph strode forward, stuck out his hand to her father and said, "M'sieu Doucet, it is a great privilege to dance with your charming daughter this night. I am called Joseph Weitz, I visit with your friend, *M'sieu* Bourque." Very formal, very French. "He invited me to attend and to bring my pitiful music for your pleasure. I hope it did not offend your ears, this strangeness."

Valsin was frowning, but Simon shook the man's hand with courtesy and a small smile. "Your music was as charming as my daughter, M'sieu."

Joseph smiled and offered his hand to Valsin, saying, "I wish you great good fortune with your mademoiselle, M'sieu, she is surely the second most lovely lady on the bayou."

Valsin took his hand, his frown wavering. "You are staying with old Bourque?"

And then, to Oliva's surprise, Simon said mildly, "Now

that you have made this gentleman's acquaintance, my son, I suppose you would like to see to *M'amselle* Guidry. We will wait for you."

At that, Joseph spoke up. "Sir, I would consider it a great honor if you will allow me to escort you and *M'amselle* Doucet home safely. In this way, M'sieu Doucet can offer his lady the proper courtesies as well."

Oliva was aware that a few departing guests lingered at the door to hear her father's answer, and she held her breath. Valsin moved off towards Marie, glancing back over his shoulder in some confusion as the group began to move out the door.

Old Bourque slapped her father on the back then, shouting jovially, "I can vouch for him, *ami,* he's as fine a brewer as he is a maker of music! Make a stranger feel welcome, Doucet, and save yourself the long pole home!"

By now, they were halfway down the bank, the people were dispersing with merry cries of farewell and promises to meet again for Mass. The night air was particularly biting after the heat of the dance. Paul Bellard was nowhere to be seen, but old Bourque hovered close to Simon, speaking low into his ear, while Oliva pretended to be very occupied with the proper swathing of her shawl and the placement of her bonnet. Try as she might, she could not make out her father's words to his *ami.*

Finally her father said amiably, "Well, then, I suppose we should make a start." He turned to Joseph, who drew his eyes reluctantly away from Oliva. "Which is your boat?"

At that, the German visibly paled. Even in the moonlight, she could see the chagrin change his face. "I have this buggy, sir," he said, his voice already full of comprehension, gesturing to a fine hack and horse hitched at the bank.

"A buggy?" Simon said softly. "Well, perhaps another time, M'sieu. We, of course, live where no buggy may go. Valsin!" he called. "Come away, we must take our leave!" Simon took Oliva's hand and settled her in her seat, her empty gumbo pot at her feet. His eyes never met hers once.

Valsin left Marie's side, casting a look of scorn at the German, and took his place in the pirogue as old Bourque laughed at the frustration on Joseph's face. "A buggy? She never told you, you must first learn to walk on water?"

As Valsin pushed the pirogue back into the current, Joseph stepped to the edge of the bank and called to her, "Tomorrow! You will be at chapel on Sunday, yes?"

Oliva gazed at him with little but her eyes showing above the layers of shawl. Holy Mary, what had she been thinking? It would never work. He was more than just a stranger, he was completely foreign! They were too different to ever come together, to make a life on any sort of common ground. A buggy! She nodded once, then turned away, as though her eyes, too, were required to find the pirogue's way home in the darkness.

Valsin poled a while in silence, as the tumult of the fete died away behind them. Finally he said, "You were shameful tonight, *certainement,* and I will hear them speak your name each time I am in the village for the next fortnight."

"Oliva regrets her behavior," Simon said quietly. "We need not hear of it again."

"Well, perhaps we need to speak of something else, then," Valsin went on boldly. "You should forget this *allemand, cher.* He is not one of us. He comes from a world you would never like, *non.*"

"And how do you know what I would or would not like?" she replied with icy calm.

"I know you'd not like his German papa!"

"He has none," she said firmly. "He has no one at all. And as to what I would not like, one thing is sure. I would *not* like sleeping alongside M'sieu Bellard for the rest of my days!"

"You made sure the whole village knew of that, my sister!" Valsin shouted, startling the silence of the swamp.

Simon frowned at him, and Valsin calmed himself with

an effort. "But no matter, it is done. If you will not have Bellard, then take another. But find somebody of your own kind. Keep to your own!"

"*Tais-toi!*"

"Oliva," her father said swiftly, "do not tell your brother to shut his mouth, it is unbecoming."

"Papa, must I listen to this chattering squirrel tell me how to pick a tree?" She jerked her bonnet down around her face so that nothing showed at all. "Soon, I'll marry anyone simply to escape his mouth."

"Good!" Valsin snapped back at her. "If you can find a man fool enough, post the banns tomorrow!"

Simon held up one hand, sighing heavily. "Peace, my children. Valsin, watch for that stump there, you come too close." He gently pulled away one corner of her shawl, so that he might see her face. "You cannot be happy with Bellard, then?"

Oliva's eyes filled suddenly, to her alarm. It was the tenderness of his voice which struck her. He sounded, at once, so old and weary and hopeful. But then she remembered the way he had laughed with the widow. I have a right to happiness, too, she murmured inside, and she returned his gaze, her eyes clear and dry. "No, I cannot. I fear there is no one for me, papa, not in the whole village. And so, I shall marry no one. I shall live in the cabin alone, or perhaps I shall hire out as a bondswoman for seven years. But I will not wed, I swear it."

Simon's face fell abruptly, and he turned away.

"What?" Valsin cried out, his voice carrying over the water, "A bondswoman! *You* will decide this without speaking to papa? Good Holy Christ!"

"I can live alone in the bayou," she said quietly. "But I hope that I may find work in the village. Because I do not wish to live with the widow or *M'amselle* Guidry, as fond as I am of her."

Struck dumb at the possibility she presented, Valsin then sputtered, "Papa! Are you going to let her—"

"Be still, both of you," Simon said firmly. "Oliva, you will not be a bondswoman, neither will you be unwed, no not if I must find the man for you myself, as in the old days. I will think on this, and then I will say what will happen."

In the silence, Oliva vowed to herself, think on this all you like, papa, and you as well, Valsin, but I will not wed someone to please you, no, not even if *maman* comes to me herself and tells me it must be. Oh, *maman,* she suddenly cried out within, help me! Intercede with our Holy Mother and bring more to Mass tomorrow than peace for my soul!

The little chapel along the bayou was the oldest building in Lafourche, for the first Acadians to come to the region had lived within its walls as they built homes for each other, attached at both its sides.

The people had a saying, "Put up the church and the village will build to it," and so it had. For many miles up and down the bayou, all were one faith. There was no thought of any other.

The French Catholic Mass was held early each Sunday evening, and at that time every house was emptied. For those few who were too ill to make the journey, each home also had a private *boîte* or shrine with personal saints, for prayers before bed and in the morning.

Simon Doucet had quietly taken down the largest crucifix above his bed when he buried his wife, but the two smaller ones remained, as well as the four religious pictures and the candles flanking the walls.

This Sunday as Oliva and her father walked up the church steps in the early dusk, she looked carefully for a certain buggy, but it was not hitched under the trees with the others. It seemed to her that more eyes looked in her direction than they had the Sunday before, and she bowed her head in confusion. Valsin hurried ahead to talk to Father LeBlanc, and she wondered if he would mention her name and tell him of her behavior at LeBleu's.

Her brother had scarcely spoken that morning, and he averted his face when she had set down his cup.

She almost touched his fingers, but she could not. She remembered how, to recall her sins in the confessional, she used her fingers, each one representing a grievous offense. She felt abased. But she did not feel contrite.

It was often so in the confessional.

"I am guilty of anger to my father," she would tell the priest.

"Honor thy father and mother."

"I coveted a girl's bonnet."

"What else?"

"I had bad thoughts. In church."

"What?"

"A man . . ."

"Ah. A venial sin," Father LeBlanc smacked his lips. "A sacrilege also. I will take it from your soul. But you must watch the hands of men. Why will you girls never learn this? Hate it—the sin, not the man. Guard the sanctity of your body, the wonderful house God gave you to live in. You should be married, Oliva, you know this is the truth." He blew his nose valiantly and lectured her for a few more moments on the responsibility of her sex, and then imposed a penance of ten Ave Marias.

Now, Oliva knelt with her rosary in her hands, praying for wisdom and strength. No doubt Joseph Weitz had thought better of his attentions last night, perhaps old Bourque told him enough to discourage him. Perhaps even now he was back with his own people, and if he thought of her at all, it was only with chagrin.

Headstrong! headstrong! Her mother used to say it often, and it was true. Now she had made a vow, one which would likely doom her to live forever with the widow or her brother, stubborn and headstrong and without hope of redemption!

Father, bless me for I have sinned, she prayed silently, fervently, I have sinned against my father, my brother, my people. I have wished for what cannot be, and in the wishing, have likely sinned against even You.

She quickly counted up her dance partners on her rosary beads, picturing each in her head. Not Claude, not Etienne, not Ovid, could she marry. Not Jean or Arcene or Marcel *would* she wed. Not a single man did she want, and few would probably want her, for true. Paul Bellard sat in his usual place at the third pew, his aging mother next to him. He glanced at Oliva quickly when she came in, nodded solemnly, and then turned away. She felt his eyes on her again, but she would not raise her head.

Ah, it was not possible! Was there no man in the bayou who could flicker a flame in her, like the one she saw in Marie's eyes when she gazed at Valsin? Was there no man in the whole village whose smile would make her happy to stand by his stove, to tote and wash his linens, to labor to bring forth his sons? Because without that smile, she would rather work for wages: anything else would be slavery of her body and her soul.

By the time the interminable Mass was finished, Oliva felt as though she had poled from Lafourche to the sea. Her arms ached with holding up her body. She followed her father down the church steps, making nods to those who greeted her, barely glancing to her left and right.

And so she did not see him until he touched her shoulder.

"Tonight, I have a boat," he said, gesturing to those pirogues tied down at the river. "Perhaps I might try *encore?*"

She felt her cheeks heat as though she faced a hundred suns. At the back of her knees, a sudden dampness sprang, despite the cold air outside. "You must ask papa," she said, her voice trembling slightly.

Simon Doucet waited at the top of the steps, watching them both. He did not speak nor extend his hand.

"M'sieu Doucet," Joseph began, "today, I have proper boat. M'sieu Bourque is kind enough to—"

"You are *Catholique?*"

Joseph Weitz bowed to her father. "As were my parents before me."

"Come then," Simon said shortly. "We will speak religious as you pole." Her father took her arm and led her to the bank, waiting while Joseph readied the pirogue for them to step aboard. When Valsin hurried away from Marie Guidry and came up to them, Simon said only, "We shall see you for supper?"

Her brother nodded in confusion, never taking his eyes off the redhead in the rocking boat.

As Simon handed her in, he murmured, "You will say nothing, *cher*. Is possible?"

"Possible, papa," she murmured back obediently.

The two men sat in the prow, her father watching closely as Joseph maneuvered the little boat into the current. The old man lifted his hand once to those who watched from the bank, a wave which looked as solemn as his final farewell to life might be. Marie lifted her hand and called out a cheerful, *"Bonne chance!"* and Oliva promised herself she would love her always, whether Valsin did or not.

The moon rose behind the tupelo bushes, double size and red like a hot branding iron. Night-feeding ducks streamed across it, their swift wings whispering.

As Joseph's boat pulled away, Paul Bellard was just helping his mother down the chapel steps. He stood and stared at Oliva, not bothering to hide his frown. Ovid Bernance said something quickly to him, a rise of laughter in his words, but

Bellard did not return the laugh. He turned his back to the departing boat as though he'd closed a door.

Oliva saw that her father had seen Bellard too, and she pulled her shawl closer, dropping her eyes. For one brief instant, she felt like shouting to this German to push to shore, to let her out, to leave her alone, for surely Bellard would turn to her again with forgiving eyes if she would have him—but she only gazed mutely at her father, willing him to speak.

The bayou was shadowed, fringed by the darker dark of the overhanging trees, with only the single oil lamp which hung at the bow for light. Oliva sat close to the fire bucket. She took the damp sack off and stirred the embers, dipping in the lightwood torch and setting it at the stern. The red glimmer of the moon played peep through the moving clouds, and the far away growl and groan of an alligator made it seem that they were moving deeper into places where one must be wary.

After a moment of silence, a silence so complete that Oliva could hear the breath moving in and out of her body, Simon finally said, "Your people are of the *Bayou des Allemands,* then?"

Joseph was keeping the pirogue close to the bank, poling carefully around stumps and low-hanging branches. *"Oui, M'sieu,"* he answered in French, "we have lands there, my brother and me. Now my father is gone, we make a division of our work so that he sells beer, and I tend to brewing."

"And you make a home together?"

"No, he has his place with his wife and children. I live in the old house, until I can build a place of my own. We mean to make over the place to a larger brewery. We make fine rice beer, the best on the river. We bring hops and barley in from Germany, and we sell all we can make. I hope soon," he said, his voice changing as though he spoke now to her alone, "to bring a wife to help me."

"Watch out for that shoal ahead," Simon said calmly, ignoring this last. "Where you learn to pole?"

"Same place I learn my French," Joseph said, speaking now only to Simon. "I count the Acadians of *Bayou des Allemands* as my friends, M'sieu, and there are as many families there who keep the old ways as here."

"Mais non!"

"You did not know this? And more coming soon, they say, from Georgia and Virginia."

Oliva did not know where this Georgia and Virginia was, but she noticed keenly that Joseph knew to pole the pirogue so that the stern slipped wide of the moss in the trees and her shawl stayed dry of nightdew. Her father asked more questions now, about the brewery and the difficulty of bringing beer to market in New Orleans, but Oliva listened mostly to the tone and timbre of this stranger's voice.

Even though his accent was difficult, he spoke as an equal to papa and did not give way before his questions, fawning and twisting like the smallest hound at his feet. She watched his back move the pole, his eyes scanning the bayou while he made his answers, and she came back to sharp attention as Joseph was saying, "I was engaged once, yes, to a young woman, but she chose another."

"You posted banns?" Simon's voice showed firm disapproval.

"Yes."

"And yet she would not wed. Why not?"

Joseph turned and smiled at her, a quick flash of teeth in the darkness, and then said levelly, "I suppose she did not want me after all, M'sieu."

Simon snorted indignantly. "Here, we do no such trifling, eh? Here, such things are decided once and for good."

"I am glad to hear this," Joseph replied genially. "Since here is where I am, *hein?*"

So he had had another! He would not bring the same pureness to his loving, perhaps not even to his bed, that Bellard would bring, Bellard who had probably not even kissed before, except the dry cheek of his mother. In a way, she pitied whatever woman this stranger might choose. But still a tension ran from her to him and back again, even as she sat so far behind, with all of her father between them.

In time the talk was through and the pirogue eased into the still water before the cabin. As Simon helped her out, he said to the German, "We thank you for your courtesy, M'sieu."

She suddenly wished that courtesy did not require him to be invited inside. She wanted only the deep, dark silence of her bed and the invisibility sleep would bring.

"You wish to come take coffee? The night is cold, and a good cup against the trip home will brace you good." Simon made the offer as easily as though Father LeBlanc stood there in the boat, instead of this Joseph-with-the-blazing-hair.

"Coffee, yes, I would like this," he said.

Somehow her hands undid the shawl, fired the stove, set out the cups, put the water to boil, all without her knowledge or help. She was not asked to sit; she did not offer to do so. She excused herself to her mother's room and took up her needlework. It was a relief to be away from all but the drone of their voices. The steady, even stitches lulled her into her favorite fantasy, and she let herself dream of the old comfort she used to conjure when she was only a girl: that somewhere, a man was searching for her, and he would know her when he found her. She fastened on her practiced thoughts of this man and his hands on her cheeks, his mouth heavy on hers, his steps to match hers somehow, his days on earth to coincide with hers, down to the last one, if she be lucky—so that the two of them might die together under a thunderstrike or a falling wall, as some old people do die together.

She must have dozed, for the lamp was sputtering when she heard her father call her. "See to our visitor's comforts, Oliva. I am weary now. Fill his lamp and wave him on his way." He stood and shook the German's hand, showing them both out the cabin door.

Behind her, the light from the stove seemed to make the bayou darker. She bent and filled the lamp from the spouted can on the dock. He took it from her and set it down. Without touching her, he spoke now in English. "We come from different stock, we two, and no one could say nay to this."

"This is true," she murmured, wondering where his words were leading.

"I once thought I want a woman who can make heads turn with her airs. Someone used to lace and silk pillows who knows a double rose-cut diamond from a throat lacet of red glass, so she could raise me up. But she would not have me. And now I see you, Oliva Doucet, I would not have her. Your father has spoken to me of making a marriage. He would have you consider me."

Oliva felt a sharp flare of anger and pride. But there was a throbbing of the blood in her, the lonely blood which impelled her to yearn towards him, made her urgent. She set her jaw against the beating of her heart. "If she would not have you, why should I?"

"Because your father wills it. And I believe you want me."

She turned to leave him, but he took her shoulders in his

hands and turned her back again. "But most of all, because I want you. We will make even the priest want us together. Even God will want us together."

"I don't think God cares who I marry."

"He cares who I marry," he grinned, "He told me so. Marry me."

"Not so long as you make a jest of God."

"Make Him stop making jest of me. Marry me."

"What did my father say to you?"

"Nothing I could not see with my own eyes. That you are a fine woman who is ready for a man. That there is no man in Lafourche you want."

"There are some," she said proudly, "who want me."

"I saw as much," he said gently. "But do you want them?"

She moaned softly, turning from him into the shadows. *"Non, M'sieu,* but I do not want you, either. Perhaps I cannot love! Perhaps I am better unwed."

To her surprise, he chuckled warmly and put his hands on her shoulders. "You will be wed, sooner or later. Why not sooner? Why not to me? It would please your papa—"

"Damn my papa!" she cried.

He put a hand swiftly over her mouth, pulling her closer. "He does his duty to you, Oliva, as he sees fit. You must not damn a man for that. But we will not speak of your father. Let us speak of love."

"I do not love you!" she wailed, wrenching from his arms.

"Not now, perhaps, but you may soon enough. I could feel something in you when I held you at LeBleu's, and I feel it now. You are a woman meant for love, no matter what you say. I will show you and make you believe it. I love you, Oliva."

"Such a lie!"

"Non, c'est vrai. I loved you the instant I held you. Think back, and you will know it. Love is like that between a man and a woman, fast and sure as an arrow. When you were a

79

child, it was all trembles and hesitation. You are a woman now."

"You do not love me. You only want me," she said, but her eyes never left his face.

"That is the beginning of love. Marry me, Oliva, and I will make you happy."

His words were powerful and strange, not at all what she had envisioned. That her father had spoken to this stranger maddened her, but she also knew that Simon Doucet acted from love. Love: it was achingly difficult to fathom! She appraised this German swiftly. He was so different from the men she knew. He was an outsider. But perhaps, so was she, in her soul.

"I want to know the truth," she said.

"About what? About love? *Une spectatrice* can never know the truth, Oliva. You were not made to watch love from afar."

"How dare you speak so to me?" she flamed. "You do not know me at all!"

He grinned now, watching her anger subside. "Marry me," he repeated gently.

"Never," she frowned. And then in a moment, "Perhaps. In time. If you can keep away from those other women who know a diamond from glass."

"I have little time to waste. And you'll have to talk to them about that," he said.

"Such a bighead!" But she could not suppress her smile. "Why should I marry you?"

"Because I want you as a man wants a woman. Because you will make your father and your brother content. And because I can make you happy in the bargain. I will make us a good life."

"And where would this life be?"

"I have promised your father to keep you in Lafourche. Sometime, we will go to New Orleans, but you will not be long from your people."

She nodded. "That pleased him, no doubt."

"That convinced him," he said. "But you will see. New Orleans is bewitching."

"But I know no one there—"

"You will know me. And there are so many new strangers, you will find it soon a friendly place. It's not so very different after all."

"I know nothing of your life."

"I know little of yours. I know to make good beer and sell it for enough money to bring me comfort. What do *you* know?"

She gazed up at him then, with all the fullness of her heart showing in her eyes. "I know how to hamstring a deer and bake his haunch in sweetened vinegar and pepper root. I know how to cut and sew a skin boot to bear a certain foot. I know the way of moonseed root for night troubles." Here she stopped and blushed hotly, for he had never even kissed her. "I know how to hold a child, how to trounce him if he needs it, how to wash him, to name him, and make him take pride in his name. I know how to make him sit still in chapel and be a man." She took a deep breath and said her last, wondering in some distant part of herself where all these words and assurance could have come from. "And I know how to content his father the while."

He took her cheeks in both hands and lowered his mouth to hers, even as she rose to meet him. The long kiss was liquid and warm and left no place in her unmoved. When they drew apart, she felt unsteady on her feet, and she put one hand on his chest for balance. "Wait," she murmured.

She went back into the cabin and straight to her father's room where he waited in her mother's rocker. He took his pipe from his mouth and gazed at her patiently.

She was trembling with fury and sadness and an urgency that made her voice quake. "It is true? You have promised me to this stranger?"

"*Non,*" he said, slowly shaking his head. "I have told him

81

it would please me if he would gain your favor." He was turning the pipe around in his hand as though seeing it for the first time. "And has he gained your favor, *cher?*"

Her throat ached with the largeness of what stood before her. "You will seek happiness, Valsin has found his own, and yet you deny me mine!"

Again he shook his head. "I pray for your happiness every night, daughter. But I know that you will not find it as *une célibataire.*"

She cringed. A spinster.

"And so. Has he gained your favor?"

Her eyes flooded, and she could not speak. She turned abruptly and walked slowly out to where Joseph waited, her chin firm once more, her head level. She took his hand in both of hers and looked at it intently for a moment. This would be the hand which would touch her for the rest of her days. "You can tell my father I will accept you," she said, her voice throaty and low.

He strode back into the cabin without hesitation. She stood, holding herself, shivering, and the roaring in her ears blotted out even the night sounds of the swamp. Fear overwhelmed her, and she felt like shrieking to the skies her bewildered pain and sense of longing. But in moments he was back at her side, holding her now, his body tight against hers the whole length of it. "We will post banns next week," he murmured against her hair. "When the moon turns again, you are mine."

There were two of her husband's phrases that she remembered most. The first was, "Even God will want us together."

As she rode in the ferry across to New Orleans, she rolled that one over in her mind like an oiled marble, feeling for the serenity she could usually conjure with those words. The second was, "You have only to wish it." At their wedding ball, he had repeated this to her again. Now as they crossed the wide river, she remembered Joseph's words that night, but she was discovering that what she would wish and what she would have were often opposite sides of a muddy river.

Their wedding was not the most lavish which Bayou Lafourche had witnessed, but it was certainly one of the most joyous, since all who attended knew a whole family was making a marriage. Simon had made his intentions to the widow known, and Valsin had already posted his banns with Marie. So why not make it a triple wedding? Why not celebrate the old man's courage as well? Why not dance three times as much, eat three times as much, and be thrice happy?

The cakes! Oliva would never forget the grand cakes, so many of them, brought to LeBleu's and set on the long table. She herself had baked six of them, and Marie, not to be outdone, baked six more. They had to soak rags in oil and wrap them around the table legs just to keep off the ants, and every *femme* in the village brought something special, some wonderful dish or sweet to help them celebrate.

Joseph's brother, Adolph, brought two huge casks of their best beer, the orange wine flowed all the night long, and the music and dancing feet made the walls of LeBleu's shake and shiver until almost dawn. Many adjourned from Le-Bleu's to the house of the widow, to charivari old Simon and his ancient bride, who had been married quietly the week before. For hours, they stood outside the widow's windows, shouting and playing and singing, until the two came out, Simon mock-stern, his plump wife on his arm, to offer the expected bribe of more wine if they would only leave in peace.

When Oliva heard the tales of her father's charivari, it seemed as though she could see him in a dream, standing at their own cabin door, *maman* smiling at his side. But then the dream slipped away. And she had so much to think of, she willed the sadness to leave her. Perhaps it was true, what the old ones said, that love was not leaving anything for tomorrow, for tomorrow was promised to no one.

More than a hundred boats and buggies gathered at the church to see Oliva and Marie step forward in their identical white dresses, orange, red, and green paper flowers in their arms, and, trooping behind, a score of gaily dressed girls. The Baptiste daughters wore fluttering yellow ribbons for luck, and each one stooped to kiss old Simon on his cheek, as he stood at the church door, the widow on his arm.

But the moment Oliva would remember all her days, she vowed silently, the one memory which warmed her most, was to look up and see Joseph standing at the altar, his stiff black suit so foreign, his face only slightly more familiar. How had she come to this point so quickly with a man she scarcely knew, from a place and a people she knew not at all? As Father LeBlanc took her hand to give it to Joseph, she pulled it back reflexively, her eyes suddenly wide with the realization of the step she took.

Joseph noticed her jerk away, saw the fear in her face, and smiled down at her. In that moment, she understood that he had been more aware of her than he was of his own feelings— that he watched her, with softness in his eyes, for the panic he must have known would come. He reached and gently took her hand, covering it with his own. "Don't be afraid," he said quietly, so softly that she could scarcely hear him. "I love you." And then he drew her hand to his lips and kissed her palm lightly.

A wave of tenderness swept over her then, for this man who was not afraid to show his love before the priest, the church, before God, and all who might hear or see him. His words and touch had calmed her, and her hand remained in his throughout the rest of the brief ceremony. All the while the priest spoke, Joseph stroked her fingers in a private signal, with a touch as soft as feathers, as though he would take all the days of his life to know that hand. By the time they were man and wife, she felt as though a promise had been made, though she could not have put it into words.

And that promise buoyed her through the next few days of so many new perceptions about who she was, who she had married, and what such a bond might mean.

In the week since their marriage, she had discovered a hundred differences between them. He was German Catholic, and even the songs they sang at Mass did not sound the same. He enjoyed his coffee, yes, but only in the morning and the evening, and the first time she set down the strong brew before him, he coughed and gagged on the black beverage which her brother had drunk since he was no higher than the stove itself. He did not know it was bad luck to kill a spider, to bake bread on a rainy day, or to open a *parapluie* in the house. He didn't even know it was good luck to spit on your bait before you threw it in the water, or to hear a cricket sing by your house. He wanted the windows open to the night air; she was appalled that he did not know how dangerous such a practice could be. If the germs and pestilence of the dark did not harm your body, then the *loupgarou,* the werewolf of the bayous, would *certainement* imperil your soul.

So much, Oliva thought, I must teach this man.

But then, she smiled a private smile, so much he is teaching me too.

On their wedding night, they had danced until she thought she could never take another step. When she expected him to suggest they retire to old Bourque's house, however, where he was lodging, he said instead that they should walk along the bayou in the moonlight. They had strolled through the quiet village, her hand on his arm, with little speech between them. They reached the edge of the houses, where the shrimp boats were docked in a cluster, and he led her still further downriver, helping her silently over stones in the path, keeping his step paced with hers. Finally, she felt so weary that she yearned to turn back to the village, and it was she, at last, who had said, shyly, "It is getting late. If we do not retire soon, we may as well stay up to see the dawn."

He had chuckled, drawing her closer to him. Then, without a word, he walked her back upriver once more, past the shrimp boats, past the silent houses, and finally to the house where old Bourque kept them a bed. Everyone had long since gone to their homes, and not even a dog barked as they walked up the gallery.

"Not a soul stirs," she said softly as they went through the house to their sleeping room, "except we two."

"For truth," he whispered, as he shut the door behind them, "it is as though we are the only two left in the world." He lit a single candle, placed it by the bed, and gazed at her a moment in the shadows. "I will go out on the gallery while you make ready," he said. "And when you are ready, blow out the light."

She stood, suddenly cold and trembling as he went out the door. She pulled off her wedding dress and draped it over the foot of the four-poster. Her cotton nightshift felt smooth and as cool as water over her skin, and her legs so relished the easy stretch of finally being prone, that she was instantly comforted. She reached up on one elbow and blew out the candle, almost hoping he would not see the signal and leave her be until morning.

But he was beside her then, stroking her hair as it spread over the pillow. "I will hold you while you sleep," he said, sliding in beside her. In the dark, she couldn't see him clearly, but she could feel that he wore the same long drawers that she had washed for Valsin and her father a hundred times. Somehow, the touch of that soft cloth made him feel familiar. "We have a million nights together," he said, as he pulled her over and nestled her against his chest. "We do not have to hurry."

She was so weary and his arms felt so warm, that she was asleep almost before she had time to feel ashamed at his nearness. And sometime in the early morning, while the dark still muffled all sounds, he turned to her with a low cry and made her want him.

In the morning, as the sunlight allowed no more hiding from each other, she watched him dress at the window, aware that she had still not seen him uncovered, nor had he seen her. But she knew the strength in his back, his arms, and legs, by touch alone, and a certain truth came to her: whatever else Joseph might be, no matter how else he might please or displease her, he was, without doubt, a man. And to hear him tell it, he was hers.

Now, as they neared the opposite side of the widest river she had ever known, the opposite side of the world it seemed, she knew that one of the feelings that were growing in her heart was gratitude.

The ferry moved steadily across the wide river, brown and turgid in the winter sun. Oliva had never seen the Mississippi before; it was like a wide sea, tranquil to the eye and yet so swift and treacherous when crossing it. The riverbanks were like small hills, and Oliva marveled at this difference between the river and the bayou. The river, Joseph had explained, was so strong, carried so much mud, that it built its own banks instead of carving them away as the bayou might. Like a slow twisting snake, it left ridges in the land, carrying away less than it left.

Joseph came to her side from where he had been seeing to their baggage.

"Look there," he pointed to the water, to a sucking mouth of a vortex which moved on the river's face like a live thing. "Must be very deep, yes?" Always, when he wanted to be alone with her in public, he spoke to her in French. He called it their *tête à tête privé* and made her laugh when he jumbled the words.

She could never get her mouth around the German words, it seemed, no matter how hard she tried. Such an ugly-sounding speech! One cleared the throat and gargled and showered a listener with spittle with each word. She wondered if the German women would be ugly, since their mouths must stretch to accommodate such harshness.

"So many changes, so fast," she sighed, leaning against him at the rail.

"This is the way it will always be for us, *liebchen.*"

"You think so? Why?"

"Because we are not afraid to take chances. To leave the old ways. To—" and here, he took her thumb and stroked the callus softly, "join hands and face whatever comes around the next bend. We will aim for something. A man must. A woman should help him. The bayou is a lazy man's country, I think. The men walk lazy there, I watch them. God gave them the richest land on earth, and they wait for Him to plow it as well. You are the only one with any—*stiffness* to you. Lazy waters and lazy people, mostly."

She frowned, about to protest—

"But you were a *fleur marécage,* blooming among the unredeemed. My *jolie* swamp flower. Look, there is our ride to New Orleans!"

Across the narrow expanse to the shore, several buggies waited, and as the passengers alighted from the ferry, drivers leaped down, shouting fares and destinations, bustling with bags, and somehow, sorting out who would go and who would not from the crowd. Oliva took Joseph's arm, again aware of how tall he was, and glad she could see him above the shoulders of most.

"You are going to have a wedding trip!" Marie had cried in joy, embracing her. "How lucky you are!"

Few newly marrieds ever left the village, even for a night away from their home, for the crops must be brought in, the traps must be set, nets must be mended, weddings or no. Besides, to waste money on such foolishness would make people glance to each other, that would be a bighead, sure.

But this was not a wedding trip, no. Of that Oliva now was sure. Joseph said they must go to New Orleans before they go to see his people at *Bayou des Allemands,* to arrange for the shipment of casks and barrels, to see someone called a broker about the new beer, and other details she could not now recall. There they would have a place only a short season, he said, high above the street.

Oliva wished suddenly, fervently, as the buggy quickly approached the city with its many houses all crowded together, that she was sitting back on the cabin gallery, and the breeze of the bayou was lifting her hair back from her face with its familiar fingers.

La Nouvelle Orléans, they called it, a city full of mansions and riches, lying between the river and lake, a magnet for the dreams of the delta people. But Oliva was most impressed by the maze of crowded streets, the upright houses painted in bright colors, and the women! Even as they went to market, they clothed themselves in velvet cloaks and damask with ribbon trim.

"So many of them are beautiful," she murmured to Joseph as their buggy approached the docks. "Such white skin!"

"That is powder, most like," her husband said dryly. "They puff and paint themselves. Those black spots some of them sport? Beauty spots. Painted on to draw the eye."

Many of the houses were built of brick from the ground up to the first floor. The second floor was often wood, with galleries wrapped all round to catch the air.

"What is that on the roofs?" Oliva asked as they rode past a block of houses painted white or yellow, with tall windows and flat roofs. Already she had noticed that her husband seemed to become more educated and knowledgeable, the nearer they drew to the city.

"New Orleans mud, they call it," Joseph grinned. "A mix of clay, lime, tar, and oyster shells. Sets like a rock and never leaks a drop, so they say." He grimaced as the driver splashed through a deep mud puddle. "They should use it in the streets, no?"

The streets were narrow and twisted, following the curve of the river. The open gutters were clogged with sewage, offal, stagnant rainwater, and the dung of passing horses. The stench rose to her nose when they swerved from the middle of the lane.

A black man walked by dressed in a fine yellow waistcoat and a tall hat. Behind him, two black brutes carried his baggage. Oliva swiveled her head to stare. *"Mon Dieu,"* she whispered, "the heathen masquerade like *gentilshommes!"*

"Gens de couleur," Joseph said quietly. "Freemen of color, they are called. Lots of them here, and some keep their own slaves."

"Such a thing is allowed?"

"There is little which is not," he shrugged.

They passed through the public square which was filled with a moving crowd. Along the iron railings were booths where street sellers offered oranges, bananas, sherbet, and *bière douce,* ginger beer. Black women, balancing flat baskets on their heads, cried out their wares, *estomac mulâtre,* the gingercake Oliva remembered her mother made. Along the riverfront, oyster stalls were crowded with finely dressed men and their ladies, waiting while the oysters were opened to eat fresh from the shell.

The docks spread out for several city blocks, laden with the bales and barrels of more than two dozen tall-masted ships which she could see at anchor. Small boats (still three times larger than her own pirogue) tended the bigger ships, holding them down with lines as though they might escape on the tide.

Men stood in bunches, haggling over goods, and others hoisted bales, loaded barges, and simply lay in the sun on the coiled ropes. Piles of crops lay on one dock: figs, watermelons, pecans, pumpkins, and other strange fruits and vegetables Oliva had never seen before.

The stream of city folk hurried past like the bayou at flood, everything in the world floating by and all of it different. Oliva was dizzied by the variety. Nuns in gray habits, their hands tucked away out of sight, fancy women who looked no better than they had to be, elegantly dressed rich ladies with their brutes carrying their parcels, swaggering gentlemen with long frock coats and silk hats, and sailors with baggy pants and bare feet jostled each other on the narrow wooden *banquettes*, what Joseph called their walkways, set above the mud. She heard a confusion of tongues: the fine noblemen and their ladies spoke French or English, the sailors spoke mostly Spanish, Joseph told her, and the brutes she could scarcely understand at all.

The buggy drove them away from the docks down a quieter street with tall houses facing to the side. A wagon was coming, a hawker with a tumbling pile of green serpent-striped melons. Beside him on the seat, Oliva saw that one was halved to show its color. "Watermelon, lady!" he hollered to her, and also up to the shuttered houses, "Red to the rind, come and get 'em, lady, fresh from the vine!"

"Where does he get such fruit in this season?" she quickly asked Joseph, turning to stare.

"Off the boats from Cuba," he said blandly. "In New Orleans, you can get most anything, anytime. If you have the money to pay."

She marveled at that, and at the houses they passed, the horse assuming a decorous pace, as though he knew that respect was required.

"We will live here?" she asked quietly.

Joseph shook his head. "This is the Creole part of town.

Too rich, for truth. They think themselves *sortis de la cuisse de Jupiter,* and will not lease to outsiders."

She thought this over in silence. The Creoles thought themselves a piece from the thigh of Jupiter, he said, a strange thing to want to be! All the gates on the houses were closed, and the gardens invisible from the street. They made her feel invisible as well. She squirmed her toes in her hard traveling shoes, hoping soon to be free of them.

They turned up and down smaller streets now, which were not nearly so wide nor straight. Finally, they pulled up before a low white house with a single door. Joseph helped her down, and she noted to herself the narrow little strip of garden on one side while he collected their bags. Nothing much would grow here, she realized, with such a tiny space. More dirt under her gallery at home than in this yard, yes? And houses so close, shoulder to shoulder like a row of teeth.

But by night they were settled in the little house, their clothes tucked into small cupboards, a candle burning on the table beside the bed. She was trying to decide which of Joseph's clothes must stay in the trunk, for he had more than she did and little space for them. He worked on papers at the little table, which teetered when he leaned his elbows on its edge.

She glanced over and said, "These Creoles. These who think they are so very much in the eyes of God. Do they make marriage with those who are not of themselves?" She spoke in English to him, which somehow seemed more fitting in this place.

"Never," he said, while one hand moved a scratching pen over the ledger book. "It would never endure if they did."

"Why?"

He looked up at her. Already she had learned that sometimes her husband got this look, where he pinched his red brows together and stared past her, and she knew she should keep still at those times. But she never seemed to do so.

Actually, when he had those brows together, it only made her talk more.

"Why would it not endure?" she asked again, her hands stilled now but deep within the folded clothes in the trunk.

"I know these people well, me," he replied in French, "and we get along in business. But they would never take in a stranger. Not for very long. They would not allow such a thing. And just as well, for truth, because they are so different."

"They speak French?"

"Their own kind. You would scarcely understand them, *cher*. And they would not want to understand you. Suppose you met a Creole *gentilhomme*, and he took you home to meet *maman*. She would never allow such a match, to *gens du commun*. Two people, so different, could never really know one another."

"As we know each other?"

"Yes, *cher*. As I know you."

She sensed a growing impatience in him, a desire to return to his papers, but she pressed on. "But if they loved each other?"

"Such a child you are!" he smiled at her kindly.

"You are only twenty-five," she said quickly. "Do not sound like *un vieillard.*"

"I'm not an old man, but I know more about love than you, *'tit chou.*"

"*Vraiment?*" she asked archly. "I await enlightenment, me."

"*Regarde, cher.* How could two people love each other if they are so different, *hein?* Sooner or later, those differences will out."

"Different," she said, her hands moving again now, her head down. "Not the same, like us."

"Yes, different," he said, a little shorter now.

"So you wouldn't have married me if I were Creole?"

"For God's sake, Oliva, what is this?"

93

"This is what you said, no?"

"No. This is ridiculous. I would not have *known* you if you were Creole. I know Acadians, these differences I know, but Creoles? We would never have met, we two."

"Suppose we did. Suppose we did meet and I was a Creole girl, not Acadian."

"But you would not be you!"

"Suppose I was. Suppose I was a Creole girl, we meet, we love. You will marry me then?"

He dropped his eyes, and she felt his anger.

She rose from her knees and went to him, touching his bent head, his shining bright hair. "Well? Will you marry me then?"

"I'm thinking."

"No more thinking, Joseph. Yes or no. It is simple."

"It is *not* simple."

"Yes or no."

"Sweet Mary, Oliva, this is maddening. All right. Since you insist. No."

"Ah," she said, her voice low and strangely satisfied. "No, it is then."

She left the room indifferently, with her back straight and her chin high. He went back to his papers, equally indifferent. But she knew she had hurt him.

She walked out on the small gallery that went round the back of the little house, looking up at the sky. The night was clear, and the stars plentiful. She wondered if Valsin and Marie stood and looked into the night as well at this moment. Somewhere a dog howled mournfully, but the sound was as much a part of this night, this place, as the crickets and frogs were on the bayou.

So this is something to learn about marriage, she thought firmly. One must keep oneself apart somehow. A piece of the heart must not be given, else love would grow fat and bored, like an overfed hog.

And yet, when she thought of the pleasure he gave her in

the darkly private nest of their bed, she knew that she was now part of a great mystery. One gave one's body. Sometimes the heart followed along like a horse to bit and spurs, whether one would or not. She could not say she loved him. Not yet. But she could feel the tendrils of tenderness wrapping around her soul like insistent spring vines, tugging her gently to lean towards him, as a flower turned to light. He made her furious. He made her feel powerful and helpless all at once. He also made her yearn for the feel of him against her, in her.

This was why Father LeBlanc used to sputter so, and froth at the young maidens to keep the boys' hands from their bodies. Because he knew that once they discovered the power of their passion, they would not, *could* not deny it. But why did *le bon dieu,* if that is indeed what He is, give us such joy, if it was not meant to bind us, each to the other?

Joseph came then to her side, with one arm around her shoulders.

"Forgive me, *liebchen.* I will make it up."

"How?" she asked.

He held her closer, whispering into her hair. "I will marry you."

She pulled slightly away. "Ah, we will see then. Go to bed. I will come in a moment."

He left her. She waited. Then she walked back from the gallery, dropping her clothing in the darkness, approaching the door to the little bedroom, her bare skin prickling in the night air.

"Blow out the candle," she said softly.

"What?"

"Blow it out."

He leaned over, blew, and the room was suddenly, overwhelmingly dark.

"Oliva?" he asked, his voice a whisper.

She did not reply.

He sat up, but she knew he could not see her. Her heart was pounding as it did their first night together, the way it did when she woke in the night in the bayou and wondered what creature had made that noise so close to her bed and waited to hear it again—and she moved silently across the room towards him. A stranger.

In 1788, New Orleans was the capital of a vast network of shipping, a glittering city of commerce, and a cesspool for most of the vices of America and Europe combined.

The Mississippi, a river which would determine the destiny of not just its native country, but of several more besides, was the Nile of North America, and it drew men and women from all over the world to see what they could glean from its muddy depths. Oliva soon found that Joseph's gleanings would last far longer than the few months they'd originally planned.

Every morning he would leave her in the narrow, storied house to go to the docks and do there what he did. At first, she tried to understand exactly how he spent his day.

"You go to the offices of the man who buys? And there, you—?"

"The factor. He is at the customs house, and he manages our imports. From there, we ship in molasses, hops, rice, some lumber, a little wheat, and plenty of hogsheads of sugar—"

"And you ship out the beer?"

"Some. Most of it we sell here in New Orleans, but we have to pay the customs man, and he takes a pretty penny for slipping it through with as little trouble as can be managed."

Her eyes widened. "You *corromps* this man? You are a *contrebandier?*"

He grinned. "If it's smuggling to be sure our tax man stays content, then I guess I'm as much pirate as any smuggler on the seas. And if an extra barrel of our best at his Christmas table is a bribe, then I stand guilty. But so does every importer in New Orleans. It is business, *cher.*"

"So the beer comes from *Bayou des Allemands* . . ."

"And hence to the French Market, the shops along Saint Phillip and Royal, some of it to Baton Rouge, to Natchez, and Santo Domingo. If we're smart and very lucky, the dollars go to our accounts man, and then to your pretty *poche* for sweetmeats and your new damask gown. Why all the questions, *cher?*"

"I wish to know what you do with your hours," she pouted, dropping her eyes. "You are gone so many of them, and I am here to polish the same tables day after day, and Anise says that her husband spends all his time at the café . . ."

"Anise is a fool to complain. Her husband keeps her in one of the finest houses on the block. I wish you would find other friends, *cher,* she is a harridan, with only ill to speak and gossip to spread. Why not call on Madame Pinckard? She is only four doors down and a fine lady."

"She is *américaine.*"

"Of course she is, some of the best businessmen *are* these days, and her husband has one of the largest warehouses at *La Place des Armes.* All the more reason to make her acquaintance."

"She does not speak *français.*" She frowned. The truth was that Madame Pinckard drove such a fine carriage that Oliva could not muster the courage to address her on the street, much less call at her home.

"She speaks *français,* she just does not speak bayou *français.* You must learn to speak better English, *cher.* English is the future of this city. It's the future of our business, as well—"

"It's not *my* future," she said firmly. "And it is a waste of time to make talk with a woman I will scarcely see again in a few months, in a language few in Lafourche will comprehend!"

"If it is *our* future, then it is *your* future, Oliva," he said indignantly, "and it would not hurt you to extend yourself on our behalf!"

"When are we going home?" she demanded. "You promised my father. You promised *me* that we would live among my people!"

"I said that we would be in New Orleans for some time, I *told* you that clearly, so do not remind me of my promises, I'm well aware of them—"

"I will remind you, Joseph! While you are out among your compatriots day after day, I must sit here alone—"

"That is your choice, Oliva."

"That is *not* my choice, it is my curse!" Her anger turned abruptly to frustrated despair. "I am so *solitaire ici!* I have nothing to fill my days—"

"Don't be silly, *cher,* you have all of the city before you," he said, taking her in his arms. "What would you do with your days in Lafourche? No one keeps you imprisoned in this house, you can come and go freely, there is ample to keep you occupied. In fact, if you would turn more attention to these cuffs—" he added, holding out a slightly frayed shirtsleeve.

"In Lafourche," she said, "I would have my garden to weed, my chickens to tend, here I can fill our larder without scarcely leaving the house, from the *vendeurs* in the street. In Lafourche, I would have the cabin to sweep, the gallery to scrub, here the dirt—what scant dirt there is, I cannot raise a radish in this yard—never comes above the first floor!"

"And of this, you complain? Do as the other *femmes* do, Oliva, receive callers and make fine friendships—"

"Do useless fancywork and make flowers of wax to put

under glass bells, make *macramé* and play *les dominos* all the day long! I want to go home!" She began to weep, trying to wrench from his arms.

"Ah, *cher,* you must be patient! I am making a life for us, as I promised. I do so that you may be content—"

"I am lonely!" she wailed, crumpling in his arms.

He sought her lips with his own, murmuring endearments, running his mouth over her cheeks, her neck, her brow, and finally stopping her protests completely, fervently, with kisses which grew deeper, more slow and languid as she calmed.

Finally, she raised her eyes to his and whispered, "But I thought you had important business to attend, *cher?*"

"Let it wait," he said throatily, pulling her upstairs with one hand and loosening his cravat with the other.

Oliva was soon able to count four full seasons away from Bayou Lafourche. Sometimes she raged, sometimes she wept, other times the days went by in easy contentment as she found pleasures to occupy her hours.

For truth, she had to admit, the early spring days in New Orleans were golden. The parks and the opera beckoned, gala balls were held each week, and a hundred shops offered the most intriguing delights from France and Spain. Cotton was booming, flatboats skimmed back and forth, and the riches of a dozen states floated to the city. It was a roaring river port, a seaport, one of the world's least tariffed trading spots, and a jumping-off place for hordes of adventurers.

The disapproving called her a witch city, a wanton. Others called her the Paris of the New World. To Oliva, the city seemed a grand lady, part American, part Spanish, more French than either. Both *grande dame* and *gamine,* New Orleans enjoyed laughter, appreciated a good show, but loved the gallant gesture most of all. Joseph liked to say that in most of America, business sometimes paused for pleasure, but in the Queen City, as the new influx of Yankees called it, pleasure sometimes paused for business.

In time and almost reluctantly, Oliva learned to find her way around the *Vieux Carré,* exploring streets that bent as the river did, passageways where strangers might lose their way for hours, and natives often discovered shortcuts they never suspected. And always, behind her, was water: the lake, the river, a canal.

Joseph said he intended to stay only a few seasons in the city, then on to *Bayou des Allemands* and back to Lafourche. But he kept receiving word from his brother, Adolph, that all went well at the brewery, and that in fact, the partnership would likely benefit from his presence in New Orleans more than it would from his return home. New Orleans was, after all, the hub of most of the business the Weitz brothers—and most merchants—would arrange for the entire season, and her trading rooms controlled all that moved up and down the great river. Soon it was necessary for Joseph to purchase a warehouse down at the docks, to hold all the goods the Weitz brewery imported and the large inventory of beer which was stored before being sent to market.

One night Joseph came home and announced that it was time they entertained some of his business associates and their *femmes.* "I think supper would be too ambitious," he said, "but perhaps you could make a fine *crème brûlée* or a fancy *pâtisserie,* eh? I had an excellent one last week at the Fourniers, and some cordials, perhaps a good claret—"

She noted once again how very polished he was becoming. Where did he learn the difference between a good claret and a poor one? "You wish to have a soirée?" she asked anxiously.

"Nothing *très grande,* but simply to recompense all the invitations they've extended to me."

"*I* have not been a party to all these invitations."

"That is because they have not met you, *cher.* Once you meet them, they will invite you. It is important that I begin— that *we* begin to be seen in the best homes. It is one thing for me to attend with my associates in the café, it is quite another thing for us to be part of their *coterie.* "

"But I do not know how to cook such things as you suggest," she said. "Perhaps a *gâteau?* You remember the ones for our wedding? I could do such a thing with lemon ice—" She saw his frown and stopped.

"That is not quite elegant enough, I think. Perhaps we can hire a cook to help you, *cher?* Just for a time, until you can learn."

Her anger rose swiftly, surely. "That is a good deal of trouble for a single, simple invitation. Do you plan to invite these associates many times?"

Now his anger erupted as well. "Your jaw looks just like your father's now! Yes, perhaps I do intend more than one invitation, is that such a sin? I do not ask much of you, Oliva! Is it too much to expect that you might take an interest in that which keeps you in fine linens and buggy rides? I even offer to get help to do all the work for you, and still you frown and roll your eyes and act as though I asked you to host the Governor and his Lady for Holy Week!"

She moved closer to him and flounced into his lap, her eyes still snapping with anger. "Hush then!" she hissed. "You shall have your soirée, invite the whole *coterie* for all I care! I will litter the table with a thousand *pâtisseries* to dazzle the most jaded tongue. And then, I will take the first boat back to Lafourche!"

"Stop nagging me, Oliva. Your threats are empty and your words drive me mad."

"Empty, are they? You will see how empty—"

"You cannot go alone, no pilot will take you. It is too

dangerous and the trip is too long for a woman unescorted. There are still river pirates, you know, and the tides are high this spring, but go, go! If you cannot be a helpmate willingly, then run away to what you think is paradise instead."

She put a single soft hand over his mouth and pressed up against him. "I said that I would give your *gala, cher,* and I will. Now, stop your shouting, or Anise will tell all the neighbors that you assault me nightly."

He began to calm, as her hand came off his mouth and she nestled closer. "Good. I do not think it much to ask."

"And so it is not. Now, to my request. When will we leave this place?"

He sighed wearily, crestfallen. "Soon enough, I suppose. Perhaps next season, when I get the next shipment sold." He shrugged her away. "I get very tired of that question, Oliva."

She appraised him carefully. It was true, she had badgered him mercilessly. It was also true that he was becoming a satisfying husband, despite his stubbornness. He made her laugh, he piqued her curiosity, he was shrewd in ways which would likely keep them more prosperous than many.

And he could still catch and keep her eye when he moved across the room, when he bent to take his linen off the bed, when he stood before the glass and brushed his red hair until it shone like a stallion's flanks. But did she love him?

She could not say. Sometimes, she felt an enormous rush of warmth, of tenderness, even of a pulsing desire which swept her heedlessly into his arms. Was this love? She still did not feel—would she ever?—that she would give her life for him. She did know, however, that she likely could not leave him behind, no, not even for Lafourche.

Oliva put her arms around his neck and nuzzled his lips at the corner, gently insinuating the tip of her tongue between them, softly and surely gathering his mouth into her kiss. He resisted her for a moment and then let himself be wooed into returning her embrace. As he lowered her onto the divan, she began to laugh delightedly. As he moved over her, parting her skirts, her linen, and into her, she cried out with abandon.

"Hush," he said thickly, "or Anise will tell them that I assault you nightly."

She lifted her face to his and pressed into him, feeling the passion between them transform her, in her mind, from an ordinary *femme* who was cross and disagreeable to a woman of power, of magic, of secret and magnificent myth.

And so, Oliva watched a second spring come to *La Nouvelle Orléans,* and she soon came to know its markets and *banquettes* well enough to negotiate its eccentricities, to speak its English, even to understand its abysmal French. But no matter how well she might manage, she never once stopped listening, even among the clatter and bustle of the docks, the streets, the promenades, for the silent peace of the bayou.

On long warm evenings when Joseph was down at the docks, she would sit out on the gallery, listening to the sounds of the city, missing the cries of the birds, the hum of the insects, even the sigh of the wind on the water.

And this new water took some getting used to, she found. The Mississippi water, which was collected for drinking in large stone crocks and sold by the hawkers in the streets, was for her at first impossible to consume. A glass filled with it appeared to deposit—in just a few moments—a layer of sediment equal to almost a third its depth. New Orleans believed, however, that the river waters were miraculous in their healing powers. New Orleans *femmes* believed, moreover, that the river water was a source of fertility. When Joseph would occasionally bring home a buyer for supper, often the man would refuse to follow his meal with anything but a full glass of the Mississippi.

"Why, it'll purify you," she heard more than one of them claim, "and if you got a stomach ailment? Four or five glasses of the river will drive off a fever or a quickened pulse. The most wholesome water I ever drank!"

Joseph began to think seriously of building a new brewery on the west bank, to take advantage of the belief that these waters could cure most ailments, cleanse the blood, and generally keep a man fit, inside and out. A second Weitz warehouse was under construction, and so they could increase production profitably.

When he spoke of this plan, however tentatively, Oliva reminded him that the bayou provided the same water with a lot less mud. And she refused to speak of anything which would extend their stay so long. Instead, she began to wonder aloud how much longer her father might live and whether or not Valsin and Marie's first child resembled her mother. Occasional letters were no longer enough.

Though she was now more comfortable traveling the city, what Oliva actually liked best was their own small house, even if it did almost touch shoulders with two more just like it. Deeper than it was wide, with a gallery wrapping round the sides and back of delicate ironwork and waist-high railings, the house seemed cozy and spacious all at once. Its low-hanging roof shaded batten blinds, and its walls *briquetés entre poteaux,* bricked-between-posts, kept off the glare of the spring sun. A small courtyard in back sheltered a banana tree, whose sheathlike leaves guarded unripened fruit, green and bulbous.

Once she entered the door and closed it behind her, she walked through a flagstoned passageway, cool and dim. The house and yard was not a neat and precise place. Like the city itself, its beauty came more from its bounty and casual grace. Next to the house, a magnolia tree cast a circle of shadow and dropped fragrant, creamy blossoms. Sometimes Oliva would sit on the *banquette* outside, and listen to the patois of the housewives calling up and down the street in their soft slurring French. Over them all floated a pungent aroma, day and night, that of coffee dripping in a pot and a spicy gumbo.

Of all the differences between New Orleans and Lafourche, however, the one that caused her the most concern was the way the men felt themselves somehow above God and his laws. The women? Yes, they were sheltered enough. *Maman* and *les jeunes filles,* if they came from a good house, would keep within rigid confinement, escorted if they left the house and protected within privileged safety. But the men, in their cafés, their saloons, gambling palaces, and other places which Oliva could only imagine, could do largely as they wished.

And from what she could see, New Orleans *gentilshommes* seldom confused themselves with monks.

The Creole women were elegant and beautiful, wore fashionable clothes, and draped their heads in lace and feathers. But did their men appreciate their beauty? It seemed to Oliva that they appreciated more their gaming tables and their taffia, the strong rum made from the sugar cane. Most of all, they appreciated the private balls where they might meet the exotic quadroons and octoroon women, the ones with a quarter or an eighth of the African or Haitian blood which gave their lips a seductive fullness, their cheekbones a slightly foreign slant.

There was a frantic gaiety to their *joie de vivre,* even on Sunday. After Mass, they took it as another day of pleasure. All the shops were open, the people thronged to balls and theaters and danced into the night. On Sunday evening, she could see the fine ladies walking barefoot through the muddy streets on their way to a ball, their dresses pinned up nearly to their knees, their shoes borne by slaves following at a respectful distance.

While these temptations might not have worried her another time, now Oliva wondered, for with the coming spring, she realized that a child was blooming in her. The sense of it gave her a heady mix of joy and sharp alarm. A baby was finally coming to them, made of their passion, something she had watched for, waited for, wondered if she would ever know.

Part of her dreaded this intruder, part of her had worried that she might be unable to conceive at all. For nearly two years, they had been married, and no sign of what she had thought would come within a few months of sharing the same bed. Lately she had taken to drinking more and more of the Mississippi water to increase her chances, without having really decided if she wanted the water to work or not.

Now she carried life. She sensed the coming child connected her somehow to a weaving of a million women who had gone before her, who would come after, in a tangling, a thicket, and bramble wilderness of private joy and pain. From this point onwards, she knew that what she would know would be unknown to men but known to all other women, a cycle of living and loving intertwined with rabbit runs and burrows and lairs, where mothers and children are refuged together. She would never be the same.

Now that the child was coming, she could no longer rest easy, wiling away her days in this strange place. He has lain with me, she thought, and now I am someone else. Someone else in the pulse that will beat in the pulse of my own body, and in the breath that will mingle with my own breath. Now my belly is not my own, nor, perhaps, is my heart.

Each evening, she decided to tell him of her expectancy, and each evening, she could not bring herself to share the news. Finally, with the sense that she brought him at once a miracle and also a vast possibility for worry and pain, she waited until he had his supper and was seated with his pipe and his papers. Then she said, "Joseph, I have something to say, can you put those aside for now?"

He glanced up warily. "These accounts have to go out tomorrow, *cher.*"

"Never mind, then," she said calmly, "it can wait."

He peered at her. "No, no, go on and tell me." He pushed aside his papers. "I am listening."

She hesitated. "I don't know what you will say," she finally said softly.

He was instantly alert. "The only way to find out is to tell me," he said.

She stood and went to him, so that she looked down into his face. "I am with child."

To her great surprise, his eyes widened, his mouth stretched in a wide grin, and he threw his arms around her waist, burying his face in her skirts. "Ah, my love! This is wonderful!" He pulled back and looked at her, "You are certain? You are *enceinte, vraiment?*"

She laughed at his delight. "You are pleased?"

"Pleased! I am overjoyed! I thought you were going to nag me again about Lafourche or even tell me you were leaving, but praise God, you are with child!" He pulled her down in his lap gently, holding her close. "I have waited so long, *cher,* wondering if we would be blessed. I did not speak, for fear of upsetting you, but I was worried—you know, almost two years we've been wed. I am so very happy," he murmured now in her neck, "and I love you."

She put her arms around him and held him close. "It will come in September, I think. We must talk of when we will go home now, Joseph, for I want to be with my people when the child comes. No more promises, no more delays, we must speak of when—"

He hushed her softly, rocking her back and forth. "And we will, *certainement,* we will plan our departure soon. I may not be able to go immediately, but we will go soon, rest assured. The new warehouse will be finished, and I can hire a foreman to oversee our sales. I want you to be calm and happy, *cher.*" He gazed in her face. "Are you happy?"

She smiled. "Yes, I am happy. Perhaps a trifle fearsome, but I am content."

"And," he asked tenderly, "do you love me at last?"

She had anticipated this question. He had asked her only once or twice since their marriage, and each time, she was able to gently demur, tease him away from her answer, or distract him with a passion which he would read as a declaration. For in truth, she did not know if she loved him, did not know if she ever would. But she was ready. "Yes, I do," she said gently. "I do love you."

With that, he put his head to her breast, and she could feel the intensity of his embrace. She reached up and softly stroked his hair, crooning to him as she imagined she would soon croon to their child.

As spring came to the city, Oliva's yearning to go home, to be among women she knew, grew stronger with each passing day. She could no longer content herself among strangers. She was no longer able to be patient with long evenings waiting alone, while Joseph was at a meeting of associates or customers. And one such evening, New Orleans itself made the decision for her.

The night was steamingly hot, though it was only March. Oliva took her cup of coffee out on the front gallery to catch a breeze from the river. As she sat and rocked, she hummed a small phrase of French to the child within her. *"Fais dormi, ma p'tite minette,"* go to sleep, my little one, until the years to fifteen have run, when the fifteen years have fled, then my Kitten will be wed, an old song she remembered her mother singing.

There was a humming of noise down the street. It sounded as though it came closer, but Oliva could not tell what it was. The noise rose and fell, and she rose herself, set down her cup, and over the setting sun strained to see what made such a clamor.

A faint glow appeared over the row of pecan trees behind the houses. It was puzzling. As she watched, it grew brighter. The sky was darkening quickly now, but it was pinker towards the docks. She looked to the right and left. No one else was on the galleries. When she looked back at the sky, it was turning dull red. Suddenly, a huge spear of flame shot into the darkness. Oliva felt her heart lurch along with the flame.

The docks were burning! As she watched, the flames went higher and higher and widened rapidly into a broad ribbon of red. Now the noise was louder and louder, she could hear the rumble of carriages and horses' hooves, and the women came out to their galleries to stare at the sky and then rush indoors once more.

Joseph! He was at the trader rooms, down at the docks! A whole block of houses must be burning. The hot breeze brought to her now the smell of smoke, and she whirled inside. She fled to their bedroom and hung out the window for a different view. The sky was now a hideous orange color and great swirls of black smoke billowed overhead like fast-rushing storm clouds. The smell of smoke was stronger now; she could smell it in her own hair.

Instinctively, her hands went to her belly, wrapping around the child within with clenching bands of protection. Though there was little swelling there yet, she was able to think of little else. But she must! Think, think! she told herself feverishly, he'll be here soon surely, what must we save, what must I do? She rushed to the cupboards and began to pull his clothing out onto the bed. She strained to push the heavy trunk to the middle of the room, wrenched it open, and began to stack his papers within. Suddenly, a terrific explosion knocked her onto the floor, and she shrieked, clamping her hands over her ears.

Was it war? Was it the end of the world? Again and again, explosions rang out now, and she realized that barrels of oil, of liquor, of all sorts of fiery fuels must be going up at the docks. And houses, too! Out the window, she could see buggies rushing down the street, wives screaming to their husbands, men hollering instructions, and Holy Mary, where was Joseph! What should she do! The house, the ground itself seemed to tremble with the explosions.

She raced down the hall, careening from side to side,

holding her belly and rushing into the kitchen. Dishes, they would need dishes and linens and glasses and shoes! Joseph's shoes he set such store by! She raced back to the bedroom, threw some heavy buckled shoes in the trunk, and ran back again to the kitchen to continue hauling pots and plates out of the cupboards. Another rending explosion ripped the air, and she dropped a china plate, shattering it to bits. With that, she clung to the edge of the cupboard, and deep shuddering sobs almost took hold of her. But she said aloud, "Stop this! You're not burning up yet!" and squeezed her hands together until they hurt. Then she shook them vigorously and continued to unstack the china plates.

The sound of a buggy clattered close, and she dropped another plate to whirl to the door. Joseph was quickly climbing down, throwing the horse's reins fast over the post.

"Thank God, thank God!" she cried, throwing herself into his arms. "What's happening! How close is it!"

"Too close for comfort," he said, embracing her firmly, "we've got to get out fast. It's already taken five blocks from the docks to here, and—"

"The warehouse!"

"Not yet, but it's close. We may lose them both—"

Another deafening explosion jolted them into each other, and before their eyes, a house at the end of the street burst into flames.

She shrieked, her hands to her mouth in terror. Horses and buggies were racing down the street; shouting men and screaming women, some of them running afoot, were streaming past them.

"Stop it!" he said, shaking her by the shoulders. "You've got to help me now!"

She stifled her cry with her fist, nodding furiously. The heat was unbearable, the smoke was too thick to see clearly, and the horse began to whinny and wrench at the reins.

"Have you packed?" He took her arm and dragged her into the house, turning her head away from the holocaust.

"Yes, yes, a few things, but I didn't know what to—"

"Well, whatever you've done will have to do. Go take five minutes—count aloud, Oliva, count with each step—five minutes only—I've got to hold the horse, else he'll bolt. Throw whatever you must have in the trunks and the rest must stay—go now!" and he shoved her into the house, his voice swift and rough.

She counted aloud, the sound of her voice so strange in the house, the heat seemed to bulge the walls now, and she raced from room to room, grabbing a lamp there, a lace tablecloth here, a piece of china, and threw them into the trunk. It was a small buggy, not much room for more than the two of them, and where did he get it? No time, no time, she almost shrieked when her steps slowed or galloped in the wrong direction, she felt she was a rat in a maze, her own small house suddenly huge and foreign. Another explosion—this one so close! And the rooms were brighter than day with a garish lurid glow that seemed to say the walls were burning from the outside even as she brushed around them. If they lost the warehouse! Many men might have stayed to save their goods, but he had raced to save her—two hundred, two hundred and fifty—

"Now!" she heard Joseph shout. "Right now, you must come!"

She rushed out, pulling a shawl around her shoulders, though her arms and legs were damp with sweat.

"Hold him!" he called, tossing the reins to her, and she braced herself, tugging on the horse who tossed his head and danced in panic.

"There's a trunk in the kitchen, too!" she shouted, and she heard him curse and cry out, "No room!" Another whoop of too-near thunder, a hissing crackle of falling timber, and another house, closer this time, exploded into flame. The air was so heated that she could scarcely breathe, so close and searing that she feared taking it into her lungs. She screamed and yanked on the horse, who almost lifted her off the ground, tossing his head and plunging.

Then Joseph was there, throwing the trunk on the buggy as though it were kindling. He took the reins in one hand, speaking soothingly to the horse and to her at once, "Step up, Oliva, climb on fast. I can't help you and hold him, too." She stepped up, but the horse danced, and she slid off again, banging her knee and her side sharply against the buggy, but she scarcely noticed it, jumping up again and grabbing one rein when she was in the seat. Joseph was quickly up and beside her, turning the horse away from the house now, and as they trotted off, the horse barely held in check, two more houses, no more than a quarter block down, were flaming at windows and roofs.

The sky, the world itself, was an inferno of flames and noise and ear-splitting explosions as the earth trembled beneath their racing buggy. Torrents of sparks shot into the sky and then drifted down on them like lazy, blood-colored rain. The clouds of smoke were black and boiling, shot through with furious flames.

They raced through the square, pulling up sharply to avoid a dozen buggies scattering in all directions. The St. Louis Cathedral was illuminated by the flames in a glare brighter than day, monstrous and sharp-spired amid the billowing clouds of smoke. For an instant, Oliva thought this must be what hell looks like; the cathedral's gothic windows were fiery eyes of a huge looming demon. Then they jerked around the corner to see the Cabildo threatened by flames and that route cut off.

Joseph cursed, yanked the horse around, and circled the square, edging past panicked crowds and jostling carriages. There was a crash of falling timbers, she heard a shrill scream, and towards them came a group of volunteer fire-fighters pulling a small pump on a cart. People raced past carrying buckets full of sloshing water. Smoke burnt her nostrils and her cheeks streamed with sweat. She cried out, "Hurry, hurry!" but she knew he couldn't hear her.

They raced down several blocks, pulling up only when the flames were farther away. Still they could see fire roaring up above the trees and buildings, the street was brighter than the hottest noon, and monstrous shadows fell and twisted around them. She turned to Joseph and saw that his face was pale, his red hair damp and askew over his brow.

As she reached back to brace the trunk, a sharp pain went through her and a moan wrenched her mouth awry. His hand reached back to steady her, his eyes still on the horse and their route. She clutched her abdomen, her eyes going wide. Another pain, sharper still. And then a third, dull and insidiously deep. *"Sacré nom,"* she breathed, beginning to sob.

"It's all right now," Joseph called to her, "we're safe. I'll find a place to leave you, and then I must go back to the docks." He was still struggling with the unruly animal and had not seen her face.

"Non!" she gasped, and she slumped against him.

"Jesus, Oliva!" he shouted, staring at her now, wrestling the horse to the side of the road. Nearby, flames were encroaching closer; it wasn't safe to stop, yet stop he did, as smoke billowed thickly near. He held the animal with one hand and pulled her to him with the other. "Oliva! Are you in pain? Is it the child?"

For answer, she could only scream, bend double, and clutch her stomach in agony, for she knew as surely as she would never see that little house again, that she was emptying inside, could feel the life run from her, and nothing she could clench to, could grasp, would hold it back.

She woke in a small room, her memory blurred by a haze of pain and blood. For long moments, she lay quietly, trying to sense the loss within her. She felt only a deep throbbing cramp, an empty ache which sharpened with the slightest shift of her hips. In one corner, a nun came forward, her white wimple winged about her face, her gray habit swishing over the stone floor.

"You are awake, child?" she murmured.

Oliva could see now that other beds were in the room, other women, she supposed, who were either sick, bereft, or dying. "Did I lose the child?" she whispered hoarsely.

The nun nodded. "But it was a clean loss," she said quietly. "And you will have another, if God wills."

"Where am I?"

"You are with the Ursulines."

The large, gray convent on the other side of the city. Oliva could recall seeing the nuns coming and going from behind the walls to the market, always in twos, always with their faces hidden behind their veils. "My husband?"

"He waits outside for you to awake. I will fetch him."

Oliva closed her eyes, gathering her strength. The sky outside, that small patch which she could see outside the convent walls, was dark with smoke. Somewhere, the fire still raged.

"Oliva," Joseph said softly, taking her hand.

She opened her eyes and focused on his face. His dear

face. Suddenly, the loss overwhelmed her, and her resolve to be calm crumpled into ragged sobs. "It's gone!" she wept.

"Yes, I know, *cher,*" he said, his own eyes filling. "I am so sorry! Perhaps the fire, the fear, all the rushing—"

"I fell! I lost our baby!" As her sobs rose, the nun came to her side to calm her, but she pushed up on one elbow and grasped for Joseph's arms. "I want to go home now!" she cried. "You must take me home!"

"Oliva, I promise, I'll take you home as soon as you can travel, I swear it! Let us see where we stand first, though, the house, the warehouses, I must see to the inventory—"

She fell back then on the bed, sobbing so that she could no longer speak. He tried to pull her up into his arms again, but she shook her head and wrenched away, turning so that her face was hidden in the pillow.

"Oliva, we'll have another child. Please, my love, please don't injure yourself—" he plucked at her, trying to cradle her closer.

"My baby is dead!" she shrieked at him, "don't speak to me of another!"

Now he ignored her clawing hands and pulled her against him, heedless of her fists. "My baby is dead, too," he said painfully. His words reached her then, and she began to subside. Finally, they wept together until they could only hold each other's hands, silently pressing palms for whatever comfort they could find and offer.

Five hours was all it took to burn New Orleans to the ground. The worst disaster the city had suffered in a hundred years left scores of homes destroyed, more than eight hundred

115

buildings—including Saint Louis Cathedral, the Cabildo, and the Presbytere—demolished. Most of the dockside warehouses were gone, ruining more than two-thirds of the city's merchants.

So fast, Oliva marveled. The good God could twist life around like a coiling snake in the blink of an eye. They lost their warehouse and everything in it, including the one which had not even been completed . . . all in the space of five hours. After the nuns released her, warning her to rest and stay quiet or the bleeding could begin again, she insisted that Joseph take her back to where they had spent their first two years of marriage.

She sifted dismally through the blackened timbers with a length of wrought iron railing. Everything was gone. She found four metal buckles and an iron skillet. Either the flames or the foragers had taken all else.

"Thank God we didn't own it," Joseph said soberly.

"We owned everything in it," she said sadly.

"Still, we're better off than some. Much of the inventory was shipped, and we were paid for that, at least. We lost the recent deliveries and that last shipment of rice and sugar, but we're lucky, compared to many, this is a good lesson to keep our assets in several different cities—"

"I want to go home," she said wearily, woodenly. She averted her face, picking through the greasy, black debris.

"We will," he said gently. "We'll make the trip as soon as you're strong again."

"I'm strong now."

"Well then, I'll arrange passage tomorrow or as soon as I can. Business in this town will be impossible for six months or more anyway. We'll concentrate on Baton Rouge and Natchez. I'll consult with Adolph, and we'll plan what to do."

She looked up at him. "Are we *ruinés?*"

"No, no," he said, "and you are not to worry about that. We have lost much, yes, but we are not bankrupt. We will survive. Perhaps even flourish." He forced a smile. "After all, we started from nothing, my brother and me, and so long as people drink beer, we will prosper."

"Now is the time to leave," she said.

"And we will, I told you—"

"*Non,* not to *Bayou des Allemands,* to Lafourche."

"I know, I know," he said, taking her arms, "and we will go to Lafourche for awhile. Baton Rouge can handle the next few shipments, I guess. But then I must see my brother. And you have a new home waiting in *des Allemands!* Or will soon enough, once I can get back to begin the construction—"

"You promised," she said, low and determined. "You promised my father; you promised me. I am going. If you love me, you will come."

"Of course I love you. Please don't upset yourself, Oliva. We have lost a baby, but we have not lost each other."

"We *will* lose each other if you do not keep your promise."

"God in heaven, Oliva! Can you not try to understand? I have—I have lost a good deal, too, after all! Do you think you are the only one who is bereft? All I have worked for in two years, my dreams and plans for us!" He dropped her arms and turned away in despair.

She pulled him around to face her. "I *do* understand, Joseph! I have lost my dreams, too. But I cannot build new ones here, and neither can you, at least not now. Let at least one of us be content, *cher.* Take me home, as you promised, or I shall go alone. Yes, even if it means I must live in my father's house again, that would be better than in this city of strangers."

"And what will I do in Lafourche?"

"You can farm rice there as well as in *des Allemands.*" Her face began to brighten as she saw the possibilities. The Weitz beer depended on the rice, Joseph always told her. They bought the best rice the farmers could grow, and from it they made the beer, a fine light beer using imported hops and wheat from Germany. The secret to their success was the sugar they added to the brew—that and the fact that they offered the only beer in the Territory.

"Joseph, papa would give you the land, for truth! The widow's land is his, no? You could grow the rice, let Adolph run the brewery, and pay your factor to sell the beer here in New Orleans. What you would save by growing your own rice, you could pay him plenty, and still make more money than you did by buying all the rice you use."

"Grow rice? Be a farmer? Is that what you think I am?"

"You always said, if you could get more rice at a good price, you could make more profits. Why pay others to grow what we can grow ourselves? And you could put up a *sucrerie!* Take half for every load of cane you press, and you would not need to buy sugar from the farmers in *des Allemands* at all! Guidry is putting in cane next year, Marie says in her letters, and Benoit already has those forty arpents planted. They need a mill and—"

"I see you have given this some thought," he said quietly.

Actually she realized she had given it very little. Always she said only that she wanted to go home. She had not envisioned what that might mean for Joseph. He had promised, and that was enough. But now her thoughts flooded upwards in a waterspout of hope. "Enough to see that it is possible," she said urgently. "You said it to me often enough, *cher,* anything is possible. I have only to wish it." And she smiled.

His answering grin surprised her. "I see I will rue that remark a hundred times over, in the years to come." He embraced her gently. "But it is good to see you smile at last." He looked over her head at the destruction around them. "If you can smile in the midst of this horror, we will make it."

"We will go home?"

"Yes, but only until we know what else we can do."

"I told you what we can do—"

118

"You told me, yes, I know. And we will see for a few months, all right?"

She nodded mutely, resolving that she would think no further past those few months for now. There was too much pain here for them, that much she knew. The pain of loss in all directions: a baby, all their worldly goods, so many months of hard work and dollars invested in the warehouses . . . even the loss of their innocence. Never again would they be so young and hopeful as they were in New Orleans. But surely, in Lafourche, the pain would recede. Silently she vowed to make him so happy there that he would not wish to leave. She could not see how his mouth was twisted in disappointment above her head.

Now Oliva could remember that pain vividly if she sought for the memory. She picked up the pan of corn meal and went out to the chicken yard, calling to her favorite black leghorn hen. When Anise came running, the other twenty hens looked up from the grass at the edge of the bayou, squawked in alarm, and came flapping in around her ankles as well.

She called throatily to her favorites, clucking to them, spurning a few aside with her bare foot as they got too feisty with each other, holding the small of her back with one hand for support. It was getting harder and harder to stand for long periods now that her belly grew out beyond her toes, but at least her fears that this child, too, would be lost were finally eased.

It was the fear, she figured, that lost the last one. The fear, the shock of the flames, the jolting of the horse, the up and down and all around flurry of frightened packing—and all she had to show for it was a pile of charred timber, a single trunk, and an emptied belly.

No fear now. Nothing here that could ever make such panic in her heart again. She straightened up awkwardly and eyed the steep roof of the newly finished little house set back among the trees. Joseph would have to get her loom down from the attic. This was the last month she could safely climb those stairs.

It was a good sturdy bayou house, built by her father, Valsin, Joseph, and others, who held the ladder and cut the cypress. As she'd suspected, it took only a week at the widow's house before Joseph consented to build his own. The high-pitched roof was timbered with stout shakes against the rain, the walls were strong and straight, the chinks between the clapboards were tightly stuffed with moss and clay, and the mud chimney would keep them warm in the coldest months. When they held the daubing bee, more than a dozen families came to help plaster the walls with mud. She had two bedrooms, a sitting room, a kitchen to the rear, and even a *garçonnière* for many sons up the side stairway to the attic. A good house. One which would keep them together, she prayed.

She had prayed more in these last ten months than at any other time in her life. As soon as they arrived in Lafourche, before they selected the site for their cabin, she had consulted Marie about the most likely saint.

"Saint Ursula is good," Marie said confidentially. "She grants boons all the time, and usually does not require more than a dozen candles and three or four nights of prayers."

"But can she do the most difficult miracles?" Oliva asked anxiously. "I mean, even the almost impossible wishes?"

"No one but God can do those things, *cher,*" Marie answered solemnly. "What do you wish to ask?"

Oliva turned away, ashamed. "I need to be with child again, in a hurry. So that Joseph will not leave Lafourche."

Marie smiled. "He will not leave you, *'tite,* whether you give him a son or no."

"Maybe not forever, but he likely will leave here quick enough if I cannot find a reason for him to stay."

"Your papa is going to give him some of his finest lands! Is that not reason enough?"

"Not nearly. Now," Oliva said grimly, "you must tell me the truth. For a miracle, no matter how many candles and how many nights of prayer and days of fasting, which saint is the best?"

"Well," Marie answered doubtfully, "perhaps Saint Matilde would be better then. Do you not wish to consult Father LeBlanc?"

"No, no. Saint Matilde, you say? And how many candles will she require?"

"To get you with child?"

"Yes, and for one other miracle, besides."

"A smaller miracle?"

"I cannot think it would be so difficult as a child," Oliva nodded.

"Then perhaps . . . yes, perhaps three dozen will do," Marie said.

That night Oliva went to the chapel and bought six candles, lit them, and knelt before the Holy Mother, running her rosary through her fingers until her eyes were leaden and her knees were stiff with righteousness. Silently and fervently, she repeated the same prayer over and over: Holy Mother, intercede for me with Saint Matilde and direct her to hear my plea. If you would keep my husband at my side, you must get me with child. Make haste, Saint Matilde, and hear my prayer. And if you cannot get me with child, then make my husband stay in Lafourche!

Outside, Oliva could hear the sounds of the bayou night, the call of the owl, the songs and belches of the frogs. Inside, the chapel was silent, except for the creak of the floor and the occasional hiss and sputter of a candle. Those who came and went did not speak, for it was understood that the evening solicitors came to God on errands which were somehow more secret and soul-rending than the beseechments of the daylight faithful. The chapel smelled dank, like the damp and softened coffins of a hundred old ones. The odor of incense did not completely drive away the smell of age.

Nonetheless, Oliva was determined to be faithful to her task. For six nights, she went to the chapel and prayed thus, lighting six candles each night. Her absence required some subterfuge, and the candles required almost all of the money Marie had saved from her netting and her chickens, but Oliva vowed to return her twenty dollars as soon as she could. She did not feel guilty about the dollars. But she did, sometimes, feel ashamed at her request: to make her husband stay in Lafourche. She realized, too late after three nights of prayer, that she had not prayed for his contentment in Lafourche, only for his presence. She supposed that asking Saint Matilde to take away her husband's will would seem evil to many, but she resolved to remain steadfast and rely on Saint Matilde to deal with the sin, if there be any.

After all, he made a promise, she told herself. I am only helping him to keep that promise. Sometimes men are weak and need some borrowed strength to do what they must. She told herself this nightly as she repeated her prayer. And she resolved not to examine it carefully henceforth.

To her great relief, within three months she was able to come to Joseph and announce that she was once more with child. She watched him carefully as she said the words, looking for some sign that he recognized and resented his entrapment.

But he only held her tightly. "My love," he said, "this one will be fine. You will be blooming and beautiful as a spring flower, I will guarantee it. I want you to do nothing from now until the child is born, and I want you to think of nothing but your well-being."

A passionate sense of relief and gratitude washed over

Oliva in that instant, and she embraced him long and fervently. Curiously, swiftly, she desired him more than she had for weeks, and then the feeling passed and she was left with a vast tenderness. "I love you, my husband," she said quietly. And for perhaps the first time in their marriage, she meant each of those words in every far-reaching corner of her heart.

Now Joseph had planted the new acreage to rice, the *sucrerie* was nearly finished, and her belly had grown to where she felt less a blooming flower than a ripening melon. As the months lengthened and time in the bayou slowed to a pace she recalled from her girlhood, she began to weary of the long wait for her body to empty. For a time, early on, she had felt apart from all who might touch her, dreamily alone and solaced by the magic flow of the days, feeling only the palpitating presence within. Then the child would kick, an uneasy impact jarring her vitals like a great foreign heart beating. She would place her hand tenderly to the spot and smile inwardly, filled with a dark, potent knowing.

When she was finally grown huge, heavy, and slow, she moved with a tender deliberateness. Her habits were almost animal. All of her past seemed unreal, and only the present had any power. Early on in her expectancy, she had wondered what Emile Arceneaux was doing in that moment. Was his wife swollen with child as well? Had he heard of her marriage? If he returned to Lafourche, would he seek her out? And Paul Bellard. She thought of him as well, wondering if news of her coming child brought him painful thoughts of what he lost when she refused him.

But as she grew larger and larger, she no longer thought of Emile or Paul, of *papa* and *maman,* of Valsin or Marie, finally scarcely even of Joseph. She thought only of herself and the child. While sinking into the utter exhaustion that came each night, she stretched her legs deliciously, turning about and about on the cool sheets. She drank deeply of the cistern water. The flavor of ripe oranges or sour pickles assumed a new fullness, and her mouth filled with saliva when food touched her lips. Life took on a certain largeness which made all else seem unimportant, intrusive. She felt an irresistible flowing within her like the bayou itself.

Joseph alternated between being tenderly gentle with her and her belly and exasperated by the distance between them. Just lately, he had stopped touching her in the night altogether.

"I don't want to hurt you," he murmured.

"You won't."

"There doesn't seem to be any room for me anymore."

"There's always room for you."

"Well, I don't feel it."

She took his hand and placed it on her mounding belly. With both of their heads down on the pillows, her stomach looked like one of those Indian mounds of shells—high, white, and almost sacred in its remoteness. He took his hand away. And then he began on a refrain he'd been repeating for months.

"When the child is born, we should go to *des Allemands.* At least for a while. I can't stay here, there's nothing for me here."

"The rice will be ready for harvest soon, and the sugar will come in soon after."

"Adolph needs my help."

She chuckled lightly. "More than your wife? More than your own fields?" She took his hand and placed it back on her stomach. "More than your own child?"

"When the harvest is in, I will need to go to Baton Rouge. And perhaps to New Orleans, as well. I cannot depend on our accounts men to do everything, or we'll be robbed blind. By now, the docks will be rebuilt, and we should find new warehouses again. And when the cold weather comes, little here will need my direction . . ." he talked on quietly, planning his future as he spoke of it.

Oliva was silent. Truly she scarcely heard him, so conscious of her moving womb was she. It seemed to her that she

124

carried a whole village within her, she could sometimes swear she heard their voices, could feel their feet stamping softly. She no longer needed Joseph, and when she thought of this she felt a flash of fear. Yet her body still needed him, and when he was gone upriver, she was fretful and without tranquility. His body sometimes seemed so imprinted on hers that her skin retained the memory, his touch so essential that she felt breathless and arid without him near.

And so she understood how he felt, for she too wished for their life back together. A few more weeks, the midwife said. She stretched once more, trying to soothe her back's ache, throwing the corn in a wide spiral for the flapping chickens. A late arrival rushed into the flock, a fat guinea hen followed by six black downy chicks. That one was hatched the first week the roof was on, she recalled. And now she has a family of her own.

She now is more than simply the sum of her parts. As am I, Oliva thought. Soon, I will be not only daughter and sister and wife, I will also be mother. If he comes to me and says *des Allemands* again, I may refuse not for my own sake, not even for the sake of his promise, but also for the sake of his child. He will not leave us. This much I do know of Joseph Weitz.

But much else, she shook her head in silent exasperation, I am still learning. She looked up to see Deborah, the Choctaw squaw Joseph had hired, coming down the steps of the little house with a basin of dishwater.

Another compromise: was there never an end to them in marriage? She could move Joseph to Lafourche, but she could not, altogether, move Lafourche into his German heart. It was the custom to keep goats bedded with sheep in *des Allemands?* So then, the Weitz goats slept with the Weitz sheep, no matter if no other Acadian family mixed two such different bedmates. It was the German custom to make of the Birth of Christ a holiday of raucous noise and gifts rather than holy prayer? So then, Joseph would awaken Oliva with gaily wrapped parcels and accordion music on Christmas Day, when all neighbors in every direction were trooping in solemn reverent silence to Holy Mass. But then on New Year's day, *Le Bonhomme Janvier,* when all children looked for gifts, fruits, and fireworks, he wanted only to dance with her and sing sentimental songs. It was the custom to hire, for the *frau,* a servant to help with the cleaning and cooking, if one could afford such a blessing in *des Allemands?* Then a Choctaw squaw named Deborah would plague her days and trail her steps, even if every Acadian *femme* likely whispered behind Oliva's back.

Sacré nom! No one had ever warned her what a foreign territory marriage could be. She spoke with Valsin about it sometimes, with Marie more often, but neither of them was less than content with their lot. No one else seemed to feel, sometimes, that they lived with a stranger. She glanced down. Her swollen belly reminded her forcefully of one common ground where all differences ceased: on those nights when Joseph turned to her, naked and proud in his manhood, she felt the neighbors, Lafourche, the bayou itself, slipping away into oblivion. Nothing then mattered but his body against her own. She twisted the simple gold band around her finger absently. It would barely move for the swelling of her fingers.

She glanced up at the crape myrtle bush. A large spider-web beaded by soft feelers of mist hung above her. A very beautiful sleek spider sat in its center, and her tiny mate of the moment was at her side. How lucky she is, Oliva thought. She owns her world securely, rules and uses her husband, and then eats him once his purpose is scattered over her eggs. If her world is ruined, she merely remakes it to her own design. So lovely. So strong. And when the new web is finished, she arranges the next series of consorts like a movable feast.

She walked to the riverbank and slathered mud on her hands to soften them, as her mother had taught her. Here the huge buttressed cypresses were draped with long gray draperies of moss, the brown water was mottled with patches of bright green floating with imperceptible slowness, resolving into slow, curious, ever-changing patterns. They eased her mind, as always. The bayou mud was like creamy fudge on her fingers; the color was a soft reddish yellow, smooth, with a fine, tawny sheen. Rubbed on her skin, it was as bland as salve, more effective than any sweet New Orleans soap, and left her skin with a bit of its own rosy glow.

Two weeks, maybe less, Madame Lascaux, the midwife, said. A big boy, bigger than Simon Doucet, bigger even than Valsin, she said. So get ready, *cher,* and rub that hog fat over your belly every night, every morning, loosen that skin for his coming, eh?

And once he came? Could she then keep his papa here to get him raised?

"*Frau!*"

Oliva sighed and turned her back to the bayou. The Choctaw squaw's voice raised again with that ridiculous word, the one she'd been trained to call in *des Allemands* when she had a question.

"*Frau!* You come!"

Oliva wondered why, after ten months, the squaw's calls still sounded more like commands than questions. She went towards the house. "I am here," she called back wearily, answering the Indian as she always did, in English. Little enough Deborah understood of that, but more than the German Oliva had managed to learn.

The squaw was holding up two hands. In one was a squirrel carcass, in the other, a gutted catfish. No doubt she'd managed to wipe both against her dirty skirt. "Which one you want?" she called out, slapping the squirrel against her chest casually.

"Neither do I want out in this dust!" Oliva snapped back. "You can not wait until I return to ask me this, *hein?*"

As she reached the squaw, Oliva took the squirrel from her hand. "I will cook it myself, Deborah."

"I clean it."

Oliva rolled her eyes silently. Perhaps when the baby came, she would welcome Deborah's two helping hands, but till then, they only cluttered up the little house. And the thought of the Indian sleeping back with her baby in the little room which would serve as nursery! But Joseph would not hear of her dismissal.

"You set her to do the chores you don't want to do, *cher*. You want to cook? Fine, nobody says you mustn't. But she can do the laundry. She can haul the water, feed the stock, hoe the garden. Surely you can find enough to keep her busy."

Almost as though her stomach had been in league with the midwife, Oliva's labor started one evening two weeks later. As her hour approached, she was resigned, quiescent, feeling like an inert shuffling mass of hot swollen flesh, incapable of laughter, wrath, or pain. What did it matter? What did anything matter? She ran her leaden fingers through her hair. They came away joyless and damp and she did not care. Her leg, propped ungracefully on a chair edge, would slide off and thud inertly on the floor, like wood, and she did not care. She wanted only to be left alone, not to be talked to, not to be looked at. She felt it was indecent for Joseph to compel her to look at him, speak to him. Once she felt like asking him to dig her a lair on the riverbank for her to crawl into, hidden from people and things. His face was to her remote, meaningless, and unreal.

But in a matter of hours, her first pains changed her torpor to keen alertness. When the small ones began, like thin threads tugging at her inside, she suddenly sat up, made wry faces, joked with Joseph, and insisted that he not leave her alone.

He picked up his accordion and sang to her,

> Si je meurs, je veux que l'on m'enterre,
> Dans la cave, où il y a du vin
> Les deux pieds contre la muraille
> Et la tête sous le robinet

She joined him on the verse,

> If I die, I wish to be buried,
> In the cellar where there is wine,
> Both feet against the wall
> And my head under the faucet,

and then they laughed until she gasped for breath.

All her mental dullness was gone. She felt girded for a battle. Deborah was jarring figs. The air was sharp with the odor of cloves. The midwife came, and almost immediately the pains made Oliva give up her jokes and begin to moan. Soon she was screaming great peals of pain, which she knew must be heard miles down the bayou.

Somewhere she went away for a while, someplace where the pain could no longer tear her, and when she came back to herself, the midwife was shouting about twins. Two healthy squalling identical faces peering up at her from the bloodied sheet. Joseph went out on the gallery and shot off his gun. One shot for a girl, two for a boy was the tradition. Oliva lay and, with the last of her strength, counted four shots. The midwife said she had never seen such perfection in boys.

"Usually," she sighed, "it is the *filles* who break your heart, yes? But these two! They will break their share before they bait their first hook! You don't make babies easily, *cher,* but those you make are *très beaux!"*

Oliva slept deeply then, remembering how she used to believe that she could make all winds blow in her direction. That she would be her own good luck. It was true. Two sons! And they would learn to make their own good fortune, as well.

Once the twins came, she was thankful more than once for Deborah's clumsy hands. In time, she became comfortable to let the squaw hold one while she nursed the other, to let her bathe one while she wetted the other, even to let her take both into the garden that Oliva might have a small slice of peace.

Her father came then, almost every afternoon, to hold the boys and watch them on their blanket on the gallery. Rocking away the hours, he would tell Simon, his namesake, and Samuel, named for Joseph's father, of the old days and ways.

In the evenings, Valsin and Marie would often come with their three children, and Joseph would play the accordion. It was Marie who first noticed that Simon and Samuel, from the time they could first clap their hands to the music, always clapped in perfect unison.

"See how they do it, without even looking to see what the other does?" she marveled. "As though they were four hands on the same body."

Samuel and Simon sat in their favorite place, on a beaver skin Valsin had given them when they were babies, sprawled before the fire. Two little black-haired heads close together, two pairs of laughing eyes, four chubby hands clapped at their father who played and winked and japed for their amusement. Their favorite song was

> Pov' piti Mamzelle Zizi!
> Li gagnin bobo dans coeur!
> Pov' piti Mamzelle Zizi!

Poor lil' Mamzelle Zizi!
She's got a pain in her heart!
Poor lil' Mamzelle Zizi!

The twins understood little of the song, of course, but they loved to shout out together at the chorus, "Po' Zee-zee, po' Zee-zee!"

After Joseph got them thoroughly excited, he would scoop them both up, one under each arm, and dance about the room, jostling them gently up and down and stomping in time with his boots. Then Oliva would leap up and pretend to try to wrest them from him, to save her boys from his big bear hug. Valsin's children would join in, racing about the little cabin with Joseph chasing them, and the twins yelling like catamounts. Of course, the harder he stomped, the more she shrieked, the more they crowed with laughter, and even old Simon must wipe his eyes to see them so full of joy.

During the long warm days, the twins followed her out to the garden where she taught them to pluck the weeds that crowded her beans and squash. One day she noticed that they had their own system, one which seemed to have been agreed to without their ever speaking of it.

Samuel started down the row pulling rank grasses from around the bean plants, and Simon followed closely behind, resettling the dirt around the bean, patting it back into place. Each twin scooted on his knees, bending over the dirt as though in prayer.

This alone seemed scarcely unusual, but then Oliva saw that without a signal, Samuel would suddenly leave the plucking to his brother and assume the responsibility of re-planting and repatting any disarrayed bean. Down the beans they went, taking turns at each task as each tired, never bickering or even clarifying their duties, until they reached the end of the row. Then without a word, they would turn in unison to the next row and begin again. It was like watching musicians who had played together so many times that

131

they did not need to watch the others' hands to know when to stop or start.

"It almost seems they have one heart and mind," she said that night to Joseph, while she lay in his arms. "Sometimes I watch them, and I feel that they are speaking without saying a word, yes?"

"I know," he murmured. "The same with their food."

"*Ma foi,* that is for truth! They will eat only what the other eats, and no more nor less! If Samuel pushes aside his *cous cous* in a tidy pile to the side of his plate, Simon does the same without even tasting to see if he likes it. If Simon will eat only four beans, Samuel will never eat five. And they do this without watching."

"Have you tried separating them at supper? See if they will—"

"Only once and never again! When you were in Baton Rouge last, I tried to put Samuel at one end of the table and Simon at the other, so they could not see each other's plate so well. Such a squalling, as if I cut one finger away from the fist! *Non, vraiment,* I would rather have them starve than break their hearts."

"They're hardly starving," Joseph chuckled, "they grow so fast, it's as though they have a plan for that as well. But you must make them obey you, *cher.* I see them bend you around their fingers. One cries—"

"One never cries alone," she grimaced.

"Well then *both* cry, and you go to your knees before them like a nun before the cross. They need to mind you, *cher,* and you need to make them."

"Oh, you're one to talk," she grumbled, burrowing deeper under his arm to nuzzle against his ribs. "Half the time, you are either in the fields or on the river, and when you're here, you cannot say them nay!"

"I do so. I slapped both their backsides good for them when they spilled the kettle in the hearth. I told them once, and then I showed them I meant it."

132

"Yes, and then you held them and rocked them until they stopped crying, promising them each they could ride old Ned twice round the yard, when that mule had a passel of better things to do than give two twins a bouncing for half a day."

He grinned. "For truth, the one who loves them best, if making them mind is any measure of it, is their squaw. That one only need cast an eye on Samuel, but Simon yells bloody hell, and vice versa."

"I'd yell too if that Choctaw cast me an eye." She mock shuddered. "Such an ugly eye, that one."

"Well, I didn't take her on because she was comely, *certainement*. But she takes care of the twins, you must admit. And she seems to love them as her own. Often I have seen them bring their little treasures to her, and she croons and marvels as though they brought her rubies and diamonds."

"It is strange," she said thoughtfully, "that they speak so little. Have you noticed?"

"They are only two."

"And a half. Marie's children talked more than the twins."

"They talk. If they don't talk so much, perhaps it's because they have each other," Joseph said drowsily. "And so they do not need to speak to others so often."

"Deborah seems to understand their prattle almost as well as I do," she added.

"She cares for them."

"She surely does," Oliva granted him. She let her voice yawn away to a murmur. "I'm glad they have each other," she finally whispered. "They will never know loneliness at least."

When the twins were three, Oliva began to notice just the slightest differences between them. Nothing that anyone but a mother would see, merely single shiftings in the same shadows. For instance, both boys were sweet and loving. Hearts full of wonder and love for trees and flowers, for birds and dogs and horses and other people, and everything under the sun. They shared with each other anything they had, as though each thought nothing of such division and did not feel their own share diminished in the slightest.

But Simon would urge Samuel to share his portion with somebody else as well. "Save that for *grandpère,*" he'd say to his twin. "He likes Mama's cakes."

"He can get some then," Samuel would say calmly. "There's plenty left."

"But he likes it better if you give it to him," Simon would confide. "Put it in your pocket for when he comes."

And Samuel would put aside stray pieces of cake or bread to give to his grandfather when he arrived. Often he would forget, and Oliva would find damp, twisted balls of dough or crumbled bread in the folds of his little pockets. She rarely found such forgotten foods in Simon's pockets, not because he did not save them, but because he did not forget to give them away.

Sometimes, for a special treat, Oliva would let the twins touch her mother's feather robe. They were not allowed to put it on the cabin floor, as much as they wished to roll on it. But she would drape the gloriously colored cape over the

134

back of a chair, and they would stand and stroke it for long moments, murmuring to each other of the things they could see within.

"This is eagle," Simon would say confidently. "Smell it, don't it smell like eagle?"

Samuel would bend down and gently rub his nose on the long, white feather. "Smells like goose to me. Maybe swan."

"*Ma foi!*" Simon scoffed. "This is eagle for sure."

"This is the neck of a hummingbird," Samuel maintained.

Simon looked doubtful.

" 'Tis, I can tell it, me."

"You're right," Simon generously conceded. "Hummingbird."

Samuel beamed triumphantly.

Joseph watched them carefully, smiling to himself and only speaking if they rubbed the feathers too roughly. Later he said to Oliva, "They even take turns being right, you notice? It's almost unnatural."

"It's not *anormal,*" she said calmly, "it's twins."

Joseph was traveling to Baton Rouge on the morning that Oliva felt a certain warmth coming from Simon's skin. At first, she thought little of it, setting the twins outside to play quietly with their collection of oyster shells which Valsin constantly replenished for them.

But in an hour, Samuel came running to her, his eyes full of alarm. "*Maman,*" he cried breathlessly, "*S'mon tombé malade!*" He only spoke French when he was tired, cross, or frightened.

She hurried out to the shaded gallery to find his twin leaning wearily against the side of the cabin, his small sides moving in and out much too quickly. When she lifted him, he seemed loose as a sack of rice and his skin was hot to her touch.

"What is it, *cher?*" she asked, gathering him close and taking them both inside. "Deborah!" she called to the squaw. The woman shuffled from the back storeroom where she'd

135

been cleaning skins. "Simon's got a fever," Oliva said calmly, lest his brother's eyes grow even more fearful. "Bring some cool water and my herbal."

She quickly got Simon's clothes off his skin, tucked him inside the bed he shared with his brother, and said to Samuel, "Did you eat anything, *cher?* Outside, did you put anything in your mouth? Did Simon suck on the shells, perhaps?"

"Non, maman," he said, *"rien, vraiment."* He looked anxiously at Simon. "You put him wrong," he said fretfully.

"What do you mean," Oliva asked, already turning back to the fevered boy.

"That's the wrong side," he said, his voice rising.

"Ma foi, as if such a thing matters," she scolded. "This side or that side—"

But Simon, hearing him, was already trying to move to the other side of the bed. "This side," he said wearily to his mother. "I sleep on this side."

Samuel sighed with relief as Simon rolled to where he usually slept. He went to stand beside his brother's head and he whispered something low to him.

"What is that you tell him?" Oliva asked.

"That he can have all my shells," Samuel said solemnly. "Even the *monstre* ones from the *poulpe.*"

"The octopus does not have a shell," Oliva said, busying herself with the basin of water and her leather bag of herbals which Deborah had set by the bed. She put a wet cloth on Simon's brow and took his wrist in her fingers.

"Oncle says they do," Simon said faintly. "The biggest ones in the sea." With that, he closed his eyes and a fine sheen of sweat came onto his face, as though it erupted from his pores.

In that instant, Oliva was struck by a cold fear. Cleoma died of just such a heat when she was little younger than Simon. Her only sister. And no matter what Lebanon Doucet did to ease her, to physic her sickness, she could not hold on to life. She glanced at Samuel. He was watching her closely, his eyes darting from his brother's still face to her own.

"*Il est vraiment malade?*" he asked with a voice filled with wonder, as though such a thing could never be allowed in any world run by God and mothers.

She decided at that moment to be truthful with him, no matter what. "I do not know," she said firmly. "But we will find out soon enough. Can you be strong and help him?"

He nodded unhesitatingly.

"Good," she murmured, touching him on the head and smiling. "Then surely, he will be well soon. Go outside now, *cher,* and I will call you when I need you to help your brother."

His face fell. "I want to stay here."

She turned away, rummaging in her bag. "Deborah, go to the garden and pick some of that winterberry. I'll need a good bit of the bark, the darkest part of it. *Cher,* I cannot take time for you now, so go on outside until I can come to you."

"No," he said firmly.

She turned to him, surprised. His voice, in that instant, had sounded startlingly like his father's. "Why, Samuel!"

"In case he wakes up," the boy added, this time with the voice of a child. "I will help."

She appraised him quietly. Perhaps he was right. Perhaps to separate them now would do more harm than good. Of course whatever this sickness was, he would get it soon, they always had shared every baby illness from colic to croup. "All right, but you must keep back and out of our way. Go and sit at the table and be very still."

He scurried away obediently and perched at the table, his eyes never leaving the bed.

Deborah took over Samuel's care without needing to be told, feeding him, bathing him, keeping him busy with the paints that Joseph had brought the boys from Natchez. Oliva, meanwhile, went from cool cloths and tisanes to heated blankets by the fire, when Simon's chills grew so violent that they racked him from his deep sleep.

"What is it?" Deborah asked.

"The fever," Oliva said shortly. "There are a score of them to fight, and some are as deadly as rattlers."

"Is this one?"

Oliva moaned softly, an echo of the piteous moan which was now coming out of Simon, almost less from his mouth than his chest. His eyes were clamped tightly shut, his mouth a thin line of exertion against the heat which came and went, leaving him besieged and unknowing, with heaving lungs and clammy skin. "I don't know," she murmured, her hands soothing him, gripping him, holding him. "I just don't know yet."

She sent Deborah to get Marie finally, who brought with her the *sage-femme* who knew of women, children, and the fevers and ills which came to both. The closest *docteur* was in Thibodaux, more than twenty miles downriver. He had been in Lafourche only a half-dozen times in Oliva's memory, and usually when a whole family was sick unto death. But Madame Belizaire, the treater, was a familiar face to any *femme* with children.

She bustled in, quickly bent to greet Samuel and ruffle his black hair, and then hurried to Simon's side. She opened one of his eyes, listened to his chest, and felt all over his arms and fingers. The poor boy lay quiet and still under her hands, wheezing with a labored breath. She took a finger and ran it under his nose, dampening it with his sweat. She then put her finger in her mouth, pondering for a moment.

"The fever has not reached its worst yet," she said gently, pulling out her large silver cross on its dangling chain. Oliva saw Samuel move closer out of the corner of her eye, his mouth open in wonder. Madame took Simon's wrist and held it in her fingers, making a cross over his forehead. "*Au nom du Père et du Fils et du Saint Esprit.*" Then she made another cross, this time taking up his other wrist. "*O, respire je te*

138

conjure du Saint Esprit. " She ended by tracing a cross on Simon's chest, murmuring, "Amen."

"Samuel," Oliva said softly, "come no closer, *cher.* "

"Maman," he said plaintively, "I'm so hot."

She whirled on him, scooping him into her embrace. "You are sick *aussi, cher?*"

He nodded sadly.

"Ah no, no!" Oliva cried, lifting him up and holding him close.

"Put him in bed with his brother," Madame Belizaire said.

"No, he will get worse! If the contagion has not gripped him yet—"

"Put him in bed with him," she said firmly. "You will see."

Bereft, Oliva gently slipped Samuel's clothes off his body and tucked him alongside Simon, who still had not stirred. Already, Samuel was beginning to shiver slightly, the first sign that he was taken just like his twin.

So began the longest night of Oliva's memory. She brewed endless tisanes, spooning them down first one throat, then another. She heated blankets and cooled cloths, changing them as they grew useless. Marie cooked her good gumbo, forcing a plate on Oliva as the night drew on. "You must not get sick, too," she said kindly. "Eat this now while it still has good strength, yes?" Oliva also gratefully swallowed the strong, black café Marie kept pouring into her cup.

Madame Belizaire tied ribbons around each boy's wrist, wads of dampened tobacco on their brows, and heated poultices of raw liver mixed with garlic on their shivering chests. At their feet, she put hot rocks wrapped in linen; at their crowns, she put damp rags cooled by bayou mud. And always, for hours on end, she prayed and made the sign of the cross over them in the air, on their palms, and on their breasts. Deborah hovered as near as she dared, watching and obeying every command without question. For once, Oliva was grateful for her loyalty, and scarcely jealous at all when Samuel once opened his eyes, murmured to Deborah for water, and then closed them again.

Sometime close to dawn, as Marie had fallen asleep in the backroom, Deborah had taken to her pallet, and Madame Belizaire dozed in her chair, Oliva stepped out onto the gallery for a breath of air and listened to the fading sounds of the bayou night.

Joseph was gone upriver. Now when she needed him most, he was elsewhere. She must depend on a Choctaw squaw and a sister-in-law to help care for his sons. If he were here, he might have gone for Monsieur le docteur—

Ah God, she sighed, leaning heavily on the gallery railing. Simon had the fever, perhaps the killing fever. Samuel may have it as well, or simply be in a *déclin* because his soul was sick for his brother. They had been so before. When one got sick, the other did almost instantly—she could not say, often, whether it was sympathy or contagion. Mothers said that was sometimes the case with brothers birthed close together, with sisters who loved more than most. How much more true might it be for twins?

And Joseph was not there when she needed him. More and more, he found business to take him from Lafourche. The fields did not keep him busy every season; the *sucrerie* only needed hands during the press, but the beer—damn the beer!—it must be marketed all the year through.

She put her head in her hands, infinitely weary and heartsick. What if she lost one of them? Likely the other would pine to his death. It was as though life for them was a load with two widely separated handles, and neither could quite bear it alone.

Like love, she thought suddenly. It was made to be carried by two people, and one heart could not carry it alone. Perhaps that is how one knew real love, after all. She had long ago reached the place where a whole day might pass without her thinking of her mother, except when she woke up or before bed at night. When she remembered her, a mild longing was revived, a sorrow fleeting as a cloud, a regret that stung but did not burn. Would she eventually forget a lost child in the same way? She doubted she would. Doubted, in fact, that she could survive such a grief. And yet, mothers did.

In some way, it made her feel serene to know that love could be forgotten. She had almost forgotten Emile, perhaps in time she would approach forgetfulness with her mother. But the knowledge that love could be forgotten saddened her also. Because such forgetfulness brought the only true death.

Ecoute, Joseph, she said in her secret heart, I will not forgive your absence this night, not for many years of our life together. I will not speak of it, likely, for what could I say that you could not defend? You must go to make our livelihood, you have told it again and again. You have said there is little for you here and yet you stay for us. For me.

And so, I must face this long night alone.

She heard a small cry behind her and whirled back to the cabin. Inside, Samuel was sitting up on the bed beside his brother. He had pulled Simon upright under his arm, and the two had their heads together. At first, as Oliva hurried towards them, she thought that Samuel was weeping, and her heart lurched, *Ah! le bon dieu,* he is dead, he is dead! But then she realized with a start, that the twin was laughing lightly, his mouth very close to his brother's ear. Simon's eyes were open, and he was smiling weakly at Samuel's words.

Wordlessly, Oliva embraced her sons, pulling them to her breast. Madame Belizaire came forward to say, "The fever has broken, *hein?* That is good, I knew it would by dawn. I knew one brother would lend the other his strength."

Marie and Deborah stumbled out sleepily towards the bed, full of questions and surprise.

Oliva asked Simon, "What woke you, *cher?*"

"Sam'l woke me," he said suddenly yawning hugely. "He said he would give me his octopus shells . . . " he looked around curiously at his aunt and his squaw and the strange Madame, with little of the fever in his glance save two red spots on each cheek. "Is papa home yet?"

Oliva's eyes filled then with relief and joy, hugging them both fiercely until Samuel squirmed out of her arms. "Let us make a pirogue to send him a message," he said briskly, hopping on the bed. He took his brother's hand and added, almost shyly, "You can write it to him, yes?"

By the time Simon and Samuel were four, Oliva no longer feared that one day their father would announce a departure from Lafourche. He seemed to have settled into the farming of rice, the pressing of the cane in the season, the shipments to *des Allemands* with his regular trips to New Orleans and Baton Rouge for buying, selling, and diversion. Adolph managed the brewery with skill, and the new brewmaster they'd hired recently was making some of the finest beer the Weitz Brothers had ever stored in barrels.

Their year was coded to the seasons now, and they followed the patterns their neighbors had followed for generations. Cane was cut and pressed in late October, and the winter months of November, December, and January were for trapping. Then the village galleries were filled with rusty jaws, broken springs, chains, and pans. Muskrats were everywhere in various attitudes of death, piled on benches, in the pirogues, along the docks. Gutted carcasses lay bunched up in every yard, and more pelts hung on racks outside, the sun glinting off the guard hairs. Joseph was soon able to skin two rats a minute, almost as fast as Valsin.

February brought the oysters in season, for two months

of dredging, shucking, salting, and brining. In March, the rice plants would be set out, for spring came early to the bayou. In a few weeks, the marsh turned green, the birds began to nest, alligators were cruising the waters, and the levees started to dry up. Life moved more quickly then, for the rice must be tended and irrigated, the sugar fields plowed, nets and pirogues must be mended. The crawfish grew abundant, and ducks and geese thronged the waterways. In May the shrimping began; in June and July, there was no rest, for each day brought its own chores. August meant roofs had to be tightened against the storm season, preparations made for the harvest, vegetables to dry, fruit to put up. September brought the rice harvest, which sometimes carried into October when the cane turned red and ripe, and then the year began again.

The bayou provided. A chicken neck tied to a string got a bucketful of crabs in a half hour. Catfish bit on anything. Oysters lined the banks, shrimp filled the pans, rabbits thrived in the woods, the waters were clogged with ducks and geese, and the earth yielded as many as three crops a season. The patterns of their lives were as familiar as the calls of the birds moving overhead, and Oliva felt warmed by their cyclical anticipation.

One September, almost four years to the day since the twins were born, however, she feared she might never feel safe in the bayou again.

The hot summer days boiled by on the heat that rose from the earth and water and the swamp that was both; the vegetation grew as if blown up by the streams of heated air. The golden days of orange wine and early sunrises were at their peak when Oliva woke to a rattling against the shutters, a beating and rushing among the thicket of willows at the bayou edge. She slammed the shutters tight and went back to sleep. She woke to a rainswept morning, but that was typical for September, the storm season. "It's just a squall," she told Joseph, and sent him to the fields. Simon and Samuel went to the levee to play once the sun came out again.

But Valsin mentioned to her, when he came for his afternoon café with his father, that the river was up for this time of year. " 'Course, the wind is from the south," he said easily. "When she changes, the bayou will drop again, you watch."

But the next day, Oliva walked with the boys to the levee and looked for herself. The bayou was high, no doubt about it. But the fishermen didn't seem worried. They continued to caulk their boats, their women to mend the nets, as they always did in this season. Fishermen said the waves were high, but perhaps . . . when the wind changed . . .

They woke on the twenty-ninth of September to dun-colored clouds that hung low and sped by like dark horses being whipped. The wind pulled at the little house, first from one direction, then from another. Streamers of rain beat against the grasses by the bayou, poured into the chicken yard, filled the irrigation ditch for the garden, and flooded out her squash. As Oliva watched from a window, she saw a panther slinking along a high limb of a tupelo gum, its body gleaming wet. It leaped to the branch of another tree and from there to the earth, in a slow majestic arc of movement. She held her breath as it vanished from sight. Rarely had she seen a panther, certainly never so close to her window.

"I think we better get ready for a blow," Joseph said quietly.

Oliva quieted the boys in the back room with Deborah, and together, the couple went from window to attic, filling cracks, gathering candles and buckets, and driving nails into loose shutters. She looked out the attic window at the bayou beyond the yard. It was higher now, gray blue and surging, half way up the willow trunks. Shore birds rushed by in low flight, giving cries that sounded almost like human terror.

"Holy Mother," she breathed, pointing to the sky.

Joseph came quickly to her side, following her finger.

"It's the man o' war bird," she said, her eyes large with realization.

"So?"

"So, he is not called the storm bird for nothing, *cher*. When we see him fly low and north, we know something fierce comes behind him."

She rushed downstairs and kneeled before the holy picture and saucer of holy water in the little entry shrine. Behind her, Simon and Samuel huddled wide-eyed on the bed with Deborah, watching their mother's every move. "Lord Jesus," she prayed softly, "keep my children safe. Watch over us now, in the hour of our desperate need, Mother of God pray for us now and at the hour of our death—"

"Oliva, bring the buckets!" Joseph called from the bedroom.

She hurriedly crossed herself, rose, and rushed to him with two large oaken buckets. But the bedroom was already in three inches of water, with more rushing under the door. It was the lowest point of the house.

"We should leave?" she asked.

"To where?" He pushed his hair back from his forehead. "I should have seen this coming. I dare not take the boys out in the pirogue, I have to believe we'll be safest here."

"Should we go to papa's?" Her father and the widow shared one of the most substantial houses on the river's edge. Built of brick, it boasted a wide upstairs gallery and a tiny third story, fully ten feet higher than any other house in Lafourche.

"If we must, we will," Joseph said, "but for now, let's see if we can wait this out. Perhaps it will blow over soon."

The wind changed to a high-pitched wail, and from the back of the house, they heard a heavy boom. They rushed to see the back of the porch fallen to the ground, two supports toppled by the rising waters. Simon began to cry, a high bewildered wail not unlike the wind. She went to him and held him, while Samuel watched them both carefully, his eyes wide and wondering.

Joseph took up his accordion and played while she sang to the boys,

> Fé dodo, mo fils, crab dans calalou
> Papa, li couri la rivière
> Maman, li couri péché crab
> Fé dodo, mo fils
>
> Go to sleep, my son, crab is in the shell
> Papa has gone to the river
> Mama has gone to catch crab
> Go to sleep, my son

Joseph heard the sound before she did. He went to the window and she followed. He whispered, "Listen to them. Lord, listen to them."

The noise seemed to come from the branches of the swamp trees themselves, an eerie sound. It was unmistakable: the bird calls had changed. These were not mating cries nor flight notes as those heard from a flock of geese on the wing. Instead, all the birds together were calling at the same time, herons and blackbirds, ibises, warblers, ducks, and geese all at once, with a sharp edgy sound like a wail. There was an ugliness in the collective cry, like a child on the brink of hysteria.

Noon approached, an hour of darkness. Deborah set out some cold corn *couscous*, but no one touched it, except Samuel, who managed to eat a few bites. All round them, they could hear the torment of trees, the cracking of the willows and cottonwoods. Against the walls, things crashed and thudded, they never knew what. At one window a crack grew and water poured in. When Joseph approached it with hammer and nails, it ripped off in his hands and the wind carried it away. Now the rain beat brutally in fierce curls and streaks, hissing and lashing like whips of water, and so they closed off that room, huddling together in the nursery. Oliva began to pray aloud, her voice a low murmur of unceasing rhythm, interrupted only when she started at something else crashing against the nursery walls from outside.

The birds were now completely silent. Instead, they could hear a constant and a growing gurgle. Samuel pointed to the floor. A stream was coming in from one corner, from under the house. Joseph grabbed a brace and drill and began to bore a hole in the floor.

"What are you doing!" Oliva cried frantically. "You let in the river on us!"

He was working on the second hole now. "I got to steady the house. If I don't it'll pull right off its pilings!"

They sat then on the bed, watching as water bubbled up in pools, but it did not seem to rise above a certain level. Oliva felt herself on the smallest, most precarious island in the world. By now the wind was an endless shriek, rising and falling. She looked out and saw a large dark object—now she could see with some difficulty—a black bear, lumbering slowly against the wind, leaning into it, between the house and the bayou. On its lee side, a smaller shape, a cub huddled against its dam, and then both disappeared in the lashing streaks of water. She could no longer see the bayou at all.

Abruptly the wind changed to a savage roar. The water rose quickly then, and Joseph shouted, "We got only two choices! We can go to the attic and pray, or we can try to make it to your father's!"

"Oh God!" Oliva cried over the screaming wind, "Let's go to papa! There we will be safe!"

"No guarantee of that! No guarantee we'll even make it there!"

But as he spoke, they could hear the creaking moan of the upstairs timbers. It sounded as though the roof was being peeled off by a giant hand, slowly and painfully. There was another giant thud, the largest so far, as though a fallen tree

147

had battered the bolted door. Water was rising swiftly into the house, now almost at knee level. "We can't stay here!" Oliva cried, pulling the boys to her. "We must get to higher ground!"

Joseph reached over and hugged her hard, squeezing the two boys between them. "We will try!" he shouted, "I should have taken you sooner!"

She squeezed his arm hard, no time now for remorse, and they struggled together off the bed. She carried Samuel, and Deborah reached out for Simon. For an instant, Oliva hesitated. But Joseph was grabbing the musket, his accordion, and the blankets he could carry. She closed her eyes and handed her son to Deborah, remembering all the times the Indian had crooned over him. "Same boys are good luck," she often said. Perhaps the good God would hear her now.

They opened the door to a hammering from hell. The wind was so severe, they had to bend into it from the knees, and still must cling to each other and the walls for support. Clustered against the house was a trio of snakes, each about three feet long. Cottonmouths. One opened its mouth. There might well be more in the waters around their feet.

Miraculously the little boat was still tied to the strongest oak, though its anchor line stretched on a gray sea all the way into the chicken yard. Joseph herded them into it, grabbed an extra pole, and stuffed Deborah and the two boys in the back. With a length of rope, he tied Samuel and Simon to each other, then to the squaw's waist. Throwing a pole to Oliva, he shouted over the wind, "Keep logs away from us if you can!" He took up the oars and cut the boat's tether.

Instantly they were swept away from the house by the roaring wind, the waves slapped hungrily at the boat, and the sheets of rain made vision almost impossible. The sky was gray, then black, then gray again, like shifting blankets, and the churning water shoved them away from the protection of her father's house.

O, if it only still stands! she prayed aloud, unable to hear even her own words. The twins were silent, ominously so, normally she would hear their squalls over the most savage wind, but now they huddled in tight balls of blanket, two dark mounds next to the larger one of Deborah. Logs threatened to ram them and swamp the boat; she frantically pushed them aside, using all her strength, scarcely seeing ahead more than a few feet in the swirling current. Trees along the levee were bent to the ground, their long branches pulled in one direction like the hair of mourning women. On the top of the levee, she could scarcely make out a house—

Then the wind shifted, the darkness lifted for an instant, and in that moment she could see that it was two houses. One had leapfrogged the other, and both were destroyed. She thought she could hear cries on the wind, animals or human; it made little difference, these were the sounds of the lost.

The waves rose higher still, and Oliva gasped when a cold drenching slap of water hit her face, almost choking her. Joseph was fighting the pole, straining with all he had to turn the boat, but it only turned in a stubborn circle, battered by the currents. "It's no use!" he shouted. "We can't make it!"

"We can't go back!" she screamed, "there's no shelter to go back to, maybe nothing to go forward to, as well!" but she could not tell if he heard her.

"To the levee!" he was shouting, and one free hand pointed her eyes upwards to a distant stand of oaks which still stood erect in the wind and rain. Three of them, it looked like, still rooted. Joseph turned the boat, letting the wind whip them freely now, and the small vessel lifted up off the water, whirled violently, and slammed back down again, almost upsetting Deborah into the waves. She screamed once, threw herself flat, knocking both boys down with her.

In that instant, Oliva felt the boat scrape the levee, and she braced herself, reaching for Simon, who was closest. Joseph threw the pole to her, shouting, "Keep hold of that!" He took the rope, tied it to a whipping tree branch, and snatched the back of Deborah's coat. His knife wickered, the rope to Simon's waist slackened, and Joseph half-dragged, half-shoved Deborah up and out of the boat, up the levee, carrying Samuel in his arms, leaning hard against the wind.

Now Simon began to howl in terror, as he saw Samuel taken away. With one hand, Oliva held him down out of the wind, with the other, struggled to hold onto the line keeping them fast. "He'll be back for us!" she screamed to her son over the storm, "papa will be back!"

She could dimly see Joseph climbing the levee, pushing Deborah in front of him towards the shivering oaks. There was some shelter there, Oliva was sure of it, surely more than in this tiny boat, and they had no choice, whatever their fate. She prayed fervently, her lips moving over the words with a passion she hadn't felt for years. If they would only be safe, if they would only be safe, she would follow him anywhere, leave the bayou, go away from it all forever, if they would only be safe!

He was struggling back now, hunched over against the wind like an old man, leaning to grab onto branches as he came. She met him at the bow, Simon in her arms, and as she felt Joseph's arm clamp her waist, she was flooded with relief, though she could scarcely see to place her feet on the rising levee. They fought to the oaks, shadowy twisted thrashing forms higher up the bank, and it seemed to take forever to get to them, forever in the wind and the rain with the savage buffeting all around her.

And when they reached the darker shadows of the oaks, the slight lee provided by the twisted branches, she screamed once. She threw back her head and screamed again, again, again. For Deborah and Samuel were gone. The tree where they had waited was still there; intact, the branches still hung over in a sort of canopy, however inadequate, but the Indian squaw and her son were not where Joseph had left them.

Once the storm was diminished enough to allow them to stand upright, they searched. They searched in the dark, in the rain, though the wind blew their words from their mouths. When they could, others joined the search, up and down the bayou, along the levee, in every shelter, in every twisted wreckage of floating log and uprooted bush. Joseph, Valsin, and others stayed out more than five days combing the swamp for Samuel, coming back only when the night grew so dark that they could no longer tell water from land.

Paul Bellard came to her, his hat in his hand, the first time she had spoken to him except in passing since her wedding. He was married to Adele Naquin, and she was carrying his third child. "I sorrow for you," he said to her quietly. And she brushed aside his hat and embraced him, sobbing on his chest.

As the floodwaters ebbed, they all continued to search. Marie kept Simon for days while Oliva poled the pirogue past every high piece of land, seeing many animals who also waited for the waters to return to their channels. A bobcat and a large swamp rabbit shared one such mound, sitting only a few feet apart, unconcerned by the other's presence. Both simply stared fixedly at the flood, and as she passed, neither took any notice of her.

Finally, she must stay at home with Simon, while the men searched for another week. The child had been almost mute since his brother was taken. He would not respond to his cousins or to Marie, no matter how they coaxed him. Eating barely enough to keep alive, sleeping more hours than he was awake, he had long since sobbed out the last of his tears. At first, Oliva was grateful she no longer had to listen to his rhythmic weeping, his incessant questions, "Sam'l will come back? Papa will find him? Sam'l is not *mort, maman?*" Over and over, she tried to reassure him, but of course, he could see her own tears and would not be comforted. Then she almost wished for his questions back again, rather than the blank silence with which he greeted each new day and the beginning of each new night.

Finally, in exhaustion, he stayed in his bed, only occasionally hitching in dry sobs. He showed little interest in food, though he would obediently swallow whatever she urged on him. His eyes were swollen and dull, his cheeks pale with sorrow. When she took him in her lap for long hours, he burrowed deep into her body, as though he wanted to return to the silent refuge of her womb. He did not speak of Deborah; after many long days, he no longer spoke of Samuel either. He no longer ran to the door at every noise or step, and the night came at last when he did not even rise to greet his father on his return.

Oliva tried to keep up her spirits, if only for the sake of Simon. Alarmed at his rapid descent into numb grief, she sang to him, told him stories, and offered to play every game which she thought might bring a sparkle to his eyes and a lilt to his voice. She even brought over a small puppy from Marie's bitch and placed it in his bed with him, heedless of the dog's fleas. But Simon scarcely seemed to care for anything at all.

Oliva divided her time between her son and her attempt to put her house back in some semblance of order. She listlessly cleared up the debris, carted away fallen timber, and shoveled out mud. The cabin still stood, miraculously, but it would be long in disarray. She fought down an overwhelming desire to set fire to the place and run, mad and screaming, into the night. Sometimes it seemed to her that she was being punished by God for having prayed to Saint Matilde for such a selfish boon: she had lost her son because she had sacrificed her husband's contentment to her own. But did God punish children for the sins of their mother? The questions, the guilt, the fear swirled in her from the moment she woke, until she stopped dreaming with exhaustion in the darkest hours of the night. What kept her sanity together was the knowledge that if she allowed herself the refuge of madness, her only remaining son would follow her to that hell and likely not come out alive. What kept her going was the belief that if she kept a fulcrum about which they could balance, sooner or later Samuel would return to her. God and the Holy Mother would surely reward her for her efforts and forgive her sins. It was not possible that such a loss could be endured with no hope.

And then finally the night came when Joseph returned to tell her they could search no more. Samuel was gone.

He held her tightly when he told her this, and she let him hold her. "It's no use, *cher,*" he said quietly. "He is in the arms of God."

"If I could believe this," she moaned softly, "then I could be at peace."

"Where else would you have me look?"

Her chin hardened. "Look in the arms of the squaw, my husband. She has taken him."

He embraced her fiercely. "You must let him go, Oliva. The storm took them both."

"And left nothing for us to find at all?"

"This happens. Many have been lost without a trace."

"Non," she said, shaking her head, "I know he is not dead. I feel it." She turned to Simon who sat watching them on the bed with the widest eyes. *"He* feels it."

Simon silently plugged his mouth with his thumb, a habit he had renewed since Samuel's disappearance.

Joseph dropped his arms away from her, shaking his head. "We have searched and searched. There is no place else to look. Her own people have given her up for dead, *cher*. We must do the same."

"She always said twins were good luck! She always wanted them close to her! She took my son!"

He turned away from her then, staring out the window at the bayou, still high and black in the moonlight. "God took your son, Oliva. And even I cannot get him back for you."

"Then you must tell his brother," she said. "You tell him that Simon is lost, and that you will look for him no more."

Joseph's face fell, but he went resolutely to his son and sat on the edge of his bed. "Simon, you know that the whole village has been out looking for Samuel," he began gently. "*Grandpère* and *oncle* and *papa* and every man we know brought boats and lanterns to help. We went out every morning and searched every day, all the day, until we could not see anymore. We called and shouted and sent messages up and down the bayou, to see if perhaps someone else has seen him." He put one hand on his son's shoulder. "*Cher,* we think Samuel must be—" his voice thickened, but he cleared it and went on, "he must be drowned."

Simon turned wondering eyes to him.

"We believe Samuel is with God, son. And so, in a way, he is not lost. He's not cold or hungry or wet. He is safe with God."

Oliva burst into tears. "He is not drowned! He is not dead!"

Joseph put his face in his hands. "What would you have me say then? What would you have me do?"

There was so much pain in her heart in that moment that she could scarcely breathe, could not speak. Part of her wanted to embrace her husband and comfort him, as she tried to comfort Simon. Part of her wanted to rage at him to go back out into the night and find her son which he gave into the arms of the squaw and the storm. But she knew, as she looked at Simon and Joseph through the ghastly veil of blind, unremitting despair, that the only hope for them—and for Samuel—was if they survived. The family must survive. And in that moment, she found a small raft of strength to cling to which allowed her to say, "Here is what we will do."

At the new tone in her voice, both boy and man looked up at her.

"We will keep a lantern burning at our door every day and every night. Simon, it will be your job to do this. That way, when Samuel is able, he may find his way back to us. We will pray together for his safety, and we will ask God to bring him home." She took a deep breath and began to see it in her mind even as she said the words. "We will ask everyone on the bayou to watch for him, and we will send messages as far away as Baton Rouge and Thibodaux to help us find him. Simon, you must help me write the messages, yes? Joseph, you will post papers in every city you visit that we have lost our son. And we will stay here until he comes home again."

Joseph looked down in helplessness, his face twisted with frustrated sorrow. "But he is gone, Oliva," he said hoarsely. "We must face this. Perhaps we should leave here and start someplace new, where I do not have to leave you and Simon alone so often—"

A small voice suddenly interrupted him. "Sam'l will come home," Simon murmured quietly.

Oliva rushed to her son and enveloped him in her breasts. *"Certainement, cher,* your brother will return to us. We must have faith and wait here for him. Will you help me to keep a light on for him? And write the messages?" She looked over his head at Joseph, with a mingled and desperate gaze of yearning and determined anger. "For I cannot do it alone."

"Oui, maman," Simon sighed. "I will help you."

At his son's words, Joseph bent his head in his hands once more and began to weep, sobs of exhaustion and hopelessness. Oliva felt so cold, so arid and dry, that she thought she might never weep again, might never be capable of enduring another person's tears. But she heard a voice in her heart say *Go to him, hold him, you must heal them both*. Before she could bring herself to touch him, Simon wrenched from her arms and scooted across the bed to pat his father awkwardly on the shoulder, murmuring low words of comfort. Joseph whirled and took his son in his arms, burying his face in the boy's neck. Simon looked over his father's head at his mother, his arms trying to get around his father to hold him.

The sorrow and the compassion she saw there in Simon's gaze was the final and irresistible spur which thawed and moved her then to embrace them both as fiercely as she was able.

They called it the Territory now. The Louisiana Territory. And in the years from 1795 to 1810, the people of the delta saw more change than they had known in the previous fifty.

Steamboats began to ply the river waters, moving vast fortunes up and down as people rushed to fill the land. Some men believed they could build their own civilization on the bayou; others merely wanted to escape from any civilization at all.

Rice became the staple of the river people. The growth called for a flat moist ground, covered frequently with water. The crop required little outlay in capital and no great labor force. All a man need do was scatter the seed. When high waters came, he had good irrigation; if he needed more, he dug a small canal and the river complied. At harvest, he threshed by hand and hulled with a pestle and mortar. The fluffy grains went into every soup, gumbo, stuffing, and bowl.

On the larger farms, indigo spread over vast acreages and built huge wealth, but then a worm infested the crops and drove many planters into bankruptcy. Cotton and sugar cane prospered to take its place.

These were the golden years of Spanish rule in New Orleans, but finally, Spain must hand Louisiana back to France. New Orleans had barely finished her celebrations when Napoleon, unable to dominate both his colonies and also the British Army, made a horse trade to Thomas Jefferson, and the Territory was flooded by Yankees flocking to the delta.

Amidst all the change and glittering promise, a small note of warning was sounded: a slave insurrection in 1811 occurred a scant thirty-five miles north of the Queen City, with over three hundred escaped blacks running rampant, burning five plantation houses, and terrifying the countryside. Militia from Baton Rouge put them to flight, slaughtered sixty-six of them, wounded fifty more, and drove the rest into the swamp. Eventually, fifty more bodies were found.

On the bayou, such rebellion and the changes from Spanish, to French, to American flags did not alter the harvest, the shrimping, or the take from the muskrat traps. Marriages were still made, old ones passed on, babies took their place, and even the deepest wounds, if they do not kill, eventually heal.

Oliva must, finally, turn her attention to her husband, her remaining son, and to her daughter, Emma, who was born a year to the day after Samuel was lost to the storm.

The Great White Egret circled the black water slowly before settling on a certain palmetto stand, close to the bayou's edge. In this place, he knew, bull alligators built winter tunnels in the bank. Fledglings had been lost, even an occasional unwary adult—eager to forage among the bright green shallows—had disappeared in a flurry of cracking jaws and foamed water. But the way had been long and his wings were weary. He chose a spot and let his heavy feet brake him in the mud.

Rha was a fully mature male of seven years, almost four feet from the tip of his black bill to the end of his white aigrettes, the long white plumes and barbules which marked him a Great White of the Egret clan. When he spread his wings, they spanned more than five feet. For five seasons he had made the courtship dance in this bayou. Five nests of fledglings raised, five mates farewelled in the migrations which scattered families to the winds. This season, he felt in his legs as they reddened with the juices flowing through him, would be his strongest so far.

He assumed the feeding stance which was at once the most effective and most dangerous. Standing with his back to the sun, Rha pulled his great wings over his head and bill to form a canopy which shaded the water. Standing motionless, his wings created shadow and also cut the glare. Now, peering directly down into the shallows, he could see the fish clearly. But of course he could see nothing else around him.

Normally, Rha would never make the Canopy in such a place. Fledglings were forbidden to feed in such a stance at any time, no matter where they were, but it had been too long since he had a full gullet. He cautiously probed the mud shallows with one foot, hoping to stir up a meal quickly. On his toes, as all egrets stood, he was poised for launch into flight at the first alarm.

Some of his clan were rebelling against the Great Flight, the migration each spring to the northern territories. Some were staying the whole of the year in this marshy land, clustering with the herons and the bitterns, clouding the spring skies with white and the trees with their droppings, until the nests were so fouled even the gulls would not use them.

Rha sensed the clan's confusion in the crowding fights for

feeding territories. Many of the best mates were already danced and nested. He was late. Hungry and late. Usually by this time in the season, by the time the dogwood flowered, he had finished with courtship. Normally, his mate would be building the nest with the twigs he provided, soon to be filled with a clutch of four pale blue eggs.

But this year, the bayou was so crowded that the feeding territories were as vigorously defended as the females. For the first time, Rha had not been able to drive away interlopers.

He saw a small green frog, swiftly gigged it, and slipped it down his kinked neck. Too many nesting now. This was what came of rebellion. Always, many were lost in the Great Flight. Now, those many merely added to the flocks, until no one could feed in peace.

The smallest splash caused Rha to yank his wings down and flex his knees, in preparation for flight. It was only a red-eared turtle slipping from a log into the water. He resumed his hunt, stabbing at a minnow and swallowing it fluidly.

The urge to be nesting kept him from feeding peacefully. Nesting was hard enough at the best of times. Six weeks trying to feed four insatiable appetites, stalking the waters constantly for fish, frogs, whatever crawled, swam or crept, never eating enough himself, watching his mate become ragged and gaunt. Every morsel they gathered must be stored, partially digested in their gullets, until they came back to the nest. He hunted all the day, returning many times to four ravenous young who clamped a scissors hold on his bill and shook it up and down to make him regurgitate his find.

In other seasons, he had raised chicks so strong and aggressive that they had clamped his bill too strongly to let him release the food. One or two even shoved him right off the edge of the nest, so fierce were they in their hunger. Where were those chicks now?

And if it were not the fledglings themselves, then there

were the spring storms and floods to contend with, the hawks, the raccoons, the snakes. Alligators liked nothing more than to circle a tree filled with twigs and chicks and swat it with their tails, tumbling a few birds to their death.

This year the best cypresses would be crowded with more than a dozen nests each. Ample lure for even the laziest alligator.

Another splash, a louder one this time, and Rha turned to face the intruder with an aggressive bill snap of warning. It was a female, all white and shining in the dappled light. She had landed across the water and downstream. A young bird, she still had the paler soft feathers and paler legs of youth. She glanced at Rha once, then quietly began to feed.

She was too young, too young his senses told him, yet every barb and barbule stood erect without his willing it. His crest and courtship plumage blossomed whitely and wide, and he forgot his empty gullet as he watched her move gracefully in the Walking Slowly stalk in the water. Her neck swayed to and fro, her head perfectly level. With a low *cuk-cuk-cuk,* Rha lifted off the mud and flew up above the water, wafting his wings so as to circle her slowly.

She never looked up once as he did his aerial display, an in-flight stretch of neck and bill and head, quite the best he had done for two seasons, and his wings gave a loud *whoomp!* as he passed over her. He landed gently downstream, a few dozen yards away.

He gave the courtship call, *rha-a-a,* for which he had been named. Still, she walked silently on.

Was she so young she did not know to even give out with the customary *rhoo-oo* in return, the common greeting call? Perhaps she was one of the new rebels. Perhaps she would have to be driven away after all. He approached her quickly now, his head up, ready for the Supplanting Flight and the Forward Display, if necessary.

To his astonishment, the female began a delicate fishing motion with her bill, dipping and bobbing, completely ignoring his advance. He stood still to watch her. Now she bent her knees and moved lower to the water, her feathers fluffed and softening all the lines of her neck.

Was this a courtship after all? Rha moved closer and gave the Advertising Call, *Skeow!*, clappering his bill nervously.

She moved closer to shore, still not glancing his way. With studied motion, she pretended to pick up a twig and shake it gently side to side. As she walked sideways, her attention on the invisible twig in her bill, a large tawny streak rushed out from the cypress growth; a snarl of attack, a panther leaped from cover to grip the female by the downy neck. Rha squawked a warning, the female's head snapped up just in time to escape the panther's killing swipe, but the claws caught her breast and tumbled her down to her knees.

In that instant, Rha threw himself on the panther's back, pecked viciously at the cat's skull and eyes, gripping the fur with strong claws.

The female shrieked and fluttered upwards, one wing bent and dragging at an injured angle. The panther turned to take a swipe at Rha, she reached a lower cypress branch, and Rha leaped as high as he could in the longest stretch display he'd ever tried. When he gained a higher branch, he called to her desperately, for she was teetering precariously close to the panther's reach, one wing dangling loosely.

Rha knew that the cat could leap high enough to snag that wing and drag her down in a flash. She returned his call and tried to fly but could not. Rha saw the cat gather his haunches for the leap, called once more, and the female gave one last effort, fluttering up and grasping a higher branch, where she scuttled out over the water to the end of the branch, locking her claws around it, crying *kra-a-ack!* in terror.

Now the panther's cry of frustration echoed through the swamp. He stretched up as high as he could reach, snarling at the two birds and clawing at the cypress. But the tree was too spindly to hold his weight, the branches too far over the water. He lowered himself to the ground, growling in anger. After a few moments, he stalked away, his tail twitching spasmodically.

The female was huddled on the end of her branch, her feathers bunched around her as though enduring a downpour. Gingerly she preened her clawed wing, attempting to fold it back against her breast.

Rha called gently to her, *rhoo-oo,* the cry of greeting.

After a long moment, she answered him quietly. She stood then, spreading her wings out and carefully flapping them. Her injured wing moved well, but several of the flight feathers were angled strangely and bent.

Rha flew down to her branch, lighting closer to her. He bowed his head and erected his plumage. She folded her wings about her primly and turned slightly away. He bent and snapped a twig from the branch, shook it side to side, and presented it to her.

She hesitated.

Perhaps she was too young, after all. Perhaps he could do better than an immature female with an injured wing. Nesting was not for cowards, that much Rha knew, and if the lunge of a panther was enough to frighten her beyond all reach, then—

She suddenly turned and gripped his bill firmly in hers, gripped both his bill and his twig in one snap, and gently shook his head back and forth.

Rha gave a soft *rhaa-aa,* fluttered his wings over her back, mounted her, and mated her, there on the cypress branch.

Simon was nearly ten before he stopped looking for his brother behind every copse of cottonwood, stopped hearing his voice in the wind which moved through the swamp. Daily, he lit the lamp to lead Samuel back to their cabin; nightly, he filled and lit it again. Finally, he almost could not remember why he did so. It was for Samuel, that much he knew. But he no longer ever expected to hear a knock at the door which would answer their prayers. In fact, his mother had stopped praying long ago for Samuel's return. On those few feast days when she knelt at the altar, she simply prayed for all of them, and Samuel was included as naturally as Tante Marie's youngest boy.

It was more than a score of years before Simon could forgive the bayou and feel safe there. But by the age of twelve, he could pole a pirogue as well as his papa, for truth, though not so well as his uncle, Valsin. He knew the bayou well enough to idle there for hours, unseen and unheard, when he should be busy at skinning or picking greens. Papa would scold, but *maman* never set her mouth against his idling.

Through the long bright days, moping days, too, when time must be counted and his brother was gone, he somehow grew to be a boy alone. Emma, his sister, was both too young and too different from him to be much company, even if she would have encouraged a deeper friendship beyond the bonds of kinship. Simon spent most of his hours on the bayou. It was in those times that he would note a bird's blue flight in crisp white air, like a sharp blade cutting through the past.

Or he'd see a fussy quail with a new brood of chicks, weaving and ducking through fern, over a low hill of sand. And he would wish to be, for a moment, that last chick, two inches high and eat what he ate and be child to a hen with great warm wings, and walk through a world where grass blades and seedling flowers were gods—and the devil was only a black snake or a hawk, and heaven an early dark and mother's wings, and every brother safe within.

He grew used to hearing *maman* and papa speak of Samuel as though he were still there. Sometimes they spoke of Simon as if he were not. Once, he heard them, low in the night.

"He's not taking hold," Joseph said sadly. "I look to him to plow that last five arpents, and where is he? Dreaming off some swamp gas folly, poling over to where no call can reach him."

"You have Ben and Varsh to help you. Seems like two brutes should be enough for forty arpents, yes? Perhaps if I gave you more sons . . ."

"I don't need more sons," he said quickly. "I just need to have the one I got."

"Valsin says he traps as well as any man he knows. Says he can find rats where no sign shows, and that he could feed half Lafourche with his fishing pole. Must he farm, then, to please you?"

"No. Not to please me," his father said quietly, "but to make his way in this world, he needs to know more than this bayou, *cher*. A man must learn to cast anchor in any sounding, and let it drag if it must. Take him away from Lafourche and what do you have?"

"An empty heart," his mother replied. "And then he's no good to anything at all."

Emma, thin and somber with her dark hair and eyes like his mother's, moved like a quiet wraith through Simon's life. His sister rarely left the house, except to feed the chickens or work in the garden, and then her *garde-soleil* wrapped almost entirely around her face, as though she would not see the world at all. She did not seem to Simon to be unhappy; neither could he actually claim her to be happy. Emma simply accepted. Only at Mass did her face take on a sheen and radiance, which caused some of his friends to look at her twice. But she never returned their gaze.

Once Simon took Emma to the swamp, to some of his favorite places, that she might perhaps find them as wonderful as he. A sister, even five years younger, was better than nothing, he thought, and he loaded her carefully in the boat almost like a courteous swain.

"Tell you what, *cher*," he said to her as they reached a place he knew well, "I'll get you a clothes bag for traveling. For when you're a fine lady and go to New Orleans. I know where a big bull gator lives that will do just fine."

But Emma looked alarmed. "I don't need no clothes bag," she said quickly. "And such vanity is sin anyway."

They passed under a hanging cypress, and he heard a cooing from high in the tree. He stopped and pointed out the mourning dove to Emma. It was a brownish gray bird, sitting on its nest.

"The doves make more nests than any other bird in the bayou," Simon told her quietly. "Four times a year, two eggs to each nest."

"We should be smothered in doves then," she said, gazing upwards at the bird.

"They don't do a good job at it. The nests fall down in the smallest wind, they build too low and the snakes get them." He shrugged, "I guess it's God's way."

As they watched, the dove fluttered to the bank near the trunk of its tree. It fell in an awkward heap and for a moment lay still as though stunned. Then it began to flop and hobble along, in a frantic effort to get as far away from them as it could.

Simon smiled. "She thinks we want her eggs. She's trying to pull our eyes from her nest."

Once they passed, they looked back to see the dove pull its wing into shape, puff itself out like a pouter pigeon, and fly straight back to its eggs.

"Does that trick work on a snake?" Emma asked.

"Perhaps. But then the snake will take her and her eggs will die anyway. She doesn't think about it, she just does it. It's her mother's heart that makes her."

Emma shuddered and looked away at the moving water.

They changed directions many times, but Simon never lost his way. The streams they followed had an almost mesmerizing flow; the sluggish tempo of the bayou had taken over. The plants they saw seemed to grow faster than the streams themselves moved. The magnolias were in full bloom, and their scent was strong.

They came to an arch of shadows. Oaks and willows and cypress on either side of the stream formed an interlocking canopy above. The water was motionless, dark brown, and the moss and leaves overhead nearly blotted out the sky. Tall reeds, a few jack-in-the-pulpits, and wild dandelions dotted the mud banks. A swamp rabbit sat up and looked at them, then calmly went back to feeding. There was a stillness about the place. An airlessness, as if the whole earth held its breath.

Simon beached the pirogue and got out on a bare, sun-dried mud bar. He took his gator hook and rubbed a fallen tree limb with it, back and forth and back and forth until the limb trembled and jarred the water, the land, too.

"This angers them past endurance," he told his sister. "Watch now, they'll come out of their dens and you can make your choice."

Emma held tight to the bow of the boat, as far from the rim as possible. Her eyes never left the black depths.

Simon got back in and poled them to deeper water. Sure enough, just then three gnarled gator faces slid into view. They were hissing like meat frying. Black and rough as rotted stumps, their heads broke the surface, their nostrils flared and red.

Emma squealed, her eyes wide with fright.

"They'll not hurt you," Simon said soothingly. "They look big enough, but they're stupid as geese. And there's too many for these waters this season. They'd likely fight and kill each other off anyway." He spotted one whose head was smaller than the rest. "This one'll do," he said, poling closer. Simon took his gator hook and prodded his head. The gator spread wide his jaws towards Emma, as though to threaten her alone. Quickly, Simon rammed his musket down the gullet and fired off. The gator floundered, churning the water, exploding the silence.

Simon speared him neatly with the gator hook, chopped a gash in his spine at the back of his head, and when his floundering ceased, dragged him to the muddy bank. Emma stared at his musket. There was a new dent there.

Simon saw where her eyes went. "They bite down hard, *cher,*" he laughed, "but they let go soon enough."

He rolled the gator on its back, the huge tail swaying in a lazy death paroxysm, its savageness gone. A leech, black with gator blood, traveled wormlike across the leather-plated belly. Simon made his first cut under the lower jaw, and then peeled and scraped off the hide of the belly and sides. The heavy black back hide, he left. It was worthless. The gator lay now, pink and naked. He cut off the tail. Tomorrow he would drag it around the house to get rid of the fleas.

"We can take the steak home and fry it up for you," he said to Emma.

"No thank you," she moaned.

He looked at her, bewildered. "But you've eaten gator a hundred times, Emma. This one's yours."

"Never again. Now I've seen their eyes."

He could feel his heart go sad. "You don't want the skin either? Maybe for a little bag for gathering your herbs?"

"I want to go home is what I want, Simon."

He sighed and lifted up off one knee. With two hands, he sloshed the gator hide in the water and hung it on the bow.

Off a little ways, the gators shuffled and dipped in the water, smelling new blood.

"It's getting dark soon," she said nervously. "Let's do go home."

He got in the pirogue, turning it into the current. "No wild thing here will hurt you, *cher,*" he said gruffly. "Nothing has ever bothered me. Maybe a moccasin or a rattler, but the rest will turn from you in fear, more than you from them. You should know that, listening to *maman.*"

"She told me that when I was a child, and I believed it. But I don't believe it anymore."

Simon set his mouth and poled faster. It would be the last time he would share his bayou with Emma. Or maybe much else he cared for, he vowed silently.

When they returned to the house, they found *grandpère* rocking on the gallery as he did many late afternoons. He had drawn his chair close to the bend of the porch and was watching the birds in the tupelo. Emma smiled and touched his shoulder, passing him as she went inside. Simon sat down heavily beside his grandfather.

"Lot of air coming out of that belly," Old Simon said softly, his eyes still on the birds. "What does a young belly have to sigh so for, *hein?*"

"Wasted time," Simon grumbled.

His grandfather grinned. "Time makes you sigh? Wait until you have as little of it as I do."

"You know how to use it, anyway."

"And who does not?"

"My sister, for one. Me, for another. I took her gator hunting to one of my best spots. Thought she'd like maybe a little bag out of belly hide or something. By the time I killed one and skinned it, she only wanted to go home. Says she'll never eat another gator for the rest of her life." He sprawled disgustedly on his back, one leg crooked over the other. "Acted like she was scared the whole time."

Old Simon just sat and rocked. In a few moments, a light

rain began, dappling the surface of the bayou. It was one of those warm spring rains which seemed to turn to steam the moment it hit the ground. The old man stood up, steadying himself on the rocker. As Simon watched in amazement, he slowly unfastened his shirt and drew it over his head. He slipped off his shoes and stood in his bare feet, with his white skinny chest bare to the sky.

"Let us walk in the spring rain," he said.

Simon jumped up and stripped off his shirt. Already barefoot, he was off the porch and laughing back at his grandfather before the old man navigated the steps. Old Simon stepped off the last one and wriggled his bare toes in the mud.

"I believe," he said calmly, "that walking in the spring rain must be one of the best things a human creature can do."

"Should we take off our trousers, too?"

Old Simon shook his head soberly. "Not on Sunday, I think. This is enough skin for the holy day, yes."

Old Simon took his hand and they walked upriver, drenched in moments, with the sun alternately burning their heads and disappearing behind trees and clouds. The marsh grass under their feet bent, and then wet their trousers to the knees. Simon felt so overwhelmed in the splendor of the rain on his bare skin that he wanted to collapse in the wet grass. For just a moment, the world was perfect, and it did not matter if anyone else he cared for felt the same way.

Joseph and Simon were fishing off the edge of Bayou Blue one late afternoon, as the sun dipped low, bending red light through the live oaks. His father played a gentle tune on the accordion, singing a ballad softly, half to himself, one eye on his pole.

> Mo gagnin une 'tite cousine
> Qui donne moin coeur à li
> Li gagnin si doux laimine
> Nouzotte yé marié sordi
>
> I have a little cousin
> Who gave me all her heart
> She looks so sweet
> We will be married today

"Did you like to fish when you were my age?" Simon asked lazily, his eyes closed, one finger lightly on the line.

His father sighed deeply with contentment, for the air was soft and warm. "Some. But it wasn't a religious calling for me, like it is with your mother's people. We fished to eat. They fish just for an excuse to be out on water, I think." He kicked his son's leg lightly. "You take after her side, Simon."

A soft plop in the bayou caught their attention. A family of wood ducks had left a hollow in a tree and the ducklings had made it to the water, paddling busily around their mother. She was preening, running her bill up and over her wings and body. She glanced at them, then herded the ducklings several yards away.

Simon grinned. "So what did you do for fun when you were young?"

"Hunted some. Played my box. Set my cap for a few ladies here and there. But we didn't have time for much fun when I was your age. Too busy working."

"That's not what *maman* says, her. She says you had plenty of time for dancing. Courting, too."

Joseph chuckled. "By the time she knew me, I did. But when I was your age, times were not so easy. My parents came from the Fatherland when there was war and famine.

The price of bread was twenty-six cents a pound and none to be had, for that. They boiled weeds to stay alive. So many were leaving then, a *Völkerwanderung*, eh? People moving by the score. I remember my father said, he would go to a place where there was no king. 'My cap will not get worn out from lifting it in the presence of gentlemen,' he said. Here, he told us, America does not say, 'eat what we give you or starve,' but '*work* or starve.' So we came. And we worked. And they died soon after. But not until they saw Adolph and me, we made it."

"The brewery?"

"Yes, we did well. It wasn't the good wheat beer of Hamburg, but they drank all we could make. We tried corn at first for the wort, but it was so bitter. Rice was cheap, the water was good for malting, and when we added molasses, we sold even more. At first it was hard to keep it from spoiling, and we could only brew a few months of the year. But then we put the casks out in the sun, wrapped in straw and bagasse, set into water troughs. On the hottest days, we kept the beer cool enough. And we did not need to keep it long. There were so many German people then, they named the place for us, the German coast. And then New Orleans, Baton Rouge, and Natchez. I never needed to go any farther than that, I sold everything we made. You hang up a sign, you start a business. It was like my father said. No need to pay a man for the privilege or wait for someone else to die. You just worked and gave a man good value for his dollar, and you did well."

"You almost married someone else before *maman?*" Simon pulled in his line and recast off the bow into a riffle of shadow.

"You heard that story, *hein?*"

Simon smiled. "Some."

"Well, it was so long ago. She was a good German Catholic. Her parents knew my parents. We were alike. I go from *Kaffee and Kuchen, braunschweiger,* and *bier,* to gumbo, *filé,* and orange wine. You know, your *maman,* she told me when

171

we were married that I should never plow on Good Friday. The old ones say if you plow the earth on Good Friday, lightning will strike your fields and the ground will bleed." He grinned. "But Valsin tells me the fish bite quicker on Good Friday than on any other day of the year." He shrugged. "Your *maman* makes it worthwhile, eh? We are still, sometimes, *amoureux comme deux colombes,* as Valsin would put it. Two sweetheart doves. Sometimes. Other times?" he shrugged. He narrowed his eyes at his son. "You got a lot of questions these days."

"Some," Simon nodded reluctantly.

"Don't rush your life," Joseph said gently. "You'll be a long time married."

"Gaston LeBleu is promised now, you heard? They will read the banns next Saturday. Him and Lucille Guidry. And him fourteen."

"Maybe all your friends make a marriage before sixteen, but remember what your uncle says. If everybody agrees on it, it's got to be wrong."

Simon smiled shyly. "Valsin, he waited until he was older, him. And they seem content enough."

His father nodded. "Your mother was old to be a bride, too." He reeled in his line suddenly. "Let's go up and check that trap line before we go in. Valsin says you sniff out those rats like a hound."

Simon looked up, surprised. Usually, his father showed little interest in the muskrat pelts he gathered each season. But he pulled in his pole and headed the pirogue for deeper water, down along the region of the bayou where he'd set a line of traps.

When they reached the bank, Simon beached the boat and took his pelt bag up to the line of cypress where he'd hidden the first trap.

A large muskrat was held fast, struggling to free itself from where it was caught high up on the right rear leg. Gnashing its teeth, coated in mud, it had worn a circle around the trap and chain during the long night of thrashing about. It paced back and forth watching them now, lunging away in an effort to be free. When they came nearer, the muskrat whirled on them.

"Watch him," Simon said. "He can take your hand."

Simon held out the end of his killing stick. The muskrat struck at it and bit down hard. Simon raised his club, leaving the animal still biting, its neck extended. In the next second, it was writhing on the ground, blood spurting from the top of its head and nostrils, legs jerking out in all directions. Simon took the limp body out of the trap. The skin and muscle on the caught leg had been scoured to the bone.

They moved to the next traps, and Simon found a few young ones he let go. They hobbled off to shelter in the marsh grass, dazed and bewildered.

When they reached the next trap, Joseph gave a soft whistle of surprise behind his shoulder. The muskrat in the first trap had its back torn open. Parts of the liver and heart were eaten. The pelt was ruined. Simon hurried to the next trap, his father right behind him. There, in the shadow of the bank, another trap. Another muskrat. Another torn back, ripped pelt. "Damnation!" Simon cursed, scarcely noticing his father's quick glance. "Something's been at these pelts before. Now look here," he rushed to the next trap, "he's run the line. Every one's tore up bad!"

"You seen this before?"

Simon was working the mangled rat out of the trap. "Last week, I lost four, all spoiled. And look, he doesn't eat much, just takes enough to make it worthless. I moved these traps, and he's back again." Simon slammed the trap down in the mud. "*Merde!* There's no tracks to speak of, just some claw marks—" He bent and looked closer. "Talons. It's a hawk, I think."

"Maybe a buzzard?"

"They don't worry live meat much." Simon strode back

to the boat and snatched up his musket. "Well, this time he's going to get more than he figured on, him."

They moved through the marsh grimly now, deep and away from the waterway. The muskrat tunnels zigzagged everywhere under the grass and mud, and the roofs were fragile. A trapper could miss one step and fall into mud up to his thighs. Simon walked well on such terrain, loosening his knees, and when he felt himself falling, he bent and twisted to avoid falling deeper. Joseph struggled to keep up with him.

They hurried up the line, and most traps told the same story. Ruined pelts and no real clue as to the culprit. Suddenly, Simon saw a flutter and flurry up the line. He hissed and pointed swiftly—something was tearing fur at the end of the traps.

They crouched low, moving as quickly as they could through the marsh, Simon leading his father, stepping on the tufts of grass, the ridges with their needle growth and submerged green that would support a man. To step off half an inch would mean a cold bath in bayou water. Simon eased up and peered ahead. Less than two hundred feet ahead, a great eagle was struggling desperately, its wings beating down the marsh grass all around it. It fought harder as the men ran forward.

The eagle was caught in a trap, and the trap chain was twisted around the tough marsh grass. They could see its fierce eyes. The closer they got, the harder the great bird battled to escape. Simon raised his musket to his shoulder, but suddenly, the eagle took flight. The grass had torn loose in that moment, and the eagle passed over their heads, carrying the trap mired with cane reed. It flew to a stand of oaks about a half mile away.

"Christ, he's a big one!" Joseph let out his air with a gasp as the eagle pounded past them on the air.

"And his leg's broke," Simon said shortly. "Come on. We can still get him."

"You think?" his father asked.

"He's got to pay for all those pelts. He'll only come back for easy hunting more, now that he's tore up."

The men set off through the bayou for the eagle's perch, over the treacherous land where the muskrats had eaten out the banks. Their boots caught in the ooze and filled with cold water. Once Joseph slipped and fell headlong into mud which stank of marsh gas and decay, and he came up cursing. They reached harder ground and Simon began to run, his musket ready, his father behind him. The eagle watched them come, with defiant yellow eyes. Finally, as they stood below him, he flapped his gray wings and lifted off the oak branch, silhouetted against the sky. The ghastly burden of the trap and the protruding broken leg hung below him, but he did not flee.

"Look," Simon said, pointing up. "He's caught again."

The eagle rose above the branch but could go no further. The trap was dangling just below a forked limb. The tendon from the nearly severed leg gleamed white against the dark oak, holding the bird fast. At that instant, the eagle's yellow eye fixed on Simon's own, and the bird shrieked in defiance. Slowly, Simon lifted his musket and shouldered it again. The eagle stopped struggling. With those eyes which could see a rabbit from five thousand feet in the air, he stared back at the hunter. At the gun.

"Son—" Joseph began, but Simon shrugged him off. He squeezed the trigger. The musket cracked. The trap with its grisly twisted foot tumbled to the ground. The eagle lifted off the oak with powerful wings, the single remaining foot tucked up for long flight, and disappeared over the treetops.

Simon felt a relief settle over him, as his father's hand settled on his shoulder. "That's a good day's work," Joseph said gently. "He won't be back."

"If he is," Simon said gruffly, "I won't give him a second chance."

His father scanned the darkened sky with one hand shading his brow. "Do you think you can get us back before your *maman* feeds our supper to the hogs?"

"Is possible," Simon answered with a small grin. "You don't want to help me set those traps again?"

"You want to help me plow those last four arpents?"

The two men grinned at each other and set off back to the boat.

TXX

There was a time when Simon seemed to see little outside himself save the birds, the slow moving water, and the traps. Then one day he realized that he was beginning to notice people. He watched his father and mother when they were together. And Emma.

Somehow Emma was not connected with them in the same way. Sometimes it seemed that she was from a different family. Or from no family at all. He wondered if she had been born somehow knowing that she was to fill a loss, the loss of Samuel. And wondering, too, if she knew she could never fill that loss. Or if all this was only in his mind, and *he* was the one who was walking a strange path.

He heard the way his mother spoke to her, and he realized that she used a different tone with him. Once he listened as Emma and Oliva talked over the preparation of supper. Usually he made himself scarce while they cooked, outside attending to some chore, downriver in the boat, anyplace but where they might turn to him and ask him to help. But this once he sat in the corner by the spit, turning the roast and listening, though he held a book in his hand.

"Add those herbs slowly, *cher,*" Oliva was saying. "They'll burn else. You'll learn when you cook for your own husband, they notice the difference." She had been chopping onions and peppers and now she turned to the iron pot to stir the roux. "It must be browned, not never burnt," she said to Emma.

"So much trouble," Emma said wearily, "over such trifles."

"Trifles? Food isn't a trifle, not to a man."

"Well, it is to me. Just something to take in to fuel the body's fires and push back out again."

"Emma!" Oliva looked half-shocked, half-amused. "Whatever gives you such notions."

"It's true, isn't it? We spend all this time cooking it up, they eat it, then we spend so much time cleaning it up, and for what? It all has the same end. God wills it so. We should be like the beasts and the birds that take what is at hand. We should not take so much pleasure in eating. It's sinful, somehow."

"Sinful? That good capon is sinful? The little tarts I bake for your father are sinful?" Oliva snorted and turned away from the pot she was stirring. "You be glad I'm teaching you to be so sinful then. You'll make a sorry wife without such sins."

"Maybe I won't be a wife at all," Emma said dreamily. She stopped peeling the potatoes and glanced right through Simon, as though he had no more ears than the roast. "Maybe I'll never cook another meal once I leave this house."

"Of course you will. Though maybe no one'll bless you for it. Don't let those potatoes go brown. Slip them in this water."

"God will bless me for it."

"God said be fruitful and multiply," Oliva retorted shortly. "He gave us these good foods for a reason, so as not to starve ourselves and our men in the process."

"Men can feed themselves. They don't need women to do it."

Simon lifted his head at that. Where did she get these

ideas? "It's little enough, I think, to feed us," he offered quietly. "When papa works so hard to provide everything else we need."

Emma considered that. "But what if one does not want what he provides?"

"Your bed to sleep in? Your clothes to wear? You don't want such things?" Oliva moved to the table now, her hands on her hips. "You are such a dreaming child, *cher*. Too much reading, I think. Not enough work to do. If you had to do more, you'd appreciate what others did for you."

Emma shrugged softly and turned again to her peelings.

Simon thought over her words that night as he fell off to sleep. Girls were hard to understand. Even his own sister, blood to his blood, he could not say why she felt as she did, spoke as she spoke.

That year, when the Mardi Gras celebrants came to the door, Simon wondered again whether Emma had been one of those sleeping infants mixed up at a *fais-do-do* and returned to the wrong family. But which family on the bayou would have bred such a daughter?

The night of Mardi Gras came to Lafourche with the same merriment it brought each year, and the masked horsemen came to the Weitz door, begging for a chicken to make the gumbo. Twenty men were arrayed in colorful clown clothes, and their horses were dressed out with bells and ribbons. They called out,

> O, Mardi Gras d'où tu viens,
> Toute 'lentour du fond du verre,

Je viens de L'Angleterre,
Oui, mon cher, oui, mon cher!

O Mardi Gras, from where do you come
All around the drinking glass,
I come from England
Yes, my dear, my dear!

When they reached the line about being English, the Madame of the house would pretend to quiver and quake and herd her children under her skirt, like chicks from a hawk, away from these bad men.

Simon and Joseph stood on the porch and welcomed the men inside, where Oliva and Emma served them the traditional *tac-tac,* popcorn, and freshly fried *beignets* ready for them, along with Joseph's best early beer. When they had eaten and drunk their fill, they filed out, singing once again and begging for a chicken for the communal pots of gumbo.

Simon's task, one he had both feared and relished since he was a child, was to step out on the gallery and throw a chicken into the air as high as he could, then dash out of the way as the men chased it and caught it. Off they would go then, the mauled chicken in their sack, to the next house on the bayou.

The day ended with horse races and cockfights, with the men clustered under the huge chinaberry tree by LeBleu's, watching the red and black rooster of Landry who had vanquished every cock in the village.

That night everyone gathered for the *Bal de Mardi Gras,* where the chickens collected had been transformed into steaming pots of gumbo, and the music and dancing continued until no more feet could move.

But Emma would not dance.

She sat on the bench by her mother, she tapped her foot to the music, she smiled and nodded to friends. As young men approached her she turned them down, one, two, three, though many *jeunes filles* younger than she danced half the night. When Joseph saw that no more would brave her firm *non,* he plucked her off the bench and whirled her around the room in a swift two-step.

She danced with her father, she smiled at couples whirling past and her beaming mother, then regained her seat on the bench.

Enheartened, several more sons of the village came to her then. But she only smiled and shook her head. The dance she took with her father was her only promenade of the evening.

Simon could see his mother quietly entreating her, coaxing her, then finally scolding her gently—but Emma would not move from her place.

"Dance with your sister," his father told him, and he grimaced.

"It will take away her fear," Joseph said.

"She's not afraid," Simon replied. "She just doesn't like to dance."

"What *jeune fille* does not like to dance?"

"That one," Simon nodded towards his sister. Nonetheless he walked over to where his mother smiled up at him and said, "Emma, *allons promenade, cher.*"

His sister said only, "I'd rather not," and would not rise from her seat.

As Simon grew, girls became no easier to understand, but the effort to do so grew less of a chore. At sixteen, he found himself watching certain *jeunes filles* at prayer, holding his breath when they murmured the rosary to hear the sibilance of their whispers, breathing as they breathed, as though he were connected by invisible cords. The year before, the flow and grace of Father LeBlanc's ancient hands and voice had mesmerized him. But no longer.

By seventeen, Simon had narrowed his fascination to two, but he discovered that simply having fewer diversions did not diminish their power. His obsession seemed to enlarge to fill the vacuum. Marie LeVille and Cerise Guidry drew his eyes whenever they sailed into his view, and soon they drew his feet as well, to place himself where his view might be frequently assailed. At odd moments, he wondered how it was that two years before, he never noticed the velvet black of Marie's hair, the pink softness of Cerise's cheeks. It was as though they had been dropped down from another sky into Lafourche, though they had grown up along the same banks he had. One year, they were invisible. The next year, they all but made the world so to his eyes.

His distraction was quickly noticed by both parents, but they couldn't seem to agree on a response. His mother smiled indulgently, gently teasing him about his sudden clumsiness, his forgetfulness, and his frequent wanderings towards the small Guidry store, the ample LeVille fields.

"Perhaps it would be good to make over papa's black suit for you, *cher,*" she said practically. "It will fit you nearly, I think. You're almost as tall as your papa now. And it looks," she smiled fondly, "as if you'll be needing it soon."

But his father did not share her view. He seemed to need him in the rice fields more rather than less these days, and on Sunday, the day when every Acadian family with marriageable daughters expected to receive visitors, Joseph set him to reading brewmaster reports from the week before. By the time he had read the requisite number of reports, accomplished the weekly cleaning of the pirogue, and been to Mass, he must choose between one girl's gallery or another, not both.

One day Simon was walking slowly down the bayou bank, his cane pole in his hand. It was one of those days he relished most, a warm languid afternoon when the hum of insects and moving water combined to lull him into a sense of peace. But today his contentment was pricked with a certain sadness. Often Gaston Le Gros came along when Simon searched for perch nests, but not today. Gaston was getting married tomorrow, and his womenfolk had set him to so many preparations, he would not surface for the whole day. Perhaps not ever again, the same Gaston.

Married forever. When he thought of Marie and Cerise, he could lose himself in the happy possibilities. But what would it be like to choose one alone? To belong to one girl only?

That was the way it was with his people, Simon knew. Others might desert or abandon their choice, but in Lafourche, once wed meant always wed, for better or worse.

He had heard that some men went to visit New Orleans for other pleasures. There were women there who made it their business to provide such things. But few men in Lafourche made such visits, of that he felt certain.

There was a *jeune fille* upriver, a Jeanne Savon, he had heard, who entertained some young men more often than her neighbors would approve. It was said by some that she had no reins on her wantonness. But if Gaston or Pierre or other of his friends had gone to her cabin after dark, Simon did not know of this. And if Gaston's new bride heard such a rumor, it would be cause enough to break their banns.

Simon sat on a stump overlooking the wandering water. It was quiet here. Only old Benoit's horses and the white egrets came to this part of the bank. A pasture stretched behind him, the water before him, and it seemed to Simon in that moment that he stood on a high place seeing all of his past and all of his future at once.

His father had said, "You're married for a long time."

His mother seemed to want that long time to commence as soon as possible.

And Emma had expressed the opinion that if such a time never came to her at all, she would be well content.

Part of his heart wanted to join with something, someone, larger than himself, to change his life abruptly, once and for all. Part of him, however, wanted to stay always the same. To feel forever as he did now at this moment, watching the waters wend to the sea.

Perhaps the problem was that he had not chosen. If he had only one girl who drew his heart, surely he would find it easier to make the picture complete in his head. The two of them, side by side, sharing a marriage bed, for the rest of their days.

The cypress stump grew more uncomfortable as Simon pictured Cerise's willowy walk, the way she touched her lips with one finger after she laughed, as though to make sure they were still on her sweet face. Other images of Marie's black hair and the way it smelled—warm, fragrant, animal— came to him.

Both pictures were interrupted by the sound of horses' hooves thundering closer. Simon turned to see Benoit's gray mare chased by a huge red stallion. It was LeBeck's red, a frequent outlaw up and down the bayou. He was out of his fence more than he was in, and now he drove Benoit's gray ahead of him, closing on her fast. The mare darted and whinnied, running hard, away from the bank and into the boggy area upriver, where Simon had seen Benoit set traps for coon.

She passed only a few feet from him, her eyes wild and wide. She was in season, but of course she ran nonetheless, looking nothing like the gentle filly which carried the Benoit buggy to Mass. Her mane flowed out behind her, her tail stiff and defiant, and she kept her head twisted as she ran to see if he followed. Suddenly she stopped in the mud and the stallion covered her. Rearing up on his back legs, he gripped her surely, thrusting his haunches at her. She moved forward, but he neighed wildly, retaining his hold, his eyes flashing.

Wide and dark, his nostrils flared, and his breaths came in ragged gasps. He gripped the mare surely, biting her on the neck, and entered her savagely, screaming out his urgency.

The mare stood still, as the stallion danced and plunged, positioning himself. Suddenly Simon heard a snap, and the stallion screamed, this time in pain. One of the red's hooves had hit a cypress log and crashed through it, splintering the wood to sharp, jagged edges. Simon watched in horror as the red pulled at his hoof, all the while buried in the mare. The only way of release was for the stallion to back out of her.

She moved forward, and with a scream of rage, the stallion followed, still unable or unwilling to separate himself, dragging the splintered log. It sawed at his hoof relentlessly, back and forth as she moved, and blood spurted from the ragged tear on the stallion's leg. It mottled and speckled the marsh grasses, as the mare moved inexorably forward and the stallion followed. He screamed, but she did not stop. He kicked and stamped his hoof, but could not release it, would not release his hold on the mare. Finally there was a drumming, ripping crash, and the log was left behind them. Simon rushed forward to the log to find, wedged in the crack, the hoof. It was a bloody mass, with white tendons still writhing slowly at its center.

He followed the horses. With each hobbling step, the stallion stayed on the mare, his blood streaming onto the mud. Finally, he fell away, panting. She walked on, unconcerned. Bewildered, the red looked around as though seeing the world for the first time. In moments, he dropped his proud head, and gradually sank to his knees. Not far away, the mare grazed. As Simon watched, the stallion fell over into the mud, his eyes wide and dark. For what seemed like an eternity, Simon watched, until the stallion died with a terrible gasp, the blood finally running more slowly, then stopping altogether.

Simon walked home slowly, dazed by the savagery of the scene. Perhaps Emma was right all along, he thought wonderingly. Perhaps this was a lesson he would need to remember.

A month later, Simon sat on Marie LeVille's gallery. Inside, her *maman* cooked Sunday gumbo. Two of Marie's small sisters scampered from the porch to the kitchen, giggling and carrying snatches of their conversation to whoever would listen within. Simon strained to think of something to say to her which would have a private meaning. Something she would understand but no one else would, even if it was passed along by a laughing *p'tite*.

Finally he murmured, "I discovered something upriver a while back. A hidden place."

"Oh yes?" Marie smiled.

"Up past Bayou Blue. I don't think anyone else has seen it."

At that, Lucie LeVille, the youngest of four daughters at six, called out, "Is it pirate treasure, Simon?"

The child had ears like a ferret.

Marie touched his hand gently. "Go on. Pay her no mind."

Simon took her hand boldly, opening the small palm and gazing down at its softness.

"*Maman!*" shrieked the second-smallest daughter, Lisette, and raced for the door to report.

Madame LeVille finally took pity on the couple. "Marie," she called loudly, "I need more okra, *cher*. You go fetch some, you."

"You come, too," Marie said quickly, rising off the hard swing. She shooed off her two sisters and led him to the back of the yard, where the kitchen garden sprawled nearly to the chicken house. There she moved gracefully among the rows, bending to pick the okra. "What did you find in this hidden place, Simon?" she asked. "Was it the largest muskrat in the delta?"

He moved behind her, a little stung. "No, not a rat. Something beautiful." He touched her hair lightly. "You would like it, *cher.*"

She stood and faced him, her skirt full of okra. "I would?"

"For truth."

"Will you show it to me?"

He took her arm. "We could go now, if you like."

At that moment, Madame LeVille stuck her head out the back door. "Marie! The gumbo will boil away to mud!"

He snatched back his hand as though it had been scalded. She hurried to the cabin, flinging back over her shoulder, "Perhaps another time, yes?" And she did not beckon him inside.

He turned away, mounted his courting pony, and headed down the road. The two sisters watched him from the house, giggling behind their hands. Marie came to the door and waved. "Come again, Simon!" she called. But he did not feel appeased.

On a whim, he turned the pony's head towards Guidry's store. There, at least, a man could get something cold for a dry throat. To his surprise, Cerise met him outside at the hitching post.

"Papa says I must take these sausages to Madame Benoit," she said breathlessly, the color rising in her cheeks when he gazed down at her. "She's ill with the *grippe.* Will you come along?"

Madame Benoit lived downriver on the edge of the levee. Though it was possible to reach her door by horse, the pirogue tied up by Guidry's dock would be the most dependable way to get there. Simon said, "With pleasure," tied his pony, handed her into the little boat, and poled away before fate could take back this rare fortune.

They slid around the bend of the bayou, partially hidden by the live oaks which bent over the water. Simon traveled slowly through the part of the conversation they seemed to repeat every week: how was her family, his family, those friends they shared, and whatever gossip they could add. And then he said, "I've found a special place upriver. You'd like it, *cher*. It's very beautiful."

"Is it far?"

He was instantly alert. "Not so very. It's a secret place."

"I love secrets."

"Would you like to see it?"

"Have you shown it to . . . anyone else?" She was trailing her hand in the water, her eyes averted.

"No. It wouldn't be a secret then."

"Well, then. Perhaps we could see it sometime."

"Today?"

She hesitated. "I must be back soon. Papa will wonder."

He turned to her fully, letting the pole down for a moment. "After Benoit's I could show you. It's halfway there." It was rare that young girls were allowed to be alone with a man, and he knew suddenly that if he did not ask, she would never offer. He might not have this chance again. "Before it's gone."

She dimpled. "What is this special place that might disappear, if I do not see it today, Simon?"

He grinned. "I cannot tell you. I can show you, though."

She settled back, drawing her cloak a little tighter around her shoulders. "Well then, pole faster. For I cannot be gone too long."

His arms ached by the time they reached Benoit's, for he never made the distance so swiftly. They delivered the sausages to the croaking old woman, made their courtesies, and got back into the pirogue. Now the sun was a little lower towards the water.

"I don't know if I dare," she said, her voice a little plaintive.

"It won't take long," he said firmly, shoving the boat off the bank, in the direction of the bayou rather than towards home. He did not look at her now. For if he had, he might have been swayed by her doubt. He began to sing a song as he poled, an old ballad about lovers and death which he knew she loved. He put all his shoulders into the pole. Soon she was singing softly along with him through the tangled verses.

A rush of egrets rose in a cloud of flashing white. Simon pulled his musket up, sighted across the flintlock, and shot. A bird fell, its wings frantically fighting the long fall onto the bank. Simon went ashore and took it up. Luckily, it had fallen on dried brush and leaves. No mud or blood stained its tail plumes, long and silken and drooping. With a quick hand, he took his knife and clipped out the four tail plumes. He laid the plumes in Cerise's palm.

"Oh, the quills are small as hairs," she said softly.

"In some places, they're as precious as water pearls," he said. "Four make a pretty frame on a lady's cap. I've seen a cap like that."

"Where?"

"In New Orleans. I've been twice with my father. Once to Baton Rouge, too."

She sighed. "Is it as wonderful as they say?"

"Not so very," he frowned. "This is prettier, to my mind. Nothing in New Orleans to best what I see right here."

She smiled and tucked the feathers carefully inside her cape.

Through the tree-hooded wilderness they passed, on black sloughs, pushing past concealed rivers widening among reeded islands. Loons took to the air at their passing. Gators shuffled down into the water as they rounded bends, leaving slow foam on the black surface, dipping sullenly out of sight. Simon knew every marker, every eagle's nest in the oldest cypresses, and he pushed harder, watching the lowering sun.

They had barely spoken, but each time he turned to gaze at her, she met his eyes without turning away. He felt a current running between them, a connection which was broken when he looked away. Suddenly, he brought the pole down hard, and eddied the boat to rest against the shore.

"Shut your eyes now," he said softly. Looking back, he saw that she had. She waited, her mouth quiet and slightly open, scarcely breathing. He moved the boat slightly to another angle and nudged it into the bar. "Open your eyes."

Heaped in wild profusion before them was a bank of flowers, a low hill of color and tangled glory, big as tin mugs and crowded together like a thick carpet. It looked as though all the flowers of the swamp might have been born here, naked and unashamed, with few to see.

"Oh!" Cerise breathed, as though in pain.

"I doubt any other eyes have seen this," he said, helping her to her feet. "I never see a track."

They left the boat and walked knee-deep into the blooms. Cerise bent and buried her face in them, breathing deeply of their drowsy sweetness. Her eyes were closed in pleasure.

She opened them. "I would never have believed it. It will seem impossible when I go home, to tell them of such a thing hidden away."

He took her hand, suddenly shy. "You mustn't tell them. No one should know. This will be our secret place."

She turned to him, her eyes wide and dark. "And you've never shown this to anyone?"

For answer, he took her by the shoulders and pulled her gently to him. Instantly, as he felt the length of her body next to his, her breasts, her legs through her skirts, he needed her closer still. She did not resist his embrace, but seemed to yield into him. Their mouths were very close. He could feel her breath on him, small quick breaths, and his heart pounded nearly into his throat. He dropped his mouth to her forehead, tracing his lips over her brow, over each eye. She closed her eyes. He continued his mouth moving down her cheek until he finally found her lips. Gently first, then more insistently, he kissed her, parting her lips with his own. He almost teetered with the power he felt in his loins, down his arms, and he had to stop himself from squeezing her too hard to his chest.

She pulled her head back and gazed at him in wonder. She murmured his name and dropped her lips to his neck, a wet softness like deer nuzzling dark water, and he moaned, a painful longing overcoming him. He pulled her down into the flowers, so deep they were over their heads, and he could no longer tell which scent was hers, which was theirs. Her touch was sweet and scalding, wild and tender. Quickly, they were skin to skin, eye to eye, and breath to breath.

Now, of course, Cerise was his. He made his farewell to Marie, a painful scene he did not like to recall. He stood on her gallery, refusing the glass of sweet coffee she always offered. Refused, too, the seat he always took. With hat in hand, turning it round and round by the rim, he told her that he had asked for Cerise Guidry's hand. He didn't look away from her eyes. He owed her that much. Later he wished that he had not seen her own well up, the fist come to her mouth, the painful twist to her lips as she wished him, with faltering voice, every happiness.

She had stood there still as he rode away. Ramrod straight, she stayed without running, and managed to smile, raising one hand in farewell.

He shook his head now as he thought of it. Women were stronger than men, he would never believe anything else. Their spines were stiffer, no matter how soft their skin might be. Their souls were larger, somehow brighter. Even Emma, perhaps the smallest darkest female soul he knew, gave off a certain light he felt he never radiated. He remembered the stallion in the marsh often, but when that image came up, he pushed it away. All around him was ample evidence that love most often meant fruitfulness, birth, and renewal. Not a bloody death in a lonesome place.

When he came home from Marie's, his grandfather and uncle had joined his father on the gallery, as they often did on a Sunday. They watched as dusk gathered over the bayou and the women inside readied for Mass. There was a certain silence to the water then, as though even the currents knew to rest.

"I've asked Cerise Guidry to marry," Simon said as he settled on the porch next to his father's chair.

Valsin gently laughed and shook his head. "Well, I just lost ten dollars then, because I wagered with Prejean you'd take the other one, me."

"And I'd have wagered you'd have the sense to wait until you can support a wife properly," his father said grimly. "You are too young."

"Many marry a lot younger," Simon said.

"Many don't have your opportunities. You should get out of this backwater, get up to New Orleans, learn more about the brewery, see a little of the world before you settle down into one stagnant little village—"

"Are we talking about your life now, or mine?" Simon asked quietly. "New Orleans is not my idea of Eden. Neither do I want to spend my days ladling malt into the kilns."

"What do you want to do then, *cher?*" his grandfather spoke up out of the depths of his rocker. "A wife is not kept with egret plumes and gator hides."

"Especially one the likes of *M'amselle* Guidry," said Valsin. "That pretty face is used to smiling, I think."

"My trap lines alone could do for us, and my share of the

mill receipts will keep us when the rats don't. We don't need to have the best buggy on the bayou."

"And what about when the children come?" his father asked. "They will, you know, before you're ready for them."

Simon glanced at Joseph quickly, to see if he suspected that Cerise was already his, but he saw no accusation there. He shrugged. "I hope they do, and more to keep them company." His father averted his eyes. "And when they come, we'll do for them like Valsin and Marie, like Gaston and Celeste, like Ovide and Odette, and like everyone else does, *hein?* We'll do our best."

Joseph shook his head sadly.

"Surely you are not surprised, papa," Simon said formally in the old tongue, so that his grandfather could follow the words. "Like my father and my grandfather before me, I must find my own way. Would you have me do otherwise?"

With that, he felt a hand on his shoulder. Oliva had tepped out into the shadows, listening to their talk. "He's not surprised, *cher,*" she said gently, "just saddened to see it come so soon. Do you love her?"

Simon hesitated. "I cannot keep away from her."

She looked from her son to her husband. Her hand moved from Simon's shoulder to Joseph's. "Well. Perhaps that is love, after all, who can say? You will post the banns next Sunday, Joseph?"

"Perhaps you should post the banns, if you approve of this," he retorted sharply.

She laughed softly in the darkness. "Whether I approve or not, the marriage will be made, I think." She dropped both arms around her husband's neck. "Will you post them?"

"You are sure of this?" Joseph turned to his son.

"I have told her so."

"Well then," Joseph said quietly, "may *le bon dieu* give you joy of her."

Simon found Emma back on her bed, reading as usual. Her Bible was open along side her, and her catechism book was in her hands.

"I have asked Cerise Guidry to marry," he said, his head in the door.

She brought the book down slowly from her face, her eyes wide and calm. "You have?"

He nodded solemnly. "It is time for me to take on a man's responsibilities."

To his surprise and chagrin, her mouth turned up in a rare smile. "It is? Well. And what did *papa* say about this?"

He shrugged. "He says I am too young, but—"

"You are too young. Do you love her?"

"Yes," he said firmly, instantly.

"Is she with child?"

His mouth dropped open with shock. That his little sister should know of such, should *speak* of such! She looked suddenly much older to him, and he wondered vaguely how she had grown without his notice. "*Non, certainement,*" he said indignantly.

"Then why do you rush to wed?"

"I do not rush," he said, his anger rising slightly. "I love her and she loves me."

"So you said," she answered calmly, "but why must you marry to love?"

He rolled his eyes. "I never knew a girl with so many strange ideas, Emma. Where do you get such notions? One loves, one marries, one makes a family, *hein?* You think you have a better plan?"

From behind him, Oliva came up quietly in time to hear Emma say, "I will never marry, *moi.* Likely I will never love. But if I do, I surely will never marry."

"I, too, made such a vow," Oliva said shortly. "And your father changed my mind quick enough. Perhaps *M'amselle* Guidry made such a vow as well. And your brother has made her forget whatever promise she made to herself in her maidenly bed. That is the way of the world, *cher.* That is the way of men and women." Her mouth suddenly softened as though she were seeing a long time ago to another place, another person. "You are too young to understand, perhaps, but don't be afraid. You will find someone to love when you're ready." She smiled up at Simon. "Just like your brother, yes?"

Emma said gently, mirroring her smile. "I'm not afraid, *maman.* But I will not marry."

Oliva glanced at Simon, saw his frown (so much like Valsin's) begin, and she ushered him quickly out the door. "Pay her no mind, son, she does not mean it. You go to bed now and get your rest, for you'll need it for tomorrow, likely. *Ma foi,* when your cousins hear your news!"

When he had left, she pulled the door closed behind her and sat alongside Emma on the bed. "Why do you speak like this and ravel your brother's joy? He comes to you and tells you he has chosen a bride, and you tell him that there is no need to marry? Emma, sometimes I wonder what you are thinking in that head of yours." She tapped her daughter's head bemusedly. "Although I must admit, I had thoughts like yours when I was old enough to know better."

"You did?" Emma had pulled slightly away from her, but now she turned her face to her mother openly.

"Oui, vraiment, I made just such a vow to your *grand-père.* I said I would never marry."

"Why?"

194

"Because I could find no one to love. Ah, but then your *papa* came to the *fais-do-do,* and I forgot my vow quick enough. You'll forget yours, too."

"I don't think so, *maman,*" Emma said quietly. "For even if I find someone to love, I don't want to marry. I don't want to be a wife."

"Why not, *cher?*"

"I don't want to do what a wife does, for truth."

Oliva took Emma's hand gently. "And what is that?"

"Cook and clean and have the babies. I don't want to have babies at all, me."

Oliva chuckled. "I understand how you feel. I felt the same way once. But you will change your mind. Just don't go up and down the bayou telling all who will listen that you will never marry, because then when you want to change your mind, no one will believe you."

"I won't change my mind," Emma said staunchly. "Why do you think I will? Because you did? Why do you think I must do as you did, *maman?* If you had the same feelings I do, as you say, then you should understand."

"I do understand, *cher.* But I also understand men and women."

"Perhaps," Emma said softly. "Or perhaps you know one woman and one man. You and *papa.* Perhaps that is all any mother can know. And from that, they want all their daughters to do as they say, even if they themselves would not take their own advice."

Oliva drew back and gazed at her daughter with some alarm. What sort of girl-woman was this, who spoke sometimes with the words of a child and sometimes with the flash of wisdom of *une vieille?* She shook her head sadly. "Emma, I know that you are my daughter, for I took you out of my body with my own two hands. But when you speak like this . . ."

"You do not know me," the girl finished calmly. "I know. I have felt it always."

Oliva said indignantly, "Of course I know you, *cher.* You are my child. And you must trust me when I tell you that you will change your ideas in time. And that until you do, it is no kindness to yourself or to others to announce them to the world."

"*Oui, maman,*" Emma answered obediently. "I will keep them to myself, then."

"No, you may speak to me of them," Oliva said, "but to no one else."

Emma turned away, pulling the quilt back from her pillow. "I'm tired now," she said.

Oliva appraised her daughter keenly. Likely, she would not speak of this again. "Good night, *cher,*" she said tenderly. "Try to find a little more joy in your life, yes?"

"Yes, *maman,*" Emma said, yawning. And she turned over to the wall, closing her eyes.

Six months later, Simon stepped to the door of the cabin where he had been born and set his empty traps down on the gallery, wiping his hands on his cape. The rain made the three miles between his house and his father's house seem twice as far. It would have been good to spend this wet morning in a warm bed. Good, too, to have his coffee at his own table with his sweet wife. But it had become his habit to be at his mother's table every working morning for breakfast. That way, Cerise didn't have to stir herself earlier than she liked.

As usual, his father was reading by the fire; his mother cooked behind him. With a smile, she set Simon's cup down at the table full of fragrant heat. "Any sign it will stop?"

"Looks like it's got its mind made up for the day," he said, hanging his wet cap on the door hook.

Oliva put a plate of sausages down before him. "Cerise is well?"

He nodded, his lips on the coffee cup.

"She has finished her sheets?"

Sheets. It seemed to be a casual question, of course, but it was not. He could remember standing with his bride in the nave of the church so clearly. The enchantment of the curls that fell around her face, the full bodice of her dress that pulled taut against her breasts. With so pretty a face to greet him each night, who cared that she did not get up to prepare the morning meal? With so rich a body in his bed, what mattered that she had not finished the number of sheets in the armoire that his mother felt necessary to begin their marriage life? Still, he wished the question had not come. Again.

"Not yet, *maman,*" he said quietly, "but we have plenty of time for sheets."

She put a light hand on his shoulder. "That's a bad tear starting on your sleeve. It'll rip all the way to the back if it's not fixed."

He picked up his arm and examined it.

She put out her hand imperiously. "Give it to me, and I'll do it right."

He slipped off the shirt and sat bare-chested, suddenly a little abashed to be partially naked before his mother. As though sleeping next to Cerise had somehow changed him visibly, in a way she could mark.

The wedding had certainly changed him inside. Of that he was certain. After the church, the flower-decked buggy had waited for them, the horses patiently pulling the long grass. "Let's go!" Cerise had whispered to him, the minute they were at the horses, and he felt himself harden at the light glowing from her eyes. One old woman muttered, half-aloud, that no bride should look so ready for the marriage bed. But when Simon looked back at his parents, his mother standing within the circle of his father's arms, he knew that the love he and Cerise would soon celebrate was still being celebrated by his parents after all these years. Would God that they still feel that rich passion, as their marriage aged!

That night they lay in the bed Simon had made, on the mattress Oliva had stitched. The moon shadow fell across Cerise's nakedness and revealed more than it hid. And though he knew Father LeBlanc had only that morning pronounced them man and wife, made what they did together now holy, he could not help but feel he was lying with a stranger. A stranger who held his heart in her hands as surely as she held his hips with her lithe legs.

Emma came into the kitchen with a towel, to dry her wet hair by the fire, nodding good morning to him. "The chickens are fed," she said quietly, "but I can't see your black guinea, *maman,* she must be setting in the woods again."

Simon watched her over his second corn fritter. She was thirteen and of a marriageable age. Yet he could no more imagine her in bed with a man, could no more picture her body in the positions of love as he could vividly see Cerise in his mind, than he could imagine his mother riding the back of a gator. With a private shock, he realized that he had never seen Emma embrace anyone other than Oliva and Joseph. Not *grandpère,* not Valsin, not Marie, no, not even himself in recent memory.

There was a quick knock at the door and Cerise hurried in, wrapped in an oilcloth cloak, her hair a wide black halo around her head. She looked stricken. He half-rose to meet her, and she rushed into his arms, weeping.

"They just brought the news," she sobbed, her eyes turning to Oliva first. "I am so sorry, so sorry! It is Old Simon, *ma mère,* he was taken in the night. The widow found him this morning. He is gone."

Emma quickly crossed herself and murmured, *"Grandpère.* Poor old man."

Oliva sunk into her chair. She covered her eyes with one hand and reached for Joseph's with the other. "Who came to tell it?"

Cerise left Simon's arms then and went to Oliva, wiping her eyes with her cloak. "M'sieu Bellard, with my brother. Father LeBlanc is with the widow."

"Valsin?"

"They went to tell him."

"He will come here," Oliva said quietly, her voice catching. "He will come here before he goes to see him. I must get ready for Valsin." She stood up, swayed slightly, and caught herself on the table.

Joseph rose to embrace her, but Cerise reached her first. Without tears now, she held Oliva and steadied her. "It is very sad to lose him. But the good God gave him a full life and a quick passing, yes? You gave him a place in the sun, as he wished. No man could wish for more."

Oliva looked as though she might pull out of Cerise's arms for an instant, but then she relaxed into the young woman's embrace. She seemed to take a calm strength from it, finally releasing herself and accepting Joseph's arms as well.

"We will pray for him now," Emma said quietly, soothingly, and they knelt together as she led them in a prayer for Simon Doucet's soul.

As Louisiana stretched south towards the Gulf of Mexico, the dark swamp sanctums of bayou country gave way to a vast marshland. No longer backwaters, these meandering stream-lets merged with treeless patches of wide wetlands. They were flat and open to the sky, seemingly changeless except for the breezes which moved up the gulf, swaying the grasses in rhythm.

But their monotony was deceptive. These five million acres of marshland supported, year-round, as intensive concentration of plant and animal life as could be found anywhere on the continent. The bright sun, the unvarying temperatures, the thick black soil, and protected brackish waters made a home for more than a third of all North American birds—indeed, birds who bred a continent apart came together to feed here, for differences were softened in the delta.

Land and earth were often indistinguishable, fresh and salt water blended in a mix that changed with each tide or wind shift. Salt and fresh water fish swam side by side; dryland animals became swimmers and aquatic animals moved easily up and over the grasses. As in a family of quite different siblings, the whole was made stronger by the variations in the individuals.

By the turn of the Nineteenth Century, man had made few changes in the delta. Hunters saw fewer jaguars, red wolves, and scarlet ibis, but their diminishment went almost unnoticed in such fertile, crowded pastures. When human eyes looked upwards, the skies were still massed with birds, and a man could see no end to them. The delta seemed ever a kingdom of plenty, where a heron soared in an ecstasy of pure freedom, high above trees that were at once his home and his prison.

Out in the wetlands, a large male alligator swam towards the shore. It was past the hottest part of the day, and his blood needed to absorb some of the sun to warm his inner organs.

Lacking warm blood of his own, he was solely dependent on the sun or the cool water to keep him comfortable. He moved up onto the shore a distance of about fifteen feet, turned in a half circle so that his snout and tail were pointing towards the water, and then allowed his small legs to lower himself to the ground. He slept.

Few creatures would have intruded into his resting space. Twelve feet long, with his mouth partially open, most of his eighty teeth—yellowed and sharp—lined his upper and lower jaws in a deadlock display.

His largest teeth of all did not show. Unlike the long and sharply tapered snout of his cousin, the crocodile, the alligator's snout was very broad and smoothly rounded at the end. It did not hide his upper and lower jaw teeth, but the greatly enlarged fourth tooth on each side of his jaw—his gripping teeth—fit neatly into a special pit in his upper jaw and were not visible at all, unless he chose to expose them.

His rough skin, even his leathery eyelids which now closed over his protruding eyes, was a deep grayish brown, almost black when his body was wet. As he lay in the sun drying, his skin took on the look of dull craggy mountain rills. The skin of his belly was a dark, deeply yellowed ivory color, shading into deeper tan. It was his belly skin that hunters prized most. And he would fight to the death to keep from exposing this most vulnerable side of his body.

He was not alone in the wetland of course. All over the delta, up Lafourche, down the Teche, in Terrebonne and Barataria, anywhere where water was deep enough to shelter them, his kind thrived. In breeding season, so many congregated that they could clog the river itself with their backs. If they would tolerate the close proximity of their kind.

Large as he was, this alligator was not the largest in the bayou. One nineteen-footer occupied waters several miles away, and few would venture into his territory. Certainly no other male would ignore his hissed warning.

But twelve feet had earned this alligator the right to doze

in the sun unmolested. Even asleep, his hearing and sense of smell were still remarkably keen. When awake, he could follow the scent of an animal on the water, and he could tell without seeing which creature might be splashing in the bayou at some distance and whether or not it was in trouble. For now, the silence of the swamp soothed him as much as the sun on his back.

It was just before dusk when a noise awakened him. It was a subtle, regular splashing, different than that made by a wading raccoon or a muskrat. At once he raised himself high and, with incredible swiftness for such weight, ran to the water's edge and plunged in. Despite his speed and bulk, he entered the water with little disturbance: a momentary heavy gurgling while the water rearranged itself, and then he was gone beneath the dark surface, leaving only an eddying swirl behind.

His speed underwater was spectacular, for his heavy tail swept back and forth in powerful surges that drove him up the bayou in seconds, moving him to the far side and up a watercourse only a dozen feet offshore, up where the water was only about a foot deep.

At the far end of his territory, a channel of open water moved sluggishly, cluttered with reeds and shrubs. Here, a yearling white-tailed doe had splashed through the tangle to reach the clear water.

She was slim and small, no more than fifty pounds. A pack of dogs had run her for several miles before she escaped them by crossing the bayou, and now she was very thirsty. She was hot and panting, and the deeper water tempted her to wade up to her knees.

Once in the water, she heard a faint gurgling splash upriver, but it was a good distance away. Nonetheless, she stopped and stood warily, listening, sniffing the air for possible danger. Her sides heaved with the morning's exertion, and her panic was still close to the surface. Finally, she waded further out and began to drink.

As he swam, the alligator surfaced only once, and then only his eyes and his nostrils broke the calm of the water. He saw the doe from several hundred yards away, then slid under the surface moving closer.

She paused in her drinking once more to listen and sniff for danger, but she sensed nothing. Her ears were pricked backwards in case the dogs still came on.

The alligator surfaced once more, not twenty yards from her as she lowered her muzzle a second time. This time, her head was turned slightly away from him, and she waded deeper, drinking more slowly now as she relaxed.

With a swift rush, the alligator rose from the water and clamped her snout up to her eyes. Before she could even jerk back, he used his tail to spin his body with such force that she was knocked off her feet. Struggling to right herself, with a high-pitched keening sound, her knees buckled, gave way, and he dragged her into deeper water.

Fighting desperately, lunging and bucking, she tried to break his hold, but he twisted her so sharply that her spine snapped with the sound of a large stick. In that moment she died, even before the water could enter her lungs as the alligator dragged her to the bottom.

As the doe's thrashings ceased, the alligator became calm, holding her on the bottom by his claws for long moments. Finally he released his hold on her muzzle long enough to grasp one of her shoulders and rise to the surface, carrying her limp carcass with him.

A half-dozen other alligators were cutting their V wakes across the surface as they rushed towards him, but he turned to face them fearlessly. He dragged the doe into shallow water, held down her body with two claws, and turned to his competition with a widely gaping mouth and a fierce hiss of warning.

He was larger than most of them, but together they could overpower him, should they do so in concert. Yet they paused just long enough for him to blow up his sides and belly, looking even longer and wider than his actual size. They ringed him at a distance of ten yards and waited, their jaws just under the surface.

The alligator did not wait for them to attack. He quickly gripped the front leg of the doe and twisted it over and over with all of his neck muscles. Bones snapped and tissue tore, and in moments he ripped the leg free, maneuvered it in his jaws, and gulped it down in two swallows, his eyes never leaving the waiting adversaries.

They had moved closer. He raised his snout and hissed again, a louder warning, but they did not back up. Neither did they move closer.

Again he took a grip and twisted violently, until the water churned to mud and the head of the doe ripped away from her neck. He swallowed it whole, manipulating it in his jaws so it went down nose first—another leg, a hind one this time. He had to work harder at the strong haunch muscles, and while he bent his head to the task, the largest of the waiting gators rushed in and grabbed the doe's carcass by a remaining front leg.

As though signaled, the others surged forward as well; one ripped away a hind leg and gulped it swiftly, another clamped his jaws on the belly of the remains. At once, a ferocious tug of war ensued, as the others watched and circled and hissed at one another, if they grazed too close. Bloody froth and water flew as they roared and tugged and twisted and thrashed, then the carcass split open and they all rushed in at once to grab at the spilled viscera.

The huge male swung his tail in a wide arc, savagely knocking one adversary back into the water. The doe was disappearing in a flurry, but he took one haunch and sank into the water, satisfied.

In moments, he was back on his bank, his eyes glowing in the dusk which loomed so long in the wetlands, listening for the sounds of another splashing—the sounds of the nightfeeders of the bayou.

The Choctaw woman had not intended to steal the magic boy. Not at first. Yes, it was true, she had wanted him, wanted him ever since he was placed in her arms. Either him or his same-face brother. Such magic was rare in her tribe, in any tribe, she guessed, and certainly drew her eyes again and again as she fed the two boys, changed their wet cloths, and rocked their identical cradles.

But she had not thought of taking one for her own, not until she found herself alone with the dark-eyed boy, huddling him against her breast, while all of the swamp howled around them. In that instant, he clung to her fiercely, squalling almost as loudly as his brother left behind in the pitching boat. And she knew that she could have him, if she were very quick and very strong.

It had been a long time since she had felt such strength in her limbs, not at all since she had been to the white woman's house. But now, with all the winds screaming at her to run, she did, as swiftly as she had ever run in her life. She bent her body over the boy, wrapping them both tightly in her sodden blanket, threw herself into the winds, and let them push her swiftly down the riverbank, away from the boat, away from the man and the woman and this boy's double, away from the stink of the cabin and the foul taste of the white woman's spices, away into the howling storm. With one hand clutching for safety at the trees, the other clamped tightly over the boy's head and mouth, she ran. When she heard the distant cries and calls of the white woman—even over the wind she could hear her—she lowered her head into the hurricane and pushed on.

They spent that night and another in a hole scarcely large enough to hold a family of beaver. But it was high on the riverbank, high enough so that the water did little but lap at its edges and muddy their blanket, and in time, the boy stopped shrieking. When he could only moan, hiding his head on her breast, she spoke to him softly of her village, of the many dogs he would have for his own, of the little canoe she would build for him herself, of the soft deerskins he would sleep on at night.

These things and more, she told him, and she began to call him by the name he would come to know better than his own of Samuel.

"Now, you are reborn," she whispered to him in the darkness of the beaver den. "Now, you will be called Apipolukta, He-Who-Has-Two-Bodies, so that all may know your power."

But the boy only fretted and wept, unwilling to repeat the new name, unable to let go of her arms. When he called her Deborah, the name the white woman had given her, she stubbornly turned her head away and would not answer him. By the end of two days, he was calling her by her true name, Amo-ani, She-Who-Gathers-Fruit. And she knew his true name would follow in his mouth soon enough.

She could be patient.

When the storm subsided at last, the two emerged into a world where all landmarks were swept away, all boundaries were dissolved. The river had actually changed its course in its fury, and for a day, Amo-ani was not certain in which direction her village might be. But finally they walked far enough so that the land became somewhat familiar. North, she headed, away from the river's flow. The farther they went, the less the land had been riled. Somewhere just south of the white town of the Red Stick, she turned up a twisting bayou, her mouth already set in a smile. Two more days' walk, and she came to the clearing where her people had built their shelters, had lived and hunted and made their babies for a space of too many seasons to count.

But the village was almost empty. In shocked dismay, Amo-ani saw that many more than she had gathered fruit. The whites had lured or stolen most of her people away, and only a few old ones remained. There were no men for the hunt. There were no fishers to paddle the canoes. The old ones fished for little crabs and gathered their roots and berries, but there were no men to father this magic boy.

For long seasons, Amo-ani tried to father and mother him alone. She moved them into an abandoned hut, fished for him, gathered for him, and told him the ancient stories each night by their small fire. For a time, he listened. But after a year, he grew silent. After two, his eyes grew dull and his black hair lost its sheen. More seasons passed and his arms and legs grew smaller, rather than bigger, and he ate less and less. He would scarcely speak, for all the words she threw at him. He began to turn away when she called his name, insisting that she call him Samuel.

Amo-ani began to dream that Api-polukta would die. He was hungering for something she could not find, no matter what she hunted, no matter how she foraged. She knew that if she caused his death, his other body would surely perish as well. She could not abide such a great sin, and she sensed that the gods would not abide it either.

The fourth winter came, and she sorrowed. There would be even less to pleasure the boy's shrunken belly in the coming moons. Even less to make his eyes spark with interest. Finally, with great sadness, she readied them both for their final journey together. Up the twisting bayou, she paddled their boat, placing her borrowed son in the back where he could trail his hand in the black water. As usual, he listened to the cries of the birds more than to her voice. As always, the bayou seemed to speak to him in a way it did to few others.

207

When they reached the place where the bayou widened, they walked to the great white village of the Red Stick. She knew there was a place within the village where everything was sold. Amo-ani looked neither to the left nor the right as she led the boy through the white man's streets. Her blanket almost hid her face completely, for she feared that at any moment, a white voice would howl out *Thief!*, and white hands would punish her. Almost did she grab his hand and run back to her own village, but when she saw the way his eyes moved eagerly over the white houses and the white faces, she kept to her course.

The central market in Baton Rouge was the oldest place in the city, and people who came to buy were accustomed to seeing the strangest things sold by the most motley hands. Trappers vied for space with slave sellers; Creole vendors shouted about their fresh berries and their spices; fisherman spread their daily catch out in stinking baskets, waving away the flies with wet palm branches. Amo-ani sat down on her blanket, pulling Api next to her and signaling him to silence.

She had not needed to tell him to be still. He sensed what she was about, and he wished for nothing more than rescue. By whom, he was not sure; to what, he could not say, but he knew with a certainty that he never wanted to see the Choctaw village again in his life. He sat cross-legged beside her, his skinny knees akimbo. The soles of his feet were so blackened and calloused that they looked more cedar bark than skin. His face, his hair, were as black as hers. But he still remembered that he was not her own, had never been. And he believed that someone would see that truth.

"Look at this child," he heard a soft voice exclaim close by.

Samuel didn't turn his head. It had been four years since he had heard that speech, but he remembered the nuance of English as though he had been dreaming it for years.

"He is Choctaw, you think?" a man answered. "Looks like he has the blood."

The woman said, "What he looks like is starving to death, and no older than our youngest."

Even Samuel could read the glance the man gave his wife. In it was a wary alarm and a swift stubborn refusal.

But she met his glance with one of her own, just as strong in its warmth. Their heads pulled away then, and he could no longer hear their words. Amo-ani began to rock to and fro, murmuring what seemed to be an old lament. The blur and bustle of the market place swirled around him in that instant, and he was overwhelmed by a sense of need. It was all he could do not to leap to his feet and cry out, "I am Samuel! Take me from here!" But he could not find the words, so he kept his silence, closing his eyes with an effort.

"He can work?" the man was asking Amo-ani. "I won't take on no rousters, hear?"

His wife touched his arm, but he gently shrugged her off.

Amo-ani looked up at the man once, then her eyes swiveled quickly to his wife and stayed there. Samuel saw something pass between them, almost tangible in the morning fog. Amo-ani stood up silently, pulling her blanket about her with dignity.

"What're you asking for him, then?" the man demanded. "God knows, I don't need the vexation, but I'll hear his price."

Amo-ani glanced down once at Samuel, a hot glance of yearning. Then she walked away through the crowd, disappearing as quickly, as completely, as though she walked a familiar bayou trail. She never looked back once.

"Well, I'll be damned," the man said wonderingly.

The boy got to his feet and said, "I am Samuel. Can you take me to my home?"

"And where might that be?" the woman asked gently.

With that question, Samuel began to weep as he hadn't in almost four years, as only an eight-year-old boy can weep, when he realizes that he does not know where his home is, cannot say where his parents and brother might be, and understands that he will likely be among strangers the rest of his life.

The color of the water lightened, and seemed to lighten further with every mile as the man and woman took him down the Mississippi. They were approaching the gulf by degrees, and from time to time they saw elevated islands—rises of sand, shell, and earth above the surrounding waters. On the islands were fringes of oak which clung tenaciously to those short strips of soil. *Chênaies,* the man called them, and the sound of the word sounded familiar to Samuel, far back in his memory.

The land was barren of most growth save the marsh grasses, the wild indigo that rattled in its dry pods, and stunted, dun-colored mangroves. The wide marshlands seemed to hold only the millions of screaming waterfowl— and the slowly moving boat.

Oysterman, he said he was. He and his wife made their home in the deep delta. They were the Popiches, Slavs from Dalmatia, and they had a fishing business in the Barataria Bay. Parents to four children, they always could use, they said, an extra pair of hands at the shrimp nets and the oyster beds.

"You can call us Mister and Missus," Popich told him solemnly. "I give you a bed and three squares a day, plus something for your pockets. Teach you a trade, boy, and some letters, too, in the bargain. You work longside my own, can't do no better than that. Teach you to know God proper."

"But first," the woman said firmly, "we fill out those ribs."

The Popiches had come, with other Dalmatians, from the Slavic lands of the Balkans. They had known the ravages of the Turks, the Romans, the Germans, the Italians, and they knew too well that work was all that stood between them and slow starvation. Their first countrymen moved into the delta and claimed squatters' land that no one else seemed to want, setting up small fishing cabins on the banks. They held themselves apart from the French, for they were a quiet people, little inclined to gossip, almost morose in their view of life. When they did speak, their thick, guttural tones perplexed the French, and their hulking men with the wide handlebar moustaches made the Acadian women shy away.

Where the French were willing to fit themselves to the land, the newcomers wanted the land to fit to them.

The Acadians nudged each other as the Dalmatians passed. "You look at them at sunrise and you look at them at sunset, and *Nom de Dieu*, you know they haven' stop all in between, them!"

When one Slav met another, his greeting was *"Kako ste?"*—"How are you?" The answer was "Dobro"—"Good." The French called them Kako-ste's, and then, Tockos.

They planted the oysters, sowed the seed shells in the low water, and cultivated the beds with curses and songs. That much, at least, the French could understand. Then they took the harvest to New Orleans in the shells or further up the river, dried, roasted, and pickled. They consumed vast amounts of olive oil and wine—but only after their work was done and harvest was in. The French shrugged at this waste of *la vie,* but soon the differences between them were softened, as blended as everything else in the wetlands.

It would take time for Samuel to know all these things, for when he arrived in the Popich boat, he saw only that the oyster settlement seemed peaceful enough in the burning sunlight. Gulls swept over them, screeching and mewing, and huge plump clouds wallowed slowly by. Just ahead in the water, a swift otter dove with a shell between his teeth. As the Popich boat approached, the oysters closed their shells, each squirting up into the air an irritated spurt of blue juice. Samuel laughed at that, peering down at them through the shallows.

There were several scattered cabins, painted in vivid hues, all of them perched on tall posts driven in the mud, facing the bay, draped with drying nets, flanked by skiffs and pirogues. Under each house a firm footing was provided by oyster shells piled several feet thick.

The Popich house was large and tidy, white with green trim. A wire cage under the pilings held several chickens and two piglets. As they docked, four children of various ages and heights rushed out to greet them in a babble of Slavic and English, which Samuel could scarcely understand. But he did understand their welcome, and he could see that it extended to him as though he had been expected. Warily, he stood behind the Mister and Missus until he was pulled forward into the house by eager arms.

He could abide the tumult of them only for so long, however, and he soon found himself out on the dock again, exploring the shell island around the settlement. It was a region of few shadows. A blue heron fixed him with a mild brave look, and from under the wharf piling came an odd sound which some underwater creature was repeating, a brief elusive twang, like the plucking of a string.

Popich came out and found him then, calling him back. He sat Samuel down on the dock and said, "Watch me, now." He cast a net off the wharf to the swift mullet that were moving out with the tide. The fish were heavy with roe. He carved out the roe with his knife and threw the fish back in the water, where they were taken quickly by the waiting gars. The Missus came out with a black pan, and he slid the roe into it.

"For supper," he said. "You like?"

Samuel nodded, feeling sure that if the others could eat it, he could, too. He felt how flat the waters, the world was here in that instant. He could sense the bulk of the earth all around him, the tremendous weight of space and water and sky. He would be lonely here, he knew, but he would be safe.

Within a season, he was strong and growing taller, a process which had seemed to stop in the Choctaw village. Within a year, he spoke Tocko, what they called the Slavic tongue, fairly easily, handled the nets as well as Popich's oldest boy, Daniel, and his hands were so calloused by the oyster shells, you could grate cheese on them, Missus said.

The hands of a born oysterman, Mister added.

The Popich children—and ultimately most in the Barataria village—came to call him Samuel French. He did not know his own name. He would not take theirs. And because he could remember just a little of the old Acadian phrases, often speaking easily with the Acadian shrimpers, the name French seemed to suit him.

Popich taught him his religion: oysters. He told Samuel that these creatures grew to market size in the warm brackish estuaries of Louisiana, faster than in any other place in the country.

"Best damn oyster waters in the world," Popich boasted. "Here, God make Heaven for the oyster, eh? We got the good flow of fresh and salt, and the winds mix them all together, and the Mississippi drop plenty for Mister Oyster to eat, and he got plenty warm months to eat it in. Make for more oyster than Chesapeake and Long Island put together!"

But the Popiches and their countrymen were not content to wait for Nature's bounty. They advanced upon the oyster beds with determination, ripping at the stony beds to see what made them thrive or die. They experimented, they tried new locations, and they devoted all year to oystering, something the French had never been willing to do. They developed tools to fit their purposes—tongs that were a pair of

213

hinged rakes eight feet long, operated with both hands like an awkward scissors to draw up the oyster clumps. And they built special luggers, low-hung, widebeamed, with a deep hold for large hauls.

The most successful Tockos took their catch to New Orleans for the best price. They followed the backwaters upriver as far as they could, then came to shallow water and had to wait until the tide deepened. Every delay worried them; every hour the oyster was out of water counted. On clear days, Popich would call out, "They're still clicking!": the oysters were alive in their piles. A warm fog would roll in and he'd curse, "Fog same like smoke. Inside pile, they livin', outside, die fast."

But once Popich made it to the city, the dealers took all he could provide. Best oysters, yes. They could sample them, but they rarely bothered. The Tockos had a reputation for the best. And they knew how to work.

For their part, the oysters of Louisiana were most busy from April to October, when the warming of the waters induced them to breed. Then they produced their "milk"—a time when most self-respecting oysterman refused to eat them at all—eggs in the female and sperm in the male. The eggs and sperm clouded the waters along the banks and collided to make new oyster spats or larvae, which could move about freely for only about four weeks. As their shells grew, they were dragged to the bottom, where they remained cemented to rock, old shell, or each other for the rest of their lives—or until Popich dragged them up.

At dawn, the Popich oyster lugger moved out into the gulf, towards the beds they had staked as their own. Once there, the boat began a kind of dance, circling lazily over the reef in an intricate series of movements which Popich directed carefully, shouting at his sons and at Samuel to "come round agin!"

With a large dredge, they scraped the bottom as the boat circled up and down the bayou. At times other luggers passed within twenty yards of them, but each boat knew its place. When any two luggers came near, the fierce banter between them could barely be heard above the creak and groan of the dredges.

"How many sacks you got?"

"We got six, goin' on seven."

"Too much talking over there, not enough dredgin'!"

"Hell, we're so good at this, we could go off fishing, come back, and still get more'n you'll sack today."

"And you'll be out here till sunrise, an' your woman will run off with a Kaintuck!"

"Then she better keep runnin'! While you been sitting there yellin', we got us two more sacks!"

The winch pulled the dredge up and down and must be wound by hand, two to a winch on the heavy iron handles, until the dredge was hauled aboard. Dripping with mud and weed, the oysters were dumped on deck, and the dredge went back overboard.

Samuel and the Popich sons spent most of the morning on their hands and knees with oyster hammers, cleaving apart the mass of shells and shoveling them into a wire basket. Soon, Samuel's hands looked like those of every other oysterman, well scarred by the sharp shells and roughened by the salt water. Occasionally, he'd stop to toss a crab caught in the dredge into the bucket for the evening meal. When the sacks were full, they turned for home.

A hundred sacks was worth a thousand dollars, but to get those sacks full took most every day of the season except Sundays, from dawn until dusk.

"I tell you," Popich said, "if you do well one season, you gonna do bad the next. This year, she's good. Last year, the water come up stormy and we dredged plenty, but they was all opened up. Too much silt, and they die off, too much salt and they stop eating. Not enough salt, and they not *fit* to eat. I jus' shake my head and said, we come back agin next year.

That's all ye can do. Ye can't control nothin' about it 'cept your back and your brains."

The deep delta was a place where the sense of the sea was stronger than the sense of land—or any other water. Barataria was a bay without a shore, a wide protected body of inland water bounded by clusters and clumps of islands, peninsulas, and soggy remnants of earth. In every direction, streams ran into streamlets, passes, bayous, inlets, all twisted about in rises of sand and shells. Its branchlike connections covered over four hundred square miles, and few men could know them well.

Even after four years on the delta, Samuel knew only part of the paths through the water, with dead endings and circular windings on which a stranger might wander bewildered for weeks.

Popich said you had to be born here to know it, and then you could find your way in the slow waters even in the dark.

Samuel learned enough to squint against the violence of the strong sun as he moved about his daily work, and to keep in the deep shade when the light was at its most ardent. But he never stopped thinking of darker cypress waters and mysterious mossy trees with black shadows. Of a brother, a twin, nestled against him in the warmth, of a mother's face, half-seen, half-sensed, which hovered over them both like the moon.

The delta offered more than tangled waters, however. It was a place unrivaled for smuggling. On Grand Isle, where the Popiches made their home, freebooters thrived. Calling themselves privateers, they worked alongside the fishermen, and they made amiable and profitable neighbors. Two men in particular were well favored in the Delta, famous even as far north as New Orleans.

Jean Lafitte—elegant, knowing, mysterious—and his elder brother, Pierre—sturdy and discreet—were welcome in even the most pious deltan homes. What had been a brawling inefficient trade in stolen goods became an organized and thriving business under their management. Most merchants were their customers; most fishermen were grateful for their fleet of fast ships to take the catch swiftly to profitable markets.

The Lafittes controlled the best ships, more than thirty of them, and over five thousand men. The harbor they chose in the bay could only be approached from the gulf through three narrow channels, and the widest was only a quarter-mile across, between Grand Terre and Grand Isle. The Lafittes' batteries of guns were mounted on the highest point of each island, and their two warehouses—one in Barataria, the other in New Orleans—were full of the treasures from a hundred ships. Slaves from Haiti, linens, coffee, silks and spices free of customs duties, the best wines, iron, mahogany, and gold were carried by pirogues up the delta, then by mule, and finally by flat-bottomed barges when they approached the city.

Samuel first saw Jean and Pierre Lafitte in the streets of New Orleans, on a visit there with old Popich. He was twelve. He'd been warned about the city weeks before he traveled there by Missus, and in fact she almost refused to let him go.

"It's an evil place these days, Samuel," she said quietly. "Much changed, even in a few years."

"I need him," Mister said abruptly. "It's either Samuel or Daniel . . ."

But she would not hear of her own son making such a journey.

And so Samuel was already dazzled by the time he placed his feet on New Orleans *banquettes*. His eyes moved everywhere at once, his ears almost turned on his head to catch the jostling hordes and their confusion of tongues, Spanish, French, and English. He saw posters up on the lampposts which advertised a bullbaiting to come. The lurid painting showed a black bull in a pit, pulled down by a pack of crazed, sharp-fanged curs, while spectators cheered, leaning way over the edge of the gallery. Cockfights, he'd seen plenty of, but not right in the street as they did it here! Gamblers, too, in Barataria, but they didn't stumble around drunk in broad daylight, brandishing pistols and cursing at passersby . . . passersby who scarcely paid them heed!

From out of the second-story window of a fine-looking establishment, Samuel saw colored women, light as creamed coffee and tricked out in bright ribbons, leaning way down to call loudly to the men who passed beneath them.

In one afternoon, Samuel saw two rawboned flatboatmen with their coonskin caps knocked askew, fighting with knives in the street, and also two elegantly dressed gentlemen dueling in the park. Two shots rang out, and one man slumped sideways to the ground with a moan Samuel could hear where he stood.

In the market, where Popich had his business and it was Samuel's job to handle the large crates of oysters, he could hardly keep his mind on his work. Had he really been in Barataria for four long years? And if so, did he really wish to return?

He saw in long rows more vegetables than he'd tasted in a lifetime: peas, cabbages, beetroots, artichokes, French beans, radishes, and potatoes of both the sweet and Irish kind. Indian corn, ginger, blackberries, roses, violets, oranges, bananas, apples, fowls tied in three by the legs, quails, gingerbread, and beer in bottles all crowded together—and then the oysters!

Everyone was eating them, even at this early hour, raw, fried, or boiled. Large pots of stew and chowder simmered on a dozen tables. Popich, with a pirogue unloaded from four families, had four thousand to sell and did so within a quarter hour.

The milling crowd of buyers called out with impunity, and each seemed to know not only what he or she wanted, but how much it should cost. With every purchase, the merchant cajoled and flattered, and then threw in a lagniappe—a little something extra, like a bunch of radishes, a rose, a handful of matches.

Near the pillars of the market hall, Samuel saw colored women selling coffee, hot chocolate, and smoking dishes of rice with gumbo ladled over. Other colored women circulated through the crowd with baskets of delicacies, while quadroons—some of them more beautiful than the whitest lady—their hair done up in colored cloths, offered bouquets of Spanish jasmine, carnations, or violets for boutonnieres.

Samuel could see why the Missus didn't want Daniel in such a place, but he found it much to his taste. Over in a corner, he saw some Indians selling their hides, furs, herbs, and the green powder made of dried sassafras leaves that the colored women used to make their *gumbo file*. Silent and immobile, they sat on the ground, seemingly oblivious to the commotion around them.

He turned away and looked at them no more.

Finally Popich's business was done at market, and they set out for the docks. On the narrow muddy streets, they threaded their way past gutters and canals clogged with garbage and the contents of chamber pots. Each house had a set of barrels alongside the door or within the gated yard.

"Mississippi water," Popich told him. "They bring it in by wagons, fifty cents a barrel. Imagine giving good silver for water, eh? They couldn't pay me enough to live in this Sodom."

Near the docks they passed a pink painted house with elaborate wrought iron railings all round. Two finely dressed men came out, bowed briefly at the Mister, and walked on.

"There be the Lafitte brothers," old Popich hissed quickly. "Jean and Pierre, hisself."

Samuel's eyes widened. The two seemed to own the street they walked. Those who passed bowed deeply, doffed their hats, and spoke pleasantly. Women smiled and curtsied, some of them following the men with their eyes.

"The most famous pirates of them all," Popich added quietly.

"What were they doing there?" Samuel nodded back at the pink house.

"Maspero's Exchange," Popich said, "it's their favorite. They plan their raids, make deals, run their contracts from there."

"So bold," Samuel murmured.

"No one can touch them. No one really wants to, truth be known. They can provide anything cheaper. Slaves, whiskey, silk goods, you want it, they get it. They say he's welcome at the finest tables."

"Where does he keep his goods?"

Popich laughed. "Why? You want to buy something? Maybe catch him unloading treasure in the moonlight? Put it out of your head, boy. That's the way to live fast and die young."

But Samuel barely listened. The two men walking in front of them seemed suddenly to him to represent all things fine and powerful. Jean was dressed all in black; Pierre in bright green silk. They wore handsome clothes, the cut of which revealed a certain dignity and position. Their shoes were polished leather, their black hats cocked at an angle which dared the world to do anything but bow. Without thinking, he quickened his step. Popich caught at his elbow in alarm, but Samuel threw it off. He reached the two pirates and stepped before them.

"I'm looking for a place," he said quickly, keeping the tremor out of his voice with an effort. "I can do most anything you put me to, and do it with a will. Would you take me on?" Over Jean Lafitte's shoulder, he could see old Po-pich's mouth hanging open in amazement.

To Samuel's surprise, neither brother brushed him off. Jean, the youngest, grinned amiably, appraising him up and down. "What do we have here?"

"Samuel French," he said quickly. "I was orphaned early, been with the Choctaws for a spell, and most lately been oystering down in Barataria. I can do most anything, sirs. If you take me on, you won't regret it."

"How old are you, minnow?" Pierre asked indolently, his dark eyes watching his brother more than the boy before him.

"Fourteen, sir," Samuel said unhesitatingly, and he heard Popich sputter indignantly. He knew he had to press their decision swiftly. "I've been elbow-deep in oysters for too long, and if you'll give me a chance, I'll work for nothing more than my meals and a bed for a year. After that, if you think I've earned it, keep me on at a fair wage. If not, then set me adrift."

Jean laughed. "Adrift, is it? Looks to me as though you've been adrift before."

Samuel smiled, feeling almost an equal. "That I have. But I mean to be setting a course in the future."

"This be your relation?" Pierre asked, gesturing to old Popich who hurried up to their side.

"No," Samuel said firmly. "He took me in and for that, I'm grateful, but I give him four good years. That's enough."

"What's the boy to you?" Jean asked Popich, his smile turned curious.

Popich opened his mouth and closed it again like a carp. "Why we took him in like our own! Saved him from savagery, taught him a good trade, he's an ungrateful whelp who—and he's only twelve! A stripling. A lying stripling!"

"I don't know exactly how old I am," Samuel said firmly. "I feel fourteen most days or older. My fingers are stiff and my back's humped from oyster tongs, and none of the harvest mine. I want to invest my sweat in something of my own!

This is America, after all." He grinned at them conspiratorially. "The land of promise."

"What's the boy to you?" Jean repeated, his voice silky.

Popich squared his jaw. "Not a goddamned thing."

"Well." Jean looked back at Samuel and the boy saw something decided in that instant. "Guess we'll take him off your hands then." And the two brothers turned to continue their walk up the street.

Samuel turned to Popich and said, "Please tell Missus I'm sorry. Tell her I'm grateful for all you've done, but I got to find my own way." He snatched the old man's hand, pumped it once, and ran after the Lafittes.

When he reached Jean's side, dropping back to walk a few steps behind as was fitting, Jean said only, "I won't tolerate disloyalty, French, and I shoot liars. Let this be the last I ever see of either."

"Oui, M'sieu. Merci, M'sieu," Samuel answered quickly.

Without further acknowledgment, Jean and Pierre Lafitte allowed him to follow them through New Orleans.

The Lafittes put Samuel to work unloading cargo on their Baratarian island, Grand Isle. The Lafitte stronghold was a storehouse of impressive dimensions, a well-stocked slave barracoon, a set of heavy fortifications, and rows of small protected huts to hold silks, furnishings, wine, spices, and gold. Grand Isle was naturally protected by shallow winding bays, which made pursuit impossible for those who did not know the tranasses, the marsh labyrinths to nowhere.

Samuel soon found that Barataria was a place of passionate moods. When a sweet breeze blew from the south, the work was calm and timeless, but in a moment the breeze might die, and a man'd be blistered in heat. A whistling wind would come up from the gulf, and salt spray and pelting rain would rattle the sails—until the sun came out again in moments. The people were like the climate, given to careless mirth and quick to fury. They held life cheap and were outlaws by choice. Eyeless, armless Portuguese or Spanish who had grown old at sea; silent young Americans, French, or Brits who had deserted navies and armies all over the world; and even the occasional man Samuel met who bore a good name but had traded a legacy for adventure.

Some of the men brought their women as well, stashing them in palm huts on the beach for as long as their desire or patience held out. French and Spanish women, many of them as reckless and hungry as their men, with little to fill their hours until the ships returned. Among all this, Samuel reached the age of eighteen.

Samuel saw Jean Lafitte himself only rarely; mostly, he worked for his elder brother, Alexandre. But no man called him by that name. His alias was Dominique You, and he had a reputation as a brilliant gunner who had taken down a dozen French and British ships in less than two years.

You was small and broad-shouldered, with light hair and dark leathered skin. Good-tempered, a practical joker, he sailed under a Bolivian flag with letters of marque from Carthagena. He put Samuel to work storing wine, tallying goods, and finally, keeping accounts. He had a way of fixing his eyes on a man's face as he spoke, and Samuel imagined he could see in those eyes visions of ships with sails in flames, of women dancing bare-breasted on fire-lit sand, of glittering jewels and gold.

Once, You asked Samuel, "Ever get tired of being Lafitte's storekeeper?" His eyes flickered like two candles in an open door. "Perhaps you should talk with *le capitaine*. He likes you. Who knows? He may make you rich, *hein?*"

"You mean, go raiding?" Samuel felt the question all the way to his belly.

He swiftly remembered that first day he walked behind the Lafittes down the Rue de Bourbon to the blacksmith shop. The smithy was surrounded by a high wall, its flat face completely concealing what went on within. The woman who answered Jean's knock was dark, with a beauty at once compelling and strange. "Welcome, *cher*," she said to Lafitte, scarcely glancing at Samuel behind the two brothers. He could see little in the darkness behind her, could smell an odor like spices, could hear the distant murmur of other men, and he had stepped inside the pirates' den without a backwards glance. Beyond that door lay a horizon as vast as the open sea, a tropic sun that turned men's skins dark and in whose heat no deed was too violent . . .

"Ye be man enough now, I think," You was saying. "There are plenty of big Spanish geese out there, waiting to be plucked. With golden eggs to be taken." He grinned. "We don't always wring the necks of these geese, eh? Let them fly for another day. Any fool can count these casks."

"I'll think on it," Samuel said quietly.

Dominique shrugged and walked away, as though the offer could only be made once.

Sometimes after that, Samuel felt himself tempted to leave the gulf waters for the larger expanses of the sea. But he always turned away again to the shallows. Lafitte paid him five hundred dollars a month just to count and store his treasures, and he liked the tidiness of it. Something out there seemed to him to be uncontrollable—and what he had learned—and learned most well in his years—was that he must control his life if he would keep living it.

Samuel would have known, if he had gone to sea with Lafitte, just how soon chaos was coming to Louisiana. On the sea, the Baratarians were encountering British ships more and more as their adversaries, and the King's Navy seemed determined to take over waters which Yankee ships had proclaimed their own.

France and Britain were already at war and had been for nearly twenty-five years. Jefferson had publicly proclaimed America neutral, but of course privately hoped that these two giants would gnaw themselves to the bone. When French ships found Yankee vessels on the high seas, they often stole whole cargoes, impudently ignoring American neutrality.

But Britain went one step farther. When they stopped to steal American cargoes, they also forced American sailors off their own ships to serve in the British navy.

In 1812, Jefferson passed an embargo on all trade with Britain. The Crown retaliated by barring all American ships from any continental port. Jefferson declared Louisiana a state and, six weeks later, declared war on England, June 18, 1812.

Americans and British, brothers once and now only distant cousins, never really did understand each other. The Brits rarely took Yanks seriously, and Americans scarcely took any-thing but themselves seriously. Yanks liked nothing better than a good joke, and Brits refused to be one.

Even so, war might have been avoided. Britain was still fighting Napoleon and did not really want to take on another adversary. For two years Yankee ships harassed the British Navy, but it was not until the spring of 1814, when the defeat of Napoleon's troops looked inevitable, that England decided to slap the American mosquito which had been buzzing around her ears and take the Mississippi.

It was this slap which finally woke the sleepy bayou and roused New Orleans to outrage. General Jackson, desperate for men to defend the river and thence, America's vulnerable interior, recruited every male in the delta who could tote a musket. Finally, he even pardoned the Lafittes and their pirate brethren, providing they would bring their ships, guns, and crews to the fields of Chalmette just below New Orleans, where the British were massing for invasion.

Unknown to both sides, a peace treaty had been signed at Ghent on Christmas eve, making the battle at Chalmette redundant. Yet both sides bristled for war, believing that what they did here would decide the future of the Mississippi and thus, America.

In the predawn of January 8, 1815, Samuel was huddled with Dominique You's battalion behind a fence rail and mud embankment they had hastily constructed on the field at Chalmette. The pirates sat with Creoles, Acadians, Indians, free men of color, regular army, volunteer militia, Tennessee and Kentucky long rifle troops, waiting in the damp cold. All together, they mustered about four thousand.

Across the field waited the British, some eight thousand strong, the spies said. It might have been more, but the English found the swamps tougher adversaries than they'd expected. First, their small boats took too long to transfer troops; second, no one had told them how cold Louisiana could be in winter. Two British West Indies regiments, accustomed to a tropical climate, were all but refusing to fight. Some of the newer recruits had sickened and died. The spies reported burial parties were kept busy.

The Sunday dawn was cold and damp, and Samuel felt it to his bones. He shivered, pulling the mud-spattered blanket closer. He was lucky to have it at all, he knew. Those last at the subscription wagons were crouching under boughs of pines to keep from freezing. It was a lot colder here at Chalmette than on Grand Isle in January.

He sat leaning against the log and earth embankment they'd spent the day building along the Rodriguez Canal, what the Americans called "Line Jackson." Close to two thousand yards of defensive mud.

At first, the pirates put their shoulders into it lustily, eager to show the battalions on both sides that they were as much soldiers as the next man. Led by Dominique You and Nez Coupe—as the men called old Louis Chighizola who'd lost half his nose in a saber fight—they shouted and cursed and sang as they worked. But after six hours of digging and carting dirt, six hours of feeling his fingers freeze to the shovel, Samuel had to admit that he wished the Lafittes had stayed pirates.

What was this battle to him? They were here to save New Orleans. If they failed, half of the country would fall to the redcoats, they said. But so far as Samuel could see, neither the Brits nor the Yanks had much love for the likes of them. "Pirates," the Tennessee riflemen had said with a sneer, and moved down the line. "Bandits," they added, with disgust. It was enough to cause some swift incendiary encounters before they were separated into their own regiment.

Those Kaintucks down the line, for example. A more ragtag group he'd never seen. They whooped and hollered like madmen when the wagons brought in the woolens New Orleans women had made for them. Raised hell about the provisions, too, and then looked over the pirates like they were beneath contempt, even though Lafitte had given Jackson seventy-five hundred pistol flints, four cannon, and seventy men.

It was a moonless night, and Samuel could see only part of the line in each direction. Soldiers all around huddled together, their muskets in their laps. At least here it was somewhat dry. Word was that Coffey's Tennessee Volunteers, closer to the cypress swamp, were sleeping in the mud.

Of course, no one was sleeping at all. The Brits were too close for that.

When they arrived, it looked as though men had lived on this field for months. The mud along the trenches had thawed and frozen so many times that it was ankle deep in places. Troops set fenceposts in place, at Jackson's orders, and banked it with mud higher than a man could stand. How much good that would be against the English cannons, Samuel wouldn't bet.

He remembered his last day in New Orleans. It was just as cold then, marching out of the city, towards the field of Chalmette, in a ragged file of fellow pirates and hastily armed fishermen. Over the balconies, women threw flowers down, and the words of "Yankee Doodle" and "La Marseillaise" rang in their ears.

"*Allons, enfants de la patrie!*" a woman sang lustily, dropping to her knees as Samuel went by. "Keep the redcoats from our daughters!"

He had smiled at that. Given the woman's dress and appearance, it was likely her daughters might welcome the new commerce.

As they marched, they heard in the distance ahead the sound of gunfire booming, and the explosions mingled with the chimes of the Ursuline convent behind them.

A week before they came, on December 28, the Brits had made a try at it. A halfhearted try, most said, probably just to test if the Americans would split and run. The First and

Second Louisiana regiments met them on the main line, Smith's Feliciana Troop and Chaveau's New Orleans Troop came from the rear, and the Navy ship *Louisiana* added her own guns to the fray.

Not a man bolted, the story went. The artillery on the main line was so heavy that the Brits backed up and retreated.

Emboldened by that victory, the Americans burnt down the Chalmette mansion then, saying it stood in the line of their fire. And they dug in again.

On the first of January, the Brits came on again, and this time, Samuel saw the battle firsthand. Their naval guns began to pound the main line at dawn, and Ogden's troop and St. Geme's company took heavy fire. Samuel could hear the screams of the men, but they were muffled by the curses and shouted orders of the pirates on all sides of him. In what seemed to be moments, the Yankee boats answered fire from another part of the river, and the Brits fell back.

"Pour it on, lads, send them to hell!" You cursed, and Samuel fired, reloaded, fired, reloaded, never giving thought to where his bullets landed or whether they hit home; the smoke and the blasts made it almost impossible to keep his eyes open to see what came towards them in the field. Quickly, though, the redcoats fell back again and word rolled swiftly up the line that they were in retreat.

Samuel sat that night apart from the carousing pirates and thought about his part in the fight. It had been remarkably easy. Frighteningly so. He had anticipated fear, and yes, he felt that. But the fear fled as soon as he began to work the gun. Never once did he actually see an enemy face, not so clearly that it looked like anything more than a dream coming to him in a fog of smoke and morning haze.

This then was battle. No wonder it was easy, as You said, to kill a man. One had only to point, pull, and look away to the next target. He felt isolated from his brothers though, and could not take part in the merriment that night. As though they carried a contagion, he edged away and sat apart.

The next morning, he shook himself to steadiness and walked along the line with what he felt must be a seasoned gait. Newcomers were still being added to the ranks. He felt he should stop and speak to them, tell them it was nothing to face the enemy, and not to fear the coming fight.

It was a colorful crowd. The pirates wore their best silks, as if they were invited to a quadroon ball instead of battle. The U.S. Marines down line had on full uniform and their tall dark hats. The Kentucky and Tennessee boys wore coonskins and hides, about as ragged as the Houmas and Choctaws and Cherokees who sat among them, tomahawks and hunting knives tied to their sides.

The guns they carried varied as much as their clothes. Samuel had been lucky twice—if a man could call himself lucky at all to be in Chalmette—he got a blanket and he got a decent Springfield. The musket was a smoothbore with a flintlock fire. The mountings were all iron, not a bit of brass on the gun. Looked like a trained marksman could get about three shots a minute off it, but Samuel knew he'd be lucky to get two. The bullet'd go about a hundred yards. He could only hope that the Brits would offer their usual wide target field—a thousand redcoats bunched together—making range a less vital personal imperative.

It was heavy at nine pounds and cold to the touch. The musket gave him small comfort in his arms, but it was better than the fowling pieces some of the farmers carried. He knew that when Jackson ordered a house-to-house search for weapons in New Orleans, he found so few serviceable weapons that he wondered aloud—and profanely—if the good people of the city had intended to pelt the Brits away with oyster shells.

The luckiest ones were the Pennsylvania troops who brought their own long rifles with them. Some bragged they could drop a man at three hundred yards and a horse at four hundred.

"This'll stop a bear," one old buzzard told Samuel at the fire one night. He patted his rifle as lovingly as a woman.

"That's hard to believe," Samuel said mildly.

"Believe it. It be too much for squirrel hunting. The bullet'd pulverize the animal, see. So ye aim just under him, splinter the branch. Bark the squirrel."

Macomb, a store clerk from New Orleans, leaned closer to see the Pennsylvania man's rifle. He looked with disgust at the fancy dueling pistol the clerk clutched.

"If they get past me," the Pennsylvania man drawled quietly, "that'll do ye one good anyhow."

"What's that?" Macomb asked.

"'Twill serve to blow yer brains in, afore the Brits do it for ye."

Hollow laughter rang up the line, and frosty puffs of air rose over the men's heads.

The men were working harder now, and everyone seemed to sense that the next battle would come soon. They had jammed cotton bales around the openings in the mud walls where the cannons jutted out, but these didn't work well in the last fight. Too many of them caught on fire and rendered several cannons impossible to use. But that was better than what the Brits were using, Samuel heard.

You told them that the redcoats stacked hogsheads of sugar around their cannons. Well enough, but when the hogsheads were split by fire, the sugar ran all over the ground! The Brits were mired in knee-deep molasses over there, and You told them to aim for the mud as often as the cannons, to keep them stuck until spring.

Samuel was beginning to wonder why these redcoats had such a fierce reputation. Of course the infantry was imposing, coming on as it did in regular waves of scarlet, but easier to hit, too, and the Kentucky marksmen had a standing joke about knocking down bowling pins named Tory. Or a flock of red-backed mallards. The Brits didn't seem to know a thing about surprise attack, either. They announced their charges with rocket flares and Highlander bagpipes, giving every man ample time to get ready. And now, when they might have rushed them and found the line unprepared, they waited. Quite all right with Jackson, because it gave him time to get four hundred more men down from Baton Rouge. Gave him time to get more muskets and dry powder. And gave every man there time to tell himself that he, of all his comrades, would be spared a bullet.

One night in between skirmishes, Dominique You announced that the pirates had been selected to lead a small raiding party behind English lines.

"Jackson says they won't expect such trespasses," You said, as he gathered the men around him by the fire. "We'll pick off a half-dozen sentries, and that'll break their nerves."

"It won't do a hell of lot for my own," Jack Pike snapped. He was one of You's seconds at the guns. "I wish they'd just get the cannons going an' get it done."

"Makes me shaky just to be on dry land so long," one of his mates replied.

"So they won't be expecting us? What makes Jackson so sure?" Samuel asked.

"He say, the Brits don't fight like this. Sneakylike. They think it's dishonorable."

That brought a round of guffaws from those listening.

Dominique quickly pointed to ten men. "French, since you got that beauty there in your lap, you go show them how to use it."

As the moon lowered and the night grew darker, Samuel and nine others of the crew crept past the embankment around the edge of the cypress swamp. They could hear the sounds of the British encampment clear enough and needed little light to guide them, since the tall cypresses stood as a boundary beyond which they should not stray. The birds of the night were stilled, and the dawn birds had not yet begun to stir.

It was, Samuel thought, that short time in the long night when death so often seems to come: those few hours when the best rest is past and awakening seems impossibly far. He held his musket out before him like a dousing rod and crept closer to the sounds of the enemy.

Two men walked before him, two You had chosen as most experienced in ambush, Jack Pike leading the way. Behind him, six more men followed—yet Samuel felt alone in the night. More alone than he had felt when he kneeled among his comrades and shot at advancing, faceless redcoats. Here, where the night was as much within him as without, where silence was as crucial as every heartbeat, he might have been approaching the British all alone, for the comfort he took from his comrades.

As they drew nearer still, their leader motioned them lower. Now they crawled through the damp grasses, frosty and crackling with their weight. For all that more of him touched the ground, Samuel felt he could actually be more quiet in this position. The earth seemed to support their every effort. It was after all, he told himself, Louisiana ground.

Finally, they crept so close that they could count six sentries in a semicircle, just beyond the fires of the encampment. Most of the soldiers huddled around those fires, but a few walked about, smoking, complaining, stamping their feet for warmth.

Samuel felt a warmth in the pit of his stomach, which was never touched by the chill of the grass. The tighter he gripped his musket, the warmer he stayed.

Now there were no words, even whispered. Pike motioned them to spread out and stay low. Samuel and two others inched on their bellies towards the two outer sentries.

One of the Brits sat on a log, hunched over his gun. He seemed almost to be asleep, but as they drew nearer, they could hear his teeth chattering softly. His eyes were down.

His blanket was hooded over his head. His gun was in his arms like a small child.

As planned, Pike moved closer on his belly, to the soldier's side. Samuel and the other man stayed in position, their muskets pointed directly at his chest. The long moments passed. Pike was taking his time easing himself behind the sentry. Once, a small crackling caused the soldier to raise his head wearily and look to each side. Samuel sighted on him, holding his breath. But then the redcoat sighed, dropped his head, and clutched his blanket closer.

For more long moments, they could see no movement. Then suddenly Pike loomed blackly behind the sentry, snatched his head back, and snicked his knife across his throat. The soldier groaned, but Pike's hand kept all but the guttural rasp silenced.

The loudest noise of all was when the sentry slumped sideways to the ground off the log, crackling the brush beneath him. There was no smell of blood or terror, to Samuel's surprise; the cold smothered everything so easily.

And in the darkness, even death was only a shadowed coming and going.

Without speaking, they crept to the second sentry. This man stood erect, cradled his musket, and rocked back and forth, humming tunelessly. The sound of his voice seemed to Samuel more distressing than the sight of his face. The first death had no man within it: this one seemed somehow more alive to begin, and so would likely hold onto that life with more determination. How would Pike topple such a tree with no sound?

They waited patiently for the man to move. To sit. To tire. He did none of these. Only hummed and rocked and moved his feet restlessly against the cold. The tune he mouthed was unfamiliar to Samuel, but he sensed it was one of the man's favorites. It seemed to come less from his lips than his chest, and he played with it as a dog might mouth a beloved shoe.

Pike breathed out his impatience, and Samuel saw his body tense. He readied his musket and glanced to his comrade. This one, the man's look said, might go bad. Be ready for anything. Pike was already moving.

Again they waited while his shadow slipped behind the man, in a wider arc this time, and much more slowly. He made not a sound. Moving slower than the moon's shadow, he eased himself beyond the point where Samuel could see him. They waited, breathing shallow slow breaths against their arms, so that the cold vapor of their breathing would not rise from the ground.

The sentry never stopped his slight rocking, his rhythmic humming. Each time he stomped his feet, Samuel flinched, but the soldier's body never assumed a wary tenseness which indicated suspicion. How is it that they could be so near, Samuel wondered, and he not sense their presence? How did humans become so contained within themselves that everything outside them could be so easily ignored?

Abruptly, the sentry's body changed, arched backwards, and a hissing gasp interrupted his hum. With one hand, he grappled behind him, and Samuel saw Pike's arm come round, wrench the man's body backwards still further, and press him to the earth. The knife had severed whatever control the sentry had over his knees and he crumpled, one arm still moving wildly. The musket clattered to the ground, the man gave a queer yodel, sharply silenced by Pike's hand over his mouth. It was over in seconds.

This time Samuel stood carefully and approached the two on the ground, as entangled as though Pike had wrestled him to submission. Pike shoved the dead sentry's legs away, wiped his knife on the blanket, and motioned them swiftly away.

They crawled, faster now and with less regard for silence, back the way they came. They had heard no sounds from the other two groups of raiders, no alarm cries from the British encampment, and as Samuel looked back over his shoulder, even the arrangement of the soldiers by the fires seemed not to have changed a whit. Yet they left two dead sentries in their wake.

Two dead, to be added to the four the other two groups had killed.

When they reached their rendezvous at the cypress edge, they dropped all pretense of silence, running and whooping through the night like demons. Answering shouts and shots rang out behind them now, as the Brits interpreted their retreat as an advance.

Samuel never looked back once they began to run and later, when he thought of what they had done, it seemed to have happened to him in a dream of darkness, silence, and vague shadows.

The Brits tried several more advances in the next few days, most likely enraged by the discovery of their dead sentries. Each morning the American troops tensed at the embankment, waiting for the signal rockets to warn of their attack. Each night they watched for retaliatory strikes against their watch.

One evening, as Samuel moved down the line carrying a message from You to another troop captain, he heard music from one of the fires. He ventured nearer and saw a man with an instrument he'd never seen before. The pirates were always eager for music, so Samuel thought he had surely heard any instrument which could be played by a man. But this one made the strangest, most haunting music, seeming almost to breathe with the man's chest.

The soldier was seated in the shadows on a log with

several around him, leading a song in French. The combination of the old remembered words and the sounds of the squeezebox made Samuel stop in his stride, frozen and alert as a buck at the edge of a meadow.

The song was a round, one he seemed to recall from childhood. Though he couldn't say what the next words might be, they were instantly familiar once he heard the man sing them. And though he used his old French infrequently, he had no trouble translating this chorus.

Allons à la cantine, o boite et bien rier,
Et bien se divertir,
Nous et nos amis

Let's go to the canteen,
To drink and laugh so well
And to have a good time,
Us and all our friends

Samuel joined the group singing, hunkered down on his heels, and gazed at the man who moved the instrument in and out, leading the voices in a wail of rising music.

"Simon!" one of the singers called out when he had finished, "Play *'La Jolie Blonde'!*"

The name of the player was suddenly as simply understood, as deeply familiar to Samuel as the strains of the ballad he played. He stared at the man in the firelight. He moved closer. When this Simon lifted his head and laughed, nodding at the request, Samuel was shocked to see that the music man's face was very similar to his own.

Samuel lifted his hand to his chin, feeling the new beard he had grown for protection against the January cold. The other man wore no beard. And yet their jawlines looked the same.

Through the next song, he watched the man's fingers move, watched the way he pursed his lips and closed his eyes and glanced at the singers, and seemed to recognize his own gestures and movements in this stranger's.

The song ended, and Samuel stood, touching the man on the shoulder. "Your name is Simon?"

The man nodded, leaning back to take a break. "Simon Weitz. Lafourche company. Have you got a favorite?"

"I think you've played them," Samuel said softly. "My name is Samuel French."

Simon put out his hand and shook. Samuel took the hand and turned it over, matching his own. At Simon's quizzical look, he said, "Forgive me, but I seem to know you and your music from a long time ago."

"Is that so? Where you from?"

"Too many places to tell. Do I—" and here, Samuel hesitated, wondering if the pain he felt in his heart was going to swell or fade with the next words from this man's mouth. "Do I look familiar to you at all?"

Simon stood then, set aside his squeezebox, and looked closer at the man who still held his hand at the wrist. They were so similar in height that their eyes met at the same level. "I had a brother named Samuel," Simon said slowly. "He was lost many years ago in a hurricane."

"Killed?"

"Lost. We never found him."

"How old was this brother?"

"My age," Simon said gently. "He was my twin."

With that, Samuel felt his knees roll beneath him, and he felt for the log, sitting heavily on it before he swayed. He held up one shaking hand to Simon. "Look at our palms," he whispered.

Simon took his hand and turned it over, sitting down beside him. Holding the two hands open, side by side, both men could see that in fact the two hands were quite the same. Simon had one long scar on the pad of his index finger. Samuel had a scar on his thumb pad and callouses on different fingers, but otherwise, they were a matched set.

238

"How did you get that?" Simon asked, pointing to Samuel's scar.

"Stacking hogsheads. How'd you get that?" Samuel asked, indicating Simon's scar.

"Trap caught me. How old are you?"

"I've never really known for sure. I think twenty-four. Maybe less, maybe more."

"How come you not to know your own years?"

Samuel shrugged, falling back quickly on the story he'd told so many times. "I spent some time in a Choctaw tribe, was took in by the Tockos down in the delta. Joined with Lafitte some time back."

"You're a privateer?"

Samuel grinned. "Of a sorts. I'm a land crab, though. I manage Lafitte's goods for him, down on the delta."

Simon did not look as impressed as many did with that information. He peered more closely at Samuel's face. "I can see that we've hands much alike. But the resemblance in the face . . . I'm not sure. French, you say? Perhaps a distant cousin, eh? My parents would know of any relation, for truth."

Samuel felt the ache in his heart move up into his eyes. "Your parents are still living?"

"Ah yes, in New Orleans, in fact." He shook his head ruefully. "I doubt they'll go back to Lafourche until they see with their own eyes that Jackson will not give up the city. Or their son. My wife waits with them there as well."

"You're married?"

"*Bien sûr,* a *fille* from my village, Cerise Guidry. We have three *'tits,* two boys, a girl. She did not want me to go, I'll tell you, but the elders decided and every man who could be spared from Lafourche is here," he spread his arms wide, "somewhere. They did not keep us all together as we had hoped."

"You say the elders decided?"

"We are Acadian, *oui,* and that is the way it is done in

Lafourche. The elders stood up in meeting before all of the village and told of the exile again, in the way their fathers had told them. Of the evil voyages on so many ships, of watching corpse after corpse thrown into the sea. There's not a child in the village who cannot recite the stations of our exile like the Stations of the Cross, eh? To South Carolina and Georgia where we were enslaved. To Boston, where we were indentured. To the Caribbean where we sweated and died in the sun, and to Pennsylvania, where the good Quaker Burghers passed a law forcing our fathers to give up their children as servants. *Vive Jésus, portons la croix,* we carry our own cross, *hein?* And not a soul there forgets it. So the elders decided that we would never give in to the Brits again."

"Of course these aren't the same armies."

"No, these soldiers were not the same ones who tore babies from mother's breasts and herded the fathers aboard the boats, but they serve the same army, the same line of kings. Such men should be helped to what awaits them in eternity, we think, and helped with all due speed."

"Have you killed a man yet?"

"Oui, and I will again, *moi."*

"Did it trouble you?"

"To kill such men as these? *Non, ami,* I did it easily. Gladly. Do you think they've forgotten in twenty-five years how to kill us? *Mais non,* these things one does not forget. And the land. No one forgets the land."

"Jackson says if they take New Orleans, the whole river will fall to them."

"They're planning on it, for truth. They posted flyers on every fencepost up the bayou, telling us this was not our fight, eh? To stay home and tend our fields while they save us from *les américaines.* But we have seen their tricks before. In Acadia, they told us the battle did not concern us, right up until the time the old ones were herded from the land onto strange ships to be banished forever. So we go. It took ten boats to bring us all to Jackson."

240

"And your parents followed. If you don't mind, what is your mother's name?"

"Oliva Doucet. My father's name is Joseph."

Samuel wiped his eyes with the heel of his hand. They were dry and they burned. "Jesus," he whispered, "I know those names."

Simon gripped his shoulder gently. "Perhaps you heard your own mother speak them? Perhaps we are old relations from Acadia, eh? Because your face, my friend, it is not so much like mine."

Samuel snatched the knife from his belt and swiftly scraped it across his beard, exposing his jawline and up his cheek. "It's the beard," he said. "It's the beard that hides our sameness. Does your beard grow in red?"

"Yes," Simon nodded slowly, peering closer. "It does. In the winter. A red streak across the jaw." His eyes widened. "You do look like me, somewhat." He took Samuel's hand again and examined the palm more closely. "There never was another brother for me."

"Oliva had no more children?"

"A daughter only. My sister, Emma. She has entered the convent of the Ursulines. Made her decision the same day I joined the Lafourche troop. My parents had no others. *Maman* was convinced that her son—my twin—was still living. She would never leave the bayou, even though my father asked her often. We kept the lamp burning for—ah, so many years. She never lost faith, at least not that she would admit."

Samuel felt his throat constrict. "And perhaps she was right all along!"

"My twin? Could it be so?" Simon put both hands on Samuel's shoulders. "You say you are my brother? Do you know the name of Weitz?"

"Now, I'm not sure. The first time you said it, I thought . . . "

"But now, you don't know if the memory is real or not."

241

The man had followed his thoughts exactly. "Yes."

And so they sat together in the dwindling light of the fire, one telling the stories of his past and the other trying to find parts of his own lost story among them.

Samuel figured they were as ready as they were ever going to be. The Baton Rouge regiments had arrived and were positioned, manning one of the stretches of the canal least protected. Supplies came in the night before from New Orleans, and each man had a full muster of powder, however empty his belly might feel.

The Brits are fools, Samuel thought ruefully. Any army that plays by the rules—rules that the other side won't acknowledge—deserves to be not just defeated but humiliated. He squinted as the dull rays of the sun crept over the horizon. In the semidarkness across Chalmette, he could see faint movement at the British lines. His chest felt hollow, and his hands were cold.

"They look busy," he said quietly to Simon. He had received permission from You to move down the line and fight alongside the Lafourche unit. Somehow, that was a comfort.

"They're going to be busier soon enough," Simon replied, pulling his cap down lower. "Unless they're figuring to wait us out till planting season. That's about the only way these ranks'll thin."

The sound of a shooting rocket interrupted his words. Another one answered from the edge of the swamp.

"Here they come, boys!" the call came up from the captain downline. "Hunker down, now!"

The signal rockets lit the hazy layer of ground fog that hovered over the muddy field. "You ready?" Samuel whispered to Simon, never taking his eyes off the British line. His hands trembled no matter how hard he gripped the gunstock.

"Been ready. *Le bon dieu,* what a target they make!"

The British moved out in a flanking motion now, a line of redcoats facing the field, their muskets up and out.

The sound of a horse cantering quickly behind them. General Jackson's voice whipped up and down the line. "The time has come, men!" he called, and every man heard his words clearly. "Aim well and hit your marks, let's finish this business today!" Already the stench of sulfur gave the air a bite.

The squeal of the bagpipes rolled across to them now, over the noise of the advancing troops, and then the battle began with a deafening explosion from their near right as a volley of cannon fired off. The balls screamed through the smoke and tore gaps through the line of redcoats that kept on coming. When Samuel squinted through the haze, he saw already that some of the soldiers had fallen, and now more cannon exploded up and down the line, blowing away men like leaves before a winter gust . . . and still they kept on coming. He gritted his teeth grimly.

"Hold your fire!" the captain cried over the din. "Hold off till I give the signal!"

Samuel snorted and yanked his musket down from position, saw that no one else had lowered his weapon, and hastily jerked it back to his eye again.

Now the Brits had split ranks and two advancing columns swiveled at an angle to sweep wide. Suddenly the Tennessee and the Kentucky regiments opened fire simultaneously, and a thousand explosions seemed to go off all at once. One flanking line was cut to pieces, with what looked like half the soldiers down or tottering in place. The others kept on coming. Still, most of the units held their fire.

Samuel glanced at Simon, and he turned then and met his

glance. A smile passed between them, and he could feel the same side of his lip turn up as he saw turn on Simon's mouth. Somehow that sameness was a comfort, as though there were two of him, two of them, two close enough in synchronization that no enemy's bullet could possible separate them.

The staccato drumbeat of the advancing Brits was more ragged now, but it was closer. How could they keep coming in the same way, Samuel wondered? Just keep walking forward, guns outstretched, while rifle balls whizzed in every direction, cannon bombardments sent the men right next to them flying off broken in a score of pieces, while the shells burst all around them, and the screams of the wounded men had to make their knees tremble even as they kept on coming. It was bad enough crouched behind this mud wall, waiting. Out there was a relentlessly marching hell.

Then the captain shouted, "Commence firing!" and the hell moved closer. As the British advanced to two hundred yards, the Lafourche regiment and those on both sides cut loose with a barrage of fire that staggered the redcoats in a melee of deafening explosions. Now mass confusion enveloped the enemy; some troops continued to march forward into the smoke and fire, while others turned and ran back towards the rear. The tide of redcoats came on, returning fire now, and Samuel crouched lower, seeing that Simon did the same. Both muskets went off repeatedly, as though they were attached to the same trigger, but Samuel could barely hear Simon's even though he was close enough to see him holding his breath as he squeezed off his shots.

A British officer on horseback rode forward into the volley of fire, shouting at his men and flailing about with a sword. The horse suddenly reared back on its hind legs, the officer fell from his saddle and struggled to his feet, holding his leg. The horse stumbled, almost fell, and then recovered, whirling away from the bullets.

Samuel heard a cry up the lines, alarmingly close. He rose up to see, but Simon pulled his arm, holding him down.

Someone was hit. One of their own. He heard then the flurry of activity to help the wounded man, but he turned his attention now to the Brits with a renewed determination, grim vengeance hardening his jaw. He took his time, aimed carefully, and watched as two of them fell beneath his shots. "There," he muttered aloud, to no one in particular, and he fought back his fear with a will.

"For truth," Simon murmured back, one eye closed and aiming as well. Another redcoat tumbled sideways with a sharp cry.

Farther down the line, the firepower was most hideous. Where the Tennessee and Kentuckian sharpshooters sat, lethal waves of grapeshot and rifle balls flew onto the field. Three and four deep they crouched, and at their officer's command, one line would fire and return to the back of the line, then the other line would step forward, fire all at once, and go the rear. The noise was deafening as the Brits crumpled in waves before them. There was never a pause for reloading, never a hesitation in the explosions, but Samuel saw that casualties claimed those sharpshooters as well, for each time they moved to the rear, they presented departing targets, higher than the edge of the mud embankment. Samuel pressed his belly closer to the earth.

Closer to the swamp, ground fog had allowed some of the redcoats to storm the embankment, and Samuel could hear the yells of hand-to-hand combat down the line, but two regiments turned to add their muskets to the fray, and the Brits were quickly beaten back once more. Their leaders were no longer riding about shouting orders; many of them were down, and the troops no longer held their tight formations.

Amid the noise, they heard a new howling and shouting; some of the men down the line jumped to their feet, heedless of the fire around their heads.

Simon cried out, "Look! We've shot their general!"

"Is that Pakenham?" Samuel asked, dropping his musket from his eye in amazement. Out on the field, a British officer—from the looks of his uniform and his mount, one of their highest ranking—had fallen, was being helped from the battle by four other soldiers.

"Perhaps they retreat now."

"Tell it to that lot," Samuel said, hunching his shoulders and shivering at the flare of panic in his belly. To his right, British soldiers swarmed the wall in hand-to-hand fighting.

"Bayonets up, men!" shouted the Lafourche captain. "They're coming through!"

"They damn sure ain't!" swore the man to Samuel's left.

"Make ready!" Simon shouted to Samuel. "They come!"

Three redcoats were on them then, more swiftly than Samuel could react. He took quick aim with his pistol, hit one in the chest just as he came across the mud ramparts with sword drawn, but not before he struck the man to Samuel's left in the neck. With a groan, the man fell and gasped for breath, blood gushing in rhythmic spurts into the mud. Simon hollered, and Samuel whirled in time to see the second redcoat almost over the embankment, his bayonet raised high. Simon thrust his bayonet at this new target, the man turned, and in that instant caught a stray rifle ball in the side of the jaw. His head jerked sideways, he screamed, and Samuel could see that most of his tongue had been shot off in a blaze of bits of teeth, flesh, bone, and frothy blood. Samuel stepped back, the man fell to his feet, and he and Simon turned to face the third soldier together.

Simon gave a warning shout, but his cry only drew the enemy bayonet to him, and the redcoat sliced at him savagely, catching his shoulder and opening it to the bone. Samuel shot him pointblank in the belly, his hands shaking too badly to bring the shot as high as he thought he aimed. The redcoat fell towards him, on him, a blossom of red erupting on them both, and Samuel was pinned under his weight, glaring upwards into maddened blue eyes. The redcoat's hands encircled his neck and his pain gave him almost inhuman strength. Samuel had never seen such hatred in another man's eyes. He struggled frantically to breathe, to twist the man off him, and just as he felt the determination slacken from him, felt the panic give way to a thudding, sliding unconsciousness, the man's head reeled sideways, the hands released, and he rolled out from under.

Simon stood over them both, a darkened bayonet in his hands. The redcoat lay dead beside him, his head and neck opened with a long gash of bubbling blood. There was so much blood everywhere, such a din of clashing swords and whizzing pistol shots, but Samuel noticed most the swift gray which came over the Brit's face, how it so quickly replaced the red flush of his anger, how his sightless blue eyes now filmed over with what seemed to be almost a second skin, like that which formed on a cooling custard.

But then he saw how Simon bled, and he held him, both of them staggering, calling for help. No help came, so Samuel tied a cloth around Simon's wound, binding flesh which felt almost like his own under his shaking hands. Together they struggled up the embankment to peer over the ridge and across the field.

The shots were lessening now, the noise of the battle dying off. Sporadic explosions sounded, but no more Brits were coming towards them. In fact, straggling troops with redcoats were retreating hastily back across Chalmette, and the British cannons had silenced. Relief hit Samuel at the back of the knees and almost made him crumple to the ground.

Before them lay a literal sea of red—red uniforms, red flags, stiffened, reddened cloth and skin, fallen redcoats spread over what seemed to be acres and acres of defeat. As the sounds of battle died, they could now hear more horrifying sounds of the screams of wounded men, the whinnying of horses struggling to rise with bleeding flanks or broken legs, the moans of the dying, the cries of comrades.

"*Merci à Dieu,*" Simon whispered, his voice shaking. "It is over."

Samuel and Simon stood then, Simon holding his shoulder, both of them lost in horrified disbelief, until the Lafourche captain called out, "The enemy retreats, *mes garçons,* see to the wounded!"

Samuel would remember that afternoon as one filled with the two extremes of hope and despair. He was unrecovered from one emotion when the next would flood him and leave him dazed. Now he and Simon walked among the wounded and dead, trying to help those very redcoats who, hours before, they had done their utmost to destroy. There seemed to be few Yankee casualties, so far as they could tell, but Chalmette was clogged with the torn bodies of the British.

Samuel and Simon worked side by side, turning soldiers face up where they had slumped over cannons, to see if they were dead or alive. Together, they stooped to examine the fallen enemy, now enemy no more so long as they made no more hostile moves. Once, when Simon bent to place a hand on a soldier, an arm snaked up and grasped him by the neck, pulling him down.

"Not yet, rebel!" the man cried feebly, "not yet ye done me!"

Samuel grabbed the man's arm and wrenched it off Simon, just as the death tremor shook the redcoat's frame. He died, half-in, half-out of their arms.

Simon looked into his grimy face, at the dirty blond hair hanging over his blank eyes. "You'd never know he was a Brit, if he didn't wear that coat. Could well be German," he said wonderingly.

"Like Joseph," Samuel answered.

"Oui, comme mo' père."

They moved to another body, to find that this one was still alive. Moaning, the man held up one hand in supplication. "Letter," he cried out weakly.

"Out of his head," Simon said.

"Letter!" the wounded man insisted, dropping his hand to touch his chest.

Samuel gingerly opened the man's coat, stiffened with blood. His wounds were wide and deep, exposing part of one lung and ribs. But amid the gore, a letter lay, half-sodden, half-saved. He plucked the letter from the man's chest and held it up to his eyes. "You want us to post this?"

The soldier nodded frenziedly, grappling in empty air.

"You have my word on it, man. Here, Simon, take his feet." They carried the man over to the hospital area, where most of the wounded were waiting for medical attention. After they left him among the moaning, Simon said, "You will post it?"

"After I readdress it."

"It is not legible?"

"Oh, you can read it all right, but I see no reason for his wife to find the man's last blood along with his last words."

The hospital area was filled with the dead and the wounded, and the doctors, both American and British, struggled together to help those they could. There was little anesthesia or antiseptic. Chest and abdominal wounds were simply stitched up in the hopes they would heal. For anything other than a simple fracture or a flesh wound, amputation with a saw was the only remedy. It was a soldier's code to bear pain without complaint, and all they had to offer were whiskey and rags to stop the piteous cries. Samuel and Simon left the man there, unwilling to stay to witness his agony.

As they went back to the field, Simon said, "I never thought I would see the day when I would feel pity for redcoats. So often, I have heard the tales. How the English robbed us of our birthlands, of all our possessions. *Maman* talks of it as though she saw it with her own eyes, how her *grandmère* was sent to one ship, her *grandpère* to another, and they never saw each other again. The damned *anglais!* I heard it so many times. And now . . ." he stooped to check another body, sighed, and turned away. "Now, I feel sorry for the poor bastards. Most of them will never see home again."

"I know. But I feel sorrier for those separated and yet still alive. It's a living death, of sorts. Did Oliva weep for your lost brother?"

"Weep and search and weep some more. I remember those days. What do you recall of your mother?"

"Little. I recall more of my Indian mother."

"What was her name?"

Samuel stopped then, stock-still in the middle of the field. To one side, there was a heavy thud as a horse, wounded and balancing on three legs, fell to the ground. A handful more of the British mounts still stood. Samuel recalled how grand they had looked at the start of the battle. So well trained. So noble. One particular horse he had seen carried an officer who was shot out of his saddle. He surely must have been wounded as well, yet he stood by his soldier, waiting even as the man died, to see if he would mount again. He had eventually trotted back, only to try to take his place in the charging line, riderless.

In that moment, a sudden memory came back to Samuel, one he had not been able to grasp for many years. "Deborah. I think—" he turned to Simon, his eyes excited. "Yes, I think they called her Deborah. Oh, that wasn't her Indian name, of course, but that's what she answered to, I'm sure of it."

Simon's eyes widened. "That's what my first Indian nurse was called. Deborah. *Mon Dieu,* I heard the name often enough, heard my mother curse that name after she was lost."

"But she wasn't lost," Samuel said slowly. "Neither was

250

I. She saved my life. At least that's what she told me. Saved my life when my family was lost in a storm."

"She told you your family was lost?"

"In a hurricane, I think."

"Your family was never lost." And here, Simon's eyes widened to match Samuel's. "*You* were. My brother. Is it possible?" He stepped closer to Samuel and took his beard in his fist, gently shaking it.

"I have hoped. But this is the first I've begun to believe."

"I had not even hoped."

"I understand. But would you—" Samuel hesitated painfully. "Would you welcome such a thing?" He turned away. "After all these years, the only son. The only heir. Perhaps you would prefer a cousin to a brother, eh?"

In answer, Simon caught his arm, turned the man, and embraced him fiercely. "If it is so, I will praise God. Even if it is not so, I will give thanks for a brother in arms."

"We look alike, it is true," Samuel said. For a moment, he was almost afraid to know the truth. But then he knew that in fact, there was nothing more he wanted in his life, had wanted, for too many years. He wondered how it would be to know that somewhere he had a mother again. "There is only one who can say for sure."

Simon grinned and clapped him on the back. "Then we must let her have the last word. That always pleases her."

The crowds had gathered outside the rebuilt St. Louis Cathedral in the Vieux Carré Square. For hours they had listened to the thudding explosions from Chalmette, many of them on their knees praying for deliverance from the British invaders.

251

The cold and damp drove many indoors to kneel at the altar, where they flinched from the firepower which seemed so near. Many others refused to leave their views of the skyline, watching from balconies and upper turrets to see if somehow the smoke on the wind might tell them who was winning the battle.

Finally the smoke began to diminish, the roar of the cannons was stilled. In the long hours, the citizens of New Orleans waited. Early word from the returning supply wagons was good, but few could trust it. Those with sons, brothers, husbands, or fathers on the front lines—and this included most everyone in the city—waited not only to hear of victory, but to hear the list of the dead or wounded.

A horse pounded past, the rider shouting "Victory!" and waving an American flag, but his passage only caused more confusion. Finally, finally, the soldiers began to trickle into the city, and the word spread swiftly then: Victory! New Orleans was saved! But what of each mother's son?

The women clogged the steps of the cathedral, hung over the balconies, and called out to each other as the soldiers began to arrive. Most of them were walking, still carrying their weapons.

General Jackson had given permission for some of the regiments to detach, with orders to return for additional burial detail as they were needed. The town was bursting with immigrants, since many on the bayou had feared British invasion well before the redcoats actually reached Chalmette. Families were huddled over small fires in the park, along the river, and anyplace where blankets would give them some protection against the cold. The luckier ones had found rooms early, before the fighting began in earnest.

Oliva, Joseph, and Cerise had found shelter at the inn close by the Ursuline Convent. Having just given their daughter to God and their son to Jackson, Oliva and Joseph could not bring themselves to return to Lafourche. What waited for them there? And Cerise absolutely remained steadfast in her refusal to go home, even to see her three children. "My mother, my brother, there are plenty to care for them," she said, her pretty chin out in stubborn determination. "But who will care for my husband if I leave him now?" Though Oliva might have wanted Simon to herself, she had to admire Cerise's courage, for certainly it was safer in Lafourche than in the chaos of New Orleans. In this season, a season when all of nature seemed to be waiting, there was nothing more important than the news from Chalmette.

Now they stood with the others on the steps of St. Louis, swept up in the currents and crosscurrents of tidings that arrived in the *Vieux Carré*. Many had been killed, the news came, but no! Mostly the casualties were British! Thousands wounded, others reported—medical supplies were short, quinine only to be used for the worst amputees—but once again, the word came down—mostly British? How many of our men were killed, the question was asked again and again, but no answer was clear. How many wounded? Too many answers to know the truth.

Hundreds had been brought to the Ursuline Convent, which had been turned into a hospital, the nuns serving as nurses. Oliva wondered if Emma's hands had bathed a strange body, touched a dying man, comforted a wounded. Might her own brother be among them?

"He may well not be released," Joseph said to Oliva and Cerise, holding both women's arms. "That gentleman there said they're letting them go according to when they came on."

"But he was one of the first!" Oliva cried, keeping her eyes on the street. "He's been there from the first fighting!"

"Not as early as some. They say the regiments from Tennessee and Kentucky were first on the lines."

"But they have no one waiting for them," Cerise moaned quietly.

A woman next to them spoke up. "Some of them brought

253

their women, I hear. Early on they arrived. Settled in as though they followed camp all over the territories."

"Everyone has someone waiting somewhere," Joseph said quietly.

The news rumbled up the square: a band of twenty or more soldiers was coming. The crowd pressed forward, and it was impossible to see any one set of shoulders, any singular face clearly.

"Get to the top of the steps," Joseph said to Oliva and Cerise, gripping their arms and pulling them to the back of the crowd. "If he's there, we'll see him."

The two women followed him up to the door of St. Louis, took off their bonnets and veils, and held them aloft, in case Simon should be in the first arrivals.

Cerise strained to stand as tall as she could, waving her bonnet, but then she lowered it in despair.

The faces all looked so impossibly old and begrimed! Bodies which she knew to be young carried themselves with the weariness of old age. Could she even know his step when she saw it, recognize his smile? Would she ever see it again?

His mother was waving eagerly. Cerise climbed up on a marble step and circled her bonnet in the air with renewed determination.

Soldiers arrived, were quickly swallowed up by the crowd, loved ones, women who felt compelled to embrace them, men who wanted to pump their hands, and more arrived behind them. It was impossible to see now, impossible to make out the soldiers, and behind them, the bells of St. Louis began to chime loudly, making the din almost a torture.

Oliva remembered suddenly her talk with Father Le-Blanc, when Emma announced she was taking the veil.

"You have not been to communion lately," he said to her. "Did the Lord say the Church must come to you? Tell me your sins."

She had answered him, "Yesterday I worshipped the sun."

"I'm not surprised. Your faith was never strong, my daughter. Do you believe in God?"

"He doesn't believe in me, Father."

To her surprise, the priest only chuckled and glanced at her shrewdly. "I want to know," he said softly, "what is it you *do* believe in? What is your idea of God?"

"I have days," she said, "when I think of Him as a great loneliness, living out where it is dark and cold. I fear Him. Sometimes, I hate Him."

Father LeBlanc turned pale. "Go on."

"I hate Him when he takes something from me. Like two children. And now a third. My daughter."

"Go on."

"He doesn't seem to know what He is doing or why."

"This is arrogance," he said quietly. "Your children do not belong to you, they belong to Him."

"Let Him bear them, then. Let Him suckle them and carry them and nurse them, then. What are women given hearts for if He means to break them? Yesterday I walked out on the levee. It was dark, everything was quiet. The stars were out. I passed a cabin and a woman was moaning. I heard her moaning, Father, and I felt sorry for her."

"The woman was suffering, Oliva. Another time, she will be laughing."

"She was not suffering, Father. She was in bed with a man."

The priest frowned.

Oliva said, "When I was small, I saw Ulysse Breaux being whipped. His mother said she dressed him and sat him on a wicker chair on the levee. She told him not to move. As soon as she turned away, he would be up off that chair and messing in the dirt. Every day she whipped him for that. She said he was stubborn, I heard her say it to my mother. So she had to beat him for his own good. One day she decided to paint that wicker chair. I watched her do it. She found a nest of bedbugs in the cracks of the chair. She cried and cried at that. I was angry at God. I'm angry at Him now."

"I see. And yet, your daughter loves him."

"So she says. Mothers make children, not children's hearts."

Father LeBlanc sighed. "Don't think too deeply on this, Oliva. There are clearer waters more near the surface. You like Mass, eh?"

"Ah, yes. The music, the oil, the incense. I like Mass, I suppose."

"Then let your daughter go. And try not to feel angry at God. He gives to each what each may bear."

She thought of his words now, wondering what she might be given to bear in the next few hours.

"There!" Joseph shouted to them, "there, is that him?"

"Where!" Cerise shouted, leaping up off the step to see over the crowd.

"Where, oh where!" Oliva danced back and forth frantically for a view.

"Over there by the door to the tavern! That looks like Simon!" He picked his wife up around the waist and held her higher, as though she were a child. She waved her bonnet, though she could not yet see where he pointed. Then she spied two men, their arms around each other's shoulders. Both the same height, they wore different uniforms, different caps. One sported a full beard, and the other—the other, thank the good God, looked like Simon! She screamed his name to Cerise, screamed again louder, and struggled to free herself from Joseph's grasp.

Together, they fought their way down one step, down another, but they could quickly see that they could not reach the men. They retreated back up the tallest step again, and this time, Joseph held Oliva up, then Cerise in her turn, up so high that her knees were resting in his arms, one hand gripping the door of the cathedral, the other waving her bonnet furiously.

Cerise could see the two men plainly now, and she called her husband's name over and over, shrieking as loudly as she could. Oliva screamed with her. Finally, one man's hand shot up in greeting. It was Simon! The two women burst into tears simultaneously and struggled to get down through the crowd, crying, "It's him, it's him, he saw us!"

"Are you sure?" Joseph asked.

"He saw me, he saw me, he's coming!" Cerise cried.

Joseph stood as tall as he could and called to her, "Someone is coming, that's sure. Two of them. I can't tell yet—"

"It's him, I know it!" Oliva shouted, pushing through the packed bodies with an energy she did not know she had.

In moments, Simon shouldered through the crowd and half-picked his mother off her feet, and she laughed with joy to feel his arms again. He kissed both her cheeks, then braced himself for the whirlwind of embrace which was Cerise, hurling herself into his arms. He held her tightly, his head dropping on her neck, kissed her fervently, then embraced his father. When all the embraces had been shared, he reached behind him and drew his companion forward. A small crowd had formed around them, as though each person on the steps wanted to take away some of their relief and pleasure for themselves. Simon gripped Samuel's arm and said, "*Maman,* do you know this face?"

Oliva smiled broadly and took the soldier's two hands in her own. "Clearly the face of a friend. Were you comrades in arms?"

"Tell her your name," Simon said gently.

Samuel looked into the woman's eyes, felt the memory flicker in his heart, and said thickly, "My name is Samuel."

Oliva gasped and drew back, her hand over her heart.

"And your family name?" Joseph asked quickly.

Samuel stared at the man intently. "I no longer can remember. But I do know that a woman named Deborah was once my mother for a time. A Choctaw woman. She gave me a name, which I don't remember. But she told me it meant, He-Who-Has-Two-Bodies."

Oliva moaned softly, then steeled herself. She took his face in both her hands, feeling over it as though she were blind. She took his palm, turned it over, and examined it silently.

Joseph asked, "Your age?"

"I don't know exactly. But all of my life I've believed that I had another life that was waiting for me to discover it again." Samuel bowed his head, wondering if he dared believe at last. He squeezed his eyes shut to stop the tears. The silence seemed so cold now, after the welcoming embrace he had imagined. And then he felt wetness on his hand. He opened his eyes and saw that Oliva's head was bowed over his open hand, her tears falling on his palm.

"It is my Samuel," she said, her voice small as a girl's. "Our son, returned to us."

Joseph took Samuel's hand from her and held it firmly between his two. "Do you remember?" he asked him.

"*I* remember," Oliva said, her voice stronger now and graveled with pain. "It is my son. Look at their hands together, look at his eyes, his face."

Joseph looked to Simon instead, helpless bewilderment on his mouth. "But the beard. How can you tell—"

"He is my brother," Simon said firmly. "It wanted only a mother's eyes to be certain."

"Yes," Cerise said immediately, "and a mother's heart."

Oliva turned grateful eyes to her daughter-in-law. For the first time, she saw that Cerise was more than just a lovely woman. She was also the mother of her son's children.

"But how can you be certain?" Joseph asked.

Oliva took both of Samuel's hands in her own, ignoring Joseph's words. "What—" she began, her voice faltering. "What was your favorite comfort as a child?" She looked only at Samuel.

"He can scarcely recall such a thing," Joseph said gently, "if he cannot recall his own name."

"Think of it," Oliva said urgently. "I know you can remember. Perhaps . . . perhaps something you used to love to touch? An old blanket?" She looked at Joseph and then back again at Simon. They were both hushed, their eyes wide. "Think," she said again to Samuel. "Can you remember?"

Samuel looked over Oliva's head to the massing crowd, a swirl of color and noise and movement, and a woman brushed by with a brilliant green cape about her shoulders, rushing to meet a soldier. In that instant, his eyes widened and he said, almost without knowing what words would come, "A magic blanket," he murmured. "A blanket of feathers. Bird feathers? I—I seem to remember touching something like this—the softest covering of a thousand feathers." He looked down at Oliva, bewildered. "Not a comfort, really, more like a dream. Something I was very taken with, I think. But could such a blanket have been?"

With that, Joseph gasped and clenched Samuel on his shoulder. "My God," he said, "you could not have guessed such a thing. It wasn't a blanket, but a cape! Lebanon Doucet's cape of feathers!"

"My mother made it," Oliva cried. "It was your favorite, yours and your brothers. You would stand and touch it, making up stories about it." She took his face in her hands. "My Samuel. I knew you would come home to me!"

With that, Oliva fell into Samuel's arms, weeping on his chest. Simon embraced them both fiercely, laughing and weeping all at once. Samuel carefully lowered his cheek to rest on her hair, and only when he felt Joseph's arm reach round his shoulders and pull them both close did he allow his own tears to fall on his mother's head, murmuring *maman* over and over.

It was only after many years that Oliva realized that those tears were the last she ever saw Samuel weep. To be sure he had reason to, at least three more times over the next decade, despite his good fortune.

When the war was over and the Lafittes could no longer so easily raid foreign ships, they were generous to those who had served them well. Samuel's loyalty earned him many rewards, any one of which would have done much to start any young man on his way to prosperity. But the one gift which became the most valuable, particularly when the Americans banned all slave trade, was the score of slaves the Lafittes gave Samuel when he left their service.

At first, Joseph and Simon would not have the brutes on their lands. But as Samuel showed them what a dozen black hands and backs could do with fertile bayou soil, they grudgingly accepted their presence. In less than a decade, Samuel's new plantation house, thrice the size of his father's and brother's combined, was built at the edge of Weitz fields, on some of the richest lands in Lafourche. Built not in the old Acadian style, but in the Creole style of the delta, Samuel's house rose as fast as sugar prices did, and his energy to drive himself and his slaves made Oliva feel he was trying to make up for all the lost years in the last three.

Oliva joyed in her son's joy, all the more precious for the years she had been denied his presence. But when he began to search for a woman to share his joy, it was then that she feared he would have reason to weep as well.

When the woman he loved, had chosen for his bride (after sampling far too many, to her mind) turned from him and chose another man, Samuel did not weep. His jaw seemed to turn to granite overnight, and his eyes dulled, his step slowed, but he did not weep. At least not where she could see him. Oliva remembered the wedding. Samuel and Simon stood together, Cerise linking her arms through both theirs, and to see the two twins watch Mademoiselle Diana DesLondes marry another, you would never have known which one had a weeping heart.

It had been at that wedding that Samuel first met Matilde Villere, the eldest daughter of the richest Creole planter in the parish. Monsieur Villere owned lands up and down the bayou, some of which bordered the fields Joseph had just planted to cane.

A neighbor with a marriageable daughter, a son with a will to wed and no bride in his heart . . . ah, Oliva recalled with a sigh, perhaps she should have seen the easy danger there. But Simon and Cerise seemed so happy in one another, she could not endure her second son alone. When Joseph spoke of a possible union, she agreed readily to encourage Samuel to think of Mademoiselle Villere as more than a winsome dancer and amicable neighbor.

Matilde was beautiful, she had a fine and graceful figure, a thick head of luxurious black hair which she wore *à la mode,* she was convent-educated, was likely well versed in the management of a large estate—these opinions Oliva aired at the table the morning after the wedding where Samuel did not weep.

"Did you find her charming?" she asked Samuel innocently. "I noticed that many of her partners returned for another waltz, you were lucky you were able to claim Mademoiselle Matilde at all . . ."

"She is charming enough," Samuel said calmly, "though I found her voice a trifle overbearing."

"*Ma foi,* you're just used to that whispery Diana, I could

261

scarcely understand her half the time. Matilde at least speaks up and makes her mind known, and a good mind she has, too. Villere has bred no *imbéciles, vraiment.*"

Samuel smiled, rather sardonically as she recalled. "No indeed, *maman,* one cannot fault the breeding at Villere's stables. One might hope, however, to find something more than simply a competent mount. One might hope to find a filly with a certain gentleness around the mouth, maybe a flash to the eye and a sheen to the coat, something that makes one's heart go fast as her heels—"

"You are hopeless!" Oliva shouted at her son, stifling her laughter. "You deserve whatever you get!"

Samuel stood up from his now empty plate and tipped an invisible hat to his mother. "And who does not?"

She shook her head ruefully when she remembered his words. Likely she should not have pushed Matilde Villere on him, but then, was he destined for happiness at all? Once a heart is broken, can it ever truly love again?

The day he married Matilde, she seemed to have happiness enough for the both of them. She brought joy to Samuel then, and the walls of the plantation seemed to expand to hold the friends, the family, the children of Cerise and Simon who clattered in and out, the card parties, the dances and dinners by candlelight, when Matilde took out the Limoges she had shipped from France and the crystal sent from Spain. Samuel wanted his family always near, and he built a summer house out behind the big house, for when Joseph and Oliva came to visit. Now when Oliva thought of Matilde's young, shining face in those days, she could scarcely find that memory in the face Matilde wore today.

The second time Samuel did not weep was at his father's grave. He stood again by his brother, this time with his own wife's arm linked through his. Simon and Cerise wept openly as the Father spoke the words of eternal rest over Joseph Weitz, she herself was scarcely able to see for her tears, even

Matilde held a delicately embroidered linen to her eyes, but Samuel did not weep.

He did not weep for loss, and he did not weep for gain, when his father's will gave Samuel and Matilde the bulk of the cane fields along the bayou, for Simon did not wish to be a planter. Happy with his small fields, his traps, and his larger part of the *sucrerie,* Simon and Cerise always seemed to have one child more than they had beds.

Samuel and Matilde called their new plantation Beausonge, for the dreamy memories of Joseph's music. Now Oliva lived in their summer house alone, and so she was there the night that Matilde presented Samuel with his first son.

That night, Oliva remembered vividly, they seemed happy at least. That night they argued over Samuel's name for the infant, Andrew Jackson Weitz, for his beloved General, but the argument was softer around the edges than usual, vibrant with hope for the future Matilde held in her arms.

Matilde had never looked so lovely, Oliva thought, nor so ripe with satisfaction.

The third time he should have wept, when even the stones on the grave seemed wet with grief, was when he buried Andrew behind Beausonge, alongside his grandfather. The child wore his first pair of long trousers to cover his wounds.

Even today Oliva could scarcely think of Andrew without her throat aching. Too young to go to the bayou, his mother had said, too young to trap with his uncle.

Nonsense, his father replied, Simon's boys were out in the swamp before they could string together a sentence.

Samuel and Matilde had had one of their usual skirmishes, but this one she lost. "I won't have him be a spoiled fop, a rich planter's son, who idles his days away with high-strung horses and high-stakes poker," Samuel declared, and gave in to his son's clamor to join his cousins in checking the trap lines.

They'd be out only a week, Simon reassured Matilde. He

would be watched over by every pair of eyes, and he would learn more about the bayou than he would in the next five years.

Matilde had turned a cold shoulder to Simon's words, and she would not help ready her son for his adventure.

When Simon carried the boy back in his arms, both legs near-severed and broken from the trap teeth, Matilde screeched as though she had lost her mind. And the next morning, when the doctor's amputations were too much for that small, shocked body to bear, Matilde grabbed hold of Andrew's cold shoulders and shook him, slapped him, to try to get him to come back to the living, still screaming at Samuel, Simon, at God himself to give her back her son.

Through it all, Oliva never saw Samuel weep. His shoulders slumped, his spine seemed to cave in on itself, and he grew older by a decade in hours. But he did not weep. Even when Matilde told him that his twin brother would never be welcome in her house again.

Oliva turned these memories over and over in her mind as she did her rosary, waiting outside Matilde's boudoir. Inside, she could hear the doctor moving, his voice rising and falling, and her daughter-in-law moaning loudly. Downstairs, she heard nothing. Samuel waited, she knew, with his brandy and his manservant in the library. Since Simon was no longer allowed within Matilde's sight, Ulysses was the master's most faithful companion.

The moans from within rose to a new level of shrieks, and Oliva knew it was time. Matilde would finally have herself something of her own or die trying. The upstairs wench bustled out with a bloodied basin, her eyes wide and white.

"Is comin' now soon, Madame," she said to Oliva, "doctor he say she near split herself, but she strong an' willful—"

A resounding scream came then from the boudoir, and Oliva dropped her rosary into her skirt pocket and pushed into the room. On the bed, Matilde lay with her legs akimbo and her black hair spilled wet and mangled over the pillows.

The doctor's shoulders were moving rhythmically, and he said, "Here, then! once more, Madame, here he is!" and he pulled a squalling, red and slippery infant up to her knees where Oliva could see the shock of black hair, the contorted monkey limbs and squinched face of Samuel's second son.

Matilde opened her eyes, gazed at the child, and then saw Oliva at the door. "It is a son, Madame," she said, her voice surprisingly strong. "A son for Beausonge."

Oliva moved closer, smiling and holding out her hands for the infant. "And a beautiful child he is! Samuel himself was no prettier when he came—"

"Give him to me," Matilde said quickly to the doctor.

The doctor had left her open legs now and was tending to the afterbirth. "Let me just get him wiped clean—"

"I'll wipe him," she groaned, her strength wavering, "give him to me!"

The doctor handed the whimpering child to his mother, and Oliva instinctively stopped, dropping her hands to her sides. Matilde took the edge of the embroidered linen, dragged the fine sheet up in a handful, and wiped the infant's mouth and nose clean of the birth blood.

Behind her, Samuel came into the room, his eyes eager, his hat in his hand. "It's a boy?" He started forward and then stopped, as though for permission to enter.

Matilde settled back on the bed, the infant in her arms. She had pulled the linens around her body so that little of her nakedness showed, though her legs were still high and akimbo. "My son," she said quietly.

"She is well?" he asked the doctor.

Oliva thought it so strange that Matilde did not beckon to Samuel, that he did not go to her readily, but she had given up trying to decipher the signals between these two . . .

"Madame is well, the boy is well, and she will likely have many more to follow," the doctor said jovially. His was the only mouth smiling, Oliva saw then.

"Many more," Matilde said evenly, "and they will be yours and mine together. But this is my son. Mine."

Samuel drew back as though he had been struck. "What are you saying?" he asked, his voice incredulous.

"That you have had your son. This one is mine. If we have another, he will belong to us both. But this one belongs to me."

Oliva turned to go, her heart wilting in pain at Matilde's voice, at her face. She was almost a little mad, but then many women are at the time of birth, she would surely change her mind, recant her words as she healed . . .

"Madame, you are my witness," Matilde called after her.

Oliva turned once more at the door. "I wish I had never witnessed such words from a wife—"

"This is absurd," Samuel said gruffly, approaching the bed now and attempting to embrace Matilde. "You are my wife, this is my son, let my mother be witness to *that*."

Matilde let herself be embraced, but stiffly. "She is your mother, *vraiment*. And I am your wife. But this—" and here, she held up the infant so that his eyes were close to hers, his face turned from his father. "This is *my* son. You killed yours."

Oliva turned and went out the door, closing it softly behind her. She wept then, for Matilde, for her newborn son, but most of all for Samuel, who could not weep for himself.

PART TWO
1835–1865

"A mulatto is the child of a white and a Negro;
a quadroon, of a white and a mulatto;
an octoroon, of a white and a quadroon;
a tierceron, of a mulatto and a quadroon;
a griffe, of a Negro and a mulatto;
a marabon, of a mulatto and a griffe;
a sacratron, of a Negro and a griffe . . ."

"In search of escaped slave, Mary, bright mulatto, almost white with reddish hair, passes for free, talks French, Italian, Dutch, English, and Spanish. No doubt in the vicinity of Lafourche, where she has children at two plantations."

New Orleans Daily Picayune, June, 1842

"Moreover of the children of the strangers that do sojourn among you, of them shall ye buy, and of their families that are with you, which they begat in your land, they shall be your possessions."

Leviticus 25:45

While the rest of America became sturdily Anglo-Saxon, the deep delta grew a region within a region, the heart of which was French, African, and Creole. The Creoles were the white descendants of the first settlers, a mix of French and Spanish blood and more ... they seemed to be almost a product of the soil itself, that black and fecund, bottomless alluvial earth deposited by the Mississippi, stirring with life.

As the steamboats slid down the river in spring and the flood waters rose to the top of the levee, men and women stood at the rails, shielding their eyes against the hard sparkle of the waves and the fervent sunlight. What they saw along both shores was one of the great spectacles of the American scene.

For three hundred miles up and down from New Orleans, the sugar and cotton plantations rose in a double file of splendor. Serene, proud, and pillared, the extravagant residences soared far past the neat precise order of Yankee Connecticut or Massachusetts. Every few miles the steamboats halted in midstream. They could traverse on even the narrowest bayous with their paddle wheels at the rear for more maneuvering room, and it was said that a good pilot could float a double-decker on a bucket of beer suds.

Bells clanged; on shore a slave waved a cloth in signal. Someone in the Big House had business, goods, or a passenger to send downriver. Gliding into place with a wash of water, the steamboat would pause, and if the vessel seemed to be bowing and curtsying before the estate, it was only fitting, for on the river, the plantations ruled.

The men who owned the Big Houses had tried tobacco, myrtle wax, saffron, and rice. Indigo did well for a time, though the handling of its poisonous leaves tended to kill off the slaves. Shortly before 1800, a Creole, Etienne de Bore, perfected the secret of sugar granulation, and about the same time, the cotton gin appeared. Now the state's fate was sealed, and society crystallized as well.

Up from the Red River, cotton was king. The lower reaches of the deep delta belonged to sugar, for the cane thrived best when its feet were damp. At the beginning of the Nineteenth Century, eighty planters were raising the Big Grass; by 1835, more than eight hundred were making their fortunes with vast acreages planted to cane in the parishes of Iberville, Ascension, Assumption, Plaquemines, St. James, Lafourche, and St. John.

Nowhere else on earth, they said, could money be made so fast; it poured out like the pale yellow juice from the fragrant kettles over hands, black and white.

In the bayou, there was a time of day when a strange quiet reigned.

During most of the daylight hours, there was almost constant movement, however slight. Muskrats swam and burrowed, gray squirrels scolded and scurried, alligators hissed and grunted, and the birds came and went in a bright flurry of noise and color, with an endless chorus of trills and chirps and croaks and quacks. Under it all like a backbeat, was the ceaseless drumming of the woodpecker, as he perpetually hunted for borers and beetle grubs in every tree.

At dusk the prowlers by night began to stir. Flying squirrels and great bats launched themselves into the evening, and they filled the night with squeals and squeaks. The owls took up the hunt and hooted through the swamp, and the skunks, foxes, opossums, and raccoons moved under the cover of the hum of night insects and frogs.

It was the time just after dawn, when the predators had settled for their rest, and the wading birds—the herons and egrets and ibises—left their roosts in great flickering clouds and sailed off to feed in the mudflats, that quiet came to the bayou. The waters were flat and calm, and spiders silently repaired their dew-spangled webs. The long strands of Spanish moss swayed slowly, sinuously, and the drone of the insects was muted for a time, until they were roused by the warming sun.

Now there was a heaviness in the air and a tranquility. On a sweet gum log, half-in, half-out of water and resting against a cypress, the rising sun could begin to warm the wet wood and coax the log's inhabitant out into the humid still morning.

This was her favorite resting place. Because her coloration so nearly matched the black log, her full five-foot length was hard to detect. Only the in-and-out flicker of her long, sensitive tongue gave away her presence.

She was a water moccasin, better known as a cottonmouth to those few men who had crossed her path. At eleven years of age, she was just over ten inches at the widest point in her body, but she had lived only about half her allotted years.

There were six other kinds of venomous snakes in the bayou, but her kind was the most numerous . . . also, the most deadly. While a man might well survive the bite of a copperhead or a rattlesnake, her powerful poison could kill the strongest field hand, and quickly.

She was wide-banded with dark olive; she carried two facial pits on either side of her vertical pupils for detecting prey, and her mouth, when she gaped it in her characteristic threat posture, was cottony white and startling in its warning.

Halfway between her spade-shaped snout and her elliptical eyes were two dark facial cavities—the trademark of the pit viper. Here were her unique heat-sensing organs by which she could tell, even in the ink black bayou night, the presence of and distance to a warm-blooded creature.

Less than a hundred feet away was her birth spot, though she no longer remembered it. Part of a brood of fifteen live young, she had since given birth four times herself, yet had never once crossed paths with a sister or daughter, so large was the bayou around them.

She had known man well, since she was only a foot in length. Once she was taken by a farmer for his child, a boy who thought to render her weaponless by removing her fangs with pliers and gloved hands. She was to be his harmless toy, unique among the play-pets of his friends.

What neither the farmer nor his son knew was that she grew fang sets in reserve, and as the front fangs were broken off, the set behind them gradually moved into position. She struck the boy when he handled her one morning, and as his mother screamed and rushed around the cabin, she quickly slid across the floor and into freedom once more.

Now she knew better than to let a hand touch her without biting instantly, savagely, in retaliation. Her kind rarely turned and fled, nor did she feel compelled to hide at man's approach. She stood her ground, gaped her warning, and if the intruder did not retreat, she was willing to narrow the distance between them swiftly with an aggressive lunge.

She lay half-in, half-out of the warm waters, waiting for what she knew would come. It was the season of mating, and this was her time. Only once every two years had she waited thus, and each time, the bayou provided. She had sensed his presence in the thicket for a day and a night, but she had not gone searching for him. In another time, she might have found him, fought him, and forced him from her territory. But now she waited, feeling the readiness within her for the mating.

Her tongue, forked at the end and very black, slid more than four inches in and out of her mouth and trembled in the air for long seconds. Though her eyesight was fair, she relied on her tongue and her Jacobson organ most of all, a pair of small pits within her jaws on either side of her snout. Each cavity had a duct which led to the roof of her mouth. As her tongue flicked in and out, she picked up minute odorous particles out of the air and from the ground. Drawn back into her mouth, her brain translated them to an image she was able to track, on any trail, even over shallow water.

A movement in the tall grasses caught her eye. She lifted her head slightly, her tongue gathering information from the air. He emerged slowly now from cover, lifting his head well off the ground to face her. Black he was, nearly as dark as she, though he was not wet from the swamp. For a long moment, he only gazed at her, and she did not move. Then he lowered his head and slid out of the grasses, his whole length of four feet coming to rest in the mud bank a few yards from her log.

The bayou breezes ceased and the water was quiet. An oriole landed in the branch above her, cocked an anxious eye at both snakes, and flew away with a warning squawk. Even the flies seemed to still in that moment.

He moved closer, and still she did not coil or threaten. Closer still, and she finally swiveled leisurely on her log, sliding her length down the wood, down the roots of the cypress, until she was on the bank beside him. Without preamble or posturing, he curved around her body, arching up and over her, twining his smaller length around her and moving up so that his parts penetrated her, gripping her with his strong side muscles so that she could not escape. She writhed, but she did not attempt to fight. Once her mouth gaped involuntarily, but her eyes never left the grasses. Locked together, the two snakes made looping circles in the mud, and their musky odor rose above the dank smell of the decayed vegetation, warning away all who might trespass.

Save one.

As the male withdrew himself from her, loosening his grip, she saw a quick movement in the grasses. Her facial pits swiftly picked up the scent of danger. It was a peculiar flavor on her tongue, acrid and unpleasant and ominous. She hissed a warning, moving away from the male and coiling swiftly. From out of the grasses burst a large dog fox, his red tail stiff and his mouth open in a rictus grin.

Now she understood the rancid flavor on her tongue, the acrid odor in her facial pits. Any other fox—indeed any other of her enemies—would never approach so imprudently, facing her when she was coiled on open ground. But this one had the sickness: his eyes were filled and matted, his coat muddied and slick, and his jaws stiff with slaver. It was the sickness which sometimes ran through the swamp in the hot summer months. Likely the dog fox had been bitten by a raccoon or a weasel, and now his own bite would spread the sickness until he died of it in a slow, painful thirst.

She saw swiftly that he would not be warned with her usual threat posture, would not be turned away by fear of her venom. In his present state, he knew no fear, and so he was more deadly than she.

The dog fox growled loudly, lowered his head, and barked at the two snakes, raking the ground before him with his claws. She put down her head to run, turning towards water, but he was on her in a flash, snatching her midsection with powerful jaws. She writhed and struck at him, catching his upper shoulder with her fangs, sinking them deeply into his muscle, and he yelped, snapped his head back and forth violently, and dropped her on the muddy bank.

Her mate had fled instantly into the tall grasses, she saw, and she tried to follow him, but something was wrong with her lower muscles. She could not gather herself for a second strike. The fox had staggered a few paces away from her and was once more growling and barking, snapping at his shoulder, twisting his mad eyes at her as though to charge again. All at once, his odor changed, and she knew that her strike had gone home. She had not taken prey for two days, waiting for the male. Her venom reserve was high. If need be, she could kill more than once.

But she could see now that there would likely be no need. The fox was beginning to quiver and whine, sinking to the bank with bewilderment. She painfully gathered her strength, trying to crawl to cover, but she could not command her lower body to her will. Calmly she watched the fox's quivers turn to convulsions and then to rigor, as he bled from his eyes, his nose, and his ears. When all movement had ceased, she tried again to crawl, but she was too broken. Flies now gathered at the fox, some of them impudently gathering around her as well. She gaped once in pain, sensing that the mating was her last.

As the sun rose hotly over the bayou and her body temperature rose past her endurance, she stiffened and died.

Celisma was only fourteen when she first came to Beausonge, though she had been a woman for more than two years. Sold from Rosewood by her master because he had no need for one more upstairs nigger, she came to Samuel Weitz's Big House in that spring of 1835 with no small relief. Better to leave her mother at Rosewood, than to be sent to the cotton fields. Better to sleep in the great pink bedroom of Matilde Weitz and eat white bread, than to sleep in the slave quarters and share cold pone with too many brothers.

Better to go and be most anything, anywhere, than to live in the field cabins where the hands lolled, with half-closed eyes, like so many cats and dogs against a sunned wall, dozing away the short noon hour in mindless ease. Nothing else to do and no will to do more.

Beausonge meant beautiful dream, the slaves said, and so it seemed to Celisma when she first saw the golden house. Larger than Rosewood by half, with cane fields stretching wide up and down the bayou, the sugar plantation of Samuel Weitz was one of the loveliest landmarks on Lafourche. The slaves said that M'sieu Weitz got his money from pirates, that he had fought with Jean Lafitte, and was a pirate himself. But Celisma knew if you believed everything the slaves said about those in the Big House, you'd believe in haunts and swamp lights, too. She believed what she could see with her own two eyes. And what they told her was that M'sieu Weitz had an eye for beauty.

The main house soared as tall as its flanking oaks. Painted light yellow and fronted by fat pillars which were bigger around than most trees, Beausonge dwarfed other homes on the bayou. The pillars started at the gallery and ended up at the second-story roof, with a matching gallery running around all four sides. On each side of the house stood smaller houses for the many guests who stopped at this river refuge, for visiting members of the family, and for the men to keep their late hours, smoke their cigars in peace, and tell their loud jokes without disturbing the women. Behind the house sat more buildings: the office house, the separate kitchen, a *garçonnière,* the summerhouse for the hottest evenings, and two pigeon cotes two stories high, for the master's squabs, pigeons, and doves.

Her pass gave her leave to walk, and so she did, taking the chance to glimpse the dairy, the laundry house, some of the stables for the horses, the pens and barns for the pigs and cattle, the granaries for corn, tobacco, and rice, and the smokehouse with the three brick ovens for curing the game and hogs. She skirted by the blacksmith's barn, the carpenter's shop, and the weaving house with its rows of flax and hemp drying in the sun, the tannery, and malt house, and finally round back to the back door of the Big House once more.

Everywhere she looked, black hands were working, black faces turned to look back.

A group of hands were walking a path to the cane fields, led by an old driver carrying a whip. Forty or more women walked together, all dressed in the same blue cotton shift, their lower legs and feet bare. Each carried a hoe and strode with a powerful swing, calling out to one another. A laugh carried back to Celisma, and then they were lost in the dust roiled up by the troop of mules coming behind them.

And then she came to the slave quarters, a double pathway of small whitewashed cabins, each like the other and set in close rows, divided by a wide dusty avenue.

When the morning sun rose over the river, the Weitz plantation turned pink, then yellow gold in the light. In the late afternoon, with the sun behind it, the Big House was the color of a gold Spanish coin.

"You come to it now, gal," ol' Ulysses told her on that afternoon she arrived. He was the tall, gaunt, grizzled boss of the house niggers, the first one Madame called to if something displeased her, the last one to check the locks each night. "Your massa at Rosewood got to be one rich cotton planter before he be startin' as a poor sugar man. Massa Sam, he not the richest, but he might near close. Massa Midas, more like. You got trainin'?"

Celisma met his scrutiny calmly. "I can do what needs doin'."

"Cook?"

"Not cookin'."

"Washin'?"

"Maybe lady's dainty wear."

"Scrubbin'? Ironin'?"

She swiftly remembered the long hours spent ironing at Rosewood, the six flat irons in a row on the hearth, their smooth surfaces turned to the blaze. The metal cylinders went into the fluting irons, hot and sizzling to the skin. Sprinkle the clothes, iron, turn the creaking fluting irons with care so that the ruffles would be crisp and yet soft, the tedious heat of the ironing shed, standing and pushing the irons for ten hours at a stretch . . .

She smiled a private smile. "I do for the upstairs, more. I know roots an' medicinals, washes an' yerbals, an' I can read an' write. At Rosewood, I take personal care a' ol' Miss an' her closet."

"At Rosewood," Ulysses said firmly, "you be huntin' up your Massa's specs an' fannin' off the flies at supper, I 'spect.

Your hand never touched ol' Miss nor her closet neither, gal."

"I was trainin'."

"You was wishin', is what you was doin'. Where you learn to read an' write?"

"*Maman.*"

"Where she learn it? Never mind that, you keep that close, gal, white folk don' want no house nigger round who knows her letters. It agin the law, an' even if some white folk hold to it, Madame sure don't. You probably jes' make your mark, anyways. You too green an' pert for Rosewood's ol' Miss, an' I 'spect you too green an' pert for Madame, too. But we kin try you out." He gazed her up and down. "We got six to do for here at Beausonge, missy, an' that be Massa Sam, Madame, Ol' Madame, Young Massa Pierre, an' the two young Misses, Thérèse an' Amélie. Young Massa, he near grown, nigh eighteen. Two young Misses, they be 'bout your age, I 'spect. You nigh fifteen?"

She smiled her most womanly smile.

Ulysses frowned fiercely at her. "You older, then. Miss Thérèse, she fourteen, an' Miss Amélie, she younger by a year. Then they all the cousins an' relations that come callin', Beausonge holds a pack o' them most times, but 'specially round grindin' time. Both young Misses already got their own wenches to do for them plenty, an' I misallow that Massa Sam paid your massa for givin' those two gals something else to spar over who gets what. You do fancy work?"

She shook her head. "But I can learn most anything."

Ulysses scowled. "Wal, I don't know what Massa Sam got in mind for such a useless gal, but I 'spect it my job to find a place to tuck you where you won' hunt up trouble. You say you know roots an' yerbs an' suchlike? Maybe Madame put you to work makin' her powders an' paints, she got plenty for two hands to do there." He peered at her a little closer. "You 'bout the yallerest gal we had at Beausonge, anyways. Your mama yaller, too?"

Celisma lifted her chin and said quietly, *"Maman is a femme de couleur."*

"You speak that French, that be fine. Madame likin' that fine." He appraised her slender height, her dark hair which lay in two smooth coils about her head, her slender nose and full lips, and her skin which was the color of light bourbon whiskey. "Your mama might be black, but your papa sure weren't."

She narrowed her eyes and tightened her lips. Such things were not spoken of in the finer houses, that much she knew.

Ulysses chuckled to take away the sting. "Never mind, gal. We see what Odette say. She do for Madame, an' she be the one to say who else be doin' for her. Maybe you be sleepin' in the pink room yet."

With that, the old man led Celisma up the winding wide staircase to the upstairs chambers. She held her hands against her skirts so that they would not tremble, and lifted her chin as high as she could and still see the stairs beneath her feet. At least I don't come with my bare feet flapping, she told herself firmly. She glanced down at the scuffed brown kid slippers she wore, passed to her by ol' Massa's youngest daughter in a moment of kindness. She had been saving these kid slippers for just such a moment, praying she would not outgrow them before she got their use. She gripped with her toes on the unfamiliar stairs, willing herself to hold her head as though she carried something more precious than the most useless, yellowest head at Beausonge.

Odette met Ulysses at the massive door of Madame's chamber. She was a huge black woman, near as wide as the door. Her skirts bunched at her waist, held together with a man's belt that carried four sets of keys, jingling with every jerk of her apron. She was jerking at it now, wiping her hands with energy.

"This the new chick?" she called out to Ulysses before he could speak. "Don' be draggin' her up here to plague me now," she added in a tone that obviously was used to being obeyed.

"An' where else I be draggin' her then?" the old man grumbled, his voice raised loud. "She ain' no downstairs wench, she ain' no cook nor laundry gal, she cain' do fancy work, an' the young Misses pull her leg from leg, fightin' over who she do for, so I 'spect Madame best say what she do an' where she go!"

Odette met his noise, decible for decible. "Look to me like Madame be wonderin' if you got too old an' foolish to do your job then, you askin' her to do it for you! Ain' fit to tote guts to a bear. Next you be askin' her which chicken for the pot." She frowned ferociously at Ulysses, all the while dropping one eyelid in a slow wink at Celisma.

Celisma felt the thrill of conspiracy and comradeship warm her belly, the first slice of welcome she'd felt since she came up the steps of Beausonge. She kept her face grave, her eyes lowered, but her hands gripped each other in front of her skirts as though in prayer.

Ulysses blustered, "I done waste too much time on this piddly chile already this mornin'. She goin' to be upstairs gal, that the word with the bark on it, an' you don't like it, *you* tell Madame!"

"Tell Madame what?" an imperious voice asked right behind Ulysses. "Half the household can hear you two scolding like spring jays up here, *c'est dommage, c'est vrai,* when it is such a crisis that I must come all the way from the gallery to settle it."

Instantly, old Ulysses fell back away from the door, his head bowed and silent. Odette managed to maintain her composure better, but she too fell away from the approaching woman as though she deserved the widest passage. *"Excusez-moi, Madame,"* she said quietly, "we done settle it, *s'il vous plaît.*"

The short sparse wisp of a woman swept past them both and into the pink chamber, lifting her skirts away from the floor as though the cypress boards themselves were offensive. "It does *not* please me, Odette, not at all. I have left M'sieu Prejean alone on the gallery in a most inhospitable manner, simply to come all the way upstairs to sort out the disposition of a new nigger? *Non, vraiment,* it does not please me at all. This is she?" Madame glanced once at Celisma and then at Ulysses.

"Yes'm," the old man said, now having once more attained his full height, "this be Celisma from Rosewood, newcome."

"And she does—?"

Celisma spoke up then softly. *"S'il vous plaît, Madame, je fais tout."*

Madame Weitz turned her full attention now to this tall slender girl before her. Celisma decided to take a rare risk. She did not drop her eyes before Madame, as she had been trained to do before all white women. Instead, she met the woman's gaze and smiled, bending to a deep curtsy.

She saw the swift look of pity in Odette's eyes even before Madame spoke.

"An unskilled and impudent nigger wench he has purchased?" the woman asked sharply of no one in particular. "One who brags she can do anything but who can likely do little at all? How old are you, girl?"

Celisma dropped her eyes instantly and murmured. "Fourteen, Madame."

"A yellow wench too young to breed and too old to train. *Sacré nom!* Must I do everything? Make every decision or see it spoiled before my eyes?"

"She can speak the French—" Ulysses tried to plead her case.

"Does that, then, make up for her insolence and her uselessness?" Madame had a way of speaking the sharpest words with a gentle tone, which somehow made Celisma feel as though a cat was slowly clawing her leg and she could not move it away. The woman came nearer to her and looked at her closely. "She'll have to go to the fields. There's no other place for her here."

Celisma stifled a gasp, flushing deeply. No mulatress ever went for a field hand, that much she knew for certain.

"Perhaps," Odette began softly, "the wench might do for ol' Madame. She know the way of roots an' medicinals an' things. Ol' Madame can speak the French to her. An' she be needin' 'nother gal since Gabriel took sick. This gal do for her, leastwise 'til Madame decide."

"Or maybe," Matilde Weitz said, scarcely listening, "she should go to the nursery. We've got a dozen suckers this season, way too many for that old midwife to mind alone."

Celisma closed her eyes now in horror.

"She too young, Madame," Odette said calmly. "Ain' no milk comin' from those buds for a few seasons, anyways—"

"Oh all right, all right, take her to *Mamère*, but if she doesn't want her, send her to the quarters. I'll not have a yellow wench serving at my table, and we scarcely need another useless hand at the pukha fans." She glared at all three of them and swept out. "See to it, Ulysses, and next time you might consider how such a *débâcle* appears to such a man as M'sieu Prejean. I doubt highly that Madame Prejean must leave her guests to settle the affairs of her niggers—"

And she was gone out the chamber door and down the stairs as quickly, as regally as she had arrived.

Celisma followed Ulysses out the door, but as she went, Odette touched her bare arm gently. "Don't let her fright you, chile. She got her own cross to bear. You do good by ol' Madame, an' you be back in the Big House soon enough. See can you learn somethin' with those big eyes when you by her." She rolled her eyes at Ulysses. "Maybe this one got *la bonne chance* an' don't know it, yes?"

The old man shook his head in weary agreement and led Celisma down the backstairs towards the rear of the Big House. The sun hit her bare head like a hot hammer, making her wince and drop her eyes to the ground. The heat shimmered around them, and the locusts buzzed and sang in the grass. Now she saw the slave quarters at a closer hand, between bedraggled rows of corn or squat bushbeans they sat, a double row of cabins the same washed-out color as the dusty earth. As *maman* would say, so small you couldn't cuss a cat without catchin' a mouthful of hair.

She shuddered, clutching her skirts. At fifteen, she could be given to a man who lived within those cabins, given as his own to bear his children and work alongside him for her lifetime. Unless ol' Madame took her in.

Ulysses said, "Massa Sam got hisself a handful with Madame Matilde, sure enough. That woman got eyes all over her head an' mouths enough, too. Young Misses comin' up just like her, I 'spect, an' not much to do 'bout that. Time was, Madame was a little thing, all smiles an' easy to please when she come. Massa say she brung the sun with her to Beausonge. Them was good years, 'fore they lost that boy-chile."

"Their son?"

"First one. Madame took it hard. Never was herself agin, if you ast me. Now, seems like nothin' much please her most times, 'ceptin' the fancy folk who come to call an' the fancy frocks they wear an' the fancy—" his voice fell away as though he realized he'd forgotten his station. And hers.

"But you best please ol' Madame, gal, an' please her fine. Gabriel never did tend her near good enough, to her mind, so if she never gets past that consumption, ol' Madame won't miss her much. You please ol' Madame, an' you please Massa Sam, an' then Madame won' worry you none. Keep out her way, is all. You lookin' to find yourself a husband?"

Celisma said, "No. I druther not."

"Um. Wal, married got teeth an' she bite. You learn that quick enough, I 'spect. Massa Sam, he got him a marriage of convenience, but don't look to me like it be all that convenient most times."

"A marriage of convenience?"

"The best folk do it, gal. Say Madame got a hundred arpents o' good cane ground, an' Massa got a hundred more neighborin', it be right convenient to bring the two together, see? I 'spect that be the best kind o' marriage, if marriage you got to have. Folks say women be the weaker vessel, but that a lie. That piece o' red flannel you got 'tween your jaws is equal to all the fists God ever made for men. I seen a woman jes' take an' ruin a man with her tongue. So I never did think much on it, myself. Ol' Madame 'bout the onliest widow I ever see who hated to wear the weeds."

"She a widow lady?"

"For more'n ten year. Massa Joseph, he pass quick an' leave her fixed. Madame Oliva Weitz, mama to Samuel, *grandmère* to young Misses an' young Massa. An'—" here he allowed himself a rare grin, "thorn in the side o' *young* Madame. Ol' Madame got 'nother son, Simon Weitz, an' he live down the bayou. He run the *sucrerie,* an' got a wife an' fambly o' his own. But he ain' no Midas like his brother, no, I ain't never seed two brothers so different from the same litter. When Massa Joseph Weitz die, ol' Madame, she live at Beausonge. I 'spect Madame wish she go live with her other son, but here she is an' here she stay. Best Madame can do is keep her out back, away from the fancy callers an' their doin's. Least ten times a year, young Madame allows how ol' Madame might be more happy livin' in New Orleans or some other place. But she won't leave this bayou. Ol' Madame, she no fool. She know what she know an' get what she want."

"She speak *français?*"

"She speak English. But she speak it in French. Now walk pert, for she ain' deaf, neither."

The old man led Celisma up the steps of the summer-house, a smaller version of the Big House. Likely it had been built before most of the other buildings, for it had a softening to its frame, an easy elegance which the larger house lacked. Heat and damp had worked to melt down the lines of the summerhouse, to tone down its shades, and the honorable stain and mold of many decades showed through its yellow paint like a melting wedding cake. The effect was that of a once-lovely matron, no less beautiful now that she was matured.

Ulysses knocked softly and called out to the old woman, leading Celisma into the darkened shadows of the cool gallery. The ceilings were vast, more than three times the height of a man, and the windows stretched as tall as the walls. They were thrown wide, as were the folding doors, and the breeze went everywhere. The floor was bricked, not marbled, and cool moss grew in between the bricks. Heavy live oaks shaded all sides, and honeysuckle vines pressed against the walls.

An old woman came down the stairs to Ulysses' call with a light step, her hand sliding down the worn white banister.

"I brung the new gal, Madame. This here Celisma from over Rosewood. Massa say, she do for you, if she please you."

Celisma watched the old woman carefully, but this time from lowered eyes and a bowed head. She could still see the girl in Madame's face, though her pale skin was wreathed in lines and the planes of the aged. Her hair was mostly dark, with bands of white at either temple. If she had ever been beautiful, it no longer showed, but there was a grace and symmetry to her features which made the eye believe that it would not be a waste of time to linger on such a face.

"She did not please Matilde, you mean," the old woman answered quickly. There was little of the croaking bite of age in her voice. "Well, let us see, then, Celisma, if we can please each other, yes?" She tilted the young girl's face up so that she could observe it plainly. "Why, she is *charmante*. Can you sew, *cher?*"

Celisma said, "I tell you now, Madame, I don' know sewin' nor weavin' nor lace-makin'. I never did for a lady before, an' I likely be useless, they say."

Ulysses sputtered alarmingly, "She say she useless 'bout

286

every other mouthful, Madame, but she be knowin' all 'bout roots an' yerbs an' such, an' Massa done brung her—"

Oliva laughed a gay, rueful laugh. "Nobody's useless, Celisma. Not unless they work at it harder than I intend to let you work at it. My husband used to say that anything is possible, you have only to wish it. We'll get by, you and I. Ulysses, go tell Matilde that this *'tite jeune fille* will sleep at the foot of my bed until I change my mind. And tell my son I will want to see him after supper tonight."

"Yes'm, I sure will do that," the old man said, bowing himself out the open door.

And so, Celisma stayed that night and many more after in the large white airy room at the top of the stairs with Madame Oliva Weitz, but she still never passed the slave quarters without a frisson of wariness skating up her spine. As long as she was at Beausonge, she knew she kept from the quarters only at Madame's whim.

Ol' Madame wasn't hard to please, Celisma quickly learned, so long as you didn't call her ol' Madame. Matilde was happy enough to hear her mother-in-law called by such a name, but to Oliva Weitz, there was only one true Madame of Beausonge: her daughter-in-law could make do with the name of Mistress, until Oliva joined her husband in the plantation graveyard. After all, Oliva told the story again and again, it was Joseph Weitz who purchased the first five hundred arpents along the bayou, who put his own hands to the plow clearing the land for cane, and who put a small fortune in his son's hands—ready enough to split it between two sons, but one would have nothing but the sugar mill and his trap

287

lines—so Madame of Beausonge she would stay until she no longer wished to hear the word. And once invited by her son, Samuel, to live permanently where she and Joseph had once seen happy days, she had no intention of vacating to suit Matilde.

Celisma's duties were light, and her days were long. Meals were carried across the open pathway from the back kitchen to Madame's summerhouse in covered dishes; Celisma had only to set the dishes on the table and serve the old woman what she wished. The bedclothes were carried out soiled and carried back again clean from the laundry shed, and the hardest chore Celisma had was cleaning out Madame's copper bathtub once a day.

At the Big House, Monday was wash day, Tuesday was ironing, Wednesday was mending, Thursday was planting and hoeing in the garden, Friday was cleaning, and Saturday was baking day. Sometimes, she was called to do for others, but mostly, Oliva kept Celisma by her side.

The rhythms were easy. Soon Celisma felt she could know what Madame wanted without her asking for it, sensed how she felt without being told. An early riser, the old woman woke, dressed, and walked along the river every morning, Celisma a few yards behind. She might gather wildflowers or simply watch the birds, but she wanted little speech to intrude on her meditations. After the heat of the day, she walked the river again, a different path this time, as though she expected to see a new slant on the world. At night, Samuel Weitz often came to see his mother, to read aloud some passage from the newspaper or to play pinochle, and Madame retired as the moon rose, sleeping through the night with Celisma tucked into a pallet in the corner.

At dawn, the bell rang out and rolled back to the slave quarters. The hands and the Big House began to stir, and in the mule pasture, Celisma could see the mules let out a collective breath like a sigh, turning their heads all together in the same direction to the stable to wait for the drivers. At noon, the bell called out again to supper. The field hands left plows abandoned where they stood, trace chains released from the wagons, mounted the mules, and came at a quick trot towards the barn. From noon to three, they ate and rested in the shade, then at three, the hands went back to the fields, and the white ladies slept behind the closed window shutters with pukha fans softly billowing their mosquito *barres.*

At dusk, another bell pealed out from far away, the call of the Catholic Church downriver to prayer. The Angelus softly echoed over the fields, and Madame had trained all hands, black and white, to stop for an instant, bow their heads, and pray.

On Sundays, the young Master and Misses accompanied their father, to carry ol' Madame to Mass. Dressed in the more somber clothing of the holy day, the two daughters seemed still wreathed in light, their wild fiery hair piled and curled round their head and barely controlled with pins and combs. Amélie and Thérèse could scarcely sedate their chatter and gaiety, even when their father frowned his impatience at them, tucking them tightly into the carriage amidst their yards of billowing skirts, petticoats, and crinolines.

Young Master looked less like his father than either of his sisters, with dark hair and eyes that seemed to move everywhere at once, and a lithe, easy grace and stride. Pierre rode behind the carriage on his black courting prancer, Houma, handling the horse's dancing steps with tight rein and a ready crop.

Celisma rode next to Madame in the carriage, across from the two young Misses, and for all the notice they took of her she might as well have been one with the golden brown velvet of the buggy seats. It was their private time with *grandmère,* and none of the three seemed to miss Matilde, who preferred to attend the later Mass alone.

It was her one morning to stay abed, she liked to say, and

she was sure *le bon Dieu* would not begrudge her the peace and quiet.

Celisma relished the once-a-week departure from Beausonge, indeed would have eagerly anticipated any destination at all which allowed her to see new people or places. But to watch the white folk at prayer seemed to her to be a peephole into their most private souls. Hail Mary, full of grace, blessed art thou among women and blessed be the fruit of thy womb, Jesus. The church smelled of wax candles and flowers, and the murmur of the soft French patois lifted above her head made her listen for secrets. She never tired of wondering what they thought when they kneeled and sang and took communion in the white-spired church downriver in the town of Thibodaux.

She had never heard God's voice nor felt His presence, but she felt sure that He spoke regularly to most white folk. Certainly, He must be a common visitor to Oliva Weitz, for never had she known a person who seemed more sure of what God intended than Madame.

Maman rarely spoke much of church, truth to tell. She told Celisma of the *loupgarou,* the werewolf who lived in the forest, about the goblins who came in the night to water the horses, about ol' white Letitche, the ghost of the dead unchristened child who haunted the chambers of children, and about four-leafed clovers and horseshoes for luck, but little about Jesus. She told her that crabs were fattest at the full moon, that birds fly low just before a storm, that wild geese flying meant a cold spell was coming on, and that a ring around the moon meant rain, but not much of God.

Celisma began to understand that there were folks who knew God well, and folks who hadn't managed to catch His eye. And that was fine enough with her, since she'd already learned that somebody taking notice might be a powerful hurt as well as a powerful help.

Master Samuel Weitz was the one who made Celisma go still and small as a forest creature at the passage of a hunting eagle. He was kind enough, yes, but he took little notice of her save to see that she had what she needed to care for his mother. The house slaves of Beausonge did not fear him, nor did they speak behind his back with amused contempt as they had her master at Rosewood, but neither did they think of ways to please him or catch his eye. It was as though the man had a secret wall in him, which all could sense but none could scale.

Celisma watched Samuel Weitz at prayer and saw that often, when eyes all round him were closed in reverent meditation, his own were open, restlessly moving from window to wall as though looking for a private answer.

Once she was gathering sweetflag at the riverbank for a tisane to soothe Madame's indigestion. As she walked through the brush, looking for the tiny green yellow flowers which grew part-in, part-out of the water, she saw a figure sitting downriver, facing the brown bayou. She moved carefully, making herself small among the shrubs, placing her bare feet soundlessly on the moss. It was Master Samuel, fishing off the bank.

At once, she sensed that Master did not care if a creature took his bait. His eyes did not linger on the line or the water; he didn't fondle the pole, tugging gently at it as most men did when they fished. His eyes stayed on the cypress across the bayou, seeing little, so far as she could tell. She wondered what such a man would be doing fishing, with so many who could be put to the chore for him.

She could have melted away in the ferns and grasses unseen, she knew, her *maman* used to say she could move through the woods quiet as a rat pissing in cotton. But something made her make just enough noise for him to look up.

"Who's that?" he asked, and his voice sounded as though it came from far away.

"Celisma, Massa Sam," she said softly. "Madame's gal."

"What are you doing?"

She put both hands in her apron pockets and drew them

out full of small flowers. "Sweetflag, suh. For Madame's wind."

"Come let me see that."

She walked shyly over to him, her hands out before her like an offering. He stood up, set down his pole, and took one of the flowers in his fingers.

"This little thing will cure a bellyache?"

"Mais oui, M'sieu," she nodded, "an' more complaints besides. There be something here in the swamp for most anythin' ails a body, if you know where to look."

He peered at her closely. "And you know where to look."

She smiled. "I know 'bout dandelion for the bowel, an' wild carrot for fixin' a man's water, an' foxglove for the heart. An' pokeweed an' wild yam an' snakeroot—"

"Your mama taught you all this?"

She nodded, dropping her head again, suddenly overwhelmed by her own boldness. "This *'tit* bit, suh."

"There are plenty of herbs and roots out here that'll kill quick as cure, aren't there." It was not a question.

She felt the swift thud of panic in her breast. Of course there were poisonous plants, and she knew just which ones would likely do murder, and some without a trace, but never could she admit to such a knowledge, her mother had warned her. If the white folk guessed she knew such things, no telling what their fear might lead them to do. If she daren't let on about her letters, she surely could never say such a truth to this white Massa, no matter how kindly he seemed. She kept her face bland. "She never learned me such, Massa," she said, "if she even know it."

His laugh startled her, and her glance flew up, her mouth gaped. "She learned you plenty, I wager," he said, "enough to know when to act the fool anyways. Don't fret, Celisma, I don't worry you'll poison my mother. Since she's all that stands between you and my wife. You don't strike me as a stupid wench, whatever else you may be."

Confused, she murmured, "No suh."

"It's good *maman* has a gal who can do more for her than fill her plate and smooth her sheets, yes? So long as you have her permission to be out here, I'll not say more. You *do* have her leave to wander, do you not?"

She nodded, her head still down.

"Good. Then go about your business, gal."

She turned to go, but something made her hesitate. "Why you fishin', Massa?" she asked, wondering where she found the courage. "Dan'l or Tim be proud to do such." Daniel and Tim were the two yard niggers she saw most often.

"Because I like to do some things for myself," he said firmly.

Still, she hesitated.

"What is it?" he finally asked, with a touch of impatience.

She lifted her chin and threw over her shoulder, "Only that there ain' no fish in this branch, Massa. Best try your luck over yonder," pointing to the place where the bayou forked, slid into shadow, and out to a swifter rushing stream. She scampered off then, her bare heels flashing, tucking her grin into her mouth until she was far enough away that he could not hear her low chuckle.

Celisma was surprised to discover that few other slaves at Beausonge knew what she knew about the ways of healing. Word spread through the quarters that the pert yellow gal brought nothing short of magic in her herb bag. Soon it was common to see her moving through the dusk to a cabin to see to some hand's fever, or arriving with the first pains to a woman in her childbed. But in three seasons at Beausonge, she had never been called to the Big House to treat one of the white folk. The doctor came in his black buggy if one of the young Misses took a chill or young Master took to his bed with one of his sick headaches. Only ol' Madame would have Celisma's hands on her and swallow her tisanes without complaint.

Once, word came from the quarters that a woman was sick with a high fever, likely caused from hoeing cane in the sun. Celisma went to her quickly, for she knew sun fever could kill quick as a canebrake rattler.

She found Passi, one of the younger women, on her straw mattress, her husband standing alongside, frowning with worry. "She never been took like this afore," he said, his voice vexed and anxious. "She ain' with chile', is she?"

A tremor passed over Passi, contorting her jaw and throat. She was a handsome slave, her face tawny and her eyes luminous, even with the sickness. She gripped Celisma's arm with hands made strong by the constant work in the fields. "It somethin' I eat," she said, her voice harsh and throaty. She was bathed in sweat, and her long legs thrashed under the rough covering her husband kept trying to keep about her.

Celisma spoke low and soothing to her, feeling for her heartbeat and the strength of its rhythm. This did not look like a case of field fever. Her face was not pallid, her skin was not clammy, and the woman seemed strong enough to take a day's work without heat exhaustion. But her jaw was rigid, her lips tortured, and water came profusely to her mouth.

A shadow fell in the doorway, and Massa Sam stuck his head inside the cabin. Instantly, Passi's husband moved back from the bed as though he had no right to attend his own wife.

"What's this I hear, Passi? You took sick?"

"Tain' nothin', suh," Passi's husband mumbled, "ain' no call for you to bother yourself—"

"Celisma, what's wrong with our gal?"

Celisma had been pressing on the thumbnails of Passi's

hands, watching as the blue moved back and forth under the tissue. "I cain' say as yet," she said quietly. "She say it something she eat."

Now Passi began to writhe and clutch at her stomach, sweating more than before. She moaned and her eyes rolled to Massa Sam, then away.

"You got pain in the belly?" Celisma asked, pulling the woman's hands away and pressing her abdomen. Her answer was a louder groan, rising to a shriek.

Massa Sam's face fell and he moved closer. "She sounds bad," he said anxiously. "I thought it was only sun fever."

"It more than that," Celisma said, her eyes on Passi's tremoring limbs. "Seem like some sort of poison, maybe."

At that, the master drew back, his mouth tight with concern. "What sort of poison? Can you tell?"

"Acts like snakebite," Celisma said. "Passi, you been bit?" She began to uncover her arms and legs, searching for puncture wounds. "Spider, maybe?"

Passi's husband still said nothing, watching Celisma and Massa Sam with eyes that grew wider and whiter with worry. His wife began to thrash again on the bed, her mouth and chin now covered with drool she could not control. Tremors stiffened her spine, arched her back, and then released her as suddenly as they came on.

Massa Sam put out one hand and touched the slave's shoulder as though to lend comfort, but then withdrew his hand and clenched his fists together helplessly.

Another shadow fell inside the open door, and Madame Matilde glided within, her skirts making a rustle louder than Passi's twisting straw mattress. She looked directly at her husband. "*Ici encore?*" she asked coldly.

"I heard we had a woman down," he said quickly.

"Yes. A field hand, is she not?" Madame approached Passi's bed and gazed down at her calmly. "What are her symptoms?" she asked Celisma, turning away from her husband.

"Fever," she replied slowly, not wanting to make a mistake. "Trembles in the limbs. Stiff jaw an' sore throat." She took the cloth from the bucket, wrung it out again and wiped Passi's face. "Water come from her mouth somethin' hard."

At the touch of the cloth, Passi opened her eyes for an instant and seemed to see about her all at once. She spied Madame peering down at her and shrunk away, her mouth gaping in a rigid shriek.

"She's out of her head," Madame said. To Passi's husband, she added, "Get some fresh water quick." As the woman's husband hurried out, she said to Massa Sam, "It seems to me that Celisma can handle this slave well enough without us, Samuel. Unless you want to send for Dr. Comeaux?"

He seemed to hesitate. Celisma knew that rarely did the white folk's doctor ever treat a slave. Maybe, if a skilled smithy or carpenter was took, doctor might come. Or maybe, if a sickness drew down half the quarters, then the doctor might be called, for hands down at grinding could ruin a crop, but certainly for things like fever and childbirth and bonesets, they did for themselves or called a conjure woman. Especially for a field gal.

Passi's head was moving back and forth on the bed now, back and forth as rigid as wood, her eyes wide and unseeing, her mouth flecked with pink foam where she had bitten her tongue in a tremor. Celisma thought in that instant that the girl had been poisoned, sure. Nothing else made that foam. She stared at Massa Sam, willing him to see the need in her eyes. Yes, she wanted to say, send for the doctor quick, for I cain' save this one, most like.

But Massa Sam rose suddenly and walked out into the sunlight without an answer, passing Passi's husband as he left. The black man hurried to the bed with his jug, holding out a tin cup of fresh water. As he held it to his wife's mouth, she jerked in harder spasm, twisting away from the water and convulsing violently.

"It's the rabies," Madame said firmly. "You see the way she fears the water. *La rage. Hydrophobie.* I should have seen it at once."

"No'm," Passi's husband protested, his voice cracking in fear, "Passi ain' been bit nohow, ain' been round no coons nor hounds!"

"*You* do not know where all she's been," Madame said coldly to the man, "I tell you, it's the rabies on the woman. Celisma, you call Daniel and Tim here at once."

"No! No!" Passi's husband cried, half-throwing himself over the jerking body of his wife. "It somethin' she eat! She be fit by mornin'!"

"Celisma," Madame repeated gently. "Do as I say."

As Celisma reluctantly left Passi's side and went to the door, Madame added, "Tell them it is the rabies, *certainement,* and that she is suffering."

Celisma nodded, wide-eyed, and ran out the door to the Big House, up to the yard where Daniel and Tim were cording wood. At her words, they looked grim and dropped their tools. She followed them to the gallery of the summerhouse where they picked up one of the largest mattresses off the summerbeds and carried it between them down to Passi's cabin.

They could barely squeeze the feather mattress within the little door, and once they did, the huge bedcover and their shoulders nearly filled the small room. They looked at Passi and then at her husband, who moaned and rolled his eyes in the corner.

"We must bring her God's mercy," Madame said to the two slaves, beckoning them forward.

Celisma had heard of such things, knew that every Master and Missus had their own way of dealing with death in the quarters, but she had never seen this before. As she watched in horror, Daniel and Tim gently laid the feather mattress over Passi, over her head, over her breasts and her jerking limbs, both of them pressing down on it with all their strength. Once she cried out, a muffled shriek from under the feathers; once her husband answered her shriek with an agonized cry of his own, and then all was silent in the cabin. They waited a long moment. Then, slowly, the two men peeled the mattress off Passi to reveal her motionless body beneath it.

Her eyes were still open wide, her jaw stiff. But her breasts did not rise. Her struggle was over. And her mouth would be silent forever.

"I am sorry," Madame said softly to Passi's husband, touching him briefly on his shuddering shoulder. "Her suffering is finished. She is with *le bon Dieu, non?*" When he did not respond, she waited patiently. Finally, he forced himself to nod slowly. "You are a good man. You come to Master this evening, and he will give you something for yourself."

She gestured Daniel and Tim towards the door. As the three moved into the sunlight, she said, "See to it that she is buried quickly and deep. Away from the quarters and to the back of the fields. Burn the feather tick and the straw she lay on. Celisma?"

Celisma went reluctantly to her, for clearly this woman could do as she willed, and her will might move her eye to anyone who displeased her. Or who pleased Master.

"Did you feed her? Give her drink?"

"No'm," she answered softly.

"Well, go up to the house right now and tell cook Passi has ended her suffering. Tell her you nursed her. Get the turpentine and scrub yourself all over." She pointed a finger in Celisma's face. "I mean all over, you hear? And then burn that homespun you have on at once. Every stitch."

"Oui, Madame," Celisma said. "At once."

"I see you do not wear your *tignon.*"

The *tignon,* a piece of colored cotton that the black women used to cover their nappy wool, had been given to her along with her work shifts when she arrived. She chose not to wear it, for her own hair was long and lustrous with a

298

reddish tinge. Instead, she only bound it back and left it uncovered. *"Non, Madame,"* she said softly.

"You will wear your hair under your *tignon* from now on."

"Oui, Madame."

"And next time you are called to the quarters to tend to sickness, if Master comes, you send for me. We cannot have Master falling ill, can we? If a slave needs more tending than you can provide, I must know it at once. Is that clear?"

"Oui, Madame," she said, "if I see Massa in the quarters, I call you at once."

Madame smiled gently. "Good. Then we understand each other." With that, she led the two slaves back up to the yard to set them to work building a box for Passi.

Sugar was a year-long obsession at Beausonge, as it was at every plantation up and down the river on both sides. A tropical plant forced to survive in a semitropical land, sugar cane needed more coddling than cotton, but it brought in more cash.

Late in September each year, the field hands moved over the black earth, tilling rows, making furrows, and dropping stalks of seed cane in the ground. Soon, shoots pushed up from the joints of each seed stalk, the first tender hints of spring. All round the shoots, the choking weeds fought for soil and space and had to be grubbed out by hand and hoe. Over the months, the field slaves worked to keep the cane rising thicker, stronger, and taking from the days of pounding rain and steaming heat, its juicy vigor.

The sugar leaf took in carbon dioxide from the air and

formed it into sugar, storing it in the stalk at night. Thus it was said that sugar came from the air, not the soil, and that the cane was a factory and a warehouse as well, open round the clock. The cane was planted every fourth year. One plant provided three crops, and of each crop, the planter took sugar, blackstrap molasses—a crude syrup fit for only cattle or slave fodder—and bagasse, the crushed cane fibers for fuel.

Around July, Master Samuel rode his two thousand arpents daily on his white horse, Valcour, and the stalks were in tassel above his head. Like a green lake, the cane spread out in all directions, so thick it hid the ground and sheltered a host of varmints, snakes, and birds. Now was about the only time when the cane could be left unprotected. The crop was laid by to grow at will, and the slaves were sent to fix the levees, cut shingles, build the hogsheads, and tend to whatever else around Beausonge they had not been able to attend when the cane called them.

As the hot summer weeks ebbed into autumn, the big grass took on a purplish tinge, and Samuel began to watch it with furrowed brow. If they cut too late, he might lose the whole crop to an early frost or storm rains. If they cut too early, the juice would not be sweet. The cane could never fully ripen in Louisiana, for the season was a few months shorter than it needed: the best they could hope for each year was a balance between the weather and each planter's judgment.

Finally, Samuel had waited as long as he dared and he gave the order, usually sometime in early October. At once, Beausonge leaped into a frenzy of action. The cutters, loaders, and haulers worked day and night, the men and the women both out in the fields with their cane knives. One flash of the blade and the leaves were stripped off one side of the stalk; two flashes and the cane was bare. A third flash took the cane off at the ground, a fifth cut off the unripened joints at the top. A toss to the side and *whack, whack, whack,* the cutter moved on to the next. It was a rhythm, a dance, a bobbing movement that the best cutters could keep up most of the day without rest, and they did so for sixteen hours a day through all of October and November.

The Weitz mill sat at the boundary of Samuel and Simon's properties, serving Beausonge and a few small farms in the near vicinity. Simon had greatly enlarged it from the smaller factory Joseph Weitz had built, and now it was a large brick building with a tall chimney which the steamboats could see from a good distance. The cane carts pulled up overloaded with stalks in a steady line for two months solid. Slaves fed the cane to the grinders and mules dragged themselves in unending circles, pulling the huge beams that rolled the cane out flat. The juice ran into kettles; the leftover stalk or bagasse fueled the fires. The heavy furnaces boiled the kettles until the juices foamed and steamed. In the glare of the fires, the slaves moved continually in the sticky sweet air, feeding the furnaces, stirring the kettles, ladling the boiled juices into tanks, where the molasses separated out, and brown sugar crystals gradually formed. When the sugar was finally declared fine, it was poured into hogsheads which held one thousand pounds each, loaded on plantation boats, and sent to the Weitz factor in New Orleans.

The factor, or the business agent, took the crop and sold it at the best price he could get, taking two percent for his pains. The remainder of the profit was credited to Samuel's account with the factor, after the mill portion was paid, and when Samuel ordered supplies or needed cash, he wrote a draft on the factor. In return, the factor charged interest if the bills were larger than the crop. In that way, plantation accounts could often be spread from crop to crop, year to year, and it was sometimes difficult to say who made how much.

But that sugar was highly profitable, few would deny.

Good sugar lands were worth up to one hundred dollars an acre; slaves might fetch as much as one thousand per head. Every planter, therefore, had to figure the expense of working

301

the land as at least equal to the expense of buying it. What with the mill, tools, work animals, slave housing, and the Big House to run, a planter might well have more than two hundred thousand dollars invested in his estate . . . but even then, it wasn't difficult to make ten percent on his investment each year.

And the end of the year was the reckoning. This was the grinding, the season of tension, when all hands worked until they could barely grip. Guests came for sugar-house parties to smell and sample the *cuite,* a thick syrup almost at the granulation stage. They dipped pecans in the syrup to make candy and drank sugar punch well fortified with whiskey.

The sugar parties at Beausonge were famous, and wandering groups of young people came to sample the syrup and eat from their picnic baskets under the cane shed with Amélie and Thérèse. Master Pierre and his friends often slipped a jigger or two of whiskey in the juice, and the girls then danced and dozed in the shade until called home by their drivers.

When the grinding was over, the slaves had their only celebration of the year. Usually soon after Christmas the sugar was made and barreled. Then they had their gifts, their extra food and drink, and their own music and dancing.

The last carts to come in off the fields were gaily decorated with cornstalks and flags, and the mules' whips and harnesses ornamented with flowers. Each hand was given a small poke of coins and called himself "nigger-rich," at least for a few days. The *vincanne,* a potent rum of fermented cane juice, was rolled out in great barrels, and as the last cane was crushed, the hands put up a cheer, tossing their straw hats into the crusher. The straw hats, they said, added something extra to the sugar flavor. A final blast of the mill whistle, and they all trooped to the Big House to be praised by Massa Sam.

With the start of the new year, it was time to hoe and

302

plow the newly planted fields for the next crop, and the cane cycle began again.

The first month of the year was also the time when slaves were sold off Beausonge, traded to another planter, or married to each other, if they were of the marrying age. Often a half-dozen marriages took place all at once, for after the grinding, Master would be most generous with new homespun lengths for the gals, new shoes or trousers for the boys, fresh pork, and a few new cabins for the mated pairs.

A wedding breakfast was part of the festivity, and for one day, the slaves sat down to groaning tables full of grits, thick loaves of French bread, fried oysters and shrimp, eggs, ham, gravy, milk, and butter. They ate deep and murmured to each other, "You think white folk eat like this ev'y day? Cain' be, they bus' apart, if they do!"

Celisma thought to herself that only hands who lived all the rest of the year on meal and bacon could appreciate such feasting.

The music makers strummed up after breakfast, and the slaves began their dancing which would go on until after dusk. Master Samuel and his wife gathered to watch, his son and daughters around him. Flanking them were the house niggers, who only joined the field hands in the dance as the tempo became so intoxicating they forgot their pride and position.

That New Year's, Celisma stood with Odette, watching as the black bodies swirled and stepped around the open yard. They jigged and they shuffled, dancing all at once in springs and flings and a shakedown of thumping ecstasy. From somewhere, they got horns and drums and one-string fiddles to add to the musicians' clamor. The joy of movement infected them to sing the old songs and dance the old dances: the calinda, the bamboula, and the pilchactaw, where the woman stood still and the man kneeled and writhed around her.

Celisma was wearing the new frock ol' Madame had

gifted her with this season, a simple peach-colored home-spun, but it had a bit of ivory lace round the throat and cuffs. She stood tapping her bare foot to the music, her eyes glowing and eager. Tim came and caught her arm, pulling her into the circle. She danced one whirling jig with him, then remembered herself and pulled away, sliding back to stand alongside Odette again.

"Ain' 'nuff young gals to dance this year," Odette said to her, "these bucks need more does, I 'spect. That boy put his foot good yonder. You stand here long 'nuff, an' they say you biggety-head for sure."

"I see you still standin' like you rooted," Celisma answered her back. "Step out then, *cher.* "

Odette laughed, a deep-throated bark. "It ain' these old bones they wantin', gal." As Daniel danced past, Odette pushed Celisma playfully at the man, causing her to almost stumble into his arms. He caught her, whirled her around, and then when the dancers separated into groups again, she spun off to another part of the circle.

Pierre stood there, watching her. He grinned.

She ducked her head to him politely and watched him from under her lashes. He was tall, this only son of Massa Sam, with dark hair and eyes more like Madame than his father. As might be expected from the only man-child to a Master rich as Midas, he wore his arrogance proudly, cocking one hip forward as though he straddled the world.

"Got yourself a new frock?" he asked her.

She nodded, glancing to where Odette was standing. The old woman was where she left her, her broad bosom jiggling as she stamped her feet in time to the music and clapped her hands.

"You look mighty pert in it," Pierre added.

"Ol' Madame give it to me," she said softly. "It got the lace round the neck and arms."

"I see it does. You look like a spring peach, Celly." He

304

had taken to calling her that lately, and his two sisters picked it up quick enough.

She preferred her own name, truth be known, but if he chose to name her hound, she must answer to that, too.

"Soft and ripe as a juicy peach."

She stiffened warily and averted her eyes at the changed tone in his voice. No mistaking that tone, she had heard it enough before from men, masters and masters' sons alike. Now she must tread carefully through this quicksand.

"I thank you, suh," she said politely, moving away as though to join the dancers.

He gripped her arm, keeping her by him. "Stay and tell me the words to that song they're singing, Celly. You must know the thing; I can't make it out."

She looked to her left and right as though for rescue, but the slaves on either side had melted away as Pierre spoke to her. Most were dancing and clapping and leaping about the yard now in a frenzied joy, a few of the more brazen couples slipping away into the lengthened shadows.

"Sing it to me," he said again, his voice more determined.

"Mo' té ain négresse," she faltered, her voice as small as she could make it. "I was a Negress, mo' beautiful than my mistress, I steal the pretty things from Mamzelle's armoire." She stopped in confusion, realizing that the verses became more and more dangerous as they progressed. "Dance, dance, dance, Calinda, dance, dance, dance!" She stopped singing and stepped away from him again.

He grabbed her shoulder this time, turning her with his grip, and she felt the chill of hate and fear weaken her legs.

"Please, suh—"

Odette's booming voice sounded almost in her ear. "Chile, you fixin' to get yourself whupped? Ol' Madame been callin' an' callin' for you, loud 'nuff for even *these* ol' ears to hear. Cain' you hear over the drums? She say that all the dancin' you need for one year, an' to get yourself into the house quick."

Odette then turned to Pierre politely, "Suh, *pardon-mo'*, your *maman* ask for you, young Massa. She say come." Odette turned and pointed to where Madame Matilde stood by Master Sam, watching the dancers. Celisma had not even noticed their arrival, but now that she looked back over her shoulder at Madame, she could see the dark eyes snapping. Something shrunk within her even further, and she clenched her fists to keep from trembling.

"Your pardon, suh," she said quickly, sliding out of Pierre's grasp and hurrying towards the summerhouse. As she got beyond the dancers, she picked up the skirts of her frock and ran to the cool, shadowed refuge of ol' Madame's commands.

Madame had few visitors, but those who did step up to the gallery of the summerhouse were made to feel as though time stopped when they arrived. In fact, Madame often had Celisma halt the hands of the old grandfather clock in the hallway on a visitor's arrival and start it again on their departure, just to make that point.

Her favorite visitor was her brother, Valsin. Once a week he came to sit and rock with her and speak of the old days. He was bent with age, this brother, but he still had the grin of a younger man. "Celisma," he would say to her each time on arrival, "did you drink up all my sister's orange wine yet?"

"Non, M'sieu, pas encore," she would invariably answer with a smile. It was an old jibe between them, one he appreciated most in French. Of course, he would then begin to improve her accent and insist she was born to speak no other

tongue—no pretty girl was—until Madame would beg him to leave her in peace.

Celisma would then withdraw to stand quietly to the rear of the sitting room, behind Madame's chair, where she might see the old woman's slightest gesture and respond with a filled cup or a removed plate. From her post she could look out the louvered windows to the garden, could watch the glowbugs capering around over the dark grass, could smell the pungent sweetness of the honeysuckle and the cool dark of the bayou beyond.

One night, Valsin was speaking about Simon, Madame's other son, and Celisma drifted her thoughts back to listen. She had met Samuel's brother only occasionally, most recently on the occasion of Madame's private birthday fête which she held on this very gallery for select callers, and she had wondered then why Simon did not visit his *maman* more regularly.

"And how is his health?" Madame was inquiring.

"He is well, *cher,*" Valsin said, chuckling at her. "Does a woman ever stop being a mother? Your sons are middle-aged now, past forty-five!"

"And does this mean he stops needing a mother?" she asked tartly. "*You* could have done with one a little longer, for truth, my brother. *Maman* would have taken off some of those rough edges, made you show some respect."

"Yes, I suppose she might have," Valsin said wistfully. "Do you still remember her, Oliva?"

"As though we buried her only yesterday," Madame answered gently, taking his hand. "And papa, too."

They spoke in French to each other, in fluid half-voiced thoughts, as though each knew the mind of the other almost before they finished the words. Celisma could follow most of what they said, but she knew she was barely touching what they felt.

"Well, Simon is fine, at any rate," Valsin went on, "as is Cerise. She will attend at the birth of your great-grandchild, *grandmère,* in a month or two, I'm sure. Tidings is grown huge and complains that she can barely see her toes."

"I always thought that such a strange name for my first granddaughter. Glad Tidings. A name that a Calvinist Yankee might pin on a child. I wonder what possessed Cerise."

"You never did take to her much," Valsin grinned. "The *jalousie* of *maman* when her chick finds another nest he likes better than her own! If she had named the first 'Oliva,' you would have found something to grumble about. She heard the name in New Orleans, I guess, and liked it. If it suits Simon, it shouldn't stick in your gullet."

"Anything that woman did would suit Simon. If ever I knew a man who thought a woman was made out of pure gold, that man was Simon and that woman was Cerise, hardly a woman yet after all these years and four children grown, for truth. Did I tell you she let those *'tits* run over the fields bare as robin's eggs until they were nigh to communion age? Naked bottoms every summer!"

"You are truly losing your mind, old woman. She let them go without their hippins on the hottest days before they were weaned, yes, and that makes good sense to me. Fewer laundry tubs to fill. No wonder she does not beg you to visit, *belle-mère,* your eyes would find plenty for your mouth to fault!"

Oliva grinned ruefully, acknowledging the smallest portion of truth in his words. "Ah, you're as foolish as both my sons. I never saw a pretty woman yet that wouldn't make you forget any good sense you ever had, and you a widower for a dozen years!"

"Well, you needn't worry about Simon. The mill does well, his traps are still busier than most on Lafourche, and his children are making you great-grandchildren."

"I must make the trip to see them soon. But it's harder for me to go there than for them to come here."

"You know Simon is not much welcome here," Valsin

said quietly. "Even after all these years. Matilde does not forget."

"No one does. But she must forgive, if she is to heal. Such *colère* she has, for everything, for everyone . . ."

He shrugged. "It has eaten her up, *certainement*. Cerise believes her mad."

Oliva scoffed. "She is not mad, she is only mean, and her pain has made her so. One must stand up to her, as I do. She does not trouble me."

"She troubles Samuel," Valsin said gently.

"Samuel must stand up to her as well," Oliva said stubbornly, "and Simon should come, whether or not she wants him. This house belongs to my son! And much of the land under it belonged to my husband. She has a right to her sorrow, yes, but she has made of it a crusade. Simon should come more often. I am his *maman,* and I say it."

He put his arm around her shoulder. "You know where he is, *cher,* and you know I'll take you there anytime you say. The bayou is not so long or wide as you make it. Remember when you used to paddle your own pirogue? Samuel seems glad enough to see his brother when he comes. They are busy men, both your sons, as different as two strangers sometimes. But do I need to tell you this? You're *maman* to them both—"

"Sometimes I wouldn't think so, if I hadn't seen them born."

"I know, I know, they have always broken your heart in little ways."

"Big ways, too. Biggest way was when I finally knew that brothers or no, twins to the very lines on their palms, they were somehow less alike in their minds than some cousins I see. The midwife told me when I birthed them that they would break hearts, but I never supposed one would be mine. Simon, he is stiff-necked, yes, even I must say it as *maman*. Truly, he never could forgive his brother taking slaves. No matter that the fields must be plowed and hands brought to

309

plow them, no matter that his own father had a few brutes in the early days. Simon turned a piece of his heart against his brother the day Samuel brought home the first work gang."

"His father's brutes were more like family. His brother's brutes were slaves, pure and simple, and he thinks that a great wrong. Even as a boy, he knew his mind and said it," Valsin said. "You can respect such a thing."

"I do respect it. Same as I respect his sister for her piousness. But Samuel has more to suffer than Simon, to my mind. So with him, I stay. He needs me. He is the only one who does." She sighed and leaned back, fanning herself with her linen. "*Maman* used to say that daughters come back to you *finalement,* but when the sons go, they're gone forever. Sometimes I wonder how I got such children. One so stiff-necked and one so pious, and me with my pagan heart." She grinned wryly, softly smiting her own breast. "Two twins. I bore them each alike as two dove's eggs, and I know they would die for each other, if asked. But they can't live like each other, or by each other. And I blame Simon more than Samuel, *vraiment,* for Samuel . . . he has had to come through so much. Each time I think what he must have known before he found us again, I want to weep. And he, no doubt, has long ago forgotten it. But Samuel has never known the—" she struggled for the right word. "He has never known peace as Simon has. Contentment."

"Ah, *cher,* they must make their own way. Look at you. Could either son take a wife to please you? *Non,* you find something to frown at with Cerise, you find *plenty* to frown at with Matilde—"

"As would the Sainted Mother," Oliva snapped.

Valsin chuckled gently. "Of that, I am certain. But when you complain about your two stubborn chicks, I got to say the eggs didn't fall far from the nest. And it wasn't the rooster they took after."

Oliva smiled ruefully. "No, Joseph was not a stubborn

310

man, *certainement.* He was a good man. A hard man to know sometimes, but a good man. I wish . . ." she sighed then, reaching across her slack breasts and hugging herself absently. "I wish he were alive to see to his two sons today. He could be a bridge between them, perhaps. God took him from me too soon." She grinned. "Just when I was beginning to like him well enough."

"You liked him well enough to start. Lord, I can remember how your cheeks flushed!"

"It is true," she laughed. "Always, when I looked at Joseph, I saw a man. But—well, he was hard to hold close, that one."

Valsin took another sip of his wine. "These are your only regrets, *ma soeur,* two sons who do not always see eye to eye and a husband whose memory does not always warm you? Sounds to me as though life has not been too grim to bear."

"*Non, cher,* not my only regrets. But it is not over yet. Not while I can still beat you anytime I choose at any game *you* choose. This Saturday, you call for me and we will see if Cerise still has not learned to cook *beignets* properly, eh? Tell them I come."

"You want them at home? I tell them nothing—"

A heavy step on the outside gallery silenced Valsin until he saw that it was Samuel joining them. Celisma hurried to fetch him a glass and the decanter of his favorite bourbon. Valsin stood and embraced his nephew in a bear hug.

"Your ears must be burning," Valsin grinned. "Your *maman* been talking about nothing but sons this night. Maybe I can have some decent conversation, me, now you're here."

"Conversation! That's the last thing I come here for, Uncle, when I see your hound waiting outside on the gallery. A little drinking company, mayhaps, and a laugh or two. I get enough conversation," he added, rolling his eyes ruefully, "at Matilde's table."

"Matilde entertains tonight?" his mother asked carefully.

311

"Her whist club. A covey of six fat quail, scrabbling over penny bets and whatever worms of gossip they can scratch up between them. I excused myself for some air." He took a drink of bourbon. "I daresay they won't miss me."

Oliva's eyes gleamed with mirth. "For truth."

"They're all a-twitter over the big event next month. *Maman,* you must be sure to set aside the night."

"The magnolia fête?"

"Same as every year. And Valsin, this time you must honor us with your presence. It's quite a sight to see."

Celisma swiftly remembered last year, her first at Beausonge, when the house had welcomed the best planters and their families on the river for a huge gala *bal.* The tables overflowed out onto the gallery, the dancing went on into the late hours, every bed was filled, musicians were brought up from New Orleans on the steamboats, and the house niggers twined garlands of magnolias for hundreds of yards up the gallery, the staircase, and along the hallways.

"Ah, you must excuse me again," Valsin was saying to Samuel, "but this is not for me. Have your fine friends, and then I come over a few nights later, and you can complain about them to me over your bourbon." He softly clinked his glass to Samuel's.

Celisma heard the clink and came forward quietly, thinking perhaps they needed something. Oliva looked up at her and smiled. "You needn't stay up if you're weary, child. We need nothing more, I think?" She glanced at Samuel.

"I guess not," he said, leaning back and looking up at Celisma. "That reminds me, I've had an inquiry about you, gal."

"Suh?"

"Yes, indeed. A proposal, more like. You know William, the smithy?"

She nodded mutely, her limbs tingling with dread.

"A likely boy. Skilled worker. Worth a good deal at auction, now he's trained," Samuel said to Valsin. Then back to Celisma, "Well, he's asked for you special. He's ready for a wife, I know, and he's a good man, not too old. What do you say?"

"I don't want no husband, Massa Sam," she said quickly.

There was silence at the table. Finally Samuel said, "You don't want *this* husband."

"No suh. I don' want no husband a' tall. Not never."

He frowned slightly. "And why is that, Celly?"

"Don' want no man to tell me how to do. You get a husband, you gets another master, sure as gun's iron."

Oliva said, "Of course you know that what you want makes little difference in this, child. Matilde will not have unmarried gals at Beausonge for long. You're nearly sixteen, yes? Plenty younger than you are already made mothers. Master Samuel did not bring you all the way from Rosewood just to tend to an old woman's needs, I'm sure—"

"Are you displeased with her?" Samuel asked.

"*Mais non, cher,* Celisma suits me well. But she can still suit me well and suit a husband, too. I suppose Matilde will have her in the quarters sooner or later."

"I rather like the idea of her sleeping here with you," he said, "but, of course, it's customary to have them mated off before sixteen, makes for less trouble all around . . ." with that he glanced up at Celisma and made a noise in his throat of surprise.

She stood slightly behind his chair, still as golden marble, tears making twin tracks down her cheeks. Oliva and Valsin noticed her at the same instant.

"There now, Celly, there's no reason for this. If you won't have William, then I'll tell him so," Samuel said mildly. He reached out and lightly squeezed her wrist. "Go on up now and get your rest. It's been a long day for all of us."

Celisma nodded silently and left the gallery. As she went through the door, she heard Valsin say, "You're good to them, Sam. Plenty would marry them off and get them bred fast as the fields need them."

"Well, I can't see the advantage of making them miserable. You know, I'm trying the task system now, just to see if it works. Instead of a gang system, where they all work under a driver—you know I've had to hire and fire four different overseers in the past three years, they're all a scurvy lot—I'm experimenting with what I call a task system, where each slave has a specific daily work assignment. If he works well, he quits early. Helps motivate them, I think, also helps weed out the poor workers."

"Gives them pride in their work, I would say," Valsin said thoughtfully.

"That's the idea. Of course, it might not be as efficient, I don't know. I'm still trying it out. They do like to specialize themselves, no matter what sort of system you put them to. The cook never wants to enter the house, and the upstairs gal won't set foot in the kitchen. The wash gal won't touch an iron, and the ironing wench never puts hands in a laundry tub. It'll drive you mad just keeping track of their own caste ranking, but you get to see the sense in it and respect it."

"It makes a difference, I think, not being raised with them," Oliva said quietly. "We weren't, my sons weren't, and so to us, they are people. To Matilde, who was raised with them at her command, they are . . . furnishings. Like her clothes, to wear out as needed. But Celisma's a good girl, I would miss her."

Celisma had stopped to listen in the shadows, and she saw Samuel turn to look where she had gone for a long moment. He could not see her, she knew, but there was a question in his eyes which she could not read. Then he turned back to the table and said, "Yes, well, we'll put this aside for now. Did you hear, *maman,* about Pierre's latest scape? He must take after you, Valsin. He was courting the youngest Landry daughter, you know, and challenged his rival to a duel. The young fool! When I heard, I went to Landry myself—"

Celisma left the drifting voices behind her as she slowly mounted the stairs in the darkness. This would not be the last time that they would try to bridle her to a man. William. He was a tall, strong set of shoulders with a nap of black wool and black sweating skin, that's all he was to her. Once he called to her as she passed the forge, to come see how he made rose nails with only four hammer hits. The nail rods were gleaming red, steaming and hissing, and he grinned as she backed away, taking her wariness for awe.

Now he followed her with his eyes as she passed on her way to the laundry, but many eyes followed her, and she took no more notice of them than the gnats at the corners of her mouth when she was root-hunting in the cool shadows.

Her tears had turned his heart. He was set on it, Massa Sam was, until he saw her cry. And then he reached out and squeezed her, telling her to go take her rest.

She reached the top of the landing and looked down at her wrist, slim and finely haired, expecting to see his mark on her skin. The moonlight coming in the window made her flesh glow as though it had an inner heat, and she felt it down to her fingers.

Preparation for the magnolia fête began more than a month in advance of the event itself. Each year, Madame Matilde tried to arrange something so special that her guests would remember this night at Beausonge more than any other. For this soirée season, she selected an English garden theme and set the slaves to building the Beausonge Mountain, a hillock twenty feet high. In a land as flat as a lake, her creation easily became the only mound of its size for miles on each side of the river.

She sent away for a Chinese pagoda to top Beausonge

Mountain, with stained-glass windows and hundreds of tiny silver bells to tinkle in any breeze. When guests were seated within, they could look out on a vista of promenades, a small silver blue lake, and swans gliding in serene beauty. The hillock had a perfect grotto carved within for lovers, but since the grotto could be seen clearly from the upstairs gallery, it offered no real privacy.

"We must get doves for the grotto," Matilde said to Samuel, over a late supper three nights before the ball. "I've sent to Baton Rouge and New Orleans, and there are simply none to be had."

"I guess everyone's using doves this year," he said, picking through his collards to avoid the onions. Onions disagreed with his digestion, but they invariably turned up in every dish of greens, no matter how he might mention his preference to Matilde.

"Nightingales!" she said with a burst of inspiration. "They're rather Chinese, aren't they? Perfect for a pagoda, much better than doves, in fact."

"And where do you propose finding nightingales at this late date?"

"That is something your agent will have to worry about. I'm sure he can manage *that* small detail. God knows, I've done everything else. He's there in New Orleans, he knows everyone, I'm certain he can find them quick enough."

"Graham's job as my factor is to broker the crop, and he does that admirably. He is not obliged to secure furnishings for your soirées."

"*My* soirées! Don't delude yourself, my heart. I don't wear myself out like this for *my* pleasure, but because it is a responsibility, given our position. People expect a fête at Beausonge to rival any on the river, and I don't mean to disappoint them. And as to Graham, he procures all the other supplies we require, I don't see why he should not be expected to fulfill that same function for our social obligations." She cut a small piece of beef even smaller and chewed

316

it vigorously. "Besides, I cannot do everything, it's too much. If you would give me even the slightest help with this, Samuel, then perhaps I wouldn't have to impose on Graham. As it is, he'll simply have to take up your slack."

Samuel's eyes narrowed and his jaw firmed. "Matilde, I said nothing when you took six of my best hands away from the levees to build your moronic mountain—though I fail to see what possible contribution such an effort will make to a pleasant gathering of friends. I also said nothing when you blocked the canals and floated swans over an acre of seed cane. You're spending forty percent more on this extravaganza of yours than you spent last year, and I still don't quibble. So don't tell me I haven't made a contribution. But nightingales! What is so damned important about a pagoda anyway—"

"It is not the pagoda, of course, it is the fête itself. I intend for the parish to remember this magnolia festival more than any other at Beausonge, and if you paid attention to the fact that you have two daughters nearing marriageable age and a son who has not yet found himself a partner, you might applaud rather than hinder my efforts."

"Oh for God's sake, Matilde, if you worried a trifle more about Pierre's temper and a trifle less about fêtes, he might have found himself a woman by now."

"He has his father's temperament," she said smoothly. "And with it, his father's passion."

"He goes far past any passion *I've* ever allowed myself, certainly past any you've allowed in your presence for years—"

She gazed at him pointedly. "I said he has *his* father's passion."

His jaw steeled. "And I am to interpret that in any way I will, as always." He passed a hand over his eyes in an effort to calm himself. "Madame, you have never once, in two decades, allowed me to consider the boy my own. Whether he is actually my blood or not—"

317

At her swift gasp, he dropped his voice and the words into a weary and more practiced cadence. "At any rate, now that he is grown, I can scarcely call up the concern you might wish that he is so far unbetrothed. And as for the girls—"

"Don't you dare speak of my girls," she snapped.

"Oh, are they your private property now, too?" He shook his head. "Nightingales. You go past the bounds of good taste, my dear, and I fear you'll provide amusement for our neighbors all right, but not the kind you intend. They may smile at your gaucheries, but it'll be behind your back." He set down his napkin and got up as though to leave the table.

"Don't you dare say such a thing and walk away," Matilde said, her voice low and full of venom. "You have the effrontery to question *my* good taste?" She set down her fork and flattened her hands on the table as though to hold it down. "Let me see. This is the same man who rides uptop the buggy with Ulysses each Sunday to Mass, rather than following behind on his best mount so that the whole congregation can see he'd rather merrily chat away with his ol' nigger than ride alongside his son. The same man who will excuse himself from the presence of any number of prominent and fascinating supper guests to go out and drink his bourbon with his swamp-rat of an uncle, an old woman, and a useless yellow wench." She stood now, bracing herself on the table, her eyes pinning his. "The same man who thinks he can sneak down to the quarters to whore after some nigger night after night and not have all of Beausonge see him come and go, to the deep personal mortification of his wife and two daughters. Do tell me about good taste, Samuel. I'm so anxious to take a lesson from your book."

Samuel blanched at this last, recovered, and pulled himself to an aloof and dignified withdrawal. He guessed that she had likely observed his occasional visits to the quarters, but he also knew that such visits were not uncommon for men in his position. What was uncommon was for any wife to speak of such aloud.

behind her to see that the door to the corridor was closed and lowered her voice. "He his mama's chile, that one. She let on that he ain' none of his papa, but thas' jes' somethin' she say to torment M'sieu with her punishments. I know, I be with her since she come to Beausonge. Ain' no man been with that woman 'cept her married husband. An' Pierre be all o' Massa Sam, even if she won' let him think so. She take his son 'cause he took hers, jes' for pure spite. But she ruin him, sure. That boy got too much too soon, you ask me. Got his own buggy when he only six, an' a nigger to polish his boots. Got his own steamboat—" at Celisma's exclamation, she added, "Yes, chile, an' more niggers to float it, too! Got the box at the o-pere-a, they say, an' nother one at the *musicales.* Think hisself *le grand M'sieu,* sure 'nuff, but he don't work at much round Beausonge. 'Cept fixin' up more trouble for Massa Sam to mend over. He do take after his *maman* in that, *certainement.*"

"He got a smilin' eye," Celisma said softly.

"I see he put it on you, too," Odette replied with a snap of the shears. "If I was you, gal, I be lookin' aside from that eye each time it fall on me. Ain' nothin' good in that eye for you."

"I know that," Celisma answered.

"You be glad you got ol' Madame to stand 'tween you an' him, else he take what he want an' he make out like you want it, too. Then you catch Madame's eye and be sold at Baton Rouge or worse, 'fore you can spit."

"Well, I guess ol' Madame might got somethin' to say 'bout that," Celisma bridled, just a little proud. "She like to say she cain' get by without me, nohow."

Odette barked her laugh. "She might have somethin' to say all right but it won' make no nevermind when the wind blow hard. We know who gots the hardest blow in *this* house. An' little ol' blooms like you get trompled in the storm, no matter who say what." She frowned now and lowered her voice more. "I seen it more'n once, chile, an' I warn you.

Madame don' have no scruples when it come to riddin' herself o' what troubles her. You jes' think on Passi, an' you wonder if you that much smarter than that poor gal was—" She stopped and cocked her head at the closed door, as though it had ears. Suddenly, her manner changed. Rising and fluffing out the skirt she was hemming, she called out brightly, "This be the pertest red I ever seen. Make young Miss look like a rose in June, sure 'nuff."

And she said no more that day.

The night of the magnolia ball, Celisma was set to hanging the wraps as they were brought to her by the gals at the door, and so she sat in a back room surrounded by more than a hundred matched pairs of corsages and boutonnieres. Madame did not want her out where the guests might see her, but as the house niggers brought back the shawls and capes, she was to hang each one carefully pinned with a different colored corsage. The matching corsage or buttonhole flower was then carried back to the guest to wear and for claiming the wrap later.

The advantage of her post was that she would likely be needed only at the beginning and the end of the evening. In between, she was free to watch out the window at the strolling couples around the swan lake and in the gardens, or to creep to the top of the stairs and peer down at the guests while hidden in the masses of magnolias which banked the balcony and stairwell. The white *tignon* she wore about her head almost exactly matched their creamy hue.

The bustle below her of elegant heads and fine white shoulders swathed in brilliant colored silks and satins was at first too much to take in all at once. The noise of their greetings and laughter and banter! As though a hundred peacocks and peahens were suddenly set loose in the house, they bobbed and elbowed and gently careened off one another, calling above the din of tinkling ice and glass, the blare of the musicians from the ballroom, and the comings and goings of carriages beyond the open doors.

Massa Sam and Madame stood at the entryway, welcoming folks as they alighted, calling out to favorites and beckoning them within. They each stood on opposite sides of the doors and never looked at each other once, so that folks stepping up had to make a choice to go to one or the other, parting in the middle like a surging tide and then spilling over into the ballroom or the gallery where the heavy tables of steaming food were spread.

Miss Amélie stood a little ways back from her mother, embracing special friends and bowing to gentlemen. Miss Thérèse stood at her mother's elbow, Pierre right behind her, and it was her laugh and rising voice which could be heard most clearly over the fiddles and the pipes.

Massa Sam stood with his mother at his side, and Oliva seemed as beautiful and strong as Celisma had ever seen her. She did not wait for hands to reach out to her, but stepped forward to embrace and welcome with an energy that belied her years.

Each time Caro or Mignon, the house niggers, started up the stairs with a cloak or shawl, Celisma had to duck back from her magnolia thicket and scuttle to the wrap room, then she'd slip back into hiding to spy down on the party.

As the evening wore on, few folk lingered in the entryway below the stairs, for the ballroom and the gallery held them fast. Once Celisma slipped down and peeped into the ballroom to see the whirling couples. She saw ol' Madame dancing with an ancient gentleman with a beard like a goat, her heels moving as swiftly as the youngest pair in the hall. But then Celisma hurried back to her post, lest she be spotted down among the guests, and leaned on the balcony, stretching her neck to see what she might see.

From out her upstairs window post, she watched Pierre enter the grotto in Beausonge Mountain and sit himself down, as though he waited for someone. It was dusk, and Celisma could scarcely see his face, but he lit a cigar once inside, and she could follow the movement of its glowing tip.

After a few moments, a nigger gal approached, and Celisma thought for an instant that she had been summoned, she hurried so. It was Polly from the laundry, a young wench new-brought from Baton Rouge. A few feet from the grotto, she stopped and looked about her, slowing her pace and swishing her skirts. She ducked inside the grotto and Celisma could not see her clearly, but Massa Pierre came into the fading light then, and she saw him shake his head and shoo her away.

From down the path came a young white lady, a pert and beribboned miss in dark blue ruffles, and this one, Pierre welcomed inside the grotto's shadows. When they had not emerged for long moments, Celisma went back to her balcony post.

From there, she watched as the guests milled back and forth: men stood with their heads together, discussing politics and crops, their stiff white shirts puffed and ruffled, their voices rising and falling in steadfast opinions; women whispered and laughed behind their fans, occasionally calling out gaily to pull another into their tight ring of white shoulders; niggers dipped and weaved around them bearing trays of syllabub and sack, almost as invisible as the shadows; and Celisma saw it all.

Just about the time she was weary of watching, Pierre and a young miss slipped into a shadow by the door, shielded by the huge grandfather clock from view of the gallery. She was speaking low to him, and he had his hands on her shoulders, trying to keep her from going. But she was clearly having none of his hands, and finally, she wrenched herself away from him and Celisma heard her say, "I should have listened, they were all right about you, all of them. You're faithless and not worth the tears!" With that, she began to shed them, putting her hands to her face.

Massa Sam walked through the entry at that moment, saw the two, and stopped. He turned cold eyes on his son, but his voice was gentle to the young miss. "Vivette, my dear, let me fetch your wrap for you and the buggy. Pierre can escort you home, if you wish."

She took her hands away from her eyes and fell against the master's chest, sobbing softly.

"Go and get her wrap," Samuel snapped as he removed her flower from her shoulder and tossed it to Pierre. "Be quick."

Pierre glowered at his father but he turned and strode up the stairs, Celisma fleeing silently before him. She plucked up the shawl and turned to hand it to him when he came in. He stopped, glared at her suspiciously, and then turned around back down the stairs again. Celisma waited—one breath, two breaths—then slid out behind him to her spy post. She saw Massa Sam usher the two out the door, patting the young miss on the shoulder softly with not a word to his son. He turned then and moved swiftly towards the stairs, looking directly at her instead of his feet, as most folk did as they came up.

She froze, unable to move.

Massa Sam came up to the landing, a few yards below her. "Celisma, I see you there."

She emerged slightly, dropping her head in shame.

"You've been there all evening?"

She nodded, clasping her hands before her.

"Madame doesn't need you to serve?"

"She don' like for me to be with the folks, suh," she murmured. "Say for me to stay up here with the shawls an' such."

"Come out here in the light where I can see you."

She lifted her head and stepped out from her camouflage. She did not look away as he gazed her up and down.

"Well, I don't know why she wouldn't want to show you off to our guests, you're certainly one of the handsomest gals in the house. Grace should never be hidden away where it shines unseen. But then, I've never pretended to understand Madame in all her decisions."

Celisma allowed herself a small smile.

"Has it been a good fête, do you think?"

"*Très élégante, M'sieu,*" she said quickly. "The finest I seen."

"And you've seen many?"

"Not so many, Massa Sam."

"I don't like it when you call me that."

"*Non?* Then what, suh?"

"M'sieu is good enough, I think. I don't own you after all, my mother does. I gave you to her a few months back, didn't she tell you?"

Celisma smiled with pleasure and surprise. "*Non, M'sieu, merci, M'sieu!*"

"This pleases you?"

"Ah, yes! Madame is good, suh."

"Well," he said softly, "I'm glad you're pleased. And you'll take good care of her faithfully?"

She looked at him then with all her heart in her eyes. "Until I die, M'sieu."

He chuckled gently. "No one could ask for more than that, then. You may stay here watching, if it pleasures you, but take care not to stand too tall. The top of your *tignon* gleams like ice in this light."

She dropped a curtsy as he turned and went back down the stairs. Then she fled to the wrap room in flushed confusion.

Later that evening, Oliva came up to the room and went directly to the window where she could look down on Beausonge Mountain and the grotto within. Celisma saw anger form on her lips, and she was about to go to her to thank her for taking her on from Massa Sam, when Madame Matilde swept into the room, her dangling ear-bobs glistening in the moonlight. Celisma drew back into the shadows quietly.

"Ah, there you are, *ma mère,*" Matilde said coolly, "M'sieu DeLonge is taking his leave and has asked for you especially."

Madame turned from the window. "I'm surprised he asked for anyone from this household, considering the way his daughter has been treated this night."

"Why, what do you mean?"

"If I saw it, I imagine half of our guests did as well. Pierre was shameful this evening, Matilde, shameful to Vivette De-Longe. So shameful that Samuel had to interfere and have her carriage brought round. Really, Matilde," she said, her voice growing more indignant. "You must speak to Pierre! He has insulted more than a few of the young ladies in the parish, I believe. Perhaps more even than you know. If you won't speak to him, I will, for I won't have the daughters of my dear friends brought to tears in my own house!"

"*Your* own house?" Matilde smiled, but there was little of joy there.

"My son's house, then. If you cannot deal with him, I will ask Samuel to do so. Else the time will come when no man will let his daughter be escorted by Pierre Weitz, no matter how many mountains you build in the cane fields!"

Matilde laughed lightly, adjusting her gloves so that they once more covered her elbows. "*Ma mère* you make too much of a simple lovers' quarrel. It is a pity that the girl has so little poise, *vraiment,* as to let a young man make her weep at a fête where all can see. But I see no reason to apologize for Pierre's behavior. After all," she added confidentially, "you know it is the woman who controls these things. Perhaps her *maman* needs to teach her a trick or two about handling a man of . . . passion. For certainly, Pierre can be handled. By the right woman."

"Oh, you would excuse him if he set fire to Saint Louis," Oliva snapped. "I can see I am wasting my breath. Samuel will know how to deal with him. I will make my apologies to M'sieu DeLonge, and I will ask Samuel to do the same."

"You may apologize to whom you choose, but it will do you as little good to speak to Samuel as it will for him to speak to Pierre. Samuel can do nothing with him." She turned to face Oliva squarely. "He never has."

"Because you will not let him," Oliva said. "Why, Matilde? Why do you punish him still? You are punishing your own son as well."

"I doubt Pierre feels the lack," Matilde answered calmly. "I do not punish Samuel, *ma mère.* I gave him two other children, did I not?"

"But no other son. You would not let him have his son."

"His son. That is true. He had one son and gave him up. I will not give up mine." She swept from the room, her head high and defiant.

"Matilde—!" Oliva cried out after her.

Matilde turned at the door. "Madame, you of all people should surely understand. You would not give up your son, no not even to death, not when your own husband told you that he was lost. Am I to be less of a mother than you? I let his father have his will with one son, I will not do so again."

When Matilde had gone, Oliva turned once more to the window and Celisma could see her shoulders slump with weary despair. In that moment, she could see the woman's age about her like a heavy, musty cloak. She heard Oliva sigh and saw her pass a hand before her eyes, as though to wipe away an old memory. She shrank back into the shadows again and out the door to let her madame have the silence, undisturbed.

When Simon Weitz came to visit, Madame made a special flurry of celebration to welcome her other son. He tromped up the gallery steps to the summerhouse carrying his accordion box, and she enfolded him with embraces and chattered scoldings all at once. Celisma smiled to see her so excited, almost like a young miss with a beau who had been neglecting her—but was still a favorite.

She sent over to the Big House for platters of fried shrimp and oysters and catfish, fussing at Betzy that the *beignets* must be made just so for the man, sending back a batch before she was satisfied.

Samuel joined them, and she sat with her sons, drinking more coffee than she should, leaning towards them and smiling into their faces, as Simon played her the old songs again and again.

Celisma was fascinated by this mirror of Massa Sam. She had seen twins before, but not whitefolk twins who were full-grown men. The two looked much alike, but she could tell the difference right off.

Simon had his mother's gestures, his mother's voice, and accent; Samuel only had his mother's face.

"There's been some smallpox in Lafourche," Simon was saying. "Cerise is worried for Tiding's *bébé, vraiment.* Mostly, it only troubles the young ones or *les vieux* these days, but it is still nothing to take lightly. Downriver to Terrebone, they tell a tale, for truth."

"Tell it, tell it," Oliva touched his hand eagerly.

Samuel laughed, "If I got half of New Orleans to come tell her the latest gossip, she'd still rather hear what goes on downriver."

Simon shook his head with his brother in rueful agreement and went on, "You know old Guidry's granddaughter? The one the women said is no better than she has to be? Colette, she is called."

"Not to speak to, but I remember old Guidry well enough. If she is anything like him, she wouldn't care what they called her," Oliva replied.

"And so she did not," Simon added. "Well, she took up with the husband of Inez Martinez, you remember her? And

Martinez, he couldn't keep away from that Colette, no matter how his wife she weep and the priest, he scold. But Martinez, he come down with the smallpox, and that kept him to his own bed well enough. Inez, she nursed him and nursed him, praying for *le bon Dieu* to let him live. He had a bad case of it, they say, and nobody in Terrebone would come to their cabin for fear of it. But nobody told Colette. She was up in New Orleans and then come back, looking for her old Martinez to keep her company again. When he didn't come and didn't come, she goes right to his cabin, looking for him."

"*Sacré nom!*" Oliva said, her hand to her breast. "Such shamelessness! Never in my day—"

"Well, Inez met her at the door. She says, it's good you came. He's out of his head and calling for you, and I want him to die a happy man. Colette says she knows how to make him happy all right, and she goes into the cabin, all smiles. But when she sees those white sores all over Martinez, she turns to run, screaming. But Inez, she wrestles her to the ground, snatches a rope she had to tie Martinez to the bed in his fits and fevers, and hogties Colette to the bed beside him."

"That's murder," Samuel said wonderingly.

"That's justice," Oliva sniffed.

"For four days, Martinez don't wake up, and Inez keeps Colette tied to the bed, no matter how much she curses and screams and begs to be set free. Inez just nurses her man, feeds them both, and never sleeps. Finally, Martinez comes to just enough to see Colette and then dies a happy man. By now, Colette, she don't feel too good, *non*. Inez washes her man and buries him and then sets Colette free. But Colette is too weak to run. By morning, the white sores are all over her body."

"Did Inez leave her to die?" Oliva asked.

"She nursed her, too. Buried her right by Martinez a week ago."

Oliva's eyes were wide and gleeful with the tale. She gestured Celisma forward, her eyes never leaving Simon's face. "Have you ever heard of such goings-on, Celisma? You think my son made up this tale just to shock me into a swoon?"

"I think if he did, he should come with 'nother one soon," Celisma said, smiling. "I don' see you so happy in a month."

Oliva rearranged her mouth. "I'm not happy, why do you say such a thing, child? Such misfortune!"

Celisma laughed, touching her mistress lightly on the shoulder. "No need to be shamed of smilin' at such stories. I got to smile, too, an' I don' know any folk downriver. Mos' wives be smilin' at such stories, I 'spect. Maybe mos' husbands, too. Onliest one not smilin' be the gal got between them."

"Well, there's certain truth in that," Simon said. "This one's got a wise head, you better keep her around."

"We intend to," Samuel said heartily, looking up at Celisma with fondness.

Because he was looking at her, he did not see that ol' Madame and Simon caught his look and exchanged one of their own. But Celisma saw it. She ducked her head in sudden confusion as the heat rose up her neck.

Her answering smile was as timorous as her heart.

In May, Simon came to take Oliva on her once-yearly trip to New Orleans to visit her daughter, Emma. For the first time, Celisma was selected to accompany Madame, for as Oliva said, "I'll not have those city wenches handling my things again, the last time half my clothes were mildewed by the time we got back to Beausonge, not a single tissue among them! You needn't drag that huge trunk in here, child, the smaller one will do. A week in the city is all I can stomach."

The trip up Bayou Lafourche was exciting enough, since Celisma had never been on a steamboat before. It pulled right to the Beausonge dock, whistling and blowing like a mighty white stallion, and the three of them stepped aboard, clutching the rails against the movement from the ship's own wake. Pennants fluttered from its double stacks, and the rolling paddle wheels reflected the still water at the dock. A huge white layer cake with blazing lights, the steamboat took them away then, and they went to their cabins.

Celisma peeped inside the grand salon when they passed. Red velvet hung from the walls and green palms stood in the corners. The bar was as long as one gallery at Beausonge, and the orchestra was already tuning up in the corner for the grandly dressed ladies and gentlemen who strolled around the decks, bowing to each other and gazing at the plantations going by and the towns of Labadieville, Paincourtville, and Donaldsonville.

If the bayou was a sleeping water, then the Mississippi was its rolling mother, the widest, mightiest, muddiest stretch of water Celisma had ever seen. She had heard of the Big Muddy, of course, but never seen or felt its silent power. The steamboat turned into its tide and south to New Orleans.

The river pulled them along, and she saw the way the waters had eaten away at the earth, exposing the raw roots of the oaks in great gulping bites of flood times. The bare red soil laced with the roots looked like the inside of a man's body with his white muscles showing, fearful and sad-making in her heart. Next flood, she thought, the waters will rise and cover it all with mud again . . . and once again will eat it away.

For a day and a night the engines steamed and the vessel slid through the water. The salon was filled always with men at poker—wide-hatted, broad-gesturing planters and quiet sharps with soft voices and hard eyes. Sporting ladies swept past the railings and dark-frocked matrons drew their skirts aside, whispering to their men. Couples danced in the ball-room to violin music, and river boatmen sprawled on the upper decks, drinking their whiskey and telling their coarse jibes.

Celisma heard as well, from the reaches of the ship, the soft low songs of the niggers, throaty and muted, matching the rhythms of the pulsing wheel as they fed the furnaces and the white folks, too.

When the steamboat closed on New Orleans, Celisma had to step back from the rail, for the white folks crowded forward to see the city sprawled white and pink before them. The wind was brisk and heavy with the sweet smell of molasses, the pungency of spices, and the waters near the docks were flecked with wisps of white cotton floating on the tide.

So many folks packed the walkways along the river!

"What you think, Celisma?" Simon asked her, bringing Madame up to the rail to see. "They say Paris is no finer."

"Paris," she murmured. "That French city, I hear of it. Cain' be no grander than New Orleans."

"Might smell a bit sweeter," Oliva sniffed, holding a square of linen to her nose. "I always said I wanted to make the wind blow my direction. *Ma foi!*"

Now they could smell the odors from the docks, the mix and mélange of a thousand barges and bales. Spoiling fruit stacked in the sun, tobacco, hemp, skins of animals, salted meats, kegs of pork, barrels full of pickled foods, rum, tar, coffee, and always cotton: bales of cotton piled high, white, and gleaming on the open wharves.

"If it rains?" Celisma asked, pointing to the exposed crop.

Simon shrugged. "Thousands of bales every day coming downriver. A few hundred spoiled don't matter no more than last season's bird nests."

Vessels crowded in everywhere of all sizes, shapes, and colors: sassy little plantation boats getting in everybody's way, slaveboats off-loading gangs of shackled blacks on their way to market, floating bawdy houses with big gaudy banners and red shutters, shanty boats of peddlers rowing up and down with their wares. Grandest were the steam-packets like the one they rode, white and big-shouldered, edging against each other at the landings along Canal Street. On one side were the ocean-going ships, gray sails furled, gangplanks letting down sailors in the garb of a dozen different nations. On the other American side of the Quarter, the flatboats and keelboats huddled together like gulls, ready for a sale or a fight, whichever happened first.

Simon led the way off the ship; Oliva followed, with Celisma carrying Madame's smaller valise behind them. A dock nigger carried the trunk to a waiting buggy, and they climbed in, settling themselves for the ride to the Ursulines.

To Celisma, it all seemed a din and a hurry of folks going all which ways at once. Yankees with wide grins and strange beards moved by the crowds with slower-ambling Creoles. Some Kaintucks argued over a horse tied before a café. In the narrow passageways between the streets, tin-roofed shanties sold sailors' trinkets, and grogshops were so crowded with customers that new folks coming must line up outside. Here and there they passed an oyster stand, with a man holding up open shells to display his wares. Blind men played fiddles, children jigged for pennies, Spaniards hawked flowers, and nigger women waddled by, their hair wrapped in colorful *tignons,* calling out to customers about what they carried in the baskets on their heads.

"It makes my head ache," Oliva leaned over and said to Simon suddenly. "The everlasting jostling and babble. Listen to them! Swearing and whooping and halooing. Crying, cheating, and stealing—"

"You ever live in 'Nawlins, Madame?" Celisma ventured.

"Mais oui, cher, too many years ago to count. I never liked it much then and I like it less now." A thundering wagon went by close to their buggy, and she covered her ears

and winced. "I bet they never hear the birds sing in these streets."

Celisma thought that a likely wager. On each side of them, heavy clattering drays pulled by braces of mules raced down the thoroughfare. They sped ahead of the carriage and then blocked the next turn in a tie-up with two other carriages. The drivers leaped out and shouted and threatened, as more carriages and drays pulled up and could not move forward. A few swept by at the edges, missing the fruit stands by inches, making folks jump back, colliding with others trying to sneak by in the same direction.

It was hotter in New Orleans, with the rains late, yet stagnant water stood in the gutters, in shallow ponds under the houses, and along the outer swamplike reaches. The mosquitoes seemed to be worse in the city, as well, with little breeze to keep them off. M'sieu Simon told her that men in their offices erected frames over their table and chairs and worked under *barres,* the mosquito netting they had to use at Beausonge only a few months of the year. Here in the city, housewives must even put sacks of muslin over their heads and arms to do their work, and cover their bird cages with netting lest their canaries be devoured alive.

Celisma had never slept under a *barre,* never knew a slave who did. The skeeters didn't trouble dark skin so much as white. Madame had to be tucked into her bed with the netting all round her each night, and Celisma would wake, sometimes, and hear them buzzing, trying to reach that white skin without success. They might then fall on her as second-choice, but she rubbed her skin with one of her salves, and they didn't feed long.

The convent of the Ursulines rose before them, gray and massive in the shadows of overhanging oaks. They could see the rows of dormer windows two stories above the street, set in graceful curves under the cypress roof. An entire village could be housed here, Celisma thought, and she tried to picture the rows of nuns within, with their stiffened linen cowls and wimples.

Madame did not hesitate but approached the iron grating on the door as though she had a right to be there. On the other side sat a nun on a plain wooden chair in dim light.

Madame spoke to her in a low voice. "Wait," the nun said.

Celisma heard the ssh-ssh of her skirts as she moved to open the door, which let in a wide line of light to a garden within. She felt herself pressed down to sober silence by the height of the walls and their blue gray mass . . . a place where even the sun hesitated to intrude. She could dimly hear a murmur from within the convent, a string of *Aves* and *Paters* from unseen voices, all female.

And then another nun approached them. Madame stepped forward and embraced her, was embraced in turn as they touched cheeks. Simon held the nun softly by the shoulders, kissing both her cheeks and hands.

"Emma, you look well," Oliva said heartily. "A bit more plump than my last visit, I think. Did you enjoy the preserves?"

"You mustn't bring more of those temptations, *maman,*" Emma scolded lightly. "You know I cannot resist them, and then I must say a penance for my weakness."

"Then you will be on your knees for a fortnight," Simon teased her, holding up a basket which Celisma knew contained more of Betzy's fresh strawberry preserves and a carafe of orange flower wine.

"Ah me!" Emma moaned, wringing her hands. "Come, you must tell me all the news," she said, taking her mother's arm and strolling down a garden path.

Simon hesitated for a moment, then set down the basket on a low brick edging and gestured Celisma to the bench. He sat down beside her. "I cannot imagine living a life here," he said, almost absently. "But my sister's been here since the war. I guess she's happy enough. Never seemed to want anything else. *Le bon dieu* calls those He wants most, yes?"

She knew that he didn't really expect her to answer.

"You are good for my mother, you know?"

She smiled gratefully.

"My brother tells me that she depends on you."

"It is good to hear that, suh," she said softly, feeling shy around this man who looked so like Massa Sam.

"He has much on his mind, it is good he needn't worry about *maman* as well."

"She kind to me, suh." Then, sensing that she might dare, she said, "Young Madame don' like me much though."

He looked closely at her, as though seeing her clearly for the first time. "That does not surprise me," he said softly. "But you shouldn't let it trouble you, Celly. She doesn't like much of anybody."

"No, suh. Why that be?"

He looked away, hesitating. "Matilde is not a happy woman. Things haven't worked out for her the way she wanted. Regrets and losses. I guess, by her lights, life is not fair."

Celisma smiled wryly. "She say a truth there." Her smile dwindled. "But she can rage more than any woman I seen."

"Yes," he said faintly, "she has a talent for it."

Emma and Oliva were rounding the bend of the brick pathway now, and came to stand before Celisma, gazing down at her with a smile. "So. This is the little wench who sleeps at the foot of *maman's* bed these days?"

Oliva patted Celisma fondly on the top of her head. "She is a good companion," she said warmly. "Good hands and a good head. I haven't been lonely since she came."

Emma took something out of her pocket and pressed it into Celisma's hand. "Then we must reward her for her loyalty, yes?"

Celisma opened her hand and found a small carved cameo brooch of coral hue and beautiful delicacy. "Oh, Ma-

337

dame!" she breathed, glancing from Oliva to Emma. "*C'est vraiment à moi?*"

"Yes, it is for you to keep," Emma said. "From what I hear, you have earned it."

Madame patted Celisma again and then said to Simon, "Come and walk and tell Emma about Tidings and the *bébé!*" Simon rose to walk with them while Celisma carefully tied the brooch in her deepest pocket. She watched him move from sunlight to dappled shade and thought that he was somehow much shorter than his brother, something she had not noticed before.

It was planned that Madame and Simon would visit Emma for five days, once after matins in the morning, and once before prayer in the evening. They were lodging at the inn across from the Ursulines, where the proprietor apologized that the furnishings were not up to the standards of Beausonge. But Madame seemed not even to see the faded counterpane and the frayed curtains. She sat for long hours before the window which faced the convent, daydreaming and watching for the nuns passing within.

Once Celisma remarked quietly, "What you starin' after, Madame? Can you see their faces?"

Oliva shook her head slowly. "I'm looking for an angel, I think." She did not turn from the window. "I lost a baby here long ago. In this town, close to this very street. I always thought it was a girl-child."

"You birthed a baby dead?"

"I never birthed it at all." She vaguely waved her hand. "Too many years ago to count. But I still remember. And I guess I think I'll see her hovering over those walls, or maybe walking past them if I look long enough. One of my few hard regrets." She smiled and glanced up at Celisma. "I guess that sounds *'tit fou, non?* The old woman has lost her mind."

Celisma smiled and touched her shoulder lightly. "Ain' nothin' crazy 'bout missin' a babe who should have come to your arms."

338

"That is so. Some women *do* lose their minds." She rose and dusted off her skirt. "Don't you want children of your own ever?"

She thought for a moment. "Maybe someday. But it ain' easy for a yaller gal to hope for such. We a mingled people, us niggers, but we got our pride, same as white folk. They cain't slave our wishin' none. Ain' no *femme de couleur* gointa take up with a black man, les' her babes be blacker than her, takin' one step back 'stead of forward. Ain' no white man gointa 'nowledge no son o' mine, an' so long as I belong to Beausonge, I cain' be traipsin' to find a likely husband where he might lie." She dropped her hand and turned away slightly. "So, even if I wants the babes, I may not have 'em. No sense in feedin' on heart meat over that one."

"Sometimes I think your people hold yourselves back just as much as slavery holds you down," Oliva said gently.

"That's a truth," Celisma said. "Sometimes we like a passel of crabs in a basket. The minute we see one climbin' too high, the rest of us got to reach up an' grab him an' pull him back. Ain' no one of us gointa get nowhere if the rest can help it."

"Well," Oliva replied, turning back to her window. "You're young yet. There's plenty of time for you to change your mind."

Celisma said, suddenly brisk, "Now, Madame, there ain' no reason we cain' be visitin' longer, if you want. M'sieu Simon, he can go on. We can pass here awhile, an' take passage home without him."

Oliva only smiled. "A week is long enough. I only miss her when I'm with her. The rest of the time, I do fine."

But in three days, they had to change their plans after all. Simon came with the news.

"They're talking of it in the saloon," he told his mother, "and soon, it will be in the streets, if it is not now. A ship came in from Rio de Janeiro with some dead. Two days ago, the *Northampton* docked with a hold of Irish laborers, and they had sickness on board. Last week, a rigger came in from Kingston, and at least seven more were taken off with the fever. I fear Bronze John is on the city."

"Is it not just ship's fever?" Oliva asked soberly. "You know how such sailors live. If it were yellow fever, surely the doctors would know—"

"I think if we wait, we will not be able to leave in time."

"Well, but I must say good-bye to Emma. Who knows how many more Mays I have left?"

"Fine, but we leave soon after."

The next day, however, the rains began in earnest, heavier than usual, hours of savage downpour that filled the gutters to the *banquettes*. Thunderstorms beat the earth, splitting the skies with lightning. The rain continued for four days, and nothing moved from the docks. When the rains finally ceased, the earth steamed in the heavy sun. The heat quickly expanded to a fiery peak, and even the dew felt hot. The heavy drops slapped down and lay on leaves and stems of grass, until the sun simmered them away by eight. Mosquitoes came out in hoards.

The *Picayune* reported two cases of yellow fever down at the waterfront. A later inconspicuous paragraph admitted that a few more cases had been found elsewhere, the number unspecified. Doctors had declared that there was no cause for alarm.

That final line was sufficient to inspire hundreds of knowing readers to make swift plans to leave the city. Meanwhile, the heat was rabid, menacing, and not a breath of air moved Oliva's light curtains.

Simon spent that morning down at the docks, searching for passage, and when he returned, his face was grave. In a period of only six hours, panic had hit New Orleans. People were scarcely seen on the streets; shops were already raising their shutters, and every road out of New Orleans was reported clogged with departing buggies.

Simon raced Oliva and Celisma to the wharves, only to face lines of agitated men and women, begging to be taken aboard any ship at all that was departing the city quickly. As usual in the warm season, few steamboats docked along the levee. Then news came into town that up and downriver other cities were declaring embargoes against New Orleans passengers and shipments. Armed guards were posted in Baton Rouge to be sure Bronze John kept his loathsome distance, and no incoming ships were allowed in New Orleans port.

Now citizens rushed by the hundreds to leave the city however they could. Carriages, wagons, buggies, and carts were in sudden short supply. The poor trudged miles to escape, women caught up children with one hand and their skirts with the other and scurried after their men. Don't fight with the landlord about the rent, leave the stuff there, just *go*. No, we don't know where we will go, but we must be gone! Some of them already carried death and, within a day or so, found themselves in agony wherever they were.

Simon managed to hire a driver and cab at more than ten times the normal rate to drive them upriver, so that a boat might be sent for them from Beausonge across the Mississippi. As they left the city, Oliva complained of a headache. By the time they reached Crescent Rose—a plantation where the boat from Beausonge might put in—she had a slight fever. As they ferried across to their own landing, she began to thrash about in discomfort, her skin hotter than before.

"She got the fever bad," Celisma whispered to Simon, trying to calm her mistress with a cloth wet in cool river water.

"Perhaps it will pass," he said, watching as the Beausonge dock grew larger. Samuel stood there, waiting.

Daniel carried Madame to her own bed, her two sons by her side. Celisma busied herself collecting what she would need to comfort Madame. When she looked closely into her eyes, she felt a deep pang of fear. The old woman's eyes were bloodshot, and the whites were yellow and thick-looking with sticky liquid.

"I've called the doctor, *maman,*" Samuel was saying, her hand clasped between his. "You're going to be well quick enough now you're home. You always said that city was a pestilence, now you've proved it."

"Emma," Oliva said weakly.

"Emma will be safe enough," Simon said. "She has been through these epidemics before, yes? God will not let his Sisters fall to such a plague."

"Emma!" Madame repeated with more energy.

"You want me to fetch her?" Simon said, leaning down low over her. "She's safer behind those convent walls than anyplace else in the city. If she leaves, she may well catch the contagion, *maman,* but if you think you need her—"

Celisma stepped forward with a poultice she had mixed and more cloths. "Madame, you lie quiet now," she said firmly. "I be takin' care of you, anythin' you need. We don't want Miss Emma fallin' sick longside you, *non,* an' the doctor tell you the same thing when he come." She pressed the cloths to the old woman's head, wiping the rheumy eyes and mouth with a gentle hand. After repeated salvings, Oliva seemed to calm, and her fever no longer rose with each moment that passed. Her eyes closed, and she drifted into a heavy sleep.

Samuel gestured Simon and Celisma away from the bed. "No sense you waiting here all night," he said to Simon, his voice low. "Unless you want to, that is. But I know Cerise will worry once she hears about the fever in the city. Go on home now, why don't you, and come back again tomorrow after the doctor has seen her. I'll send Tim or Daniel if she takes a turn for the worse in the night. Celisma," he turned to her, "do you think you can ease her any?"

"Suh, I know some 'bout this fever. I do my best, an' *le bon Dieu* do the rest."

He gripped her forearm gratefully. "You know her better

than anybody else. If she's going to—" he hesitated but his eyes never left hers—"if she's going to pass, at least I want her to be eased. I don't want her to suffer or to know. Can your herbs keep her easy in her mind?"

She nodded gently. "She won' feel no pain."

Simon said, "I should stay. I can send word to Cerise."

Samuel shook his head. "Not a thing you can do. Only Celisma can comfort her now until the doctor comes. The longer you stay around her, the more chance you'll take it home with you, and you've got Tidings to think of, and the new baby. Go home to your wife, and leave mother to Celisma for now."

Simon glanced at Celisma, who nodded in agreement. He bowed to her and left. Samuel watched him go and then turned to Celisma again. "Are you afraid?"

She smiled gently. "No more'n you, suh. I got to die some time. No better way than servin' Madame, *vraiment.*"

With that, he leaned down and kissed her lightly on the forehead. "Best business I ever did, the day I brought you from Rosewood."

"Best business you ever did, givin' me to Madame," she said quickly, before she thought.

He smiled. "You didn't like belonging to me?"

She looked full into his eyes, and her gaze made his grin falter. His eyes dropped to her mouth. "Celly—" he started, but she stopped his words with her finger. A delicate touch, the merest graze of skin against lips. He leaned down then and kissed her lips very gently, barely touching, holding her shoulders away as much as pulling them closer. He pulled back and looked into her eyes. Then he leaned forward and kissed her again, and she felt her lips tremble under his, could not keep them from trembling.

A call and a light approaching from outside, and the doctor followed Tim up the gallery steps. Celisma broke from Samuel's grasp and went instantly to the door to lead the doctor to Madame's bed, holding her skirts quiet and glancing only once at Samuel, as the three of them were gathered around the sleeping old woman.

Samuel followed her, standing at the other side of his mother's bed, watching Celisma all the while.

Once before, Celisma had seen a man die of yellow fever. It was when she was young, only ten or so, but she never forgot Clapper and his sickness. His fever went high, and he thrashed about like a crazed dog. He screamed for water until he was hoarse, then the delirium broke and he struck out at his brothers, who tried to hold him down. Her mama was nursing him, and she shoved Celisma out the door, but she peeped in around the corner and saw ol' Clapper's face go as dark as a plum, and the veins stand out on his neck. Blood oozed from his gums and lips, and when he retched into the tin bowl they held, it was dark, too. Black vomit, they called it, and Clapper died that night in agony.

Madame would never suffer such, Celisma vowed silently to herself, as she watched the doctor do his best. He forced limewater down her throat until she coughed it up, and he pressed cups to her skin to bleed her. The cups were set in with razor blades that cut and let the blood flow. Celisma caught the dark blood in a basin, until Oliva was white in the face and her breath came shallow.

All the while, Samuel stood by. Matilde brought the young Misses and Master once, their faces covered with gauze against the contagion. They stood at the door of Madame's room, whispering to each other with fearsome eyes. Simon came and went, more often longside his brother than not, and Valsin kept vigil in a chair at her feet. Madame was never alone as she slipped in and out of sleep.

Sleep was what Celisma brought her, no matter what else the doctor did. She made a strong syrup of nightshade root and poppy juice, finding the red flowers and cutting them on the slant as her mother had shown her. Every few hours, she returned to the plant stem to scrape off the soft material which collected there, mixing it with her roots and adding a little of M'sieu Sam's fine bourbon. The syrup soothed Madame's cough and slid her into sleep, smoothing out the lines of pain on her forehead so that she looked, in the dim light, like a young girl again.

When she woke, she moaned softly, "I wish you could warm my feet, Celisma. Yes, I know you have a hot brick there, but I cannot tell it. The cold is creeping upwards." She shivered and was still, and for a moment, Celisma thought she had ceased to breathe. But no, the old heart was still faintly beating.

The second night, she called her sons to her and whispered to them as they bent low over her wheezing breasts. Celisma could not hear much of what they said, of course, but there was no mistaking the sadness in their murmured tones. Valsin slumped in his vigil chair, looking older than his years.

On the morning of the third day, Oliva slipped away too deep to bring her back. Celisma had been dozing in the chair longside Madame's bed and she woke suddenly with a start, sensing a change. She leaned over and saw that Oliva's spirit had passed. Death had been gentle and swift, sneaking up behind her so that she didn't know until hands slipped over her eyes.

Celisma woke the doctor, who woke her sons. While they bent at her bed in prayer, the young girl stood in the corner of the room quietly weeping. She felt in that moment more bereft than the day she left her own mother.

"I couldn't save her," the doctor told Samuel and Simon

sadly. "Few make it through this yellow fever, and fewer still at her age. But she didn't suffer much. She had God's blessing in that, at least."

They asked God's blessing again for Oliva Doucet Weitz as they laid her into the family burial ground at Beausonge, to sleep once more next to Joseph.

Samuel and Simon stood together with Valsin, and each one spoke of Oliva and his memory of her, occasionally reaching out to touch one another's shoulder, as though to keep themselves upright. Emma had managed to escape the ravaged city, and she stood like a tall gray ghost in her habit, her face hidden and bent in sorrow. Matilde, Cerise, and Oliva's three grandchildren stood alongside, moving the rosary beads through their fingers, their faces veiled in black.

The slaves sang a final resting song for the woman they all knew as ol' Madame.

> I'm gonna drink that healin' water, gonna drink
> that healin' water, gonna drink an' never get
> thirsty some o' dese days! Lord God knows it!

And then Celisma stepped forward to the edge of the grave and looked down at the box which held her mistress. The rest of the slaves fell back with respect, for they all knew she had been the last one to lay hands on ol' Madame.

It was a bright day, she saw, as she lifted her head to the bayou beyond the graveyard, the kind of morning that Madame always loved most. She could smell the dark tannin of the water, the swampy, soggy smell of the roots and leaves soaking up the sun and mud, and she knew that Madame could smell them still, would smell the water and hear it through eternity. She began to sing softly, and as she sang, Odette and Betzy, Clara and a few of the others took it up.

> Fé dodo Minette,
> Trois piti cochons du laite,

Fé dodo mo piti bébé
Jiske lage de quinze ans
Quan quinze ans aura passé
Minette va se marier

Go to sleep, Minette
Three little suckling pigs,
Go to sleep, my little baby,
Until the age of fifteen years
When fifteen years shall have passed
Minette will then marry

At the final notes, all the family was singing as well, with the voices of the two brothers rising above the chorus, strong and even together.

And then, Samuel stepped forward to the grave, and Celisma caught her breath, for her throat ached with pain for him.

"This is a time of sadness," Samuel said, and the slaves behind him moaned in agreement, "but it is also a time of joy. We know that my mother, your first mistress, is set free today from the bonds of her earthly business, to do the business of God."

Ulysses sighed, "Yea, Massa, He hear you."

"And as she goes to her reward, I want to speak now of another who deserves a reward as well."

Odette cast a quick glance at Celisma. She raised one eyebrow slightly in question, but Celisma looked back at Samuel, waiting for his next words.

"Celisma has labored day and night to care for my mother in her time of need. With no rest and little regard for her own safety, she tended her final hours as she might have tended her own mother. She has earned a reward. And because I am grateful to her for all she has done, I will give her the highest reward any master can offer. As of today, Celisma is a free woman of color. I emancipate her before you all as witnesses."

The moaning from the slaves rose to a high shriek of glee and amazement, as they crowded around Celisma, patting her back and pumping her hands. She could scarcely see Samuel for all the shoulders and grinning faces, but she did catch a glimpse of Matilde clearly—her face was frozen in a sharp and angry smile. Emma nodded to her sadly, making the sign of the cross on her wimpled breast. Pierre grinned at her in open disdain. Only Amélie and Thérèse looked truly surprised and pleased for her, returning her hesitant smile.

Then Samuel turned and looked at her, and she bowed her head, the tears overwhelming her. Before she could speak her gratitude, Odette swept her in a broad embrace, almost lifting her off the ground. "You got *la bonne chance,* gal, I said it the first day!"

"I be free?" Celisma turned to Samuel, "truly and always?"

Matilde moved closer to him, taking his arm in hers.

"That was my mother's wish," he said firmly, "and she told me on her deathbed it had been her intention. I must respect her wishes."

"*Merci,* M'sieu," she stammered, ready to say more.

But before she could, Matilde swept him away, and the rest of the family followed them into the Big House.

One by one, the slaves filed by the grave, tipping their hats and making their courtesies, until finally only Simon, Valsin, and Celisma stood by to see Tim and Daniel pick up their shovels.

"You did not know?" Simon asked her then.

She shook her head, mute with emotion.

"He planned it this way, I think, *longtemps,* him," Valsin said. "Where will you go now?"

She heaved a huge sigh, feeling the lightness leave her. "I got no place to go, *vraiment.* No place to be save here, I 'spect. I can work for wages, maybe. M'sieu Sam, he tell me."

Simon said, "You don't need to ask directions now from anyone, not even him. But you got to have some plans, for truth. The law says you got to leave the state within a year of freedom."

She gasped. So this explained why Matilde would agree to her freedom. "Where I go?"

Valsin shrugged. "The law say only you got to go, *cher.* You don't know this?" At her look of despair, he added, "Don't seem like a fair trade, *non,* but some would take it, no matter."

She sank down on a cypress stump near the grave, her head in her hands. It was not just the grief. Celisma had the sudden feeling that she had disappeared with Oliva Weitz into nothingness. If she was not ol' Madame's gal, who was she?

Emma came out from the house and walked over towards them. "What will you do now, Celisma?" she asked.

At the gentle look of peace on the nun's face, Celisma felt her will crumple. She fought back the sobs. "I don't know!"

"Have you no family?"

"*Maman.* But she can't keep me, she can't keep herself scarcely. She had a hard life. All day, she belong to ol' Miss, and at night, she got to answer to the Massa sometimes. Didn't have her ownself no time. She never had nothin' but me, an' they sent me away soon as I grew enough to help her some." She shook her head sadly. "I can't go back to Rose-wood."

Emma looked up at Simon. "That is perhaps one of the worst sins we have visited on them," she said quietly. "We took away their families along with their freedom." She put her hand on Celisma's shoulder. "You must ask *le bon Dieu* for help. And if He wills it, come to me. I will do what I can."

"*Merci,*" Celisma answered, bowing her head.

Simon also touched her shoulder lightly, awkwardly, and said, "*Maman* wished for only your happiness, *cher.*" Then they left her as Daniel and Tim covered Madame for her final rest.

Finally Celisma raised her head and looked around. In the damp foliage, she saw the slightest movement, something red was glinting and shivering. She turned her head slowly, so as not to scare it away. First she thought it must be a flower, but then she saw that it was a sundew.

No bigger than an inch across, the flower rose from a single thin stem. It was red and shaped like a starfish with many legs, each ending in a round pod covered with a score of tiny little fingers, all in motion. At the tip of each finger was a single drop of a glittery, sticky-looking syrup. Like some giant lady's brooch, it was, Celisma thought, something that Madame Matilde might wear to a fête.

In the middle of the pod, caught fast and kicking, was an ant. It was raising its legs one by one in a struggle to get loose from the crystal drop of syrup. As it fought to get free, the sticky syrup grew all around it, dripping faster and faster. The flower began to close slowly, relentlessly, no matter how the ant writhed. Finally, the ant was buried deep within the pod, closed tight as a red fist.

Celisma looked around and saw more than twenty of the sundews in the brush. Most of them were closed and feeding. She found one open and twitched it with a twig. Nothing happened. The plant knew it couldn't eat that stick and would not be fooled.

She turned and looked again at the grave, soon to be smoothly covered and graded by Daniel's careful shovel. In three months, it would flatten and green up. In a year, only the carved marble angel and headstone would mark Madame's rest.

And that was right, Celisma thought, right as rain. Everything had a place, even death. And there was no loss so important that grass would stop growing, river would stop flowing, or life would stop feeding.

I am free, she thought then, free as the river, free as the

air. Where will I go? Up North, they say folks think slave meat is good for eating and they kill them right off, first sight they have of them! She remembered all the times she had stood and looked up at the night sky, wondering where run-off slaves got to, after they lost the patrollers, after they went North or whichever way freedom was.

I have lost the one somebody who kept me safe, and I have no place to go, she thought, but I am free. What will life bring me now?

Soon enough, Celisma knew what freedom would not mean, here at Beausonge. Odette told her Madame vowed to have her off the place before the month was out. "Ain' seen her so waspish since never, *non,* ain' nobody can calm her on this one. All she do is eat those pecan fudgies by the hour an' set like a broody hen. She gettin' fat as ol' Betzy. You be out of her sight, hear, or you be sorry."

"I never crossed her," Celisma said. "Don' know why she take such a hatin' to me."

"She say you put bad ideas in nigger heads, with your airs now you got 'mancipated. She won' have you in sight, *non,* not even in the quarters."

"What M'sieu Sam say?"

Odette only shrugged. "What he gointa say, him? They don' talk, them, he do what he wants, she do what she wants, an' they don' do much together, for truth. Might be, you can ask him. Might be, he got a plan. But don' let her see you."

Celisma waited in the summerhouse for three nights after ol' Madame's death, waited for M'sieu Sam to come to her and tell her what to do, where to go. When he didn't come, she took to sitting in the shadows of the gallery, listening for his footstep, letting the moonlight wash over her bare feet. Finally, on the fifth night, she recognized the sound of his boot coming across the graveled path.

He came into the lamplight and stopped, halfway up the gallery stairs. "You by yourself?"

"*Oui,* M'sieu."

"Feel like company?"

Such a strange question. As though the world had flipped over like a river turtle and now she had the right to deny him trespass to his own summerhouse, just because she sat on the steps in the shadows. "You must please yourself, suh," she said quietly.

He came up the gallery and took a seat by her, following her gaze out over the wide strips of moonlight, the rows of live oaks, the dappled lawn. "What are your plans, Celisma?" he asked, settling himself as though he intended to stay for a time.

"Got no plans. Got no place to go, for truth."

"You're free now to go wherever your fancy takes you."

"Ain' got no fancy to go, suh. I be thinkin' I work for wages for you, did you need me. If you don' want me, I got no plans."

"You can't stay here, I guess you know that."

She looked away sadly. "I been told."

He thought for a moment in silence.

She gathered her courage. "What am I to do, suh? You 'mancipated me. You got to tell me."

He laughed ruefully. "I got to tell you? I don't have enough troubles of my own? No, Celisma, no one's got to tell you anymore. I should think you'd want to leave this place forever."

"An' go where? I got no people. I got no way to earn wages—"

"You could get hired up north, I'm sure. You know your numbers and your letters, do you not?"

She hesitated. Such an admission was dangerous, she knew. But now she was free. "I do," she said. It felt good to say it.

He thought for a long moment. When he turned to her at last, she could see a cautious hope in his eyes. "I guess I do have an idea or two. A plan, maybe, that might work."

She turned away from his eyes, the better to hear his words.

"I've been thinking about building a guest house out by the docks, to take advantage of the steamboat trade. A place where paying visitors could stop to rest for the night and have a meal in comfort and safety. There's nothing for two-days' travel up or down the bayou, and more folks are traveling all the time, too many strangers to have at Beausonge, even if Matilde would welcome them. I need someone to train the help, to welcome the guests, and to see to their comfort."

She held her breath, turning to face him again.

"It could be a paying proposition. Could you do such a thing, Celisma?"

The pictures he made in her head made her close her eyes, they were so powerful. Standing on the gallery of a fine place, speaking to the folks and showing them inside, setting them down to a meal, and then welcoming them to a clean, safe rest. She had heard of free women of color doing such things, running their own little dressmaking business or making fancy hats for the white ladies, but mistressing a house for white folks, that was the biggest picture she had ever seen in her mind. It blinded her, truly, and when she opened her eyes she saw only his face.

"At first, we'd take in only five or six at a time, see how it goes, maybe just have four rooms. As the word gets around, we might expand. But anyway, it would give you a place, something to do, it would use up that useless bit of land that's too sandy to plow at the bayou's edge, and it would help pay the taxes now that sugar prices are down."

"You pay me wages for this?" She looked up at him with all her hopes shining in her eyes.

"Certainly. And you would live on the place, of course, and oversee the slaves. You'd need your own cook, an upstairs gal, a downstairs gal, and likely a good lad to fetch the trunks and do for you. Could you keep them in line?"

"Oui, M'sieu, but—"

He waited, watching the way the moonlight made the angles and cheekbones of her face glow softly.

"Madame never allow it." She dropped her head and the light went from her face.

He touched her hand carefully. "Madame will have no say in this, Celisma. I am master still at Beausonge, whatever else Madame might think. You have earned a place here. My mother wanted it for you, and I can do no less."

"But they say I got to leave here. Leave the whole state of Louisiana forever!"

"That is the law, it's true, but it's a bad law. And there are ways around it. I have friends, a judge or two . . . so long as you stay on my lands and make no trouble for other slaves, I think we can work it out. What do you say?"

Suddenly, all the woe and hope of the last days overwhelmed Celisma, and she felt her insides tremble, her mouth dissolve from the pain and the joy. She slid to the gallery steps at his feet, embracing his knees, and she sobbed.

He put out his hand and touched her head softly. Then he stroked her face, her neck, and finally pulled her upright into his arms. When he kissed her, she felt every hidden place within her open and swell. She opened her lips to him, tasting her own salt tears and the strangeness of his flavor. She pressed against him the whole length of her legs, her body, yearning for him to feel her gratitude. He gathered her closer, she felt a heat come from him, and she let him draw her into the shadows, wanting only to be closer still.

In the bayou when the light began to fade, the chirping of the crickets was the first signal of the end of day. Then the frogs began to sing in chorus, all along the various streams and inlets; the song mingled and rose, until by full dark, the land itself seemed to vibrate with the sound of night.

Every denizen of the bayou knew to listen to the frog song, for it was a signal of warning, of weather, and of the rising or waning of the life of the swamp in all seasons. Mating, birthing, dying, hibernating for the next cycle, all could be read in the frog chorus.

Only the male frog vocalized, to attract the female, and each species had a different song, even each frog a separate and distinctive way with that song. All year round, in these waters, some frog or another was singing, but the chorus was at its most insistent from spring through summer, which in Lafourche was March through August, and then the frogs sang even in the daylight hours. In those hot months, every creature heard the deep resonant hum of the pickerel frog and the *quonk-quonk* of the green tree frog. The gray tree frog sent forth a sharp *brill-brill-brill,* and the cricket frog sounded like the rattle of a handful of river pebbles clicking together.

More than twenty different types of frogs made up the bayou chorus, from the raucous-sounding bullfrog which gave out rumbling bellows that carried a half mile or more, to the grunting of the pig frog, to the tiniest *chirr* of grass frogs. One of the last to call each summer night was a midget, the oak toad, with a high-pitched whistle that sounded like a baby chick peeping.

The frogs warned of man's intrusion into the bayou, but not every creature heeded their call. Or heeding, might then allow stronger urges than fear to move them into the path of danger.

Daniel knew this. He showed Celisma the tracks of the male turkey in the mud edge of the clearing, and she hunkered down quickly, surprised to see them so close to the two-story white guest house. Surely the noise and bustle of the building going on for two seasons, should have driven away even the most stupid tom.

Daniel raised his hands to his mouth and uttered a long, low, plaintive cry. She waited, carefully adjusting her knees and her breeches. She was finally used to the trousers, and they certainly made it easier to gather her herbs and reach deep within thickets for the ripest berries.

Daniel slowly raised his musket to his knee and readied the flint. She said, "This ol' tom—" but he shushed her swiftly.

"Ain' easy making that ol' tom come callin'," Daniel whispered softly, his hiss scarcely loud enough to hear, though she kneeled right next to him. "Cain' too many make the call jes' right. Turkeys, they got ears like a cat, an' the hen make one call, maybe two, an' then she be quietlike. You got to be still as death, once you call 'em. That call carry through the bayou to some tom, an' he leave his other hens to come see what hen wan' him now. Then he find her, strut her good, spread his tail, an' jump her." He put his hands to his mouth and made the call one more time, the sound of a turkey hen in season.

The quiet was broken only by the crickets and the frog chorus. A distant blue jay cawed harshly, but it was not a call of warning. Daniel put a finger to his lips, his eyes focused out on the thicket beyond.

Celisma felt her left leg falling asleep, and she eased it out, careful not to rustle the brush on either side. She was about to call Daniel back to the guest house, for the wood out back needed stacking, when she saw something move over his shoulder, and she settled back.

In the space between two oak trees, a big and strong-looking tom turkey was scratching at the ground. He looked up and began to strut. So slowly that she could scarcely see the movement, Daniel raised the musket up to his chest. The tom stopped and looked around.

Celisma suddenly felt an overpowering urge to sneeze. She tried to stifle it, but only halfway succeeded, and she made a low choked sound, barely a noise at all. The tom melted into the brush and disappeared.

Daniel looked at her and rolled his eyes hopelessly. He set down his musket again and made another hen call. For what seemed like the longest hour, they waited once more, and then another tom appeared. He was larger than the first one, more determined in his strut. With a slow-motion fan of feathers and a stamp of feet, he passed closer to where Daniel watched with his musket to his eye. A quick blast of thunder, and the tom fell in the leaves.

Daniel jumped up and ran to where the tom dropped, lifting his heavy feathered body high. "This one feed folks for four suppers, Miss Celly!"

She smiled, standing up and stretching her legs one at a time. Between the fish lines, crab pots, the rows of vegetables she had out back, and Daniel's keen eye with a musket, she had no trouble feeding as many folks as stopped at BonReve.

"Good Dream," M'sieu Sam had called the guest house at the farthest edge of Beausonge lands. And good dreams she had there, too, now that she no longer worried herself to death over what each new day might bring. What she had learned in three seasons of mistressing BonReve was that each new day brought something new indeed, but nothing she could not know and hold familiar, once the day was through.

She left Daniel to clean and bring the bird to the kitchen, and she walked back to the house. At some distance, she stopped and gazed at BonReve, seeing the way the heat waves shimmered around the white eaves.

It was a tall, narrow, two-storied house, with four rooms above, a wide and spacious gallery wrapped all round, and within, on the bottom floor, a long dining room and reception hall. It was here that she met the folks getting off at the dock, here that their bags were brought by Daniel until she could escort them up to their rooms. Out back, attached to the house by a narrow breezeway, Sally Red, Betzy's younger sister, worked in the kitchen to fill the dining table with victuals that might pass good words up and down the bayou to hungry travelers. And out back, too, just off that same breezeway, Celisma slept in a small room with a window to the river. It held only an iron bed, an armoire, and a basin, but it was the first time she had ever had a room of her own. Just going within each night and closing the door behind her made her feel easy in her heart, no matter what work might have plagued her through the long, hot hours of the day.

There was a small whirring rustle in the sawgrass behind her, and she leaped sideways and away without looking or thinking. She turned to see only a red squirrel scurry up the live oak, even more startled than she.

She waited for an instant for her heart to quiet. It had been thus for three seasons, that she flinched at any sudden movement. And no wonder.

She thought back to the first warning Odette brought her, not a month after Oliva's death.

Samuel had the carpenters busy on the frame of what was to be BonReve, and she was at the site most of each day, helping to clear brush, to dig flowers from the bayou and carefully set them in place along the pathway from the dock, to till the earth to get a garden started, to gather the white oyster shells for around the gallery steps. There was so much she wanted to do to make the white house at the edge of the water something which would lure all eyes up and down the river.

At first, it was hard to tell Daniel, Tim, and the others what she wanted. She had never given an order in her life. But soon she saw that they wanted to hear her direction, and as long as she started each command with "I think that—" or "Likely, it be good if we—" they stepped to her bidding gladly.

So each day, she hurried to the building site, watching the house grow and watching for Samuel. He came early and stayed late, occasionally pulling her into the shadows of a cypress or touching her at the waist or cheek when no one could see. She had never worked harder in her life and never been happier. And she went back to the summerhouse only to rest each night, her eyes on the rapidly growing guest house first thing each morning.

But Odette came to warn her one evening, meeting her in the dusk as she returned to the summerhouse.

"You think that BonReve, it be far enough away that Madame not know you here, *cher?* You cain' be so foolish, *non*. If that BonReve be clear up to the big water, it not be far enough away. She know where Massa Sam go in the day. She know where he go in the night, *même chose,* an' that woman not sleep 'til she make sure you gone, one way or other."

"M'sieu Sam don' go nowhere in the night. Not by me, leastways."

Odette smiled gently. *"Cher,* don' make no matter to no one but Madame where Massa Sam go or don' go. If he not be with you, he be out, an' Madame blame you for his goin'. I tell you, the woman be raged."

"Do she rage at him?"

"Most any time she see him. She used to be nigh 'rascible, now I think she nigh crazy, older she get. An' flesh on her like a fall shoat. So no wonder, the man he go out. But she tell him she not stand for no yaller gal in her sight, she holler that no yaller gal welcome folk to Beausonge or any *piece* a' Beausonge."

Celisma frowned, her chin firm. "Well, I guess that be for M'sieu Sam to say, *vraiment.*"

Odette shook her head at Celisma's ignorance. "I declare on God, you sure is something I ain' never seen before. I b'lieve you think that light skin make you white as they is. Either you a fool, or you crazy. You think that man see everythin' an' know everythin'? You think any man can? 'Less he send her away, she mistress here, an' she make happen what she want. You jes' keep your care 'bout you, is all I want to say, *cher.* I hate to see you get 'mancipated an' buried all in the same year."

Celisma did not forget Odette's warning, but after days went past and she neither saw nor heard more of Matilde, she began to believe that, indeed, M'sieu Sam had settled her rage somehow. And then one night, she went to her bed in the summerhouse, and she bent to smooth a wrinkle from the bottom of the bedclothes.

The wrinkle under her hand jerked and coiled, and the tip of one fang poked through the covering, almost snagging her palm. She gasped and jumped back in the room, watching fearfully as a large moving mound uncoiled and moved under the counterpane, dropping out from the bottom of the bed and onto the cypress floor. It was a writhing black moccasin, nearly twice as long as her arm.

The snake coiled again when it hit the floor, gaping at her with its white mouth open and angry. She backed slowly until she felt the wall at her spine, then she slid alongside it away from the snake, keeping her bare feet as quiet as possible.

The snake moved towards her swiftly, its head raised slightly and unafraid. Celisma felt the panic all through her legs, her stomach, the chill of her neck, and she froze, knowing that if the snake chose to strike again, she likely would not survive the night. Then she remembered something her mama told her once, that the moccasin was a ragin' snake, most likely to take it into its head to bite for no other reason than it wanted to, unlike the copperhead or the rattler, which would usually try to get shut of man, if he could.

To freeze, then, was no surety of safety. She stared at the snake in horror, and it returned her stare, both of them for that instant frozen in the fascination each species had for the other—and in that moment, she leaped high over the snake, her bare legs clearing its head by more than two feet, and landed on the bed, standing on the mattress, leaping into the air up and down and unable to stop herself.

The snake looked no more at her, but slid quickly out the door of the room. Celisma stifled the scream in her throat. She knew in that instant that no scream would bring the help she needed, no other soul could guarantee the protection she must have. She could only depend on herself. And a scream would be heard by ears which were waiting for just such a satisfaction.

Celisma waited long moments and then carefully stepped off the bed. Watching the door of the room, she moved slowly to it, and then leaned to peer out, looking up and down the shadowed corridor. She saw the end of the moccasin disappearing down the steps and to the gallery. Following it gingerly and at some great distance, she finally watched the snake slip under the screening at the gallery door and into the grass outside.

She stood at the door and looked at the Big House in the distance, with all the lights ablaze. There was no doubt in her mind how the moccasin got itself under her bed covering. There was no doubt that, having failed at its mission, it might well be followed by another, or some other danger which she could not now see clearly.

Celisma grimaced in the darkness. I am here, she told herself angrily, and I am going no place else. Let her do her will. She will never again take me by surprise.

A hatred began to grow in her heart and the fullness of it frightened her. She remembered her mother telling her about hating the white folks, how it was useless as a raindrop hating a hurricane. Just worthless and useless to itself, even. Only kept a body down, feeding on that rage.

The next night, when the moon was thin and dim, Celisma went to the swamp to search out further fortification. Behind the woodpile at BonReve, she built a small effigy of swamp mud, needles, hair, and the small bones of a green chameleon. From out of her red herb bag, she drew her most powerful gris-gris, the "bitter bone" which she had from her mother.

She held it in the moonlight and looked it over carefully for signs of decay. It was the bone of a black cat, boiled and then passed through the mouth of a hoodoo woman, carried by her mother close to her heart, and then finally passed to Celisma with many words of caution.

"Don' never use it 'less you mean it, *cher,*" she had told her then. "Like de nable-string, it ain' nothing to mess with 'less you willin' to carry through. De bitter bone do murder, sure as gun's iron, an' it keep murder from bein' done, if that's your wish, but it 'xact a price for all it do, an' that price come from you." Her words were hypnotic, almost like a singsong chant in a dream, but Celisma could still hear them clearly.

She completed the mud and bone effigy, carefully modeled the hair, and took the thin ribbon of lace she had in her pocket and wrapped it about the doll's waist and neck. It had come from a piece of Matilde's underlinen, slipped away from the laundry cabin the day before.

Celisma took the cat bone out of her mouth and began to chant over the effigy, sprinkling it with herbs and red pepper dust, until she could feel the power resting and waiting. She repeated the words from the Catholic hymnal which her mother had taught her: "Be not deceived, chile; God is not mocked, for whatsoever a man soweth, that shall he reap, *vraiment* and amen."

"Now," she murmured low into the night, "she be

warned. If she trespass me again, she find that's a corn I be willin' to grind."

Many seasons later, she was still watchful and wary. But she never told Samuel of the moccasin that night, nor did she ask for his aid. She merely watched and waited, certain that she, like every dog, would have its day.

She had told Odette that Samuel did not come to her in the night, but it was a lie. The first she had told the woman. The lie almost stuck in her throat, refusing to come out, so much did she want to share her joy. But she could not bring talk of him among the slaves and risk his happiness, simply to share her own.

Not often did he come. At first, he seemed to ask her permission with his eyes as he saw her during the day. She came to know the look that meant he wanted to be with her, came to sense that the look was coming before it did. And then she would smile at him and glance away, but somehow he knew that he was welcome.

As the weeks of building went on and BonReve rose to completion, it became a play-game between them, and she would smile at him in invitation before he asked with his eyes. On those nights when he came to her, their hunger was greatest.

He would slip into her room—as silently as though a hundred Matildes listened for his footsteps—and come to stand by her bed, a tall shadow in the moonlight, while the wind was redolent with anise and whispered through the moss-hung cypress. Sometimes, she would roll over and open her arms to him silently, only her sounds of pleasure indicating that she was awake and waiting. Other times, she would deliberately play possum, and he would play that he woke her with his caresses, until she came to life under him like a rousing cat, stretching and moaning.

Once, a time she would always remember with flushing pleasure, he had come to her almost roughly, covering her mouth with his hand like a thief in the night, taking her silently, except for the harsh whispers of desire in his throat. That time, as she tried to speak his name, he silenced her, his lips on hers as though he claimed new territory, and they let their passion take them to strange dark places they had never known. Then he slipped away as silently as he came, and she was left to throb for him alone in the small bed, smiling in the darkness, scarcely believing that he could seem such a stranger and yet at once altogether loved and familiar.

The population along the bayous and in New Orleans seemed to double, triple in the years from 1835 to 1845. To watch the traffic in the ports along the wide river—vessels two and three deep waiting to dock—was to believe that most of America was moving to the delta. Crop prices leaped, land prices trebled, and thousands of slaves were being imported each month to this golden highway of America. Men in every other region looked to affairs "down around New Orleans" to see what prosperity should look like in these years.

But sugar required almost a factory of workers and most of a bank's credit line to stay prosperous. Inevitably, prices began to drop, and the winnowing process began.

The price of slaves increased alarmingly, for the slave trade was outlawed in so many seaboard states. As slaves became more valuable, the agitation over their ownership grew. Harriet Beecher Stowe wrote the popular Uncle Tom's Cabin, *and the play made from her book opened in New York to wide audiences, with separate seating for "respectable Negroes." Sojourner Truth was speaking in the Midwest about the evils of the South's "peculiar institution," and after resigning his Senate seat to protest the Compromise of 1850, Jefferson Davis was named Secretary of War.*

Valsin Doucet died in his bed, an old trapper past seventy-five, and was buried out in the bayou under a wide-spread cypress.

Freedom gave Celisma walking time, and she began to widen her horizons past the boundaries of Beausonge. Though it was dangerous to be on the road, she sometimes even went as far as Rosewood on occasional evenings, to visit her mother's cabin.

But now that she was a free woman of color, her mother treated her as a guest in her old home. She found it hard to tell her of Samuel, of her fear of Mathilde, and hardest of all to ask her advice about much that mattered.

She did venture once, "I tried that ol' cat bone you give me, *maman,* made it out o' clay an' hair."

Her mother peered at her shrewdly. "You made a hoodoo o' his wife?"

Celisma looked up, surprised. News crossed the bayou as easily as the breeze. She nodded miserably. "I don' know why I done it. Ain' no sense to it. If I got to believe, I should be prayin' to God."

"Do that, too. But the hoodoo won' work less you wan' it, chile. What you wan' it to do for you? Kill her dead?"

Celisma flinched, horror on her face. "No'm! I jes' wan' her to leave me be!"

"Wal, you start it, it take off its ownself. Cain' tell what it do now."

Celisma glanced around at the squat cabin, the shadowed corners, the single candle guttering and smoking on the rickety table. "I don' believe in all that hoodoo," she said firmly.

Her mother chuckled. "Yassum, you do. You give your hands to it, an' you believe."

"What gointa happen, happen. Ain' no hoodoo make it happen. God make folks do what they will."

Her mother shrugged. "Maybe. Maybe white-folks god, maybe black-folks god, maybe all the same but different way o' prayin'. I tell you, chile, it works its way. If you don' want what it do, leave it be."

Celisma never knew if it was the power of her effigy or simply the grace of *le bon dieu,* but within the space of weeks, word came from the Big House that Matilde's bags were being packed. Moreover, so were those of Miss Amélie, Miss Thérèse, and Master Pierre. Pierre was entering one of the largest brokerage houses in New Orleans, and the young Misses were to be married in a dual ceremony at St. Louis Cathedral to the two sons of Armond Gaspeau, a neighboring planter. Matilde, of course, must oversee the details of both events.

"How long she be gone?" Celisma asked Odette.

"The way the trunks loaded, I 'spect she take in the season while she there. Massa Sam goin' for the weddin', o' course, but then she stayin' on."

"Wonder that the young Misses ain' making the weddin' at Beausonge," Celisma said unthinkingly.

"Ain' no wonder to it," Odette grinned dryly. "She can make out like BonReve ain' nothin' more than a bad dream to her ownself, can make believe she cain' see it sittin' here

366

if she take it in her head to hunt it up, but she cain' make out like *other* folks cain' see it. She say it the shame of the fambly, this here boardin' house, takin' money for makin' folks feel welcome. An' no other Massa up an' down Lafourche got to do such a thing, she say, an' she don' care to have quality folk see it up close. So the young Misses, they be weddin' in New Orleans, where she can hold up her head." Odette rolled her wrinkled eyes like a wise elephant. "An' it ain' no wonder that Massa Sam hurry back here, chile, there ain' nothin' for him in New Orleans."

Celisma cast her a quick warning glance.

"What? You think I won' say it? Big talk don' change what you doin', gal, you cain' clean yourself all over with your tongue like a cat. Folks ain' blind, black nor white."

"Is my business," Celisma said, her voice cool. "You got no call to speak of it, *non,* not to me nor to other ears."

"Is your business, yes, an' I don' fault you none when you got no say-so in the matter," Odette gently replied. "But now you got a choice. You free, gal, an' that be somethin' more precious than gold. You got a choice an' you got a soul."

"I always had a soul," Celisma said shortly.

"C'est vrai, cher," Odette smiled, "but now God know that soul got a say-so, too."

Celisma sighed and brushed her hand against her eyes. "Then maybe God can show how to stop a heart from wantin', if it ain' right to want."

"That ain' the way He work. He cain' take you out o' Sorrow's kitchen. But that don' mean you got to lick all the pots."

Celisma dropped her head and said quietly, "M'sieu got nobody but me. He all alone."

"That be true enough," Odette nodded. "Now his ol' uncle pass, he ain' got much kin left. No mama nor papa nor much o' wife an' chillen neither. One brother he don' see but 'ccasional. Ever think why that be?"

Celisma's jaw turned stubborn.

"Well, you can go hot as July jam, chile, but you cain' change the truth. He drive off what fambly he got, an' you the stick."

"The man's nigh fifty an' more," Celisma replied stiffly. "I guess he know his own mind."

"It ain' his mind he listenin' to," Odette chuckled, padding away down the path towards Beausonge.

Celisma watched her until she was out of sight beyond the high stone fence and the oaks which hid BonReve from view of the Big House. She suddenly wished to be anywhere but near to Beausonge, anywhere but where M'sieu Sam could lay claim to her once more, with her heart as willing conspirator.

The months rolled by as easily as the bayou waters, and Celisma was soon so busy with BonReve that she no longer waited for Matilde's return with dread. Seasons passed, Madame did not return to Beausonge, and it was easy to forget the Big House sat behind her in the distance, practically a mirage if she squinted in the sun.

She almost forgot the small clay figure out in the swamp as well. Several times she started to go find it and destroy it, but then she told herself it was only an old slave tale, no more substance than swamp fire and werewolves, and she put it out of her mind.

Folks came and went, and Celisma found in time that it was not difficult to manage slaves. Her greatest trouble came in managing her own feelings about them. She could put Daniel to a task, set Sally Red to her work with a clear heart, but the trial came when it was time to turn her back and let them do the job without a constant eye.

She found herself stepping out to the field to see if Daniel was putting in the corn rows the way they should be, slipping back to the kitchen to oversee the second batch of buttermilk biscuits, until finally Sally Red rose up in a squawking flutter and threatened to take to her bed with a sick headache if Celisma came to the stove one more time that day.

But the power of command rarely bothered her at all.

Her value to herself had changed. Before freedom, it did not matter how she spent her hours. If she tracked in dirt and had to clean it, it was something to shrug away. Her time had no value, even to herself. Now that her time was her own, she resented wasting even a moment of it, and if working the slaves would help her to get more of it, then she swallowed down her grimace of discomfort and worked them well.

But she never forgot what that work felt like, working for white folks. To bury hands to the shoulders in hot water boiling over a fire, filled with lye soap, to wash another person's dirt, for no pay and no thanks and never to be able to think, "Tomorrow I can rest. This evenin', I can rest." To cook and serve, sick or well, serving folks who don't care how you feel, never knowing what's in your mind and heart. That was what it was like for her at Rosewood, and without ol' Madame, that is what she would have known all the days of her life. So she never forgot. And she always remembered that Daniel and Sally Red were not her slaves, they were her people.

She found that with their help, she was able to do more than just collect greenbacks from folks for their bed and board. She asked Samuel for the loan of Daniel and Tim to build a bark mill in one of the outbuildings, for she heard that tannin was in high demand, and few could spud felled oaks as quick as Daniel.

In April and May, when the oaks peeled easily, she could put the man to a grove and he would peel and split a load of oak bark to fill the mill grinders in a day. When the bark was milled and covered with good bayou water, it produced a strong tannin for Cajun trappers to cure their hides. The general store in Thibodaux bought all she could tote, and she put the cash money in a flannel bag she had hidden in her closet. Freedom money, she called it in her head, and she never touched it.

In the fall she asked Samuel for a pack of dogs to run the bears. Bear grease was something the steamboat pilots asked for often, swearing it was harder and harder to come by. Hunters claimed nothing else eased their muskets so well, yet few were willing to chase the summer-fattened bears to ground, even though one carcass brought in more than ten bales of cotton.

Celisma set Daniel to traipsing after the bears. Sometimes she had an urge to be with him and the dogs, tramping through the bayou, hunting down whatever they could find, sleeping on soft moss at night with the flickering fire keeping off the wild things, hearing the hoot of the owl above their heads as they slipped into dreams. Wild dreams, they would be, like the wild things around them.

But then she thought of her smooth clean bed and Samuel sometimes waiting for her in it, and she dismissed any sense of traipsing right out of her head. Besides, she told herself firmly, you a mistress now. Do what is fittin'.

The early months of spring came, and Pride of China trees bloomed. Celisma planted marigolds, prince's feather, lady slipper, immortelles, and portulaca round the path leading to BonReve. The Cherokee rose by the door grew in wild abandon all over the gallery rails, and as the first flowers began to show themselves in the bayou, Celisma felt stirrings within to match their blossoming. The herbal tonics and simples she usually dosed herself with in this season did not work their expected magic. She felt at once lazy and restless all together, with an urging which sent her out to the river often, only to stand and gaze at the slow-moving water in confusion, wondering why she felt so compelled to come.

A whirr of wings above her head, and she glanced up to see two cock blue jays zigzagging through the air, one in desperate flight from the other. She followed the duel with her eyes, sensing that in the concealing foliage nearby a motionless little blue jay hen was watching it, too. Eventually one of the jays ran off the other and, with a perceptible swagger, flew back to the nest which he had just defended— or invaded.

Along the levee, a black colt was tearing along at breakneck speed, and a flock of geese with goslings in tow had to waddle fast to get out of his way. Two calves cavorted with such foolishness that Celisma laughed as she watched. She was filled with a sense of spring joy, and she recalled how the old ones used to say that the bayou gave a special gift of fertility to all who touched it. It was the water, she knew, more than the season, which was the source of her happiness and the life around her.

Once, as she returned from the river on just such a woolgathering, Pierre met her on the back path that led from the corn rows to the kitchen, the first time she had seen him in almost three years.

She smiled hesitantly at him, quickly wondering where Daniel was, how close to calling distance Sally Red might be. "Good day, M'sieu," she said to him, thinking he might let her pass without comment.

But he stopped her in the path, blocking her way. "Well, look at this wench, all growed up and sassy. I guess you think you just about got the world by the tail, don't you, *Miss*

Celly," he said, his voice dark and sarcastic. "Setting yourself up mighty high, looking for a fall. Making your share of enemies, too, in the process, *Mistress,*" he deliberately came down hard on that last word. "I come to tell you something. Lest you think you're fooling anybody with these fine airs, you better know that BonReve is likely going to be more of a nightmare than any fancy dream you're having. I come to tell you my mother will be on the next steamboat from New Orleans. And I want you on it, off Beausonge for good."

She ducked her head and tried to go around him, stepping off into the cucumber rows. But he grabbed her arm and she stumbled in the soft dirt, falling partially against him. He shoved her off as though she were unclean.

"Please, suh," she murmured, trying to keep her voice under control.

"*S'il vous plaît,* don't you mean? Isn't that the way you talk these days when you want something? Isn't that the way you siren my father?"

When Pierre mentioned his father, something hard and dangerous stiffened in Celisma's heart, and she stepped back from the man, crossing her hands before her chest and planting her feet. "What you want then, suh? Speak it an' leave me."

"Oh, you giving orders to white folks now, too? You find giving orders to your liking, I hear. Can't get enough of bossing your own nigger gang day and night." He grinned, a nasty crooked thing. "At night most of all, I'd bet."

With that last, Celisma knew she must get back within the safety of the house; she wanted that more than she wanted to fling his words back in his face—but would even the house be safe from Pierre? There was really no place on Beausonge land that she could go and be sure he could not follow. She fervently wished in that instant to be an ugly, black field hand nigger who was invisible to his and every other man-eye on the plantation.

She tried to push past him once more, this time ducking

as he reached for her and flinching away, but he caught her again by the shoulder and whirled her around to face him. "You'll stand and listen, you yellow wench, until I give you leave to go. I don't care what my father says, I want you gone from Beausonge, do you hear? There's a law made just for sluts like you, and I want you off this land and out of my mother's sight once and for good."

"Or?" Her head was up, her spine stiff and unflinching. In one part of her head, she was measuring the distance from where he stood to the house, measuring the distance a full-throat scream would travel. But what ears would hear and what feet come running?

She felt a strange flutter below her heart at that moment, a movement that was as though some small creature fought to get out or to get deeper within her for refuge. And she knew in that instant why her tonics had not gone down as easily as before.

"Or I'll make you sorry you ever set eyes on Beausonge, Miss Fancy, ever set your hussy eyes on my father, too. Did you think we'd simply let him set you up here for all Lafourche to witness? Did you think my mother would tolerate his concubine in her own backyard forever? She gave him every opportunity to right himself. Now, I'm going to do it for him."

"Suh, I believe you best speak to your father 'bout this, not to me—"

"I'll speak to whomever I please, woman!" Pierre shouted at her then, suddenly enraged beyond control.

For the first time, she felt real fear before him. She turned to run, but he grabbed her from behind, grabbed her around the neck and the waist and pulled her to him fast. "By God," he swore, "you'll stand and hear me, I don't care if Christ himself set you free, you're a yellow whore and nothing else, no matter how many keys you wear at your waist!" He ripped at her apron, tearing off her kirtle and her jangling keys to BonReve's pantries. With that, she screamed as loudly as she could, protecting her breasts and belly and face with her arms and hands, screamed again and again as she tried to wrench herself from him.

A scuffle behind them, and Samuel's voice suddenly pierced her terror. She heard him shout, "Leave her be!" Celisma felt Pierre's arms loosen from around her, and she spun to see Samuel and Pierre grappling with each other across the pepper rows.

She had stumbled and fallen in the plants, and she rose slowly now, her eyes on Samuel's angry, incredulous face.

"How do you dare!" he shouted at his son. "With your pockets full of my money and your horse taking his leave in my stable! While your every pleasure comes by *me,* how do you dare to do this?"

"How do *I* dare?" Pierre shot back. "How do you dare speak to me of fit behavior? My mother weeps every night in shame, my sisters can scarcely even bring their new husbands to their own home, none of us can meet the mocking eyes at spring fêtes, and you put your whore up higher than all of them, installing her here in her own white castle like some sort of courtesan under our noses, and you complain of *my* manners?"

"Celisma, go to the house," Samuel said, never glancing at her.

"Yes, Mistress, go kneel at your chaste maiden's bed and pray for your soul. For you will need all of God's forgiveness in the days to come," Pierre cast after her as she fled, his words sharp with scorn.

At that, she stopped and turned to him, her eyes blazing and her fists clenched. "I be askin' Him to forgive you as well, *mon ami,* for there be plenty times you lust for this same whore you take up stones against now."

Samuel's eyes narrowed, but he still never glanced at Celisma. "Be gone," he said to Pierre coldly. "There's no reason for you to be here at BonReve ever again. I'll not stand here in the kitchen rows, justifying my actions to you. And if I ever hear of you molesting this woman, I'll send you packing from Beausonge as though I never had a son at all. Then you can see what living on a broker's salary will do for your manners. *Tu comprends?*"

Pierre whitened, his lips curling in disdain. As he stalked to his horse, he threw back over his shoulder, "You needn't bother, I'll not be back. You're not only an old fool, you're deaf to all reason. You better join your wench at prayer, papa. Pray for a very long life. Because once you're not here to defend her *honor,*" and he all but spat that last word, "it'll be up for sale faster than she can shuck her skirts. Likely, she will be, too." He mounted and galloped away.

Celisma watched Samuel gather himself and calm his anger as deliberately as he might have buttoned his waistcoat, one restraint at a time. He took her arm to lead her to the house, and she could feel the muscles in his arm tremble with the effort for control.

"I am sorry," he said to her sadly. "I never thought he'd dare approach you again. You're a free woman."

"I never be free while I be on your land," she murmured.

"This is your place."

"By whose leave? You say it be my place, but to them, I'm trespassin'. I always be nothin' but a thief to them."

"I'm sorry!" he cried out suddenly. "I know what it's like to feel you never belong anywhere, I felt that way for most of my life. My youth taught me well enough that love wasn't to be trusted, and now I'm teaching you the same hateful lesson!" He held up his hands and looked at them, his face contorted with self-loathing. "I still have the calluses from working for something that wasn't mine. Someplace I didn't belong. Beausonge is mine, at least. Here, I'm working for something I can keep. I learned I had to do that—had to control my life if I wanted to keep it—and I never wanted my son to have to learn that lesson. But he's no son of mine." He looked away painfully. "He never has been."

She took his hands and pulled him towards the house, murmuring comfort which she knew he scarcely heard.

In the shelter of the gallery, he embraced her, holding her close and dropping his lips to her neck. "It will get easier," he said. "It'll just take time."

"I got less of that now," she said faintly, smothered in his chest.

He pulled back and looked at her quizzically.

"I be with child," she whispered, her mouth close to his.

"Oh my God," he moaned softly.

She went on determinedly. "And so I got to ask you what I wouldn't ask before. Is he to be born on his own land? Or is he always to be under Madame's thumb, waitin' on her pleasure?" She searched his eyes, looking for the joy she hoped to find there. "I don' look for him to have your name," she added, her eyes sliding away from his, "but I do look for him to have somethin' of his own some day." She tried on her best smile and found that she could keep it in place only with an effort. "Any mother wish for *la même chose, cher*. You cain' ask me to be wishin' for less for . . . your chile."

He held her for a long time without speaking. Finally he asked, "When will the child be born?"

"I ain' reckoned that yet. Maybe by grindin'." Again she sought his eyes and smiled. Let him be pleased! Her heart ached with the hope.

"Well. I should have expected this, I suppose."

She stiffened slightly. "I be happy, *cher*. Cain' you find some joy in this comin'?"

"I will," he said, smiling ruefully. "You must give me a little time to make a space for it in my head."

"In your heart, more like," she answered.

"Yes. And elsewhere." He put her away from him gently, moving to stand at the edge of the gallery, gazing out over the dock to the water as though he might peer into the past and the future all at once. "You know, there may well be a way."

She went to stand behind him, rubbing his neck as he liked. He sighed and moved under her hands, leaning into her palms as if for comfort.

"Cotton prices are going down, you know, and sugar's soon to follow. Talk on the river isn't good; even those who think that God himself eats Louisiana sugar at his table of hosts, they're worried."

"You worried, too?" she asked. He rarely spoke to her of his business. What she knew, she had by listening well. She yearned for him to take her in his arms and speak of the child, but she listened patiently.

"Some. We can hold out longer than most, if prices fall, but nobody can hold out forever. Taxes can eat up a place faster than a field of locust. You know, I've been thinking about this before, Celly, but now it looks like an idea to consider. What would you say to buying BonReve?"

She laughed, never stopping her hands. "I'd say that be jes' fine, an' while I be at it, might as well buy me the moon an' have done. 'Bout as likely I be ownin' either one."

"No, I'm serious," he said, pulling her from behind him and seating her in his lap. "It would keep at least something safe from the revenuers, it would drop the taxes on Beausonge, and—"

"It make Madame foam at the mouth like a mad dog," she said. "Pierre say she come back soon, an' likely, she start ragin' again. So don' talk 'bout me buyin' BonReve, that crazy talk. Ain' no yaller gal goin' to own nothin', leastwise a fine place like this. But I thank you kindly for the smile you give me."

"It's not as crazy as you think," he said, warming to the idea. She could see it take him and run. "Freed people of color are legally able to own land if they can buy it. Of course, no white man can leave land to his black mistress, that's against the law."

"More law. Why this one?"

"To protect the white wife, of course. A whole passel of

377

them must have got together and yanked on some politicians' shirttails for that one to pass, because most of those same politicians got themselves some sweet little—" he stopped and glanced up at her curiously. "You ever think why I took up with you, Celly?"

She dropped her eyes. "Lots of gentlemens got their gals, I 'spect."

"That's true. And most of them got good reason. See, the majority of white Southern males were suckled at some black breast while their white mama kept herself dainty in her glassed-in parlor. So naturally, when these men get to be big enough for pleasure, they can't help themselves, they think of black wenches every time rather than their prissy white wives."

"An' that why you with me?"

"Nope," he grinned. "I just happen to like you better. But that doesn't mean I can just up and deed you BonReve, even if the law would allow it. You can sure in hell buy it, though. Why I heard there's a mulatress downriver who has over a hundred acres and a dozen slaves to work them, bringing in a cotton crop same as her neighbors."

"A woman of color *owns* slaves?"

"You got a right to own whatever you want, now you're free. Only problem is the transfer of it to you. But I think I can get around that. I'll sell the place to Simon, and then, in time, he can sell it to you. And when BonReve is out of my name, they'll lower the taxes on Beausonge, and you'll have some security for you and the child. Of course, you'd have to pay the taxes on it, but at least you'll have someplace of your own no matter what happens to me."

"How I pay the taxes?"

"By the dint of hard labor, of course," he said, "just like the rest of us. I'll sell you some slaves, too. Prices are going up for prime hands all the time, and taxes are going up on them, too. I paid twelve hundred dollars for a field hand five years ago, and that same hand'll cost me eighteen hundred today, but I got plenty who can't work what the tax man says they're worth. There's a perfect mania for slaves, and everybody thinks the prices are going even higher."

"So much I was costin'?" she murmured.

"Not quite so much. Women bring less. You were worth, oh maybe a thousand when I gave you to my mother. But a crash is sure to come, I can feel it. And when it does, we'll see land and slaves going under the sheriff's hammer. With you owning BonReve, you'll be safe. So will the child."

"And it all be his?"

"Sooner or later, it will be. All yours and his. Just you and the revenuer, like every other parcel of ground in the state."

She frowned, suddenly frightened of his words. It was one thing to be out here at BonReve, almost hidden out of sight, not flaunting herself under Matilde's nose. It was something else altogether to own a piece of Madame Weitz's land, against her will. It was too much for Celisma to fathom, though she sensed that there might be a kernel of glee hiding under this bushel of worry somewhere.

"Celly, I should think you'd be happy as an oyster at high tide. Don't you understand? You'd be more than free. You'd be safe."

"Ain' no safe in what you proposin'," she said softly, "not for me nor the babe. Ain' nothing safe at all here for me an' him. But we got no place else to go an' nothin' else to do. *Maman* used to say, might as well jump at the sun, chile, an' even if you miss it, you cain' help grabbin' hold of the moon. I got somethin' I got to ask, though, if you want me to be happy with this plan." She twined her arms around his neck. "Do you want me to be happy, suh?" She called him this when she wanted to tease him.

"If it doesn't trouble me overmuch," he grinned.

So she nestled down on his chest and told him what would make her feel lighter in her heart.

BonReve soon came to be known up and down the river as a refuge for travelers, where the beds were always clean and the food some of the best to be found along Lafourche. At first, Celisma let Sally Red cook her own recipes as she saw fit, but soon she realized that she could put her own hand to that task as well. The bayou was full of herbs and roots which would bring new piquance to any dish, and those she could not gather, she grew in the herb plots behind the house.

In short order, not an egg went on Celisma's table that was not redolent of tarragon, and not a shrimp curled, pink and succulent, without its bath of bay leaves.

Rumor had it that folks traveling to New Orleans who had friends in the big houses sometimes chose to stay at BonReve instead. It was worth the few dollars, they said, to eat at that table.

As her belly grew, Celisma did her best to disguise her expectations. She wore her apron loose and higher, finally adopting the shapeless shift that Sally Red wore so that her stomach barely showed at all. As the months wore on, however, it was harder to hide her condition. Soon she was unable to greet folks at the door and had to depend on Cassie, the downstairs gal, to serve at the table.

If Sally Red and the others noticed her swelling, they never spoke of it to her face. The time came when she took most of a half hour each morning, binding her stomach as flat as she could, and still she did not feel easy with white eyes upon her.

Finally, Samuel asked her, did she not wish to go to her mother for the rest of her confinement?

She laughed ruefully. "I can jes' see *maman* an' her big eyes now. She not know to look at my face or my belly. No, I druther stay here, leastwhys if I can manage." She peered at him closely. "Unless you want me to go, *cher.*"

She had noticed that he still was drawn to her, even with her belly growing large between them. But no telling what went on in that man's mind of his. "I ain' shamed," she added.

"Most women would be," he said carefully, "with no husband to stand for the child."

"Havin' a husband ain' no guarantee 'gainst shame," she said quickly. "I seen plenty women havin' babes which don' look nothin' like those men who give their names. Seems to me that's more shame than I got. I am free, yes? My child be free. If I marriage to a man, he got to be free, an' that man be hard to find on this river. So I stay in my room an' I look hard at Sally Red if she fixin' to say somethin' she oughtn't, an' I bide my time. Won' be long now, I hope."

When grinding came that year, Celisma had all but disappeared from outward eyes. She rarely left her room except for an early evening walk down to the river and back again. The child pressed downwards, always downwards, and made her feel so connected to the earth that she could scarcely stand to pick her feet up off of it.

And then came the night when she could not walk at all, felt she might never walk again, for the pains came hard on her, and she sent Sally Red quick for Odette. The waddling black woman came carrying Minou, Thérèse's old tabby cat.

"What the news?" Celisma called out to her gratefully when she saw her, gasping between the pains.

Odette answered with her usual reply. "Oh, the white folks still in the lead, *cher.* Why ain' you up an' walkin'?"

"What fool thing is this now?" Sally Red asked indignantly, pointing to the cat. Finally admitted to Celisma's birth room, she was loath to give up her new power.

But Odette only took the cat to Celisma, beckoning to the rocking chair. "You ever see a cat have her kittens?" Odette asked, speaking only to the woman writhing in pain. "She bears 'em purrin', not screamin', *cher,* and so perhaps you holdin' her for a bit will help you to feel the pains less."

Sally Red snorted in derision, but Celisma took the cat on her belly gratefully, and when it began to purr, she felt somehow comforted for the moment. But then the pains made her double over, and she had no more faith in Odette's birth magic.

"You got to walk," Odette said firmly. "Sally Red, you go ready the swaddlin' for this chile. Put the water on to boil, an' it be ready soon enough, I 'spect."

"First one never come that quick," Sally Red hurrumphed.

"I seen 'em come faster than water boils," Odette snapped back. She pulled Celisma out of the rocker and said, "Here, chile, lean on me an' walk it out. You got to walk as long as you're able."

"So tired," Celisma groaned.

"You be more tired afore long," Sally Red offered.

"Get that water!" Odette hollered, bending over with the full weight of Celisma on her arm.

Celisma tried to walk then, tried to stand upright, but she could not force herself to straighten. Each time she did, the pain caused her to buckle and writhe, though her legs tried to hold her.

The hours dragged on slowly. Sally Red fell asleep in the chair by the window. Odette walked up and down with Celisma, only letting her rest occasionally, when she begged piteously with tears and even curses to be left alone. By the depths of the night, Celisma was paler than Odette had ever seen her, and her face was drawn around the edges. Now Celisma stumbled, barely able to put one foot in front of the other. Again and again, she retched and vomited, at last bringing up nothing but bile, but she could not seem to stop retching. Odette forced an herb simple down her throat, which she gulped thirstily, but then she retched again and again.

"She jes' like Sukie, you 'member Sukie, that lil' ol' gal who used to do for Massa Roberge? She puke like a dog all through her pains," Sally Red observed.

"It don' mean nothin'," Odette said to Celisma quietly. "Jes' the pain makin' you lighten your load."

At last Celisma could walk no more, and Odette let her lie down, gasping and biting at her lips with the pains which came now in waves.

"I seen it a hundred times," Sally Red said to Celisma solemnly. "Might be, this chile too big for your belly an' won' never come out at all."

Odette murmured to Celisma, "Don' listen to her fool mouthin's, she don' know nothin' 'bout birthin'. Once we brung your fine babe, I beat her good."

Celisma managed a tight grimace at that, almost a grin, at the thought of Sally Red and Odette pummeling each other out in the kitchen rows.

In an hour more, Odette had her up kneeling upright on the bed to help the child slip from the womb. Celisma slumped, and Odette called for Sally Red to help hold her. She seemed almost lifeless between them, too exhausted to do more than convulse and fling her head back, her mouth squared with unvoiced screams. The linen was blood-flecked and wet with the birth water, and still no head crowned. Then Celisma began to shake and retch more violently, sobbing as she fought them blindly, struggled to get away from them.

Sally Red took a firmer grip under her arms, Odette supported her sagging back, and Celisma screamed each time, any place they touched her. Suddenly, there was the sharp smell of blood in the room, and Odette pulled something from beneath Celisma's body, dark and shrivelled-looking.

"You got a fine man-chile," she crowed triumphantly, her voice ringing through the room like a raspy trumpet. She bent over him, breathing into his tiny mouth. Celisma heard a sharp, outraged cry, the sound of a newborn boy shrieking in fury at the cold world into which he had been forced.

"Look, look!" Sally Red called out, "he white as the day is long!"

But Celisma lay collapsed in Odette's arms and could not even open her eyes to look at her child.

The baby lay washed and swaddled at her breast, and Celisma had swallowed a cup of hot milk with honey and herbs against the bleeding. Now she lay drowsing, not even stirring as Odette put a cool hand on her brow.

"No sign of fever, that be lucky. I seen women take longer, but I never seen one work harder, chile. That boy be a wonder, I 'spect, for all you had to do to bring him forth."

"Is it mornin' yet?" Celisma struggled to say.

"Nigh 'bout."

"Where Sally Red?"

"I sent that chicken-headed fool back to her cookin'. She have some good strong beef broth for you when you ready to take it. Leastwhys, she can do *that* right enough."

Celisma smiled weakly. "I don' listen to her."

"That good," Odette said heartily. "Neither did that fine boy, there. What you goin'ta call him?"

"I may let his papa have his say in that."

Odette smiled sadly. "Don' wait for him, chile. This mite needs *one* name o' his own, anyhow."

There was a quiet knock at the door, one which scarcely could be heard if one were not listening for it. Odette smiled again, this time more sadly still. "I go now, *cher,* leave you alone. You send word if you need me, hear?"

She went to the door and admitted Samuel, dropping a slight curtsy to him as she went out and closed the door behind her. For a moment, Samuel just stood in the room, gazing at Celisma without a word. She could not make out his expression, but she saw his eyes scarcely take in the child at all. She held out one hand to him, using most of the strength she had reserved for this moment.

He came to her then, bending down and touching her cheek softly with his palm. For the first time, he seemed to take in the boy nestled in the crook of her arm.

"He give you much trouble?" he asked gently.

"More than he worth, for truth," she smiled.

Samuel carefully tucked back a corner of the child's covering and looked at his face for a long while. The boy made a soft mewling sound but kept his eyes closed. "He's so fair," Samuel said at last. "I guess I should have figured that."

"He may darken down," she said. "Or not, hard to tell now."

"What will you call him?"

"I thought to ask you."

Samuel looked at her then and she saw bewilderment in his eyes. How tight the man keeps himself reined, she realized. So careful with his loving, like he plans on pain from every pleasure he takes from it. If he truly does love. Likely, he is fond enough of me, but will never love. Won't let himself. Maybe loves no one at all. It was strange how folks could have hearts that beat alike, but have such different things in them. They say all people love, but she sometimes could not believe that. Some, she knew, had such a small bit of love in their hearts, like a little puddle, that dried up with orders from their minds. Then some had so much love they love things and folks they don't even know. She felt a strong pity for Samuel in that instant, and knew the power and pull of caring for a wounded man. In some ways, his pain balanced the power between them so that they were more equal. Perhaps, she thought, this child will be something he can love in time, to take away his sadness.

He truly does not know what to do, she saw then, and I must help him now.

"Pick the boy a name," she said firmly, with what strength she could summon. "It be fittin' that you do."

"Something from the Bible, perhaps?" He frowned in hesitation.

"No."

"Something from your own family?"

She shook her head, pulling the child's blanket back even further, so that his father could see the fragile blue veins under the creamy skin. "I thought to call him Sun, 'cause he shines so bright and he is your son."

"That won't do," Samuel said. "Sounds like a darky name."

She smiled. "You choose, then."

"Well. I always liked the name Alex. It's a good strong name. Doesn't sound either Creole or American, really, not one thing or the other. Which will give him a chance to decide which he might be when he's of a mind to choose."

"I thought you might say Andrew," she said quietly.

He glanced at her searchingly and then away. "You know about that, then?"

"Just what Odette know. You had a son, an' he die in the bayou. Cut his legs on a trap, she say. M'sieu Simon take him an' bring him out."

He was silent for a long moment, as though remembering. "So. Then you understand about Matilde."

"*Non, cher,* I don't understand. I see why she grieve, *vraiment,* an' I see why she grasp ahold to her other son, but

386

I don' see why she rage. Women birth babies an' women lose babies, an' they keep on lovin' an' livin' after. Why you never speak of him?"

"I guess because I never could. We haven't . . . spoken of him." He passed a hand over his eyes briefly, and his voice hoarsened. "I haven't said his name since we buried him. Matilde would not hear it."

"Well," Celisma said gently, "here you say what you will, *cher*. Ain' nobody really dead if they still live in your heart. You want to call this nubbin after him?"

Samuel shook his head. "Alex would be good, I think. Does that suit you?"

"Do it suit him?" She held the child up and gazed in his face. "I think it do. Alex. We try that one on for size."

The child was a month old, and already he slept through most of the night. Celisma counted herself lucky, yet she would have willingly picked him up several times before dawn, just to have those moments with him.

He was a gentle, quiet boy, but his eyes never stopped moving. As though he saw things clearly and early. No matter how many times Sally Red told her that his mouth movements were only gas pains, she knew in her heart that he was working up to a smile. And she also knew that once he smiled on her, she'd be lost to him forever.

One night, she came back from the kitchen to check on him before locking up and found Matilde standing in the middle of her room, bending over his cradle. The woman had grown hugely fat, her head a small haired ball on a mountain of flesh.

Celisma froze in instant terror, her stomach tightening into a solid mass of sick helplessness.

Matilde turned to her calmly. "Did you think I wouldn't hear of him?" she asked without preamble. "Did you think you could hide your little bastard away out here in the cane fields like Moses in the bulrushes?" She turned back to the cradle and gently moved the blanket off Alex's chest. "He looks white, all right, just as I heard. Whiter than you."

Celisma saw that in her other hand, Matilde held something which shone briefly in the lamplight. A glass something. She held her breath, not daring to move. From where she stood, she could just see into Alex's cradle. He was watching something over by the window, barely aware of Matilde's intent stare. His tiny white chest looked mottled and fragile.

"Strange, though," Matilde was saying, her voice low and almost confidential. "He doesn't look a thing like Samuel."

Celisma finally found her voice. "Ain' so strange," she said quickly. "He ain' Massa Sam's chile."

Matilde turned now away from the cradle and stared at Celisma, putting both hands behind her back. "Not his child? That's not the word I heard."

Celisma moved slightly nearer the cradle, but stopped when Matilde brought her hands out before her. She held a glass jar. Something dark moved within it.

Sweat broke out on Celisma's brow, but she wrenched her eyes from the jar and said softly, "I know what they say, but they wrong. You can see for yourself, Madame. This chile ain' his."

"Whose then?"

Celisma shrugged helplessly, but her voice never wavered. "Don' rightly know, Madame. The white gentlemens, they come an' they go, you know."

Matilde smiled a fierce, tight smile, one corpulent hand on the top of her jar. Her eyes were mad. "You whore. You lying, yellow whore."

Celisma shook her head. "Ain' no lie. That chile no son of Massa Sam."

Matilde turned leisurely and examined the boy again, unscrewing the lid of her jar slowly. "Well, little man," she said gently to Alex, "this is a fine tale your mama tells, isn't it? Have you ever heard such nonsense in your short life?"

Celisma took a step towards the cradle but froze again as Matilde held the open jar over Alex's bare chest, tilting it slightly towards him. Now it was clear what lay inside.

The moving mass of black rearranged itself and the light hit it just so that Celisma could see the spiders easily. More than a hundred of them, she swiftly guessed, clambering over each other for escape. More than a hundred glossy black widow spiders.

"I've been feeding these lovelies for a good while," Matilde said, "thinking sooner or later they'd come in handy." Her hand held the jar so that the spiders fell slightly forward, their black hinged legs inching up the edge frantically towards freedom and the open air. "Likely, it would only take one bite, he's so young. You know, the very young and the very old are most hit by the poison, I find. Most adults can live through the bite of the widow, though it's brutally painful, I'm told. But a single bite would probably kill an infant. And of course, a swarm of bites would surely be certain."

"Please, Madame," Celisma whispered, her voice a whistle of fear in the dark, "let me take him away. He ain' nothin' to you, I swear it. Jes' a yaller pickanniny with no name. We be gone before sunrise, if you let me take him."

"Oh, but it's too late for that now," Matilde said quietly. "You should have left way before this. Now if you leave, my husband may well try to find you. Or even join you. For of course, he likely believes the child is his. You *have* told him this, have you not?"

Celisma nodded, her eyes never leaving the jar. "He think the chile is his, yes'm. But I lie to him. You can see the truth, he cain'. The chile don' look nothin' like him."

389

"Frankly, I don't give a damn what he believes or doesn't believe. But no bastard freeborn child is going to survive to lay claim to Beausonge. I have a responsibility to my own children. To *my* son." She turned back and crooned at Alex in a soft voice. "You can surely understand a mother's concern, can you not, little man?"

"Please, Madame," Celisma gasped, "he won' make no trouble. I tell M'sieu the truth. I tell him this boy ain' no seed of his."

"As I said, whore, I don't give a damn what he thinks." She tilted the jar forward again until three spiders were within two inches or less of falling out into the cradle. "But if you go, he'll know I chased you off. No, Celisma, I no longer care if you stay or go. I no longer care what *he* does, so long as he meets his responsibilities. But if you want this child alive, you'll swear he'll never lay claim to what is mine and my children's rightful reward."

"I swear it, I swear it," Celisma moaned.

"You'll do more than that," Matilde said. "You'll swear it in writing."

Celisma bowed her head in defeat. But then she yanked her head up again without hesitation and said, "I will, jes' cover the jar."

Matilde turned and set the glass jar on the table without its top. The spiders slid down again, one on top the other in a jumbled mass, climbing up the slick jar sides and clawing at the air. She opened the Bible next to Celisma's bed, the same one the young girl had been given the day she arrived at Beausonge.

"I'm sure you never even glanced at the pictures," Matilde said, ripping out the blank frontispage. She turned to the little desk in the corner and reached for the inkstand and quill. She bent over the paper for a moment, writing. Celisma closed her eyes firmly, steeling herself anew. She opened them hastily, glancing from Alex to the open jar near his head.

"Make your mark," Matilde said, holding the paper out to Celisma.

Celisma took a deep breath. Now she must gather all her wits. "What it say?"

"It says that you swear this child is a bastard born of an unknown father, plain and simple."

"That all it say?"

Matilde swooped and picked up the jar again. "If it says that you are a lying whore and that you promise to feed your child to the gators at dawn, you'll sign it anyway, I suspect. But yes. It says only what I said."

Celisma glanced at the paper, saw that indeed it said only what Matilde claimed, and added, her voice wavering, "Well, I got to take your word on it, Madame."

"That's right," Matilde grinned.

Celisma took the quill and made a broad X on the line below the writing, passing it back to Matilde with all the reluctance she could feign.

Matilde examined the paper and then folded it up in her expansive bodice. "I'll keep this safe, you may rest assured," she said, reaching for the jar and capping it, "and these, too, in case you change your mind." She turned once more to Alex, who looked up and gurgled. Laughing softly, she swept from the room.

The instant she was out the door, Celisma yanked Alex out of the cradle and held him tightly to her bosom. She stepped to the door and peered out. Matilde was gone. She slipped down the hall, out the back door, and into the garden. Way off down the path she could see Madame walking leisurely back to Beausonge, her lantern by her side. When she could no longer see Matilde, Celisma turned to the woods, still clutching Alex.

It took her long moments, but finally she found the log where she had hidden the clay and bone effigy she had made years before. It was still safe within the hollowed-out gum tree, the lace ribbon tight around its neck and waist. She laid

391

Alex down on her shawl in the grass, wrapping him tightly so he could not roll. He promptly fell asleep.

She took the effigy to the edge of the bayou and crouched with it in a small eddying pool. Calling up out of her mind the old remembered chants her mother taught her, she began to lave the effigy with water, ever increasing wavelets that she pushed over it, over its body and head, until it was soaked, then softened, and finally, it began to dissolve away in the splashings she poured over it. When it would barely hold together with the clay and bones, she held it aloft in the moonlight and shouted the rest of the spell. Her voice seemed shockingly loud in the bayou night, startling the crickets and frogs to silence.

But she no longer cared who heard or saw.

There was a time when the jaguar roamed the bayou in abundance, along with many red wolves, smaller cousins of the gray wolf. When the Spanish government placed heavy bounties on them, however, both magnificent predators went south into Mexico and Central America. In 1850, though, a hunter could still occasionally see the red wolf, easing through the swamp as silently as smoke, and its pelt was in high demand among the trappers.

The scarlet ibis and flamingo, too, made the bayou their home in the middle of the last century, flocking in great numbers as they moved south to the gulf and their South American roosts. But as man encroached into the deep swamp, they, too, no longer made the delta part of their flight path. In the same way, the roseate spoonbill, the swallow-tailed kite, the whooping crane, the passenger pigeon, and the ivory-billed woodpecker also left the bayou. Some of these species quickly became extinct, once deprived of their traditional winter grounds.

Those birds which survived were species which did not attract man's eye with their color or their plumage. Those which thrived were those which could, like good street fighters, adjust to changing, crowded conditions, and make them their own.

The bird approached the rookery, almost dragging his wide wings with exhaustion. Even to his eyes, the nest seemed a bulky, sloppy affair, thrown together loosely and ill-kempt. But there was no help for it. He swam towards the leaning tree on which the nest rested, moving through the water with more speed, watching the far bank all the while.

He paused at the point where the trunk of the tree entered the water and then angled his long, snakelike head upwards. His strong claws and webbed feet gripped the tree trunk, and he went eight feet up to where the three lumpy eggs lay on the leaf lining. All three safe. Ugly, untended, but safe.

Hesh, himself, had few attractive characteristics. He was a snakebird, one of the more numerous birds of the bayou. Called the water turkey, the darter, or the *anhinga*, he nested among the herons and egrets but looked nothing like them.

From the point of his tapered beak to the tip of his long brown-banded tail, he was three narrow feet of black wing and mostly all neck. His neck had so many extra vertebrae that he could literally tie it into a knot without discomfort. His beak was a five-inch dagger, and his head was scarcely wider than his neck. All together, beak, head, and neck made up more than a third of his length.

Normally he would have been returning to find his mate and relieve her in the tiresome incubation of their eggs. But several days after the laying, she had been taken by an alligator while fishing in the shallows.

Now that he was reasonably dried, he clambered clumsily atop the nest and settled himself over the eggs. It would take him almost twice as long to hatch this clutch alone, but he was determined to do so. Determined, too, to provide for the fledglings until they were able to leave the nest and hunt for themselves.

He sat until late in the afternoon, but he could not sit still. Restlessly he turned, jerked his tail up and down, and writhed his neck in snakelike fashion, rearranging twigs and bits of leaves as much in boredom as for tidiness.

As the shadows grew longer, he became more nervous and finally stood up, climbed out onto the branch, and poised himself. Then, with a fluid movement, he lowered his head until his beak slid down his breast, past the branch, and even below his tail before his feet left their grip. Almost bonelessly, he slid into the water without a sound, and with no more of a ripple than if a dagger had pierced the surface.

He flashed through the waters with great speed, his webbed legs pumping like pistons, and he located his prey swiftly. A cordon of bass hovered near the submerged stump of an old cypress tree. As he approached them, Hesh pulled his neck back so tightly that his head was nearly at his shoulders. The fish scattered, but he selected his victim, maneuvered the fish away from the cover of the stumps, and then, with incredible speed and accuracy—much like a striking snake—he shot his head forward with a lightning thrust. His beak plunged completely through a fish and held it fast.

The bass struggled frantically, but each wiggle only caused Hesh to tighten its impalement. When the floppings weakened, the bird used the fine, toothlike serations of his beak to grip and hold the fish broadside, returning to the surface.

He had been under only six minutes, though he could have stayed under much longer. Now he swam to a nearby sandbar, and there he flipped the fish into the air, deftly caught it head first, and swallowed it whole. The outline of the fish's body as it slid down his throat made it look as though it actually swam to his belly.

The snakebird shook his head, preened his breast and wing feathers, and started the swim back to his nest. Suddenly, he saw the ominous snout and eyes of an alligator swiftly cutting the water towards him.

Hesh instantly lowered himself into the water, so that only his eyes and nostrils remained above. With no telltale wake and looking very like a cottonmouth, he swam rapidly towards a tupelo that had toppled into the water.

The alligator headed to the place in the water where he had last seen the wake and the bird. But no bird remained. No wake followed what seemed to be a snake swimming away. The alligator circled several times in the area, while the snakebird clambered up the sloping tupelo trunk. Finally, reluctantly, the alligator gave up and drifted back casually towards the opposite bank, moving his snout this way and that to scent the disappeared prey.

Hesh opened his wings and tail once the alligator was gone. He shook the water from his plumage, waiting for his heart rate to slow. He could not have flown so wet or so frightened. The sun was just setting when he flapped his wings vigorously a few times, did a hopping jig from one webbed foot to the other, and then flung himself into the air.

He had to beat his wings swiftly to rise above the trees, for he swam much better than he flew. Finally he caught an air current and was able to glide above the bayou, his sharp eyes watching for the movements below. He saw the deer awake and begin to browse; he saw the egrets and herons return to their roosts for the night. He watched the muskrats and the nutria amble out to feed on the tubers along the bayou edges. The marsh rabbits and the flying squirrels, the raccoons, the skunks, and the owls below him all began to stir for the foraging and hunting ahead.

He was most alert for another colony of his kind, a grouping he might join for the evening feed. If he could find such a colony, he might also find a lone female willing to adopt the eggs, share the incubation chores, and take on the chicks as foundlings. He had seen this happen before, when one mate or another was taken, though it was late in the nesting season.

But he found no colony in the twelve-mile radius he flew that day.

Only when dusk was deep did he arrow back to that portion of the bayou where his nest waited. He knifed into the water a hundred yards away, for he preferred to come to it from the water rather than from air.

After drying himself once more, he settled down over the eggs, lulled by the chorus of croaks and chirps from the frogs and crickets all around him, into a fitful sleep.

Each year Madame Matilde had taken the family for the season to New Orleans, and then on to Isle Dernier. The southernmost island off the Teche, Isle Dernier, or Last Island as it was called by the wealthy who flocked to the resort, was a cool respite from the heat of the bayou in the summer months. Also, it was one place at least where the Bronze Jack did not care to go. Something about the saltwater kept off the fever, they said, and the planters from up and down Lafourche made the pilgrimage first to the city and then to Last Island to see and be seen.

In 1856, Matilde announced that Samuel would be accompanying her for the first time for at least part of their holiday. Celisma heard the news well before Samuel confessed it to her, for Sally Red had it from Betzy that the Master's trunks were being packed as well.

That very night, Samuel came to see Celisma put Alex to bed, an event he rarely attended. The boy was five years old now, and it was clear he would have his father's slender nose and light complexion, no matter how else his hair might darken down. He was bright and inquisitive, if a little shy with strangers. Celisma loved most the gentleness in her son, a trait she felt he must have got from his father, who long ago had to hide it behind so many other things. Alex ran to the door and laughed, clapping his hands when he saw Samuel approach.

"He knows his *papa,*" Celisma said, smiling. "No one else gets such a welcome."

Out of his pocket Samuel took the bit of caramel he always brought for Alex. "No one else bribes him so well," he grinned ruefully. "I believe he'd clap for a gator if he carried a caramel in his jaws."

He dandled the child for a moment, hefting him up and feeling his weight as he always did, drawing cries of glee from Alex. Celisma laughed, filled with a secret joy to see Samuel's face relax into happier lines when he saw the boy. She finally took him from his father's arms and settled Alex once more, leading Samuel out of the room and into the light.

He wasted no time. "Matilde has it in her head," he said gruffly, "that I must accompany her south this season."

"Why this season more than last?"

He shrugged. "She says that now the girls are gone and will not accompany her, she can scarcely go alone."

"They went all the years before."

"They have their own families to see to now. It's too much to ask that their husbands wave them off for two months or more without question. Even if they wanted to go."

"So. She has it in her head, then. And what is in *your* head, *cher?*"

He frowned. "Of course, I don't wish to go, Celisma. You know that, I scarcely need say it. But if I refuse outright, I will pay for it over and over for the rest of the year."

"You feel you owe her." It was not a question.

He sighed. "I always have." His mouth twisted ruefully. "So does she. But look, maybe it's easier simply to accede to her wishes this time than to battle her to a state of siege. She has," he added, "been unusually docile of late. I don't want to get her riled up again."

It was true, she had to admit. If she had not known that Beausonge and BonReve shared a boundary, she would never have felt Matilde's presence. The wife had been silent since that evil night of confrontation. Clearly, she felt she had what she wanted. Now, almost as if she willed Celisma and her child invisible, she had ceased her ranting and threats.

And yet, Celisma felt a strong uneasiness at the thought of him going. She wanted to ask him to stay, but she dared not.

"How long you be gone?" she asked carefully.

"No longer than I must. I suspect she'll get bored in a week or two, and certainly I can't stay more than that, no matter what she wants. Let us say three weeks. Surely you and Alex can manage without me that long." He smiled gently to take away the sting.

She smiled back and saw then in the lamplight—with a bit of a shock—how old he had become since she first loved him. Now the silver in his hair was prominent, but she could recall the first few gray hairs he found and how he had grimaced at them. Now, his shoulders which were once so stout—broad enough it seemed to her to hold all of Beausonge and even some of the world beyond—these same shoulders were shrunken and curved, as though seeking refuge somewhere within his own chest.

I am stronger than he, she realized suddenly. I have been for a good while. I must be and so, I am.

"*Vraiment, cher,*" she said calmly, "me an' Alex can manage fine. It is the slow time for folks to travel upriver. Mostly, they go where the breezes keep the bugs off. When you go then?"

He stood and walked to the window, gazing out at the darkness of the river. "She wants to go tomorrow."

She turned quickly in her seat. "And if I be weepin' an' beggin' you not to go?"

He turned to her with a smile. "I knew you wouldn't, Celly. You never do. I can count on you."

She went to him and embraced him, pulling him gently towards her small bed in the shadows, a refuge he visited rarely now. "Yes. Everyone can count on Celly."

Last Island lay nearly due east and west and seemed to be, from the approach of Bayou Teche, the last piece of land that Louisiana had to spare, thrown boldly out to sea to protect the land itself from the surging waves of the gulf. It was the last of the chain of islands composed of Grand Terre, Grand Isle, and Cheniere Caminada, all of them clustered west of the Mississippi. Behind Last Island was a fine bay, ten miles in width, always calm and clear as an inland lake. In front spread the vast expanse of the gulf with mountainous waves that pounded the shore.

On one side was peace; on the other, the war of the elements.

In the summer of 1854, a fine hotel rose up three stories, soon followed by more than thirty private and lavish homes. These were only occupied during the summer months, as the planters sailed down to escape the heat and mosquitoes of the bayou country.

The beach at Last Island, more than twenty miles in length and smooth as a white mirror, teemed every evening of the summer season with visitors. Dignified old gentlemen strolled with their carefully coiffed and bonneted wives. Young men in red flannel shirts and duck trousers and their ladies in green, red, and gray bomazet bloomer bathing costumes teased each other in the water or rode spirited horses up and down the sand. Carriages whirled by on the boardwalk, each more gaily decorated than the last.

The St. Charles Hotel, though not as lavish as its sister in New Orleans, still managed to delight guests with feasts of oysters, turtle soup, and fish of every variety.

Last Island held onto some quaint customs, and the least popular was that the St. Charles restricted dances to only twice a week. Further, the sum of one dollar was assessed each gentleman who led a lady to the floor.

"But what else can you do?" expressed a swain. "There is no other game in town, and the belles from Terrebonne and Pointe Coupee! You will not find more beautiful anywhere in *Lousiane.* It's worth a dollar just to see them move their legs!"

The summer of 1856, Matilde had booked them at a new hotel, the Muggah, which sat at the western end of the island, facing the gulf.

"The St. Charles is getting *passé,*" she said firmly, "and it will do them good to be reminded that they are not the only shell on the beach. The Heberts and Dupuys will be on the island while we are there, Samuel, and I expect we should bring Odette and Tilly with us, don't you think? I understand the help at Muggah's is not quite what the St. Charles offers,

400

but then the rooms are larger and the atmosphere more what I'd prefer."

"And what is that?" He looked up from his papers with ill-concealed boredom.

She raised her brows and stared at him a moment. "I don't like that tone, Samuel," she said calmly, "and I'll thank you not to use it with me again. The St. Charles is catering to the likes of the Swanbecks, those upstarts who bought that beautiful old plantation on the Teche and then ruined it, simply ruined it with all their Northern furbelows. I don't care to spend my season around annoying trash like that. Now that I think on it, I believe we'll need Ulysses and perhaps Profit as well, so do tell them they'll be going along." And then she turned and went out of the room, as though her words were a slamming door.

Within days, the Weitz entourage was en route, making the trip to New Orleans and from there, on the Morgan Rail Road to Bayou Boeuf, thence by steamer down the Atchafalaya River into the gulf, and up to the dock of Last Island.

That August at Last Island, the crowds were thick. The summer had been hot and damp, so the sugar was laid by early. Work around most plantations was at a minimum, and many who might not have been able to come south did so, to catch the last cool breezes before grinding set in.

But the breezes the week Samuel and Matilde arrived were almost annoying. The wind grew insistent and strong, whisking sand about in bathers' eyes and making the horses skittish.

By August 8, the wind had increased to where the waters of Caillou Bay were crowding the north shore of the island. Large swells with sheared tops were coming in from the gulf. Conversations at the supper hour turned to the excitement of a possible storm at sea. It would be great fun to watch it, a few of the young men told their ladies, from the top *gallerie* of the St. Charles.

By dusk, the sunset over the gulf was full of color and

drama, and the St. Charles gallery held as many as could fit and lean over the rail. The waves were running higher and faster with a great variety of form, almost as if they were vying with each other for an exhibition of beauty and power.

"They seem to be speaking to us," a young woman said in wonder, "with the roaring voice of God."

"Well, they're making it nigh impossible to bathe," her escort answered with no small disgust. "I'm a strong swimmer and I had a good bit of trouble making it back to shore. I don't recommend going in until they calm down, that's certain."

There was a ball at the St. Charles that evening, and Samuel insisted they attend, for the guest violinist was an old German who was famous for his delicacy with the instrument. When the ball broke up about midnight, the sea was churning and heavy. Word came to the dancers that the steamboat *Star* was due in from Bayou Boeuf that night on its regular passenger run, but had not arrived.

"Probably sought a safer mooring," Samuel said to Matilde, watching the sea with a frown. They sat out on the gallery, listening to the last few waltzes being played. They had shared some wine, and he felt particularly tender towards his wife this night.

"Do you think it will get worse?" she asked, following his eyes out to the waves.

"If it does, there's no way to get off the island unless the *Star* lands," he said. "But perhaps she'll try to dock at dawn."

"Well, I had it from Monsieur McAllister that the Muggah has withstood many storms before. He says it'll stand a tornado, so if the ship doesn't come, we'll be safe there, at least. I'm glad I insisted on the Muggah instead of the St. Charles. These floors are all but rotting away beneath us, I can hear them creak when we dance."

Sunday morning dawned gray with heavy rain. The wind continued to rise in strength, and still no sign of the *Star*.

Samuel went out walking that morning, bracing himself against the gale, and he saw pieces of driftwood lodged in dead cypresses all over the highest points of the island—which were no more than five or six feet above sea level. Clearly, Last Island had been swept by storms before.

By mid-morning, the call came up that the *Star* had been sighted. A huge crowd watched and waited on the beach as she tried to beat her way towards the island, but the wind forced her onto the north shore. There she went aground before the eyes of the crowd. Now there was no escape.

Samuel hurried Matilde back to their rooms in the Muggah Hotel, and there they collected Odette, Ulysses, and the others around them. "The storm is coming in hard," Samuel said to them solemnly, "and there's no way to get off the island. We must get ready for it as well as we can." He made them collect all the trunks and mattresses in that one room and pile them against the windows. To his surprise, his wife did not whimper or rage against their fate, but only put her shoulder to the mattresses alongside Odette, calling to Ulysses to help her drag a trunk in place.

The wind was howling outside with a ferocity that whipped the water and sand into the air until it was almost dark; they could hear an occasional scream or cry, the desperate lowing of the penned stock almost right beneath their gallery where they had been brought for shelter, and the yawning creak of the hotel walls. When one particularly strong gust came, the whole top of the roof lifted off as one piece of timber, and the room tilted crazily more than five feet to the front. They hurried to pull the mattresses on top of them for protection, and Samuel caught Matilde's arm as she rushed by in the wind. He pulled her next to him, under a mattress, calling out to the others to hold on for their lives.

"Will the waters reach us?" Matilde screamed at him, her eyes wide and white with terror.

For answer, a rushing wave of water swept through the roofless room from the outside gallery, splashing them full in the face and lifting them off the floor. Matilde shrieked then, as did the others, and Samuel shouted to them that they must hold to each other, to anything at all to be saved.

"I cannot save you now!" he added to Matilde above the din, "we are in God's hands!"

She threw her arms around his neck, and he could barely breathe for the strength of her grip. In the room, he could hear the shrieks of the slaves, the cry of Odette to Ulysses to grab hold of a timber, the crash and swirl of water and wood, and he knew that death was all around him, would likely take them all in moments.

"Say an act of contrition!" Matilde cried in his ear, "ask God for forgiveness, Samuel, or you'll die with sin on your soul!"

Before he could speak, the sea-facing side of the room caved in on them and the waters rushed in with a fury. He rolled over and over, taking in great gulps of sea water and choking, saw Matilde swirl by in deep water, barely visible in the wreckage and debris, Odette went by with the current, and he thought in that instant of Celisma, her face calm and strong before him, and he could bring no act of contrition to his mind at all. God will have to understand us, he told himself, and what she brought to me. It was the last thought he had as the waters closed over his head.

The hurricane that struck Last Island roared up the bayou, flattened cane crops, ruined cotton, and flooded New Orleans to her second stories. News from the gulf was slow to come, since severe weather for several days kept most mainland boats in their berths. When a few rescue boats did arrive at

Last Island, they found less than two hundred had survived, scarcely a third of the island's visitors. Lists of the lost were rushed to New Orleans, and from there the news came to the bayou.

Celisma was bathing Alex in his copper tub when Daniel came and stood in the kitchen door. She saw his face and instantly pulled her son out of the water, holding him to her though he was dripping wet. He gave a startled cry and fell silent, his large eyes taking in his mother and Daniel, who stood staring at each other.

"You have news?" she finally asked faintly.

He nodded, his head down, his hat revolving in his great black hands.

She shuddered, a great wracking shiver that started at the base of her spine and made her head almost rattle in its ferocity. Alex whimpered, pulling back and sliding his thumb in his mouth. "He is gone," she said, her voice flat and final. It was not a question. She did not need to ask. She suddenly felt his loss as keenly as though she'd seen him take the final gasping mouthful of saltwater herself, had let him slip away from her rescuing arms right before her eyes.

Wordlessly, Daniel stepped forward and held out his hands to Alex, and she placed the child in his arms. Freed, she threw her hand over her face and slumped to the floor, rocking and groaning.

Was it possible that the hoodoo took him, that God took him to punish her? Lord Jesus, she moaned, the one most punished'll be my son, who will never know his father, maybe never learn to grow a strength to go with his gentleness . . .

"They both gone," Daniel said, his voice full of pain. He followed her to the floor, sitting alongside her with Alex in his lap, one arm awkwardly around her shoulder, while she wailed out her grief like the storm itself.

It did not take long for the children of Beausonge to finish their mourning and remember their rights. Samuel and Matilde were laid alongside Oliva in a funeral cortege which called out carriages from as far away as Baton Rouge. Celisma stood dry-eyed at the edge of the crowd, holding Alex in her arms. Dressed in black, she stayed by the rest of the slaves, as she saw Ulysses, Odette, and the others set into the ground. The bodies of Profit and Tilly had not been found, but their souls were given comfort, she knew, by the murmurs of all who stood and bowed their heads.

Within days, she was summoned to attend the young Madames and Pierre in the drawing room. She gave Alex over to Sally Red and, wrapped in a silk shawl which Samuel had long ago brought her from New Orleans, she went up the front steps of Beausonge for the first time in over ten years.

Pierre met her at the great entry, his face grim and hard. "Who gave you leave to come by the front door?" he asked.

"You did," she replied calmly, "when you invite me to come."

"This isn't a social gathering," he said, ushering her inside to the coolness of the gallery.

Of course, she knew that. The two Misses sat waiting in the large wicker chairs which once held Samuel and Matilde. At the sight of them, she almost faltered, so much did Samuel come to her mind's eye. But then she steeled herself. Behind them stood the family solicitor, Monsieur Desobry. The man

did not return her bow but only nodded his head in acknowl-
edgement.

"Please come in, Celly," Thérèse said evenly. "We have
some business which concerns you, and we thought it best to
talk it over face-to-face, rather than simply let you hear of it
through Monsieur Desobry." She gestured to a small chair
to one side.

Celisma took her time arranging her skirt and her shawl
once she was seated. When she raised her head, she looked
directly at Amélie and smiled. The woman smiled back involuntarily, then caught her sister's glance and her smile
faltered.

Pierre did not take a seat but stood before the three
women, his hands clasped behind him as though in oratory.
"As you know, Celisma," he began solemnly, "we were never
agreed as to your status here at Beausonge, and in fact it's
against the laws of Louisiana for you to stay. For a long
while, you've been aware that no one wanted you here after
your emancipation."

"Your father did," she said firmly. A long pause followed
wherein all three siblings met her eyes and took her measure.

"Well, far be it for me to speak ill of the dead, but my
father wanted a lot of things that I could hardly stomach. Be
that as it may," Pierre finally went on, "it is my responsibility
to take care of the place as *both* our parents would have
wished, and to that end, I'll be consolidating our holdings so
as to manage them better and selling Beausonge in the near
future. I'm selling BonReve as well, so you got to find yourself another place. Say, by the end of this month. For now,
I'll be closing it down to further guests for a proper period
of mourning."

Celisma almost gasped aloud, but she stifled her response
with effort. She waited, letting her thoughts settle like riled
water. Then she poured liquid silver into her voice as she
said, "I be sorry to see Beausonge go to a stranger. That cain'
be what your *papa* would want if he here to say so. But

nothin' I can do 'bout that. BonReve is not yours to sell, though. I be stayin', as M'sieu Sam promise. BonReve don't belong to you."

As Pierre began to sputter, Monsieur Desobry broke in with a cultured drawl that crawled as smoothly as a snake across mud. "Why whatever can you mean, Celly? Who does BonReve belong to, then?"

"BonReve belong to Alex Weitz. M'sieu Sam make that promise to me before my son were born."

Amélie's face fell and she began to weep quietly, covering her mouth with one hand.

Pierre said, "You signed a paper that your bastard is no kin to us. My mother told me—"

"Your mother be mistaken. I tole her what she want to hear, but it ain' true then, an' ain' true now. I never signed no paper."

"It has your mark!"

"I don' make my mark," she replied calmly. "I write my name. Alex Weitz is son to Samuel, same as you."

"How dare you tell such a lie," Pierre said, his voice frozen. "And use my father's name. So many lies! You can't prove your bastard is kin to us. He could have been fathered by a hundred men, and each of them slept under your roof!"

"Perhaps we are getting away from the point of the discussion here," Monsieur Desobry said gently, his hand on Thérèse's shoulder. She had turned a white smoldering glance on Celisma when first she spoke. Her eyes blazed, but she said nothing, except to hush her sister once.

"The issue at hand," the solicitor went on smoothly, "is not the parentage of a child, but the ownership of certain lands and assets, is it not? Can you produce a legal deed, Celisma, proving that your . . . progeny has rights to Bon-Reve?"

"No suh," she said quickly, "but M'sieu Sam tole me he made such a thing. He sold BonReve to M'sieu Simon, an'

M'sieu Simon sell it to me. All this be with his other papers, I 'spect."

"There is no such document," Monsieur Desobry replied easily. "Perhaps you were mistaken about Monsieur Weitz's intent."

"No suh. He give BonReve to my son. He give it to Alex forever."

Pierre chuckled mirthlessly. "There's no such thing as forever, Celly, even you should know that."

"Let me understand this," Thérèse said, speaking for the second time. "This mulatress claims that her boy is—" and here, her mouth wrinkled in disdain, "my half-brother. She also claims that this child has some sort of right to my father's property. And yet she has nothing to prove either claim." She looked up at the solicitor and her brother, from one to the other. "Are these the circumstances?"

"That's about it," Monsieur Desobry reassured her.

Thérèse rose suddenly, gathering her skirts around her. "Then I see no reason to continue the conversation. Celly, I believe you understood my brother clearly. Please be off our land before the month is out." She reached down and took hold of Amélie's hand, pulling her up out of her chair as though to go.

"I can prove what I say," Celisma said, never budging from her seat.

"How could you ever prove such a pack of lies?" Thérèse asked coldly. "I wouldn't believe Jesus Himself if He swore it was true."

"Would you believe the tax man?" Celisma asked. "I got records provin' I pay the taxes on BonReve these many years past. They be in my name. M'sieu Sam take the money an' pay for me an' give the rest to M'sieu Simon for buyin' BonReve."

Thérèse froze, sinking back into the seat, her spine as stiff as the marble column behind her. She lifted her eyes to Monsieur Desobry in supplication.

"Paying taxes on a piece of property does not prove ownership, Celisma, did you think it did?" the solicitor answered smoothly. "Why I can pay the taxes on any number of parcels up and down this river, and it doesn't give me the right to claim ownership. If I were so stupid as to be convinced to pay somebody else's taxes for a year or two, it still doesn't give me the deed in my hand. Without a deed in your hand, I'm afraid you've got nothing but receipts to show for your efforts. And while it was good of you to take the profits of BonReve and pay a share of the taxes—"

"I pay *all* the taxes, every year!"

"That may well be, but they were paid from profits on property you did not own. Profits which rightfully belonged to the Weitz estate and heirs, either Samuel's or Simon's. In a sense, you're mighty lucky they don't ask you to account for those profits for the past years. Since you're only an employee working for wages, they'd have every right to do just that. Surely it didn't take all the profits from BonReve just to pay the taxes?"

She shook her head, her eyes wide in disbelief. "I be buyin' BonReve, he say!"

"*You* say, he said. But what did you do with the monies left over, after the expenses? What did you do with the monies which belonged to Monsieur Pierre and Mistresses Thérèse and Amélie?"

"M'sieu Sam, he saw to that," she said quietly. "He give me to buy what BonReve need, an' he say to pay the taxes. I sign the papers an' I pay, jes' as he say. An' he give BonReve to his son."

"If you say that again," Pierre shouted, "I'll have the sheriff arrest you within the hour for theft!"

Celisma gripped her hands before her in a fist and shut her eyes tight.

"It's not necessary to make ugly threats," Monsieur Desobry said calmly. "Celisma is a free woman, and I'm sure she understands what her rights are and are not in this situation. Unfortunately, we have no proof of her claim that her son owns BonReve. She cannot even prove that her son is entitled to own property."

"What do you mean?" Thérèse asked, her eyes suddenly bright and glittering.

"I mean that her son cannot legally own property if he is a slave."

"My son is free!" Celisma cried.

"You say," Monsieur Desobry continued, "but we have no proof of this, do we? If your son's father is a slave, he may well be a slave also, depending on where he was fathered and when, regardless of your own emancipation. He may well have been fathered by—"

"Daniel," Pierre said quickly. "By Daniel or Tim or any of those niggers she bossed around BonReve."

"Alex be white!"

Monsieur Desobry shrugged. "The courts long ago stopped trying to prove parentage by the color of skin, Celisma. That can be, as you know, such a quirky thing, what with throwbacks and all. Any number of lighter infants are born to colored parents and dark-skinned babies show up in white folks' cradles often enough to make it impossible to judge. No," and here he formed a steeple with his fingertips, "the courts recognize only one fact. Who is the child's father and mother. Mother is easy enough to say, most times, but the father is a whole other kettle of fish. Now, if the mother is free and the father is free and claims him, then the baby is free as well, no matter what color. If the mother is free and the father is not, that child could be free or could be just as much slave as his father, it just depends, even if he be snow white as a river egret. Because, as you know, the Louisiana legislature just made emancipation illegal this year."

At the shocked look she threw him, he said, "Yes, Madame. Even your own claim to freedom might well be in jeopardy, the way the wind is blowing these days, particularly since you did not leave the state as the law demands.

There are precedences for re-enslaving emancipated slaves who do not vacate, not to mention any offspring born during that period when they were breaking the law. But back to the gist. Do you have some sort of proof of what you claim, Celisma?"

Once again, she shook her head slowly.

"Then you can hardly expect that Monsieur Weitz and his sisters will accept such a supposition on your word alone? Neither will any court, of course. And unless you can prove your son's claim to freedom, he cannot own land. Furthermore, I think I can say without fear of contradiction that unless you agree to Monsieur Pierre's request that you leave BonReve within the month—no, let us say sooner than that. Let us say that you will be gone in one week, Celisma. Because if you do not agree to leave without making further trouble, I will, of course, have to counsel Monsieur Pierre to collect the rest of his property as well, using whatever force is necessary."

Celisma raised her head and stared at the man with cold fear. She saw that Thérèse and Pierre were smiling now, making no attempt to hide their satisfaction. Only Amélie turned away, unable to meet her eyes.

"And that property would, naturally, include your son, since he was likely fathered by slaves owned by Beausonge and during a time when your own emancipation was in jeopardy."

In the brief gasping silence that followed, Celisma thought she would fall from the chair, slip sideways and hit her head on the cold marble floor, never rise again, never open her eyes on such despair—but she said, hoarsely, "I kill him first."

Pierre now had adopted the solicitor's soft tone, with none of its gentleness. "Then we'd have the sheriff arrest you for murder as well as theft." He leaned back against the marble column. "I think we've covered all the ground we need to, Celisma. No doubt you've managed to squirrel away plenty of money from my father in the last few years, and that'll be enough to get you started someplace else. We won't take it from you if you close down BonReve and be off within a week. You can keep that much of our property, anyway. As to the other piece of property Monsieur Desobry referred to—Alex, you say you've named him?—I'll have to give that some thought. A male slave, even a child, fetches a pretty price these days in Natchez. 'Course he's too white for the field, they'd likely kill him there, but he's not too white for a house nigger. He's what, about five? Too late to feed him off a black tit, but I expect if we put him in the quarters, he'd likely darken down in time. That's all the talking we're doing, Celisma." With that, he extended an arm to each sister and escorted them off the gallery.

Celisma rose slowly to her feet. As she reached the door, Monsieur Desobry spoke gently from the shadows behind her. "You're a smart woman, Celisma, you wouldn't have come this far if you were not. You come out of this with more than most in your place would have, likely. You come out with a fine son and your freedom, if you do the right thing. Plenty wenches in your place, who did what you did, get the lash and worse."

She turned and gazed at him with all her fear in her eyes. "God see what you do," she said.

"Yes, He does," Monsieur Desobry answered after a pause. "And I expect you've got plenty to thank Him for."

"What I thank Him for, in all this trouble?"

"Thank Him," the solicitor said, "because He saw fit to take Madame Matilde along with Master Samuel, my dear. Or you would find yourself in hell instead of simply in limbo."

Celisma could scarcely rise the next morning. She was so suffused with terror and despair that she got up only long enough to get Alex washed and fed, and then went back down again to her bed. What should she do, what could she do, and who could she call on for help? She clenched her fists together at her breast and wept harder than she had when Samuel died. Could such a thing be that her son might be taken from her? Could they both be slaves again? Would God permit such a torture as the mere taste of freedom—only to yank it away? Before God, she vowed, I *will* kill him before I let him be taken by that devil, Pierre! I will kill them *both* and let them hang me for it!

The thought came again, as it had a dozen times in the night, that they must run away. She feverishly counted up again the money she had hidden, surely enough to get far from Beausonge, far north to wherever freedom was sure. But would the patrollers stop her? Would they take Alex from her right there on the road? Would they whip her, beat her, chain her up like a dog? And what of BonReve?

When she thought of all the days, weeks, months she had worked to make the house a place where decent folk would come, when she thought of all the dreams she had—the dreams that Samuel had!—she could only weep and writhe on the bed, holding herself in fear.

He had promised, he had promised! she chanted to herself over and over, moaning in disbelief. No papers, the man said, nothing to prove his promise. Nothing to prove that Alex was born of his seed, that there had ever been anything between them but the common ugly lust of a master for slave.

She rose finally and took Alex in her arms, heading for the river. Up and down she walked with him, her eyes cast to the water, her mind racing over the doom that seemed as inevitable as the pull of the current. Was there nothing fair in this world, under the eyes of God? Was there no time when she might say, "This, then, is mine at last to keep and hold forever"? After hours of walking, she finally exhausted her fear and from its residue, slowly, anger began to flow.

She thought of the many colored wenches, some of them black, others various hues, who had been taken by white lovers. Mostly, they got something out of the arrangement they could hold to their heart. The wench usually got some frocks, maybe some gewgaws for herself, or a little piece of swamp land. Something for her children, too. She got these things, even if she had a black husband and children by him as well. Her black husband couldn't do much about her white lover, of course, he was gelded by the same white man who had neutered his white wife, keeping her in her fancy drawing room, breathing the smells of magnolias, musty portieres, and pride.

The only one who took his pleasure with no payment, really, was the white man.

But Samuel had been different, she knew that even as she felt the anger in her heart. Not a perfect man, Lord knows, maybe not even a loving man, all told. But certainly a man who wanted love. A man who surely kept his promises, she breathed in a whisper of hope.

At first, she could think of no place to go, no one who could possibly help her. But she knew that somehow, there was an answer, and she must find it. All of her life had taught her this lesson, if she had learned no other: that she would come out on top sooner or later and that everything that happened to her, no matter how fearsome it might seem, would ultimately be for the best.

Finally she sat and willed herself to think, forced herself to stop weeping and steel herself for battle. She dandled Alex on her lap, offering him a pat of mud when he fretted, for it did not seem fitting that he should disturb the silence of the bayou. He immediately sat down on the bank and began to build mud houses, telling himself a murmured tale which she could not follow.

She wished suddenly that she had named him herself. He was growing so fast now, getting taller and thinner almost as she watched. He had an inward eye, this boy, that made him seem to see private worlds more clearly than the world that was. Should have given him a river name, she thought, a name not bound to anything, just like the waters ain' bound to anything. When a woman birth a child, her waters break, she flows him forth, and he runs free. He must be free!

The shadows grew longer as she sat, and still she was motionless, watching the river swell and ebb and swirl away. In the drifting current, she saw a strange thing. A ball of fire ants was rolling along the surface of the river, tightly packed as though they were one living creature. In the center, she could see that worker ants carried the white pupa cases of their children, the blind helpless future of the whole swarm. And the ball of ants rolled and rotated constantly, so that no one layer of ants was ever under water for long. In this way, they all reached the other side of the river safely, and no layer of ants was sacrificed. What was important was that the young were protected and carried to the other side to live without harm.

By turning to each other for help and confessing their need, she thought wonderingly, they took strength from their numbers, as one arm cannot lift a burden alone and instinctively calls on another arm to pick up the load.

Though the evening was coming, she knew now what she must do and she knew she must waste no time. She gathered Alex into her arms, pulled her shawl tight round him, and set off down the bayou with more strength in her step than she had felt in two days.

Two mornings later, back at BonReve, she sat down to pen a careful note which asked for another audience with Monsieur Pierre and the two Misses, together with Monsieur Desobry. She signed her name with a flourish. Then she waited. At the end of that day, Betzy came tapping at her door, eyes wide and wondering, to tell her that Monsieur Pierre would expect her the next afternoon.

Celisma thanked her and lay down on the bed, pulling Alex to her side. Another low knock came then. Sally Red stuck her head in the room and glanced around curiously. "You not packin'?"

"Not yet," Celisma said calmly.

Sally Red's face crumpled. "I hear the news, don' try to spare me, *cher.* I hear we all to be sold, me an' Tim an' Daniel an' all of us, Massa Pierre, he say so." She covered her head with her apron and wailed. "I wish I go with Odette an' Ulysses! Better be dead than on a block in Baton Rouge!"

"Stop that weepin'," Celisma said firmly. "M'sieu Pierre don' got the last word on what goes on at BonReve, not yet anyway. I tell you when it be time to weep."

Sally Red lowered her apron and fixed Celisma with a shocked stare. At the fierceness of her face, she backed out of the room, wiping her hands on her apron and shaking her head in wonder. "The day you come," she murmured, "I tole Odette, that chile goin'ta make the wind blow her way. Yessm', I say jes' that." She quietly closed the door behind her.

The next afternoon, Celisma once more walked up the front steps of the big house. But this time, she did not walk alone. Behind her, his shoulders bent with age, his hair silvered on his head, walked Simon Weitz. Together, they stood on the gallery facing Pierre and Monsieur Desobry.

"I did not expect you, Uncle," Pierre said courteously, extending a beckoning hand to a vacant chair. He ignored

417

Celisma completely. "Did you wish to discuss some of the details of the disposition of my father's estate?"

"Actually," Monsieur Desobry spoke up, "it would be best if we dispense with Celisma's visit first, and then we can speak freely with Monsieur Weitz about any concerns he might have. Rest assured, Monsieur, that no sale of Beausonge will take place without your consultation."

"It is not the sale of Beausonge I come about," Simon said easily, "but the sale of BonReve."

Pierre glanced quickly at his solicitor. "And how does that little place concern you, Uncle?"

"It does not concern me at all anymore. But it does concern Celisma, and so I have come on her behalf."

With that, Pierre sat down in the larger wicker chair, feeling with his hand behind him to hold it steady.

Simon Weitz reached into his vest pocket and withdrew a letter which he carefully unfolded and placed in his lap. Then, from another pocket, he withdrew his spectacles, almost identical to the pair that Samuel had worn right before his death. Clearing his throat and lifting the letter, he said, "Celisma has told you that my brother intended BonReve to belong to his son."

Behind Pierre came the sound of whisking taffeta, and Thérèse and Amélie stood behind their brother. Thérèse moved forward to place one hand on the back of his chair.

"I said you needn't bother yourself with this," Pierre said, his voice low.

"Clearly, we *do* need to bother," Thérèse answered, her eyes never leaving the letter in Simon's lap. The two women sat quietly, spreading their skirts with practiced motions.

Simon nodded to them cordially. "I have a letter here from my brother which proves her claim," Simon said simply, with formality. "And, of course, I knew you would want to see it yourself, since you will want to do what your father wished."

"And which claim does this letter address?" the solicitor asked carefully.

"Actually," Simon said, adjusting his glasses and reading the letter, "it clears up both claims she makes. 'I have deeded BonReve over to you to be sold to Celisma in her name,' he writes here, 'and now that my son is born, I want the place to be in his name as well.'" Simon looked up. "He goes on to name Alex and to say that he wants him to have the security of BonReve as his own." He ignored Pierre's outstretched hand and passed the letter to the solicitor. "I think you can see that Samuel's intent was clear, Monsieur."

Pierre's face was pale, but he did not speak. Monsieur Desobry read the letter carefully, taking long enough to read it more than once. He said, "Well, his intent seems clear enough, but men do not always accomplish their intent. We still have no deed."

"I have the deed," Simon said gently. "He sold me BonReve more than five years ago."

"But you've not sold it to this wench, surely, Uncle," Pierre said quickly. "And we will make you a handsome profit on it. It should, rightfully, stay with Beausonge, it's part of the land and part of my father's estate, no matter whose name is on the deed."

Simon took the letter back from Monsieur Desobry and turned it again and again in his hand silently.

"And, of course, we have only your word that this is, in fact, your brother's signature," Monsieur Desobry added.

"Let me see that," Pierre snatched at the letter.

Simon carefully handed it to him so that the bottom signature showed plainly.

"That could be *your* signature, just as well as my father's," he said.

"It is true, our signs are much alike," Simon said mildly. "But why would I forge such a document? I don't want BonReve."

Celisma felt the ache begin again in her throat, the ache

419

which she knew would surely choke her to death if it did not abate.

"No, I think if I swore in any court of law, I would be believed. And, of course, there is still the other claim which the letter proves," Simon finally said. "Alex has the same rights to BonReve that his other siblings share. As his father's son, I mean."

Pierre stiffened. Thérèse shook her head at Amélie, who only turned away.

Celisma looked up swiftly in time to see a hard glance pass between the solicitor and Pierre.

"In fact, as that goes, Alex has the same rights of inheritance to *all* of Beausonge, along with his half-sisters and half-brother. The judge will have to decide, I suppose, what rights those might be, but I'm sure that this letter will entitle him to share in all of his father's property, at least to some extent." Simon leaned back and folded his hands on his chest. "It will be interesting to see just what the court will make of such a claim. It *is* a legal claim, is it not, Monsieur?"

The solicitor opened his mouth once and shut it again. Finally he said, "One would suppose."

"Yes," Simon continued, "one would suppose. And, of course, once BonReve is his, he could then press his suit for some portion of Beausonge as well. *C'est vrai?*"

Monsieur Desobry ignored Pierre's gaping mouth. "Yes, that is the truth as well."

"This is outrageous!" Pierre shouted, rising and glowering at Simon. "You are not going to deed BonReve to this wench and her bastard!"

"I already have," Simon said, "as my brother wished."

Simon gazed up unflinchingly at Pierre, unfolded the letter in his lap and read aloud. "Celisma has blessed me with a fine son, and I must say he favors me more than Pierre. I always did wonder if Matilde had perhaps betrayed me, and each time I look at the man she claims is my blood, I wonder again, he is so little like me in all ways, my brother. You know she told me he was not mine at his birth. I have sometimes wondered if, in fact, she told the truth after all. I could only say this to you, for you understand how much those family resemblances mean, how much they are inescapable. No matter how our lives are different, we will always be two halves of a whole. And no matter how much our lives are the same, Pierre and I will never be father and son as I would wish. Perhaps this new child will bring me the filial pride he never did. Celisma has asked me to keep it secret, for she fears reprisal, and I shall, but to assure his future, I've decided to deed him BonReve, with your help—"

"There is still the issue of the law," Monsieur Desobry said swiftly. "She has broken the law which demands her departure, whatever else she may claim."

Simon did not raise his head but kept on reading. "I've spoken to Judge Beauregard, and he assures me that so long as she is a landowner and on the tax rolls, they cannot require her to vacate the state. I have left a copy of the deed with him, in case there's any question as to my intent. And should any member of my family attempt to block my wishes, I ask that you, my brother, act as my executor and take the portion of inheritance which would belong to that malcontent and distribute it to my son, Alex."

Pierre, white-faced, turned on his heel and slammed out of the room, with Thérèse, weeping, right behind him. Amélie rose slowly, stiffly, as though she were suddenly aged. She bowed her head briefly to Celisma with a slight smile. "I wish you *bonne chance,*" she said softly. "*Grandmère* always spoke so well of you." With those words, she glided gracefully from the room, her head tilted to one side as if she heard a murmuring tune from a distant instrument.

Celisma got to her feet, feeling more weary than she could recall since Alex was born. She bowed stiffly to the solicitor and turned to go. As she and Simon reached the door, Monsieur Desobry asked, "Madame, do you intend to pursue your claim against Beausonge?"

She said quietly, "I only want to be left alone with my son an' BonReve. Tell them that."

"And if I may ask, Monsieur," the solicitor turned now to Simon, "what is your interest in these proceedings?"

Simon smiled. "Just what your interest is, I'm sure, Monsieur. The truth. And to know that my brother will rest easier, knowing those he cared for will be cared for in turn."

"And you choose this—this woman over your own kin?"

"I do not make the choice," Simon said carefully, "my brother did. I do this for him. And for the son he chose to name in his heart. A hard choice, to be sure," he added, lowering his voice, "and one I did not undertake lightly. But he was my only brother, yes? *Mon jumeau.* And this woman's son is all I have of him now."

He bowed solemnly to the solicitor, extended an arm to Celisma, and walked from the house.

Celisma kept her composure until they neared the end of the drive, until they were sheltered from any eyes at Beausonge by the long row of live oaks. Then she took Simon's hands in both of hers and, weeping, bent over them and kissed them, murmuring her gratitude.

Embarrassed, Simon gently pulled them away. "You were good to my mother, Celisma, and you were good for my brother. You deserve whatever goodness you can get back in return."

"How can I thank you?"

"Well," he said smiling, "you might bring that boy by to see us once in a while. We never got to see much of Samuel's kin, you know, thanks to their mother." He dropped his head. "And maybe she had good reason."

"Never good enough reason to keep kin from kin," she said.

He looked up and gazed at her. "Well, if you feel that way, I'm taking my own to N'Orleans to see Emma soon, I'd be happy to cart Alex along with his cousins to see the big city. If you trust me with him."

She smiled. "His father would 'a liked that."

"I believe that's a truth. Maybe this one get to know his Uncle Simon, eh? And his *cousines,* as well."

"I never been *en famille, moi,*" she said. "Never had no one, really, but Samuel. And now Alex."

"No need for him to know that same emptiness."

She put her arm through his. *"La famille, c'est bonne."*

He started her off again towards BonReve in the distance. "Family is all, *cher.* Even this old man knows that much."

The bee hives out front of BonReve were stout and crowded with honey and wax, and the tannin house produced each spring. The kitchen rows behind the house thrived so that Sally Red could have fed a third of the bayou from her harvest. Anytime Celisma looked around and could not see Alex, she knew to trace his steps out to the garden, where she could find him among the cucumber rows or shaded under the bean stalks, puttering in the warm soil and murmuring to himself of small-boy plans.

He now had free rein over most of BonReve, and he stalked the wild creatures everyplace they flew and swam and climbed. She had learned to step carefully around his bed, for he might have any number of crawling, creeping bugs stashed away in jars or flour sacks, waiting for him to draw them carefully in his journals, number them, and discover their names before they could be set free. Likewise, she must dust around handfuls of bird feathers which needed to be examined and recorded before they could be discarded.

He was not allowed to play, however, in her herb plots, for they did more than enhance the suppers served at Bon-

Reve. Celisma's herbs and her knowledge of how to use them to heal or comfort were earning minor fame in Lafourche, as well as bringing in extra greenbacks. Each Sunday after Mass, she disappeared for an hour. No one saw her go to the small stone wall, count along twenty paces, and dig up the tin box where she had moved her savings once the red flannel bag got too tight. Not even Alex knew of this new hidey-hole, and she smiled as she thought of what the growing pile of green and silver could do for his future.

Now that her property was secure, Celisma looked to its edges to see what could be used more profitably. Within the year, she had a small stand of cane growing back from the river. Daniel could only clear three acres, but the small crop they harvested that first year and hauled to Simon's sugar mill added still another pile to her tin box.

Celisma always drove the cane wagon herself to the mill, for there she felt closer to Samuel than in any other place. The great black wheels and grinders in endless motion seemed to her things of strong beauty and power. She sniffed the golden dust with delight, drawn to the fragrance that poured out of the open doors. The sour-sweet smell of the boiling juice and the lime, and the sulphur which cleaned it, seemed better to her than the jasmine, for she remembered how proud that smell made Samuel, and she seemed to take in his memory as she took the aroma into her nose and mouth.

And, of course, she thought of him each time she saw her son leap up the steps of BonReve, taking two at a time.

In 1860 when Alex was nearly ten, a crew of Irish workers came to the bayou close to BonReve to work on the widening of the river so that vessels might move more easily up and down Lafourche. Plantation owners wanted the work done, yes, but they would not risk their slaves in such dangerous labor. Between the gators, the snakes, and the fever, a man could lose ten slaves a week out in the swamps. But the Irish? Maybe the whiskey in their veins kept them safe, and if they did die, one less Irish gave the world little to mourn. His life was his own to lose.

So the Irish crews were a familiar sight along the roads and byways of Lafourche that year, as the levees extended into the lower reaches of the delta region.

Celisma saw the first bunch that spring, camped alongside the riverbank next to BonReve. With their shirts stripped off to expose darkened skin, they were carting earth over the banks and setting up rows of tents among the cottonwoods.

"Ces Eereesh," she called them when she answered Alex's questions, "they will be gone when the earth is moved where they want it, *cher.* "

"Can I go see?" he asked, his long legs already moving down the road.

She thought for a moment. "You take the men a pitcher of *citronnade,* yes? An' tell them if they tire of campstove cookin', we servin' fresh catfish at BonReve tonight."

He grinned, a boy who marked the success of the day by how many chairs pulled round the supper table at night, and ran to Sally Red to tell her to fill the pitcher full.

She watched out the window as Alex raced down the levee road pulling his wagon behind him, loaded down with lemonade, a dipper, and tin cups. He would come back with his pocket full of pennies, that one, and likely a new word or two he'd learned from some Irish pickman.

Two new faces shared the plates at BonReve that evening, and two more followed soon after. Sally Red bustled about the kitchen, peering out through the swinging doors at the new arrivals. "Them Eereesh fellas can tell a joke!" she chortled to herself as she saw the plates passed up and down. "An' such blue eyes!" She rolled her old black eyes suggestively as she waddled back to the stove.

One man in particular, the one who called Alex, "Kiskadee"—from his habit of asking, *"Qu'est-ce que tu dis?"*— passed the plates with more gusto than most. Celisma watched him and thought ruefully that she would scarcely make a dollar on him, this Tom Kerry ate so cheerfully.

And drank as cheerfully, once supper was cleared. He sat with his companion out on the gallery, lifting his glass as often as she would fill it.

"These Eereesh must make good cash for diggin' levees, *certainement,*" she said to Sally Red as she passed back to the kitchen for a second bottle of orange wine. She opened her palm and showed her a handful of silver coin.

"No women, no gamin', nothin' else to spend it on," Sally Red nodded wisely. "Ask the *bon Dieu* to make the shovels slow up some."

Celisma returned to the shadowed gallery where the two men sat, and she stood back in the darkness beyond the reach of the oil lamp. They were telling tales on their bossman, punctuating their stories with lilting laughter, and Tom's laugh rose above his comrade's, drawing her closer to listen.

"And so I told ol' Maloney, he could take the gator, and I'd take the lady, by God, and I never heard another word out o' the man!" He turned at her step, even though she came quietly. "Ah, there she is, our fine mistress with another bottle of her magic elixir." He held up his glass and beckoned her forward. "Come on then, lass, and fill us up."

Celisma came into the light of the lamp and smiled at this Tom with the wide grin. She poured out more of the orange wine, dipping in a graceful curtsy. He was brown around the edge of his collar and shirtcuffs, and his shoulders were nearly broad as Daniel's. His hair was red and tousled, as though he sat in a perpetual wind. One of the smallest noses she'd ever seen, she thought, wondering how such a large man could take his wind out of a narrow passageway as that, and those blue, blue eyes . . . she realized with a start that she had been staring at him and he had noticed.

"May we know your Christian name, lass?" he asked.

"I be called Celisma," she said softly.

"And you are mistress of this fine house?" Tom's eyes

dropped slowly from her face to her neck, her bodice, down to her waist and up again.

"I am, suh," she answered. "M'sieu Sam, he 'mancipate me long ago, an' give me BonReve."

"Well," Tom said after a pause, "you must have done him good service for such a reward."

She smiled. "He a good man. But he gone these five years an' more."

"So you've been alone all that time?" Tom asked. "A handsome lass like yourself?"

She frowned, inwardly annoyed at her confusion. "Not alone, suh. I got a whole house to do for, an' folks who come to stay." She set the bottle down and turned to go. "No time to be alone, *vraiment,* I got too much to do."

As she walked from the gallery, she heard Tom's companion say something to him in a low voice, and Tom returned his chuckle ruefully. She narrowed her eyes and as she went by the kitchen, called to Sally Red, "If these *gentilshommes* wish somethin' more, you fetch it, *cher,*" scarcely heeding Sally Red's weary groan of agreement.

It was very late when Celisma finally found her bed, after checking over every lock and every door as she was wont to do. Alex slept peacefully just inside the small compartment off her room, and Sally Red had long ago shut down the kitchen and banked the coals.

The moon was so high that it seemed far away and aloof, as though it could scarcely share light with the world. Even the frogs were stilled, for it was that time when even they pulled in their bug eyes and rested.

For some reason, Celisma could not sleep. She thought of Samuel and the way he had come to her on this bed. It seemed so long ago, as though she were an old woman long left alone by love. She lay restlessly tossing in her light blanket, thinking over the past and her choices. To her, this night, it seemed that she had made some which had almost guaranteed her soul would be burdened with sadness. That she would be alone most of her natural days. It looked as though her life stretched out ahead of her long and wide as the Mississippi, with no one to float alongside.

There was a small noise outside her door, and she stiffened. Sometimes, the boarders got up and walked in the night, and she had learned to tell which sound meant which door was opening. She had not heard a step descending. The noise came from the outside of the house. She glanced at the lock on her door. Shut tight, as always.

But then, an almost soundless knock at her door. She rose and pulled her wrapper around her shoulders, glancing at her sleeping son. She pulled the door closed between them. Perhaps someone had taken ill? Needed something for their rest? Rarely was she disturbed at such an hour—

She cracked the door and peered around the edge. Tom Kerry stood there in the darkness, smiling softly at her.

She started to speak and then stopped. No need to speak. She knew why he was there without asking. Almost without willing it, her arm swung the door wide enough for him to enter. He stepped inside and she shut the door after him. Wordlessly, he stood and gazed at her, with a soft warmth that seemed to seep under her wrapped like sunlight. Wordlessly, she went into his arms, pulling him against her body and enfolding him closer.

He was the same size as Samuel and fit so easily to her. She felt the strength of his arms kindle an answering strength in her own. When they found the bed together, she did not ask herself why he had come or why she welcomed him, she listened only to the hot hammer of her heart urging her to move her hands over him, to move her body under his, to rise and fall and rise and fall, until she could no longer tell his flesh from hers.

In one moment of white cold clarity she thought, since I was fifteen, I know what a man can do to me if he chose. Each time he climb on top of me, I be trustin' him with my life. He can break my arm 'twixt his fingers or snap my neck with his hands. That be the same for all womenfolk, black or white. We each know the sour taste of gratefulness when he don' hurt an' even bring some pleasure. But we never stop watchin' for him to change his mind.

His movements then pushed all such thoughts from her, and she rose in rhythm with him silently, praising him with her body, and all without a word passing between them.

She never regretted that one night of silent yearning and completion. She never understood why that man and not any other who had passed under her roof, but she knew that she would carry the debt of that one night, of that one man, for all of her days. Not a month passed since Tom Kerry's crew moved up the bayou, but she realized she was with child.

Forty years old and carrying life again, surely for the last time. Carrying the seed of a man she scarcely knew. One part of her mind was horrified at her impulsive need. Another smiled tenderly at the memory, knowing that somehow he had come when she wanted him most and left again, leaving her no regret nor untidy ends. He will never know, she told herself firmly, no need for that. This child will be like a virgin birth, and no man'll have a say in its raising.

As she swelled and showed in the months that followed, however, it was more difficult to ignore her coming. For it was a girl-child, of that Celisma was certain. So different from Alex, and not just because her womb was older. This one would be a daughter and likely have the red hair of her father . . . the only legacy from him she would ever know.

When Celisma was so mounded under her apron that even the loosest shift would no longer hide her, Daniel came to her with his proposal. She was somehow not surprised.

"Miss Celly, I come to say a thing to you," he began, quite determined it seemed to her, with his head up and his jaw out.

She leaned against the door and waited. He had caught her in the gallery where the cool shadows gave her ease. She had the notion he had been watching her for a while, waiting until she was alone and at peace.

"You with child again, looks like." He did not move his eyes from hers.

She felt a quiet respect rise for him. Before her stood a piece of her property, but also a man resolute in his chosen path. "Looks like," she said calmly.

"Well, I come to say a thing, and I got to say it. You can turn me out if you like, but give me leave to speak afore you do."

"I give you leave," she said. One hand dropped to her lap and she plucked aimlessly at the fringe of her apron. She sensed what was coming, but she wanted to hear him say it nonetheless.

He cleared his throat and rocked a moment on his heels. Now that he had her leave, his courage seemed to have winnowed away under the force of her steady gaze. "Well," he started, "it ain' good for a woman to be alone. Not with one boy an' 'nother chile comin' fast."

"I be alone most all my life," she said gently. "You know that, Daniel."

"I know it, Miss Celly, an' it pain me to see it go on. You ought to have better." He twisted his old scuffed hat in his hands and gathered up the speed behind his words. "I know I ain' no blue-ribbon, but I be strong enough to take care of you an' BonReve an' most anybody else got need to be cared for. I ask you to think about me as a husband, Miss Celly. I wan' to marry you an' give this chile a name."

"Your name?"

"Yes, Miss, an' if you 'mancipate me, I care for you an'

430

yours like they was my own 'til the day I die." Now that he had it out, he seemed to gain in height before her. "Ain' no body gonna wag they tongue over you, Miss Celly, not while I be here to keep 'em stilled. Ain' no body ever come to trouble you again. You give me my freedom, an' I bound myself to you an' yours forever."

"But," she said delicately, "you be mine already, Daniel. You be mine jes' like BonReve be mine. If tongues wag, they be waggin', no matter if you take me to wife or no." She paused and looked away to give him time to compose himself. "Is this more on account of your freedom or this chile, Daniel?"

He shrugged, a huge mountainous movement of shoulders and neck. "I figure I free already, truth be known. I work an' I work good, you know that, Miss Celly. But if I don' wan' to work, you ain' gonna whup me. If I lay down in the dirt an' refuse to budge, you ain' gonna send me to the block in Baton Rouge. You ask me to work, you don' tell me. Ain' no body tell me since Massa Sam, an' he ask 'bout as much as he tell. So no, Miss Celly, ain' my freedom. It be this chile." And here he stumbled. "An' o' course, your ownself. It be good to be free, for truth, but it be better to be your husband."

She smiled gently. "That's a fine thing to hear, Daniel, an' I thank you for askin'."

"Will you think on it?"

She hesitated and then decided that the fastest way was the kindest. "I tell you what. I think on 'mancipatin' you, Daniel. That seem to me considerable to think on for now. But I won' think on marryin'. I thank you, but I cain' be wife to no man."

"Why not?"

It was her turn to shrug, but softly. "I don' want to. I don' need to. This chile don' need me to, neither. The world got more to worry 'bout than one little chile born to Miss Celisma, I 'spect. So we don' speak of marryin' again. I think on the rest an' I let you hear when I'm done thinkin'." She rose and gathered her apron loosely around her, not caring for once that her belly tightened the cloth so obviously. When she saw him wince and lower his eyes, she could not keep from smiling and patting his shoulder as she left the room.

Manon was born in the last of the summer, when all the bayou seemed to be offering up harvest enough to fill each set of arms. She was a small child, even from the first, with blue eyes which followed Celisma about before she could scarcely focus. Those blue, blue eyes were opaque and somehow glacial, with little of the warmth Celisma had seen in her father's.

But she was a beautiful girl-child, lighter-skinned than Alex and finer of limb. Quiet and alert, she lay in her cradle and smiled readily at her brother when he leaned over her, dangling a handful of Queen Anne's lace.

"Look, *maman,*" he would say, "she likes to smell the flowers!" And he would laugh and gently tickle the infant's cheek with the soft white clump.

"If you get her fussin', you got to hold her," Celisma said from behind him.

"She never fusses, she only farts!" he laughed. Manon laughed, too, as though in agreement.

"Alex, if that be her first word, you in trouble," Celisma chuckled. She was once more filled with wonder at her two children—so strong, so smart, so beautiful. Alex spoke now with a soft drawl, half her own, half words and patterns of speech he had picked up from his many cousins and Uncle Simon. Twice a week, he played outside their bayou cabins

432

and shouted with them up and down the swamp, until sometimes she could scarcely tell his speech from theirs.

He joined his cousins in the old schoolhouse, bending over primers, and then out into the drowsy warm days riding their ponies and romping. They showed him every bird nest, taught him every bird song, and told him to tie pieces of meat on strings at the ends of short poles and sit patiently for hours on the riverbank catching crawfish. They helped him harness the huge black grasshoppers, called "devil horses," and make carts of matchboxes for races inside a circle drawn in the bayou mud. Together, they gathered driftwood and flowers and blackberries, hunted quail eggs, slid the levees, and raced past the shaded gallery where Celisma sat, her mending in her lap, listening to Cerise and Simon tell of the old days.

This was something Alex had which she had never known, this feeling of being part of a whole: a family. Just watching him made her feel less lonely for what she had never had.

And in many ways, the folks who gathered at her supper table became like distant relations as well. Each night Alex heard visitors from New Orleans, from the Teche, from Plaquemines and Baton Rouge, even from as far away as Natchez, arguing politics and passing pleasantries as they passed Sally Red's good biscuits and chicken.

In these days, the arguments most often were about slavery and states' rights, and Celisma thought if she had to hear one more oratory about the cause of the South, she would spit in the soup.

One night Monsieur Kane from Natchez was staying over, and he held forth about the real cause of the "incivilities" between the North and the South until he had roused most of the other men at the table.

"Why Lincoln himself is for states' rights," he finally said, "and lest we forget, he's said so often enough. One of the finest intellects in America, if you ask me."

"When did he say such a thing?" a man from Georgia

asked indignantly. "I've never heard the man make any sense at all on the subject. Long, gambling uncouth son of an ape! Have you seen his pictures? *Foi*, what an ugliness!"

"It was just after the war with Mexico, I believe, but I do recall his words most clearly. He said that any people anywhere being inclined and having the power, have the right to rise up and shake off the existing government and form a new one that suits them better. If that doesn't sound like an excellent argument for the cause of the South, I don't know what."

"Lincoln said that?"

"He most certainly did. One of the best minds in politics today, I said."

"These hostilities, if they come—"

"There will be no war," his wife interjected swiftly.

"You're likely right, honey, but if it does, it won't be to free the slaves. That's just a lot of pretty words for sentimental hearts. The hostilities are over economics, plain and simple. No, this war, if it's fought, will be because the North doesn't want to lose our rich land, our tobacco, our sugar, our cotton. But to rally Yankee soldiers around a flag stitched up of greenbacks would be impossible, so your smart Mister Lincoln sounded the cry to free our poor benighted black brothers."

"You're saying the fight is just so much hot air? That what you're trying to tell us? Before God, I find it hard to believe—"

"Not hot air, but just a different wind that's blowing. Now I got to say that no man alive loves the colored man more than I, when they deserve loving. I revere the memory of my black mammy, and I cherish the laughing, humble nigra friend I had in boyhood. I rejoice in the happy laborer out in our fields. But I know and you know that they are not equal to any white man alive. Go to the Bible of our fathers, my friend."

"That's right, it's all in the Good Book."

"Yes, sir, where any man can read it. The black man shall be a hewer of wood and a bearer of water. Go to history. In every age, in every clime, the black man has been a benighted, inferior race, incapable of self-government or greatness. We in the South know this. We know how to handle our problems. And by God, we *shall* handle them."

"But you're saying the nigra is not the issue in this conflict."

"I'm saying it's a mask for the real issue of economics. Mister Lincoln thought that people had a right to free themselves from government, when he was part of those wanting freedom. Now, he's trying to prevent the South from doing exactly what he said was right to do a few years back."

"You talk about protecting our cotton. Have you seen the way they farm in the North? They got machines that'll do the work of fifty men. We don't have machines like that, we can't put our capital in machines, we got it tied up in slaves. Why, Louisiana doesn't have a single cotton mill, sir!" the man at his elbow responded. "We send it all to Liverpool, to Boston, or to New York, and we get it back in the form of nankeen, sailcloth, or Indian cloth. What do we do when they blockade?"

"We don't need machines and manufacturing in the South! We don't need to become a lot of factory workers and shopkeepers to survive. So long as we got cotton, plenty will step forward to make cloth. There's lots of places to make the nankeen, sir, but few damn places that'll grow cotton like we can!"

The discussions went round and round for months, and just about the time Celisma despaired that folks would ever talk of anything else, the men in charge made a decision which even she felt was too ominous to ignore. In that year of 1861, Louisiana seceded from the Union.

"And why not?" they argued at the table then. "We might as well go the way of South Carolina before us! Her cotton crop hit two billion pounds this year, no better time to declare for the Confederacy. Sugar's up, you watch, we best get out while we can still keep a passel of it for ourselves!"

Not everyone was wanting war, and not all who came to BonReve were eager to join the Confederacy. Once at the table, a guest from Pennsylvania suggested, "What about a free labor system? They got such a thing out west, and I hear it works—"

"No, sir," he was answered swiftly by a visitor from Terrebone, "our blacks are different down here."

"How's that?"

"Why, they're too lazy. They don't care about pocket money!"

"Well, I heard you say you got a blacksmith who's the best you've seen. Surely, he's bright and wants to make something of himself."

"It still won't work. You got to understand, sir, that sugar is a crop not native to this state. It's a forced crop, you see. In Cuba, you put it in the ground, and it grows up fine. Here, we got to coddle it, to plough it up and hoe it, we got to guard it from frosts and grind it before it's ripe to get the sugar set right. Now, I don't hold with harsh discipline, personally, but the black man needs it occasional. In the grinding season, we got to work day and night to get the crop in, and we need to have dependable labor. Got to know we can get sixteen hours out of a man when we have to have it, or you Northerners would have to—"

"Give two cents a pound less for sugar than we do now."

"What do you mean, sir?" the Terrebone man asked, appalled.

"I mean what you likely know, of course," the Pennsylvania man replied, "that Louisiana only grows about a quarter of the sugar we use in these United States and the rest comes from Cuba, slapped with a heavy tariff so that all over the country, we pay two cents more for every pound so that you can raise what your soil was never meant to raise. And then you want us to support slavery, so you can make it profitable as well!"

The wife of the Terrebone man spoke up then quietly, to her husband's discomfort. "I think slavery is an evil," she said, "because we smother the nigras with our orders and take from them their will, and they in turn smother us with pleasure and give us so much shame. The cage we put round the nigra is round every white child as well. Each is on a different side of the wire, but each is pinioned there. What cruelly shapes the one, is as cruelly shaping the other. We think we're making them like us, but they're making us like them. A people can only tolerate brutality for so long. We're overwhelmed by them, drifting on a black tide and smothered by them."

"Madame," her husband said, "you simply do not understand the politics of the situation."

Events swirled around them, but BonReve seemed somehow in an eddy, out of the main current of war and secession, except for the folks who brought it to them over each supper. The Cotton Belt will secede as a block, they said, and take Sugar states with them. State after state was joining the Confederacy after South Carolina; Mississippi went next, then Florida, Alabama, and Georgia.

"And Alabama didn't just secede! She declared war on the whole rest of the United States!"

"By God," a man murmured in a hush of admiration, "we can scarcely refuse to stand with her!"

Two months later, the Yankees bombarded Fort Sumter. President Jefferson Davis, leader of the Confederate Union, declared war on the United States, and Mister Lincoln called up seventy-five thousand troops to quell the insurrection.

"They still don' call it war," Sally Red said, grumbling at the news.

"They jes' as well call it hell an' be done," Daniel said, "'cause that be what it is, soon as them troops reach the bayou. Ain' no Lincum sojers can chase a rabbit through there, much less a secesh sojer. I 'spect we in for it now."

Celisma came into the kitchen in time to hear the two of them and said, "They took New Orleans, *cher, M'sieu* Donald just come an' told it. The Yankee Navy sailed right in an' took it fast, an' Yankee troops are bivouacin' on the steps of St. Louis!"

"Lawd Godalmighty!" gasped Sally Red.

"Now, it come," Daniel shook his head.

But for a long while, it seemed BonReve might escape the horrors of war. The hated General Butler took New Orleans, yes, but the skirmishes rarely reached as far south as Lafourche. Tales of New Orleans did, however, and they were enough to make Celisma grateful for the many miles of bayou between her family and chaos.

Folks told stories of when Farragut's ships came up the Mississippi, sliding past the forts which were the city's last defense, and men rushed out to climb upon the levees, straining to catch sight of the Yankees steaming up the river. At the same time, anyone who was part of the government was heading out of town in retreat, along with remnants of the Confederate army. Ladies sewed up their jewelry in their petticoats and took to the road in whatever would carry them. All the steamboats at the docks were seized and loaded up with anything military in the city, to send upriver to escape the Yankees. As they retreated, the army burned all of the thousands of bales of cotton that still remained on the wharves and in the warehouses.

"That cotton burning was a sight to see," a supper guest told Celisma, "never seen a sight to match it. Wagons, drays, anything that rolled they piled high with bales and burnt them on the commons. Nigras ran around, cutting the bales open, and setting them afire. Or they rolled them to the river, all ablaze!"

"What 'bout the sugar?"

"Burned that, too, threw it right on the pyre, all the

molasses, everything. And the planters stood around, watching the work of the whole past year going up in smoke. So many floating burning bales, the whole Mississippi's nothing but a sheet of flame!"

Merchants figured that the Yankees would plunder their shops, so they opened their doors to the citizens, inviting them to take what they wanted. Men pulled wagons up to the doors and made off with sacks of coffee, hogsheads of sugar, huge barrels of beans, hominy, cans of fruit, barrels of potatoes, hams, and butter. Hundreds of women and children were refugeeing out of the city, some bareheaded and in all sorts of motley costumes. Young girls were all alone, white and black mixed together. Lots of slaves carried bundles for their owners. Some white women simply sat in the dirt and sobbed, wringing their hands.

Farragut began a continuous bombardment of Fort Jackson on the Mississippi, pressing forward and upriver. Finally breaking through the blockade, he steamed up past levees lined with men and women, white and black, past rows of slaves who looked frightened and joyous all at once. New Orleans' bells clanged, and the city knew it was taken at last. Major General Benjamin Butler was assigned to command the occupation.

Butler the Beast, folks called the invader, and he terrorized New Orleans for more than seven months, even hanging a man who pulled down the Federalist flag. Yankee troops paraded in the streets, and Butler demanded the unconditional surrender of the whole town.

His most hated edict was called The Woman Order. Butler was tired of hearing complaints from his Union officers that women of the city refused to show them respect. They wore Confederate colors, they pulled their skirts aside when they passed a Yankee uniform, and they got up en masse and departed from restaurants and churches when a Yankee officer entered.

So Butler issued an order which said that any woman of

New Orleans who showed contempt by word, gesture, or movement towards any officer or soldier of the United States was to be treated "as a woman of the town plying her vocation."

"An' what is the penalty for that, suh?" Celisma asked her guest when she heard the news.

"Why, if she's arrested, she'd have to spend the night in jail and be brought before a judge to pay five dollars. Just like a common sporting woman! By God, the Beast has gone too far!"

Protest was violent in the city, and when President Jefferson Davis heard of the insult to New Orleans women, he promptly put a price on General Butler's head.

But the women of New Orleans had their own revenge. Many took a portrait copy of the General and placed it in the bottom of their chamber pots. When Butler heard of this united effort to humiliate him, he systematically raided house after house in the city, confiscating every chamber pot he found. Word had it that he was so enraged, he beat most of them to pieces with a hammer himself.

Meanwhile, New Orleans responded to invasion with debauch. Houses of prostitution flourished, particularly in the streets of Gravier, St. John, Basin, St. Charles, Chartres, Royal, and Canal. Men reported quietly that there was not one block in the city which did not shelter a thriving house for women. And prices were low—fifteen cents for Negro women, up to ten dollars for the finest white ladies in the Quarter, but the latter came with a bottle of French champagne.

Celisma saw that prices were dropping everywhere, not just in New Orleans. And folks were stopping by BonReve less and less, for the Yankees now controlled all of the delta, all the way to the sea.

Yet, if you didn't know what to look for, Celisma thought, you might never know it was war. The town of Lafourche was under Yankee troops, of course, as were

Houma, Thibodaux, Labadieville, Paincourtville, and all the other villages up and down the bayou. The buildings still stood, though, and the churches were intact, though no new buildings were going up.

Twice in the bayou, rebels sought to wrest their lands back from the invaders. They built a fort of mud and straw on Bayou Grand Caillou, set up some cannons, and tried to keep the Union steamboats from passing upriver. But after a quick battle, the fort was destroyed and the rebels captured. Celisma heard they were sent north to fight against their own kind in Union armies.

Another time, a group of planters in Houma ambushed a party of Yankee soldiers on their way to Grand Caillou, killed them, and buried them in the Houma Court Square. When the Union troops heard of this, they chased the planters out of Houma into the swamp, burned down their houses, and captured their property. They then ordered the people of Houma to dig up the Yankee bodies and give them a proper burial.

Necessities quickly became scarce, and Celisma turned more of her energy to making do, thanking *le bon Dieu* that winters on Lafourche were short and seeds sprouted as early as March. She plaited palmetto and sewed it into hats, which she traded for needles, thread, and buttons. Leather was impossible to buy at near any price, so she put Daniel to tanning squirrel hides which she traded for salt. She made laudanum from her poppy patch, plucking the ripe bulbous heads, piercing them gingerly with one of her precious needles, collecting the opium gum, and trading for shot and powder.

Hardest of all to stomach was the scarcity of coffee. At sixty dollars per pound, she vowed she'd drink bayou mud before she'd pay such a price. Sally Red tried browned okra seeds, burnt sugar, burnt corn, and dried peas for coffee, but none of them satisfied.

"By the time this war over," Celisma grumbled, "I take to strong drink."

"Take to this then," Sally Red grimaced, passing her a cup of anise and parched yams she was drinking, "it strong enough to fell a mule."

Finally, the day they dreaded dawned, and Yankee soldiers came up the levee road to Beausonge. When Celisma saw the vast dust cloud and the army of blue uniforms coming, she moved her bee hives close to the house, pulling them under cover of the climbing roses. The troops approached with the noise and rumble of a city in motion and finally stopped along the river. An officer rode up on a scraggly mount and strode up the steps of BonReve. Celisma met him with her apron on, Sally Red behind her, frowning fit to frighten his horse.

"Ma'am," the officer said, doffing his cap, "Lieutenant Williamson of Perkins Troop C of the Massachusetts Cavalry. Are you the mistress of this place?"

"I am," Celisma said, eyeing him carefully.

"Then you would be the mulatress who owns this boarding house?"

"It called BonReve," she answered, lifting her chin. "An' I hold the deed."

"Yes, Ma'am, we know something about your situation. How many slaves do you own?"

Celisma glanced at Sally Red who had ducked back behind her the first time the officer spoke. Manon and Alex were tucked away in the upstairs attic, hushed to silence and threatened with capture or worse if they made a peep. Daniel was crabbing downriver, thank the Good God, and the others were hiding out back. "I don' own no slaves," she said calmly. "My people work for wages."

"That's not the information we got," the officer said.

"Then your info'mation ain' right," Celisma replied with the heaviest black drawl she could manage. "We jes' runnin' a place for folks travelin', suh, an' tryin' to make it in hard

442

times. We be happy to share whut we got wid yore men, but we thank ye to leave us in peace after."

"You, gal," the officer said, peering around Celisma and pointing to Sally Red. "You a freed slave?"

"Yesssuh," Sally Red croaked at him, "I be free."

"You damn right you are," he said firmly. He thought for a moment. "That big house back yonder," he said then, gesturing to Beausonge, "that the Weitz place?"

"Yessuh," Celisma said. "But Massa Weitz, he dead these five years past. Madame, too, she gone. Only maybe Massa Pierre be there to greet you."

"Oh, he's there all right," the officer said grimly. "And no doubt expecting us. You signed the loyalty oath yet?"

"You be the first to come through," Celisma said.

The officer drew himself up with dignity. "Ma'am, I'm authorized to spare this place from destruction on two conditions. First, you will provide what provender you can for these troops, and second, you will sign a loyalty oath to the Federal government of these United States of America. Do you agree?"

Celisma narrowed her eyes at the man but nodded her head without hesitation. "I sign." She turned to Sally Red. "Go get what we got for 'em, *cher,* an' be quick."

"No need to be quick," Lieutenant Williamson said. "We plan to stay a while. I am authorized to commandeer half of your stores, Ma'am, and by your leave, I'll send in my men to do so." He pulled a paper from his breastcoat and offered it to her. "You got to sign this."

She bowed her head to read the paper and when she lifted it again, he was thrusting a pen at her. "What it say?" she asked.

"You don't know your letters?" he asked, pulling the pen back in confusion.

She shook her head.

"Well, Jesus Christ," he said in abrupt annoyance. "My report says you do—"

443

"Wish I do, suh."

He peered at her suspiciously. "How you run this place, then?"

She shrugged. "We get by. Ain' no call to read an' write if you can count, suh." She smiled. "But I sign, if you wan'."

He took the paper from her reluctantly. "No use to sign if you don't know what you're signing. Anyway, I got my orders. This place stands for now. But if we hear of you aiding and abetting, we'll be back, you understand?"

"Yessuh," she said meekly. "Won' be no 'bettin' at Bon-Reve."

He replaced the cap on his head and mounted his horse, pulling away from the porch with a rattle of reins. As soon as he rode towards the gathered men, Celisma rushed over to the bee hives and turned two of them over, spilling the swarming bees out into the air. They rose in dual black clowds of angry, stinging insects, joining above her head as she hurried back to the porch, her apron over her *tignon*.

She stood and glared as the officer called to six men who followed him back towards BonReve. Slipping inside the door, she watched from a window as they approached. The two in the front began to slap at themselves and curse at the air, and the officer called them all back again. From a distance, he shouted, "You think you got the first bees we seen in the South? Damn fools! All we got to do is wait, and we can do that a sight better than you can!"

With that, the officer and his men stood just outside the ring of bees, glaring at the house and the windows as though they could see Celisma and Sally Red glowering right back at them inside. A quarter hour passed, by the grandfather clock in the hallway. Celisma saw the officer lead his men forward again, and this time, they swept through the bees, right up onto the porch, and banged open the door.

She stood stonily at the foot of the banisters, but they ignored her, sweeping past her and right behind Sally Red who fluttered before them like a racing chicken, into the kitchen, down into the storeroom, and left again with their mess bags full of flour, meal, beans, and salt meat.

"You ain't got much, sister," one of them said as he passed her again on the way down the steps. "But we left you half of it, anyways."

"Thankee, suh," she said coldly, watching them ride back to the spread of blue uniforms now stretched along the levee.

She watched them most of the day, as the troops paraded up and down in a display of power and noise. At one point, a unit of black soldiers marched right past the gallery, singing to the tune of "The Battle Hymn of the Republic,"

> We be done with hoein' cotton,
> We be done with hoein' corn,
> We be colored Yankee sojers,
> As sure as you be born,
> When Massa see us shoutin',
> He think dis Gabriel's horn,
> As we go marchin' on!

By dusk, the troops had moved into position flanking Beausonge on all sides, with cannon in place and mounted soldiers with bayonets at their sides. They seemed in no particular hurry, as though the fate of the big golden house was already decided.

Celisma held Manon in her arms, kept Alex by her side, as she and the others crept out to the edge of the cane fields where they could see the front gallery of Beausonge and still be hidden by the waving tall grass. Daniel said only, "They so many of them! Like a host of angels!" and then he was struck to silence.

From their watch post, they saw three officers ride right up to the front steps of Beausonge and call out.

"Where everybody be?" Sally Red asked with a shiver. "Like a ghost house."

Daniel said, "They all took off dis mornin', I heard them

445

say they goin'. They seen the Lincum sojers, an' they take off runnin'."

"Will they be back?" Celisma wondered.

"No'm," Daniel said. "They be free, they say. Ain' never comin' back."

She looked around her in awe. Slaves had been leaving Beausonge for a month or more, slipping away in small groups, Sally Red told her, more and more brazen. Most of the house niggers were gone, and only about twenty field hands were still in the quarters. The cane was laid by and growing strong, but it would freeze and rot in the ground without hands to take it down.

A figure came out on the gallery. It was Master Pierre.

"Wha's that he got?" Sally Red asked.

"A gun," Celisma said. "*Sacré nom,* the fool!"

As they watched in horror, Pierre faced the officers and the troops, shouting something they could not hear, and gesturing with his arms. He raised the musket and a shot seared the air, horses shied and whinnied, and when the confusion ceased, Pierre lay on the gallery motionless. An officer went to his side and said something to his comrades, and they pulled him inside Beausonge.

"He dead!" Sally Red whispered, "they killed Massa dead!"

Then the soldiers came forward and they could see them carrying out bushels of salt, rice, grist, crockery, the great grandfather clock, curtains, velvet chairs, and anything else they could strap to the wagons or lash to their saddlebags. From behind the barn, they drove the mules and the horses before them, lashing up the buggies and the wagons and adding them to their caravan. The moon was high overhead when they finally stopped pillaging Beausonge and drew back from her high pillars as though to gaze at her one more time.

Four men carried out a sheet-draped figure, and Celisma saw them take Pierre Weitz round back to the family burial plot.

Then a flame flickered in an upstairs window of Beausonge, a second one in the parlor, a third on the gallery.

"There she go," Daniel said, the first words he had uttered in hours.

As they watched, Beausonge blazed in a brilliant light, the flames leaping higher and higher, taking hold of the oaks on each side and leaping from pillar to pillar.

Celisma would never have believed it could have been over so quickly. She must have dozed, sitting there in the cane with Alex and Manon dead asleep against her legs, and when she awoke, it was almost dawn. Beausonge was nothing but a steaming, hissing pile of charred timbers and smoking black slags of ash.

Celisma put the children to bed and lay down on her own counterpane, falling into deep exhaustion. She did not get up again for twelve hours.

After that, the bayou settled down to occupation. There was little else to do. Up and down the river, slaves walked past in droves, house niggers and field niggers all together for once, roaming the levee road, sitting in the dust, and moving, moving, Celisma could never tell where. They grabbed at strangers passing, asking them where they came from, where they had been, who they were, who their mama was. Some just sat, crying. Some laughed and others just walked along, holding themselves, rocking to inside songs as tears ran down their faces, nary a sound coming from their lips. When the grinding time came that year, few crops could come to harvest, for those slaves who hadn't already taken off did so then, shouting and hollering jubilation, and the crops rotted in the ground.

It was October when Daniel came to Celisma and said, "Massa Linkin done freed me, Miss Celly. I be takin' my leave, I 'spect."

"Oh, Daniel! But you belong here!" she cried, holding Manon to her breast. "We cain' make do without you."

He gazed at her long. "Well," he finally said, "I guess I cain' help that. There ain' nothin' for me here."

She set Manon down in her cradle, absently noting how the child instantly settled herself, cocked her head, and turned her hands to something else which might please her. "There's a home," Celisma said, "an' folks like family. Is that nothin'? There's a bed an' a plate with your name on it, is that nothin', too? We made BonReve together, you an' me, an' I cain' keep it goin' without you. I set you free official, an' I do it gladly. I should a' done it before, I know, but I figure you know you free, an' I never think of you like a slave no more. Now you ain' a slave, an' I sign whatever paper you wan' me to sign an' 'mancipate you today, but please don' go way an' leave us."

Daniel put his two huge hams of hands on the top of his head, as though to keep himself from toppling. "You ain' got to sign no paper, Miss Celly. I ain' yours to sign away no more. I be a man, like any other. An' they be callin' for men now, to go an' fight for the Yankees. They say they need us to see to the horses an' mules an' such, an' dig the trenches. Maybe even to fight Confederates Massas, too. They pay us, an' show us places!"

"I can pay you," she said swiftly. "Stay here with me an' help me keep BonReve, an' I pay you good. Wages an' Sally Red's rhubarb pie, an' you be your own man, *vraiment.*"

"How you pay me? We ain' got 'nuff folks stoppin' these days to keep the rooms full, an' cash dollars is scarce as hair on a tater, anyhow."

"We got enough to keep food on the table an' pay a good man what he worth. What you got to have to stay?"

Daniel dropped his arms and paced the length of the room once. As he passed her cradle, Manon squealed and held up her hands to be lifted. He had always been able to get her to laugh. He stopped and touched the top of her head, smoothing her dark silken curls. "I don' know. They say we all free. We don' have to stay or go where we don' want. But

I got no place to go. What you goin' to do if folks stop comin' all together?"

"Then we still got a roof an' the garden an' the bayou to provide," Celisma said fervently. "Ain' nobody goin' to starve on BonReve. But I hear plenty folks starvin' in Vicksburg an' Natchez." She glanced at the new shoes he wore, shoes she had bought for him before the blockade. "Lots of them walkin' round in bare feets, too. I wan' to plant cane again, leastwhys as much as we can manage. Even one acre better than none, an' prices got to come back up soon enough. What you got to have to make you stay?"

He straightened up and gazed out the window towards the bayou.

She followed his stare. The water was black beneath the live oaks, moving slowly, imperceptibly, as though her world were not crumpling before her and the day was as a million before it.

"Daniel," she said softly then, "I need you. Alex need you, too." She put a grin into her words. "Even this *'tit chou* need you," she added, glancing at Manon, " 'cept she don' know it yet."

He turned back from the window, his mouth set. "You need me 'nuff to marry with me?"

Her shoulders slumped and her smile faded. "I don' want to marry with no man, Daniel. I tole' you that. If I ain' needed to marry so far, I don' see why I got to now. I offer you a home an' a wage an' a place to stay when nobody else want you. If that ain' enough, then I guess you got to do what you think right."

He heaved a sigh. "Tha's right, Miss Celly. Tha's what I got to do." And with that, he walked past her, out of the room.

She stood at the window, watching him go down the steps of BonReve, shoulder a small bag of goods, and walk towards the river. When he got to the live oaks and the road leading up and down, he stopped for a moment, looking first one way

449

and then the other. Finally, he turned and went upriver, towards New Orleans. She watched him until he was out of sight in the bayou shadows. Never once did he look back at BonReve.

Celisma missed Daniel more that season than she would any other. Folks who stopped to stay were few and far between now, and the news of fighting came to them only in bits of gossip and hearsay, sometimes from old Simon and his family, sometimes from the occasional riverboats that still docked to take on water and fresh greens. Celisma kept little packages, the little she could give away freely, stacked next to the front door ready for the slaves when they come knocking up from the road. She asked questions and she got answers. She learned one side was winning one day, and the next day the other side was winning. Few knew the truth, but they said the South must be losing, because of the things happening to their old masters and big houses. No one had cash dollars, that much was certain.

Money and time, she realized, worked like the sand and grass over at the marsh's edge. Whatever stood on it slipped down and finally disappeared. Not so fast you could see it going, but still, after a while it was gone. Time was forever cutting off things behind you and then finally, all you remembered of those things, and leaving you just a little narrow spit of present and the near past to stand on safe.

Celisma was able to gather some of the greenbacks she needed by selling her herbs and simples to the ladies on the rare steamboats that stopped, and she got a bit more by selling moss she gathered, cleaned, and combed from the live oaks for folks' blankets and saddles. Without Daniel, she had no tannin to sell, but her honey bees still filled their hives for her as though they knew there was too little sweetness in the world. So few folks traveled in these days of chaos and war, however, that she never knew if she could collect the tax money for BonReve or not.

When she could, she sold what her kitchen rows produced, for she heard that lettuce was nigh to one dollar and a half a head in New Orleans and a peck of green beans more than twelve dollars. But this wasn't New Orleans, and folks could do without or grow their own.

Still, Celisma felt life was good. Maybe even better than in the easy times. She sensed she was eating her white bread now. Both were sent on this earth—the fine white bread to enjoy and the dry cornbread to be eaten with hard silence or soft tears—but you had to eat whatever was sent, of that she was certain.

As the long days of the war wore on, she used up, made do, and finally did without most everything she once took for granted. Lamps were left unlit at BonReve, for the oil was too dear and hard to come by, even if she'd wanted to spare the dollars to buy it. Alex wore trousers patched and re-patched, until finally she had to make him a pair out of Sally Red's old dishtowels, held up with a waistcord. The Yankee bummers came through and took the mule team, but they left the chickens. Then the Confederates, those still hanging on and hiding out in pockets of the swamp, they came through like a swarm of hungry locust and took the chickens.

"I gettin' mighty tired of catfish," Sally Red said over supper one night. "I 'bout to grow whiskers if I got to eat one more this week."

"Me, too," Alex sighed. "But the crabs won't get in the pot, no matter what I try. If I just had an old chicken neck or a piece of hogfat . . . " It was Alex's chore to do the fishing each day, and it was taking him farther and farther into the bayou to fill their plates each night.

"Be grateful we got meat at all," Celisma said shortly. "Plenty folks wishin' for what we got right here."

"Well, they can come get mine," Sally Red snorted, pushing back her plate.

Celisma glared at her impotently. She'd been sassy and flounced enough before, but now she worked for scant wages she thought herself too fine to bear. For one picayune, Celisma thought, I tell her run after Daniel to hell and back. But she knew she couldn't manage BonReve alone, no, not with the big garden and the canning, the preserves, the herbs, and taking care of Manon, too.

Manon reached up and banged on the table with her spoon, her favorite way to get attention when she sensed more heat over supper than she liked. *"Non!"* she cried, grinning ear to small, pink ear. "Nudder! Nudder!"

"She say mother?" Sally Red asked.

"Nope, she's saying nother—another," Alex said firmly. And with that, he reached over and set half of his fish on her plate.

Celisma, watching them, wondered where two such beautiful creations had come from and what she had done to deserve them. Alex was past twelve now, a strong stocky boy with his father's jaw and hands. Manon was only just emerging from baby-camouflage, but already there was a glint in her eye which was far too mature for two.

She recalled with a cold thumbprint at the base of her neck the last time Yankee uniforms showed up on the road to BonReve. Coming from downriver, they had been on her before she'd known they were there, and she had no time to whisk Alex and Manon out of sight as she usually did.

This time, Alex stood in the row of beans and he was one of the first they saw, coming from the backwoods.

"That boy's old enough to tote a gun," Celisma heard one of the uniforms say.

"Naw," said another, "I got one at home older, and he couldn't hold a musket if you tied it to him."

"How old are you, boy?" a sergeant hollered to Alex.

With all the proud bluster of a twelve-year-old, he answered back, "Nigh to thirteen, sir!" And he grinned.

Watching from the kitchen window, she almost died on the spot. From that day forward, she took pains to watch for uniforms coming from any direction. Alex had strict orders to keep hidden, did he see them approach. If he was seen, he was to disappear; if questioned, play mute.

"And if they ask your age," she told him soberly, "then you got to lie."

"That's a sin, you told us," he whispered, impressed to near silence by her grim face.

"Any other lie, it be a sin. This un' have to be told, an' told well. You ain' but ten, if they ask. Big for your age."

"Do they take boys like me?"

"Only if catch them," she said. "An' I die 'for I let them catch you. Run for the swamp, if they come, an' I find you soon enough. Stay off the trail, hear? Go to the ol' bee tree downriver, but keep hid 'til I come for you."

Though she wanted him to believe her warning, Celisma really could not fathom them taking a young boy his age. Surely, she reasoned, they could not take him, not for several years, and the war would be over by then. Indeed, some folks said it was running down even now.

She was so busy watching for Yankee uniforms that the approach of nearly any strange man at all quickly raised her alarm. On the day the trio of patched and scruffy rebels ambled into BonReve's garden, pulling at corn and plucking out ripe tomatoes, she did not hesitate. With a flap of her apron as though huge chickens molested her rows, she bustled out the back door and shouted at the men, "Hey you there! We got to eat, too, you know!"

She had already seen Alex take out from the front of the house towards the swamp, so her courage flared up high. She strode down towards them. "If you come ask politelike, I be glad to serve you, but to come stealin' like coons in broad daylight—"

"Damned if I got to take sass from a yellow wench," one of the men growled to the others with a hard grin. "We might be near licked, but we ain't got to lick ass, too."

"You best go back inside," another of the men told her gruffly. "We ain't in no mood to be turned away."

She studied them for an instant, holding on to her temper. News up and down the river was that the Yankees had won. Of course, they had won here in Lafourche so long before that the question of winning and losing hadn't meant much for a long time. More important was when would cotton and sugar go back up, how would they get the crops in, and what markets would still buy.

The Confederates had plagued the delta almost as much as the Yankees, truth be told. They came in roving bands, always hungry and usually more irritable than those armies who came from victory. Now she realized that she faced the last of a losing breed. But since Alex was likely well hid, she had little reason to keep from doing her best to save her own greens.

"*Attendez*, get your boots out of that patch there, you stompin' all over my radishes. Now, come on up to the house, an' I give you what I can spare—"

"I'm tired of taking what folks can spare!" one man shouted to his comrades. "Ain't you, Wallace? I'm tired of fighting for these niggers and then turn around and listen to them taking what white men need. Hey—" the man stopped and turned, glaring at her. "Ain't you that one they tell of, that got her own niggers?"

She drew herself up with some dignity, still watching her tomatoes going into one of the knapsacks. Two plump peppers followed, quick as a blink. "I am Celisma, suh. I own this place, legal. BonReve is mine. But I 'mancipated my slaves long time passed."

"You got a boy by some rich planter, I hear tell," the

same man grinned at her. There was nothing of mirth in that grin.

She said nothing. But she felt the anxiety crawl up her spine a little higher.

"Yeah, I heard such a tale, too," his comrade said. "Might be, we should take the boy along. He can tote our pokes and mess for us. Where he at, wench?"

"He gone away to school," she said shortly. "His *papa* send him to New Orleans."

The three men looked at each other and back to her appraisingly. One of them said, "That so?" His eyes scanned over the back of BonReve as though to see through the walls. "That means, you all alone here, just you and this big old place?"

"I got my people," she said, and she turned to call to Sally Red. The fat old woman appeared at the back door, scowling.

One of the men burst into laughter. "I see you do, sister! She look like the best cook in these parts!" he said to the others, gesturing to Sally Red's huge belly. "I say, we partake of this lady's gracious hospitality, boys," he went on. "We sleep a night or two on clean sheets and load up on some biscuits and white gravy, for once."

"I say," his comrade frowned, "they'll know we're here inside of six hours. We best bivouac in the woods."

"Shit, I'm tired of sleeping on wet ground. Le's us keep a close watch out and we take one night, anyway, to eat and sleep good." He glared up at Celisma. "You be happy as a clam to have us, right?"

She glowered right back at him. But she could see she had little choice. The Yankee guard troops were more than four hours downriver. If she fed these strays what she had and bedded them down, they'd likely take off of their own accord come sunup. "You be welcome, suh," she said. Turning to Sally Red and ignoring her gaping mouth of amazement, she said calmly, "Get supper started for our guests, *cher,* an' I go downriver an' see can I get us some crab."

"Get a mess of good she-crab!" one of the men hollered at her departing back, "them's the best damn eating in these parts."

Celisma bound up her skirt and put on her river boots, tucking cold biscuits and cheese into her pockets. She tucked Manon into her cradle and stuck a sugar tit in the child's fist. That would hold her until Sally Red could tend to her. She was out of the house in a flash of skirts, heading for the river. She knew if she did not find Alex, he would likely venture home soon and run smack into the arms of these scoundrels.

It was still hours before dark. *Dien merci,* she breathed gratefully, for it would have been harder to track Alex in the dusk. As it was, she had to follow the trail closely, for it was overgrown with creepers and sawgrass. She lost her way once; it had been months since she'd ventured this deeply into the swamp, but then she found the trail once more and, keeping her eyes to the ground, headed through the brush in the direction of the bee tree.

She dared not call out, she knew, for fear that one of the men followed her. Or that they might hear her call and wonder why she would call out if all she was doing was catching crab. She prayed quickly that the crab pots had a little something in them she could collect on the way back, just a small blue-back or anything else to keep the men satisfied. Not too satisfied, of course, but something just to flavor the gumbo—

The bee tree was just ahead, she could see its tall branches pulling up out of the lower palmetto scrub and cottonwood. There was a clear spring somewhere around here, she seemed to remember, one which she had drank from a few times before. She was so thirsty, she realized. Fear always made her so. There it was, right off the edge of the path.

She knelt quickly to cup her hands in the trickling water, bending next to the pool which formed below it and then ambled to the river over the damp ground. There was a sudden dark movement, and she faltered, but her movement was forward towards the water, and her balance was tilted. The thickly coiled moccasin struck at her swiftly from its waiting place by the spring, catching her on the cheek. She felt the deep embedment of its fangs in her face, and her first thought was that it was lucky the snake missed her eye. Her immediate second thought, as she pushed herself back and flung herself away and to her feet, was that she now had no reason to keep quiet, was surely too far away from BonReve to be heard, and she screamed, a high keening wail, falling backwards away from the snake and the spring, feeling her cheek puffing away from her skull even as she screamed, feeling the poison flush over her in a wave of burning heat with a cold core. Alex was there in an instant, his face bending over hers in horror, and she heard his voice calling to her as though from far away.

Celisma cried, "Watch out for the snake, *cher!*" and her own voice was hollow inside her head. Now she could not see out of one eye at all for the swelling, and the other was closing fast. She tried to gesture back to the spring. "Cottonmouth, by the water," she gasped.

"*Maman! Maman!*" Alex screamed, and she shushed him with the last of her strength.

"Don' go back to BonReve 'til they gone," she murmured. "Rebs holed up there one night, maybe two. Sneak to the backdoor, see Sally Red, an' then get to your Uncle." Then she stopped, for a vast rushing sound was coming to her from somewhere, she couldn't say where. From within her? Without her? The pain was strong, she knew that much, but she could not feel it as she might have thought. Not like a stab through the belly or a burn on the skin, but a pain which cramped her gut and stiffened every muscle, even her skin seemed to stiffen—but her mind was somehow free of it.

Alex was weeping, she could tell that though she could not see him. Could not see anything now. He was wresting his sheath knife from its holder, she heard its wicker, dimly felt the slice of tissue and knew he cut her face, sensed blood slide from her eyes, her nose, down her neck, but she felt nothing more.

Celisma heard a bird song from the bayou, and for some reason, it caught her fancy and carried her up with it, higher than the cottonwoods, higher even than the bee tree, and she spasmed with joy at the pureness of its beauty, the shining of the water below her, the roundness of the curve of the world . . . and she left that place and never once looked back.

PART THREE

1877–1927

Down the Yellowstone, the Milk, the White, and
Cheyenne;
The Cannonball, the Musselshell, the James and the
Sioux;
Down the Judith, the Grand, the Osage, and the Platte,
The Skunk, the Salt, the Black, and Minnesota;
Down the Rock, the Illinois, and the Kankakee,
The Allegheny, the Monongahela, Kanawha, and
Muskingum;
Down the Miami, the Wabash, the Licking, and the Green,
The Cumberland, the Kentucky, and the Tennessee;
Down the Ouachita, the Wichita, the Red, and Yazoo—
Down the Missouri, three thousand miles from the
Alleghenies;
Down the Ohio, a thousand miles from the Alleghenies;
Down the Arkansas, fifteen hundred miles from the Great
Divide;
Down the Red, a thousand miles from Texas;
Down the great Valley, twenty-five hundred miles from
Minnesota,
Carrying every rivulet and brook, creek and rill,
Carrying all the rivers that run down two-thirds the
continent—
The Mississippi runs to the Gulf.

Pare Lorentz, *The River*,
a New Deal Era film on flood control

The Civil War left Louisiana a ravished wasteland of ruined plantations, impoverished farms, and fallow fields. All railroads were destroyed, two-thirds of the livestock stolen, one-fourth of the adult males were killed or maimed, and 300,000 slaves worth two billion prewar dollars roamed the countryside without resources.

Reconstruction arrived in the bayou early, bringing frequent race riots and the Northern carpetbaggers who descended on New Orleans like hungry fleas. The same year the slaves were freed by the Thirteenth Amendment, the Knights of the White Camelia added their violence to the already powerful Ku Klux Klan, and in one of their more infamous night rides in 1873, an entire Negro village in Colfax, Louisiana was massacred.

Between the carpetbaggers, the Southern scalawags, and the "Satraps"—Federal generals set to command the South under the Reconstruction Acts—political chicanery flourished. As Governor Warmouth of Louisiana declared in frustration, "Why, damn it, *demoralization is a way of life down here, and corruption is the fashion!"*

Amidst plunging prices and ruined crops, John D. Rockefeller formed Standard Oil and began to buy up bayou land; the Robert E. Lee *and the* Natchez, *two of the fastest steamboats on the river, raced eleven hundred miles from New Orleans to St. Louis as thousands cheered along both shores; and the first steel truss bridge crossed the Mississippi at St. Louis, a union of both banks once thought impossible. In 1877, the last Federal troops withdrew from New Orleans, Reconstruction officially ended, and the Queen City began her recovery with the nation's first and richest "Golden Octopus": the lottery.*

It was September, a time when the tides ebbed low in the great river and down in the delta, a "sook" or female crab was making her way with stubborn annoyance into more brackish water.

Annoyance was her usual state in this season, for she was nearing her time to molt, and her hard shell felt like stiff walls around her body, like anchors on her jointed legs. Sook was two years old, and she had already molted more than fifteen times. As a young blue crab, she molted as often as once a week, eating voraciously and growing quickly. Now she molted only a few times a year, but the process never pleased her.

Sook scuttled her six-inch body down the riverbank, darting in and out of the reeds for protection. Under her shell, she could feel the soft cover growing over her organs, the mantle which would barely hold her insides together when she was in molt as a softshell crab. During this brief time, she was completely vulnerable to any predator, including all waterfowl, an alligator gar, or even another cannibalizing crab. But for now, her claws kept danger at bay.

Sook moved swiftly downriver, snatching at small shrimps and bits of decayed fish washed up in the foam, until she came to a bend of the bayou she instantly recognized. Bunches of reeds grew close together here several feet from shore. It seemed an ideal place for molting, a perfect refuge to hide for the twenty-four hours it would take her hard shell to grow back over her body. She saw that many younger sooks had taken advantage of the cover to nestle among the dense reeds and await their growth.

But Sook turned away from them and downriver once more. Last molt, she had stopped in this place and narrowly escaped with her claws intact, for the reeds were no refuge at all. Fishermen had tied clumps together to imitate safe cover, taking up hundreds of the molting crabs in their nets.

Further downriver, she nestled deeply within some swamp grass set a few feet within the gently lapping waters and waited. In half a day more, she split the seams of her carapace down the side and across the bottom rim of her shell and backed out like semisolid paste out of a tube. She waited a while more, feeling hunger but knowing that she could not venture forth to feed. Within her, a restlessness grew to replace her annoyance. She had found solitude, yet she was not safe.

She began the swelling process just as soon as her hard shell was gone. This was the part of her molt which usually made her most irritable and willing to snap at anything that floated past, for her internal organs stretched and grew to almost twice their normal size within only hours. But this time, she felt a certain peace come to her, and she waited, puffing and blowing past the swollen discomfort.

Another crab, a female, suddenly swam into her line of

sight and turned towards her hidden refuge. Sook crouched lower into cover, trying to blend into the camouflage of grasses. But the female intruder sensed her, moved closer, and was on her in a flash, catching one soft claw between her pinchers and swiveling into Sook's snout with a ferocity born of hunger as well as territorial ire.

Sook took a deep breath through her filtering orange gills and dove into the muck beneath her, trying desperately to escape the claws of the other crab, but her own claws had not yet hardened sufficiently for defense. She bubbled frantically and tried to cover herself with matter and muck, but the female snapped off her soft claw with one quick snip and came in to cut her in two.

In that moment, a jimmy crab, a male with full armament intact, scuttled from the deeper waters, moving swiftly towards the female attacker. He was almost half again as large, twice as aggressive, and came on snapping and clicking for battle. A wide blue with one small and one over-huge claw, he did not hesitate, but quickly grabbed the female around one leg and snatched it from her body as though it were the smallest shrimp.

The female turned for battle, saw she had no hope of victory, and backpedaled off through the gentle current. The jimmy approached Sook boldly, straddled her soft, swollen body, and turned so that he faced outwards towards the open river, backing deeply into the reeds. He cradled her in his fierce claws gently, his one oversized and his second smaller one gripping her surely. For many hours, he held her safe.

Sook now relaxed and let her developing claws tuck inside, giving herself over to his grip completely. For eleven hours he held her fast, and after this lengthy foreplay, finally inserted enough sperm in the pocket under her abdomen to fertilize several million eggs—eggs she would ripen months later.

Sook felt her carapace harden after more than twelve hours in his grip, and she eased away from his claws. He carefully released her, leaving the reeds ahead of her to check for predators. Now her claws were firm enough for defense, and she clicked and snapped them aggressively to test her stamina.

Another season's molt was finished, another season's eggs fertilized. In months, she would burrow down in the bayou mud to hibernate and let her sponge, or egg mass, develop properly.

But for now, she barely glanced at the jimmy who had saved her life. She spied a small pink shrimp drifting on the current and scuttled off to snatch it away from a pickerel.

Two nights after his mother died, Alex was certain she spoke to him, quietly and without warning, from a cypress tree which waved in a soft breeze right outside the bedroom window. For two nights, he had waited for her voice, certain she would come if she could. She always used to tell him that death was nothing more than a new beginning—"for the folks which is left, same as the soul which goes on," she said. And certainly, she must be as right about the nature of death as she was about everything else, Alex told himself. For a new beginning was what he and Manon had now.

When Sally Red took them to Uncle Simon's to stay until decisions could be made, Tante Cerise said that Celisma was still watching over them. *"Le bon dieu* may take a mother's life," she said gently, "and she might be resting safe alongside your father in her grave, but He leaves her eyes alive to watch over her children wherever they go. She sees you, Alex, and she smiles on you." She swept Manon up with one thin arm—Cerise had never run to fat as so many bayou women—

and with the practiced gesture of a woman who was born to mother, lodged her firmly on one hip. "And on this *'tit chou* as well. People die, even the good ones. But love goes on forever."

When Alex did not, could not speak, she put a gentle finger under his chin and added, "Your *maman* would have wanted you to get past your grieving and get on with her plans for you, *cher,* just as soon as you feel able."

"*Oui, tante,*" Alex said, wishing with all his heart that he might refuge in her arms as Manon did now.

That night, his mother's voice came as clearly to him as though she stood over his head. He could almost feel her hand on his brow in the moist, warm breeze that blew in from the bayou. "My son," she murmured, "you cain' stay here long."

"*Maman?*" he whispered. "Is that you?"

"*Oui, c'est moi,*" she rustled with the boughs of the cypress. "Do you hear me?"

"I hear you. Are you dead?"

"*Vraiment, cher.* I be killed, but not lost to you. No, nor to your *'tite soeur.* I be with you."

"That's what Tante Cerise said," he answered with awe.

"She knows. Listen to her, *cher.* And listen to me. You cain' stay here long."

He moaned, exhausted with grief and the need to be so grownup so quickly. "Why not?"

" 'Cause you made for better. *I* made you for better, and your sister, too."

Alex glanced over at the trundle bed in the corner where Manon slept soundly. She did not seem to understand that *maman* would not be coming for them ever again. She wept but she did not—here, he stumbled for the difference in his mind—she did not grieve. She wept in the same way she slept: she was sad or she was tired, but she did not seem to think ahead to the next day. Alex knew in his heart that in a few years, Manon would scarcely remember her mother at all, whereas he . . . he would never forget her. He saw that the counterpane had slipped off Manon's shoulders, and he rose to pull the covers back up to her neck. She sighed and rolled, unaware of his touch. He clambered back into bed.

"What must I do?" he asked wearily.

"Simon will tell you," she whispered, her voice falling away as from a great height. "Listen to Simon—" and a sudden gust of wind pulled the words away from him into the darkness.

"*Maman!*" he cried out, his heart torn with fresh grief at her going—

But there was only the susurration of the cypress in the breeze.

For a long month, Alex waited for his mother's return, but she never again spoke to him. Each Sunday Simon and Cerise took the children to visit her grave, where she lay alongside Samuel Weitz in the family burying plot, but she did not rise from the earth nor did she shake the trees or sing in the leaves. Nonetheless, he felt her presence all about him, and his sorrow began to ebb, slowly and surely as the autumn gave way to winter. Simon told him that Sally Red had gone to find her folks, that BonReve was locked up tight, and that soon, he would have a choice to make.

"You can stay here and welcome," his uncle told him, "but with winter coming on, I'll be out with the traps for weeks on end. You might think what your mother wanted for you."

Alex stared at his only kin as Cerise set a plate of *couscous* down before him and added, "You're old enough to have a say, *cher.* Your sister's decisions will be made for her, of course, but you're—nearly a man." Here, she smiled gently. "What do you think is best for you both?"

In that moment, he saw clearly how very old his aunt and uncle had become in the last few years. Simon was bent and silver-haired, and Cerise looked as fragile and powdery as a silky dandelion globe. A cough racked her in the morning and again as the damp came on with the night. "*Maman* wanted me to go to school," he said slowly. "She always said that."

Simon nodded. "*C'est vrai,* that was her dream."

"But what is yours?" Cerise asked.

He thought a long moment. "I would like to go to school, I think," he said slowly, "more than just the village school. *Maman* always said that was the mark of a man." And then he remembered his mother's words the night she came to him. "Where should we go, Uncle?" he asked Simon. "*Maman* said to listen to you."

"She did?" He hugged his arms and rocked back in his chair. "Well, if I was your *papa,* I'd tell you that Gerard, your aunt's nephew, is making the trip to New Orleans in two weeks. I will take him, me. He goes to the *lycée de science* to study the architecture, yes? Perhaps this is what your *maman* wanted for you as well?"

"Architecture?" Alex asked. "What's that?"

"How to build a building. But there are many other *apprentissages* there, if that does not suit you. You are younger than Gerard, but they would take you, I think. Celisma taught you your letters well and your numbers—"

"I can read and do figures, *certainement,* but it would be good to learn more than that. What about my sister?"

"Well," Simon said slowly, "what do you think we should do about her? She can stay here, of course, if that is best. What would your *maman* say to this?"

Alex shook his head, suddenly sure what the decision must be. *Maman* would not want them separated. "We should be together," he said.

"But she is so small," Cerise spoke up, touching Simon's arm. "Surely, I can—"

"*Cher,* she will be too much for you, here alone. And then you cannot go to stay with Tidings, as you like to do while I trap." He looked at her with soft eyes and then at Alex. "I think we should take her to Emma."

"Who's Emma?" Alex asked quickly.

"Your mother did not speak of her? Your father's sister?"

"I don't remember."

"She is a woman of God," Cerise said. "Of the Ursulines." She shrugged reluctantly. *"C'est vrai,* the child would be safe there. There is no place safer."

"What is this place?"

"A house of the faithful."

"For—" he could scarcely bring himself to say the word. "For orphans?"

"Yes," Cerise said gently, "but also many of the fine families send their *jeunes filles* there so that the nuns might teach them the graces." She sighed unhappily. "If she cannot stay here, that is the next-best place for her. At least then brother and sister can remain closer. I would want this for you, *cher.*"

Alex pushed himself back from the table and strode over to where Manon played quietly with a handful of feathers by the fire. The lights from the flame caught the black of her hair and made it gleam. She saw him, laughed, and reached out to be lifted, as always. He hoisted her into his arms, and she shrieked happily, curling her hands on his collar as she was wont to do. "Do you think this best, Uncle?" he asked, using the formal French and turning to face him.

"Non," he said, shaking his head. "Best would be that children stay together. Best would be that your *tante* would be young and strong enough to raise this *'tit* as her own, but if one cannot have the best, one must choose wisely from the rest, *hein?* It is a new beginning, *vraiment.* One which I think your *maman* would approve."

"Then tell Gerard I join him in two weeks," Alex said calmly. "And write the letter to my father's sister. I shall sign it."

Cerise's eyes welled up with tears. "There speaks your brother's son," she said to Simon.

469

He smiled, shaking his head in rueful wonderment. "I never doubted it for a moment."

It was easy for Alex to tell himself that this was a new beginning rather than an ending as they journeyed to New Orleans. He had never seen so many new faces, new ships, new places as he did in the three-days' journey from Lafourche to the Queen City of the Delta.

As they neared New Orleans, Alex sensed the sea even in the mile-long width of the vast river, pulling him nearer as the tides pulled the Mississippi. The air lost its bayou thickness, and his nose deciphered a faint tang, a salt edge to the freshening breeze. Closer still, and the birds became more numerous and varied: screeching gulls with wide, dark-tipped wings, slow and indolent cranes, flocks of ponderous, fat-billed pelicans. And then, out of the green horizon rose the dark wharves and tall buildings of the looming city. Although he had never felt large in the bayou, standing on the docks of New Orleans he felt not just small but invisible. Nonetheless, he took Simon's hand with a determined grin and followed him along thronging streets.

He stood like a man before the walls of the Ursulines, gazing upwards at their vast, gray cliffs, stood alongside his uncle with his new traveling suit cramping the skin around his neck and stifling his arms. He sat like a man in the cool, shadowed antechamber where Emma Weitz greeted her brother, scarcely flinching at all when she bent to graze his cheek with her parchment lips, dodging the edges of her white sailed *coif,* even managing not to stare too hard at the heavy bronze cross that lay on her chest like a sword. Manon, too, seemed transfixed, sitting unusually quiet on his lap.

Simon had told him before he met this Sister that she was not to be confused with the nuns who lived at the little chapel in Lafourche. "Sister is *une Règle Vivante,* a Living Rule," his uncle said with some pride. "It is said by her sister nuns that if the Holy Rule of their Order were ever lost or destroyed, you could see it still alive in her face, she is such a perfect nun."

She must be an angel, Alex first thought when he saw her, so effortlessly did she seem to move across the stoned floor of the cloister. They passed down a long corridor to meet her, and he peeped into a small chapel as they went by. Within, more than two hundred nuns knelt in soldierly rows down the long nave. A miniature city within a city.

What he noticed next, as they greeted the Sister and took their seats, was that she kept her back as rigid as the high, gray walls outside the convent, with a space between her cloak and the back of the chair. Yet she seemed gentle and relaxed.

Uncle spoke so long to Sister that for a brief time, Alex was almost able to will himself out the high window, down to the streets of the city, to wander at will among the intriguing shops, staring at the passersby without himself being seen—until they spoke of Manon. Then, his attention was riveted back to their words.

"It is not that she is without means," Emma was saying quietly, "for we have many who are less dowered than she. But she is so very young—not even four years old."

"You have others this young?"

"Yes, but they do not stay for long. Perhaps only a season, while other arrangements are made."

"We may well make other arrangements, but for now, this child needs care, and Cerise is not strong enough to chase after her all the day. Besides, her brother will be here at *école*

471

and it is good they are at least where they can visit, yes? Their mother would have wished it so."

"Poor woman," the old nun said gently. "You scarcely see one of her kind with such dreams!"

With that, Alex spoke up firmly. "My father provided for us. If you need money, I can pay for my sister."

Emma smiled at him. "You are the image of your father, *cher*. What do you mean to study at *lycée*?"

"Whatever I'm good at," he answered promptly.

"Samuel all over," she confided to Simon. "Well, then we shall take your sister for a time, until we can make other decisions. And you may come to see her when you wish."

The sense Alex had of a new beginning was suddenly and agonizingly shattered as Emma put out her arms and gathered Manon into them. His sister, as though sensing that this was not a casual embrace, turned to him and shrieked in a way she had not since she was an infant. With arms outstretched, she wailed, "No, no, no!" and tried to climb out of Emma's hold.

"It is better if you leave quickly," the nun said firmly, gently, "and then come back again, perhaps tomorrow. She will be *plus contente* once she cannot see your face."

Simon took him by the shoulders and turned him out the door and, like a man, Alex walked down the long flight of stone stairs, from shadow to sunlight, out the garden gate, and onto the steps of the Ursulines, where he suddenly turned and buried his head in his uncle's stomach, sobbing like a young boy.

The *lycée de sciences* where Simon took Gerard and Alex was not considered the finest in the city, but it was the school where most of the Acadian boys were enrolled, if school was something their parents deemed necessary. Since the *lycée* also accepted the quadroon sons of freed mulattos, the sons of the finer Creole families went, instead, to *École des Arts* or abroad for their studies.

Because Gerard was three years older than Alex, he boarded with another boy from his own class, and Alex was assigned a small room on the third floor of the *lycée* with the son of a shrimper from the Bayou Teche. Simon embraced Alex as he left him at *lycée* with the admonition, "Work hard, *cher,* and make your *maman* proud." Left alone then with his new friend, no less bereft at the departure of his father, Alex sat on his bed and stared at his new suitcase with two handwoven suits, four pair of trousers, two shirts, and his underdrawers.

Although he had intended to go to the Ursulines the very next day after class, he found that the *maîtres* had most of his hours planned. He was not only responsible for his studies, he was also expected—as were all the students at *lycée*—to help maintain the institution itself. Assigned to the groundskeeper, Alex was put to the rake and hoe for a two-hour stretch after classes and sent to the garden to help with the weeding and seeding.

He considered himself fortunate. At least he was able to be outdoors, and the pleasant odors and touch of the soil reminded him of his mother's rows behind BonReve. The work involved his hands, not his mind, and he sought refuge in daydreams of a more ordered past and a more hopeful future.

It was five days before he was excused from duties long enough to make the trek across the city to the Ursulines. Alone he faced the high walls of the convent once more and asked for his great-aunt by her bride name, *Soeur Soumis*. After interminable shadowed moments, she arrived in the garden to greet him. Gracefully, she swept over the cobbled stones, her skirts dusting the ground, her shoulders precise and straight, unbent by her age.

"Ah, Alex, you look taller since I saw you last. Are the *maîtres* treating you well?"

"Oui, Soeur," he said, bowing as he had been taught in the first day of school. "But the lessons are harder than I thought. Where's my sister?"

"She is in the nursery with the other *enfants.*" She smiled, almost mischievously. "Your uncle did not warn me that she was so *adroit* for her age. If we let her, she would have organized *tous les autres* for *la revolution!* Would you like to see her?"

"Oui, vraiment," he said quickly. But then he hesitated. "Does she still weep?"

"Of course," Emma said calmly, "and likely will for a few nights more. This is to be expected, I think. But it will not hurt her to see you, *cher*, in fact it may make her feel less *abandonée.* Come. You can see for yourself how she fares."

Emma led him to a large room up two flights of stairs, which opened up onto the courtyard below. The ceiling was high, and the light flooded the walls, making it a far more agreeable place, to his mind, than the rest of the convent he had seen. More than a dozen children played within, some of them on the floor with blocks of colored wood, others with rag dolls and bits of fabric. A row of gray-covered beds lined one wall, immaculate and unwrinkled as slabs of marble.

474

Three nuns watched the children, answering questions and forestalling struggles over this play-toy or that.

In one corner, surrounded by three other *jeunes filles* about her size, Manon sat with her head bent close to the others, as though she whispered to them of the most intricate secrets. As Alex approached with Emma behind him, Manon did not look up, so concentrated was she on her story. Only after two of her compatriots raised their head in curiosity, did she stop her tale.

When she spied Alex, she at once threw herself into his arms, wailing as though she were suddenly scalded.

"What is this?" he scolded her. "You were content enough until you saw me, *chou*. What a *pleurard* you are!"

She took her fists and pounded on his chest. "You left me!" she cried, throwing herself backwards in his arms until he had to strain to hold her.

"I had to go to school, *cher,* and you had to stay here. But look, you have new friends already, yes? And the nuns are good to you? And I'm back again already."

Manon stopped wailing abruptly and peered down at her two friends, her face lighting up impishly. "This is my brother!" she crowed to them. "He comes from a far place just to see me!"

"Not so very far," Alex started, but Manon had lost interest in berating him. She struggled to get down.

"I have a play-dolly," she said, pulling at his hand, "come and see, her name is Gabriella!"

Alex let himself be pulled along into Manon's game and her tales of her adventures, while Emma smiled down on them both. After an hour with his sister, he was both weary and relieved. "Where does she get this frock?" he asked Sister. It was a garment he did not recognize at all, and it made Manon seem even more separated from him.

"The good people of New Orleans bring clothes, linens, even playthings for our children here."

He blushed furiously and looked aside so that Manon would not see his dismay. "*Charité.* For the orphans."

"Charity, that is true," Sister said calmly, "one of His greatest commandments to us all. But not only to those without parents, but to all those children who are in our care." She smiled gently. "For you see, there are some here with *famille,* and they still have less than you do."

Her words lightened his heart somewhat. Finally he told himself, *maman* would be pleased, after all. My sister is safe, I am safe, and we both are putting down new roots in old mud. She used to say that was the best thing to do when life made you take a turn. Be bendable, *cher,* like a willow, not fixed like a cypress, *maman* said. The first tree to go in a flood is that cypress, for it cannot give way without giving out.

As he watched Manon draw the other children around her, Alex was struck by the truth of his mother's words and also something Sally Red told him once: better to be dough to be kneaded by life than be clay, to be broken.

When Manon cast her mind backwards, she could recall few firm memories of those earliest years at Ursulines. The nursery, the nuns, the studies, the refectory, the masses, the catechism drills, the prayers at dawn and dusk and at every meal, all flowed together in her mind's eye as a dim, shadowed time of cool order and gray sameness. One of the first words she learned was the word obey. It had *audire* at its root. *Audire:* to listen or give ear. For such a place of silence, there was plenty to listen to, no matter how many times Sister reminded her that she should be still, inside and outside, for "interior silence was the power of God."

The bells alone were an everpresent incantation which she seemed never able to escape. Time in the Ursulines belonged to God. The bronze bell in the chapel campanile announced every single activity of the day, calling the nuns to duties and devotions and was as stringent a taskmaster as Jesus himself, Manon thought. No matter what they were doing, what they were saying, when the bell tolled, on the instant of the first peal, the nuns stopped in mid-voice, mid-air, their gestures frozen, their words silenced, to turn to their devotions. To do otherwise was to commit an imperfection against obedience.

So many times, a glass was being handed to her, a fork just to her lips, or her teacher was completing a lesson on the chalkboard, when a bell would ring. The glass was instantly set down, the fork averted, the chalk dropped to leave the *y* without its tail, the *t* without its cross—and the nun would be gone.

At first, Manon's frustration smoldered, and she wailed her dismay. But soon she learned to accept, and the time came when she would unconsciously stop her lips, set down her pen, or obediently close her eyes the moment she heard a bell.

An early recollection—she guessed she would have been about six or seven—was walking in the garden with *Soeur Soumis,* the nun who took a special interest in her. She knew, on some level, that this old woman was somehow kin, but she did not know what that meant, exactly. She said to call her *Soeur,* and so Manon obeyed.

The garden was one of Manon's favorite places, for the many different kinds of flowers and greenery, the cool, shaded stone walkways in the hot summers, the formal geometric plantings, the tinkling of the fountains, a cheerful place even in the grayest days of winter. She was sometimes allowed to discard her many-laced shoes—usually the source of endless trial to her—if she had been very good. Then, with her feet bare, she could occasionally wheedle *Soeur* into letting her dip up to her ankles in the fountain.

On one hot afternoon, *Soeur* sat doing her lacework in the shade while Manon collected colored pebbles and washed them in the fountain, setting them in rows to dry in the sun. *Soeur's* hands were never idle, and she had taught Manon early that even small hands could always find something useful to do. A crowded gaggle of *jeunes filles* trooped down the steep stairs to the gate, all demurely veiled and shawled for their *excursion* outside the convent. The trio of everpresent nuns—never only two, lest they become too fond of each other and forget that all were equally sisters—three nuns flanked the girls and ushered them out to the street with frequent hissed warnings to keep together, to lower their eyes, and to still their tongues when on public streets.

Manon had seen the older girls leave in this fashion, but she knew that she was not allowed to leave the convent until she was eight years old. She picked up her skirts and ran to the gate to peer down the street at the lucky departing immigrants.

Soeur called her back patiently. "It is not seemly to clutch your skirts about your legs like that, daughter," she said mildly. "Nor to run and spy on passersby. If Reverend Mother were to see such behavior, she might wonder if Manon should be allowed the freedom of the garden after all."

"*Soeur,*" Manon called, ignoring her admonition, "where do they go today?"

"Likely to Saint Louis," the old nun said, "or perhaps to *l'hôpital* to tend the veterans."

"Do they ever go anyplace to play?"

"To play?" She smiled. "They are young ladies now, and ladies do not play."

"What do they do, then?"

"Many things, *cher,* all in good time. Some may go on to *l'université.* Others will make a marriage and raise daughters of their own. Some may even return to their sisters here and join us for the rest of their lives."

Manon grimaced in ill-disguised horror. "Is that all?"

Soeur laughed softly, a surprisingly young laugh for a woman of her age. "That is enough, my daughter, believe me. And when you are of an age, you will find your paths as rich with choice as they do now."

Manon flounced back to the fountain and her washed stones. She took a palmful of water and splashed them again to make them glitter in the light. "I will never make a marriage," she said firmly. "I will be very rich and have many houses where all my friends will come to stay."

Soeur looked more stern now. "God does not wish to hear young *'tites* declare what they will and will not do," she said. "He will direct your life as He sees fit. Perhaps more concentration on your prayers will help you understand His plan for you."

"And I'm not coming back here either," Manon said, unconcerned. She rose and began to skip around the fountain as fast as she could in a dizzy circle. "I shall go and live with my brother and take care of him, and we will have a fine house with a red door. And I shall eat *glacé* whenever I wish." Manon had recently discovered the luscious fruit sorbets the vendors sold outside the gates, for Alex had brought her a lemon ice on his most recent visit.

Soeur reached out without warning and yanked Manon off her feet, to sit firmly beside her on the bench. "I am certain that God has heard enough this day of what one impudent daughter will and will not do."

Manon stumbled and banged her leg smartly against the marble, but she did not yelp. She had learned that the old nun would comfort her kindly if she were truly in pain, but if she had disobeyed, she could expect no solace. She sat still, keeping her leg against the cool stone, easing the scrape. The moment Sister's hand was once again in her lap, however, Manon darted up and away from her reach, laughing delightedly at her minor triumph. She raced for the steps to the cloister, knowing that Sister could never catch her before she reached chapel, where she would find her on her knees in prayer, asking God for His patience and forgiveness. One more set of *Aves* avoided. As she ran, she called back over her shoulder, "God wants me to be happy, *Soeur,* He told me so!"

Many years later, when Manon recalled that moment between Emma and herself, she wondered where she had found the courage to speak so to the old nun. She could only suppose it came from a decade of learning that for every obedience, there was a reward—and it might not be the reward of God's love, but a minor freedom instead. So there was no doubt the nuns taught her courage—even if it was a different sort of courage than they might have designed. And they also taught her that with every wound came an in-creased strength. But she could not relish their fortress as they did, no. Even after the passage of many years, the smell of a quiet garden, the splash and glitter of a fountain in the sun, put her in a mood of rebellion rather than quietude. She was surprised to discover that most found the sound of run-ning water a soothing thing; it only made Manon restless.

More than a decade and a score of busy blocks separated the Ursulines from the three-story house at 717 Orleans Street. As though the convent was an island of another century, a foreign land, it ignored Orleans Street and its saloons and *palaces de dance* with a consummate disconcern that few wives of New Orleans could imitate. As they came and went from the *Théâtre d'Orléans,* even the most secure wife could not help but notice the close proximity of 717 Orleans Street. But no wife ever stepped foot inside; indeed, most cast their eyes away upon alighting from their carriages for the opera with their husbands, for this three-story and ornately furbished house was where the Quadroon Balls took place.

On the lower floor, the rich and well-dressed gentlemen could enjoy their favorite games of chance, and sometimes, if they were very unlucky, their losses would mean that they would not be welcome again on the second floor, even if they could pay the two-dollars' admission.

On a hardwood ballroom three-cypress-layers thick and edged with loges for onlookers, the dancers took up all of that second floor. It was the largest ballroom in all New Orleans, airy, handsomely paneled with huge glittering chandeliers, fronted by an ironwork balcony overlooking Orleans Street, and flanked by a cool courtyard reached by a curving stairway.

Here waited some of the most beautiful women in the world, men said. *Les Sirènes,* the Creoles called them. White wives altered the epithet to "serpent women," but could do little to discourage the private fêtes which ranked among the city's most seductive scandals.

Manon d'Irlandais stood slightly apart from the rest of the beauties, holding a champagne goblet in one graceful hand. Up and down the staircase to the gardens, women draped themselves in artful repose, taking the air between dances.

But Manon held herself alert and erect. Discreetly, with an infinitesimal shrug of her shoulders, she adjusted her bodice so that the cleavage between her breasts deepened. She knew he would seek her out, and what she said and did in the next quarter-hour could alter her fortunes forever.

As though she had directed his steps, he appeared then at the top of the stairs, his eyes moving quickly over the gowns, the women, and finally stopping when he saw her. He came down the stairs with a studied grace, and she smiled at him, her head high, her lashes veiling her eyes.

He held two glasses of absinthe in his hands.

"*Mademoiselle* Manon," he said, "I see you have already been served."

Manon's smile never wavered. It was a slow triumphant smile, implicit with the luxurious mastery of surrender. She simply extended her hand over the edge of the balcony and let go her champagne goblet. No need to follow it with her eyes as it crashed on the brick courtyard below, she had surveyed the scene to be sure no one stood beneath her. Monsieur Booth grinned at the sudden shrill shrieks from the closest women and handed Manon the glass of absinthe.

"Now," she said softly, "now, truly, I have been served." She took his arm and eased him away from the balcony, upwards to where the music streamed out of the ballroom doors, before too many associated the crash of glass with her, for she knew that only the best-mannered, most refined quadroons were welcomed night after night. She could not afford to be turned away by the elderly mulatresses who arranged the balls with skill and discretion, and the white wives of the city need be given no excuse to demand the doors of 717 Orleans Street be closed once and for good.

She picked up her heavy lace skirts with one hand and handed her glass to Monsieur Booth, so that she need not let go of his arm.

" 'Manon d'Irlandais,' " he was saying, watching her face, "a most beautiful name, Mademoiselle, in a garden of beautiful names. It means 'Irish,' does it not?"

" 'Of the Irish,' more exactly," she murmured, "*Merci, Monsieur.* I am glad it pleases you."

"It does, indeed. It is not your own, though, that I'll wager."

She slid her eyes away from his with a Cheshire smile. Ah, these Americans, their boldness intoxicated her, made her feel so vibrantly alive, that she did not care if a score of mulatto *mamans* glowered at her. "Of course, it is my own," she said with a taunting lilt. "I chose it, after all."

"From your mother's heritage?"

"From *papa.*"

"I would very much like to meet your mother," Monsieur Booth said as they stopped just outside the ballroom and the orchestra began the opening strains to a waltz. "Where is she seated?" He glanced around at the rows of ambitious mothers, like so many setting hens, scrutinizing the dancers.

Manon turned into his arms with a swirl of lace. "She is not," she said gaily. "Come, let us dance!"

As he dipped and turned her around the room, she surveyed the mothers in their evening dress with their fans and pearl chokers. Like *grandes dames,* she faltered inwardly, *grandes dames* of fat, dark flowers, waiting for the best flies their honeys can entice.

Most of the lovely quadroons dancing around her performed the steps more surely than their rich, white partners. And why not? They had been trained for one thing: to attract and please a man. Sent to small schools or convents to learn to read and write, a little sewing, a smattering of singing and poesy, much grace and deportment, and then set at their mothers' feet to perfect their voices to low, dovelike tones, their manners to exquisite refinement, these women were the jewels of their caste. And each one was assuredly a virgin, Manon knew, or had learned the art of seeming so. For therein lay her hope of future security. No man waltzing at Orleans Street wanted damaged goods.

Some of the wary mothers eyed Manon carefully as she and Monsieur Booth swept past, but she tossed her head and shone such a smile on her partner that his eyes widened with pleasure and he did not notice their stares. If she were very careful, they might never realize that she was likely the one motherless dancer among them. She had no protector, no chaperone. But that would not keep her from success, she vowed. After all, she had seen it done often enough to manage the affair herself.

An introduction was generally arranged after several dances. *Maman* would accept the man's bow—even the darkest mulatress had a right to be there accepting attentions on her daughter's behalf—*"Oui, Monsieur,"* she had seen Monsieur before at Cathedral, *"Oui, certainement,"* she was acquainted with his second uncle, ah yes, she would give permission for her daughter to stroll downstairs with Monsieur for a cool sangaree in the shadowed courtyard.

Once the couple walked away, the mothers' heads dipped together, comparing notes about his prospects, his family. If things went well, the young man and *maman* might then continue a discreet conversation where the suitor would promise to settle a flat sum, say several thousand dollars, or he must make certain guarantees, *non?* He must care for her daughter for some specified time. He need not be rich, but it helped. If the dancing daughter liked him, well, and it could be arranged. And perhaps she might better her arrangement once she became his *placée.*

The waltz ended, and Manon knew she must bring about a *dénouement,* or Monsieur would find another. "Perhaps," she said a little breathlessly, "it is cooler down in the gardens, away from the lights." She turned her eyes on him now, her blue eyes which she could alchemize warm or cool by will and whim.

"Yes," he said, his voice lowering to match her own. "Yes, we should try the gardens in the moonlight."

Once past the rows of dancers and chaperones, Manon began to relax, to watch this man with more pleasure. She had felt drawn to him the moment he embraced her for that first dance. Tall and long-armed, he wore his trousers tight across the thighs in the American style. His hair was darker than her own, his skin darker, too, but his blue eyes were lighter, almost as the sky above the gulf, where hers went gray in the corners. He came with Monsieur Auburd, a frequent guest at the quadroon balls, and so she guessed he must be rich enough.

But it was necessary to know.

They passed a serving wench with a tray of canapes, selected two apiece, and then went on down to the trellised yellow roses.

"So, your mother is not present, Mademoiselle?" Monsieur Booth took both canapes in one bite and briskly wiped his mouth with a snatch of white linen.

Ah. He had not been completely unaware, then. She bent her head, nibbling at one morsel. "*Maman* died when I was quite young, Monsieur. To be truthful, I have no near relations here this evening."

"Is that not rather unusual? I mean, for a woman of your—" here, he broke off and began again. "I would have thought that it would be awkward to be alone."

"*Mais non,* I am not alone," she smiled up at him. "I have many friends, Monsieur. Many who are happy to escort me to my carriage."

"Ah, I see. Well, if a man should wish to see you again, where might he call?"

She hesitated, running her tongue carefully over her lips to both sleek them and clean them of errant canapé crumbs. Carefully, Manon, she told herself, and her heart was thudding. The Creoles had a phrase to describe the things one should have said but didn't have the presence of mind to say at the time: *l'esprit d'escalier, or staircase wit.* She must now be Creole in her head. She murmured, "And does this man wish to see me again?" She leaned against the wall of the garden, feeling the heat from the disappeared sun still in its stones.

"Most definitely," Monsieur Booth said, moving closer to her.

His hand touched her waist. When she did not move away, it slid slightly around her.

"I find you the most beautiful, enticing creature."

She thought swiftly of what she knew of Monsieur: the mothers said he was married to the daughter of a planter in Donaldsonville, had a home there for his wife and two sons and another home for the winter season in the Quarter. A box at the Opera, a thriving export business with an office in town and another at the docks, well-connected with the Governor's office, no more than forty if he was a day, and likely worth more than twenty thousand a year. Married, that was better. He would not wish too much of her time. But could he afford her? Would he think her worth the investment?

His hands intrigued her. They were narrow, finely shaped, but full of power.

"*Monsieur,*" she said demurely, dropped away from his hand only slightly, "because *maman* does not sit with the others does not mean she is not watching, nonetheless." She cast her eyes upwards in case he did not catch her meaning.

He missed her point. "And if she were watching," he said, leaning closer, "what would she wish for such a lovely daughter?"

"The question is," Manon replied, "what does Monsieur wish?"

"Call me David," he said, taking her wrist and gently gripping it with three fingers. "David Booth, new-come to grace."

She laughed, a low trill of delight. "New-come? Or merely new-minted. For surely, I have seen you at the balls before."

"Then I have not seen you. For I would have made you mine at once."

She tilted her chin up at him. "And this is what you wish to do *maintenant?*" She held her breath.

He brushed her lips with his, and she felt the cool overlaying a warmth from within. "Most assuredly," he whispered.

She drew back and appraised him with what she hoped seemed a poised detachment. "There is a small cottage on Saint Philip Street, white with a blue roof. You would be

486

welcome there tomorrow afternoon for a little *déjeuner,* shall we say between two and four?"

"I will be there," David said, gazing into her eyes. "But this evening?"

She removed her wrist from his fingers delicately. "This evening is for dancing. Shall we have another waltz before you put me in my carriage?" And she led him out of the shadows, up the stairs, and across the full and watchful gaze of the mulatto *mamans.*

The little blue-roofed cottage on Saint Philip Street was one in a long line of unprepossessing lodgings, most of them owned by merchants on Canal who collected the rents with prompt dispatch. The white house which Manon shared with her brother, Alex, was one of the tidiest, however, with a small garden in front and to one side, filled with neatly trimmed palms and cascading bougainvillea in shocking pink and purple. The lace curtains in the front windows hinted at a subdued elegance which somehow lifted the lines of the little cottage above those of its neighbors.

Manon surprised Alex by rising just as early as he did that morning, greeting him at the kitchen table with a full cup of *café noir* and a plate of hot *beignets.*

"Is it a holiday?" he asked wonderingly, setting down his slim body in his favorite chair and peering at her over his horn-rims. "A holy mass in the middle of the week? Or are you only just now getting in from last night?"

"*Très amusant,*" she grinned at him over a powdery bite of pastry, not bothering to remove the white mustache. "I wanted to talk to you before you got away."

He assumed a pained look, and she settled her elbows on the table firmly. Long ago, Manon had learned this about Alex: he might be her only male relation and ten years older, but he was so naive about life and its workings, he was as a boy. At twenty-seven, he showed no interest in marriage, no passion for anything but his mining inventions and his birds, and she had only to steel her jaw and narrow her blue eyes to get him to bend to her whims. She loved him more than she wanted him to know, but someone had to tend to the details of their lives.

After a decade with the Ursulines, Manon had felt the high, gray walls were smothering her. Once Uncle Simon passed away, even Sister could see the virtue of her departure. By then, Alex had excellent employment with the Delta Mining Company and was able to secure comfortable lodgings. He found an old quadroon woman to care for Manon, and Fasse quickly took over where the nuns had left off. To Manon's cloister education, Fasse added the training which any *jeune fille* would need to attract the attention of a *gentilhomme généreux,* as she liked to say, with the same care she had given her own three daughters, *toutes belles et toutes comme il faut.* So long as Manon seemed content, Alex asked few questions.

Alex had lived as a bachelor for so long, he scarcely noticed whether he ate at noon or midnight, whether his waistcoat frayed at the edges, or whether his hair crept down past his collar. Manon lost no time in rearranging his boxes of books, his scientific tools, and dusty journals, and making of the cottage a home of some comfort and graciousness. But she could do little with his waistcoats and his haircuts.

So long as she did not trifle with his workbench and bird drawings, however, he was content. So long as he paid the rent and did nothing more than absently cluck at her décolletage and late hours, she was serene. But she knew they could not—*she* could not—continue this way together forever.

"I'm actually glad you came down this morning," he was saying, "because I have something to talk about as well."

"You go first," she said, amiably. Might as well let him get his news off his chest before she had to upset him.

"Well, now that the Federals have pulled out, Ned McIlhenny's going to put in a new shaft out on Avery Island and rebuild the salt mine properly. The Union troops burnt the old operation nearly to the ground. It'll take some capital, but his family's got it, and he thinks I've got some good ideas."

"And so you do."

"He wants me to come aboard."

"Would it mean more money?"

He nodded happily. "And it would mean we could get out of this sumphole of a city and down to the bayou again. Get a place on the Teche, maybe in New Iberia or on the island, itself. Ned's going to be putting up some decent digs, he says, and he's looking for good men. You know, I think that salt deposit might be as much as a hundred miles long, maybe the biggest in the world; it'll be the tallest mountain on the delta before we're done digging. Why, we could—"

"*Ma foi,* you want to move down on the Teche?" Her eyes grew wide and she placed her *beignet* carefully on her plate.

"Well, I can't very well live here and work a hundred miles south. Oh, I know you like New Orleans, but Iberia's a pretty little town, and if you don't like that, there's Jefferson Island, it's smaller but—"

"*Attends, cher.* I'm not leaving New Orleans," she said, her voice rising slightly with soft determination.

"I can't support two places, Manon. Even if Ned buys my new drill patent, it won't be enough to keep you here in lace and dancing slippers. Besides, you can't live here alone."

"I won't be alone. That's what I want to talk to you about." She smiled brilliantly to infect him with her optimism.

489

He took off his horn-rims and carefully polished them, looking at her with a slight squint. "If you're about to bring up that ridiculous idea of taking in boarders again, you can save your breath. No decent woman can do such a thing, I told you that, Manon, not without a husband. It was one thing in *maman's* day, under her circumstances and during the Northern aggression and all, but you can't do that in this city, not as an unmarried *femme de couleur.*"

She shook her head impatiently, and two small tendrils of dark curling hair fell down to the line of her jaw. She tucked them back behind her ears. "A gentleman is coming to see me this afternoon," she said calmly. "*Monsieur* David Booth."

"Who is this? Another 'investment' man? Manon, I've told you, we don't have enough left from the sale of BonRev to pay the taxes on a place, much less buy anything outright. Before Uncle died, he warned you to remember everything *maman* went through to get us where we are today. You have a good education—"

She snorted indelicately. "I've learned more from Fass than I ever learned from the nuns and their dusty primers."

"Well, you had an opportunity, at any rate, however you may have squandered it. How many freed men of color have the chance to do the sort of work I do? I have a good job with Delta Mining, and I mean to have a better one with McIlhenny. That salt deposit could be one of the richest resources this state will ever see, not to mention the migrations I can study while I'm there. But we aren't rich, Manon, and we never will be, so get used to the idea. *Maman's* estate has supported us for fifteen years, but it can't last forever. And especially if you keep dumping bits and pieces of it into these crazy money-making schemes of yours. How much do you spend on lottery tickets each week? That last stock you bought in that gambling club out at Pontchartrain—that ship cost us plenty before it sank without a trace. Perhaps I best

490

stay here this afternoon and tell the Monsieur that we won't be dabbling in any more speculations."

"No, you will *not* be here, my brother," she said gently.

Now his eyes narrowed, and she could see the strong resemblance to their mother, a resemblance she knew she shared.

"This gentleman is not a broker," he said.

She shook her head again.

"You don't mean you're still considering *placée?*" His voice dropped to a shocked whisper.

She smiled sadly.

"Then he is not a gentleman at all."

She brushed aside his comment with a shrug and another sip of her coffee. "But, of course, he is, *mon frère,* and your ignorance is showing abysmally. Some of the richest, most highly placed gentlemen in Louisiana keep their mistresses just two streets over. Can you pretend you've never noticed?"

"All of New Orleans notices, but that doesn't mean I ever intend to have my sister kept on such a street."

"What *you* intend? I believe the war is over, *cher,* and we are slaves no longer. Just as you wish to reach for your opportunity, so do I. Monsieur Booth is a gentleman, he is well received, and I will receive him here this afternoon. If we can reach an agreeable settlement to both of us, you need not worry yourself about me further." She drained her cup and set it down, whisking away a few small crumbs from the table linen.

Alex's mouth drooped sadly. "I will always worry about you, Manon. From the day *maman* died, I've worried."

She reached across and took his hand, cradling it softly. "And has it done you any good, my heart? Not a whit. So stop worrying and let me do as I will. I am past seventeen, and I must make my own way. Like *maman,* after all, and she was happy enough."

"Times were different then."

491

She laughed. "Not so very different, *malheureusement*. Men are still men and women will still love them, yes?"

"Why do you not simply marry? Find a freed man of color, marry him, and raise his children with pride. You are beautiful, you have wit and charm, you could get your pick of any colored men in the city."

"I do not *want* any colored man in the city."

"Why will you deny what you are? You are a Negress, Manon, even if you could pass for white in any city north of Atlanta. You have your mother's blood in you, and so will your children! Why will you break your heart? For what—this Monsieur takes you as his mistress and keeps you in a dark little house on Orleans Street! You'll get a cook, probably a maid or two, but you'll have to earn every picayune you take from his hand. You'll have to keep yourself beautiful, your figure trim, keep a smoothly running *ménage* just as he likes it, learn to talk about his interests, keep a smile on that pretty face. You'll be faithful to him? Of course, you will, but he won't be faithful to you. You may take his name and call him your husband—so may your children. But he will always have someone over you. His real wife and children will always take first place. And when he leaves you?"

"Many gentlemen are faithful to the death." Her voice was low with hurt.

"Some are, I hear, but many more go on to replace their aging *placée* with a younger, more spirited mount when she can no longer keep up the pace."

Manon's face whitened slightly with anger. She narrowed her eyes. "*If* he ever leaves me, *then* perhaps I will take any colored man in the city. And only then. And he will be proud to have me under any circumstances, for I'll bring with me children whiter than either of us, children who have been sent North or to Paris for their educations, I'll bring property and my investments—"

"You'll bring him some white man's castasides."

She stood up briskly, dropping his hand. "Believe me, if

the arrangement does not please me, it will not come about. If it does, I will be settled, and you can go to your birds and your salt with a light heart." She turned then and went from the dining room, unwilling to witness his disappointment in her, unwilling to listen to the echoes of doubt his sadness raised in her own heart.

Manon could recall so clearly the day Alex came to take her away from the Ursulines forever. Though she had awaited the day for what seemed long years, once her departure was at hand, she felt a sadness to say good-bye to the sisters who had been her only family for more than a decade. *Soeur* gave her a copy of the Epistle, wherein she had underlined, "When I was a child, I spoke as a child, I understood as a child, I thought as a child . . . "

"Now," Sister said gravely, "you are become a woman. And you must put away the things of a child." She took Manon's cheeks between her palms. "One last reminder," she said softly, her voice quavering with age or sentiment, Manon could not say which. "Grace will come to you if you will pray for it, my daughter."

"Oui, Soeur," Manon replied, pain suddenly filling her eyes.

Sister sighed and murmured low to her, as though she spoke more to Manon's soul than to her ear. "It is not easy to be a nun. It is a life of sacrifice and self-abnegation. A life against nature. But it is not easy to be a woman outside these walls either. I will pray to the Holy Mother to guide your way." She took her thin thumb and made the sign of the cross on Manon's forehead, adding a benediction in Latin. Then she turned and walked away, lifting her serge skirt from the back as she always did, so as not to fray the hem on the stones.

To be embraced then by Alex felt almost like a violation of her body. But that feeling quickly swept through her and out again, followed by a giddy exultation at being free from the gates, the high walls, and the bells of the cloister.

Alex took her out to the streets, to have a sumptuous lunch with a dozen succulent pastries and creams, to buy a new frock with a matching parasol, and a pair of red leather shoes with dainty heels. The intoxication of the liberation so completely overwhelmed her that she was unable to sleep for three consecutive nights in the little cottage he had leased for them. Through the dark hours, she woke regularly, to listen for the breathing of the sleeping girls around her, for the sound of the bells, and the silence echoed in her heart and haunted her.

Now, she thought back to Emma often, wondering what counsel she might offer in her soft dry voice, as Manon planned this new twist to her destiny. She used to say that God sends us what our hearts ask for, which we draw to ourselves with our own stubbornness or weakness or rage. "We ourselves fashion our lessons," she would say slowly, thoughtfully. "According to our own needs."

What is it I am needing then, *Soeur,* which causes me to fashion Monsieur for myself? Is it, perhaps, only love? And could love ever be bad?

That afternoon, she met Monsieur Booth in her most beautiful day gown, her black hair carefully coiffed to softly frame her eyes and chin. The bodice of the gown was loose and silky, suggesting languor, and the lace panels down the skirt gave a sensual feeling of transparency. Four hours it had taken her to be ready, but she had been able to do nothing with her hollow stomach.

The requisite inquiries had given her the answer she needed: he could afford her. Only one question remained.

He carried in a large box, gaily bedecked with ribbon. "I saw this in a shop on Bourbon," he said, taking off his hat and setting it on the tapestry chair. "I could not picture it on any other woman in New Orleans, now that I've seen your eyes up close."

She opened the box and took out a wide flowered hat, inwardly grimacing at the large blue roses all round the brim. He had American tastes, to be sure! But she put it next to her cheek so that he could see how nicely the blue did pick up her eyes. "It's lovely, *Monsieur, très charmant.* But of course, I cannot accept such a gift. You must take it back and let some other pair of blue eyes be made so beautiful."

"Never," he said, taking the hat from her hands and setting it alongside his. He drew her closer. "And you must get out of that habit, Mademoiselle."

She cocked her head at him pertly. "What habit is that?"

"Of telling me no. I don't want to hear the word from your lips again."

She felt a distinct thrill at his touch, but she laughed gaily, pulling away from him and circling the room. "Then you must needs go deaf as a post within the next quarter-hour, for I'll surely be saying it again!"

She sat him down on the settee and served him coffee and thick slices of chocolate cake and apple pie. American fare. Guessing rightly that this man would not prefer dainty pastries and thinly sliced watercress sandwiches, she was pleased to see him eat of both desserts heartily. They bantered back and forth of this and that, and she carefully kept the conversation impersonal. When finally he set down his plate and his cup, she knew that the time for silence had come. She dropped her eyes and waited.

"How long ago did your mother pass?" he asked.

"When I was still in my cradle. I scarcely can remember her now."

"And you're all alone?"

"Mais non," she said gently, "I have a brother and many other relations."

"And would it be to this brother that I would go to make certain . . . arrangements?"

She gazed up at him. Now was the moment. She gripped her fingers tightly. "You should speak frankly, Monsieur. You will find that I do so."

For answer, he took her in his arms slowly, pulling her face towards him irresistibly. With his mouth only inches from hers, he said, "I am married. Did you know?"

"Of course," she said softly, and she could feel his chest pound against hers.

"And yet I am drawn to you past all reason. I will never tell you that my wife and I don't get along, for we do. I won't tell you she is cold or turns away from me in our bed, because in fact she makes me quite happy. God help me, I'm not an easy man to please, and she tries. But despite her best efforts, I deliberately went to the quadroon ball, searching for something more. And I found it." He traced a gentle finger down the line of her cheekbone and jaw, down further over her neck and to her collarbone. "I want you for my mistress, Manon. I know this sort of thing is done all the time, but it's the first time for me." He took a deep breath as if diving into black, cold water. "Are you agreeable?"

She let her eyes almost close. "To what terms, Monsieur?"

He kissed her then, probingly. She let her tongue trace delicately against his for an instant, then withdrew slightly.

He shuddered, and his grip tightened on her shoulders. "Would you want to stay in this cottage?"

She thought for a moment. *"Certainement.* That would be pleasant."

"I would pay the rent, furnish you with help, take care of you—"

"Non," she sighed, leaning into his arms and letting her breasts flatten against him. "I must know that something here is mine. Just as you will know that something here is yours."

"Then I will buy the place for you. Is that what you want?"

"Oui, David. That would be more agreeable."

Now he kissed her again, more deeply, and she felt a hunger begin in her for this man. Her fingers twined the hair at the back of his neck, and she lifted her arms to get closer still. She must not forget what she wanted!

"Perhaps we could consummate this bargain between us?" he murmured.

"Ah, but we have not yet concluded our terms," she whispered.

"What else do you want?"

"What every woman wants, Monsieur," her lips grazed his. *"Sécurité."*

"Suppose," he said slowly, "I were to deposit five thousand in an account in your name today, with a promise to do the same on the first day of each new year we are together. Would this make you feel more secure?"

She smiled and trailed a half-dozen light kisses down his neck. "This would help."

"And perhaps we could discuss more details at another time?"

Her smile did not falter, but she said, "I can see you are not acquainted with our customs. In *affaires de coeur,* we do not muddle love with business. First one, then the other, *non?* After all, once I am yours, David, I can be only yours. It is best to take care of all these details now." She kissed him deeply, letting her tongue and her lips promise all she was feeling.

"You are so wise. Wise beyond your years. How old are you?" he whispered.

"Eighteen."

"Good Lord," he moaned.

"Does that trouble you?"

"Of course, it does," he said, his lips still inches from hers.

"Don't let it bother you, *cher,*" she murmured, "I was never really young. I could not afford it, none of us can. This is what I was born for, *vraiment,* and were my mother with us today, she would say the same. For years, I have been taught to be what I am, the perfect mistress for a man like you."

He kissed her once more. "And I have found you."

"*Oui,* we have found each other. Go now," she whispered, "and do what needs to be done so that I can truly belong to you. One week from tonight, I shall devote myself to your happiness. Until then, I will wait impatiently for your return." She moved gently away from him, gathering her strength for what she feared might be a bit of a tussle.

He grinned at her. "So this is the way it works? Even in the capital of sin, it is business before pleasure?"

"Pleasure," she said, "is always first, *mon coeur,* but its success is best secured by attending to business." She took his face in two hands and murmured, "But I tell you that never before have I wished time would fly as I do now."

During her wait, Manon began preparations for her new life. It was as if a marriage had been settled. Word of her good fortune spread quickly among the quadroons, and friends gave her small intimate soirées to announce her match and offered special gifts of linen, wines, and tableware. She sent Fasse back to her people with a light heart and began happily to interview several cooks, selecting a woman who was as dark as midnight and as silent as the stars. Alex shook his sorrowful head over her decision, but past a few pointed remarks, he said no more. He left for the coast wishing her well. Manon wept bitterly that night with loneliness. Fasse was gone, Alex was gone, and she had never felt so adrift and abandoned. But by the next morning, she was back to setting her house in order with a will.

One week later, when the deed to the cottage and five thousand dollars had been safely secured in Manon's box at the bank, she welcomed David Booth to her boudoir once more. When he first came in, he wrapped her in his arms, and she held the largeness of him, the broadness of his back, the strength of his body, and she felt at once as frightened and as safe as she ever had in her life.

But with little hesitation, she pressed herself against him and sank into him, her head on his shoulder. As she slipped her arms around him, she began to feel linked to this man in the strangest way, as though she had planned for this moment for years and finally could enjoy, in peace, its consummation.

Her hair was against his cheek, her hands on his lower back, and she felt her body mold to his as though it had long practice in that pose. The warmth of his skin came through his waistcoat; his scent filled her senses.

He put a hand under her chin and lifted her face to his, pressing his lips to hers. It was a kiss which seemed at once electric and strange, longed-for, and also familiar and long-known.

Finally, he broke their kiss, and she pulled away slightly to look into his eyes, suddenly less afraid than shy. "You are finally here," she whispered.

"I could not keep away," he said, and his voice was low and bristling with desire.

"Come and see how I have arranged for your comfort." She led him into the small bedroom up the stairs, smiling at him and feeling as quivery as any bride. The brass bed was polished and banked with potted ferns. Fragrant magnolia blossoms floated in crystal bowls. She had candles burning in all four corners, despite the shuttered heat and sunlight of the day outside.

The bed was a nest of clean white linen and fat pillows, and a dressing jacket in what she had guessed to be his size lay strewn across the foot. Fasse's lessons rang in her ears more stridently than any dozen cloister bells.

He laughed and pulled her to him, and she sensed some shyness in him as well. "Are you sure you haven't done this before?" he asked her, peering at her teasingly. "Or perhaps taken lessons in mistressing at the convent?"

She was inwardly shocked at his irreverence, but she could not help but laugh at the pictures he made in her mind. Now that they were actually in the doorway to the bedroom, all her plans seemed to leave her head. For a moment, she was completely awash in doubt. Was this a mistake? Was *he* the mistake? Perhaps she should have gone to Jefferson Island with Alex after all—

With one hand, he gently untied the ribbons at her bodice, opening the gauze over her breasts and lowering his mouth to them softly. Moving aside the fabric with his lips, he licked first one nipple, than the other, lovingly.

She watched him watch her, felt her nipples swelling, and her doubts left her in that moment. "I love you," she said, meaning it.

He pulled back and gazed at her with surprise. She could see the hesitancy in his look, but she felt none in her heart. In only those few days, it seemed she had fallen in love not only with what he represented, but also with his face, his body, the wit and boldness of his mind, his courage in taking such steps with little thought beyond his will and what he would have, with the way he walked, the way he smelled—

"Is this, too, a part of your customs?" he asked softly. "These are not words I say lightly."

"Nor I," she said, leading him by the hand to the bed. "I have never said them before in my life."

He bent and kissed her throat, and she felt the throbbing of her pulse all through her chest and lungs. She kissed along his nose, his jawline, his eyes, his ears, and his hands were moving over her body, removing her garments carefully.

Her mind was racing almost as fast as her pulse. She did not know how long she had loved him, some part of her was shocked, even appalled that she had said and felt such an abandonment so quickly, and she could not say when the admiration she felt for him had altered to something finer and more powerful. She could not think clearly, she could not pin down at what moment she knew she felt love. She knew she was swept away, and she also knew that this condition was foreign—even dangerous—to her.

Nonetheless, as he lowered his naked body down on hers, she knew she had never wanted a man before this. Suddenly, she needed to have him inside her, couldn't breathe until he was holding her firmly, couldn't keep her body still under him. His arms felt lean and hard, his skin smooth as her own, but with firmly defined muscles under each layer, and as he slowly thrust inside her, she felt astonishing pleasure that bordered on pain. Each stroke he took within her drove out everything else, everyone else, even thoughts of herself, until she clung mindlessly to him, amazed at her own abandon.

After, when it was over and they lay tangled in the linen and each other, in a soft fluid silent sea of satisfaction, she realized that she had lost something by telling him that she loved him. He, of course, did not feel the same. Not yet.

She vowed to herself that one day, very soon, Monsieur David Booth would love her and say so. And that when he did, she would devote her life to making him happy.

Manon found life luxurious in the months that followed. The cook and the maid attended to her needs with little effort. She was too wise to relax overmuch, however. She got up early every morning and walked about the city to keep her figure trim and to find the special market tidbits that he would savor. When he arrived, he found everything as he wished it: his favorite food and wines perfectly served, the servant dismissed promptly after the meal, good talk about his business and the local political gossip of New Orleans, her ever-warm smile, and hours of lovemaking with no thought save their mutual pleasure.

Indeed, she often smiled to herself as he left her, Madame Booth could likely learn something from her in how to keep such a man content.

In his absence, she was unfailingly and joyously faithful. And why not? she asked herself. She had all that she wished, and most all the company she needed. If she grew lonely, she had only to visit one of a dozen friends in the street who had the same sort of *ménage* with an equally successful protector. Often, they discussed less their men than their investments. From these *placées,* Manon learned that five thousand regularly deposited in her personal account could quickly grow to deeds for small parcels of carefully selected land, cotton contracts shared with farmers who were willing to pay well for her greenbacks, and rental apartments down at the docks to house the sailors who flooded New Orleans with full pockets.

Monsieur had no objection to her attending an occasional quadroon ball, so long as she sat on the sidelines and merely watched the dancers. She was only tempted to dance once with an attractive Yankee from Boston, but at the glares from the *mamans,* she quickly took her seat once more and laughed away his entreaties. Monsieur also provided her with a splendid box at the opera, one of the only prominent places in New Orleans where the quadroons and mulattresses were welcome. Since few rich white women would sit in the upper boxes, the higher tiers had been opened to *femmes de couleur.* Here, they could wear their jewels and low-cut gowns in vivid hues with that touch of daring that few white women attempted. Upstairs, near the ceiling, the blacks were seated.

It was so gay, Manon thought, to go to the Orleans Theater and see the colored layer cake of blacks, then part-blacks, then whites below. Sometimes the two "families" of a prominent Orleanian could be seen within a few yards of each other—white below, quadroon above. She always dressed immaculately for any public appearance, but at the opera, she reached for new heights of glamour. And she always wore, in the middle of her breasts, the large sapphire he had given her the first month they were together, for he said that the color of the gem so perfectly matched her eyes that he could not allow it to dangle on another woman's skin.

But still, David never spoke of love. He came to see her two, perhaps three evenings a week, always leaving before ten o'clock, never on the same evening, never with any warning.

He might be at a political meeting, he said, and he would drop by later. Or, if she expected him for dinner, he might show up several hours before the dining hour or several hours later than expected. It was difficult to have the food as perfect as she liked, when he was so unpredictable, but she never scolded him. She never wanted him to think of anything but pleasure when he thought of her—let his wife make him think of obligation.

Manon did not worry about his other life, nor did his business failures or successes concern her, except as they made him happy or morose. But one quality in David did cause her much anxiety, and it seemed to be an irascibility he shared with a great many men in New Orleans that year, particularly the Americans.

The blacks were stirring things up, of course, and Manon instinctively understood that this caused some of the problem. The riots of a few years back had quieted, but strikers still made trouble for many of the planters. David had told her of an ex-slave, one Richard Gooseberry down in Saint Charles Parish, who led a strike for higher wages.

"They're asking a dollar a day, up from seventy-five cents," David said one evening over supper, "and not a planter'll pay that."

"*Ma foi,* what makes them think they can get away with such a demand?" She poured him another cup of coffee, slipping in two sugars as he liked.

"They're paying that in Kansas."

"So let them go to Kansas."

"Lots of them are, but I'm damned if I'll buckle under to

at kind of blackmail. I'll let the crops rot in the ground efore I'll pay a dollar a day. Dollar a day or fight, they're ollering. Well, let them holler. Or let them fight."

She slipped around behind his chair and put her hands on is neck, soothing the tension out of his shoulders.

But the tension of the rebellion trickled down into too any cracks in the New Orleans nights to be healed so easily. 1en had always worn pistols in the delta, but now in these ears after the war, violence seemed to simmer, Manon hought, just below the surface of the *banquettes.*

Duels were such frequent occurrences that they scarcely ade mention in the *Picayune*. It seemed nowhere in Amer- ca was it easier to get killed. *Affaires d'honneur* had always een part of the bayou rhythm, but with the new prosperity nd easing of wartime privation, men developed an unprece- ented passion for dueling.

Ten duels a day at a certain favorite meeting spot were ot regarded as unusual. Each week seemed to bring its npromptu gun battle in some crowded hotel lobby. Most of ne quadroons who reported the news to Manon took it as ood-naturedly as they might news of rain.

But Manon feared that David, being a hotheaded Ameri- an, would one day fall in just such an encounter. And how ad it come to such a pretty pass? Why, she herself had seen . One day at *Trois Soeurs,* a newcomer to the city said he referred Northern coffee to that he was served in New Or- ans, and the next day he was run through with a sword. nother man, sitting near a fencing master, by chance or- ered the same courses for supper. The master decided he vas being mocked, called the man out, and sent him to his rave.

The men who seemed to dominate the *code duello* were he fencing masters. Gaudy swaggerers, they walked the *ban- uettes* of New Orleans with arrogance, attracting the grins f children and the stares of women. You could not sit in a afé these days without hearing tales of this one or that one:

why, it was said that one killed ten men in a row before h
was wounded once! And this one? Well, they say he maime
the wrong man and had to leave for France in a hurry.

Manon knew many women, and not only quadroons, wh
found the fencing masters alluring. This or that husband wa
aware, the whispers went, but dared do nothing openly. Wh
would match swords or pistols with an expert? Other me
kept out of their way on the *banquettes* and made sure n
to jostle them by accident. Well-dressed youths followe
them wherever they went, trying to emulate their style, re
peating their jokes.

Spoiled fops, Manon thought as she saw them pass, cur
ing her lips in distaste. How was it that the measure of a ma
came to be how he handled his *colich marde,* the Creole
favorite rapier? Prima donnas, every one of them, and letha
as rattlers besides.

Perhaps it was something in the sunlight, Manon decide
in the tropical heat, the languorous nights, that made me
dueling mad. She asked David once what would make hir
challenge another man to a duel.

"How do I know? Any number of things, I suppose. Wha
a question, my kitten, a question with no answer to it at all.

"Well," she tried again, "I mean would you feel oblige
to defend the honor of the South or New Orleans, would yo
call a man out if his eyes followed me on the street? Wha
would make you take such a step, my love?"

"Has someone insulted you, Manon?"

She could feel his irritation rise sharply. *"Non, non
cher,"* she reassured him, "but I wonder. And I worry."

"No need to worry, I'm an excellent shot."

"So are too many in this city. And even their own wome
sometimes do not know what they plan! Why, last week
Monique told me she was at a soirée, you know the Butler
I believe, and Madame Butler said two gentlemen had a smal
encounter. *Sans signification,* she barely noticed it. The
went through the rest of the evening with nonchalance, *non*

The next day, Madame Butler hears that there has been a duel and one has killed the other!"

"And so?"

"So, I wonder if even their wives knew of their intent."

"If they did or did not, it doesn't matter. There are rules to this, Manon, points of honor which women can't possible understand."

"Monique told me there are books of dueling etiquette available? These are written on how to offend and be offended, how to kill or be killed?"

He shrugged. "I suppose there are, I've not seen them. But certainly a challenge must be delivered in a certain way, a deft slap. A flick of a glove. Not a punch or any other ungentlemanly show of anger, that puts your opponent beneath notice. There can't be a duel if one is lower in social rank than the other. No, my dear, it doesn't surprise me that a hostess might not know of an impending duel, likewise a wife."

"What if an offender apologizes. Would you ever accept an apology rather than fight?"

He thought for an instant. "Perhaps. Doubtful, but perhaps. Usually, no matter what either man wants, the thing goes on to one or the other's satisfaction."

"You mean, death."

He grinned. "Why this sudden interest, *ma petite?*"

She sulked, forming a pretty pout and turning away one shoulder. "It is not so sudden that I am interested in something which might harm you, Monsieur. More than a year now, I am interested, more to the pity."

He drew her to him, muffling her face on his chest. "Then I'm the luckiest man in all Louisiana, even if I'm not the fastest draw."

She smiled to herself, feeling his heartbeat. Did he hold his wife like this? She doubted it in every fiber of her being.

Though Manon did not wish to remind David of responsibility, she was soon unable to avoid thinking of it herself. Despite her herbs and washes, she found herself pregnant one spring day, and her body told her, in every stretching of skin and ache of muscle, that this coming was going to change her life in more ways than she could imagine.

She confided in Monique that she was expecting.

"*Mais c'est vraiment merveilleux!*" her friend exclaimed. "This will surely tie him to you tightly, *cher*. What did Monsieur say?"

"I have not told him."

Monique eyed her sharply. "You are not content?"

Manon's mouth crumpled despite her efforts to keep it firm. "It is too soon. We've had so little time."

Monique thought for a moment. "Do you want to be free of it?"

"I don't know. Perhaps at another time, I might welcome a child. He might welcome it as well . . . "

"He will likely never welcome it, *cher*, but he will not turn from it or from you. This much I know of him, from all you have told me. You could go to Marie LaVeau."

Manon's eyes widened. Of course she knew of the woman of the serpent, the voodoo queen of all New Orleans. No one who lived in the city more than a few months could fail to hear of her fame with spells and hexes and charms. One could see the *nègres* in the morning, on their hands and knees busily scrubbing the *banquettes* and steps of their houses with *letanier,* the root of the palmetto, said to keep off the power of the *Mamaloi,* the voodoo queen. Indeed, many of the quadroons called her Boss Woman, claiming she had the most powerful *gri-gri* of all. "I thought she was dead," Manon murmured.

"*Non, cher,* that woman is too strong to die. She must be close to ninety, if she's a day, and she still does her magic. She could help you lose that lump in your belly, if you're certain that's what will make you content. Or . . . " here, Monique smiled in such a way that Manon could readily understand why her Monsieur had picked her as *placée.* "Or she can perhaps make your gentleman want this child and you as well."

That night, Manon took a carriage to the twisted back street of Saint Ann where Marie LaVeau had lived for more than fifty years. Candles burned in the two windows on either side of the narrow red door. A woman wrapped in a shawl was leaving the cottage. Manon paused as one might stop at a confessional, not wishing to intrude on her privacy. Her carriage was rich and well appointed, and from what Manon could see of her dress, she did not want for care. Yet such a woman would seek out the voodoo queen in the dark of night!

Manon knocked quietly at the door, and a deep voice called out for her to enter. A tall dark woman stood just inside the door, one of the largest Negresses Manon had ever seen.

"Madame LaVeau?" she asked cautiously.

The Negress gestured to the corner of the room where a tiny wizened woman sat in a high-backed tapestry chair. Her feet scarcely grazed the oriental carpet, and her face was like an apple left to wrinkle and rot in the sun. But her eyes still gleamed with a spark of wisdom. And something else.

"Madame LaVeau," Manon tried again, "I hope I have not come at an inconvenient time."

"No one ever comes to see me when it is convenient,

509

child," the old woman said shortly. "Only when it is very inconvenient, indeed, and they need something to make it more convenient *tout de suite.* Do I know your face?"

"Non, Madame, I have never been to see you."

"That doesn't matter. I know many faces who have never crossed my door. But yours, I have not seen. I would have remembered." Madame LaVeau put out her hand to the Negress without looking at her. The huge paw lifted her to her feet, and she strode across the carpet towards Manon.

Manon was struck by the youthfulness of her walk, once she was liberated from the depths of the chair. Her voice, too, seemed younger than her years. She wore impossibly huge gold hoops in ears that had stretched nearly to her chin, and her *tignon* was a rainbow of sparkled hues and jet ribbons of black. Her face and her eyes could have belonged to an ancient crone from the depths of Africa, but that her skin was more mulatto than dark.

Suddenly, she realized she had been staring. "Pardon, Madame, for the intrusion. But I have come to—"

"I know why you have come."

Manon started and pulled her shawl a little closer around her shoulders, as though a night breeze had moved over her skin.

"When they are young, it is always one thing or the other. Either love or the seeds of love, *non?* You wish one or you do not wish the other." The old woman peered at her closely. "Ah, I see with you, it is both. You wish the love and you do not wish the consequences." She laughed suddenly, a high, piercing sound of ancient mirth. "Such twin desires cost dear. But likely you can afford Madame's price, eh?"

The Negress gestured Manon to a chair, and Madame LaVeau sat down in another opposite her.

"How long has Monsieur been gone?"

"He is not gone," Manon said, a little indignantly.

"Ah. Then he has another woman, and you fear his going."

Manon slumped in her chair, nodding reluctantly.

"As well you might, *ma petite*. Most particular with that *paquet* in your belly. How long it growing?"

"A month. Maybe two."

"No longer?" Marie LaVeau pinned her with her black eyes.

Manon shook her head dolefully. "No more."

"Then you will have one of your wishes, at least." She gestured to the Negress to bring to her a dark leather satchel and from it she took a packet of dried herbs. "Take this and make a tisane, drink all of it no matter how bitter it seems. Make sure it is so hot that it burns the roof of your mouth, yes? And if you do not bleed within seven days, come back to me. But you will bleed. Be ready for that, *cher.*"

Manon took the packet from the old woman's hand gingerly, as though merely handling it might somehow upheave her. "That is all?"

Marie LaVeau shrugged balefully. "So soon, it is easy. Twenty dollars and a singed mouth, and your belly is clean as the Virgin's again. Your other desire, this is not so easy."

In that moment, Manon could not suffer the woman's nearness another moment. She felt suddenly a heat of shame, of fear, that caused her to get up violently, almost knocking over her chair. The Negress reached for her, but Manon flinched away. "I think I'll only take this, Madame," she said nervously. "Nothing more for now. Perhaps I'll come back another time for the rest—"

"There is no reason to be afraid," the old woman said, grinning.

"Never mind, Madame, I've changed my mind." She fumbled in her purse for the twenty-dollar fee, thrust it in the Negress's hand, and hurried to the door. "Your pardon, Madame, thank you so much for seeing me, but I must go." She fled out of the cottage, hailed her carriage, and only stopped to think what she had done once she was halfway down Orleans Street.

What a fool! she cursed herself. Now, if the herb did not work, she could never go back to Marie LaVeau, and if David did turn away from her in distaste at her swelling belly, she could not win him back.

She eyed the herb packet that her twenty dollars had bought. Looked to be a simple gathering of dried roots and ferns, nothing too dreadful there. But it would work, of that she was certain. Marie LaVeau did not gain her reputation by selling tame concoctions.

Unconsciously, her hand went to her belly. She carried life. Yes, it would make her swell and vomit, likely make her legs marble with blue veins and her ankles puff up like angry mottled toads. She would be ugly and misshapen, certainly not in the mood for love or its *accoutrements,* and perhaps even end up with no man to care for this child.

But she could not do it. She closed the herb pouch and lifted her hand to toss it from the carriage. But then she withdrew her hand again, settling it in her lap. No, she would not throw away twenty dollars. She might not need it now, but who was to say she never would? Or that in the future someone else might not need a piece of Marie LaVeau's magic for a price?

Manon tucked the herb packet inside her purse and settled back for the rest of the ride. She would have this babe, she decided firmly, and she would have his love, as well. If it could be, she would have it. If he needed a voodoo spell to keep his love alive, then she would learn to live without it.

Manon waited as long as she could before telling David of the coming child. She gloried in her breasts which grew larger and riper, and thanked whatever gods watched over her that she did not suffer overmuch with morning sickness. She watched her cheeks grow pinker, her hair more lustrous, and she only had to wear her chemises looser, drawing the necklines down so that his eyes went to her breasts rather than to her belly.

But one sultry twilight after an hour of slow caresses and pulsing desire, he suddenly put one large hand on her stomach and said, "You better cut back on the *beignets,* my darling. You're starting to puff out like my old mammy."

Stung, she rolled on her belly and appraised him warily. "You think I'm *grosse?*"

He grinned, reaching for her again. "Damn, you'd think I'd learn after all these years. No, my sweet, you're gaunt as a hen in a yard full of cocks."

"I am *not* fat," she said, turning back into his arms. "And this isn't a *beignet* in my belly, Monsieur."

He stiffened slightly, drawing back to look at her more closely.

She smiled. "That's right. I'm with child. Your child."

His mouth twisted angrily. "Jesus Christ, Manon, I thought you knew how to prevent such a thing."

She wanted to dissolve in hot, angry tears, but she kept her face bland. "No plan is foolproof, I suppose. Don't think

513

I want this anymore than you, David. I went to see a woman about it, but she said it was too late."

He drew back and crossed his arms, sitting up in the bed. They avoided each other's eyes in silence for a long moment. "Well," he finally said, "I suppose it doesn't matter. Perhaps it was inevitable. These things happen all the time. I'll give you enough money to care for the child, of course."

She reached out one hand and laid it on his bare chest. "He will likely be a handsome boy. With your eyes and nose." She ran a single gentle finger down his cheek.

He took her finger and kissed it absentmindedly. "I guess you'll need a wetnurse. Probably a mammy, too. How long?"

"Probably by next year's Mardi Gras. Perhaps before. But certainly not until 1879 is born."

"And you're well?"

For answer, she only pulled him over onto her again, ran her hands down to the small of his back, and pressed him so close that his desire instantly ignited, and he slid into her without preamble, as though claiming ownership.

Alex was not as calm about the coming child, however. She told him when he next came to visit, and by then, her belly was mounding perceptibly despite the looseness of her day gown.

"This was what I feared, Manon," he said sadly. "Now, will you come to the bayou where I can take care of you properly? Soon you'll be all alone with the child, and your Monsieu'll be dancing at the next quadroon ball, hunting up your replacement. You should have married your own kind."

"Name of God! And what kind is that? Some mulatto farmer with a patch of peas by some swampwater? Raise a passel of barefoot pickaninnies plagued by hookworm and head lice?" She put both hands defiantly on her belly and stretched the chiffon tight around it. "*Non, mon frère,* I thank you very much, but I don't want my own kind. I want better than that. And I'll have better than that for my child, too. You'll see, Monsieur Booth will do what is right by us

514

both. He's a man of substance. I don't need a husband to be a good mother, and this child will have all the father he needs."

"He's promised to care for the child?"

"Yes. And he'll send him to school, probably up North or to Paris, perhaps—"

"You're going to try to pass him off as white?"

She narrowed her eyes. "If I can, I will. And you will do nothing to hurt his chances."

"Jesus, of course, I'd do nothing to hurt his chances, but his chances are far greater if he doesn't live his life as a lie!"

"It's not a lie! Away from here, he could have anything he wants, be anything he chooses. As you and I could not."

"Manon, don't break your heart like this."

She started to rage at him, but then she suddenly stopped, struck dumb. "Why, you're jealous, Alex. Jealous because I have a man to love, a man who loves me. Jealous because I have someone and you have no one." She moved closer to him, her hands still on her belly. "Is that it, *cher?* Are you jealous you don't have someone like—David?"

He raised cool eyes to hers. "Don't be a fool."

Her eyes widened. "You are," she whispered. "I should have seen it before. You've never wanted a woman in your life, never frequented the *salons*—"

"You don't know everywhere I go," he said shortly.

She shook her head. *"C'est vrai, cher,* but I know everything you love. And it is not a woman, *certainement.* I should have guessed," she added wonderingly.

He twisted his mouth in disgust. "I knew you'd say this sooner or later, Manon. You, who think mostly of passion, could never understand someone who finds his passion elsewhere."

"Where do you find it, Alex?" she asked softly.

"Not where you suppose! I find it in solitude. In the pleasures of my work and the beauties of nature."

"There is nothing to be ashamed of," she said calmly,

"for we each need passion. Something to love. If you are *marrant*, well, and you are still my brother. But do not presume to give me advice about love, *cher*, not when you can only envy mine."

"Manon, I do not envy you your David, nor do I envy him you. But I do care about your welfare—and now that of your child. And so, when he leaves you, I'll forget your accusations and care for you both as our mother would have wished. Indeed, as she asked me to when you were still drooling on Sally Red's shoulder." He stood up, looking older and weary. "You have invested the monies he has given you?"

She nodded quietly, a little ashamed of herself. "Yes, and I have my eye on a little piece on Chartres. It's across from the market and should fetch a pretty rental, if it's well managed."

He reached down and gathered her under his arm gently. "You were always having your eye on one thing or another, Manon, even in the cradle. You haven't changed much. I guess people don't. I wish you the very best, God knows I do."

"I wish the same for you," she said faintly. "But more, I wish you less loneliness."

"I'm not lonely, I'm alone. There is a vast difference between the two, Manon, which you have never understood. And when I choose to be no longer alone, I have my—friends." He grinned, a sudden jaunty smile which made him look a decade younger and a rascal besides. "You'd be surprised how in demand I am in the backwaters. But I'll always have time for you and for this child, too. Whatever else he may or may not have, he will always have an uncle."

Zoe was born in late January, just as Manon had predicted. But what she had not predicted was that the baby would be a lovely girl-child, creamy white as spring magnolias. Manon spent long hours rocking her, gazing at her perfect face, her sweet and dimpled hands, crooning private love-lullabies, and planning her future as a lady of great substance. Zoe had her dark hair, her blue eyes, but her skin was more fair, with a pink undercast. Her chin and cheeks were modeled less like Manon's own slender, sharper French features, and more like David's round, open American face.

Manon whispered to her a hundred times in the first week of her life, that she would certainly combine the best of both *histoires,* but her luck would be sublimely, supremely, her own.

She kept David away for the last few weeks of her confinement, both to hide her swollen disfigurement and also to whet his appetites. When she finally welcomed him back to their cottage, the child slept peacefully in her wetnurse's arms, the linens were once again immaculate and scented, and Manon herself was slender, upright, and ardent once more. Unless the man knew where to look, she told herself, he might not even know an infant had come into their lives—except that Manon now needed far more deposited into her personal account than she had before the coming of the child. After all, as she reminded David only occasionally, she now had two lives to secure for his love.

That spring ebbed into one of the hottest summers New

517

Orleans had endured, and Zoe could not be kept quiet during the stifling afternoons without cool cloths packed round her body to help her rest. June came and went and the heat approached a fiery peak. David came to the city rarely now for it was cooler down on the bayou, and the yearly exodus of the rich out of New Orleans had left shuttered storefronts and a deserted port in its wake. The *Picayune* reported sporadic outbreaks of fever, as usual, but they were largely in the closely packed Lynch's Row at the Irish Channel, in the sailors' boardinghouses along the river, and in the marshland where the Germans persisted in trying to get livable land out of swamp.

The fierce *maringouins,* the huge mosquitoes of August, scarcely troubled Manon and her Creole friends, as they did the immigrants to New Orleans. She was used to the heat, she drank wine rather than water, and she draped gauze over her bed and her windows to keep off the unhealthy miasmas which came from the evaporated swamp water all around them, unfavorable atmospheres which everyone knew caused the fever to lodge in the pulmonary passages.

David had to meet with his factor that week, so he spent two evenings with Manon, a rare treat for which she kept Zoe up to see her father. The second night, he dandled the baby listlessly for a bit and then handed her to Manon with a sigh. "I'm blasted tired," he said softly. "I think I'll just have a brandy and turn in."

She was awakened in the darkness by a strange and stentorian breathing in her ear. She lit the lamp and saw that David was bathed in sweat beside her. She leaped to her feet and ran to check the child. She slept peacefully. Back at David's side, she woke him with wet cloths, murmuring to him that he must have some slight fever. But when he opened his eyes, she saw with alarm that he seemed not to be able to focus on her face.

"My head is splitting," he said weakly. Though the rest of his body was flushed, his face was pale.

She moved the cloths to his temples, stroking him gently. "Do you have pain anywhere else?"

He shook his head, and then a chill hit him. He shivered violently, briefly, and closed his eyes in agony.

She closed her eyes as well and said a brief prayer to the Virgin. It was the Bronze John. Yellow fever. She was as sure as though the doctor had come and pronounced it himself.

That night went slowly, and Manon slept little. Between changing cloths for David and urging cool water on him to keep his fever down, she stepped back and forth between their bed and Zoe's cradle. So far, the child showed no symptoms, but she knew that yellow fever could come and kill within the passage of only a few hours, particularly in the aged, the infirm, and the very young.

When morning light began to stream into the bedroom, she closed the shutters against the heat and met the cook in the kitchen. Surprised to see her mistress already up and dressed by eight, the cook asked few questions.

"You will not disturb Monsieur," Manon told her flatly. "He is feeling indisposed and needs his rest. Make up a tray and I'll take it to him myself, but do not open his door." For now, she wanted no one to know of David's peril save herself. She took the *déjeuner* tray to their bedside and saw that he slept fitfully. She set the tray beside him, packed more cooling cloths around his head and neck, and slipped out again.

When the wetnurse arrived, Manon had her feed the child while she penned a cursory note. There were few colored on the street at that hour, but she was finally able to hail a passing sweeper and press coins in his hand to deliver her message. She sat a few more moments with David, but he did not open his eyes. Nothing on the tray had been touched. She took Zoe up in her arms, changed to her plainest dress, grabbed a small silk pouch from her jewelry chest, and hurriedly hailed a carriage. She knew she had little time to guard the child's life. With yellow fever in the house, having sat on her father's lap and kissed him just the night before, it might already be too late to save her.

The Ursuline Convent loomed bright in the morning sunshine, a place of stoic stone which seemed to reflect and defy the shimmering light all around it. Thanks to her note, the nuns were waiting. Manon scarcely glanced at the walls; they were unchanged in her memory and in fact since her years behind them. But as she walked down the cool corridors, her steps echoing behind the nun's, she thought of how her name must be inscribed in some vellum-bound ledger in the Mother Superior's office, how the sisters passed each other bearing a bedpan or soiled sheets from the nursery, murmuring, *"Tout pour Jésus"* to each other, as though to take away the stain of human reluctance to serve. To give up the self. From the chapel, she could hear the sound of *Aves* rising to God, time for Meditations, Prime and Tierce, and she marveled how one could grow up with nuns and never really see and comprehend their secret and singular way of being. Yet they offered the only sure safety in this world.

She was led silently to the small cubicle where *Soeur* received her. It had been years since she had seen the old sister, and she had almost expected to learn that she had died peacefully in the pristine starkness of her prayer cell. But no, Emma awaited her with folded hands and a crisp white wimple, looking scarcely older than she had been on the last day Manon had seen her, the day she left the Ursulines at the age of fifteen.

Manon held Zoe in one arm and bent to kiss the hand extended to her. "Grace be to God," she murmured.

Emma's dark eyes were the only darkness in the pale face, the white linen, the almost invisible lips in the lined parchment skin. "You are well, my child?" Emma asked softly. Her voice trembled as much as the extended hand.

"I am as you see, *ma soeur,*" she said. "And you are the same?"

Emma smiled serenely. "As God wills. You have brought the child. Does she show any signs of the fever?"

Manon unwrapped the shawl from Zoe's face. "Nothing so far. But I fear for her, in a house where her father is already taken. If she could only stay with you until he is recovered, she may well survive."

"Only a few times has the epidemic climbed these walls. She will likely be safer here than outside. But as you know, we cannot take every child in New Orleans. Reverend Mother will ask me why this particular child should be more precious than any other?"

"Not more precious, only more in peril, perhaps," Manon said. "She is so very tiny!"

"As are many others."

"But she is all that I have," Manon said softly. "Emma, I came to you and Reverend Mother when I was little older than she is now. I like to believe you loved me, not only because my mother loved your mother, not only because your brother asked it, but because I was worthy of being loved. You saved my life. I ask you to save my daughter's now." With that, she pulled the silk pouch from her purse and took from it an intricately carved coral brooch. She laid it in Emma's hand. "Do you remember this? You gave it to my mother in gratitude, saying you would help her if you could. She never called on that favor. I am asking to redeem it for her granddaughter now."

Emma folded her hands within her large sleeves, and her palsy calmed. "We are *plus proches parents,* even if we share no blood, *c'est vrai.* But what of Alex? You cannot take her elsewhere?"

"Alex is down the delta, and I must stay to care for my child's father."

"And if he dies?" The gaunt simplicity of the nun's words seemed so brutal in the arching sunlight and the shadowed room.

"Then at least I will have his daughter left. If I lose her

as well, I truly will have lost him. Will you keep her safe for me?"

"It's not up to me, my child," Emma said gently.

"I know, but if you appeal to Reverend Mother on my behalf, she'll be swayed, I know she will. Will you speak for me?"

Emma turned away and gazed out of the window for a long moment. In that instant, Manon thought perhaps it would be the last time she would ever see the old woman who had taken her in, so that she might have more opportunity than the bayou and Uncle Simon's cabin might provide. Emma's time was coming swiftly. She knew it. Likely most who looked in her eyes knew it. She turned back to Manon and moved the corner of Zoe's blanket off her face. "She is even whiter than you. Even more beautiful."

"I mean her to have a better life."

Emma smiled, almost mischievously. "Yours is hardly unendurable, it seems to me, nor is it even defined as yet."

"Well? Will you speak to Reverend Mother?"

Emma sighed. "I will. But if she cannot accept the child, you must come and retrieve her immediately. I cannot be responsible without her blessing." She touched the child's cheek. "Truth be known, I can't be responsible even with it. I am too palsied to even hold her. I will do my best, of course, but she will be given over to the children's ward, and you will have to trust that—"

"I trust them. I trust them all. Please. I have nowhere else to turn."

"Then give her to me." Emma held out her hands.

Manon gently laid her daughter within the arms of the old nun, smiling defiantly to cover her pain.

Yellow fever swiftly ravaged New Orleans. Almost overnight it seemed, the city was out of control. Manon sprinkled herself with limewater and sulphur, two old Creole remedies to keep off the disease, but she had no real hope it might guard her. She stayed by David's bed relentlessly, tending to him alone. The servants had not come in on the second day; she could not blame them. Perhaps even now, they were dead or dying themselves.

When she stepped outside for short respites, either to get a breath of fresh air or to try to find some small vegetable or piece of meat to keep up her strength, she was appalled at the swift changes around her.

From everywhere seemed to rise exhalations of death and decay. Gutters were clogged with debris and dead dogs and cats, for no sweepers were working. The carcasses swelled and rotted, and green flies and mosquitoes swarmed incessantly. She heard the rumor that over on the next block, a Creole who kept a rooming place saw nine of her ten boarders die within a two-night period. A mulatto woman lost her husband, brother, sister, and five children in four days. Now she wandered about the streets, a mad and broken thing, asking the occasional passing gentleman if he had met any of them.

The bells from the cathedral tolled constantly, and the cannons at the port were fired regularly to keep off the diseased air. Vehicles stacked with bodies passed by, even on this side street, with sickening regularity. The drivers called out, "Bodies! Bodies! Out wid your daid!" Anything which could carry corpses was put to use, including cotton drays and wheelbarrows. From Manon's vigil at David's bedside, it seemed she heard only the ceaseless rolling of wheels day and night.

The sextons could not keep up with the graves, and trenches were being dug out in the swamp to cover the bodies as quickly as possible. Vandals were stripping the bodies, but no one could take the time or energy to stop them.

Once her neighbors learned she was caring for a fever victim within, they assembled piles of tar and pitch on each corner of the cottage to try to contain the sickness. The corner pyres burned day and night to purify the atmosphere, and Manon's nights were hideous with noise, dim with acrid smoke which she could not keep out of the rooms.

But her discomfort was nothing next to David's. He moaned, complaining of a fierce headache for long hours, his skin yellowed and swollen, as though his face might burst with the pressure. This stage seemed to last for half a day. Then his skin turned mottled, and he twisted and groaned, no longer able to make a coherent word to her. Delirium set in, his vomit turned black, and she could not get him to perspire, no matter how she dosed him with hot cloths or packed him in salt. And from all parts of the house, from without like a circling cat, came the menacing heat. She had taken to nursing him in her shift, her hair bound up on her head, not caring how she looked or whether she stank from the sweat that rolled off her in slow drops for hour after hour.

There was not a single breath of air, it seemed. Everywhere, in every crack and cranny, the heat waited. The birds had disappeared from the city altogether, and a hush hovered over the streets as though it waited for something.

Death, she thought, the heat waited for death. And when the two met, destruction was inevitable. She sensed that despite the combined wisdom of the doctors who advised keeping the sick ones warm, she must keep David cool at all costs.

When she ran out of ice and could find no more in the city, she kept the cloths cool by soaking them in the river water urns she had buried in the back. The water was cool for a quarter-hour or more next to his skin, then she would change the cloth again.

Finally after three days of constant vigilance, she thought she could see some slight improvement in him. He was no longer so desperate in his writhings, no longer so swollen and distended in yellow decay. At the end of that evening, somewhere before dawn, he opened his eyes and said his first coherent words to her in two days.

"Am I alive?" he asked hoarsely.

She embraced him, holding his hands in hers. "My love, you are, you are. You are going to be well." She lifted a glass to his lips, and he took a gulp of cool water. She almost wept with gratitude at that small gesture.

"Where am I?"

"You are safe. Here with me."

He seemed to focus on her for the first time. "Manon?"

She smiled widely, gripping his hands tighter.

"What are you doing here?"

Her smile faltered slightly, but she knew it would take some hours before he gained lucidity. "Taking care of you, my darling, here in our home."

He closed his eyes and turned his head away.

Worn out by even these small words, she thought worriedly, leaning closer to feel his pulse. Please God, keep him in this world with me.

She must have dozed briefly in the chair by his bed, finally awakened by a knock at the door. If this is at last the doctor after two days of waiting for him, I will turn him away with a curse, she thought, rushing to stop the knocking before it woke David from his stupor.

A richly dressed woman in a protective cloak stood at Manon's door. Behind her waited two gentlemen.

"Mademoiselle?" the woman said when Manon opened to her knock.

"Yes," Manon said with mild annoyance. She preferred to be called madame, of course, as was befitting her status, and she was anxious to get back to David's side.

"I believe my husband is within. Will you be so good as to show us to his side?"

Manon froze, her hand on the door frame, her mouth open in wonder. In that instant, all she could think was that she likely looked a sight, as did the cottage, that this was no way to have David's wife see her the first time, no way for her to see him—and then her mind stopped its swiveling. She had known all along of me, Manon realized, and her mouth closed firmly. But she cannot have him now.

She stepped aside, gesturing the three within.

"This is David's partner, Monsieur LaSalle, Mademoiselle, and his eldest brother, Peter. They have come to help bear him home."

"He is not well enough to travel," she said.

"We will be the judge of that," the wife said calmly.

Helplessly, Manon led them to David's chamber. One part of her mind screamed that she must fight them away, that they—*she*—had no right to be there, that he could not stand the movement, the shock. But the rest of her mind dully accepted that she had no choice but to let them see him, at least. Surely, when they saw him, they would know that he must stay.

The woman swept past Manon at the door to David's chamber—their bedroom—without even glancing around. She sat at his head, speaking to him softly. His eyes fluttered, opening finally on his wife's face.

"David," she said clearly. "You are going to live. I'm here now. I've come to take you home."

Manon could see no shock on his face at his wife's presence, no horror at her appearance in the bedroom he had shared with Manon for almost three years.

526

The two men moved forward towards the bed at the woman's gesture, and Manon only then found the anger and strength to move between them. "You cannot move him. He is still in danger, can't you see that? The shock will kill him."

The woman gazed at Manon with compassion. "*Mademoiselle,* I appreciate what you have done to help him. Likely you have saved his life. If I could have been here sooner, I would have saved you the trouble. But, of course, we will make the decisions about David now. You needn't trouble yourself further."

"David!" she called to him, throwing herself on the foot of the bed. "You cannot go!"

The two men began to lift her Monsieur up off the bed, and he groaned, his eyes closed in agony.

"You'll kill him!" she shrieked, trying to wrest their hands off his shoulders.

The wife gripped her firmly but gently from behind. "You must leave this to us, Mademoiselle. We know what is best for him."

Before she could protest further, David opened his eyes and looked at his wife. "Clare," he said feebly. "You here?"

"Yes," she said to him, moving Manon aside as so much baggage. "I am here for you now, my dear."

He glanced at Manon and then his eyes swiveled back to his wife. "Take me home," he said softly to her.

"As quickly as I can," she said, and the two men lifted him up as though he weighed no more than the coverlet beneath him. Cradling him, they wrapped the linen about his body, the linen Manon had selected for their pleasure, had washed so carefully of her childbirth stains, wrapped Monsieur securely and bore him from the room and out the cottage door. Manon heard the carriage drive away as though in a fog of distance and memory. It was one more in a rolling drone of moving wheels she had been hearing since the fever struck the city, one more traveling carriage to somewhere, away from her, perhaps bearing death, perhaps bearing life. Bearing David away from her forever.

Manon thought at first that her legs would never move. Surely her arms would never swing, her head would never turn, and her body would cease to live in any way that could be measured. She felt his absence as an actual physical ache, a pain that sounded like a deep iron bell being struck within her. Finally, she knew that if she did not move, she would die.

For three days solid, she cleaned the little cottage inside and out. She pushed aside every piece of furniture, washing, dusting, and waxing. She ran wet rags over every inch of wall, finding any dust, spiders, or mold. It must be clean, she muttered to herself in a fever, must be new and clean and completely free of any sickness, loss, or love. She bundled up most of her clothes, particularly those she had most preferred to wear when David visited, and she burned them to ash in the little yard. Then she swept up the ash until nothing remained but scoured earth.

That same week, she discovered she was pregnant again. She wasted no time in agonizing over how this could be, wasted no curses on a God who would let such a thing come to pass, when half of the city was facing death. She found the packet of herbs she had saved from Marie LaVeau, and forced the harsh liquid down her throat, letting it burn her mouth with some small satisfaction. When her bleeding began, she packed cloth between her legs and writhed on her bed alone, thinking that surely now the Bronze Jack would take her in her weakened state.

But she lived.

The morning came when she felt as arid as an empty pantry, as clean as the cool glazed windows around her. Her belly was flat, and the sickness was gone. Not just from her own cottage, but also, largely, from the city. With the first cool breeze of autumn, the yellow fever seemed to waft down-river and out to sea, leaving New Orleans drained but recovering. Likewise Manon's body was exhausted, but her mind was calm. It was time to retrieve Zoe.

All the way to the convent, she thought of what she might do with the child, how she would take the first carriage she could hire to Jefferson Island to find Alex. It would be good once more to care for him, to sit across the table from him over café in the morning, to watch him dandle Zoe in his lap while she stood at the stove and prepared his supper in the evening.

When at last she stopped before the tall gray walls of the Ursuline, she gazed up at the top of the convent in wonder. She had never noticed how beautiful it was. In all the years she spent there as a child, it was a place of protection, yes, but also one of confinement. Now for the first time, it seemed a refuge from the pain and disillusionment of the world on the outside of those walls. Emma had told Manon everything she knew of her mother, her mother's past, and had in that way helped to define her own future. It had been easier then to translate herself out of those women who came before. She wished fervently that she could go back to being that small girl, embraced by nuns and their piety, in a world where the largest problems were those posed by books, the most pressing imperative was pleasing God.

Her imperatives had changed markedly since then. Now it seemed to her that all of life was waiting for her, that every conceivable opportunity might for once be within her grasp, if she could only focus on what she wanted. She had cheated death and given up love and still stood strong enough to face the morning with hope.

She sat down on the marble bench before the convent, suddenly exhausted with what lay before her. She knew, in her heart, that David would not be back. She must, somehow, provide for herself, must face the city alone now, a rejected *placée* with little value to those same men who might have yearned for her two years before. The investments were good and the cottage was hers, yes, but she would need more than small coin to support it . . . and herself. Now she must steel herself to work and work hard if she would stay in New Orleans, with few of the same assets she brought to the task before.

But what was the alternative? To go to Alex and become his spinster sister, his housekeeper, his—parasite? To raise her daughter in the same backwaters which Uncle Simon saved her from nearly twenty years before?

She began to weep quietly, holding herself and rocking to and fro like a small child. To give up now was to see the pity in Alex's eyes for the rest of her life. To give in was to banish Zoe from her own future. Yet how could she care for an infant and also create a sparkling phoenix to rise from the ashes of David's abandonment? She must make this city sit up and pay heed, must take in boarders—Alex's prudishness be damned—must husband her money and multiply her investments, must still the whispers with her charm, her beauty—

In that moment, she knew that she could not retrieve her daughter. Not yet. She could not hide out on the bayou, comforting the loss of one dream with the loss of still more hopes. She belonged in New Orleans.

Manon stood and paced distractedly up the street towards the Ursuline gate. She caught her reflection in a tavern window, saw that her hair was lustrous in the mirrored light. A harsh sob constricted her throat, but she swallowed it down. Just a little while longer, Zoe must stay with Emma. Perhaps only a month or two, until Manon could get her bearings on this new course she must follow. The little one would be safe, she would be loved, and when she was older, she would thank her mother for making such a sacrifice. For charting her future full of shining possibilities, instead of sad little compromises.

For a moment stricken by guilt, Manon's eyes watered as she looked up at the shining top of the convent, wreathed by slow-wheeling doves. And then she dropped her veil over her eyes and walked away from the Ursuline in the direction of the docks.

The years from 1880 to 1892 ushered in an era of golden prosperity to the delta. Despite yet another devastating flood of the Mississippi in 1892—a deluge which prompted a construction flurry of new locks and levees—New Orleans was, in this last decade of the Nineteenth Century, a glittering mirage of wealth and glamour.

With the Cotton Expo of 1885, the Queen City announced herself a comer. The newly finished Southern Pacific line from California brought tourists in waves of fashionable prosperity, and bumper crops of cane fueled her growth. Mixed bathing was allowed out at the jazz clubs at Lake Pontchartrain, and ladies with oilcloth caps and high-necked, long-sleeved bloomer bathing costumes cheered on their men at gambling, rowing regattas, and swimming races. Electric arc lights were strung like fairy stars in the poshest sections of the Quarter, and everyone was reading and talking of the new best-selling novel, Ben Hur, *about the life of a Roman slave during the time of Jesus.*

The benefits of prosperity, however, were not equally available to those who had helped create it. In 1887, ten thousand cane workers up and down the Teche struck for higher wages. The sheriff's posse and state militiamen were called in to quell the riots, and in Thibodaux, thirty Blacks were killed outright, with many more lost in the swamps. For the next sixty-five years, there would be no increase of wages in the cane fields.

And in 1892, the anniversary of Abe Lincoln's birthday was declared a national holiday.

In the early hours of twilight, a small animal about the size of a house cat roused himself from his earthen den and stretched, wrinkling his nose in anticipation of a full belly to come. Like a house cat, he was insatiably curious, but he had little of a cat's natural wariness.

His body was covered with dense fur, dark brown, almost black in shadows, and dotted with white spots and narrow curving stripes. He was glaringly obvious among even the densest bayou foliage, a quick target for predators, and unable to conceal himself in cover. Yet even this vulnerability did not make him timid.

For he was a spotted skunk, armed with a weapon that could run off intruders from as far away as twelve feet, should they be so foolish as to ignore his natural markings.

Stamp's underground den had been used by many occupants before he moved in. An armadillo, a small gray fox, a marsh rabbit, even a canebrake rattler had at one time or another been tenants. Now it belonged to the skunk, and he shared it with no one.

His small dark eyes worked well in the dusk, even better at night, but he was too hungry to wait. He quickly groomed himself, yawned, and checked his double musk glands beeath his tail. Both were well filled with the viscous yellow luid he sprayed when threatened; he could spray, in fact, five or six times in rapid succession at will. He was practiced in aim and usually struck an attacker full in the face, most often he eyes. This caused an extremely painful and temporary blindness. He rarely missed, and he had never needed to spray more than once. He was ready for the nightly hunt.

He left his den casually, with an obliviousness to attack which few in the bayou could assume. Without looking about, he strolled to the water to drink. Watching from cover, a female gray fox instantly saw him, crouched, and ensed. It was a young vixen, with four pups hidden in a den more than a mile away. She had hunted most of the afternoon, which was very unusual, but she was quite hungry, and her pups needed food even more. She had only managed to catch two small mice, and her needs drove her out in the daylight hours despite her caution. She had never hunted a skunk before, but she was instinctively wary.

The skunk meanwhile ambled up and down the riverbank, rolling over small logs and snapping up beetles, white grubs, and crickets as fast as he could crunch them with his needle teeth.

The vixen followed at a distance, keeping downwind. The skunk seemed small enough to take without much of a fight. When he bent to another log, she pounced on him swiftly.

Stamp was not surprised. Though he seemed not to notice, in fact, he had been aware of the vixen the moment she moved from cover. He had supposed she would not attempt to attack, but he was prepared.

As the vixen moved, he abruptly spun around and stamped his feet on the ground in warning, growling at her. The vixen stopped a dozen feet away, watching him carefully. Most creatures no bigger than this one ran when she chased. She had never seen one stop and stamp in this way. She circled him warily, but kept coming closer.

Again the skunk stamped and growled, and when the

vixen came on, he raised his tail, stood on his front paws, still facing the fox, and fired his first volley right over his own head. The spray of oily stench hit the vixen full in the face. Fortunately, only one of her eyes was wetted.

Instantly, a sickening odor overwhelmed her, choking her and making it impossible to breathe. She retched uncontrollably, and both eyes stung, teared, and were blinded. One burned with an intense fire, and she howled in pain and shock, throwing herself to the ground. She rolled over and over frantically, trying to dig her muzzle in the sand and then jerking it out again, biting at the wet mud to try to rid herself of the horrible taste. She pawed at her eyes, whining and howling and rolling.

Stamp twice lowered himself to all fours and then raised himself up on his front paws again, watching to see if another shot would be necessary. Finally he relaxed and saw that the fox would not try another attack. His nose wrinkling at the strong odor which even he disliked, he trotted off quickly with scarcely a glance at the suffering vixen.

Crossing a narrow piece of the bayou by jumping small stones, Stamp turned over more rotted logs and found a whip scorpion. Ignoring its acid, vinegary smell, he cracked it spine and swallowed it quickly, followed by two crickets, a beetle grub, and a dozen termites. In a ball-shaped nest of dry grasses, he nosed up a meadow mouse. She squealed shrilly as his teeth closed over her, and then it was all over. He grunted like a small rooting pig as he ate her in moments.

Ambling out towards the dark open meadow, he came to a wide flat place which he rarely crossed. Here the earth was hard and baked in the hot months, a slog of mud in the wet seasons. But there in the center of the open pathway, a dead weasel lay strewn and broken in the rictus of death.

Stamp lowered himself slightly, stiff with caution, and sniffed the air around the weasel. Death had been here awhile. Looking about him for enemies, he moved warily closer, and took an exploratory bite of the weasel's hindquar er, for like many bayou creatures, the flavor of decay did not repel him.

Within moments, Stamp had pushed his muzzle deeper into the weasel's belly, and he ignored a distant noise growing closer. When he did look up, his nose was too covered with blood to clearly identify what approached, and his eyesight too dim to warn that the blackness looming swiftly out of the night, rumbling down the wide dirt path, was coming right towards him. At the last moment, he whirled to a standing threat posture, but the horses' hooves knocked him spinning, and the carriage wheel crushed him so completely that the driver never noticed the bump in the road.

Spring was her favorite time, Manon decided as she placed the enormous flowered hat on her piled curls. The most ludicrous display of bright hues and blossoms in silk and muslin—which might go far beyond the bounds of good taste in autumn—were completely forgiven in the riot of color that was spring in New Orleans.

And this year of 1892 would bring a more heady spring than most, she knew. Bumper crops of cotton were expected, even richer than the last two years, which had broken all records. The Weitz *sucrerie* was working overtime, prices for sugar were sky-high, and even the most parsimonious planters were putting in their own private railroads from field to mill, and adding on pillars and porches to their houses.

Manon's own investments were doing so well she could scarcely keep track of them all. From small cottages, she had used sugar profits to move up to boardinghouses, from boardinghouses to fine hotels, and from hotels she spread cautious fingers into city blocks where she owned the best restaurant and the most elegant accommodations around strategic corners in the Quarter. Always careful to court political contact as well as customers, Manon had learned that in the Queen City, *securité* was not possible without friends in high places

Now hired accountants made quarterly reports to her lawyers managed her affairs, and still she seemed to use up every day, she thought, in shooing greenbacks from one place to another. Her most profitable decision had been to turn the old boarding house on Bourbon to one of the finest private hotels in the Quarter. Home to the elite of New Orleans, their guests, and any number of gentlemen who, for their own reasons, preferred a more select accommodation than the average hostelry could offer. Manon rented only to those she knew personally, or who came with a personal recommendation from a friend. Gentlemen came for a weekend or a week they paid well for their comfort, and Manon made sure that their privacy was protected.

Money brought power, Manon had discovered, and prestige as well. The *ancien* Creole regime might not be willing to forget her lineage, but the hoards of newcomers to New Orleans had scant concern that her mother was the mulatto mistress of an ex-pirate from the bayou.

She peered closer in the glass, inspecting her face for any incipient flaws. So far, at thirty-two, her face was nearly as unlined as Zoe's. Her dark hair with its high widow's peak framed her small, slightly sharp features. Her eyes were as clear and luminously blue as Zoe's, but her nose was longer more narrow and fragile. Her wide breasts were still high, her slender neck still smooth, if a little too dark from the spring sun. She frowned and saw the familiar etching between her brows, smiled to smooth out the creases, and pulled back from the glass. Well, almost as smooth, at any rate.

Why is it, she wondered, that just as we begin to go, our daughters begin to arrive? That just as the fold in my neck begins to deepen, the fine bones of her cheek begin to sharpen? That as my skin reveals its overripeness, she opens like a small pale bloom at the end of a hibiscus?

It's the oldest story, I suppose, Manon reflected ruefully. The oldest we have on this planet. The story of replacement.

She remembered vividly a long-ago visit to Zoe in the convent, she couldn't have been over seven at the time. Alex had not come along that day, which was rare. Usually, it was his prodding which reminded her that more than a week had gone by since she had seen her daughter and then—always stricken by guilt and wondering how the time slipped so fast—Manon would hurry to see Zoe with Alex tagging along.

The child was not fooled, however. She greeted her uncle with at least as much fervor as she did her mother. The two would sit and whisper over Zoe's latest adventures and secrets for an hour or more, while Manon must hear the nun's report on Zoe's studies, on Zoe's eating habits, on her tardiness to devotions or her raised voice in the refectory. And, of course, it was not Alex who must then reprimand the child and tell her she should do better. Naturally, Manon told herself, Zoe might well prefer to see her uncle than her own mother.

But there were occasional visits when Manon had the child to herself. And for this visit, so many years ago, Zoe had seemed somehow changed from the week before. At once more poised and also more innocent, she met her mother in the refectory in a dark serge skirt, alarmingly like the skirts the nuns wore, only shorter. Around her head, Zoe had draped a white napkin for a veil. When she walked to meet Manon, she walked with the same gliding, swayless walk of the nuns, her hands hidden under her sweater as theirs were hidden within their surplice, her eyes downcast as theirs were in the habitual custody of God.

"*Ma foi!*" Manon said, kneeling and attempting to sweep her into her arms. "What is this little sister I find in the place of my Zoe?"

Zoe shied away in the same way a nun might, reluctant to be touched. *"Bonjour, ma mère,"* she said formally. "It is so good to see you."

Manon couldn't help it, she laughed aloud. "And it is good to see you as well. Have you decided to become a bride of Christ now, *cher?*"

Zoe frowned ferociously at Manon's smile, as only a child can when its pride is trespassed. "Sister says I would make a good novice."

Manon suppressed her annoyance. Would the nuns never cease their missionary work? *"Vraiment?"*

"Yes, for I am able to be still so long. Longer than the others, mostly. Except for Lisabet, but she's a whole year older, almost." She smiled proudly. "I am in contemplation of God."

"Ah. Well, that is noble, *cher*. Do you have time, in your contemplation, to think also of your grammar lessons on occasion? For Sister Marie tells me that they lack your usual attention."

Zoe sighed hugely, and she was suddenly Manon's seven-year-old daughter once more. Plucking at her napkin-veil, she said, "Sister Marie is impossible to please, *maman!* If the words are right, then the penmanship is the worst she's ever seen; if the letters are correct, then the words are all in the wrong places." She frowned, once more fierce. "I don't know why I have to learn English anyway, nobody speaks the ugly stuff."

"Perhaps not here," Manon said, "but outside these walls, you'll hear more English than French."

"When am I to come home again?"

It was a constant refrain from Zoe. She had two weeks with Manon at the Christmas holidays, two weeks at Lent, and two weeks at the end of the summer, yet she could never seem to remember how long the weeks would be between these visits. "Soon enough," Manon said cheerfully. "I am having your room repapered, *cher,* you will love it, I think.

You remember that sweet frock with the pink cabbage roses Alex bought you? It matches almost exactly—"

"Oh, *maman!*" Zoe squealed, all further thoughts of her nunlike composure now completely forgotten. "I love that dress! And will it be done by Lent?"

"Will you bring up your mark in grammar by Lent?" Manon answered quickly.

Zoe appraised her mother carefully. "I will try," she said slowly. "Perhaps it's not necessary for a bride of Christ to learn that ugly English grammar."

"Perhaps it's not necessary for a bride of Christ to have pink cabbage rose paper on her walls either," Manon replied, unconcerned.

"Did you have to learn grammar when you were here?"

"Yes, and the good sisters wondered if I would ever be passed to the second level at all."

Zoe beamed. "I will be passed, they say," she said. "I am likely smarter than you were at my age, *maman.*"

Manon shook her head and made a mock-rueful moue. "Of that I have no doubt, *cher.*"

Now, as she looked into her mirror closely, it seemed that her daughter might well be more beautiful as well, at least in time. Replacement, to be sure. And one could see it in New Orleans as well. The old was being deluged, overcome, rankled, and forever altered, finally to be replaced, at least a little, by the new.

With crops good, shipping up, and even the river nigh tamed with the new levee system, it seemed to her that the *Picayune* was almost justified in yodeling about the Queen City's Golden Age, even if it did fly in the face of all sense to continue to seduce new visitors to a city already bursting at her bustle. If the opera loges got any more crowded, they'd soon have to add the season tickets to the lottery!

"We're going to be late again!" Alex's voice came ringing up from the front door.

She took off her emerald and ruby rings, pulled on her

lace gloves, and slipped the rings back on her fingers. With a final inspection in her glass, she picked up her parasol and hurried down the stairs. Alex waited, somewhat impatiently as usual, in the foyer. The afternoon sun gleamed brightly through the leaded windows in the door, and she instantly wished she had worn her coolest frock. But Zoe always noticed every detail of her toilette, and her muslin had a stain on the skirt. Better to be too hot than to bear the mild scolding of her eagle-eyed daughter.

"Don't fuss at me, Alex," Manon said firmly, "I guess I can have one day a week when I don't have to be someplace exactly on time."

"One day!" he snorted. "Bankers, lawyers, and politicians all over the city would get a good laugh out of that one, Manon. You haven't been on time to a meeting with any of them since—"

"I pay them well for their time," she said airily as she took his arm and opened the door. "If I perturb them overmuch, they can always tell me to take my business elsewhere."

"Well, since you're going to give her bad news," he said worriedly, "at least you shouldn't keep her waiting, too."

He helped her in the waiting carriage, carefully piling her voluminous skirts in all around her. She smiled to herself to see how deftly he tucked them, taking a precarious seat on the edge to avoid crushing her, almost as though he had been married to her for years. He was a good brother, she thought fondly as she inspected his stooping shoulders for lint and his trousers for wrinkles. For once, he was quite the dandy. Usually, she half-expected to see spider webs in his thinning hair.

"Alex, I don't know why you persist in saying she's going to take this as bad news. Most young girls would be thrilled to have a proposal from one of the most up-and-coming families in the delta."

"You know perfectly well I'm not talking about the betrothal. She might be happy at that, she might not, I don't know. You don't, either. Which is exactly my point, Manon, you scarcely know your own daughter. Here, she's wanted to come home for a year now, and you won't let her, even though you sold that boardinghouse—"

"It was a guest house," she said firmly.

"It was not a place for a young girl. Nor for a lady," he replied, equally firmly, "and I praise the Virgin you no longer hold it on our books. But, at any rate, now you have an appropriate place for her to live, and still you delay her departure from Ursulines. Why, sometimes I think you've got less of a mother's heart than a common street cat. Zoe's thirteen, old enough to make up her own mind, and she might as well be an orphan child, for all the home she's had with you. Two weeks here and two weeks there, it was one thing when Emma was still alive, but now she's gone, Zoe needs her own family. Thirteen is old enough to decide for herself that she's had all she wants of convent classes and Mother Superior. *You* certainly had enough at her age, as I recall. You couldn't get out of there fast enough!"

"I was different, and times were different. Zoe is a far more level-headed child than I ever wanted to be, certainly at that age." She smirked at her brother. "Maybe at any age."

"Merci au bon Dieu," Alex rolled his eyes at her.

"And besides, as you know, it makes no sense for her to come home right now, I certainly cannot spend all my time chaperoning her, that new club will take all of my attention, and the plans for the downtown building must be seen to immediately. Once her betrothal is set she can come home, and then I can fête her properly."

"Does Henry Avery know you're about to open one of the biggest jazz clubs on the lake?" He looked out the window studiously at the streets rolling by, avoiding Manon's sharp glance.

"No, he does not," she said firmly, "and neither does Zoe. Besides, it's not the biggest, it's only the finest. I always buy quality, Alex, not quantity, you know that. And I see no reason to involve my daughter or her future husband in what is a business decision, and my private business at that. Lake Pontchartrain is going to be the biggest draw the delta has had since the steamboats quit running, and I mean to have my piece of it, even if I have to endure snubs from a dozen of the haute monde when they have to rub shoulders with upstarts at the ballet. And I should think," she added, patting his knee fondly, "that you would applaud me for it, rather than trying to make me feel guilty for taking good care of us all. I have worked hard for a dozen years, harder than you'll ever know, to make something for us all that we can depend upon. Your own pockets are hardly moth-bitten, thanks to my lack of a mother's heart." She glared at him, squeezing his knee hard. "That was a dreadful thing to say, *fou-fou,* and I think you should apologize." She used her favorite endearment for him, watching to see if he would relent.

He smiled. "Then, of course, I do." He took her hand off his knee, kissed it lightly, and put it aside. "But I reserve the right to say at least three more dreadful things before *déjeuner,* lest I lose my touch."

The carriage pulled up outside the Ursulines, and he helped Manon alight, once more dropping her skirts into place for her and looping her parasol over his arm. Shown inside, they waited in the garden for Zoe to appear.

"Ah," Manon said when she saw her small and slender daughter step into the courtyard, "she is more beautiful every week."

"And more like you every day," Alex said softly, rising to meet her as she hurried to them, her arms outstretched.

"If you had only seen her father . . ." Manon murmured. "My darling!" she called, gathering Zoe to her warmly. "You have grown another six inches this week!"

Zoe grinned at Alex over her mother's shoulder. "She says that every visit. If I grew as much as she claims, I'd be able to scale these walls like a lizard. Mother," she added, pulling back to gaze into Manon's face, "that hat is brilliantly bad. I told you that red flowers only make your cheeks look pale in comparison."

"Why, they *are* pale, my Zoe," Manon teased her, "I've been missing you all week."

Zoe embraced Alex, murmuring in his neck, "She lies so charmingly, doesn't she, *mon oncle?* I guess we'll find out just how much she misses me soon enough." She lifted her long black hair off her neck and fanned herself, pulling away and adding, "By June, it'll be too hot for embracing at all!"

Zoe took them each by an arm, steering them into the garden, and her ready laugh soon had them each joining her, as she told them of her studies and lessons and tribulations of the week before.

"I told Sister Agnes that the next time she wants to talk about unknown quantities, I would prefer to discuss the face of God than algebra."

"Keep that up, and they'll pack you out of here," Alex said. "Or worse. A hairshirt in a dank virgin's cell for a fortnight to contemplate your excesses. Your mother was bundled out quick enough for just that sort of heresy."

"That would be fine with me," Zoe said, smiling at him gratefully for the opening. "Mother, I really do think it's time for me to come home with you. I know the nuns have been good for me, but it's really not the same since *Soeur Soumis* passed. I've learned all I'm going to behind these walls. While I'm grateful to the Sisters, I want to do something more with my youth than parse sentences and learn French grammar."

"Exactly what I was thinking," Manon said briskly, "and I'm glad you agree." She turned to Zoe and embraced her fervently. "My dear, I have the most wonderful news. *You* have the most wonderful luck. You are betrothed!" She beamed on Zoe's wide, open face, watching every change of expression intently. "I know this is a surprise, frankly I was surprised as well, because you are, after all, quite young yet to think of marriage. But the Avery family is one of the finest

543

on the delta, with holdings which rival some of the older families which, as you know, are now in sad straits, most of them. The Averys emerged from the war with more to recommend them rather than less, unlike most I could name, and Henry Avery, heir to a handsome piece of it himself, has asked for your hand."

Zoe looked blankly from her mother's face to her uncle's. Her eyes narrowed, then widened in incredulity. "Henry Avery? Has asked to marry me?"

"No one else!" Manon said, almost twirling her daughter around in her glee.

"Why would he want to marry me?"

"He knows you are an intelligent, pious daughter, of course, and—"

"Mother, stop this," Zoe said, taking her arms out of Manon's grasp. "I have no idea what you're talking about. Uncle Alex, what in the world is going on behind my back? Do you know about this?" She saw her mother's face go firm and searched her uncle's eyes for support.

Alex smiled ruefully. "You mean you didn't see your mother's *annonce* in the *Picayune?* It was so tasteful!"

"Mother—!"

"Yes, of course, I know about this, Zoe," he soothed her gently. "And it's true, the Averys are a fine family. I've no doubt there are many lovely women in New Orleans who would be proud to be—"

"But I've never even met the man, have I?"

"Not formally," Manon said quickly, "but he has seen your daguerrotype—thank God we had it made!—and is smitten with you, *cher*. He thinks you are the most beautiful girl he has ever seen."

"How many has he seen?" Zoe asked sullenly.

Manon pulled up to her full height and surveyed her daughter with dignified poise. "My dear, I do not understand your frown. This is an honorable offer, an excellent match, to my mind. You are betrothed, not buried. His family is happy, your family is happy, and if you are not happy once you meet him, then, of course, I will not shackle you to him at the ankles like a slave. But consider this, child. You don't come with a plantation or a fortune, and lovely as you are, there are many just as lovely. Frankly, I think you have *bonne chance*. You will have a wonderful life with such a man."

Zoe thrust her hands behind her and walked away from both of them, her back rigid and set.

"Don't you dare walk away from me, daughter," Manon called mildly, "I know that the nuns have taught you more obedience than that."

Zoe turned, crossed her arms, and faced her mother across an open pathway of dappled sunlight. Her chin looked frighteningly firm. "They have taught me respect, that much is certain. Respect for myself, as well. Tell me, Mother, what did you sell me for?"

"Why, what do you mean?"

"I mean, which of your holdings do I take with me to Henry Avery, to make this package so enticing?"

Manon rolled her eyes at Alex and threw up her hands. "Brother, will you explain to this child that a dowry is scarcely a matter of shame? Indeed, I can think of no betrothal which does not require one." She put her hands on her hips and faced Zoe defiantly. "You'll be bringing the Averys a fine commercial building on Saint Charles and two rentals on Bourbon, and if I could give you more, I would. But you should know that the Averys consider this a love match—or at least a match with that potential—and so do I. I would never want less for a daughter of mine."

"Why would the Averys want me for their precious son? Surely, he could have his pick of New Orleans' belles, if he's as magnificent as you say."

"Tell her the truth, Manon," Alex said softly. "She should know it all."

Zoe raised her chin stubbornly. "I *will* know it all."

545

Manon sat down on the garden seat, carefully arranging her skirts around her. "Henry Avery wants you, child, for his wife. That is what you need to know. You come with a handsome dowry, nothing to sneeze at in this day and age. Your mother has offered, as well, to forgive the Avery debt on some parcels they had to mortgage some years back, and they are building you a grand estate down on Jefferson Island, where you will live as Madame Avery for the rest of your happy days. They want a gentle, conservative girl who has been raised in the strictest propriety, and your loveliness is hardly a detriment to the match—"

"How old is he?" Zoe interrupted.

"Thirty. Not too old at all."

"What's wrong with him, Mother? Tell me now, for I'll find it out soon enough."

"Nothing that is not wrong with you, as well," Manon said gently.

Zoe's eyes widened. "He is *nègre.*"

"Don't be grotesque, child. He is quadroon, nearly as light as you. His grandfather had his father by one of the most beautiful slaves on the Avery plantation, but he was raised same as the other Averys with the same advantages, and he is no less white than any of them to any casual eye. But more to the point, he comes with the same amount of land and the same claim to whatever inheritance comes to any of them." She smiled shrewdly. "More, actually, since he is his mother's favorite."

Zoe looked bewildered. "But I am only thirteen."

"Which is why I have told him that this must be a long betrothal. Perhaps two or three years. In that time, you will find out all you need to know about this young man of yours—"

"Scarcely young."

"Scarcely old enough," Manon said dryly, "to handle you, *cher.* I never thought I'd be blessed with such a headstrong daughter." She crossed the pathway and embraced

Zoe firmly. "Now, do I get a smile and some thanks for arranging such happiness?"

Zoe accepted her embrace tepidly and said, "I'm coming home with you now, mama."

Manon pulled back and looked amazed. "Whatever for? You are doing so well here, child, and you know that I cannot possibly—"

"I'm coming home with you today, or you can tell Henry Avery the betrothal is off."

Alex laughed softly as he lowered himself to the garden seat with the air of an old, tired man. "Checkmate, *ma soeur,* and deftly done, too."

"Name of God! Don't be ridiculous, Zoe," Manon said, ignoring him balefully, "we are not prepared for your arrival. My business simply will not allow me the time right now, and I must remind you that if I do not attend to our affairs, no one else will do so. Try to remember that, *cher,* when you imagine yourself so *abandonée,* yes? I do this for you. Perhaps in a few weeks, a month, you can come and welcome, but for now, I have so much to do, I cannot possibly chaperone you as you need."

"I have heard you tell me for all of my life what you must do for my sake, and I'm sick of it. Tell Reverend Mother you are taking me out of here, or I will write to Monsieur Avery myself, regretfully refusing his offer of marriage." Zoe smiled softly. "One thing they have taught me, *ma mère,* is lovely penmanship and eloquence with the written word. I'm sure that the Monsieur will never receive so graceful a rejection again."

Manon eyed her daughter shrewdly. Finally, she sighed. "You are too old for him, *cher,*" she said resignedly. "Too old for me, as well. Go tell Sister to prepare your baggage, then."

As Zoe gracefully glided off, her head high, to arrange for her departure, Manon heard Alex chuckling softly behind her. She whirled on him, about to give him a sharp retort, but when she saw his face, she could not help but smile. Sighing heavily, she slid down beside him on the stone bench. "She is all of a woman," she said.

"Indeed," Alex murmured. "A Southern woman, at that."

Manon grinned wryly. "A Southern woman. I wonder what you men mean when you say such a thing, *vraiment.*"

"Why," he hesitated. "I'm not sure I could put it into words. A certain . . . charm. A graciousness. A softness, I suppose, but underneath a certain *férocité.* A strength of will."

"Ah, *oui, certainement,* a strength of will. What you call the charm of the *belle,* is really not charm at all, of course. It is more an instinct. We do it all the time, even when we are not trying to, I think."

"Do what?"

"Make the world what we want it to seem to be. Make a man what we want him to be. And do you know how we do it? By praising him, *toujours,* for the qualities we want him to have." She smiled. "It takes a ferocity, to be sure. A *férocité de coeur.* But you must promise to never tell the secret."

"No man would believe it if I did," he murmured, shaking his head. "And not a one would want to hear the truth."

"Which is why it works every time," she grinned.

Soon, the two of them were laughing quietly together, keeping their voices low lest the nuns should be disturbed in their peaceful meditation.

Alex was reminiscing about a time he had visited Zoe and found her weeping over a book of poetry. "It was Swinburne," he said to Manon, still slightly shocked at the memory. "How she ever got a copy of it smuggled through the nuns, I'll never know. But she was weeping over the picture he painted of a gray, corpselike Christ, who could never bring as much joy to the world as a pagan goddess."

Manon wrinkled her brow. "It sounds blasphemous."

"I guess some would call it that. But what struck me was her response to it. She has never wept easily, you know, and here she was weeping—and not gently, either—over a poet's vision of the world. I can remember one line even today. 'I have lived long enough, having seen one thing, that love hath an end.' "

"I can't recall if I ever wept over such a thing."

"That love died? *I* can recall, let me tell you. The two of you were alike in many ways, but not in this. You might have wept some, but mostly you'd have been enraged. She is young to weep of such. Even to know of it. I hated most that she no longer believed in love. Maybe in God, either."

"Oh," Manon said softly, "I wept my share, I suppose. But I soon discovered it did little good to weep. Zoe will discover the same truth, and the sooner the better."

"Zoe's not you," Alex said gently. "And the sooner you discover *that* truth, the better. I know, I came to visit each of you behind these walls, and I guess I had my share of sadness that the world made such a refuge—or confinement—necessary for *jeunes filles* in your place. I think she felt safer telling me her hopes and dreams and fears, sometimes, than she did telling you. She was such a—such a lovely child. Much softer than you were at her age, Manon. She never had your spine—"

"She had a mother; I did not."

He hesitated. "Ah, well, a point I won't debate at this late date. Leave it that her dreams were different than yours."

"What kind of dreams?" Manon scoffed lightly. "I would wager the dreams of young girls are not too difficult to fathom."

Alex reached for an old memory. "I shall give you one example only. Anymore would be a betrayal of her confidence. She used to tell me that she dreamed she was a bird—"

"That's not so unusual. Any young girl in a convent dreams she has wings to escape these walls at times, it doesn't mean she was so miserable!"

"She did not dream she was a lark or a dove," he continued quietly. "Zoe dreamed she was a pelican. And not just occasionally, *cher*, but many, many times."

"A pelican? And these dreams frightened her?"

He nodded. "For a time, I could not understand the significance, but now I think I do. The pelican does not use its wings for flight so much as other birds, but for feeding, yes?"

"You are the expert on birds, my brother, not I," Manon retorted a little impatiently.

"Exactly. And the most obvious trait of the pelican is that it stores food for others in its broad beak, carrying it back to feed—"

"Its young," Manon finished for him. "And so what does this mean to a child in the care of nuns?"

"Perhaps that this child sees itself as more parent than child, yes? And that it dreams of one day being able to carry enough to satisfy others so that it may, finally, be able to hunt for itself."

"It is you who are dreaming now," Manon said, laughing lightly. "I am her mother, and I know her mind and heart better than you, *cher*. After all, we are not only the same flesh, we are the same sex."

"That is true, but I know you both better than any man alive and from my unique vantage point, let me just say that she is not you, *cher*. The nuns raised her, *c'est vrai*, same as you, but she raised herself at least as much." He put his arm around her and pulled her closer. "Just as her mother did."

The first morning Zoe was home, Manon saw that she had made an error by not taking her away from the Ursulines much sooner.

Manon sat at her toilette table, as the soft morning light came in on her bottles of perfume, of creams and oils, of rouges and paints and powders. She was applying a light dusting of white powder to her face with a large camel brush. Zoe drifted in wrapped in one of Manon's old dressing gowns, her hair tumbling down around her face, her eyes still soft with sleep.

Manon was, in that instant, smitten with the same fierce protective hunger she had felt so long ago, when she first held her daughter. Even in *déshabille,* Zoe was a lovely animal, radiating a languorous vitality.

She sat down on the puffed pillow at her mother's feet and watched the process carefully. After the powder, Manon followed with a careful tracing of dark pencil around both eyes, up her dark brows, and darkened a mole by her lips. "Why do you do that?" Zoe asked, leaning closer to examine the lash pencil.

"To make the black blacker against the white of my skin," Manon said, pursing her lips and rubbing glistening pomade across them.

"You try to look whiter?"

Manon glanced at Zoe in the mirror. "Of course. Every woman of fashion does."

"Even *les femmes de couleur?*"

551

"Particularly do *they* wish to appear lighter."

"Why do you say they? Why do you not say we?"

Manon turned to her daughter with mild exasperation. She had her perfect chin molded in her hand, ruining the line of her jaw. "I do not say 'we' because, of course, we are so close to white, we might as well be. You, my darling, are even closer than I. Should you choose, you could go to any capital in Europe and *passer pour blanc* with ease. It is only here in this city where you must even concern yourself with meaningless distinctions. But at the very least, you can minimize them." She picked up her powder brush. "Did the nuns teach you nothing of—but, of course, they did not. Glamour cannot scale the walls of the Ursulines. Emma, for all her loving heart, was scarcely a good model for what a woman should be."

"She was a good enough model," Zoe said quietly, "when she was all I had."

Manon rolled her eyes. "*Ma foi,* as though you were an orphan child! Lean forward, *cher,* and take your chin out of your fist, it makes wrinkles and buck teeth."

Zoe leaned forward and grimaced as her mother dusted her all over her face and neck with the fine brush. "It tickles," she only said. Then Manon picked up her plucking tool and began to pull stray hairs out of Zoe's untidy, thick brows. Zoe flinched and gritted her teeth. "It stings," she muttered.

"If that's the worst you have to endure for beauty, you'll be luckier than most," Manon murmured, concentrating on her task. "You know, you have lovely eyes and fine, arched brows, once we get all this hair out of them. You're too old to be running around with shaggy brows like a shetland pony."

"Ouch!" Zoe winced, pulling away. "You must have pulled out six at once!"

"Don't tell me not a single girl at the convent ever shaped her brows? No one ever showed you how to do this?"

"There's not a lot of call for perfect arches over Latinate

552

conjugations," Zoe said, pulling away and rubbing her fist over her eyebrow.

"And there's not a lot of call for Latinate conjugations in real life. At least not in any of the real lives I've known."

"Mama," Zoe said, almost wistfully, "how many men have you known?"

Manon laughed aloud, a sudden, startling, bawdy laugh. "*Mais, cher,* what a question for a young convent girl! What do you mean?"

"I know no men at all," Zoe said. "Except Uncle Alex, and he hardly counts."

"No, I suppose not." Manon turned back to the mirror and pursed her lips thoughtfully, watching herself appraisingly. "I've known quite a few men, child, but very few in the way you mean. There's been no one for me, *vraiment,* since your father. Not in my heart."

"What was he like?"

"Your father? You have asked me this a hundred times. He was handsome, he was *comme il faut,* and he was very married. He left us reluctantly, but he left us, nonetheless. What is more to say? You should put him out of your mind, Zoe, I have. And if someone asks, he has been dead a very long time. Since you were born, *n'est-ce pas?*"

"I know. You've told me that much. Still . . ." Zoe said quietly, "I would like to know a man before I am married."

Manon closed her eyes in pain. Here it was. What she feared most. That her daughter would be driven by the same passions which drove her mother, herself, perhaps too many women to count. But not a one of them finally knew happiness in that passion, so far as Manon could see. Passion was the downfall of women, she was certain of it. Passion made a woman blind to her own safety, to her security, yes, even to love.

Manon could remember with stark white clarity the moment she knew that she would never give herself completely again. No matter how much she loved, how good she felt, she would retain a little piece of her heart, a small sane corner of herself which would never disappear in a lover again. She had to be almost destroyed to know that sanity, and she was determined that of all of them, Zoe would rise triumphantly above such passions which had kept so many women down. "Zoe," she began softly, "you are too young to speak like this. You don't know what you're saying."

"I do, *ma mère*. And I know that others, some of them younger even than me, they feel the same."

"You speak of such behind convent walls?"

"The walls don't keep out everything," Zoe shrugged. "Emma told me of her own mother and of your mother, at least what she knew. She told me all about Uncle Simon and Aunt Cerise, and her brother Samuel and his wife, Matilde—"

"What did she say about them?"

"She spoke of the women, mostly. And their . . . passions."

"And little enough she would know of that!"

"She knew much of love," Zoe said, with some dignity, "and its value. And so, I will marry when it is time, if that is best, but I would like to know love once."

Manon stood up briskly, wiping her hands on the face-cloth on the gilded hook. "Love is as much a curse as it is a blessing, *cher,* and you will learn that quick enough. Each of us does. If you are fortunate, you will learn the lesson early, as I did." She strode to her closet and took a gown from within. "Now, Zoe, I think it is time you got yourself dressed and ready for business. We have a great many places to stop today, people to see."

"Am I to go with you?" Her daughter's eyes widened with pleasure.

"Of course. How can you know how dangerous the world is, if I don't show you? *Vite,* child, and cover your shoulders, or you'll be speckled as a hound pup by noon."

That day, and many thereafter, Zoe followed along behind Manon while she made her usual rounds of the offices of her investment bankers, her attorneys, and her factor for her crops. Almost every day also seemed to require a stop at a milliner, the dressmaker, or the cobbler, for Manon did not stint on what she liked to call "appearances." She was equally adamant that her daughter at all times look the proper young woman, and Zoe quickly learned how constraining that role could be.

"Not in red," Manon said as Zoe held up a gown to her chin for her mother's approval. "Not if Christ Himself came down from the Cross to tell me it was His favorite color. In pale pink, yes, or perhaps even a gray with touches of cherry about the neck and hem, but never in red—and oh, Zoe, put down that jet, you cannot wear black unless you're in mourning! Did they teach you nothing at Ursulines?"

Manon gazed at her daughter with tenderness. She seemed so achingly ripe; touch her and you'd leave thumb-prints, she looked that fresh from the oven, with her frank, open gaze.

Zoe sighed as the dressmaker measured out wide swathes of soft, dove gray, scarcely perked up at all when she pinned the touches of red-edged lace at the bodice. "Mother," Zoe said, "I see plenty of girls my age wearing more red than this. Some of them even wear red shirtwaists to the market! And black, too. Why with a string of single pearls—"

"They are not in your circumstances," Manon said cheer-fully, "and they might need to wear red to catch an eye. You don't, *cher,* I see the way men look at you when we pass on the *banquettes,* don't think I don't, and you don't need to flaunt yourself like some girls must. If anything, you need to soften a certain . . ." she paused and considered. "It's not really a hardness, daughter, for there's nothing stern about you at all, but certainly there is a . . . firmness to you, even for such a young age."

Zoe beamed at her mother's words.

Manon's maternal smile instantly changed to a look of

warning. "Don't be too happy about that, Zoe, for firm at fourteen is grim at forty."

The first week Zoe was with her mother, she met a score of politicians and men of power in the city. To each, her mother turned a smooth and polished hand, a warm smile, and each in turn paid her mother court, as though he wished for far more than simply an audience.

Zoe watched Manon move through men as though she were a sleek sailing ship in a crowded and choppy harbor. She dipped and bowed as if she were a supplicant, but ultimately, Manon seemed able to set her course around any number of lesser boats and never needed to drop anchor once to get her hold filled with what she wanted.

Zoe found herself wondering often what sort of man her father had been, to capture this woman for a brief space of time. He must have had something which most others lacked, for Manon never once seemed to consider any of these men more seriously than she considered which frock to choose for the opera.

There were times, when Zoe allowed herself to think on it, that she ached for what she had not known. Uncle Alex was dear, but what would it have been like to have known a father's protective arms, a father's advice, a father's scolding concern? Surely, a father would not have allowed her to spend a dozen years behind convent walls. *Jeunes filles* who had fathers must have a secret defense against all fear, she thought, a piece of a male heart within them which bolstered them with masculine courage when they needed to be strong.

Three generations of women with no father, Zoe realized, must leave those feminine hearts altered in irrevocable and frightening ways. Celisma, Manon, and me. Of all of us, only Emma had a father she could depend upon, and only Emma could accept the ultimate Father in his stead.

Zoe could recall vividly the one time Manon had told her about her father. Often she had asked, but her mother always brushed her questions away. But once, over the Christmas holidays, Zoe caught Manon in a reflective mood.

Most of the guests were gone, for it was the night before Christmas. Alex was due to arrive in the morning, but for now, Zoe had her mother in a rare moment of solitude. She came upon her polishing a trio of brass angels and setting them in boughs of greenery over the mantel.

Zoe came up behind her and hugged her gently. "Another year will soon be gone, *maman.*"

Manon sighed pensively. "I can scarcely believe it. You will be twelve in a few months. It seems only yesterday I chased you around the fountain at Ursulines, and your fat little knees looked like these angels' knees then. Now your long skirt covers whatever cherub is left in you, *cher.*" She turned and appraised Zoe, smiling. "Soon, you will put your hair up and you will be no more my *'tit chou.*"

"I wonder what my father is doing tonight," she said wistfully.

Manon turned and stared at her, almost angrily. "Why would you wonder such a thing? He has his own family, Zoe. I can assure you, he wastes no time wondering what we are doing."

"Are you so sure of that? Tell me again what he was like."

Manon was about to respond tartly, but something of dust and moonbeams in her daughter's eyes made her voice more gentle. "Why don't you tell me, child? You know it as well as I do."

Zoe began reciting, almost as though it were a nursery tale from her infancy, "He was a very handsome man, well connected, with a fine plantation across the river. He was married, of course—"

"Of course."

"With a family of his own. When his wife discovered that he loved you and me, she took him away. And you never saw him again."

"*Vraiment.*"

"Nor did I."

Manon watched her carefully, her eyes suddenly welling up despite her efforts to be brisk.

"Then I really don't have a father."

Manon took her into her arms. "No, you don't, *cher*. Neither do I. But a father isn't so very necessary in this world. I have discovered this truth, and so will you. He wanted to love us, I know this. His intention was to take care of us forever."

Zoe put her cheek on her mother's bosom and closed her eyes. From somewhere outside, she heard the faint sound of chapel bells, and the deep chimes soothed her sadness down to where her throat no longer ached. He intended to love us, she thought, and that is something, I suppose. But between women and their fathers, intention is the last thing that really matters.

On the Saturday after her daughter's arrival, Manon announced that Zoe would have a very special caller. Monsieur Henry Avery would be coming to their home to see his betrothed. Manon held out his card with a flourish. "He will expect to be received at two o'clock precisely, my darling, and asks that you consider a private audience for some small part of his stay."

"Why didn't he write to me directly?"

"Because that is not how these things are done. Now, of course, I'll stay with you for much of his visit, but I'll slip away frequently to fetch café and other tidbits—"

"Won't Dolly be serving?" Manon's cook, Dolly, was

single-handedly responsible for adding four pounds to Zoe's slender frame in the week she'd been home.

"She'll cook, but I'll serve. It's more gracious, especially when they know you have servants and don't *have* to serve them, but choose to, just to make them feel more welcome. And when I'm out of the room, you can see then what he's like. Now, I think your water blue silk would be best, don't you think? It makes you look so tall and poised."

Henry Avery arrived exactly on time. Zoe suspected that he had his carriage wait around the corner out of sight so that he could descend at their door not a moment late or early. A tall man with slight shoulders, he bowed deeply to Manon as she admitted him and then took the seat that she offered. Zoe watched him from the upstairs landing, keeping well out of sight as her mother had directed.

Zoe listened carefully as the initial pleasantries were exchanged. Manon directed the conversation, as usual, but Monsieur was clearly no novice at small talk. He kept his voice low, but the timbre of it commanded attention. Zoe found herself leaning forward slightly to catch what he said, and she saw that even Manon was paying more attention than usual. Finally she heard her mother call to her lightly, and she stepped out into the parlor in full view.

"My daughter, Zoe," Manon said to Monsieur Avery with pride. "You'll recognize her from her picture, *certainement.*" As he rose and offered a bow, she said, "Zoe, please come and help me welcome Monsieur Avery to our home."

Zoe walked forward and curtsied to the man, offering a hand for his kiss. She kept her voice low, sensing he would prefer it to a girlish giggle. "Monsieur," she said softly, "I have been looking forward to your visit."

Manon and Monsieur Avery beamed, though not at each other. Each gazed upon her with delight, until Manon felt she had been canonized with their approval. She was suddenly, horridly aware of her too-small shoulders, her large hands, and she wished her hair long enough to cover her breasts entirely.

They went on to speak of this and that, of New Orleans' opera season, of the price of sugar, of the influx of Haitians to the Quarter, of the weather, and when Zoe could, she ventured an opinion. Each time she spoke, her mother and Monsieur stopped and waited for her words, still beaming at her.

Zoe found it took little to keep pace in the conversation, and she examined this Henry Avery carefully. His hands were good, she liked those well enough. Large and capable, they looked as though they could hold a set of reins or a woman's body with some competence. What she could not abide were hands such as those she had seen on some of the men they visited this past week, hands which looked like they could hold nothing heavier than a stack of greenbacks or a ledger book.

His hair was a bit thin and light brown, as though his brain—for his brow was large and expansive—had sucked all the vitality right out of his scalp. His eyes were cool, his torso slender, and his legs long and ill-adjusted under her mother's tea table.

In a moment, Zoe guessed that this man was likely capable of devotion and had probably never known hardship or violence in his life.

"I'll be back in a breath," Manon was saying gaily, "with a plate full of some of Dolly's most sinful seductions."

Zoe flinched at her mother's lack of subtlety, but she relaxed when she saw that Monsieur was even more uncomfortable than she was. Once they were alone, he asked, "Have you enjoyed your first week *en famille?*"

She smiled as warmly as she could, consciously imitating her mother's glance. *"Sans doute, Monsieur,* but, of course, the good sisters are like *famille, n'est-ce pas?* I owe them every gratitude."

"Your words are to your credit," he said evenly. "So

many young women find the confines of the Ursulines difficult to bear beyond a certain age. But you did not?"

She hesitated a moment. Something told her to be scrupu-
lously candid with this man now, while she still could. She
let a small sigh escape and lowered her voice to a murmur.
"*Vraiment, Monsieur,* little of life does creep over or under
those high walls. For a decade, I scarcely noticed. But in the
last year, they were growing higher and thicker with every
month."

He grinned, an unfortunate positioning of mouth and jaw
which made his ears jut out slightly away from his head. "I
am happy you can tell me this," he said, lowering his tone
to match her own. "It bodes well for our friendship."

She dropped her head shyly. "And yet I have been told
you want a young woman of pious modesty. Of the most
conservative demeanor. Perhaps I am not the right choice for
you, Monsieur, for in all honesty, there were many with the
Sisters more pious than I." She watched him from under her
lashes, thinking that if he bolted now, she might almost feel
relieved. Almost.

But to her surprise, he only leaned a little closer to her
and whispered, "Let this be our first secret together, then,
Mademoiselle. It is true I asked for such a bride. But it is
not true that I necessarily hold these qualities more important than any other." He winked conspiratorially at her. "I
think if you confessed to a penchant for blasphemy and a
healthy skepticism, I would respect you nonetheless." When
she returned his grin, he added, "And if you also confessed
that Mother Church alone did not provide you with sufficient
passion for your soul, I could only applaud your vitality. For
that is, indeed, what I find most attractive in you, Zoe. May
I call you Zoe, when we are in private?"

She nodded, mesmerized.

"Your vitality. It is a powerful force in a woman. And if
you have half the *joie de vivre* that your mother has, you will

561

bring much delight to any man who is fortunate enough to win you."

Slightly stung, Zoe said, "My mother? You find her full of—life?"

"But certainly."

"And yet, you did not offer *her* a proposal."

Now Monsieur Avery laughed aloud, not troubling to lower his voice. "I see you have all a woman's instincts, even at this tender age. No, my Zoe, I did not." He peered at her cannily. "And do you wish I would?"

Flustered, she turned half away, seeking the tray of pastries to give her something to do with her hands. All of a sudden, she wanted him gone. As though she had read her mind from behind the walls, Manon swooped into the room, bearing a fresh pot of coffee. She bent low over both of them, her eyes moving first over his face, then over her daughter's.

"Zoe, perhaps Monsieur would like you to play for him. That new piece you were practicing yesterday? Monsieur, Zoe has the lightest touch on the piano, all the Sisters praised her deftness. Though her repertoire is not as yet extensive, she seems to have an instinctive grasp of music. Zoe?" Manon gestured to the black piano which stood, ignored and largely ornamental, in the corner of the dining room.

"Perhaps at my next visit," Monsieur Avery said smoothly. "I don't want to overstay my welcome."

Zoe rose so quickly that Manon frowned at her.

"Oh, surely you don't have to be going just yet," Manon said to their guest, but her hands were reaching for his coat. "We could pull out that old stereopticon and look at my pictures of Paris, France."

"That'll give us something to look forward to next time," he said, pulling on his coat and moving towards the door. Zoe floated after him, her hands steadfastly pinned behind her back. She felt her mother's hand on her arm and was drawn forward.

"Shall we say next week?" Manon was saying. "Assuming, of course, that Zoe has no other plans?"

Both of them turned to her then and waited. Zoe glanced up at Monsieur's gaze and flushed. "No, Monsieur, I've no other plans."

"Ah, it's settled then," Manon said graciously. "And perhaps next time, we can persuade Zoe to make some of her luscious lemon tarts for you, you'll never taste better."

"I look forward to it," Monsieur Avery bowed deeply to them both. And then he was gone.

Zoe let out a huge sigh of air, suddenly aware she had been holding her breath in as tightly as her belly.

"Come, child," Manon said gently, leading her into the kitchen and sitting her down with a cup of chamomile before her. For a long moment, her mother only gazed at her, waiting. Finally she asked, "And how did you find him, *cher?*"

"He seems like a good man," Zoe said carefully. "Tall. Light enough. Not much to his shoulders. Reminds me a little of Ichabod Crane."

"Who?" Manon wasn't much of a reader. "Oh well, never mind. Did you think him intelligent?"

"Yes."

"Charming? Witty?"

"I suppose so. Really, we scarcely talked at all—"

"Oh, Zoe, you didn't go all timid on him, did you? I told you to plan several topics of conversation—"

"No, Mother, I did not act shy." She allowed herself a small smile. "Neither did he."

Manon instantly saw the smile and beamed. "Ah, it went well, then. And next week will go even better, you'll see, my dear. By this time next year, I daresay you'll no longer be wondering what sort of fool your mother is."

"I daresay," Zoe said quietly, sipping at her tea.

Manon watched Zoe carefully that first month, waiting for signs of rebellion. Monsieur Avery came and went punctually once each week, and both seemed to find their time together pleasant. Zoe volunteered little about her feelings, but Manon assumed she had learned the habit of privacy in the convent, and she did not press her to reveal her heart.

In short, no rebellion seemed to be fermenting. It was true, Zoe sought out Alex for long walks and talks when he visited, but he either supported her destiny or helped her to see the value there, for she bid him adieu with a small slice of serenity which fed her most of the week until his return.

For his part, Alex liked Henry Avery, once he adjusted to the idea of Zoe's betrothal. The men shared a certain gentleness between them—a gentleness which was the one quality which quietly alarmed Manon. Would Monsieur be yet a second male in her household who would need help with the fiscal management of his life? She prayed not. The man seemed stable, whatever else he might not be. And Zoe seemed not to notice or care about those lackings.

But Manon did not let up her surveillance. And as May turned hot and steamy that next year, she was glad she had not.

One night as the temperature rose past midnight, Manon entered Zoe's room to offer her a chilled drink of lemon water. The child had not been sleeping well in this heat and often needed to nap during the day. Though fever was not such a danger these days, Manon could never quite rest easy when someone she loved approached the summer months in less than vigorous health.

She slipped into the dark room and went to the windows, feeling for a breeze. The soft lace curtains billowed gently back in her face, and she could smell the orange tree in the courtyard, already wreathed in heavy perfume.

She fingered the lace absently in the shadows. It was lovely and tasteful, like most of the furnishings Zoe chose to have around her. The girl had a discriminating taste for one so young. Unerringly, she seemed to select those colors, fabrics, and textures which spoke of quality, graciousness, and a quiet wealth. Such taste would serve her well as Mistress of the Avery estate, Manon mused, as she turned to see if her daughter slept on.

The shadows of the room made it seem as though Zoe were completely under the covers, highly unlikely in this heat. Manon fumbled for the lamp in the dark, holding her hand before it so as not to wake Zoe unnecessarily.

The wide four-poster rice bed was empty. The coverlet had been pulled neatly to the chin of the pillows, left slightly rumpled as though to suggest a body within, but no daughter slept there.

Manon quickly carried the lamp out the door, headed towards the privy. If Zoe had not been content to use the chamber pot, she must be feeling ill, indeed. Perhaps something stronger than lemon water would be needed after all—

But the lamp outside the back door was there on the hook. The privy was dark and plainly deserted. Now Manon went to the kitchen, to the parlor upstairs, and finally downstairs to the damp basement.

No Zoe.

Manon sat for a moment on the side of her bed, thinking frantically. Where would a young woman of fourteen go at such an hour? She had few friends and no lover, save her betrothed. In her wildest imagination, Manon could not picture Zoe running to the arms of Henry Avery.

No, Zoe had gone somewhere, and possibly not for the first time. Somehow, Manon guessed that the window in her room was open for other reasons besides the breeze.

She went back to Zoe's room with the lamp. Somewhere, on the dresser, in her drawers, in the armoire, even on her bedside, there must be a clue as to her destination. She hunted quickly but thoroughly, with the instincts of a mother not so far away from the same heartbeats of her daughter. There was a time, after all, she thought swiftly, when she had thought of crawling out the same window, to slip away in the night from tiresome Alex . . . but where had she wanted to go?

Manon's eyes widened as she realized that no clue would be as telling as her memory. She hurried upstairs, pinned up her hair, grabbed her shawl, and went out the door.

Carriages were not plentiful at any hour on her small street, but once she reached the Quarter, it was easy to hail one, even after two in the morning. She called out the destination to the driver and sat back, thinking. What if Zoe were not there? What if she *were* there, worse yet? As they neared Congo Square, she could hear the drums rising in the night, and she called to the driver to let her off well before they got to the edge of the park.

A ring of torches marked the area well, lest any casual passersby stumble onto what was the most secret public ritual in New Orleans. Secret it was, because every citizen agreed not to speak of it except behind their hands. Public it was, because it took place every Sunday evening, with full knowledge and grudging support of the city fathers, whatever the city mothers might say.

Congo Square was weekly host to the black dancers and their voodoo rituals. Since well before the War Between the States, the slaves had gathered to dance there, in the very heart of the city, on North Rampart Street. A large cannon sat in the center of the two city squares studded with large sycamores. The cannon fired at nine o'clock in the old days

566

to warn the slaves of curfew. Before the War, any slave caught on the streets after nine was arrested and whipped, as a precaution against rebellion.

Manon had heard the tales and seen the dancers many times. Most young women of the city had, at one time or another, sneaked to the white picket fences surrounding Congo Square, either by themselves or with their friends, to spy on the black dancers as they crowded the small park. While a few white folk and tourists gaped, they did the Calinda and the Bamboula and their other dances, mostly the tamer ones without much voodoo in evidence. In the old days, they might have worn red loincloths, ankle bells and knee rings, and all the cast-off finery from their masters.

Now, though, the dancers mostly wore elaborate costumes with wide colorful skirts, and no curfew ended the dances. Past midnight, and the pulsing beat continued; the drums were the same, through the years. The drums never changed.

And one thing more . . . the current queen of the dancers had always been, would always be, the most beautiful they could find, the haughtiest, the most wild. Since the War and even before it, she must never be a slave, she must always be a free woman of color who need fear neither curfew nor the worst laws of the *code noir*.

Manon passed through the picket gate, led forward by the compelling pulse of the drums. Letting her shawl dangle from her waist, she came to the edge of the crowd and shoved her way forward, ignoring the stares and mumbled complaints of those on either side, more than three hundred she guessed.

An old man sat astride a cylindrical drum, his back bent, his head down, both hands beating out a rhythm, faster and faster. Another man held a calabash with two strings, and at the end of its fingerboard was the crudely carved figure of a man or a god, Manon couldn't tell which, but it seemed to her suddenly obscene. The music was harsh, cacophonous, and brutal.

"*Danse Calinda!*" the singers cried, "*Badoum! Badoum!*"

Manon brushed her hair back from her brow, sweating in the steamy night with the dozens of bodies about her, too close to breathe easy. She tried to see around the circle of watchers, but the shoulders were too crowded. She moved once more, to have a clearer view, and the dancers were suddenly right before her.

A tribe of men and women were moving in the middle of the crowd, all of them barefoot and bare-legged, the women with their skirts pinned up high on their hips. The men, all shades of black to yellow, danced and screamed and shrieked to the drums, leaping high into the air and twisting on their knees before the women in almost a parody of love. The women wiggled and shook their bodies, swaying like snakes, but their feet never left the ground. There were a few white women among them, but most of the dancers were various hues of colored, some of them black as the African night. Many of the onlookers played pebble-filled gourds, long whistles, or violins made from cigar boxes. A few fortunates blew on dilapidated cornets or trombones. On the sidelines, children danced in imitation of their elders, and vendors cried out their rice cakes, beer, and pralines. Some sold good luck charms and bad *gris-gris,* and over all was the primitive beat of the drums.

A beautiful yellow wench stood on a box in the center of the dancers, swaying to the music, her eyes closed, her head thrown back over her shoulders as though her neck were broken. She cried out rhythmically with the music, punctuating the song with weird shrieks and moans. Her *tignon* was bright red, even brighter as she turned and it shone in the firelight from the dozens of fires burning around the edge of the circle. The gold hoops in her ears hung almost to her shoulders, and she wore only a single skirt of several dozen ed handkerchiefs. Her bosom was bare and glistened with sweat. Around her shoulders writhed a long, black snake, and she took its head and rubbed it against her cheek at intervals in the song.

Danse Calinda, badoum, badoum!
Danse Calinda, badoum, badoum!

Manon moved first to one place in the circle then to another, and finally she froze in one place, staring.

There was Zoe inside the circle of dancers, swaying to the music with her eyes closed.

Now the dance was reaching a crescendo, and a few of the men kneeled before the woman on the altar. She reached behind her and took up a bottle of tafia, the strong sugar rum. She tipped it to her mouth, filled her cheeks, and sprayed each man in the face by turns, while the crowd shouted with glee and excitement.

Manon had seen this done before, and knew the men on their knees believed that this was one way to cure themselves of a spell put on them by one woman or another. Each one held his face in his hands and writhed, moaning in either pain or ecstasy, she couldn't tell which. Meanwhile, she began to elbow her way closer to where Zoe stood.

Before she could reach her daughter, a black man danced up close to Zoe and stood before her, twisting and writhing silently. She opened her eyes and saw him, almost flinching back with the power of his gaze. He took Zoe's hand and drew her into the circle of dancers. Manon fought now to get to her, but the crowd held her in place, surging forward to see the young white girl join the moving, swaying bodies.

Zoe dropped the man's hand, but followed him around the circle, matching her movements to his. His body was dark and glistening, strong and alien-looking, even in the night. Zoe danced behind him, swaying her slender body, her head twisting from side to side, her mouth half-open in rapt concentration, her light skirt whirling about her bare legs and feet. She looked more white than the few white folks there, Manon saw, and certainly more beautiful. More fragile.

Manon reached the edge of the circle now and was about to snatch Zoe's shoulder and grab her back into her arms, when her daughter suddenly turned closer to the black dancer, gripped his hand, and pulled him to her, moving her hips close to his, then pushed him away. The voice of the crowd rose in a savage thrill at her gestures and then moaned as one body, when the man turned and danced directly in front of Zoe, almost grazing her belly with his. Zoe danced in one place now, her eyes closed, her head still, only her breasts and her hips shook in unison, her slender white arms out for balance. Her mouth, her face, looked almost as though she were in pain.

Manon pulled back into the crowd so that Zoe would not see her. She knew now what she must do. No mother's arms would keep Zoe from Congo Square, perhaps not even keep her from such a man. At fourteen, it was almost too late to save her.

Manon remembered swiftly, as though in a fever, the few times she had danced the dances and felt the heat of the bodies around her, and certainly no one could have stopped *her* on those nights, if she had wanted to go into the shadows with one of them. Only her own vision of her future had kept her from such a step.

Zoe's future was set, Manon reassured herself with a firm jaw, whether or not she saw it clearly. She must be made to want it, for New Orleans had a hundred seductions to offer, even if she were forbidden Congo Square.

A pause in the music, the black dancer reached for Zoe, but she pulled away, as though awakened suddenly from a heady dream. She snatched her hand from his, almost angrily, and Manon slid even further back in the crowd. Still watching, she saw Zoe turn from the man, push her way through the shoulders, emerge on the fringes of the mob, and move swiftly for the gate. Her daughter raised one hand and expertly hailed a passing carriage, as though she had done it a hundred nights in her life. As Zoe was climbing into the carriage, Manon stopped another one and barely reached the cottage ahead of her daughter.

From the silence of her bedroom, Manon heard Zoe softly climb into her open window, only a creak from the old sill giving her away. She sat up most of the rest of the night, watching the moon move through dark clouds over the city. When despair took her hard by the heart, she lit a single candle and gazed at herself in the mirror. Whites said that the beauty of the quadroon did not last. She had seen many who once were lovely, who once had the love of some Monsieur as she once had. But then the dark hair faded into shades of brown and red and grew more crinkled. Streaked with gray. The once-bright eyes dimmed, the irises stained with yellow. The lips thinned and grew dry and chapped. And Monsieur might still be generous, but his visits became less and less frequent. He no longer stayed the night.

She moistened her lips with rosewater, reaching for a bloom by her bedside. She crushed the red petals and rubbed them on her lips. They were still full and enticing, would likely be so for a few more years, and then her power over men, her daughter, her life would ebb like the tide. She could waste no time.

By dawn, she knew what she must do.

It was highly unusual for a mother to leave a daughter alone in the house with her betrothed. Manon knew it, even as she suggested the possibility to Zoe. She also knew instinctively that Zoe would relish the opportunity to welcome Monsieur Avery in her own way and feel, for at least that afternoon as the mistress of her own affairs.

"There's no help for it," Manon told her, feigning a distracted worry. "I must see to this account today, and it's too late to get word to Monsieur to delay his coming. You'll simply have to manage, *cher,* and I know you'll do fine. But for heavens sake, don't tell the man I'm not in the house."

"Where shall I say you are?" Zoe asked casually. She had been calmly detached since the night before, as though she had made some decision in her heart, if not in her head.

"Say I'm indisposed. He'll not ask the particulars. Let him think I'm just in the next room, even if I won't get out of my bed."

"What if he asks to make his courtesies to you?"

"He won't, I tell you. He's too much of a gentleman."

"That's true," Zoe said quietly.

Manon narrowed her eyes at her, but she said nothing more.

The little cottage on Saint Ann was little changed, to Manon's eyes, in the fifteen years since she'd seen it last. In fact, strangely enough, it did not seem older by a day. Usually, she might have expected to see rot around the windows and doors, the yellowing of the whitewash up the walls, the general sagging of frame that would indicate the natural obsolescence of any building. But the cottage of Marie LaVeau seemed unaltered by time.

She pulled the cord at the door and heard a bell ring somewhere within. A low shuffling step came close, and then the door swung open, revealing a shadowed coolness inside.

Manon was instantly frightened, for she did not know what to expect. Marie LaVeau was dead, that much she knew. All in the city knew she lay in the St. Louis Cemetery, and that her daughter, Marie, had taken up where the high priestess left off her work. But it was also rumored that Marie, the daughter, was far more powerful than Marie, the mother. Moreover, the blacks in New Orleans, who knew more of the voodooienne than any other group, believed that Marie the Second was more inclined to evil.

As the door swung open, Manon stepped back slightly, not at all sure she should have come. A tall slender woman stared at her, a woman whose eyes seemed to penetrate Manon's most secret places with little effort. She wore a red and yellow silk *tignon* and a haughty expression. Manon knew instantly that this was Marie LaVeau, the Second. And for some reason, it did not surprise her at all that Marie herself opened the door.

"Come in, *cher*," the woman said, her voice low and commanding. "I know why you have come."

Manon felt a warmth start in her throat, brim over into her eyes. She fought back a sob of relief with effort.

Marie led Manon to a chair in a dimly lit room, not a parlor, really, more like an antechamber for lesser visitors. "The secrets told to me are not so very mysterious, really," Marie was saying. "Many believe I have second sight. Perhaps this is true. But I did not need second sight to know of your pain and the reasons for it. The grapevine still serves me well."

Manon took her seat and steadied herself with her hands. "You heard of my daughter's—dance?"

"Of course, that news reached me quickly enough, but already I knew of her betrothal. Already I know of Monsieur Henry."

Manon nodded, accepting this truth. Years past, the slaves always had a secret underground means of communication, unknown and undetected by the white masters. In the world of slaves, the whites had no secrets, and little had changed since slavery ended. Now the servants shared the same secrets with even more freedom and ease. No doubt, Manon realized, Marie LaVeau could choose to know more about Monsieur Avery than even his own mother knew, if she had a need for the knowledge.

"How can I help you, Madame?" Marie asked calmly.

"My daughter must marry Monsieur," Manon said, suddenly calm herself. There was something about the woman's voice which swept away all considerations. "She is betrothed. He is a good man from a fine family, and she will be happy—"

"Of this you are certain?"

"Of this, I will make certain," Manon replied. "I know her well, she is already made happy when he is with her, I believe, and though she is young, she has an old heart."

"She did not display such an old heart at the dance, I understand," Marie said softly.

Manon pulled herself up with dignity. "Are you suggesting that my daughter is unworthy of Monsieur?"

Marie thought for a moment, pulling gently at her lower lip. "She has a certain fire. Perhaps it is he who is unworthy of her."

"That was a small rebellion of youth. Many young white girls go to see the dances and it doesn't ruin their lives. It doesn't mean they're wantons. I know my daughter. She is as the nuns made her. In time, she will see the truth of it, and until then, I mean to save her from a senseless tragedy."

"You think she may take an unsuitable lover?"

Manon snorted with derision. "*Mais absolument non!* I only fear that she will give the appearance of wantonness, and so ruin her chances."

"So you wish my help to give her the appearance of piousness, of happiness with her betrothal. Is this your wish?"

Manon nodded. "Only until she comes to herself once more, which will not take long, I'm sure. She is only a little restless right now, surely you remember the age, Madame? I, myself, danced at Congo Square one night, but I was not betrothed to an Avery at the time. I cannot let her ruin her opportunity. If she knew, she would thank us both, I am certain."

"Do you wish, then, for me to keep her only from Congo Square?"

Manon reflected for a moment. "No. No, that is not quite enough, I think. I wish for you to insure that the wedding will take place as planned."

Marie LaVeau turned away slightly with a grimace. "This is much harder, *cher*, much harder than simply taking away a young girl's stomach for wild nights. For of course, the *gris-gris* must now also bind Monsieur as well as your daughter."

"Then do so," Manon said firmly. "Bind them both."

"Once you came to see my mother, *c'est vrai?* But you did not accept her powers."

"I did accept the truth of her power," Manon said, amazed that Marie would remember that single night of panic. She could scarcely remember even taking the herbal packet and emptying her belly, so long ago did it seem. A dim, gray dream. "But I could not, finally, find the courage to take her potion."

"And this child is the result of your failure of courage that night?"

"Even so." Manon smiled. "I have never regretted that I could not kill her."

"That is well," Marie nodded gently, "that the child in some way owes her soul, then, to *maman*. This will make it easier, I think."

Manon did not know which *maman* she meant, but she did not hesitate. "So you will do it? You will make the wedding happen?"

Marie shrugged. "If this is what you wish."

She stood and gestured Manon to follow her. From the anteroom, they went to a back chamber which was fitted with the trappings of the voodooienne. Marie prepared a small altar by spreading a table with a clean linen cloth, and upon it, she placed a framed picture of St. Joseph. Before this, she set a bowl filled to the top with white sand. She wrote the names, Zoe d'Irlandais and Monsieur Henry Avery on two bits of paper and buried these in the sand. Then in the sand, she placed two blue candles, thick ones which would burn for hours. She fetched two small dolls from the cupboard and set them before Manon.

"Her hair is dark?"

"More black than midnight," Manon said.

"I had heard it said," Marie replied, taking a bit of black hair and pinning it to the head of the female doll. "And his is—?"

"Brown, I suppose. Lightish. He has little left of it on top."

Marie smiled and took three strands only of brown hair, laying them gently on the head of the male doll. Then she bound their tiny hands together with white satin ribbon, and set them on the altar before the bowl with the names and the candles.

Next she brought a dish of salt and a bottle of brandy. "You must light the candles," she said to Manon, holding out a burning taper.

"Will she know of my visit?" Manon asked, suddenly hesitant.

"Perhaps. In time. But if she learns of it, she will not mind so much. That is the way of happiness after it comes, yes?"

Manon lit the two blue candles.

"Now you must kneel with me," Marie said.

They knelt before the altar, the dish of salt between them on the floor, the brandy to one side.

"Saint Joseph, pray for us!" Marie shouted suddenly, loud enough to make the canary in the cage by the window squeak in alarm.

Manon flinched, but she kept still.

"Saint Michael, pray for us!" Marie cried out once more. *"Dani! Dani! Blanc Dani!"* She shuddered and closed her eyes, breathing raggedly as though she were laboring. "Saint Peter, help us! *Liba! Liba! L'a commandé!"*

576

At the voodooienne's call to a pagan god, Manon shifted nervously. Suddenly Emma's face, teaching her the catechism, swam before her eyes, and she moaned softly.

Marie glanced at her, narrowing her eyes. "You are not changing your mind again, are you? You regret? Do not insult the gods again, *cher!*"

"No, no," Manon panted, almost in pain. "Go on, go on, regret nothing."

"Until death?" Marie asked her. "Until death? Say it!"

"Until death," Manon whispered.

"Louder!"

"Until death!"

Still kneeling, Marie uncorked the bottle of brandy and passed it to her. "Drink. Drink until your throat burns with your vow."

Manon took a great gulp of the brandy, her eyes filling with tears at the searing pain.

Marie pulled her up, giving her a push towards the altar as she did so. She placed a handful of salt in Manon's fist, closing her trembling fingers around it. "Now toss this in the caper's flames," she murmured.

Manon released her fingers slowly, letting the salt dribble like sand over the fire.

"Good," Marie sighed. "It is good."

She left the room and came back again quickly carrying two saucers. Each had half of a black snake cooked and cut in two, divided between the two plates. She took up a piece of the snake and put it to Manon's lips. "Eat."

Manon retched involuntarily, pulling away.

"You must eat, or the spell is not finished."

"I cannot," Manon said faintly, twisting her head away.

Marie glowered furiously. "Did you think the magic came so easily, you fool? Did you think you would have to pay only gold for such a gift? Eat this, I say, or bad luck will plague you and the child for the rest of your days!"

Manon opened her lips, closed her eyes, and managed to swallow the piece of cooked snake, gagging rhythmically.

Marie, watching her, calmly ate most of the pieces on the other saucer.

She went out of the room again and came back carrying yet another bowl, and this time Marie thought she might faint. Inside the bowl was a white, maggotty-looking substance, full almost to the brim and sprinkled with some green herb.

"Oh Sweet Mary," Manon gasped, "I cannot—"

Marie snorted in disgust. "It is only macaroni, you goose, with a little parsley. You must take it to the old oak tree at Congo Square tonight, at midnight, and place it within the roots which spread over the ground towards the area where the dance takes place. In that way, you will have given the gods something in exchange for the loss of your daughter."

Manon took the bowl, her head bowed in shame.

Once more Marie shouted at her, "Regrets! You have always regrets, Madame! I do not think you have the stomach for this!"

Manon shook her head slowly. "I do. I have no regrets. Is it done?"

"It is done. She will wed Monsieur before the year is out."

Marie lifted her head in shock. "But she is still so young. Barely fifteen she will be at the end of the year. I had told him, two years or more betrothal—"

"The spell will not last that long. She will wed before the year is out or she will never wed at all."

Manon clutched the bowl to her belly and closed her eyes. "Well then, she will be wed."

When Manon returned to the house, she sought Zoe in her small room, finding her writing out a letter in her perfect, neat hand at her secretary. Zoe casually set the paper in the drawer at her mother's approach.

"And did it go well with Monsieur?" Manon asked, equally casually. She took off her hat and smoothed her hair, wiping the moisture off her brow. Some nausea still lingered, and she willed herself to ignore it.

"He did not come," Zoe said calmly.

Manon sat down suddenly on her daughter's feather coverlet. "He did not? Why, whatever—"

"He sent round a note early on, right after you left, actually, with his apologies. Evidently, some business or other entangled him. He asked to come again next week at the regular time." She smiled pertly, reaching for a gaily decorated box by her desk. "He sent these *bonbons,* as consolation. They're lovely, *maman,* try one with the hazelnuts. If he cancels again next week with the same apology, I won't be too disappointed."

Manon felt her teeth grate with the effort to keep her anger checked. "That remark is unkind and stupid, besides. If I were stood up by my betrothed, I would certainly ask myself what I had done to deserve such indifference. Did your last meeting with him go so badly?"

"Not at all," Zoe said, shrugging and rummaging in the candy box. "We are getting on quite well, I think, but he had other things to do. Why worry, *ma mère?* It's too hot to get yourself in a froth over—"

"One of us best worry, my pet, and if you refuse to see the danger here, it must be me, I suppose." She snatched the candy box away from Zoe and settled the lid on it firmly. "You say your last meeting went well? Not well enough to make the man hasten back for seconds, it seems to me. Not well enough to make him beg for a meeting sooner than a week away. Doesn't it strike you as odd that he should, so early on in your courtship, be so tepid about its progression?"

Zoe frowned and flounced down on the bed. "Oh Mother, who cares? He's tepid about everything, so far as I can see. The man is not given to passion, so I don't take it personally."

Manon appraised her daughter with a new and careful eye. There was a certain coldness to her that she had not seen before, a sure sense of herself that belied her years. This cool self-sufficiency would, Manon realized, either defend her against all pain forever, or cause her enough to make her wish she never had a heart at all.

"So. Then he will come next week. I hope you make him welcome, Zoe."

Zoe smiled thinly. "I was just writing to him now, to say that I would count the days."

That night, Manon was haunted by thoughts of Marie La-Veau and her voodoo gods. She woke in the night, chased out of sleep by the red glowing eyes of the black demons and the pale weeping eyes of the white spirits Marie had conjured. Guilt twisted her heart until she sat up and lit a candle to dispel the shadows. It was as though she could hear her mother's voice from the corner, where the palms brushed against the outside of the house. Where is your mother's heart, the scratchings seemed to ask, for Zoe, for Zoe, for Zoe?

Manon put her head in her open palms and breathed deeply, willing the fear and guilt away. She knew she was taking a terrible risk. She knew her daughter was a good girl in her soul, but she also knew she was capable—wasn't any woman?—of throwing away her future for some ephemeral passion or even just the promise of it. Some might have that luxury. Some who were rich. And white. Zoe did not have that luxury, she had only her beauty, which would not last. And her mother's determination, which would.

Manon leaped from the bed as though something within burned her legs, and she strode about the room, growing more angry by the moment at herself, at her doubts, at the shadows. She thought back to David, and she shivered as she remembered how much of herself she had given up to be what he wanted. When a man and a woman lie down together, she thought, he's thinking of winning and she's thinking of love, and so she will always lose. Always. I must protect her, she vowed to the shadows, to the scratching palms—I *will* protect her. For she is all I have, all I can never hope to be. I cannot let her throw herself away!

She went to the window and shoved it open, searching the dark for some answer. In the distance, she could see the lights of New Orleans winking and shimmering in the breeze. Out there, a thousand people cast away their nights on pleasure, only to have empty hands to show for it come morning. She looked down at her own hands. They were pale, strong, and handsome with capable, tapering fingers. Not Zoe's hands. Her daughter's hands were more slender, more fragile, as though made to hold a quill or a brush. Manon's hands were meant to hold reins.

She glanced over to the palm leaves scraping the cottage walls. It was only the wind, not the voice of fate. Not the voice of the Holy Mother, either. Let her come and raise this child, if she could do it better! Manon knew what she must do, and she also understood that her guilt must be silenced to do it well. Zoe would one day thank her for this, she vowed, and she shut the window firmly. She blew out the candle and was, within moments, asleep once more.

Manon waited a week before sending her own letter to Monsieur Avery. It took her nearly that long to decide exactly how such a note should be worded. She frowned over the paper, biting her quill in concentration. Delicacy was necessary. Without saying that Zoe needed to wed for any particular reason, Manon must somehow let him know that her daughter wanted to wed—despite the fact that, when asked, she might not admit to such a desire.

In fact, Manon's lips twisted wryly, she likely would refuse even to consider the possibility.

But the note was finally written and sent, and Manon believed that one line in particular would move Henry Avery to unquestioning speed. "I find that my daughter is far more mature than I'd previously considered," Manon wrote carefully, "and her passionate nature should not go unnurtured."

After all, Manon told herself firmly, this was hardly an untruth. Zoe was, indeed, far more mature than she seemed, and she did have a passionate nature. Anyone watching her dance could see as much.

Manon was much relieved to receive Monsieur's prompt reply. He would be at the cottage in five days, he wrote, and he would formally propose to Zoe at that time, suggesting a winter wedding date, to be celebrated soon after the cane harvest.

That night, Manon offered Zoe a glass of muscat wine after dinner, suggesting they take it into the music room.

Zoe raised her eyebrows. "Wine? You've never let me drink spirits before, *maman.* What is the occasion?"

"The occasion is your great good fortune," Manon said giddily. "To have such a fine man as your betrothed, to be planning such a wonderful life together—"

"But there's nothing new in this," Zoe said, taking the glass from her and walking ahead to the chaise in the music room. "You mean you're just relieved that I have accepted his visits? He's a nice-enough man, I guess, no reason to offend him. I must say, I haven't yet decided whether to accept his suit altogether, but as you say, there is plenty of time to decide." She sat on the chaise, leaning back and putting her feet up as though she were already a lady of leisure. The glass of muscat, half-empty, dangled rather precariously from her hand.

Manon stifled her annoyance. Her daughter suddenly seemed to her to be almost insufferable. Gazing about her with the clear and competent eyes of youth, she looked as though she never would, never could doubt her own judgment. She had power. And her power lay in her infallible self-esteem. A self-esteem which had never once had to confront reality.

"Occasionally, he bores me," Zoe was saying quietly. "That worries me some, because I have to think if he bores me now, he might flat put me to sleep after a few years of marriage. Don't you think it's important, *maman,* that one's husband seem interesting, at least at first? I can't imagine what we would talk about after a time—"

"You likely will not talk much to him at all," Manon said, "at least not after a few years. Most wives don't, *vraiment.* You will talk of your children, of course, and the neighbors. Perhaps his business, if you are fortunate. But wives and husbands do not marry for talk, Zoe, they marry for a hundred other reasons."

"That doesn't sound very romantic," Zoe said, taking another sip of her wine.

"One doesn't marry for romance," Manon replied easily. "One marries for children and land and houses and friends and having someone by your side when you are sick or old or ugly."

"Rather like an investment, you mean. You do without what you want now, on the belief you'll want it later and won't be able to have it, unless you put yourself aside early on."

Manon frowned and rolled her eyes. "It's not attractive for one so young to be so cynical. Marriage *is* rather like money in the bank, yes, but is that such a bad thing to have?"

"Not if money in the bank makes you happy," Zoe said,

tipping her glass up and finishing it. "But perhaps I'll feel differently in a year or two, who knows."

"Actually, there's really no reason to wait that long. You're quite mature enough, I think, to marry now." Manon glanced away to make her words more casual.

Zoe sat up and set her glass down on the side table. "What are you saying, *maman?*"

"*Monsieur* Henry does not wish to wait. He wants to set a wedding date now. He has suggested the end of this year, after cane harvest."

"But we agreed I would have time to consider him."

"You have had."

"I've only been out of Ursulines for two months!"

"And you'll still have six months before the wedding. Anyway, it will take that long to make all the arrangements and to get your new home finished for you. You'll find that the time goes quite quickly, there's so much to do. We'll go to the Avery estate in a few weeks, so that you can see the plans and the building site—"

Zoe stood up and began to pace. "I don't want to marry!"

Manon steeled herself. She rose to catch her daughter as she strode up and down. "Of course, you do, you silly fool. It might not be the ideal time, but it is the ideal match. Sometimes we must compromise to have what we want."

"But I don't know that I want him!"

"You have all but told him that you do by accepting his attentions. Listen to me, Zoe, stop this pacing—"

"I will run away if you make me!"

Manon slapped her daughter lightly, pulling her stiff arms close and shaking her slightly. "To what? To where will you run? To Congo Square at midnight?"

Zoe gasped and tried to pull away, but Manon pulled her closer, into her arms. "Did you think I'd be like other blissfully blind mothers in this town? I can't afford to be, and you can't afford to be like those daughters. I'm not white, and

584

either are you, and a mistake like that won't be so easily ignored!"

"I only went once," Zoe whispered. "The girls in the convent told me about it, they said everyone went at least once. I just wanted to see what it was all about before I was buried away forever."

"And so you saw. And you were seen. Do you think you're so magnificent that any man will overlook such a shameful display?"

Zoe moaned painfully and covered her face with her hands, stiffening with shock. Manon held her daughter's unyielding body and felt every tremble in her own belly. "Stop this now," she said low, her voice intense. "Do you think I don't know how you feel? Do you think I can't understand? I *do, cher,* and that is why you must do as I say. You are not a wanton, not a bad girl, but you will ruin your life forever if you seem so. It doesn't matter what you are, it only matters what you *seem* to be! You must accept this man and accept him quickly. You are lovely now, it's true, but you have little to offer on the marriage market. You will have even less if you ruin your reputation. This is the best match I can make for you, and I'll make no other, I swear it. If you do not wed Monsieur Avery before the year is out, you must look elsewhere for support. I'll not hand over half of all I worked for in these dozen years, only for you to turn your pretty cheek and humiliate us both. You will ruin your chances and mine, Zoe! He knows you are the daughter of a *placée* and he overlooks it, do you know how rare that is? He's a good man, a kind man, and he'll take care of you—"

"But I don't love him!" her daughter wailed in anguish.

Manon pulled her closer and pressed her cheek to Zoe's, fighting back her own tears. "You mean you don't *want* him! You're speaking of passion, *cher,* and passion is only an illusion. It doesn't last! It's a dream, like youth, like desire. You cannot live your life for it. You cannot make such an important choice based on it. I want so much more for you!"

585

"You said you wanted me to marry for love," Zoe sobbed "you said it that day in the garden. You said you'd never as your daughter to settle for less!"

"And it will come to you in time. You will grow to lov him in more ways than you now believe possible. Zoe, sto this and look at me!"

Zoe contorted her face, stopped her weeping, and drew back from her mother, but she kept her eyes on her lips.

"You are learning now," Manon said gently, "what ever woman learns sooner or later. The wisest, most conten among us learn it sooner. Love will not last in marriage. I you marry for it, you will be left with nothing. What *will* las is respect and affection and responsibility for one another This, Monsieur will give you. If you are lucky, he will als give you love, at least for a time. And that, my precious child is the best you can hope for, the best any of us can hope for."

Zoe began to weep again, more quietly.

"Be wise, *cher*. Give up the dream now, lest it tangl about your heart for the rest of your life, and make you fee always alone when you have every reason for contentment Tell me you will marry Monsieur as he wishes."

"*Maman,* you had love," Zoe said miserably. "Why d you deny it to me? Why do you make me settle for *content ment.*" She all but spat that last word.

Manon laughed lightly. "Yes, I had love. And I neve came closer to slitting my throat in despair when it left me As indeed, I knew it would. I would save you that pain, child You need never know it."

"Then I'll never know the joy, either!"

"You'll have plenty of joy in your life, Zoe, and what you never know, you'll never miss."

"You are locking me away from life!"

"No! I am protecting you from its pain! I wish to God I' had a mother to do the same for me, to tell me that passior is more trouble than it's worth. To tell me the same abou men—"

"You hate men!"

Manon laughed again, this time ruefully. "I love them only too well, *cher*. But I know that we give up our power to them too easily, and get little enough in return."

Zoe began to sob heavily. "I wish I had a father! Even a brother or a sister! Anyone at all to advise me, to stand *between* you and me—!"

"No one will ever stand between you and me, *cher*," Manon said fervently. "You are my only child. You are my life."

With that, Zoe fell into her mother's arms, and the two of them wept together softly. When Manon finally could, she dried her own tears and those of her daughter and said, "Now, you must settle your heart and tell Monsieur that you will marry him this year as he wishes. Will you do this?"

Zoe pulled away and went to the window, drawing aside the lace curtains. She stood for a long moment, looking out on the street below and the flickering lights of the city. When she turned back again to her mother, her face was almost calm. "Yes, *maman*. I will. But I do not know if I can give up on the dream of what love is supposed to be." She put her fist to her mouth. "It hurts so much!"

"Yes, *cher*," Manon said softly, "it is a pain worse than even death or old age, I think. But you can endure it. All of us do, eventually."

Zoe turned back to the window. "Does the night ever look as lovely again, once you no longer believe in love?"

"No," Manon said truthfully, "but the day does. And you learn to sleep at night and live your life in the day."

When Zoe finally took herself to bed, too exhausted to speak or weep anymore, Manon sat up by the window, remembering. As though he waited once more for her in the next room, the image of David Booth came back to her powerfully and poignant. That I loved him truly, Manon thought, I could never deny. I had never felt so before, likely never will again. Even tonight, I can feel the largeness of him, the broadness of his back, the strength of his body, and I can feel that same joy again.

And yet, he left me. Brutally and with no further word he was gone, taking my heart with him.

Manon knew he had not taken another *placée,* for she would have heard. He had never contacted her once, yet in some way, it seemed to her that he must still love her, must at least still yearn for her, since he had not chosen her replacement.

She remembered that she had loved him from the start far before he loved her. The love she felt was almost enough she did not need for him to reciprocate her feelings, so long as he was with her and seemed to wish to be. So powerful it was. And the despair she felt at his going was equally powerful.

We lovers, we are the *curiosité,* the misfits, she thought. The old-fashioned, the wounded who do not heal apace like others. No one tells us how long we are free to yearn and mourn, but we are always over the limits of the normal heart.

There had been a time, and she could still recall it vividly when she wanted not only to die, but to die on his doorstep to let her blood flow over the dirt under his shoes, over his shoes themselves, so that he could see how little she cared for life without him in it. She cared nothing for her dignity, her future, or even her child. Even tonight, she was not sure what had kept her from destroying herself in her despair. All she knew was that one day, she was able to leave her bed and do one simple piece of business. The next day, she was able to do two. The third day, she was able to care that others could not too easily see her despair in her face. Finally, she was able to watch the sun rise and set without wishing for death twice in a twelve-hour period. And to see that she had been in love for many reasons. David was only one of them.

Better she should have asked Marie LaVeau for a spell to make love stay that first visit, than a spell to rid herself of

he baby that would be Zoe, she realized. Perhaps then, she
would have him still.

And now, Zoe was grappling with love, or the lack of it,
as she had long ago. *Did she agree to the wedding because
of the voodoo or because of the sense of my words?* Manon
asked herself.

Regardless, her fate was sealed. *As is mine. Perhaps all
women reach this place in time, yet never speak of it to one
another, least of all to their daughters. But it is the hand that
holds the skillet that knows best the price of lard. Only I can
tell her this. Only from me, will she believe.*

*Each of us lives through the death of the dream—or does
not—but we do it alone, with little comfort from each other.
And when we emerge out the other side of this fire, we can
never love again in exactly the same way. We secretly pity
those women who still do, while we envy them their brief and
passionate illusions.*

A light mist began outside the window and quickly rose
to a patter of rain. As always, the *banquettes* filled swiftly,
and the street was wet, noisy, and iridescent with the flickering lamps of passing carriages.

Giving up the dream of love was rather like death by
drowning, Manon thought then—really a peaceful sensation,
after you ceased to struggle.

The only other time Manon heard Zoe question her decision
was when she talked with her Uncle Alex. His very next visit,
he took him aside for one of their usual long and private
têtes-à-têtes, a tradition which Manon had always respected.
Usually she trusted that the advice Alex would offer—largely

on how to get along with fractious *mamans*—was wise. Less than advice, really, he and Zoe most often seemed to speak of books they had read, articles in the *Picayune* about national politics, or the race issue—topics Manon was happy to leave to them.

But this time when Alex and Zoe ensconced themselves in the parlor, their heads together in murmured exchange, Manon felt there was too much at stake. She stood behind the opened door quietly, listening to her daughter's voice rise and fall with emotion.

"I do not want to marry," she was saying quietly. "But it seems that it has all been decided, whether or not I wish it."

"You do not want to marry at all, or you do not wish to marry Monsieur Avery?" Alex asked gently, adapting his voice to hers.

He had always been so tender with Zoe, Manon thought grimly, and this tenderness had helped to bring her to this sorry pass. She was unwilling to see her responsibility, kept expecting to be saved from some unnamed horror—the horror of a decent marriage and a fine man for a life partner! Am I the only one who will ask her to be a grown woman at last?

"I don't know," she moaned. "I do want to marry someday, I suppose, but not now. I feel that I have so much I want to experience first—"

"This is natural," Alex said, "for you have long been with the Ursulines. But, of course, young woman do not usually have your restlessness. Most often, they are yearning for exactly what you are renouncing now: a husband, a respectable estate, the prospect of a secure future."

Good, thought Manon, he is not disappointing me in this, at least.

"*Maman* says that if I do not accept him now, I will lose him forever." Zoe picked up the serviette and dabbed at her eyes. "I am so confused, Uncle!"

He reached over and patted her shoulder softly. "I dare-

590

say most young women do experience at least a little confusion with such a decision. But perhaps you should ask yourself this, Zoe. If you do not marry, what will you do instead?"

She looked up at him blankly.

"Will you take on some trade or another? Perhaps do some sewing or teach small children their letters? Bake pretty pastries for the rich and deliver them in a cunning basket with ribbons?" His voice was still soft, but the words belied his gentle tone. "You do not need to marry Monsieur, of course, for you may well make another match if he does not suit you. But will what you do with yourself for the next few years make you more or less attractive to an alternative proposal?"

"I could go abroad," she said weakly. "Perhaps study music or art."

"Does your mother offer such an option?"

Zoe hung her head. "She says if I do not accept Monsieur, she will not help me make another match."

"Ah. Well, then, that rather scuttles things, doesn't it," Alex said pensively. "I cannot stand between you and your mother. Even if I wished to offer financial assistance, all I have is entangled with your mother's accounts. Besides, I'm not even sure it would be the right thing to do. It is unfortunate, child. Not fair at all, from my way of thinking, but a fact of life. Women—even rare and tender young women like yourselves—cannot always pick their paths as they might choose. Which of us can?"

He sighed and straightened his shoulders in an ungainly manner. "My advice to you would be to accept Monsieur Avery. If you feel you can care for him in time, I would wish that time to come to you as quickly as possible, that you might grasp what you have rather than grub about for something which might never be as fine."

Zoe gasped softly. She took her uncle's hands beseechingly. "I never thought to hear such counsel from you. You

591

tell me to marry and resign myself? You who have always followed your passions to wherever they lead—?"

He shook his head gently. "Let us not speak of passion. You asked me, Zoe, and I have given you my opinion. It is only that, of course, and certainly not as important as the urgings of your own heart. But I would tell you to listen to your mother. I have learned she was often right," he added ruefully, "even when I disagreed with her most vehemently." He patted her hands. "Usually, she knew what she was about. I expect she does now."

Zoe drew herself up and stood stoically before Alex. "Well, then. I know who stands where in this household." She brushed back her hair and wiped savagely at her eyes. "I thank you for your advice, Uncle." Her voice was silvered and brittle at the edges. "I won't trouble you further with my whinings." She left him alone at the tea table and strode up to her room.

Manon heard Alex sigh again heavily and rise from his chair. She went to him gratefully, but he pushed her gently away and turned to gaze out the window. "I knew what you wanted me to say to her," he murmured, "and I said it. I only hope to God we don't both regret pushing her like this."

"She will doubtless have some moments of discontent," Manon said firmly, "but who does not? I believe, when she looks back on this time, she'll be grateful for your words. I assumed you meant them," she added, glancing at him quizzically. "You've never given her advice simply because you thought *I* needed ammunition."

"Mostly, I did mean them," Alex said, his face miserable. "I felt somehow compelled to say them."

Manon looked at him sharply. A vision of Marie La-Veau's face swam to her mind, but she thrust it aside and concentrated on his words.

"I wish I could think of other choices for her," Alex continued. "Isn't it horrid that a young lovely girl of less than fifteen would have so few?"

"If she were white . . ." Manon joined him at the window, her voice low and vibrant with passion. But then she squared her shoulders. "But she is not. And so, she must use her head at least as much as her heart." The smile she cast on Alex was a little hard around the edges. "She cannot afford the luxury of anything else."

"Tell me, *ma soeur,* did you grapple with these choices as well?"

"You know I did. But I had far less to offer on the open market. No dowry to speak of, little respectability, and—quadroon rather than octoroon, eh? Just that smallest drop of black blood, and it made all the difference . . ."

"And so you became *placée.*"

"And," she said smoothly, "Zoe will *not.* She must marry. She must not be able to be abandoned at a moment's whim." Her mouth twisted in memory. "Or a wife's. As I was."

The cane harvest was ample that year, for the rains held off until after the crop was safely in. After months of arrangements, the morning finally came when Manon could measure in hours, rather than days, the moment when her daughter would become Madame Henry Avery.

If it was not so large as might be planned for an Avery daughter, still it was to be a grand garden wedding, and carriages from four neighboring counties were expected to clog the long curving entrance to the Avery plantation. In a final touch of *famille*—one which thrilled Manon more than any number of elaborate and expensive matrimonial details—Elice Avery, younger sister of the bridegroom, had volunteered to stand beside Zoe as her bridesmaid. Manon had taken the news to Zoe eagerly, certain that she would be as flushed with pride and pleasure as she had been.

But Zoe only responded with her usual calm and gracious poise, an attitude she had cultivated since she had accepted Monsieur's wedding date.

"But, my dear," Manon remonstrated, "this is such an excellent omen for the beginning of your wedded life together. You could have any number of friends stand up for you, but none of them would send the same message that Elice Avery sends, simply by helping you with your train as you kneel before the priest."

"And what message is that, *ma mère?*"

"Why, that you are a part of the family now, of course, an Avery in spirit as well as in fact." Manon smiled winningly. "She didn't have to make such an offer, you know. The Averys are being very generous to both of you. You could be standing up there all alone before the world."

"But, of course, I *will* be standing up there all alone," Zoe said calmly. "No matter how many Averys stand up with me. It is I, after all, who will take the vow."

Manon hugged her firmly. "You're right, of course," she said, not wanting to continue what was already a dissatisfying conversation. Zoe was so self-contained these days! "Now let's make the decision on that lace for your veil," she began hurriedly, "you know we must let the milliner know whether the Brussels or the French lace is your preference—"

Now Zoe stood in the antechamber off the parlor, and her ivory wedding dress fell in graceful folds around her satin slippers. Her dark lustrous hair was bound in a lace net, up and off her face, and the effect made her appear much older and more sophisticated than her years; likewise, the towering headpiece of the veil added inches to her slight frame.

Manon came to her daughter, intensely aware that this was the last time she would *be* her daughter just in this way. She held Zoe's bouquet of fragrant orange blossoms in her hands. "The ivory was the perfect choice, child," she said tenderly. "It makes you look pale as these flowers. You are a vision, my Zoe." She handed the bouquet to her daughter and embraced her, taking care not to crush the lace of her bodice, which filled out her figure so nicely.

Zoe smiled gently, returning her hug.

"Tell me," Manon said suddenly, with a certain urgency to her voice. "Tell me you are happy, Zoe. I couldn't bear it if you weren't. Tell me you regret nothing."

She saw over her shoulder that the guests were gathering, and the pianist and harpist were beginning the music selected for the entrance of the wedding party. Madame Avery was approaching, all smiles, to kiss her soon-to-be daughter for good luck. In moments, Zoe's life would be decided, her fate consummated forever.

"I regret nothing," Zoe said evenly. "What is there to regret?"

"Then I shall weep only for happiness," Manon said, embracing her one last time and turning her to face Madame Avery. "A mother's prerogative!" She fell back from the small crowd of shoulders coming to pull Zoe along in their wake, and the ceremony began as Henry Avery took his place alongside the priest at the front of the parlor. Manon made her way to her chair in front and took Alex's hand.

"She is absolutely beautiful," she whispered to him joyously, nodding to those she recognized as they filled the chairs.

"Is she happy?" Alex asked quietly.

Manon frowned and rapped his hand as though she held a folded fan. "Of course she is, *fou-fou*, what a ridiculous question!"

The music reached a peak of anticipatory announcement, and the wedding party began to slowly wend their way into the parlor. When Manon saw Zoe reach the threshold and, shyly, drop her eyes as she made her way through the smiling throng to where the priest waited, she could not keep her own eyes from brimming over, and she dabbed at them carefully, smiling through her tears.

The words of the priest drifted over Manon like the low murmur of a cool breeze off the river, and she was unable to rivet her attention on the Latin phrases, the words of French he interspersed only occasionally ringing in her mind like a distant muffled bell. She thought instead of her own great good luck and Zoe's even finer fortune, that both of them had risen above what might be expected for two of their caste. She recalled vividly something her friend, Monique, had told her on the night she first visited Marie LaVeau, to rid herself of the belly which was to become the girl standing before the priest now . . .

"I was never a child," Monique had said. "Few of us could afford the luxury of youth. My mother told me about love and passion when I was only eight. From then, I was raised to be what I am. The mistress of my Monsieur. This is what I was born for, this is what I was made."

But Zoe was born for, raised for, made for much more. And today was the culmination of every hope Manon had held to her heart for fourteen years. She was married. She was safe. As her daughter moved now away from the priest, Madame Henry Avery at last, Manon closed her eyes and breathed a prayer to the Virgin for her serenity.

Manon was unable to claim Zoe for many moments after the ceremony, nor did she really attempt to take the new bride from her husband's protective curve of arm. So many smiling properous faces she did not know were making such an effort to get to know her daughter, she was almost sated simply to stand back and watch the procession of well-wishers flock by in a flurry of laces and satins and richly brocaded waistcoats. She saw with satisfaction that Zoe's bow to each was just the right depth, sustained for the proper moment, and held an ingrained rhythm of poise and dignity.

Alex stood by her side, smiling and nodding to those introduced. Several times Manon heard him speak of his work when asked, but fortunately, he did not go on in his usual way to bore listeners with too many details of the bird sanctuary and the salt production. When she saw that he was able to manage both an hors d'oeuvres plate and also a conversation at one time, she slipped to Zoe's side and whispered, "My dear, I have never been more proud of you than at this moment. It was a perfect ceremony, don't you think?"

She nodded quickly, clinging to Monsieur's arm. "And only just think, *maman,*" she whispered back, "Henry says we may visit our new home tomorrow. The windows are finally in place, and the doors are on hinge, likely we'll be able to set furnishings in place within the week."

A voice behind Manon interrupted. "I would like to make the acquaintance of the mother of the bride, if I may," a man was saying to Monsieur Avery, "such a beauty must have had its genesis in a fleshly reality." He was bowing to Zoe but gazing at her mother.

Manon turned to accept the courtesies of a tall man who kissed her hand deftly. "*Monsieur,*" she smiled.

Henry Avery said, "May I present Monsieur Nicholas Fletcher. Madame Manon d'Irlandais."

Manon noted the addition of the Madame before her name. Usually she insisted upon it in her business dealings. Henry knew the truth, of course, but was too well bred to have ever referred to it, even when in private discussions over Zoe's dowry. Perhaps now, at last, the issue would never come up again.

"A lyrical name," Monsieur Fletcher said smoothly, "fitting for a woman of subtle grace."

His words were perfect, Manon noticed swiftly, but there was something less than perfect about his smile. Something almost . . . appraising. As though the man suspected she might not be all she seemed. She turned up the simmer in her eyes deliberately, warming her own smile to the corresponding degree she felt appraised. "Fletcher," she murmured. "Should I know the name?"

"It's going to be a name to reckon with soon," Henry said, smiling over at Zoe who had drifted away to speak with two young women. "*Monsieur* Fletcher is well respected in Natchez, with shipping interests and a thriving export business in cotton. But he's expanded his influence to the delta now, and I expect to see the name Nick Fletcher on any number of ballots in the near future."

"Or any number of arrest warrants," Fletcher grinned.

"You are in politics, then, Monsieur?" Manon asked.

"I am *of* politics at the moment," the man said quickly. "I'm not as yet *in* politics, at least not in up to my neck. And if I can't get these local sharks to see things my way, then the New Orleans bosses will have to get along without me for the time. I'm the newcomer on the street, and you know New Orleans' *banquettes* are sometimes a tight squeeze to shoulder through. In Natchez, business and politics don't feel obliged to be such friendly bedfellows. Here, one can scarcely get a license to ship without the backing of two or three parish bosses in one's breast pocket. I find that I might as well run for office, it's likely cheaper than buying those who already hold the votes." He bowed smoothly, abruptly. "But today is not a day for such. And I can acquit myself better when I'm in motion. Madame, will you do me the honor?"

He held out his arm just as Manon realized that the orchestra was swinging into the first waltz of the evening. "*Mais non,*" she shook her head, "the first dance belongs to the bride and groom." As she spoke, Henry was claiming Zoe for their initial turn around the dance floor together, her arms on his shoulders, her face smiling up into his.

The guests quickly lined the ballroom, exclaiming and clapping softly as the bride swept up her train over one delicate arm and swooped into the first dip of the waltz. Where had she learned such perfection? Manon wondered. Zoe held her head high, gave herself to her husband's movements, and swept about the dance floor as though she had waltzed with him a dozen times.

"I believe it is customary," said a voice at Manon's ear, "for the mother of the bride and the mother of the groom to join the young couple. For luck."

Manon turned to face Nick Fletcher and grinned. "Customary? Whose customs, pray tell? It sounds absolutely barbaric, two mothers dancing away together before such a company—"

His eyes narrowed for just an instant and then widened with grudging admiration. "You are right, of course, Madame. Too barbaric to be repeated. But perhaps we might modify the custom. You could dance with me, sharing your daughter's waltz."

"And her mother-in-law?"

"Let her find her own partner," he grinned.

She took his arm and allowed herself to be led onto the floor, smiling over her shoulder at Zoe's startled glance. To her great relief, she saw Madame Avery size up the situation swiftly, grab her husband's arm, and join the waltzing couples before they had passed her twice.

"Has anyone ever told you," Nick Fletcher murmured in her ear on the second passage, "that you are a worthy adversary, Manon d'Irlandais?"

"No one needed to tell me this, Monsieur," she murmured back, tightening her grip on his shoulder. He whirled her faster as though he were a horse responding to the spur. "I was born with the knowledge, *vraiment.*"

In a part of the bayou where the tupelo and cypress were most dense, a snowy egret and his mate built a nest. Normally, these woods were so crowded that nesting sites were scarce, and common egrets, snowy egrets, and blue egrets squabbled for space among the brush. But this season, the two had been able to build with little competition.

It was a spring evening, and Cuk circled his mate—who was incubating the clutch of eggs—spreading his wide white wings and braking before landing on the edge of the nest. As he'd feared, the anhinga or snakebird was still standing too close, near the nest which balanced on a downed cypress branch. He gave a cry of defiance to the intruding bird, but the anhinga never budged. It had watched them for three days now.

Cuk's mate nervously rose and rearranged her clutch of six eggs with her long bill, clucking to him for reassurance. But he could give her little. If the anhinga would not be driven off by threat postures and croaking protests, Cuk could do nothing else. The other bird was larger, his body more suited to battle. Cuk preened his long aigrette feathers anxiously, watching the anhinga all the while.

In time, his mate stood and stretched her long bill, craning her neck to get more comfortable. She needed to feed soon; it had been many hours since she had relief from setting the eggs. She eyed the anhinga, glanced once at Cuk, and spread her wings, flying off over the swamp towards the deeper waters where the fishing was easier.

Cuk hesitated. The anhinga moved closer then, taking a hopping step to within a wingspan of the nest. The snakebird cocked his narrow head at Cuk, hopped closer once more, then stepped on the edge of the nest itself. As Cuk watched, unable to do anything but croak anxiously, the anhinga reached in and took up an egg in his bill. Cuk flapped his wings, opened his bill threateningly, and made harsh guttural sounds at the intruder, but the anhinga only dropped the egg over the side of the nest into the water. One by one, he then picked up each egg in turn, until all had disappeared beneath the surface.

Cuk moved to a nearby tupelo, flapping his wings in

agitation. As he watched, the anhinga's mate joined him. They mated quickly; she balanced on the edge of the nest, her long neck stretched out over the water, and then she settled down in the egret nest, folding her wings about her firmly. The male anhinga flew off to feed.

Cuk's mate came back and circled the swamp as the sun was getting lower in the spring sky. When she saw the female anhinga in her nest, she set up a raucous screeching and landed on a nearby tree, calling for Cuk in distress. He answered her, flying over to where she roosted. Together, they paced the tree and preened nervously, always watching the nest.

Towards dusk, the female anhinga took flight from the nest, and Cuk and his mate immediately descended upon it. Together, they dismantled the nest, working from the edge inwards, removing sticks and twigs two and three at a time, and swiftly flying them over to a dry spot on the bank. When they had almost the entire nest dismantled, Cuk's mate began to carry the twigs and sticks to another cypress she had selected, weaving some of the larger branches into the fork of the tree. It was almost dark now and too late to build. At dawn, they would begin again.

Cuk found her as the last light left the sky in the swamp, landed next to her at the building site, and roosted. He preened himself once more, watching carefully for enemies. There were none. He slept at last, balanced on his toes for light.

Lake Pontchartrain, just north of the city, was the mecca and the birthplace of New Orleans' spirit of glittery debauch in

1898. Jazz clubs sprouted around the edge of the wide water on the south side like mushrooms after the rain, and beach clubs and dance halls drew citizens and travelers every night of the week.

It was a decidedly more classy arena than that offered by Storyville, or Tango Belt, or Basin—it went by many names—New Orleans' Tenderloin, the largest red-light district in America. Legalized by New Orleans Alderman Sidney Story—hence the name, Storyville—Basin Street's bordellos finally went public. Hundreds of travelers came to point, to be shocked, and to ogle at Basin Street, the center of a broad rectangle of commerce, legally created, legally maintained, and had, as the street barkers swore, "everything."

"Everything" in Storyville ranged from mansions of erotica with mirrored ceilings, oil paintings six-feet-wide, and a charge of fifty dollars a night, to the individual gal who roamed the streets with a rolled carpet on her back and charged a quarter. More than two thousand women plied their commerce in Storyville, and many thousands more served food and drink, played jazz, and collected their rent.

Indeed, some of the most eminently respectable citizens of the Queen City made their fortunes on the proceeds of Storyville, and when they chose to spend some of those fortunes they came—not to Storyville or Basin Street—but to Lake Pontchartrain.

The crowded tables at Manon d'Irlandais's popular lakefront club, The Irish Palace, were always reserved well in advance. Like many of the clubs, the Palace provided picnics at the lake edge, pavilion dancing, contests, club parties, and private entertainments for a price. Also available for a price were the *chanteuses,* some of the most beautiful bar girls in the delta region. Madame Manon insisted that her girls be lovely, be discreetly selective, and always the epitome of high fashion and grace. Wealthy patrons of the Irish Palace knew to ask for their favorites personally, to insure an evening c gay laughter and sparkling entertainment—whatever else her *chanteuses* arranged was up to them. But they paid Madame well for their positions at the long bar, and she did not hesitate to rotate them right out the door if their evenings ceased to be satisfactory for all concerned.

The Irish Palace also had a reputation for the finest jazz musicians in town. Every Sunday, Madame d'Irlandais's club car, Smoky Mary, ran from the French Quarter out to the lake on its own private short line railroad, to carry passengers in style to the Irish Palace. One of the cars was always filled with musicians, a moving medley of blues and jazz and Dixieland; close behind in the second car lounged the *haut monde* of the Queen City, wealthy patrons who traveled in glittering comfort.

Manon often rode her own railroad just to cozen her customers, but she made her last trip one night when she got into a well-bred argument with a man from Chicago who claimed his town invented the word, jazz.

"Mais non, cher," she told him firmly, "we say it in French, *non? Le jazz hot.* To *jaser,* to chatter, to prattle like pigeons, it means. It is not jazz, but jass. You in Chicago simply pronounce it badly, yes?" She smiled, taking away the sting with her eyes.

"Hell, yes, if you say so, sister!" the man shouted, slapping his beefy hand on her thighs.

She could not rid herself of this companion for the rest of the short ride to the lake, and she vowed that she need no longer ride Smoky Mary simply to insure that her tables were full.

But most nights would find her in residence, and the Irish Palace pulled in more customers a week than other clubs garnered in a month of the best weather. Manon sat at her table, one of the largest in the club with a view of most of the lower floor and a partial view of the dance pavilion at the lake's edge, receiving guests and, as Nick Fletcher put it, doing business.

One night as Nick sat beside her, a position he occupied several nights a week, Manon received the Governor of Louisiana, the Mayor of New Orleans, and the Chief of Police of the French Quarter. Each man got her warmest smile, a glance at her deep *décolletage,* and an earful of remonstrations about what was wrong with the management of the state, the city, and those streets in the Quarter where she owned properties.

"Why, Ben, you know you've got almost more criminals on your payroll than you've got on the streets," she said to the Chief of Police. "*Assassination* can be made right under their noses, and they'll look the other way. They only raise a hand when their side is losing." She frowned prettily. "I want those fence shops and nickel and dime hotels on either side of Saint Philip closed down, so that decent *gentils-hommes* can walk the *banquette* without being ambushed."

"And so they can eat at your hotel and café in peace," the Chief grinned.

Her smile widened. "*Vraiment, cher,* you understand me so well. You always have. Now. What must I do to help this fortunate happenstance come about?"

Nick chuckled soberly. "Careful, Ben, she'll meet your price, but she'll get her money's worth out of every picayune. She always does."

"It won't be the first time Madame Manon and I have done business," Ben said smoothly. "It's not that far from Basin Street to the Palace."

"Farther than the moon," Manon said easily. "I can depend upon you then, *cher,* to roust that reeking collection of thieves? I'm weary of having my customers complain their pockets are picked before they reach the safety of my doors."

One of Manon's bouncers approached the table, bowed slightly, and beckoned for her attention. "Nick," she smiled winsomely, "perhaps you and Ben can discuss the business arrangements while I attend to some of our other guests—" She slid away gracefully, leaving Nick to negotiate payment with the chief of police, something he was far better at than he.

Though Manon wanted her way, it always rankled her to have to dicker for a price. It was far more pleasant to enjoy the illusion that these gentlemen did her favors because they saw the wisdom of her requests and wanted to please her.

The bouncer was bringing another gentleman to her now, and she bowed before him, extending her hand. *"Monsieur,"* Manon said gaily, "I have been looking forward to your arrival with such pleasure!"

John McGovern bent over her hand and kissed it. Manon watched him carefully. He was the most powerful lottery man in the state, and she needed his support. The Louisiana lottery pledged donations to charity hospitals, asylums, yellow fever funds, the French Opera—most any worthy cause to keep the reformists from trying to shut them down—and a few not so worthy. Called the Golden Octopus by its critics, Louisiana's lottery was one of the most wealthy in the nation, and New Orleans was lottery mad. Small drawings went on daily, grand ones twice a month, and grandest of all twice a year. Manon's customers talked lottery, dreamed it, bought tickets by their dreams, and sought out voodoo women to help them interpret their dreams. They went to mass to get their tickets blessed, and most boasted they had not failed to buy a daily ticket once in years.

Manon knew the twenty-five-year charter on the state lottery was almost up, and if she were to garner a share of the lottery donations, she must do so quickly. John McGovern was just the man to help her find a way.

"Well, I'm deeply shamed, Madame," McGovern said smoothly, "that I've waited so long before meeting *La Grande Dame* of the Queen City. Your reputation does not do you justice."

She gestured him to sit beside her at her table, quickly noting with satisfaction that Nick was even now glad-handing the Chief and ushering him down to the bar for a round of drinks on the house. Obviously, their *affaire de commerce* had been concluded to her advantage. "And what reputation is that, Monsieur? With my many business responsibilities, I scarcely have time to get out as much as I'd like, I fear I'm becoming a phantom to my friends!"

"Your reputation for beauty," the man answered, and a single gold tooth in the side of his mouth glinted once in the darkness.

Manon matched his smile and leaned slightly forward, signaling to her *maître d'hôtel* to bring forward the chilled champagne. "You have an eye for beauty, Monsieur? That is excellent. I had hoped you would be a man with such an eye, yes? And if, indeed, you can appreciate the subtle grace of womanhood in its most fragile flowering, then perhaps you and I—and some of my other special friends—can truly make New Orleans as famous for her beauty as she deserves to be."

In the next few moments, Manon persuaded, seduced, argued, and cajoled, until she had John McGovern's promise that a goodly slice of the lottery donation pie would be slid onto her private plate, to build one of the city's first public nursing schools for young women. In return, John McGovern's eldest daughter, due to marry in three months, would be fêted in grand style at the Irish Palace with Manon's compliments to the bride.

As she said goodbye to Monsieur McGovern and saw him ushered to the bar, she spied a small group being led to one of the front tables on the dance floor. Manon stopped, struck dumb at the sight of the tallest man in the group, and shrank back into the shadows to watch more closely. It was David Booth. She saw him take his wife's elbow and settle her easily in her chair, laughing with a man at his side, taking his seat with a jaunty shrug of his shoulders. David. The first time she had seen him in nearly twenty years.

In the dim light, she could see that he had aged more than his wife. The woman was still lovely. Mature, but lovely, with a poise and easy smile which spoke of years of comfort and security. The diamonds at her neck were, undoubtedly, of high quality. David's hair was nearly white at the temples, but still full, his face lined but handsome.

She would have known him anywhere. She would have preferred to see him for the first time in all these years almost anywhere else. The happy noise of the bar and the *chanteuses* around her made her swiftly aware that she had frozen, her face a revelation to any who might have been watching. She quickly rearranged her smile, made a passing comment to a customer on her right, and moved a little closer to David's table.

She knew she must speak to him, for no other reason than that she must. She had to see his eyes when he knew it was her, just once. But she must speak to him alone. Manon retreated to her table, more disturbed than she wanted to admit, and greeted her next three guests with less than her full attention. All the while she flirted and bargained and cajoled, she kept one eye on David's table. She saw him lead his wife to the dance floor, saw him signal to the waiter, heard, once, his voice rise above the others in an exclamation, and yet managed to give her guests the impression each was the focus of her energy.

Luckily, she saw David rise and leave the table for the gentlemen's lounge, just as she was saying *bonsoir* to the councilman from Saint Tammany parish. She waited until David was almost at the door and then appeared before him.

"David Booth," she said softly. "You seem none the worse for wear." In fact, now that she was closer to him, she could see that her statement was false. He had aged, and markedly. The pearl buttons of his evening shirt were strained with the effort to hold in his belly. The man had obviously lived well in her absence. Since his abandonment. Nonetheless, he was still a striking man, and she could yet feel his power.

He looked down at her quizzically. Then she had the vast

pleasure of seeing his eyes widen in recognition, dart uneasily to his wife's table, and then down again at her with shock. "Madame," he said, his voice faltering slightly. "Have we met?"

"Indeed we have," she said lightly. "Don't tell me you have forgotten me, *cher.* I would never believe it of you." She slid her arm through his and led him away from the lounge area, where they might not be so readily watched. "Surely you recall our little cottage on Saint Phillip? I know," she said, now turning him to face her again, "you have not forgotten your Manon." Unreasoning anger flared in her, but she did not allow it into her voice or her smile.

"Ah!" he said, nervously looking over her shoulder towards the dance floor and his party, "it *is* you, my dear. I wasn't sure . . ."

"Have I changed so much then?" She watched him carefully, feeling like a cat with a mouse between its paws.

"No, no, but it's been so many years—"

"Indeed it has. Your daughter is married now, likely soon to have a babe of her own."

He was shocked to silence. His smile disappeared. "My daughter?"

Manon chuckled gently, shaking her head. "Do you even remember her name?"

His face fell further, but his voice stiffened. "Do you mean to make trouble, Madame? For if you do, I imagine the proprietress of this place would not wish her help to harry her guests—"

In that instant, with those words, Manon knew that she would never think of this man, yearn for this man, wonder if this man were well or ill—not ever again. She put out her hand and took his warmly. "I *am* the proprietress, Monsieur. Manon d'Irlandais. The Irish Palace is mine."

He grinned, hugely relieved. "Ah, then! You have not done so badly after all. You know," he began confidentially,

"I missed you many times, dear, and so often wondered what became of you and our little girl. Zoe, wasn't it?"

"Yes. Zoe. She is well, as am I. And you, David?" She peered at him closely. "Life has been all that you wished?"

He shrugged ruefully. "Who ever has all he wishes, eh? I won't pretend that I haven't had my share of heartbreak and loneliness. I've done well, yes, but money isn't everything, you know. Although," he laughed jovially, gesturing to the crystal chandelier gleaming brightly over their heads, "it certainly looks as if you learned to turn it into everything! Tell me, Manon, did you do all this on the five thousand I gave you every year?"

Now it was her turn to laugh, and she did, with scarcely a trace of scorn in her voice. "No, *cher,* I think it safe to say there's nothing of yours here at the Irish Palace."

David's voice lowered now to a more intimate tone. "Truly?" He took her elbow gently. "Not a thing? I'd have hoped that something of mine might have remained . . . something I might revisit, perhaps, for the sake of old, dear memories? You are still a strikingly beautiful woman." The pressure on her elbow increased subtly. "And I am very glad to see you."

Manon's smile never wavered, but she felt a sour coldness in her heart. Suddenly weary of the man, the scene, the tilt and noise from the bar behind her, she said, "Are you? That's sweet, *cher.* Of course, it would have been easy enough to find me, had you wanted to sometime in the last twenty years. In fact, for us not to have seen each other in all this time almost seems as though one of us wanted it that way. After all, New Orleans is not New York. But I would guess you had others to—distract you—from whatever disappointments your life offered."

He moved his face slightly closer to hers. "I won't say there haven't been others in your absence, darling, but there have certainly been none so memorable. Do you remember the time we—"

"I remember everything," she said smoothly, moving slightly away. "Women don't forget so easily as men."

"Surely, you're not still angry at me? What could I do? When my wife follows me right to your door."

"I stopped being angry many years ago," Manon said, letting the weariness show now in her voice. "I'm happy your life has been so fulfilling." She let her eyes drop subtly to his belly.

But he missed the direction of her gaze. "It could be more fulfilling," he murmured. "Tell me where I might find you now, Manon. Let me come and see you. Twenty years, has it really been so long? I would never know it, looking at your face. We have so many things to talk about, so many old memories!"

She gently eased her elbow away from his fingers. "You may find me here, Monsieur, most any night. But I'm afraid I've no taste for old memories." She saw Nick searching for her, discreetly scanning the room for her—there, he had seen her. She flashed him a brilliant smile. "Do you see that gentleman over there?" she asked David, turning him slightly towards Nick, who was unabashedly watching her now to see if he was needed. "Smile, David, or he will come to my side instantly."

David grinned at Nick and lifted a halfhearted salute.

"He is my *protecteur* now, and a more excellent partner a woman could not wish." She waited until his eyes were back on her. "In all ways." She slipped her arm through his once more and strolled him back to the door of the gentlemen's lounge. "And so you see, *cher,*" she finished, smiling her farewell, "I am busy making *new* memories, and so you shall have to find fulfillment elsewhere. In fact, I might suggest that you find entertainment elsewhere, as well. And not the Lakeside Hotel, either, I own that one as well."

She slid her arm from his as he turned back with surprise. "For you see . . . I don't need anything from you anymore, *cher.* Not even your money." She patted him fondly, as one might pat an old, familiar hound. Then she turned and walked towards Nick, her head high and her chin tilted to the light.

"A problem?" Nick asked, watching over her shoulder to where David Booth disappeared.

"Not at all, *cher,* a solution. Has the alderman and his party arrived yet?"

"They wait at your table. Don't forget you wanted to talk with him about the taxes on your warehouses—"

"I won't, and I won't let him forget that the lease on that land next to his that he wants comes due next month, and I might be willing to let it go, if we can *fait de bonne coopérer . . .*"

"And in that way," Manon said wearily to Nick as they closed the club that night, "each hand washes the other. I wonder if they do business in Des Moines as we do in New Orleans?"

He pulled her into his arms. "I doubt even the rest of New Orleans does business as we do."

She kissed him exuberantly. No one set of lips worked quite as well as Nick's, she thought. More than two years of steady kisses, and she still felt so. Two years since their first dance. Two years of a heady love which had swept her along into his bed, his intrigues, finally into a partnership with him which had become as wildly lucrative as it was passionate. Together, they had maneuvered to become one of the most powerful couples in the Queen City—and all without benefit of clergy.

Oh, there had been moments in the past two years when

she had wanted marriage. Moments, too, when he had wanted it as well. But they never seemed to want it at the same time, and so they still danced around each other like courting snakes, writhing and intertwining their lives and their hearts, but not necessarily their destinies. Perhaps, Manon thought occasionally, it was that very separation that kept their passion alive. Neither quite knew what the other might do at any particular moment. And so, neither could bear to have the other out of sight for long.

They closed the doors, locked up, and turned down the lights, reaching for each other even as they climbed the stairs to their apartment. Manon had insisted that they keep two separate rooms above the Palace, but one was largely wasted. Nick almost always shared her bed, unless they had one of their blistering arguments. And even then, he generally threw open her doors and swept under her coverlet before dawn, either shouting down her points one by one or petting her into calm.

As they mulled over each victory and defeat of the day, she watched him stride about the room, taking off his tuxedo, almost as intrigued by his body as his mind. His was a volatile, mercurial set of movements, graceful as a fencing master, as sharp-edged at times as a weapon.

"I think we've got the mayor in our pockets finally. Damn it, I've never seen so much corruption in one place," he laughed wryly. "Honest politicians in New Orleans are as scarce as hairs on a tater!"

"It's always been that way," Manon said cheerfully. "I can remember hearing about when King John Slidell ran the Democrats all the way to Plaquemines marsh. He gathered up a covey of voters, loaded them on steamboats, and stopped at each parish downriver, having them vote each time. It was common knowledge that some of those boys voted six or seven times that day, and nobody raised a brow. It's not much different now, it just costs more to accomplish."

Nick stopped and pondered that. "I seem to recall hearing that story. That was about fifty years ago, wasn't it? You may have just dated yourself, my darling—"

She threw a silken pillow at him and shouted, "I said I *heard* about it, *mon fou!*" She had not so far shared all of her secrets with Nick Fletcher. He did not know her age of nearly forty, he did not realize the beauty mole by her mouth was an artifice, nor did he know that she rinsed her hair with coffee to mask the stray strands of gray. With luck, he never would.

Nick sat down on the bed naked and pulled her to him, sliding his hands up her thighs and between them, grinning up into her face. "Your skin is like a virgin's," he murmured, "no matter if you've got a whore's heart."

"Oh!" she laughed, pushing him back on the silken sheets, "what a rogue's tongue you have tonight! You can just sleep down the hall, Monsieur, and don't think you can come crawling back and be forgiven, either—"

He pulled her on top of him and gripped her firmly on both cheeks, beginning the movements which he knew she loved most. "Don't make me beg," he moaned, low and throaty, "for what I need, Madame. Perhaps if you could let me . . ." and here, he hooked his feet under hers and drew her legs slowly, wide apart. His pelvis now was hard against hers, his mouth an inch away from her lips, his hands holding her fast. "Only just let me inside you for a moment, just the smallest bit." His eyes glimmered, half-closed. "You know how I need it," he groaned, grinding against her, "you want to give it up to me."

"Did you see the way the chief of police looked at me tonight, *cher?*" she whispered. "Do you think he was picturing me with him, as I'm with you now?"

"I think," Nick whispered back, "the man would give his balls to be under you as I am now, and likely his soul to be—" and here, he slipped himself inside her deftly, "inside you."

"And what do you think," she moaned, moving over him

613

now and feeling him thrust deeper, "he might give to come in me?"

Nick's voice was husky and low. "Sweet Jesus, woman, he would give his life to come in you,"—she gripped him tighter and he groaned—"as would any man in the city."

"Only in the city?" she half-whimpered, half-whispered. They were moving quicker now, and he was covering her neck and her face with kisses, starting as he always did with her eyes, the sides of her nose, down her cheeks, and finally, teasingly, probing her lips with his tongue. "In the state," he panted.

"It's a small state," she murmured.

He covered her mouth with his then, his tongue swirling with hers and pulling her buttocks apart with his hands so that he could get deeper still. When their teeth grazed, he deliberately stopped and repositioned his lips so as to lock her mouth against his, her teeth touching his, her tongue entwined, so that there was no part of her mouth unkissed. Their movements rapidly became so powerful that they could not stay joined at the mouth, and as he pulled away to bury his mouth in her neck, he groaned, "The world, the world, then—"

"Yes," she moaned, arching her back as his mouth went to her breast.

"Give it to me then, Madame," he whispered, "you know you want to give it up. Give me that sweetness you save for me."

He rolled her over then, still inside her, and rose so that his chest was over her mouth, his hands on her shoulders, pushing hard and deep and swiftly in the rhythm he knew she needed. Grasping her legs, he drew them apart at the knees, and she lifted herself in abandonment, crying out in her pleasure. Well after he knew she had begun, well in the midst of her contractions, he finally let himself go to trumpet his climax, groaning hoarsely as he spent himself. For long moments after, their parts spoke to each other in small, delightful shivers and throbbings. And as always after they had made love, Manon felt the joy bubble up in her and out of her mouth in quiet laughter, as he rolled her into his arms, staying inside her as long as he could, stroking her hair and murmuring to her soft praise and subsiding hunger.

Later, as she wound around him that night, cleaving to his backside as a matching spoon in a drawer, she thought how different this man was from others she had known. So different from Alex, for example.

Alex was approaching fifty now, and still content to live his life among the fowl of the swamps. He would always be a *naïf* of the first order, she sighed to herself, his most important achievement to the world likely being the naming of a few obscure birds. He had ambition for nothing more. Yet, he treated all with unfailing kindness, particularly Zoe. In a hard world where decency did not thrive, a city thronged with brutish, greedy souls, Alex was a man of gentle disposition and great generosity. If he had failed to find in himself the ruthlessness which made Nick Fletcher such a success, he had discovered something else, she supposed. Long ago, she had vowed to ask him no questions about his private life. He evidently wished to know nothing of hers, as well. He seemed content enough.

But, she told herself as she held Nick tightly in her sleep, he would never know the passion and the satisfaction she knew. And for that, she pitied him.

Manon only saw her brother now when she made the journey down the Bayou Teche to Jefferson Island, for he rarely came to New Orleans anymore.

"There's nothing there I need," he was fond of saying, "nothing there anybody needs much at all, if they'd just get away from the city long enough to realize it."

Manon had mocked his opinion so long that now she no longer really heard him. But Zoe listened and seemed to take Alex's words to heart. Indeed she, like her uncle, had scarcely been to New Orleans twice since her marriage. And so Manon, if she wanted to see all the family she had in the world, must make the long, hot trip up the Mississippi, across the Atchafalaya River, and then down the bayou to what seemed like the end of the civilized world.

It was such a hodgepodge down on the delta, she thought, such a gumbo mix of small Acadian homes next to a vast plantation owned by some Yankee investor, beside a *grande maison* belonging to an old, respected Creole family.

Many of the best estates stood empty and forlorn, never restored since the ravages of the War Between the States. Some were deserted, slipping away toward the soggy earth and their own doom: a balcony gone, a shutter hanging desultorily in the sultry breeze, the paint peeling away like dry skin. Usually the houses were curtained and festooned with purple wisteria, yellow creeper, and a riot of green vines tangled like a madwoman's hair. Some of the older places were so jungled that the sunlight scarcely intruded, and bees hummed over the somnolent flowers and around the rotting cornices. Over it all lay the somber damp of decay and forgetfulness.

The delta seemed to lack the life force of New Orleans and it wearied Manon, not only to make the trip, but to feel the oppressive force of all that past around her.

But Zoe had given birth to her first child. A son to carry on the Avery name. At eighteen, she was the mistress of a fine, vast estate, and her letters spoke of the myriad details of running their life in such a way as to make Manon secretly wonder at her daughter's poise and balance.

For all Zoe's squalling despair, this marriage was her

destiny, Manon told herself often. However it had to come about, it was the right thing. Her happiness today proved it.

The flatboat that moved passengers and cargo down the Teche was hardly a conveyance of luxury, but its slow passage did allow Manon an unobstructed view of the delta as she passed through it. Most of all, she noted the stately rows of live oaks along the Teche, long files for several miles, double avenues with branches arching high above the heads of travelers, leaves mingling with leaves letting through only thin, dusty shafts of sunlight, hanging over the water. Some of the oaks were fantastically twisted giants, thirty feet or more in girth, of a heavy wood that seemed inviolate. Bulbous roots lifted iron fences away from the ground, and limbs clawed at the shutters. Moss hung down several yards from the huge branches, trailing right to the banks. At the bayou bank the palmettoes and the cane crowded together, and against them, the matted water hyacinths floated on their way to the gulf.

The boatman told her that the hyacinths she so admired would one day be the death of the water itself.

"Ain' a nat'ral plant, M'dame," he said. "They brought it over from Ja-pan, you know, an' give it away free at the Cotton Expo ten year ago. Wal, ever Cajun *femme* put it to root at her own front door, an' it took off wild an' spread. Now, you cain' kill it, not with fire nor turpentine, an' it strangles the life out o' the water. Mark me, Missus, they come a time when no boat at'all get through, for the blasted flowers."

They passed Shadows on the Teche, a stately mansion in poor repair, with its back to the bayou. She could still see the great, unornamented columns, outlined in the sky against the classic cornice, and along the tall, sloping roof with its three dormer windows. But the town of New Iberia had crept up on Shadows, the slave quarters were gone, and the house itself was beginning to fade and sag among its weeds and waving grasses.

The Teche made her lonely, Manon decided, or at least its abandoned opulence did. Everywhere she looked, the houses seemed to give her a feeling of life in a reflected light of abandonment in a place so obviously meant for the sound of many feet.

Until she reached ShadyOaks, the place Henry Avery had built for her daughter. Here the house was vast, the grounds ample, and the estate had a sense of life and bustle to it that lifted Manon's weariness each time she set foot on its wide dock. She had meant to come more often, but the way from New Orleans was so long. She told herself that after all, Zoe could make the trip upriver as easily—more easily!—than she could go down.

As usual, Henry met her with a half-dozen servants to carry her bags and the boxes of gifts she had brought for Zoe and her infant son. He kissed her firmly on both cheeks exclaiming over her, "Manon, you don't look a day older certainly not old enough to be a *grandmère.*"

"And so I am not," she said wryly, "and I'll thank you not to use that wretched word again in my hearing. Zoe is well?"

He loaded her in the carriage and they trotted quickly up the curving front drive. "In excellent health and spirits. She waits for you in the nursery, she scarcely leaves it for more than an hour at a time, though we have the best wetnurse in the delta."

Manon put one hand on his and searched his face briefly "And you, Henry? You are happy with your bride? Your son?"

He smiled. "I made the best bargain of my life, Madame the day I accepted your bribe."

"Bribe! I hope you never say such a word to Zoe!" she began to sputter, "it was a bonafide betrothal with a hand some dowry, and you were lucky, Monsieur, to get such a—"

He began to laugh then, helping her down from the carriage, and she subsided, turned, and saw her daughter com

618

ing to be embraced. Behind her stood a tall mulatress, holding a bundled child.

"My Zoe!" Manon cried, kissing her and holding her at
arm's length. "You look more lovely than on your wedding
day. Motherhood obviously agrees with you!"

Zoe laughed and pulled away, pushing Manon gently
towards the nursemaid. "When you saw me last I was
scarcely showing and sick as a hound every day, so I guess
I should be much improved. Come and see your new grandson."

"Just so long as you don't call me his grandmother,"
Manon said, taking the bundled infant in her arms and pulling back the mosquito lace over his face.

The child awoke then and opened his eyes with the frank,
trusting stare of the very young—or very old. Manon was
struck to silence by his beauty and the serenity of his gaze.
In that instant, she recalled vividly the first time she had held
Zoe in her arms, and she felt something dissolve in her heart,
something she had determined to keep walled in. Whatever
doubts, whatever guilt she might have harbored for Zoe's
choices or lack thereof, she let go of all of that forever. This
child was the proof, she thought dazedly, that the end did
indeed justify the means.

Her eyes were brimming with joy when she looked back
up at Zoe and Henry, standing alongside her. "He is perfection. What have you named him?"

"Alexander Adam," Henry said proudly.

"Oh," Manon murmured, "he will be so pleased."

Zoe said, "He already is."

"Alex has seen this child before his very own grandmother?"

Zoe laughed gently. "*Maman,* you have not changed a
whit. You still think time stands still if you're not using it.
He's been in and out quite a bit in the last few months, and
he's arriving today in time for supper. Now come up with

me," she said, linking her arm through Manon's, "and let me show you some of our lesser triumphs."

As Manon mounted the elegantly turned cypress staircase, she glanced down to see that Henry had already left the foyer, turned his attention to the overseer waiting on the veranda, and had called to the boy to bring round his horse. Zoe, meanwhile, moved gracefully up the stairs, giving murmured instructions to the wetnurse as she handed the child back to her arms.

Manon smiled to see her daughter and her husband so well in tune with one another. They meshed as a well-oiled machine, each partner playing a role so that the work of the whole got accomplished with a minimum of fuss. She slipped her arm through Zoe's as they went into the nursery, and Manon clapped with delight at the prancing, fanciful horses in greens and golds which paraded around the walls.

"The child will be a centaur, if you're not careful!" she laughed, "or a cowboy down on the Sabine. Did you do these yourself, Zoe?"

"Yes. I've discovered I enjoy puttering around with watercolors just for fun. Of course, it'll break my heart when he gets old enough to get tired of them and paints them over with footballs or automobiles or something."

The room was masculine and childlike all at once, with heavy dark green drapes to keep out the light and heat, but a light, airy canopy of pale green over the crib.

"Green was a smart choice," Manon said, inspecting everything approvingly. "No matter what he turned out to be, you'd be safe."

Zoe tucked the baby into his crib, and the two stood over him, watching him trace his thumb over his cheek until he found his puckered mouth. "He looks just like you did," Manon murmured.

"Really?" Zoe asked, delightedly. "I thought he was the image of his father."

"Not a bit. He's you, all over again."

Zoe gazed at Manon for a moment, as if wanting to say more. But she let the silence grow instead. Finally, they eased out of the room, and as they passed down the hallway, Manon glanced into the room next to the baby's to see that Zoe's wrapper was on the wide, high four-poster.

"Has the baby been wakeful?" Manon asked.

"No, he already sleeps through the night."

Manon stopped at the door and said, "But you're sleeping in this room."

Zoe avoided her eyes. "Yes," she said briskly, "for quite a while now, actually. I find we do better, Henry and I, if we have our privacy. We sleep better, for one."

Manon touched Zoe's arm, stopping her from descending the stairs. "*Un petit moment, cher,*" she said quietly, "you've only been married a few years, and you already have separate beds? Does Henry agree to this?"

"He's come around."

Manon hesitated. Zoe's demeanor did not invite advice. "I know many couples do make such arrangements," she began, hesitatingly. "But usually, they've been married for decades, Zoe. I hate to see you start that—*diviseur*—so early in your married life."

"Don't make it more than it is, *ma mère,* it's not so important."

"Sleeping alongside the man you love is not so important? *Ma foi,* you are too modern for me, *cher!*"

"Sleeping alongside one's husband is not so important, I said," Zoe returned patiently. "Now, can we agree that this subject need not have a maternal vote?" She linked her arm through Manon's and led her surely down the stairs, diverting her quickly with questions about the Irish Palace and her latest triumphs with the *beau monde* of New Orleans.

That night, Zoe, Alex, and Manon sat out on the upstairs gallery watching the purple martins take the mosquitoes out of the evening shadows.

"Alex, I think you'll be pleased to know," Manon said

drowsily over her wineglass, "that some of our new invest ments are getting attention as far away as Baton Rouge. Eve the Governor is intrigued by my latest plan."

"You've never had any trouble getting attention, *m soeur*," Alex said softly, "and it doesn't surprise me to see th Governor himself sit up and take notice. What've you got ou money in now?"

"Don't tell me you got him to build you another school *maman*," Zoe teased. "Soon we'll have to start shippin young ladies in from Texas, just to fill the seats."

"No, no, this is not a charity, it's a money tree. I expec we'll make more on this idea than on all our other propertie combined. We're going to lease some of those acres along th Atchafalaya to the oil companies, and if they discover oil o our land, they'll pay a pretty picayune to pump it out. W don't even need to sell it to them, they don't want to own i So we can leave the sharecroppers be and still take out a profi from the fields. And even if they don't find oil, they'll pa good money just to look!" She set her glass down and claspe her hands jubilantly. "I think it's an investment for the fu ture, and the Governor agrees with me. He's thinking o going in partners with a parcel he's got upriver from ours Nick says if they find oil, we should buy up even more lan along the bayou for the future. Because oil is likely the futur of this state."

"I thought perhaps Nick Fletcher might well have a han in this," Alex said dryly.

Manon dismissed him with an airy wave of her empt glass. "Oh you wouldn't like an idea of Nick's if it cam gold-plated with a certified stamp from Rome. You're jus ruffled because he's got a good head for business, and yo wouldn't know a bank account from a no-count if it up an robbed you. *Mon frère*, I've been handling your investment practically since I left the Ursulines, and Nick's been takin a hand to them for several years. He hasn't made a mistak yet. And my own have been few and far between."

"Maybe it's not the money, it's the politics Uncle objects to," Zoe said quietly.

"Politics! What does money have to do with politics?"

At that, both Zoe and Alex laughed aloud.

Manon grinned ruefully. "Well, I admit that politics and money sometimes set the same nest—"

"In this state," Alex said, "they *foul* the same nest. Listen, Manon, I didn't object strenuously when you put our mother's money into—"

"It wasn't our mother's money! It hasn't been our mother's money for nearly forty years."

"Be that as it may, I didn't object when you bought a jazz club out at Pontchartrain, though I knew it would mean some unsavory characters would be involved. I didn't object when you bought up those flea-bitten hotels on Basin and turned a profit on drunks and pimps."

"Alex—!" Manon began, but he put his hand up and stopped her.

"I know, I know, you cleaned them up, you said, and improved the whole tone of the Quarter. But the fact remains that there were—shall we say—less controversial ways to increase our investments. And now you want to bring the octopus of oil companies into the Atchafalaya and make them comfortable on our lands. Don't you understand what a delicate region we inhabit, Manon? The crop-lien system is doing enough to damage the bayou, the sharecroppers are leaving fallow fields and eroded banks behind them all over the delta, just stripping off the topsoil and moving on. Now the oil companies will come in and rape what's left of Louisiana."

"Oh for Sweet Mary's sake," Manon said impatiently, "leave it to an old-maid bachelor to turn a kiss on the cheek into a rape. You're mad because I'm not married to Nick and don't want to be. You don't approve of him and you never have, and I don't give two shakes. Besides that, I've already signed the lease agreement with Standard Oil, and one thing

623

I *have* learned in politics *and* business, is never go back on an agreement. Besides, do you think you're the only one interested in the future of this state? Why, I'm investing in its future right and left. We've got more than ten thousand in Southern Pacific stock, which in case you missed the headlines, Alex darling, did a while back complete the rails from New Orleans to California. If that isn't the future, I don't know what is."

Alex sighed and took another long swallow of wine. "I never could argue with you, Manon. I don't know why I try."

"That's right," she said firmly, "it only upsets you and to no good end. Now, tell me, *cher,* how are your birds and your salt mines faring?"

"Uncle is becoming famous himself, *ma mère,*" Zoe said gently.

She had been listening carefully to her mother and Alex spar back and forth, and Manon could not tell by her expression which relative she sided with—or even loved—most of all. Zoe's gentle, uncommitted smile always unnerved her. "Is that so, Alex? Have you invented a new bird now along with all your other inventions?"

"He has started a sanctuary," Zoe said, smiling proudly at her uncle. "The first in the country, likely in the whole world. For egrets. He and Ned McIlhenny, on some land Henry's mother gave them, so the egrets can nest and breed in safety. Already, they have ten breeding pairs. That may be enough to save the whole species in this state."

"I never realized it was in peril," Manon said, bewildered.

"Every time you see a lady's hat adorned with feathers *maman,* it's probably the aigrettes from the plumage of the great egret. It's the largest of the four species we have in this country and, unfortunately, the favorite of all the milliners." She frowned and shook her head. "An entire bird destroyed for the sake of a woman's vanity. But,"—she brightened—"this spring, six of the breeding pairs returned to the colony and so we have hope they'll survive."

"We? Are you involved in Alex's . . . experiments, my dear?"

"I've been helping with his correspondence, *maman*," Zoe replied. "He gets letters from scientists all over the world wanting to come to study his egrets in their natural state."

"She's been invaluable," Alex said, smiling tenderly at her. "And if I'm finally able to interest a publisher in my studies on the birds, it'll be to her credit."

"A few letters . . ." Zoe blushed.

"Your line drawings are excellent, *cher*," Alex insisted. "Delicate and lovely as the birds themselves. If we are published, it will be because of those, I believe."

Zoe said, "Well, at any rate, *maman*, Uncle will soon be having famous scientists from all over coming to Avery Island to see his egrets. So when he speaks of Louisiana's future, we best pay heed."

"You believe," Manon said with a frown of some confusion, "that the state's future lies in its birds?"

"And the rest of its wildlife," Alex said firmly. "The Cajuns have a saying, you know, 'Watch the birds. The birds know best what *le bon Dieu* brings on the wind.' I think they're right."

Manon shook her head. "I doubt highly that I could interest the Governor in a partnership of bird-watching. He sees tourism as Louisiana's best hope. That and her underground resources. He'd like to see every plantation restored and every bayou lined with refineries."

"That's one of the problems with the South," Alex said thoughtfully. "We're selling off everything, even our past. Selling it off like an old coquette auctioning off her party clothes."

"If you would put up a mock antebellum mansion on Avery, plant some camellias, and bring out belles in hoop skirts every Saturday afternoon to serve mint juleps, I imagine the Governor would show new interest in your little island refuge."

"Fortunately," Alex said, "we don't need him that bad. At least not at the moment."

"And perhaps by the time you do, our oil agreement will have made him so rich," Manon said gleefully, "that he'll happily write you a check for the welfare of your birds."

"Perhaps," Alex answered, pouring another glass of wine.

As the silence around them grew larger, Manon glanced at Zoe for a clue to her daughter's heart. But her face, as usual, was opaque.

Henry came out to the gallery then, peered at them all sitting in the shadows and asked, "Have you solved the problems of the world yet?"

Zoe looked up and smiled. "Just this little corner of it."

"Well, that's a good day's work all by itself." He pulled over the cane rocker and settled heavily into it, fatigue showing in the lines of his face and the slope of his knees. "Manon, did she tell you we've got our own railroad now?"

"I haven't had a chance to brag on you yet, honey," Zoe chuckled. "The world's problems only just now got finished up."

"Got ourselves a little ol' thirty-six-gauge steam engine, strictly for the plantation. Zoe likes to ride up and down investigating the fields."

"Well, I heard that's the latest thing!" Manon laughed. "A few of the sugar planters Nick knows put them in, too. They say, they're great for socials and squiring their daughters and beaux out and about, not too far from mama's eyes and far enough away so that the boys can steal a kiss or two."

"I hope they're good for more than that," Henry said dryly. "I mean for them to pay their way in time and foot leather saved. We're paying sixty-five cents a day for good labor now, and if Congress shuts down the spigot on sugar tariffs, we'll be in a heap of hurt this winter."

Henry had a way of taking on a backwoods air to his speech, Manon noted, when he was away from New Orleans and on his own gallery. He would never have expressed himself in such a way in her parlor.

She said, "Sixty-five cents a day is a blessing. Imagine if the colored got a dollar a day, like they asked! Why even their own hero, Booker T. Washington, told them to renounce equal rights and concentrate on learning their letters first. The Jim Crow laws have been upheld by the highest court in the land, and some of those schools they're setting up for the colored are every bit as good as those for the white children. They should be grateful, *vraiment,* and most of the better colored are. They've got it a sight better than they used to, and that's what progress is all about." Holy Mother, she thought with small contempt, I'm sounding as bayou-back-woods as he does. "Well," she patted her thighs with finality, "they lost the vote, at any rate. *Certainement,* someone in Congress knew what they were doing when they voted for disenfranchisement. Reconstruction is over, *grace à Dieu,* and I doubt we'll brook that sort of interference again."

To her surprise, Henry threw back his head and closed his eyes. He laughed once, loudly. Rudely, it seemed to her.

"Manon," he finally said, "it astounds me that a woman with your head for business can delude herself with such consolations."

Now, *that* sounded like the old Henry, Manon thought with quick satisfaction.

"If Congress continues its disastrous course of first, pulling out price supports for our sugar, and second, making it tough for us to keep our colored happy, I can see no reason to suppose that even a hundred acres of sugar will stand in this state within five years. No one can make a profit on a crop that must compete with cheap labor, if there's no cheap labor to be had."

"Every place I look, I see nothing but black faces," Manon said with pretended indignation. "Surely we have cheap labor abounding." Privately, of course, she applauded Henry's passion. God knows, she had seen it rarely enough.

627

Truth be told, she was already bored, missing the good adversarial sparrings she and Nick enjoyed, wondering what in the world they found to talk about in this backwater—

"Yes, and most of their hands are empty," Henry said. "We can't pay them enough to make them want to work, and we can't suffer their leaving. And now, they've lost the vote, so they can't even take control of their own destiny. Mark me, Manon, those black faces—and those empty hands—will be the barnacles that keep this ship of state from any speed. Sooner or later, we'll rot from the inside out."

"Not so long as we can keep on starting wars just to keep Cuban sugar out of Spanish hands," Manon said. "Who did you poor planters maul in Washington to get that accomplished? Commodore Dewey has taken the Philippines with scarcely a man lost—"

"So that now, Cuban sugar can continue to pour into this country unabated," Henry finished for her. "And if that isn't enough, we just annexed Hawaii, another place where they can grow sugar faster and cheaper than we can. I believe you should stick to Louisiana politics, *ma mère,* for the intricacies of international commerce seem to escape you." He turned restlessly to Alex. "You're mighty quiet tonight, Uncle. Is the salt trade sliding down alongside sugar these days?"

Alex shook his head drowsily. "We've just found a new deposit, probably the biggest one in the state. Maybe in the whole country. So long as folks keep eating, I guess they'll still need salt."

"That's what I always said about sugar," Henry grumbled. "Well, this old man is too tired to cure it or cuss it any longer tonight." He rose and bowed to Manon. *"Ma mère,* it is always a delight." He turned to Zoe. "Are you coming up soon, honey?"

"In a little while."

He bowed briefly to Alex and Manon and took his leave.

Alex yawned hugely. "Henry sounds more worried than

I've heard him before. Is sugar really in trouble in this state?"

Zoe shrugged. "It's Henry's job to worry, and he does it well. If sugar goes lower, then we'll plant something else, I suppose."

"Well, it's not that easy, *cher,*" Manon began, "if Henry's right, he's going to need—"

"Don't tell me what Henry needs, *maman,*" Zoe said quietly. "I believe I can divine that on my own."

Alex glanced from one woman to the other. "Well, it's time I took my leave as well, I guess," he said, rising and setting his glass down. "You two must surely have secrets to share that don't need a set of masculine ears as witness."

Zoe said nothing.

"And will you be staying out the week?" Manon asked as her brother left the gallery.

"Oh yes, *ma soeur,*" he said over his shoulder. "It'll take at least that long to finish the work Zoe and I need to do. I give you *bonne nuit.*"

"He is so pleased," Manon said with lowered voice, "about your choice of name for the baby. I could tell by his face when he told me—"

"I know he is."

"He's a beautiful boy. But I never had any doubt that you and Henry would make beautiful children."

Zoe gazed at her mother curiously. "*Vraiment?*" She gazed away, out to the vast shadowed lawn which disappeared into the blackness of the bayou. "Well, we shall likely have many."

"With separate bedrooms?"

Zoe shrugged. "As many as God grants me. In that way, I can be assured that my inevitable errors will be spread out over as many souls as possible." She gazed back at her mother. "And no one soul will suffer overmuch."

"Zoe," Manon said quietly, "are you happy, then?" She took a deep breath. "I so hope that you are happy, *cher.*"

Zoe smiled softly. "I know you do, *maman.* I have always

known that." She thought for a moment. "I suppose I am happy enough. No woman marries the man she thinks she marries, *n'est-ce pas?* No woman has the marriage she imagined for herself. But one does not argue with the angels. One learns to accept the differences, not only between the two of you, but between what you hoped for and what you finally have. One learns, I hope, to even love the differences. In time." She stood up. "And to see that in our differences lies our strength."

"So you *are* happy?" Manon urged.

Zoe laughed ruefully. "You will have your answer, won't you? Let us say that I would miss my marriage if it were gone. It's like so many things, I suppose. So many things which are appreciated more in the loss than in the having . . . including our lives."

"My darling," Manon managed, "I believe you have grown ten years in the past few."

Zoe smiled. "Did I have any choice? Sleep well, Mother, and I'll take you on a train ride tomorrow."

Zoe left Manon alone on the porch then and disappeared into the dark house. Manon sat and listened to the sounds of the bayou coming to her over the lawn, sounds of the night and the creatures which she had not heard before through the voices. An overwhelming urge slid over her, and she bowed her head and wept quietly, though she could not say why.

In 1898, the Louisiana legislature joined most of the other Southern states in disenfranchising their Negro population. Two years later, G.H. White, a Negro Representative in Con-

ress from North Carolina, introduced a bill to make lynching federal crime. It was soundly, swiftly defeated.

The Wall Street Panic of 1901 rolled over the delta, leaving many planters bankrupt and vast estates carved into share-roppers' plots to pay taxes. Standard Oil drilled the first well t Jennings, and Northern corporations rushed to follow, fill-ng local politicians' pockets for the privilege of tying up oil and mineral rights to much of the bayou. But little of the influx f capital found its way into the delta economy, and times were ard for many.

The discovery that yellow fever was caused by mosquitoes made New Orleans once more a less dangerous destination for ravelers, and crews of immigrants were sent to the swamps to trip the Atchafalaya of valuable cypress forests.

By 1912, sugar as a cash crop had declined to less than a enth of its postwar value, and men of industry in the delta earched for new ways to make a profit from the soupy marsh f Louisiana.

But the marsh was changing as quickly as the men who ought to exploit it. Even the Mississippi was changing in these ears. Always a slow and silent river, almost lazy in its quiet ower, it was beginning to flex and move the land in new ways. Rolling through the delta at the rate of sixty tons of water every econd, it appeared to be contained by the rising embank-ments, but it was not tamed. On lands so soggy that their ncestors were afraid to drive the lightest carriage across it, men were building tall buildings and bridges. The Mississippi, meanwhile, was building a second mouth in the Atchafalaya River to the north.

Until the Civil War, the Atchafalaya had been blocked at ts northern end by a permanent logjam, a raft of logs twenty miles long that kept the waters of the Mississippi from pouring down the delta. In 1855, the raft was cleared away to make he Atchafalaya navigable for gunboats. The channel immedi-ttely began to widen and deepen, and by 1910, the vigorous oung river was carrying a fifth of the flow of the Mississippi.

There was little indication that 1915 was going to be a stellar year. Manon knew it, most of her friends knew it, and the conditions in New Orleans underlined their conviction. It wasn't enough that the country was headed towards war again, and this time with an adversary who could well dam the entire Mississippi with U-boats and submarines. The sinking of the *Lusitania* convinced most in the Queen City that Germany would do anything to strangle British trade, even if it meant blockading the gulf.

Cotton prices were down, sugar prices had plummeted, and patrons at the jazz clubs and restaurants along the Pontchartrain had dwindled to a grim handful of somber tourists who monitored their drinks and limited their tips.

Many Northern corporations had flooded the city with offers to lease or buy mineral and oil rights, but most of the money stayed up North, with little lining local pockets. Manon knew several planters, caught in the downward spiral of sugar prices, who were desperate to sell or lease any square acre of land to the oil companies, but few had what they wanted to buy: swamp land in the Atchafalaya or along the inner bayous. Standard Oil built a refinery, the state's first in Baton Rouge, but it did little for the economy of the Queen City and the delta.

Tempers were high that summer, and as the hottest months came and lay over the city like a simmering syrup, men were called out with regularity for imagined slights.

Manon found the city intolerable that season. The summer months were no longer comfortable, for the stench and damp from the river and the Quarter were pervasive, even on the top floor of her vast and normally cool apartment on Canal.

"Used to be," she had complained to Nick, "if there was any breeze to be had in the whole Quarter, I got a little edge of it, day and night. Now, they build so close and high, even a gale barely ruffles my priscillas. I've got half a mind to go see Zoe and the children for a fortnight, until it cools off. The roads are passable, at least. Thank God that Cadillac's got an electric starter. This is the worst August I can recall." She threw her pillow on the carpet in a huff and flounced forward on her stomach. Naked, they were in bed, though it was only two o'clock in the afternoon.

"Why don't you then?" he said, reaching for the bottle of cologne she kept iced on the nightstand. He drenched a linen cloth and draped it across the back of her neck.

"Will you come with me?" She turned and leaned up on one elbow, letting her breasts arch and her waist curve. Even past fifty, she noted with satisfaction, her body still fell into seductive lines as though it knew no others. She grinned at him with promise.

He groaned and threw himself on his back. "Woman, it's too hot. If you had any decency in you at all, you wouldn't torture a man into tempting a stroke."

"I've been putting up with the frivolousness of a younger man all these years, just so that now—when I'm at my peak—I'll have someone who can keep up with me. Don't tell me I've been wasting my time, *cher.*" She took the cloth off her neck and stroked him softly with it, up his chest and down his groin.

Nick snorted, a half-growl, half-snarl which announced his desire, and rolled over, gripping her buttocks firmly and covering her body with his. "How long have we been doing this, Madame?" he asked as his mouth moved down her neck, riding in the sweat which beaded on her skin.

"Long enough . . ." she murmured, moving him up and into her deftly. "To get it down right . . ."

Later, they lay and talked drowsily through the early twilight, something they often did when they could. Manon asked him again if he wanted to go with her to ShadyOaks, just to get away from the city.

"Not particularly," he said lazily. "I'm surprised you want to go, yourself, it's a long damn trip in this heat."

"I don't see enough of the children," she said fretfully. "I have six *petits enfants,* and they grow so fast I scarcely know them when I *do* see them."

"Everytime you come back, you're bothered about something or other. Usually, your daughter."

"Yes," she sighed, "it's true. I never have understood her. She doesn't seem unhappy and she doesn't seem happy."

"She's content," he yawned, "why can't you let it alone?"

"Because she doesn't seem to have anything that excites her much these days. She's content, but that's about it. She has no passion in her life."

He chuckled wryly. "You got all the passion in the family, honey. Sucked up that julep to the bottom of the glass. Ol' Alex and Zoe never had a chance to get a share. But they seem satisfied enough. You're the one always wanting them to be different. Why can't you just let them be?"

"Because I love them," she said, rising up on one elbow and glaring at him. "I love my brother and he breaks my heart. I love my daughter, and she breaks my heart, too. I can't get close to either one of them, they both keep me at arm's length—"

"I think you scare them," he said calmly.

She stopped, a little shocked by the truth she sensed in his words. "What are you talking about?"

"Passionate people are a little frightening, honey," he said quietly. "They demand a response. They make other people wonder if their lives are as satisfying as they thought they were. They flat tire you out, sometimes."

"Do I tire you out?" she demanded.

"Hell, yes," he teased, wrapping her in his arms. "I'm alf-dead, mostly."

"Well, I don't get the impression I tire Zoe out," she ontinued, ignoring him. "I get the impression I bore her. hat she thinks I'm a silly, vapid *bidet,* and she'd just as soon cut my visits to every *sixth* month."

"So why don't you?"

"Because I love her!" she wailed, flopping back on the amp pillows.

"But does she love you?" he asked softly.

"Of course, she does," she snapped, "I've been a good nother, I've never done anything to make her not love me, nd I've always wanted nothing but the best for her."

He was silent for a moment. "Well, only you could be the adge of that, I guess."

"It's just that our lives are so different now," she went on, tretching and running her toes up his instep. "I should make nore of an effort. You can't just drop in on people once every w months and expect to feel like family. I should visit more ften. The children grow so fast . . ."

"A good idea. Wait until they're all old enough to make alfway decent conversation, and then I'll ferry you back and orth whenever you take the notion."

"I wouldn't take you with me now if you begged me," she aid, rolling over on top of him. "Go on. Beg me."

And he did.

But for all her teasing, finally, Nick would not make the rip to ShadyOaks that month. Too much business, he mainained, far too many adversaries to battle, especially if *she* vanted to shirk all responsibility and gad about.

Manon knew the truth. In fact, Nick never really felt very omfortable with Zoe and Henry. Though they had come to ccept him over the years, accept that he was part of her life s inevitably as they were, they still kept him at arm's length

with that gracious Southern formality which seemed to enci
cle and sequester all at once.

Nick was a Yankee, he was younger than Manon, and h
was Protestant. These taints they may have been able t
overlook, but that he had not married her in all these year
remained scrofulous in their eyes.

And so, Manon made the trip to ShadyOaks alone, t
visit her daughter, Henry, and her six grandchildren. Ale
was seventeen now, Henry Junior was fifteen, Samuel wa
thirteen, Simon, eleven, Alice, nine, and Celly was just si
this month. Manon privately wondered that Zoe could wal
upright, much less keep the pace she had for so many year

The letters and the occasional calls—now that the tele
phone lines were out to the bayou at last—these helped clos
the distance between them. Zoe had always been dutifu
about her weekly letters, from her convent days righ
through six children. Each letter made Manon feel guilty an
glad all at once. It was wonderful to hear from her, but eac
meant an answer required. How did Zoe find the time? Eac
week, two pages, never more or less, as regular as the sunse
Manon skipped one, sometimes two, then flooded her daugh
ter with six or seven pages—only to be followed by a lon
silence. As in most things, their styles were wondrously mis
matched.

Nonetheless the letters and the calls were better tha
nothing. Manon relished the lines from her daughter, read fa
too much into each phrase, and hunted for secrets in ever
word. She sometimes feared that Zoe was scarcely her chil
at all. That at the moment she was conceived, Manon becam
only a tunnel into the cosmic dance. She had done everythin
she could to keep Zoe from coming into being, if wishes hel
any sway with the universe. She almost, after all, killed he
within her womb. But nature is in such a fury to reproduc
she thought, one only has to look around to see it. The tangl
of vines which erupted each spring, despite every effort t
root them out, the throngs of insects which exploded in th

r and water, the swarms of birds which would nest, no atter how she tried to dislodge them, in every nook and anny of the Irish Palace roof. And Zoe would be born, hether she was wanted or not.

She sometimes had the sense that David had only existed, at her passion only sparked, flamed, and consumed them th, so that Zoe could get off of the clouds and down into er heart.

And so, one would think that once in Manon's heart, she ould be content to give hers as well. But something in Zoe eld herself apart, yes, even from her own mother.

There was much about her daughter she would never now, she thought to herself as she sat on the gallery of hadyOaks, watching the workers in the distant fields. Much e didn't wish to know, even if she could.

She shaded her eyes with her hand, focusing on the fields. enry had stripped out the sugar and replaced it with a new op, a hot pepper he sold to McIlhenny for his new factory. he seedlings went from hotbeds to the field in April and now ey were covered with bright red peppers. Harvested and ushed, salted and aged, they made a mash which, when dded to spice and vinegar, made a piquant sauce McIlhenny lled Tabasco.

Henry joked that between the salt and the peppers McIlenny got cheap, he could drown the world in the sauce for ss than the price of a good beefsteak.

The message came on the telephone that afternoon while lanon drowsed on the gallery. She could barely hear the uzz of the machine in the far recesses of the house, but when oe came and stood in the doorway, she knew instantly that e call had been bad news.

"It's Nick," Zoe said.

"Nick?" Manon said, rising to her feet with alarm. "Why he calling—?"

"No, it's not Nick calling, *maman*," Zoe said, taking her m. "It's about Nick. There's been an—an accident."

637

Manon stopped and her hand went to her throat. "What sort of accident?"

"Be strong, Mother. He's been shot," Zoe said, dropping her head. "I'm so sorry." She tried to take Manon in her arms.

Manon whirled away and towards the house, "What do you mean? Shot? What sort of accident? Where's the phone?"

"Mother," Zoe said, taking her arms and holding her still. "I'm sorry, please listen to me. He's been shot. Your solicitor just called."

"*Monsieur* Apton? Why in God's name—"

"*Maman,* he is dead."

Manon shrieked, her eyes wide and her mouth open in horror. She fell against the side of the house, clinging to the door.

Zoe pulled her tightly into her embrace, repeating in her ear, "Mother, I'm so sorry. He was in a duel. He was shot. He died instantly, your attorney said. Just a few hours ago. I'm so sorry, *maman!*"

"A duel! No, no, no—" Manon moaned, sinking down to the chaise with her head in her hands. "Then it was no accident at all! Who shot him? Why did he do such an insane thing? Why did you call it an accident, it's not accident, it's murder! He always avoided this when it was in fashion, he's never been called out, always managed his business without such stupidity. And now that dueling is on the wane, he let himself be killed! I knew it, I told him to be careful!"

Zoe looked alarmed. "You mean he had dueled before? You never mentioned—"

"No, no!" Manon said, "I told him, men are crazy! I told him not to wear a gun!" She stopped, bewildered. "Not Nick! It wasn't Nick, we never spoke of it. It was David. I warned your *father,* and now it's Nick who should have been warned!"

Zoe sank down in the chaise next to her mother. "You never said this before, Mother." She paused for a moment.

That might be the first time you've mentioned my father in any years." She recovered herself quickly. "But Nick had ver dueled, you said? He must have been urgently pro-ked. And even if you had warned him, he would have done hat he had to do. You know that. Your warning or lack of arning had nothing to do with his death. You know men ill do what they will do, regardless of whether it's right or w much you warn them or try to help—"

Manon yanked her hands down from her face, her mouth visted in anguish. "You don't know why people do what ey do! You don't know anything about what makes them. ly God, he can't be dead. I would have known it! I would ve felt it!"

Zoe took one of her hands. "Monsieur said he died viftly, *maman,* and never regained consciousness. Even if u had been there, you could have done nothing. There was surgeon there, and he couldn't save him. He tried but there as no chance. So Nick didn't suffer, at least."

Manon began to weep, more calmly now. "He didn't ffer. That's good. Out and gone too swift to stop him. So ke him. I doubt he's suffered a day in his life."

"Then," Zoe said softly, "how fortunate he was."

Manon nodded, scarcely hearing her. Distracted, she ood and began to pace. "I must get back right away. My od, I shouldn't have come, I asked him and he couldn't get vay, he said, but I should have been with him. He died one! Sweet Mary, he died before me, I never thought it ould happen like this. And now there will be so much to . Nick had been handling the club, he was taking care of many things for me lately, and I don't know—"

Zoe stood and embraced her. "Do you need me to go with u?"

Manon looked at her with surprise. "No," she said owly. "It's good of you, but no." She pulled away and began gain to pace. "Say my good-byes to the children and Henry d tell them *grandmère* must attend to business. Tell them

I'll be back soon, tell them a dear friend has—" she put clenched fist to her mouth and caught her breath in a sob "He was so very dear!" She closed her eyes. "I loved him. truly did. He gave me so much pleasure . . ."

Zoe looked away, uncomfortable. "I'll tell them," Zo said, leading her into the house. "If you're sure you don' want me to come with you."

Manon turned, almost exasperated. "And if I said ye: what would you do? Leave the house and the children an Henry? I can scarcely believe that you'd—"

"Of course, I would, *ma mère,*" Zoe said firmly. "If yo wish it, I will go with you this minute."

Manon's face softened, and she took Zoe's chin in he hand. *"Merci, cher.* I guess you would at that." She turne and hurried up the stairs. "Call for my car to be brough round," she cried over her shoulder, "and tell them to chec the gasoline and oil. I don't want to stop before New Or leans."

Zoe watched her mother hurry up to pack, watched th line of her shoulders straighten and stiffen as though she wen into battle. Ah, Mother, she thought swiftly, now perhap you will know grief and loneliness, maybe for the first tim in your life, and I feel sorry for what is coming for you in th years ahead. Will you be able to battle fate into submissio for much longer?

But then Zoe noticed something even more importan about her mother's figure as she ascended, something she ha not seen for the longest time, really. The wonderful ripeness the softness of Manon, the fullness of her mother's arms an hips, the lines of her bosom, saw the folds and curves of body that had been made for sexual pleasure and had glorie in it. And she envied her mother in that moment as much a she had at any time in her life.

As Manon approached the Mississippi, the sky from the south was lowering fast. She pushed the Cadillac into a faster pace, keeping one anxious eye on the clouds. A storm on those dirt roads up the western side of the river would make New Orleans an unreachable mirage by nightfall.

She thought of little but Nick as she wrenched the wheel first one way and then the other, avoiding the wagon ruts and the muddy potholes. It occurred to her that potholes in Louisiana had at least an inch of mud in them at all times, especially as they neared the river. As though the water was such an insistent part of the landscape that it had to boil to the surface at any opportunity, at the slightest indentation or abrasion, like the blood in the body.

Nick. Some part of her cursed God that He hadn't let her be there when he died. A larger part of her blessed Him, that she wouldn't have to remember for the rest of her days the way his face must have looked at the last. She wept as she drove, letting the tears roll and dry and roll again, as monotonously as the tires. It was such a waste. A decade ago, duels were common, and women worried each time their men confronted each other. But now, duels were more rare, and few men were tempted to meet beneath the oaks to settle their disputes. Had it been over her? What a fool the man was! What a waste of love!

For he had loved her, of that she was certain. Loved her as much as a man like Nick could love. Loved her with a fury and a passion and a wit that knew just enough to keep her at arm's length, lest she engulf him.

And she had loved him. With as much of love as was left in her after David abandoned her, leaving her heart like a little pool in the sun, drying from the outside in. Nick had made her love again, yes, but not trust. Never again could she trust. Never again would she try. Besides, it wasn't necessary to trust in order to love. She had proven that much to herself. And how could you—why would you?—trust a man like Nick anyway? He was so different, so flamboyant, the very things which most drew her to him also kept her heart at bay.

But she would miss him all the days of her life, of that much she was certain. And it was this aching loneliness which spread out before her like a map of a wide, empty, and arid land, that made her weep until she could scarcely keep the car on the road. Lonely, empty, alone—for lover, for friend, for family—in those moments, she yearned for Alex's arms, for Zoe's smiling face, for grandchildren around her like a warm cocoon, for someone to care whether she lived or died.

The wind did nothing to help, she finally noticed as she calmed and cried herself to steady, rhythmic hitches. The constant breeze up the river had turned to a strong gusty pattern of intermittent squalls that buffeted the Cadillac to and fro under her hands. The clouds above were rolling as fast as the automobile, dark and threatening to the south and the east.

By the time Manon drove across the bridge at Donaldson into Ascension Parish, her alarm over the gathering storm drove her grief into a different part of her mind to be consid ered later. At Saint Rose, on the outskirts of New Orleans she finally had to stop at a roadside filling station and scurry inside for shelter. She was afraid to pull the Cadillac unde the live oaks—they were creaking so in the wind—so sh parked right out alongside the highway and ran, holding he skirt and her hat against the grasping, tearing gusts.

"What are you doing out there alone!" shouted a man, wrenching her off balance as he pulled her inside the station, damming the door behind her. "Lord, lady, don't you know storm's coming hard?"

"It wasn't coming when I started out!" she said, panting and straightening herself. "Is it going to be bad?"

"Supposed to be a big one," he said, turning back to the counter. He and his wife were piling canned goods and packaged stores onto the lower shelves. "Coming up from the gulf, they said, and flattened Myrtle Grove on the way."

"It doesn't take much to flatten Myrtle Grove," she snapped, realizing that her bodice was torn in two places.

"Maybe not, but they say she's getting stronger with every mile north. You got people in New Orleans?"

"Yes," she said, not stopping to explain. "And I've got to get there tonight."

The woman turned to her with alarm. She was a dark, small Cajun *femme* with a shy manner. "*Madame, ça c'est vraiment dangereux.* You must find shelter here. Perhaps at the church, it will be safe. Come with us, it is on high ground—"

"No, I must go on," Manon said firmly. "I'm close enough to make it now."

"But Madame," the man began—

Manon did not wait to hear his protest but pulled the door open again and fled for the Cadillac, the wind now howling past her face, whipping her hair down and over her eyes. A branch had fallen down over the Cadillac's hood, and she struggled with it for long moments, her traveling suit tangling around her knees. From the station, the man came out running, helped her dislodge the branch off the automobile and wrenched the door open, pushing her in.

"God keep you!" he shouted at her through the glass, and she could barely hear him over the wind. She battled the Cadillac out to the road, set it towards the river, and urged the machine with her will. Closer to the city, as she approached a bend of the highway which swerved close to the Mississippi, she saw that the water was high, gray, and surging against its banks. She felt the first real frisson of fear up the sides of her neck and her cheeks. This was a mighty storm, perhaps even a hurricane, for nothing else could touch and swell the river so quickly. Coming from the gulf, heading upriver, it would hit New Orleans with the fury of a fist. She pushed the Cadillac to its utmost, clenching her teeth a tightly as she gripped the wheel, and in that instant, the clouds opened as a second river, and it rained in rippling angry sheets, making it almost impossible for her to see the road at all.

Into the city now, and branches littered the roadway debris and papers flew in spiraling fits of angry flotsam al around her, people pushed by, leaning against the wind and gripping their clothing, and the rain burst and swayed around them like billowing curtains. The sky was filled with threads of lightning like spider webs, and the clouds were dark green. Manon finally reached her apartment and raced for the door, frightened and cursing the storm.

It seemed to her, once inside, that there was scant refuge even behind the walls. The sides of the house were shivering with the wind, and Lucy, her maid, came running from the back of the house calling frantically, *"Madame! Madame! C'est un hurricane! Nous sommes abandonées de Dieu!"*

"Lucy, stop that unholy noise!" Manon shouted back a her. "Run quick and get all the candles you can find, fill al the buckets with water, and I'll get the blankets!"

"Oh! Oh!" Lucy shrieked, running towards the kitchen with her hands to her ears against the equal shriek of the wind from the outside.

Manon raced upstairs, grabbed what blankets she could find from the spare rooms, and when she reached her bed room, she stopped stark in the middle of the floor, struck by the sight of the bed itself. Nick's dressing gown lay across he chaise, as though he had only just shrugged it off his shoul ers. She almost threw herself down on the bed and gave way to a fit of weeping to rival the storm. But she gathered her will together and angrily yanked all the covers off the bed, bundled them against her breast, and hurried from the room without a backwards glance.

In moments, she had Lucy in the small basement, in the farthest corner away from the river side of the house. She had calmed the woman as best she could, and the two huddled together, listening as the hurricane ravaged the house, the block, the Quarter above them. They heard crashes, tinkling of glass, the thud of heavy objects being thrown to the floors, and with each, Lucy jumped and squealed as though pinched by God.

But Manon sat stock-still and stony, facing the darkness of the basement, listening to the wind. Nick, she thought, if you were here, you'd be holding me. Comforting me. Instead, I must be strength and comfort to someone else. Likely, this will be the way the rest of my life will be.

The wind had changed direction several times; they could feel it in the bulge and heave of the walls above them, sense it in the keening chaos, like the despairing wail of a thousand hungry cats. Bricks rattled down on the roof, and loose objects around them actually rose up towards the ceiling with the pressure. At one point, a mighty tearing, ripping noise shuddered through the house and the basement, and Lucy screamed frantically, clutching at Manon.

"It's the gallery," Manon said. "Next, the roof will go."

Tormented trees thrashed against the walls, and Manon counted them one by one as they fell, waiting until she could stop counting and they would stop thrashing. Water seeped into the basement from two corners, but it pooled in the deep sections of the earth, never getting high enough to make them anything but damp and miserable.

The wind turned savage within hours, a hammer of rain and blasts of power that drowned out all other sounds, all other life. Water dripped, then dribbled steadily from all sides of the basement now, and the temperature dropped so low that the blankets Manon had collected seemed like muslin sheets against the cold. The candles hissed in the dampness of the air, and the wind reached its fingers even under the earth, making the flames waver frantically.

Finally the long winds began, slowly, to lessen. Manon urged Lucy to her feet. "If we can, we must get out of here," she said firmly. "If something hasn't fallen on the door and trapped us. We must get to higher ground, in case the levee breaks and floods the city completely."

Lucy scrambled then, and they put their shoulders to the basement door to open it to devastation. It seemed that half the house was down on their heads, though fortunately, little had landed directly on their passageway to freedom. They emerged in the gray dawn, with rain coming through a hundred places in the roof. One wall was partially gone, another in the foyer was slanted in at an odd angle, as though an enormous boot had kicked it off kilter.

Manon made her way out to the street through the debris and broken glass, scarcely heeding Lucy's whimpers behind her. Canal Street was still recognizable, but many of the houses were sagging and without their roofs. Not a window was intact, so far as she could see, not a door still hinged, not a gallery undamaged. Water stood a foot or more in the street, and a thick, greasy mud lay over most surfaces.

A large black snake wriggled by down the roadway, and she shrank back against what remained of her front door. Dead fish, cats, dogs, and birds lay in pitiful piles against those walls which still stood upright.

Manon saw a man wandering down Canal Street, seemingly the only survivor except herself in the whole block. He looked dazed and shrunken, as though he had glimpsed the face of God and wanted only to die.

"Have you seen my wife?" he called out plaintively. "Madame Franklin?" He kept walking without looking at her.

"She would have had our two sons with her, I'm certain. Have you seen my wife?"

Manon went back inside and crossed herself, and her weeping began for the first time since she had arrived home.

The hurricane which struck New Orleans that September was the worst which had ever roared through the delta. The city was without power for more than three days, and food and water were almost impossible to find. Parts of the Quarter were under eight feet of water. Manon had been lucky, she discovered, compared to many of her neighbors. One woman down the street had drowned in her own basement with her three children, as a retaining wall gave way, flooding them in seconds. Five hundred people were sleeping in the Federal Building; thousands more took shelter in churches, in banks, and other well-anchored constructions. Only a few hundred houses in the whole Quarter still had their roofs intact.

As Manon and her neighbors began to move about and discover the full extent of damage, they found that most of the cemeteries were flooded, with tombs uprooted and caskets exposed. In the harbor, tugs were sunk and boats crushed against the wharf and each other.

Manon moved most of her valuables to a part of the house where the roof was still intact, then went to the mortuary where Nick's body was being held. Repairs and reconstruction could wait, she decided, until she saw Nick and arranged for his comfort.

The mortuary house was a low building surrounded by taller apartment houses, relatively unscathed by the storm. The director met her with courtesy, but his moving hands betrayed his agitation.

"Madame," he began quickly, "I hope you will understand that in this emergency, we had to move quickly. Monsieur was interred the morning of the storm."

"You've already buried him?"

"Regretfully, we had no other choice. We don't have

647

facilities for the protection of the deceased, of course, and we could not be sure—"

"Where is he buried?" She felt her rage and despair rise as suddenly as they had the first time she knew of his death. "He had no proper funeral? No flowers?"

"Of course, many families will prefer to have their funeral arrangements completed at this time, and I'll be glad to help you plan a proper grave-site ceremony, Madame, once the repairs and restoration of the cemetery are complete." He touched her arm in sympathy. "The dead will not be offended that we must turn to the living first, Madame. They, at least, are at peace."

She moved her shoulder away from him coldly. "Where have you buried him?"

"At Saint Louis number two."

"Is there a marker?"

He shook his head sadly. "There has been no time. But if Madame would like to choose the statuary or perhaps a fine vault, I would be happy to show you a wide selection."

But Manon was already out the door.

Saint Louis, one, two, and three, like most of the cemeteries in New Orleans, were vast spreads of stones, above ground tombs, and marble statuaries. The Cities of the Dead, they called them, and tourists came to gawk at such strange customs which decreed that the dead should be housed aboveground, rather than beneath it for reasons of seepage, and should rest, in fact, in as much or more grandeur than they knew in life.

Like the Creole houses, the tombs were of brick, stuccoed and whitewashed, complete with galleries of ironwork and, in some cases, narrow *banquettes*. Many were fitted with iron gates and metal garden chairs and benches, so that the dead might "receive" guests on holy days. Here was serenity without chill, even humor and hospitality. Plaster and marble statuary crowded the aisles: weeping willows and widows in bas-relief, carved angels and seraphs, soldiers, sphinxes, sheep being driven by shepherds, and even one with a heavy steamboat plying the ground as though it rode the waters.

As Manon picked her way among the toppled and tilted stones, the downed branches and debris from the storm, she felt none of the peace she normally enjoyed when she visited Saint Louis. She went to the rear of the acres of tombs, guessing that Nick would have been buried in the newer part of the cemetery.

A colored caretaker was wearily working with a wheelbarrow, collecting branches and windblown debris from the graves. With the air of a man who might never finish his task, he bent and lifted, swept and piled, and only looked up after Manon called to him the second time.

"*Mais non,* Madame," he replied to her question, "can't say where he might be 'zactly. But you be in just the right spot to look."

She wandered up and down the rows, looking for fresh gravesites, thinking that if she only pictured him as she had seen him last, only conjured up his face with enough concentration, her heart would lead her to where he rested. And then, finally, she went up a small rise and stood before a newly covered grave which seemed to her to pull her eyes. She bent and read the metal tag tied to the wooden stake at its head. "Nicholas Fletcher, September 20, 1915."

She sank to her knees at the grave site, heedless of the damp earth under her skirt. Crossing herself, she closed her eyes and clasped her hands. But no prayer came easily to her mind.

She opened her eyes and stared at the mounded dirt. Under there, was a man she loved. A body she had held and stroked and kissed in the night. A skin which, at times, seemed so close to her own that she could not say where she began and he left off. In the dark, damp dirt, he was lying now, alone and completely forgetful of his life, of all that had made him angry or happy . . . of her. She would never feel his hands again.

In that moment, she would have given ten years of her life to feel his mouth on hers one more time.

She took her hand and smoothed it over the dirt gently, mounding it more precisely under her palm. The damp earth of Saint Louis was cool and velvety under her fingers. It contoured and trickled at her touch obediently. She remembered the way the hairs on Nick's legs would lie down smooth or stand up, depending on the way she stroked them, like a cat's fur, his hair was as alive as his skin. Are you there, Nick? She willed him to hear her somehow. Can you feel me touching you still?

She lifted her head and saw the rooftops of New Orleans stretch into the distance away from Saint Louis, those rooftops which were still intact. The man who had shot Nick, a financier from Natchez who fancied himself the boss of Pontchartrain, had already fled back up North, away from her vengeance. They had insulted each other, one had died, the other was banished. Though to her, Nick was a world, he was gone as easily as sun behind a cloud. Likely, his killer had friends, relations, perhaps even a lover in New Orleans who would suffer in his absence, yet they would heal from their pain soon enough. Two men subtracted . . . a simple reduction which made not a ripple in the grand scheme of things.

The city looked largely unchanged. The living were beginning to live again. Even the storm made no difference to the citizens of Saint Louis. The diffidence of the world to her loss left her feeling numb. She could not weep for herself. She could not weep for Nick anymore. Perhaps she would never weep again.

She bent down and picked up a handful of dirt from the grave. Clenching it in her hand, she made an imprint in the earth like a set of ribs under a living skin. She carefully put the handful of dirt into her pocket, smoothing its surface with her fingers one last time. Then she went back over the rise towards the city of New Orleans.

Wending her way, she passed a tomb marked LaVeau.

Likely, Marie the Second. At first glance, it seemed no different from its neighbors, but then Manon bent and saw that the concrete was marked by dozens of red crosses made by brick. They still believe then, Manon realized. Come and make a cross and pray, and Marie or her daughter will hear. On one corner, a dish of dimes was undisturbed, full of the coins of supplicants. No one would dare steal from the voodoo queen. No one but Death.

At the top of the hill, she stood and marked Nick's place in her mind. A tomb with a tall, imposing angel would look best in that place and could be seen from a good distance. Tomorrow, she would see to it.

New Orleans seemed now to hold little fascination for Manon. Try as she might, she could not collect the energy she needed to pick up the reins where Nick dropped them. Politicians called with invitations and hints of favors, but she politely made her excuses. Two opera debuts went by without her attendance in her usual box, and the *Picayune* wondered in print when Madame d'Irlandais would venture out of mourning and grace the Queen City with her smile once more.

When Manon realized that her property managers had let three leases go unrenewed on her rentals, she knew that her inattention was costing her more than merely her reputation as the *Grande Dame* of the New Orleans Fall season. At the countless charity balls which took place immediately after the hurricane to raise money and begin reconstruction, she had been conspicuously absent. She knew that others would rush in to fill the void and that, in a very few seasons, the mention of her name would actually go unrecognized with newcomers to the city. She would be unremarked. She well knew how fickle New Orleans could be.

But she could not bring herself to care. Neither did she haunt Saint Louis and Nick's new tomb. She spent countless hours combing through her books and papers, organizing her assets until she knew to the dime what she owned. Then, she set her solicitors to quietly selling off any asset which required management to make a profit. The Irish Palace was the first on the block. Having sustained heavy damage in the hurricane, it did not bring what it might have six months before, still she cleared eight-hundred-thousand after fees and taxes. Next, she sold two hotels and three restaurants. Together they brought her an additional four-hundred-thousand. Any land unencumbered, she tucked away in her portfolio to remain intact. Stocks and bonds, she methodically converted to Treasury Notes and stored those in her safe deposit box, each one labeled with a different grandchild's name.

Then she sat down to write Alex a letter, explaining her actions, and sent him a check for his half of their liquidated estate. "I'm advising you to put this in long-term securities," she wrote cryptically, "but, of course, you might well want to get some financial advice before you decide. I will not be handling our assets after the first of the year, my dear brother. There's not much left that requires attention anyway, and I'd like to be free of this responsibility. I hope you agree I've earned my retirement."

Manon then made discreet inquiries up and down the Bayou Teche until she found what she wanted. Oaks-on-the-Teche, a plantation manor sliding into rapid dissolution, sat on forty acres upriver, less than two hours' ride from ShadyOaks. She bought it cheap, hired the best contractor she could find in the parish, and began to restore the mansion to its original splendor. After some thought, she renamed the plantation Bagatelle, and she took out an announcement in the *New Iberia News* to quell what she knew would be rabid curiosity about her intentions. "Bagatelle, formerly known as Oaks-on-the-Teche, will be restored with every attempt to honor her heritage. Vendors and craftsmen please apply to Monsieur Boone, of Boone, Appleton, and Fisher, architects of New Iberia."

Manon had thought she might wait until the mansion house was finished before she moved from Canal Street, but her solicitor brought her a heady offer from a man moving down from Georgia, and she accepted his check in a whirlwind of sudden determination. Not one more week did she wish to stay in the town. Not one more Saturday night did she want to wander up Bourbon Street, listening to the music sliding out of a dozen honkytonk doors, without Nick by her side. Even hearing the music now brought on a haze of melancholy. And Manon resolved to have no more truck with melancholy if she could help it.

She moved into the mansion, almost looking over her shoulder the whole of the drive from the Mississippi. In some vague way, she felt haunted. Could not shake her ghosts. And it wasn't only the ghost of Nick she carried with her, but the ghost of a South she seemed to have lost somehow while she wasn't paying attention.

The slow steaming afternoons and early evenings she remembered in New Orleans were changing quickly now. The shrimp boats down a sunset channel, the soft accents of the women lapping like low country creeks, the pungent scents of wisteria and gardenia, were all altered in almost imperceptible ways, it seemed to her, were no longer as she recalled. Tugboats churned the waters of the port, diesel fumes filled the air, the strangulation of traffic in the Quarter, the influx of so many Yankees that one scarcely heard the old patois in the market . . . it was time for her to get out while her memories were still intact.

Everywhere she looked in New Orleans, there was a nagging sense of something lost, something dying at the soul.

Even the elaborate wrought iron gate at her apartment troubled her. Spiders had woven their tiny webs over and around the curved design for so many insect generations, that they were encrusted and impossible to remove. In places, the iron had rusted without care for so long, it fell away to powder as she brushed by. New Orleans smelled to her now of decay instead of ripeness.

Even Mardi Gras that year did not raise her spirits as it had, faithfully as the sun rising. The Mystic Krew of Comus, the brass bands playing their primitive music as they blared by, torches blazing, the crowds surging the streets, none of it moved her to abandoned joy as before. From high on the papier-mâché floats, men and women in glittering costume threw glass necklaces and wooden beads, people fought to catch the trinkets, and after, when Mardi Gras was dead and done and the air dank with cold, she could only see the twisted streets made more ugly with broken glass and trash.

There was only one way to get herself back again, and that was to reinvent her memories, she decided. She no longer knew who or whose she was.

But the first night along the edge of the bayou, she thought she heard a hint in the whispering of the wind in the live oaks. Something, too, in the jasmine-scented night. She looked out and saw the ghost fires flickering over the water, dodging in and out of trees, the methane from so much decayed matter in the swamp, spontaneously and delightfully ignited into spiderwebs of beauty. She felt at home all of a sudden, even though the rooms had never before echoed with her steps, had never known the feet of any of her kin; this plantation, even in the throes of restoration, felt more a part of her past than the apartment on Canal which had sheltered her for a decade. She slept well and peacefully that first night, without her usual dreams of tombs and cobwebs and loss.

When the morning light came in through the gallery windows, a light like no other that bathed the worn cypress doors of her room with a gossamer glow, she rose feeling refreshed. Feeling herself and whole once more.

Zoe was coming that afternoon to see Bagatelle for the first time and to help organize Manon's goods, due to arrive by truck before noon. She had shown little curiosity about the place when Manon told her that she had bought it. Instead, she asked questions about what her mother expected to do "planted way out here on the Teche" and who she knew in New Iberia. When Manon admitted she was acquainted with only a few neighbors, Zoe had raised her brows delicately.

"I should think it'll be quite an adjustment, *maman*, from the excitement of the Quarter to the slow rhythms of our little piece of the delta. Wouldn't it be wiser to take a small place temporarily and see if you like it here, before you plunge right in with the largest restoration project on the bayou?"

"Probably wiser," Manon had said, "but I don't feel like being wise these days. It's time for me to leave New Orleans, *certainement*. And once I decide something for certain, I like to waste no time. I always trust my feelings."

"That's certainly true," Zoe said wryly. "But has it ever occurred to you that your feelings aren't facts? At least not the only ones . . ." she turned her head away, picking up a corner of the lace counterpane and smoothing it. "And what will you do way out here? I should think loneliness will eat you up inside. I can't be driving two hours in each direction two and three times a week—"

"I don't expect you to, *cher*. I am changing my life, *vraiment*, but I don't expect the rest of my family to do the same. Though it *would* be nice to see you and Henry and the children more often. I only have one daughter, after all, and so far as I know—" and here she flirted with Zoe as unabashedly as though she had been a suitor, "you only have one mother."

"Well," Zoe shrugged, "I know one thing well. You will do what you will do. You always have."

"And I always will," Manon agreed briskly. "Now, tell

me what they're saying in this little backwater about Ma
dame d'Irlandais and her Bagatelle."

Zoe smiled grimly. "Is that why you came then? To keep
the tongues wagging at all costs?"

"For truth! I ran out of ways to shock them in New
Orleans and needed new pastures. What do they say?"

"That you have no respect for the past."

Manon threw back her head and laughed loudly for the
first time since Nick's death. "Of course, they would! And
that's just fine, I suppose. Envy is a dangerous feeling to
provoke, I'd almost rather they can look down on me just a
little. Giving people a chance to patronize you every once in
a while only increases their affection. Besides, what they say
is true! I have no respect for the past and little for the future
as well. But the present and I get along famously, my daughter, and I hope to show them that the South needn't drag her
past along on her ankles like slave shackles—"

"What is it about you that makes you want to cut such
a swath?" Zoe asked, still smiling. "How did you get such a
nerve? I swear, you're never really happy unless you're building up and tearing down at the same time."

"It's the mother in me, I suppose. And don't tell me you
haven't felt the same way, why I've seen you cut a swath
through Henry Junior when he displeases you, *cher*—"

"Not as you do, though," Zoe said, her smile fading now.
"I try to prop up while I'm cutting out the deadwood."

"So do I! The deadwood and the dryrot. Speaking of
which—"

Zoe put up her hand to stop her mother's oratory. "Let's
get you unpacked, *maman*, before you take on the conver-
sion of the delta." And she turned away briskly to the house
woman Manon had hired and began to give orders in a low
gracious voice.

Bagatelle was soon the talk of more than just the delta.
Manon's connections were wide and entangled, and though
she had taken herself from the Queen City's primary stages

she still was able to seduce callers to make the trek down the Teche at her invitation. She had no more than two guest bedrooms refurnished, when the mayor of New Orleans and his wife accepted her invitation for a private soirée. As the mansion enlarged, she was able to entice the president of Standard Oil, the state supreme judge from Baton Rouge, the U.S. Corps of Engineers Levee Supervisor for the whole delta, and their entourages, to visit her bayou sanctuary.

Manon got almost as much press in the *Picayune* in absentia, as she had when she was the toast of New Orleans society. Increasingly, society came to her, if for nothing more than to satisfy their curiosity about the refurbishing of Bagatelle and her celebrated callers.

Zoe and Henry rarely attended Manon's fêtes, though she sent them an invitation to each. The duties of the plantation, attentions to the children, a sick servant, or other responsibilities usually kept her daughter on her own side of the bayou.

Once, as Zoe sent her regrets to a particularly fine soirée, Manon drove her Packard down the ShadyOaks drive to confront her daughter once and for all. They sat together on the gallery, and Manon waited until she had been brought a cool julep before she began. "Now, Zoe, I'm tired of these excuses. I guess if you won't bestir yourself to make the acquaintance of the Governor of the entire state, then I'll simply have to get the President down here for supper next. Maybe he'll bait you out of your humdrum little tedium."

"Ah, mother, my life is hardly tedious," Zoe laughed softly. "I scarcely have time to be bored."

"Yes, but do you have time for pleasure? What do you do, child, for entertainment? Do you and Henry only work your lives away? Do you accept *any* invitations? Do you extend them?"

"Of course, *maman*," Zoe said smoothly. "Why only last month, we hosted a fine supper for dear friends—"

"And I was not invited?" Manon interjected, amazed. "After all the soirées I've invited you to!"

"Mother, you would have known no one here. It was only a small gathering of special neighbors." She stopped and considered Manon for a moment, as though wondering whether to say more. "You know, you don't know everything about our lives, after all." She looked away, her gaze drifting out over the pepper fields. "We have our own pleasures, Henry and I. You needn't worry about us."

Manon sat forward and clasped her daughter's hands. "But I do worry, *cher*, I always have. I want you to be happy."

"And so I am," Zoe smiled. "But not exactly in the way you would have me be. Or for the same reasons."

"Do you and Henry get on?"

She hesitated. "Yes, of course. He tries to please me. I try to . . . seem pleased. We are—partners."

Manon took a deep breath. "Have you come to love him then? As you said you required for happiness?"

"No." Zoe's voice was calm and strong. "I never have. Not as you promised I would. But I have found happiness, nonetheless."

Manon felt as close to her daughter as she ever had in that instant of candid confession, in a lifetime of little true intimacy between their souls. She asked, "How? How have you found happiness then, without love?"

Zoe shook her head slowly. "Why will you ask the obvious? What would you have me say?" She released her hands from her mother's, but her eyes did not swivel from Manon's. "I have found love. I simply have not found it with my husband."

Manon sat back in her chaise abruptly. And then, without her volition, her mouth turned up in a wry smile. "Indeed. I should have guessed it. You are my daughter, after all." She glanced over Zoe's shoulder and saw that they were completely alone. "And where have you found it then?"

Zoe's mouth stiffened, and Manon could see the veil cove her eyes again, the private opaque filter which Zoe had use against intrusion since she was old enough to consider herself separate from her mother in heart as well as in fact. "No names, *maman,* not even with my dying breath. Suffice to say that I have quietly arranged for my own happiness through all these many years. It has been an—indelible—arrangement. And a discreet one. Which has in no way compromised my position as mistress of ShadyOaks."

"And he has made you happy?" Manon asked, amazed.

"He has given me whatever semblance of that state I hope to enjoy."

A noise from behind Zoe, a footstep, and Henry came out to join them, extending his hands to raise Manon up for his embrace. He kissed her on both cheeks hurriedly. "Welcome, *ma mère,* did Zoe show you the new foal? Quite a set of legs on her, that black stud'll breed true every time." He turned to Zoe and added, "Sweet, that new gal over in the cropper's cabin's got some sort of fever, they're saying, wonder if you could get down there to take a look at her? She's got three barely knee-high, and if it's the contagion, I think we should isolate her quick, before they spread it to every child in the fields."

Zoe rose smoothly, picking up her glass. "It's not the fever, I already saw her yesterday, honey. It's fleabites, from the filth. She won't wash those ticks no matter how much soap I send down to her,"—she threw over her shoulder— "Mother, I'll be back in an hour, why don't you go up and see Celly, she's got a new storybook to show you." She went out right behind Henry, the two of them already discussing this and other problems to be solved before supper.

It was really rather lovely to see, Manon thought with a quiet wonder. They shared a camaraderie that was, in its own way, as powerful a bond as love. They made their own beauty together, like the beauty of a well-made chair or a knife that fit just so in a carver's hand. The beauty of a form which suited its function and never aspired to more. Or less.

Here was a partnership she had never known with any

man. Here was a marriage as enduring as the soil itself, likely, and as dependable as the rains in their seasons. Did she envy her daughter? Manon had to ask herself as she watched the two of them disappear, shoulder to shoulder as two horses in harness, though one was almost two heads taller and half again as wide. No, she admitted candidly to herself, she did not envy Zoe.

I wouldn't exchange my life, Manon realized, would not have bartered my passions, for a mountain of tabasco mansions.

She went then, up the stairs, calling to her youngest granddaughter as she climbed, "Celly! Celly, *où es-tu?* Where are you, *cher?* Come and show me your new picture-story before *grandmère* must drive away once more!"

Finally, Zoe and Henry did accept one of Manon's invitations, however, and to her great surprise, Alex accompanied them as well. It was the night of New Year's, and the *réveillon* Manon planned was as glittering and sumptuous as any Bagatelle had seen since her rebirth. Most of the planters in two parishes were coming, as well as the Governor, a Senator, and Sophie Tucker, in town to sing at the French Opera.

When Zoe and Henry arrived arm in arm, Alex coming up the ballroom steps behind them, Manon rushed to embrace her daughter, overwhelmed by pride and pleasure at her beauty. Zoe wore a long spangled gown of silver, which set off her dark hair magnificently, and her white, slender neck rose out of a deep *décolletage* which was at once elegant and daring. Even Henry and Alex, in their black tails, looked taller and more dignified than she could recall. Manon took their arms and introduced them to her more important guests, beaming as Zoe made poised conversation as easily as though she had been débuted at the Versailles Palace rather than the Ursulines' *école dominicale.*

Manon set them free then, whirling between that guest and this one, and she only paused to watch Zoe once more as the orchestra was well into its fourth waltz.

Zoe had danced with Henry and Alex, Manon had noticed that much, even as occupied with Governor Ritchie's wife as she was. Her daughter moved over the floor with grace, and she was reminded of how easily Zoe had done so on her wedding day, as though she had been born knowing the steps. Now, she danced with Monsieur Lonigan, a rice planter in the next parish, and she made him seem as deft as she was, the surest mark of a skilled dancer, Manon thought, and a lovely quality in a woman.

As the music died away and another waltz began, Manon's partner left her with a bow, and now she was free to watch her daughter with undistracted pleasure. Again, Zoe danced with Lonigan, a handsome man who had been widowed for years. Manon thought idly, sometime this evening, I must take care to introduce him to Madame Tucker, there may well be someone in her entourage who will suit him—

And then she paused, her lips at the rim of her champagne glass, her eyes narrowing as she watched her daughter more closely. Zoe and Monsieur had obviously danced together often, and it was not simply her daughter's skill which made them seem so well matched.

As Zoe moved in his arms, her body leaned into his with obvious pleasure, her arms rested on his shoulders in a way which suggested not only comfort but . . . intimacy. Now Manon became alert to Zoe's smile, the intensity of her gaze into Monsieur's eyes, and in that instant, she saw him return Zoe's stare with such tenderness that her stomach grew hollow with sudden fear.

This, then, was Zoe's lover. It was as swiftly obvious to her as the fizz of the champagne in her mouth. The way they held each other, the way they danced in easy, melting embrace, the fluid motion of their limbs, the softness of their eyes as they looked at no one save each other, it was so readily apparent that Manon knew the entire company must see it as plainly as she did. She could suddenly picture her

661

daughter making love with this man, she knew how she would move in just such a way, saw how he would hold her just as he did now, and her eyes closed in sudden distaste. Then she opened them wide in panic, searching out Henry and Alex. If Henry saw his wife now, her secret would be scandalously public, for surely no one could miss the look in their eyes.

To her great relief, she saw that Henry was deep in conversation with several men at the corner of the champagne table, and as the music ebbed, Manon rushed to whisk Zoe off the floor. *"Monsieur,* you must let me steal my daughter away from you, I promise to return her in good time. *Cher,* there's someone who's dying to meet you, and if I don't bring you round at once, I won't be able to hold my head up—"

Before Zoe could balk, Manon had her out of the ballroom, up the stairs, and into the library.

"My heavens, Mother, you must have God himself hidden away up here, what in the world is all the mystery—?" Zoe was murmuring as Manon pulled her inside and closed the paneled doors behind her.

"There's no mystery," Manon said firmly, "not any more at any rate. And with another dance or two, I doubt it would be a mystery to anyone present tonight. Zoe," she said, sliding down into the overstuffed chair by the window, "whatever can you be thinking of? What can *he* be thinking of?"

Zoe stood stiffly by the door as though to run, her chin high and defiant. "So that's it, then. Another pretense. What are you talking about, Mother?"

"I'm talking about Monsieur Lonigan, of course," she said angrily. "How dare the two of you be so transparent! He is obviously your lover, has clearly been so for quite some time, given the way you two dance together, and if you don't care about the spectacle you're making of yourself out there at least think of Henry—"

"Don't tell me to think of Henry one more time!" Zoe cried out, her voice rising in a throttled shriek.

Manon stopped, eyeing her daughter cautiously. This was the first time she had seen Zoe so close to losing control. She was at once appalled and fascinated. "Then we will not speak of Henry at all," she said calmly. "But, Zoe, you must think of your position. Think of mine, if you won't think of your own. In my own house, before my guests! If Henry knew, he'd—" she shook her head, turning away with distaste. "Zoe, you said you had been discreet. I shudder to think of what you must have revealed without realizing it, if you'll dance with him like that in your mother's ballroom. It's time you ended this affair, you must tell him at once. Or better yet, you must not speak to him again this evening, *cher*. Not a word, not a glance, or I'll tell Alex and he will confront the man and ask him to leave. And then tomorrow, you must send him a letter telling him it's over between you. You have too much to lose, and you'll surely be caught, I'm amazed Henry has not confronted you already—"

To her surprise, Zoe began to laugh softly, a mirthless, bitter laugh. "Tell Alex? *Maman,* Alex has known forever. Alex brought us *together,* for god's sake. Dear Uncle Alex has provided me an alibi on any number of occasions, when I've not been where I should have been."

Manon's mouth dropped. "My brother has known all along? He—approves of *cette liaison* and says nothing to me?"

"Alex loves me, *ma mère.* He wants me to be happy. And he understands passion. God knows, he's been hag-rid by it all of his life in his own quiet way." She turned away. "He knows what despair such loneliness brings. He understands. In a way you never can."

"Of course, I understand passion," Manon said with distaste. "I have followed my passions all of my life—"

"Ah yes, I know," Zoe smiled sadly. "I come from a long line of women who understood passion. A long line of strong-willed women who followed their passion—and what a motley coven we are!"

663

"What are you talking about?" Manon snapped.

"You should have listened to Emma more, *maman,* you would have learned more than Latin conjugates, if you weren't so stubbornly blind to the past. Emma told me what she knew about her own mother and about your mother, and between us all, I guess it's not surprising that I would have a Monsieur Lonigan in my life."

"What in the world are you saying, Zoe! You're talking about the past, I'm talking about your future!"

"The future means nothing without the past, *maman!* You of all people should see the truth of that. Only think of it, and listen! Oliva Doucet, like a mother to your own mother, *her* passion was for the bayou, and she choose it over her husband, Emma says, even over her children at times. Emma's own passion was for God, choosing Him over all else. Your own mother's passion was for family, and your passion, *ma mère,* yours was for passion, itself, I suppose. Passion for its own sake, no matter who or what must be compromised in the quest." She laughed again, ruefully this time. "And me. Poor Zoe, she never even had a passion of her own. Of all the women in my past, I am the only who did not."

"It looks to me as though you've had your share, daughter," Manon said angrily. "And no doubt, he's had his share as well."

"Ah, Mother, I had hoped you might understand. You who have known the sweetness of it, you who put it first always, your passion. How rare it is, and how sweet are the gifts two lovers give each other. They give each other life. They help keep death at bay. That's what gives love it power, that passion. Nothing less than the gift of life—"

"Zoe, you're talking like a madwoman—"

"No!" she said wildly, "not a madwoman, just a woman *ma mère,* speaking to you like a woman instead of a child for the first time in my life. I thought you might understand. After all, we've all had different passions, but none of us were

664

free of its mastery. So I come by it honestly, God knows. But where is the love, in all of this passion, I sometimes wonder? I wondered it when you left me at Ursulines all those years, I wondered it when—" she faltered and turned away. "Well, I've wondered it plenty of times, let's just leave it at that." She leaned against the door wearily. "You thought I had no passion in my soul," Zoe added quietly, "you were so busy snipping and pasting, rearranging bits of my life for me. I was your play-dolly, your—work of art. You alternately ignored me and then treated me like a rare investment which must be protected at all costs. When all I wanted to be was a woman. Like you." She smiled. "I knew you felt sorry for me, sometimes. Pitied me my tedious little gray life and my empty little stoic heart. But not enough to let me love where I will." She turned, with her hand on the door.

"Then you admit he is your lover?"

"I admit no such thing. In fact, the suggestion has left me in no more mood for gaiety. So don't bother asking Monsieur to go, *maman*, I'll go instead. But I will not give him up, *whoever* he is. You don't have the right to ask me."

In that instant, Manon noticed for the first time that Zoe had aged markedly in the recent years. There were silver strands in her black hair which matched her gown. "I don't have the right? What about your children, then. Will you give him up for them?"

"What do you mean?"

"I mean, if Henry finds out, they will find out, and they will be destroyed. Perhaps he would even divorce you, Zoe, it's happened for less. Think of your sons. Think of Celly."

"Think of my daughter?" Zoe smiled. "That is especially interesting advice, Mother, coming from you. Never fear," she said over her shoulder as she went out the door, "I have not forgotten my responsibilities. Were it not for my children, I might have lived with my love the last ten years of my life." And then she was gone.

Manon gripped her hands tightly and put her head back,

stifling a howl of despair. And anger. Yes, she realized, she was furious with Zoe at that instant, deeply resentful of what she said, what she did, and her stubborn refusal to see the danger of her actions. And what was all that babble about Emma and her mother and passion and compromise—what did that have to do with Zoe's selfish refusal to give up what will someday bring her house down around her pretty little ears!

Manon stood and paced then, fanning herself with agitation. And Alex! Alex had brought them together, had pandered for them, had helped her to live this lie—oh, that was so ironically fitting, she thought, since he was so adept at camouflage himself. What wouldn't she say to him when she got him alone! How dare he encourage such scandalous betrayal!

Panting, Manon whirled to the glass and tidied herself swiftly, expertly. Now was not the time for a resolution. Now, she had guests to attend, a *fête* to make memorable, and allies to enchant. She went down the stairs in a bubble of numbness, reaching out beyond it to greet and embrace, scarcely feeling the despair she put aside in one corner of her heart to deal with tomorrow. For now, she saw that Zoe was gone, having taken Henry and Alex with her.

I hope she feigned illness, Manon thought swiftly, so as to save us both explanations, at least. As she looked around, she saw Monsieur Lonigan in a circle of friends, and she swept by him with scarcely a glance.

Manon waited a week before she went to see Zoe again but the hiatus did nothing to move her daughter to compliance. Zoe would not speak of Monsieur at all, would not allow Manon to speak of him either. In fact, when pressed, she all but claimed that perhaps her mother had imagined things after all.

"Mother, I believe you might have let the champagne go to your head," she laughed gently. "*Monsieur* and I are old friends, it's true, but I doubt we danced any differently to gether than any number of couples on the floor that night."

"Zoe, I saw you," Manon whispered, shocked.

"As did a hundred others. No one felt compelled to take notice, Mother, and I suggest you might consider the same courtesy."

"Zoe, you must give him up!"

"And so I shall. Someday. Now, you mentioned that you were having some trouble with your back lately, what has the doctor said about that?" And she changed the subject stubbornly whenever Manon tried to return to it. Finally, wearied and bewildered, Manon decided to speak of it no more. At least for the time.

In April of 1917, America was catapulted out of a domestic dream of tranquility into the international trenches. "The war to end all wars" began in the states with a burst of patriotic fervor, but little real unity about what the United States role in the conflict should be. A year and a half after America entered the war, it was over, and this country was the only one left stronger after the ordeal.

In the delta, German U-boats were first sighted off Avery Island late in the year, but rumors that Mexico would invade America—urged on by Germany—ran rampant up and down the Gulf Coast, even when shrimpers couldn't see the German submarines.

Whole fields were plowed to cotton and corn to fuel victory, and prices for sugar soared. On June 5, from seven in the morning to seven in the evening, every American male between the ages of twenty-one and thirty registered for the draft. But it was largely unnecessary in the South, where thousands of men volunteered eagerly to fight the Hun.

Zoe's three oldest boys, Alex, Henry Junior, and Samuel announced that they were going to New Orleans to sign up with the Delta Armored Division, and one hot afternoon in September, Alex came from Avery Island to escort them upriver to join their company.

Their father was knee-deep in the pepper harvest and welcomed Alex's offer to stand in his stead. "Besides," he said to his three sons, "if you're old enough to decide to go and fight, you're old enough to get to New Orleans without your papa holding your hands."

But Zoe appealed to her uncle as she had so often in her past. "Someone, a man in the family, should be there to wave them adieu, Alex. Will you take them and see them safely off?"

And so it was that the family stood on the steps of ShadyOaks to say good-bye to Alex, his young namesake, H.J., and Samuel. All morning, Manon had been weeping off and on each time she thought of the boys voyaging across the Atlantic to fight on foreign soil.

"It's not so foreign after all," H.J. reassured her. "We'll be stationed in France, they say, and that'll seem like Lafayette, I imagine."

"Can they guarantee you'll stay in France?" Manon cried, clinging to her grandsons. "They'll say anything to get you boys over there, and then they'll send you to the front!"

"Someone has to go, *grandmère,*" Alex said quietly behind his brother. "At least we'll be together."

"Can they promise that as well?" Manon wept harder. "Ah, *'tits,* you should stay on the bayou where it's safe!"

Then her brother, Alex, took her by the shoulders and pulled her gently to his embrace and off the three boys. "No place is safe, *cher,* if men will not do their duty. Boys, get that Packard loaded now, we'll need to leave in a moment."

As her grandsons hoisted their luggage onto the back of

the car, she turned and wept into Alex's breastcoat, leaning into him as she had not done in twenty years or more. "But they take our best," she murmured. "The youngest, the strongest, the ones who should never know pain, much less death—"

"Hush," Alex said softly into her hair. "Don't talk like that, Manon. Who would you have them send, your gray-haired brother? Ol' Henry with his bum knee? Stop your tears now, and straighten up. If their own mother can say farewell with a smile, so can you."

Manon turned to see Zoe come out on the gallery then, with her husband by her side. Simon ran to his three older brothers and his sisters, Alice and Celly, were close at his heels. Manon was surprised to see that Zoe was composed and calm, with no trace of tears. She embraced her sons firmly and said, "I am proud of you boys. Look out for one another, and I'll pray that the war will be short."

"We'll be home soon," Alex said on her shoulder, his voice breaking. He was the oldest and the closest to her heart.

"I know you will, son," she said clearly, defiantly. "With all my faith, I know it."

Henry embraced his sons, there was a flurry of hugs from the children, and when the four pulled away—young Alex driving, honking, Henry Junior by his side, Samuel and her brother perched in the back, their knees up awkwardly and wedged in by baggage—Manon waved frantically until the dust had settled and the hollering, waving pickaninnies had chased them clear out of sight.

She turned then to Zoe who leaned against Henry, her arm still uplifted in farewell. "You were very brave," Manon said to Zoe quietly, as the other children scattered back into the house. "I never saw you shed a tear."

"I shed my share," Zoe said, her voice sounding strained. "But I didn't want them to see me. They don't need to carry that memory away with them into harm's way."

At her words, Manon's eyes blurred again. "You're

stronger than I am, *cher*. Three! I couldn't let my children go like that."

"Oh yes, you could," Zoe answered quickly. She glanced at Henry and, invisibly, he seemed to understand her signal. He patted Manon's shoulder and left them on the gallery alone. Zoe took her mother's arm and said, "Let's walk awhile, *maman*. Soon, it'll be an oven even in the shade."

The two woman walked in silence, arm in arm, and Manon felt her heart lifting slightly, eased by the simple rhythm of their steps and the pressure of Zoe's wrist. The fields stretched out before them in a patchwork thicket, the yellow and red peppers standing up like a million pointed bulbs on tangled green bushes, the colored pickers moving slowly among them. Bent so that only their backs and shoulders showed under their broad straw hats, the workers seemed not to move at all until you looked—and then they were slightly shifted from their original place. The heat rose above the fields in shimmering waves, and the sky was a vast blue plate above them.

Zoe took a deep shuddering breath, and Manon squeezed her arm gently. Clearly, she was not as calm as she had seemed.

Suddenly Zoe spoke, and her voice sounded as though it broke through some unseen barrier within her chest. "*Maman*, Henry and I have been talking lately about sepa rating for a while."

"What!" Manon stopped and turned to face her daughter.

Zoe took her arm and kept walking, however. "Let's no stop where the pickers can watch us. I imagine this is not complete surprise to you—"

"You imagine wrong! You just send off your boys to wa and now you tell me that you are divorcing your husband!"

"No, Mother, I'm saying no such thing. I'm saying th Henry and I have agreed that we might be best apart for while. I wanted to discuss it with you sooner, but it nev seemed like the right time."

670

"And now's the right time? I've lost three, and now I'm to lose three more? What of Celly and Alice? Simon's not old enough to be without you, either. Did Henry find out about—"

"Mother, please don't raise such a fuss," Zoe said calmly. "Henry knows nothing I've not told him, and you're not going to lose your grandchildren. This is only in the planning stages, after all. We're only talking about the possibilities. If we decide, he might move to the office house, and life would then go on largely uninterrupted. Of course, the children will need to be told why their father is not in the big house, but it needn't be such a disaster. Or perhaps we might try some other plan."

"This is what happens when husband and wife sleep apart," Manon said angrily. "I told you when Alex was born, you were making a big mistake. Now, it's come to this!"

Zoe stopped and let go her mother's arm, since they were safely in the shade and shelter of a live oak. "I'm not asking for your approval, Mother. But I wanted you to know, in case it does comes to this."

"Did the boys know of this before they left? Did you send them to war with this on their hearts?"

Zoe shook her head sadly. "Of course not. Perhaps, by the time they return, their father and I will have reached an understanding."

"And what understanding is that? That you will be able to see your lover freely while still under your husband's roof? Zoe," Manon gripped her daughter's arms insistently, "what are you doing? What is it you want?"

"Just some space to breathe, *maman,*" she said quietly. 'Is that too much to ask? I have been a good wife and mother for nearly twenty years." She dropped her eyes and hesitated. Then she raised her gaze to Manon and added, "I thought perhaps I might come to Bagatelle for a time. Simon and the girls will be fine for a month or so. I could come to you until Henry and I decide—"

671

"Non, cher," Manon said flatly. "Absolutely not. You cannot come to me. You are a married woman, you must stay here and work this out with your husband."

Zoe turned away slightly. ShadyOaks shone brightly in the sun like a castle, flanked by wide, tall trees. The house looked positively rooted in the earth, as though the land itself seemed to revolve around it like a fiery fulcrum. "I cannot come to you, then."

"No. I will not seem to lend my approval to this by giving you refuge, Zoe. You are making a terrible mistake. I'm not going to make it easy for you to make it."

Zoe smiled wanly. "No, I should have known that. You never have."

Manon stood in silence for long moments, waiting for Zoe to say that it was all a stupid notion, to forget she ever spoke, that it was only a passing whim. Finally, Zoe began to head back towards the house, almost as if she had forgotten Manon was beside her. Manon trailed along doggedly, rehearsing all she would say when Zoe spoke again. But Zoe said nothing more. As they got closer to the big house, she walked faster and faster until finally she left Manon gasping in the dust. Manon would not speak out for her to wait; Zoe would not turn and allow her to catch up. She rushed up the steps and disappeared within, leaving Manon to fling herself panting, into a rocker on the gallery alone.

Thus, three of Manon's grandsons were soon in France, an their letters to Zoe bragged that they were the rage of all th French girls with their Creole accents. Over supper, Mano had a heated argument with Simon, the youngest boy, abou whether he should join the Army soon, before the war would be over, despite the fact that three brothers were all his country asked.

"Those Heinies won't last another month in France," the boy grumbled. "They're eating their own mules now, Alex and H.J. say, just to keep their strength up. They'll never cross the Marne, and I'll never get to see action at all."

"Holy Mother, please forgive this child for his blindness," Manon said, glaring at him fiercely. "To speak in such a way when your poor mother already has three in danger!" She glanced at Zoe and lowered her voice when she saw that her daughter was busy attending to Celly's plate and had not heard her youngest son's complaint. Zoe had not spoken to her privately about anything of substance since the day the boys left. She shared their letters, but she did not share her heart. For all Manon could guess, she had put away her idea of separating from Henry. "They also serve who only stand and wait, remember," Manon whispered to Simon fervently. "You might think of that next time your father asks you to lend a hand with the chores."

"Nigger chores!" Simon snorted.

Henry said quietly, "Young sir, you ever let me hear that word again, just once, and I'll make you sorry your lips ever formed it, I promise you. They are colored people, understand. Colored, yes, but people. And those who call them nigger, in just that tone of voice, make themselves less than those they try to insult. You understand?"

"Yessir," Simon nodded unhappily.

"Remember then. You'll not get a chance to hear me say it again."

Manon saw Zoe look up and smile at her husband. There, Manon thought with quiet triumph. He is a man to respect. Zoe has learned she needs him and has healed their rift.

Simon murmured, "But I got to watch croppers clear the swamp of scrub, while my brothers help clear Belleau Wood of Huns."

Henry said, "You may not believe it, but your job's going to feed more people than what your brothers are doing. Try to think of that, Simon, rather than dreaming about visions of glory. There's nothing glorious in war."

"Look away, look away," murmured Zoe. "Your father's right. The South's had enough of dreams of glory that never bore fruit. Your brothers are likely learning that lesson even as we speak."

Simon fell silent under his mother's gaze as he often did. Manon turned again to Alice and Celly. "Tell your brother that we need him here, not off in some place we can't even spell, much less find on the map," she teased.

The two girls chimed in all at once and cried out, *"Oui, Simon,* please stay here with us!"

But despite their words and the wishes of many, the letter finally came in October declaring that the family would never be the same. Alex had been killed in St. Mihiel, France. Zoe's eldest was buried in a field somewhere near Verdun, and his brothers, Henry Junior and Samuel, would be coming home alone.

The war was over in the next month, and women all over the delta wept in gratitude and relief. But there was no gratitude and little relief at ShadyOaks.

Zoe suffered more than Manon would have believed possible for a woman to suffer, and still survive. Manon wept, yes, and clung to Alex, paced the floor and wailed aloud to heaven in despair. But finally, she was able to let her sorrow subside, to sit sadly in her rocker and begin to think of tomorrow.

Zoe, however, seemed to believe that tomorrow would never come again. In stark contrast to her usual stoic calm, she fell into a depth of anguish which frightened all around her. At first, she shrieked when the messenger came, raced about the lower parlor, unable to be stopped even by Henry' grip, unwilling to lower the level of her terrible cries even when she knew that the other children would surely hear her

674

"No! No! No!" she wailed frantically, beating against the walls of the room like a trapped bird, flitting from window to window as though seeking escape. Alex sought to hold her; she would have none of his comfort. Manon went to embrace her, but she wheeled away as though stung. When Henry came and, weeping, attempted to gather her to him, to take her upstairs, she beat against him fiercely, forcing him to release her, her wails rising to a panicked scream.

The servants stuck their heads into the room and quickly withdrew, Henry roused himself from his own grief long enough to call the doctor, Manon pleaded with Zoe to go to her bed, but Zoe seemed to hear and see nothing but the black void of the loss of her son. As though demented, she sobbed and shrieked, plucking uselessly at the letter in her hands until she had raveled it away into tiny shreds. "Alex! Alex!" she called again and again, until it tore Manon's heart still further to hear her cries. Finally, crumpling on the carpet in exhaustion, she could only shiver and sob, writhing away from any hand that reached out to touch her.

Over the next night and day, Manon's awe of her daughter's grief grew as large as her own sorrow. She had never seen a woman mourn a loss so hard, certainly had never taken one so hard herself. Zoe's anguish was terrible to see and frightful to hear. By the hour, she wept and raced restlessly through the house, almost blind and deaf to any comfort. Occasionally, Celly would call to her, Simon would reach for her, Alice would trail along behind her, but Zoe paused only for a moment, and then she would fall into abject grief once more. The doctor's injection only muted her cries, it did not stop them. Finally, Henry locked himself upstairs in the bedroom with her, and Manon could hear the screams of renewed despair echo through the door and down the hall.

"Surely, she will run out of tears soon," Manon said to Alex, appalled at the sounds from the upstairs.

Alex, pale and fragile under his own sorrow, only reached out and held Manon's hand. "We cannot know what it means, to lose a child. It's not natural. It's not the way it's supposed to be, to have them go ahead of us."

"Do you think she will go crazy with it?" Manon whispered, finally allowing her worst fear expression.

He shook his head. "She can stand it. But she has to get this out, I guess, to be able to survive."

By the next morning, the upstairs was silent. Manon, Alex, and the children tiptoe through the rooms like ghosts, terrified of waking Zoe's grief once more. Henry came down for a tray of soup and disappeared into the bedroom once more, haggard and aged by a decade. Finally, she emerged.

Manon hesitantly embraced her. "My God, Zoe, I feared we might lose you as well."

Zoe bent and pulled her three children into her arms. Weeping still, but now softly, contained, she put her cheek on Celly's head. Mother and daughter rocked each other gently, and none could say who held whom.

Two more days passed, and Zoe began to emerge from her grief. She was finally able to speak of Alex without breaking down into blurred sobs. She began to put his room in order, packing up his clothes for the poor, and placing his pictures around the house. She sat silent for long stretches, gazing out over the fields, responding only slightly to Manon's attempts at comfort.

She said, "It seems like a dream now."

"Yes," Manon said. "It seems like the letter came so long ago."

"No," Zoe said, almost absently. "I mean his life. And mine. Not like he died at all, but that he went away. No funeral, no body, he's merely gone. In some way, that's easier, I guess."

Manon stayed with her that week, watching the comfort Henry and Zoe took from each other. Almost did she envy them now, for she could find little understanding of death at her age.

Indeed, Manon's greatest consolation and pleasure was

being with the youngest member of the household, little Celly. She thought she saw something of herself in the sprightly, spirited girl, heard something of her own laugh in Celly's pealing giggle. Often, as she walked the edges of the pepper fields, trying to understand the reason for war, for loss, for death, Celly would slip up behind her and ease her small hand inside Manon's, squeezing it and tugging her faster up the rows to see this new bird nest or that blooming flower, and her face would ease into softer lines, her back straighten and strengthen again.

The early Twenties brought dramatic change to the delta, as these years did to the whole country. Maxwell House Coffee replaced the strong Creole brew at many tables, Frigidaire made the old iceboxes obsolete, and women who had never read a newspaper in their lives now had the vote. Though the bayou was more isolated than most regions, even here, an occasional skirt rose to the knee and a few women bobbed their hair.

In 1919, the Volstead Act made liquor illegal, and over a period of only a few years, bootleggers and smugglers moved into the bayou with impunity, establishing outposts and secret warehouses in every backwoods waterway.

Those in the bayou found prohibition a personal insult. For years, they'd been fermenting their own orange wine, at least as potent as whiskey, and selling it to visitors traveling up and down the delta. Now, the people of New Orleans traveled farther and farther to get it, for the wine of the backwater Cajuns made an excellent martini base, a fine champagne when carbonated. When a government agent crossed into a parish, the few telephones rang off the hook and children ran up and down with the message, so that the goods could be hidden away in sacks, weighted down in the river. But gradually, the cars from up north came less and less.

Depression followed fast on the heels of the 18th Amendment, and bankruptcy became as common on the delta as juleps once were.

The Depression barely touched Manon at all, however, and skidded past Alex, hardly leaving an impression. Their investments, solid government securities, continued to provide them an income, and they needed little to live comfortably on the delta. Prices dipped and swayed for crops, but Henry and Zoe managed to remain solvent, even if some of their neighbors had to let go their servants and sell their surplus automobiles, stock, and land. More and more plantations were whittled down to smaller parcels, but life on the delta still moved at the slow pace Manon had come to prefer.

Alex's bird sanctuary had become, more and more, a tourist mecca which drew travelers, scientists, artists, and naturalists from all over the world. His refuge on Avery Island, which he had developed with M'sieu Ned McIlhenny, now wintered more than five thousand nesting birds. Unfortunately, however, "Bird City" had been discovered by more than the herons and egrets.

Bootleggers found that the low banks, extensive brush, cypress cover, and numerous tidal inlets were perfect camouflage for their smuggling operations from Cuba. Armed men in small skiffs moved in and out of Alex's sanctuary at night, no matter how many signs and fences he put up to discourage them. When he found nests destroyed and fledglings abandoned because of human intrusions, he finally took to camping out nights on the beach to fend off the pirates. Still physically able and vigorous for his age, Alex was determined to keep his sanctuary safe.

Henry Junior and Samuel often joined the old man, to

help discourage the skiffs from docking on the nesting side of the island. When Manon expressed alarm that her two grandsons were tangling with bootleggers, Zoe asked if she had a better plan.

"Let Alex stay out there a few nights alone, that'll show him the folly of putting the safety of some birds over his own skin; he's nearly seventy years old!" Manon retorted. "Or let him hire some thugs to fight thugs. But there's no reason to expose the boys to that sort of danger. What if they're armed?"

"They are armed," Zoe said. "So are Alex and the boys."

Manon gasped and clutched at Zoe's arm. "I cannot believe you'd allow such a thing!"

Zoe put one hand over her mother's hand. "The boys are grown now, *maman*, haven't you noticed? I must let them make their own decisions about what and whom to defend. I've spoken to Henry about it, but he feels that if they want to stand alongside their great-uncle, he can't discourage that kind of loyalty. There's too little of it in the world as there is, he says. The bootleggers simply laugh at an old man standing on the beach and cursing them, waving them off his birds. But three men standing together, they tend to dock elsewhere. In time—soon, I hope—they'll find other places more hospitable to their trade."

"But they could get hurt!"

Zoe nodded. "It's one of the hardest things I've had to learn about being a mother. If I want them to be independent, I have to let them make choices, even if they're the wrong ones." She looked hard at Manon. "That was one thing you never did learn, *ma mère*. But," she said easily then, looking away, "times were different then, I guess."

"And you were a girl." Manon said shortly. "Damn Congress, damn all the prissy bluestockings! They've made criminals out of every man who likes his liquor, and brought gangsters into the bayou!"

The spring rains came that year with a vengeance, and the

679

backwaters were unusually high with runoff from the Mississippi. Zoe more often found snakes close to the house, and Manon's favorite row of camellias, a hundred feet back from the riverbank, were rotting in a foot of water.

The river had always had its own natural cycles, usually flooding in the spring and again in early summer, to carry home the spring rain and melted snow from the north, then settling back into its bed during late summer to await a new season. For as long as Manon could remember, certainly as long as Alex could remember, too, the river had never been so high.

Henry was part of the planters' association that tried to keep the river inside its banks. As farmers built along the bayous, they built dikes and levees, attempting to control the waters. Each planter tried to make his levee stronger than his neighbors', but they finally got tired of the competition and organized. Then the battle was not against a man's neighbors, but against those farmers on the other side of the river. As in a poker game, one side would raise and the other would call. The stakes were high, for if the levee on one bank caved in, the other would be relieved of pressure. Sometimes men would destroy a levee across the river or downstream from their own crops to protect their fields.

But for years now, the river had been docile. The levees had grown to tall walls of earth. In 1926, the Chief of Engineers surveyed the levee system and declared it adequate protection against all floods.

The spring of 1927 brought heavy rains up and down the Mississippi Valley. The cypress forests which usually might have slowed and soaked up the runoff had all been logged, and the woods had all been cleared for crops. When the rains poured into the streams unchecked and on to the Mississippi, the river was the highest it had been in two hundred years. People up in Ohio sent down nervous word that the river was so blocked that the Ohio was actually flowing upstream.

Manon was at ShadyOaks in April, visiting the grandchildren before her every-other month trip to New Orleans. Zoe and Henry had been watching the waters with concern, and at supper that evening Henry said, "I expect you'll not make it across the Atchafalaya for awhile now, *ma mère*. They're saying a crevasse will come any time, but they don't know where."

"I read that the Atchafalaya levee is one of the strongest," Manon said.

"I don't care what they say," Zoe said, "There's not enough dirt in the world to hold back that river if it wants to break. Mother, you must stay here with us, at least until the danger subsides."

"If you really think it's that bad, I should go back to Bagatelle immediately!" Manon said. "I should be at my own house—"

"We sit on higher ground," Henry said. "I think if it comes, every foot up will make a difference. Besides, we're better off all together in an emergency."

"I'll need you to help me, *maman*," Zoe said, glancing at Celly.

After supper, they walked together out to where the bayou was lapping at the edge of the fields. In places, water was trickling between the furrows as though God himself decided to lend a hand with the irrigation. There was a tension in the croppers' cabins, however, and no singing came from the fires that twilight. Groups gathered here and there, glancing at the whites and then away. When a black worker came up to Henry, hat in hand, Zoe stayed alongside her husband to hear his answer.

"No, John, I have no news yet. They say it'll hold, but would be ready for the worst. Have you gathered together something for Jane and your boy, should you have to get out fast?"

"Yessuh," John nodded. He gestured to the other cabins. "We been packin' up vittles an' blankets. Thomas say he think the other side's safer."

681

"Well, I would doubt that," Henry said, "for both sides are just as swamped. But, of course, you're free to go where you think best. I wouldn't go north to Iberia, though. They've taken the boys out of school to work on the levees, they're that worried."

"The white chillen?"

"Yes, indeed. How does Thomas figure to get across the Teche?"

"He say, the bridge at Iberia be holdin' fast."

Henry grimaced at that. "I hate to see you try such a crossing. No trains are crossing that bridge now and haven't for some time, for fear it'll give way."

"Yessuh," John said, turning away. "I tell him that."

The man turned and hurried back to the group of workers, and they all left for their different cabins to spread the news. Henry started them back to the house.

As they reached the gallery, they heard a shout and looked back out to the fields. A solid tan-colored wall of water about six feet high was rolling from upriver with a roaring growl down the Teche and out both sides, sweeping everything in its path. They raced inside and up the stairs to the top floor, where they could look out and see the water sweep by the sides of the house, pushing trees and brush and lumber and debris ahead of it, and as it passed, ShadyOaks sat in brown foaming water more than five feet deep.

"The levee must have blown at Iberia!" Henry shouted, herding them to the back stairs.

They made it to the small motorboat Henry had prepared, carrying what they had wrapped in extra blankets and linens. Even as they loaded into the boat, with Simon poling to keep it as steady as possible, the waters were rising higher and higher.

Zoe's face was grim, and Manon held Alice and Celly close to her, settled in the back of the boat where they would be out of the way of Henry's maneuvers. Simon sat in the middle, close to his father, and at their feet were boxes o

682

canned goods, bottled water, towels, blankets, Zoe's emergency first-aid kit, and anything else they could grab in a hurry.

Celly cried out and pointed at something going down the Teche, blocked in a clump of uprooted cypress. It was part of the roof of Manon's small garage, where she had stored her Packard. Painted bright blue only the year before, it was one of the most distinctive sheds on the bayou, and now the glistening color could be clearly seen above the shifting currents.

The garage had stood on the highest ground at Bagatelle.

"Sweet Jesus," Manon gasped, "the whole house must be gone."

"Maybe not gone entirely," Henry said, "but I think you better be ready for some disheartening damage." He pointed to the gallery of ShadyOaks. Already the water had risen to more than eight feet high and was lapping hungrily at the second story of the house. The porch pillars were leaning precariously.

Zoe began to weep quietly, pulling her daughter closer to her.

"It's only a house," Manon said to her, trying to comfort. "We'll simply rebuild it, bigger and better than before."

Zoe shook her head. "I don't give a damn about the house, Mother. But my family!"

Manon whitened. She had not even thought. Somewhere south of them, likely where the water was headed next, Alex and her two grandsons, H.J. and Samuel, were waiting on Avery Island with only a small skiff and limited supplies.

Henry maneuvered the little boat—with all they might ever see of their world again—away from the wide vast lake that was ShadyOaks, turning south towards the gulf. Often he had to turn off the motor and row, while Simon poled, for the debris all around them was perilous.

"The closer we get to the sea," he said, "the more shallow

the water will be, I figure. It'll have more places to go and spread out, and the land's flatter."

"If the land's flatter, how will we find any that's dry?" Manon asked.

"Do you want to try to pole against the current? We've talked all this out," Zoe said. "Henry knows what he's doing, Mother. Let him steer the boat."

Manon settled back and tried to get comfortable, wrapping the blanket about the three of them firmly. The boat rocked back and forth as they hit eddies and swirls, sometimes more violently than others. They were in constant danger from floating brush and jagged stumps of trees, uprooted and blocking their passage, but somehow they managed to keep constant progress in the direction the water flowed.

The water flowed swiftly at first, almost too swift to control the skiff, but then began to slow after several hours in the same direction. They could see few buildings, only the tops of what must have been tall estates, and only the tops of the very tallest trees. In any clump of trees or on any roof, people were crowded together and holding for dear life, waving flags of shirts or blankets at them as they went by. Occasionally, they saw another boat at some distance, sometimes could hear the lowing of cattle or the shrill whinny of horses as they swam by, looking for high ground. Once, a poor cow swam clumsily right to them, lowing pitifully as though she expected them to do something to save her. Henry and Simon had to fight her off with the pole, or she would have tried to clamber into the boat. Alice wept then, as the cow swam off exhausted and bewildered, towards a moving clump of logs. But that was the only time Manon saw any of Zoe's children succumb to tears.

The sun traveled lower in the sky, but there were none of the usual twilight shadows, for there were no trees, no buildings, to cast them. Manon could not fathom how Henry could navigate or even tell which way was generally south but she dared not question him. Besides, she had no suggestion to make, so she decided on silence. She watched his broad back move the pole up and down, sometimes resorting to the paddle, when the tide was too deep to allow even the ten-foot pole to touch bottom, and they made their way over the water as they could.

Finally, in the distance, they saw a high point of ground, and Henry began to row to it. As they approached, they could see that many people clung to a dome, which was glistening in the light from the water.

"It's the salt dome," Henry said in wonder. "God almighty, I never thought of that. But, of course, Avery Island would be one of the tallest points, with that old mountain of salt built up. The only mountain in the whole delta."

The cypress trees around the salt dome were taller than most in the vicinity and their tops intruded out of the water. Boats of all types—skiffs, fishing boats, luggers, motorboats, canoes, and pirogues—bumped and jostled for space to tie up, and more were arriving from the east and the north. Folks were hollering back and forth, telling of their plight and asking after friends and family.

Henry tied up to a clump of trees and brush at the rear of the dome, and Zoe and Manon helped the children to get out and spread their bundles around them to dry.

Henry began to speak of tying up to a cluster of treetops soon, if they could not find land which was high enough. "I doubt the water's going any higher," he said wearily, "but we can't be sure. If this is just from a break in the Atchafalaya, and the Mississippi's still to go, we could be lost. But we got to figure this will be the worst we'll see."

Manon was struck in that moment with his strength and the calm way he directed Simon to organize their scant belongings, the way he comforted the girls and Zoe, all the while watching the horizon and marking the coming of night. Manon took his suggestions without murmur, as the children did, and was grateful that he seemed to have a plan. The trees were crowded now with nesting birds, and more were coming through the skies, seeking shelter. Because of the waters, the people and the birds found themselves in close proximity; nests and boats had to share the same small refuge.

It was such a relief to feel dry land under her feet that Manon allowed the fatigue to overcome her along with the darkness. By the time night was on them, the children were fast asleep on the bundles. Henry had walked over to another section of the island where some of the rescued had built a fire and were sharing news of the flood. Zoe sat silently, her hooded cape pulled over her head, her eyes invisible.

Manon stood, straightening her knees painfully. Nowadays the damp bothered her joints more and more. This night she felt a decade older than her sixty-seven years. Nearer to Alex's age, though he scarcely seemed to slow down in his traipsings.

Alex. Was he safe? Had he and the boys been on their way to ShadyOaks for refuge when the crashing waters overtook them? Or up at Jefferson Island, where the land was low and there was little shelter?

If she lost him, she would be so lonely! They were tied together in their past because of memories: the little house on Saint Phillips, Simon's old bayou cabin, certain streets and places in the Quarter—all these places existed in their minds and in no others. He moved in the same mental spaces with her, Manon thought, and if she wanted to reminisce about her past and he were gone, she would have no one to help her make the memories come alive. Her past would die with him in some significant way.

She moved closer to Zoe and sat down again, moaning slightly when her knees had to resume their bent position. Zoe gazed at her calmly from within her hood, her eyes quiet and fathomless.

Always, Manon thought, she has been older than her years. Wiser. Even now she takes whatever comes and rises to meet it. "Henry said that boat over there," Manon ges tured, "came all the way from Donaldsonville. Imagine what they saw!"

"Yes, I heard him," Zoe said softly. "I expect he'll come back with news of refugees from all over the delta."

"He was terribly clever to get us here safely," Manon said. "I would never have thought him capable of such courage." She glanced at the sleeping children. "He saved our lives."

Zoe said nothing.

"But I guess you are hardly surprised at his competence," Manon continued. "You've seen him perform miracles under duress before, I suppose."

"It won't be the first time he's saved me."

Manon smiled, bewildered. "Really? I guess there are stories you've never told me, then."

"Oh," Zoe smiled sadly, "you know them well enough, *maman*. No marriage gets as old as ours is without both spouses saving each other several times, I'm sure. Why, you set the pattern for us when you called on him to save me from myself, remember?" She gazed away over the black water. "So many years ago," she said faintly. "I can scarcely remember who that girl was now."

Manon felt a small fear in her stomach. "I remember that girl well enough," she said. "By the Virgin, you *needed* saving, *cher*. God only knows what you might have done if Henry had not swept you up into respectability. You were becoming a—"

"Woman?" Zoe pierced her with a stare.

"A wanton," Manon said, her voice low.

In the long silence, Zoe finally laughed softly. "I doubt that, *ma mère*. But we shall never know now. You couldn't keep from imposing yourself between me and whatever I took it into my head to reach for in this world. It always had to be good enough for me, and then *you* would go and get it for me. You and your spells took care of whatever choices I might have had quickly enough." She turned her eyes away. *"Maman et la voodooienne."*

The fear in Manon's stomach flowered now into cold panic. "I don't know what you're talking about." She stretched her legs out painfully and almost rose to her feet.

"Of course, you do," Zoe said calmly, "you're hardly senile, and I doubt you have managed to forget such an ordeal. I'm sure it was a difficult decision for you to do such a thing." She shook her head slowly with measured contempt. "Marie LaVeau. Such desperate measures. But at least you did have a decision. A choice. Henry and I did not."

Manon settled back again. Here it was at last. Finally after all these years, she could confess her trespasses and perhaps have some warmth and forgiveness from her daughter before she died. Or not. But at least they could speak of it. She turned towards her daughter determinedly and said, "Well, then you know. I should have guessed you did, I suppose. Why did you say nothing before?"

Zoe smiled. "That is so like you, *maman.* Ever into the breach. When in doubt, try the good offense."

"How long have you known?"

"Since right before the wedding. Dolly came to me and told me what she knew through the grapevine. You remember old Dolly? She was always a good gal. More faithful to me, really, than to you. She said she could not see me hexed into something I didn't want to be hexed to, that's the way she put it. Said if I knew you had spelled me, that me simply knowing could break the spell, if I was strong enough."

"So why didn't you call it off once you knew?"

Zoe shrugged. "It was too late. And I hoped you were right, that I would learn to love him."

"You have," Manon said firmly. "You just don't know what love is."

Zoe laughed mirthlessly. "Well, that wouldn't be too surprising, since I never had the chance to learn it for myself." She turned and her face seemed to glow inside the hood. "Mother, you wronged me terribly in so many ways. Too many to forgive easily. You made the world look so dangerous. I guess it had been, to you. I have tried all these years to forgive, and I almost have succeeded at times, but the one wrong I can never forgive is that you taught me to fear and mistrust love, without ever letting me discover for myself its sweetness."

"You looked to me like you discovered it well enough," Manon said quietly. "You told me you had, anyway."

"Yes, I did. But in all this time, I have never been able to trust it. I could never give myself to it. I always held it at arm's length, because you told me love hurt, it was an illusion, that I had to learn to sleep at night and live my life in the days, remember?" She shook her head sadly. "Love wasn't something to build on, so I kept it that way. Always at the shadows and fringes of my life. You told me that men wanted something from me, that they'd take away my will. So to save me from that, you took it away yourself. You knew—but you never let me see—love's softer sides. You feared your own passion and you feared mine. You taught me to fear my own nature, to fight it down until I could drive it into hibernation. So I settled."

"What did you settle for, Zoe?" Manon asked, her heart twisting with pain.

"I settled for contentment. As you wished me to do."

"Name of God, Zoe," Manon cried out, "then you had more than most women ever find! What did passion bring to me? Abandonment, that's what. The worst loneliness and despair I've ever known!"

"I wish I had a nickel for every woman who complained about men and how to protect herself from them. The ones who complain the loudest go right back to the fire again and again, it seems to me. I know that everyone has to draw a line between love and self-protection. But I think every woman needs to draw it for herself. And I don't think you can speak of loneliness," Zoe said slowly, "until you have lived with a

689

man for more than thirty years, have borne him five children, have buried one and possibly lost two more . . . all without passion. And the tender sweetness, the love that springs from that passion. All the time wishing—aching—to feel more than contentment."

"But, Zoe, you *do* love him! You must."

"Must I? How would I know? Perhaps I do love him all that I can. I had a gift for love once, I know it. A gift for passion. Emma said all of us do, and even you saw it. You said as much. But I never had a chance to use it. So I've never been able to give myself fully to either love or contentment." She smiled sadly. "I also had a gift for music once, you said. But I never got to discover that either." She held out her hands and looked at them in the rising light of the moon. A wan moon which slipped in and out of hiding. "It wasn't my colored blood that held me back, Mother, but another part of my heritage altogether. The fear my mother willed me. Who knows what these hands could have done, given the chance. Who knows what this . . . heart might have felt." She stood then, thrusting her hands back inside her cape. "Well, anyway, I should go and find Henry if I can. Will you watch the children for me? I'd like to see how many neighbors found their way here safely."

As she passed, Manon caught hold of her cape. "Zoe, why did you pick tonight to tell me all this? Why, after all these years?"

"Because," Zoe said softly, "we are all getting too old to keep secrets any longer. I may be burying more sons by daylight. Perhaps I'll stand at my lover's grave when the water recedes. And if I do, I'll need you to stand alongside me, Mother. No matter what, we women need to support each other, Emma told me that much, too. If I lose another someone I love, I might well go mad. So I'll need to forgive you enough to let you help me survive my losses."

Manon watched, appalled, as Zoe walked away into the darkness. She glanced at the sleeping children, feeling nothing more than a strong urge to get away from there that instant, to never have to see her daughter, her grandchildren, their father—anyone at all—ever again. Ah God, she cried out in her heart, I have been such a fool! Such a meddling, bossy, manipulative, mothering woman! I have wronged my daughter, her husband, my whole family with my love. Or what I chose to call love. In trying to live their lives for them, I have stolen the most valuable asset any heart has—its right to love, even at its own peril.

She wept then, openly, clutching her hands to her eyes, her mouth, so that the children might not hear. She rocked, weeping and muffling her cries in her cloak, hating herself in that moment with a desperate urgency that made her bones burn with shame.

Zoe was older and wiser than her years? Naturally, since she had never been allowed to be a child, to make the mistakes of childhood. I asked her to be older and wiser almost at her birth, abandoned her just as I had been abandoned, and then denied her the love which might have healed her. I knew she had a passionate nature, and I quelled it. I taught her to mistrust love as I had come to mistrust it. I knew the gentleness and softness of love with Nick, but I never told her anything but how it could hurt her. I asked her repeatedly if she were happy, but I never wanted to hear the truth. Not really.

I brought evil into my heart when I visited Marie La-Veau. It wasn't her voodoo that was evil. What was evil was my desire to make Zoe's choices for her. And it was futile all along. As is all that goes against nature, human or otherwise.

All we fight for, build, and strive to grasp, all of it is so easily swept away by time, by loneliness, and finally by an angry river, she realized, a mile-wide muddy mess of uprooted hopes and drowned dreams.

The two things I wanted to be in my life most: a lover and a mother—I have failed at both. I have aborted both. And if the flood had taken me, who would have keened at my grave? Not my brother. I've scarcely shown him much understanding or appreciation over the years. Not a lover. I've never let one get close enough, and now, at past sixty-five, I am alone. And not my daughter.

Manon wept until she could barely hold up her head with exhaustion. Finally she thought, Zoe was right in at least one thing she said, that it's our differences, not our samenesses, which give us strength. I did my best to make her over in my likeness, make her what I thought she should be, but it's where we are different that she's the strongest. Alex and I are so different, but it's our very differences which make us strong together. In a marriage, in a family, perhaps its our very opposition, instead of our unity, that makes us stronger. And I have fought that process most of my life.

Sometime in the darkness, she curled up against Alice and fell into a leaden sleep, her breath hitching with half-drawn sobs like a small child.

The birds knew the coming of dawn before most of the bedraggled refugees. As the first light came over the island, their jostlings and cries woke even the most exhausted, and people in their clusters began to wake and move, searching in their packs and bundles for items of comfort.

Manon woke to see Simon up and arranging a small pile of firewood which he had evidently gathered. He made a gesture of silence to her, nodding towards his mother and father who slept alongside one another, both of them covered under her hood. Alice slept on as well. Celly began to stir, sat straight up, rubbed her eyes, and called, "Good morning, *grandmère,*" softly. Manon beckoned her over and the two of them walked down to the water's edge. Bending to wash their faces, Manon was struck with the memories of last night's pain.

She stifled a sob in her throat, concentrating on Celly's chatter about her dreams and the strangeness of where they now stood. Perhaps, perhaps, Manon thought with a riffle of hope, it is not too late to make amends. The old Creoles say the bitch never bites her pups to the bone. Perhaps with the next generation. With this child, if with no other.

Celly reached up trustingly and took Manon's hand and a flood of gratitude washed over her then for the smallest bits of beauty at her fingertips, at her feet, even in the deluge. The cry of the waterfowl, the brilliant washed colors of the swampgrass, the shine of a little girl's hair in the sunlight. A hymn of praise rose in her throat, unbidden, and her mind said thank you, thank you, thank you, over and over. She felt her strength returning to her, and she praised that as well, knowing that somehow, she would surmount what seemed to be losses now.

The cycles of her days were clearer to her in that moment than ever before: there were those who had gone before and had prepared the way for her, whether she was aware or not. In turn, her present life would give way to new cycles which Celly would celebrate in her time. Thus it had been and thus it would be forever. Somehow, her mistakes seemed less important, in all that. If she would just be allowed to reach out, to keep reaching out and bringing in, for the children, for the children's children.

Emma used to say that after the long winter, after the season of planting, after the long time of tending and growth, the harvest finally comes. Every woman knows that. And every woman takes peace from it. Manon knew the truth of this now.

In that instant, Celly shouted and pointed out over the water. An answering shout came across from a small boat coming towards them. Manon peered across the mist which rose from the brown water along with the dawn light and saw two young men standing in the front of a skiff, one poling, the other wielding a paddle. Behind them, rising on creaky knees and holding onto one man's shoulder, an old man raised one hand in greeting.

Alex's white hair was the first thing she recognized. Before him in the boat stood Henry Junior and Samuel. She hollered back, waving both arms, as Celly called and jumped beside her.

Manon felt a hand on her shoulder, and Zoe was there, Henry alongside her. "Thank God," Zoe cried, calling and waving as the boat drew nearer. "Oh Mother, they're safe!"

Manon turned and buried her head in Zoe's neck, holding her daughter close. Her eyes filled as she felt Zoe's answering embrace, as strong, as full of hope as her own. And over Zoe's shoulder, as the herons jostled for space in the crowded, partially submerged cypress, sending their throaty cries over the water, Manon knew that there were few places in the world where the rising sun would look more warm and welcome.

Afterword

BAYOU is a work of fiction, of course, and as such, has had to sometimes subvert historical accuracy for thematic and plot purposes. Those who are expert in delta history may notice minor alterations in dates and places, heroes and heroines; however, the bulk of this novel is as historically true as smooth fiction could allow. For example, the well-respected McIlhenny and Avery families, naturalists and producers of the famous Tabasco sauce, did not, so far as I know, have any descendants such as I have described. Henry Avery is a fictional character, as are Manon and Zoe. However, as a long-time lover of the delta region, I would hope that I might be forgiven some liberties with the dry facts of her lineage.

The Creoles have a saying. *Dans le pays des aveugles, les borgnes sont rois.* In the country of the blind, the nearsighted are kings. I have taken a nearsighted look at the delta, but what the region needs more today is a farsighted vision, like the vision of Simon and Alex and, yes, even Zoe. Just as the delta is a metaphor for the whole Mississippi, the Mississippi is, in turn, a microcosm for the whole nation.

If we lose this, our largest wet and wild ecosystem, we will feel its death in every state, from coast to coast, for a thousand years to come.

As a single example of all the species driven to extinction since World War II, the brown pelican is an ironic symbol, since it is the Louisiana state bird. In 1931, the delta had eighty-five thousand or more of the spectacular bird with the seven-foot wingspan. By 1961, the population was less than two hundred breeding pairs. Poisoned by insecticides both in the water and in the tissues of fish, the brown pelican had not been sighted since 1963, until a breeding sanctuary was set up deep in the Barataria Bay, using borrowed Florida birds.

As a single example of the fauna destroyed by contaminants, Spanish moss, once festooning every live oak in the delta, so plentiful that the Cajuns turned the stuffing for mattresses and furniture into a two-million-dollar-a-year industry, now can scarcely be found. The moss is an air-feeding plant, an epiphyte, its long gray strands another symbol of this most southerly of the South. Sensitive to chemicals, it first slowly disappeared from the delta along the Mississippi, where the petrochemical plants line the banks. Today, even in the deepest bayous, the moss is rare.

The loss of habitat for species is at least as destructive as the poisoning of that which remains. In the past, the sea and the river have engaged in a battle, thrust and parry, always a close contest, but the victor over the long run has been the Mississippi as it slowly, with the patience of the geological clock, has withstood the sea's continual chewing away to build the land of Louisiana.

Today, however, the Mississippi is unable to construct land as fast as the sea erodes it, for silt is channeled off between levees to protect oil refineries and orange groves. Louisiana has the highest rate of land loss in the United States—forty square miles a year—and the rate is accelerating.

Louisiana has harbored more chemical dumps than al

most any other state in the nation. The people of New Orleans and all the surrounding cities drink water that flows past more than sixty refineries and chemical plants, most of which bury their wastes on landfills or lagoons sold to them by families who could not support the acreage and its taxes any longer. Many farmers traded an uncertain future with crops for a steady paycheck from companies twenty-five miles above New Orleans which will impact the river for generations.

Now New Orleans is one of the nation's cancer capitals. Despite the thousands of grocery shelves and coin machines which dispense bottled water, the delta holds America's records for the highest rates of bladder, stomach, and intestinal cancer.

And yet, progressive improvement is being made by some—increasing with every day—who wish to turn farsighted eyes on the delta for her own good. As in every part of the country, we can find those who are trying to turn back the ravages of the past. It has been my hope that by focusing on that past and its unique heritage, I might help to swell the numbers who seek to preserve it . . . and Louisiana's future.

For the delta and the river are inextricably wedded, as are all of us to one body of water or another for survival. The Queen City and Old Man River have remained faithful to each other since destiny first joined them together. She has stayed his queen through fat years and thin; now his consort in ornate palaces, now a tired helpmeet eating red beans and rice. With the Mississippi, the delta will live to the end, so long as we allow it in this country of the blind.

The story of the bayou is far from over.

References and Acknowledgments

The following are selected references from my own research which the reader might enjoy.

Part One—1786–1815:

Agnew, Janet M. *A Southern Bibliography of Historical Fiction, 1929–1938.* Louisiana State University, 1940.

Bergeron, John W. *Cajun Folklore.* Abbeville, LA, 1980.

Brasseaux, Carl A. *The Founding of New Acadia, 1765–1803.* LSU, Baton Rouge, 1983.

Cable, George W. *Creoles and Cajuns.* Doubleday: New York, 1959.

Chambers, Henry E. *A History of Louisiana.* Vols. I, II, & III. American History Society: New York, Chicago, 1925.

Childs, Marquis W. *Mighty Mississippi.* Ticknor & Fields: New York, 1982.

Conrad, Glen R. *The Cajuns: Essays on Their History & Culture.* Center for Louisiana Studies, Univ. of Southwest Louisiana: Lafayette, 1978.

Daigle, Jules O. *A Dictionary of the Cajun Language.* Edwards Bros., Inc.: Ann Arbor, MI, 1984.

Deiler, J. Hanno. *The Settlement of the German Coast of Louisiana.* Genealogical Publishing Co.: Baltimore, 1975.

Johnston, Margaret H. *In Acadia: The Acadians in Story and Song.* Hansell & Bros.: New Orleans, 1893.

Kane, Harnett T. *Deep Delta Country* and *The Bayous of Louisiana.* New York, 1944.

LeBlanc, Dudley J. *The True Story of the Acadians.* 1932.

O'Neill, Charles Edward. *Church and the State in French Colonial Louisiana.* Yale University Press, 1966.

Pitot, James. *Observations in the Colony of Louisiana, 1796–1802.* LSU: Baton Rouge, 1979.

Post, Lauren C. *Cajun Sketches.* Baton Rouge, 1962.

Reilly, Robin. *The British At the Gates.* Putnam: New York, 1974.

Saucier, Corrine L. *Louisiana Folktales and Songs.* George Peabody College: Nashville, 1923.

Savoy, Ann Allen. *Cajun Music, Volume One.* Bluebird Press: Eunice, Louisiana, 1984.

Saxon, Lyle. *Old Louisiana.* Rober L. Crager & Co.: New Orleans, 1950.

Saxon, Lyle. *Lafitte, the Pirate.* D. Appleton & Century Co.: New York, 1930.

Taylor, George Rogers. *The War of 1812*, Greenwood Press: Westport, CT, 1963.

Voorhies, Felix. *Acadian Reminiscences.* New Orleans, 1907.

Wall, Robert E. *The Acadians.* Bantam: New York, 1984.

Whitfield, Irene Thérèse. *Louisiana French Folk Songs.* LSU: Baton Rouge, 1939.

Part Two—1835–1865:

Blassingame, John W. *Black New Orleans: 1860–1880.* University of Chicago Press, 1973.

Bragg, Jefferson Davis. *Louisiana in the Confederacy.* LSU: Baton Rouge, 1941.

Bush, Clara Goodyear. *The Grinding.* Henry Holt: New York, 1921.

Clinton, Catherine. *The Plantation Mistress: Womens World in the Old South.* New York, 1983.

Craven, Avery O. *Rachel of Louisiana.* LSU: Baton Route 1975.

David, Edward. *The Story of Louisiana*. Three volumes. New Orleans, 1960.

Dufour, Charles L. *Ten Flags in the Wind, The Story of Louisiana*. Harper & Row: New York, 1967.

Fortier, Alcee. *History of Louisiana*. Four volumes. New York, 1904.

Hepworth, George H. *The Whip, the Hoe, and the Sword*. LSU: Baton Rouge, 1979.

Kane, Harnett T. *Plantation Parade*. Morrow: New York, 1945.

Kennedy, R. Emmet. *Black Cameos*. Albert & Charles Bird Publishing: New York, 1924.

Lindeg, Carmen. *The Path from the Parlor: Louisiana Women, 1879–1920*. Center for Louisiana Studies, Univ. of SW Louisiana: Lafayette, 1986.

Myers, Robin. *Louisiana Story: The Sugar System and the Plantation Workers*. National Advisory Council on Farm Labor: New York, 1964.

Northrup, Solomon. *Twelve Years A Slave*. LSU: Baton Rouge, 1968.

Scarborough, William Kaufman. *The Overseer: Plantation Management in the Old South*. LSU: Baton Rouge, 1906.

Tallant, Robert. *Voodoo in New Orleans*. Macmillan: New York, 1946.

Touchstone, Samuel J. *Herbal and Folk Medicine of Louisiana*. Folklife Books: Princeton, Louisiana, 1983.

Webb, Allie Bayne Windham. *Mistress of Evergreen Plantation: Rachel O'Connor's Legacy of Letters, 1823–1845*. State University of New York Press: Albany, 1983.

Part Three—1877–1927

Asbury, Herbert. *The French Quarter: An Informal History of the New Orleans Underworld*. Knopf, 1936.

Bertrum, Wyatt-Brown. *Honor and Violence in the Old South*. Oxford University Press: New York, 1986.

Castellanos, Henry C. *New Orleans As It Was*. LSU: Baton Rouge, 1978.

Crete, Lilian. *Daily Life in Louisiana, 1815–1830.* LSU: Baton Rouge, 1978.

Daniel, Pete. *Deep'N As It Comes: The 1927 Mississippi River Flood.* Oxford University Press, 1977.

Dominguez, Virginia R. *White By Definition.* Rutgers University Press: New Brunswick, New Jersey, 1986.

Jackson, Joy J. *New Orleans in the Gilded Age.* LSU: Baton Rouge, 1969.

Moe, Christine. *Yellow Fever in Nineteenth Century New Orleans, Necropolis of the South.* Vance Bibliographics.

Moore, Diane M. *Their Adventurous Will: Profiles of Memorable Louisiana Women.* Acadiana Press: Lafayette, 1984.

Morrison, Betty L. *A Guide to Voodoo in New Orleans.* Gretna, Louisiana, 1977.

Prose, Francine. *Marie LaVeau.* Buckley Publishing: New York, 1977.

Saxon, Lyle. *Gumbo Ya-Ya.* Houghton Mifflin: Boston, 1945.

Tunnell, Ted. *Crucible of Reconstruction.* LSU: Baton Rouge, 1984.

Animal Lore and Naturalist Sources:

Eckert, Allan W. *Bayou Backwaters.* Doubleday & Co.: New York, 1968.

Feibleman, Peter S. Editor. *The Bayous.* Time-Life Books: New York, 1973.

Hancock, James and James Kushlan. *The Herons Handbook.* Harper & Row: New York, 1984.

Meanley, Brooke. *Swamps, River Bottoms and Canebrakes.* Barre Publishers: Barre, MA, 1972.

Special thanks to the reference staff at the Stanford Graduate Library, to the reference staffs at the New Orleans Public Library and to Louisiana State University, and to the staff a Louisiana Public Library, Lafayette. Thanks also to the staff at the New Iberia Public Library and the Houma Public Library. I appreciated help offered by the Louisiana Natur and Science Center in New Orleans as well as the Lafayett

Natural History Museum in Lafayette and the McIlhenny Company of Avery Island. My gratitude, also, to all the wonderful Southern writers who preceded and inspired me: George W. Cable, Grace King, Ada Jack Carver, Lyle Saxon, Harnett T. Kane, Lafcadio Hearn, Hodding Carter, E.P. O'Donnell, Gwen Bristow, Roark Bradford, Robert Tallant, J. Hamilton Basso, Kate Chopin and Shirley Grau; thanks to the staff at the University of Louisiana in the Southwest, for their invaluable Acadian collection. Most especially, I'd like to thank Tina Pilione of Bluebird Press in Eunice, Louisiana, who welcomed this author and her mother for an evening of genuine Cajun music and dancing. You were right, Tina, the two-step wasn't so tough, after all. Thanks also to the fine hosts who offered Southern hospitality and welcome to this Yankee usurper, as well as intrusive phone calls when she got back to her notes and discovered she needed yet more. To my family and my extended family with love; to Judy and Chris and Sandy, for reading drafts; to Roz Targ, the best of friends and agents, for ten years of love and partnership; and to Ann LaFarge, a savvy and intuitive editor with an author's heart, who has given me refuge in more ways than one.

A special heartfelt gratitude to my mother, Pat Jekel, to whom this book is dedicated, who drove every mile with me, even into the teeth of Hurricane Hugo when schedules were too tight to delay.

And finally, to my husband, Bill. *Vraiment, je t'aime tou-ours.*